# STAR TREK®

# ADVENTURES IN
# TIME AND SPACE

For orders other than by individual consumers, Pocket Books grants a discount on the purchase of **10 or more** copies of single titles for special markets or premium use. For further details, please write to the Vice President of Special Markets, Pocket Books, 1230 Avenue of the Americas, 9th Floor, New York, NY 10020-1586.

For information on how individual consumers can place orders, please write to Mail Order Department, Simon & Schuster Inc., 200 Old Tappan Road, Old Tappan, NJ 07675.

# STAR TREK®

# ADVENTURES IN
# TIME AND SPACE

## EDITED BY
## MARY P. TAYLOR

POCKET BOOKS
New York   London   Toronto   Sydney   Tokyo   Singapore

An *Original* Publication of POCKET BOOKS

POCKET BOOKS, a division of Simon & Schuster Inc.
1230 Avenue of the Americas, New York, NY 10020

Introductions, commentaries, and compilation copyright © 1999
by Paramount Pictures. All Rights Reserved. Novel excerpts
copyright © by Paramount Pictures. All Rights Reserved.

STAR TREK is a Registered Trademark of
Paramount Pictures.

This book is published by Pocket Books, a division of
Simon & Schuster Inc., under exclusive license from
Paramount Pictures.

All rights reserved, including the right to reproduce
this book or portions thereof in any form whatsoever.
For information address Pocket Books, 1230 Avenue
of the Americas, New York, NY 10020

ISBN: 0-671-03415-4

First Pocket Books trade paperback printing August 1999

10  9  8  7  6  5  4  3  2  1

POCKET and colophon are registered trademarks of
Simon & Schuster Inc.

Cover design by James Wang

Printed in the U.S.A.

*To friends, who make life joyful*

John Ordover
Delia Marshall Turner
Kit and Bob Simon

# A FAREWELL

As this book was going to press, word came of the untimely death of DeForest Kelley, the wonderful actor who portrayed Doctor McCoy in the original *Star Trek* series and in the six movies with the original cast. The editor of this book and everyone here at Pocket Books offer our deepest condolences to his friends and family. He will be greatly missed.

# ACKNOWLEDGMENTS

I would like to extend thanks and acknowledgment to friends without whose love and support life would be much less fulfilling, and this project would have been impossible:

John Ordover, incredible friend and terrific editor, who asked me to read all these wonderful books again and share my favorites with the rest of the reading fans ("What do you mean, John, Pocket will actually PAY me to read all these books again?!");

Delia Marshall Turner, who is the very definition of the word "friend," and who read and commented on this work while maintaining a busy writing, teaching, and saber fencing schedule (Delia is an incredible writer—go read her books!);

Bob and Kit Simon, who have always been there for me through good times, bad times, and the absolute worst times;

Hilary Elizabeth Black Winiarz, a special friend who read this work and provided very helpful critique, particularly on Chapter One: The Captain's Captain: James Tiberius Kirk;

Bernadine Turner, who gave me much needed moral support and encouragement through this entire project; and

Milt and Judi Black, for more than words can express.

# CONTENTS

# INTRODUCTION

STAR TREK HAS BEEN A PART OF MY LIFE FROM ITS VERY BEGINNING, nearly thirty-three years ago. I was one of the first fans, having discovered *Star Trek* during its initial three-year run on NBC. I was captivated by my first sight of that magnificent ship, the *Enterprise*, NCC 1701 (no bloody A, B, C, or D), and its incredible multi-racial, multi-ethnic, and mixed gender crew. At a dark time in our nation's history, *Star Trek* spoke to me of a better place and time when the problems that were tearing us apart no longer existed. Star Trek brought adventure and glory and purpose to an otherwise mundane adolescent existence. My friends and I played Kirk, Spock, and McCoy (I was always Spock), and we wrote our own adventures during summer rerun season. When *Star Trek* ended, we were devastated, but we moved on with our lives and left our galactic adventures behind.

We never forgot Star Trek, though, and we always longed for its return. "Star Trek lives!"—the slogan of fans during the dark times with no Star Trek—was a hope and dream. When Gene Roddenberry toured colleges and universities during the early 1970s, I dragged my somewhat reluctant roommates with me to hear him speak and to see "Devil in the Dark" on a large screen. I was entranced anew at the message of tolerance for differences and celebration of life represented by Star Trek. I longed for the return of Star Trek with an intensity that surprised me. Through my busy years in college and law school, I read and re-read my copies of the *Star Trek Reader,* the James Blish adaptations of the episodes published by the Science Fiction Book Club; to this day, I have both my original paperback copies published by Bantam Books and my SFBC editions. I read the Bantam Star Trek novels and wanted much more.

I was in the theater for the opening night of *Star Trek: The Motion Picture* and have seen every subsequent film on its opening night. Although I agreed with much of the criticism of *TMP,* I enjoyed every second of it. *TMP was* Star Trek, and it had been so very long since I had seen the *Enterprise* and her crew. As I shared Kirk's emotions at seeing the *Enterprise* again, tears clouded my vision. I rejoiced at the reunion of our crew, at Spock's epiphany, and at Vejur's discovery and rebirth to new life. I felt as though I had returned home.

The same year *TMP* premiered, Star Trek fiction was introduced by Pocket Books. Fans embraced the books and the new adventures of the *Enterprise* crew. I have read each of the books, and they have given me more hours of reading pleasure than I can count. The novels filled the gaps between the films and provided an endless supply of adventures for Kirk, Spock, McCoy, Scotty, Sulu, Uhura, Chekov, and the fans who love them.

Upon the debut of *Star Trek: The Next Generation, Star Trek: Deep Space Nine,* and *Star Trek: Voyager,* Pocket began publishing adventures for their crews as well. At the time of this writing, Pocket has published more than 250 original *Star Trek, TNG, DS9* and *Voyager* series novels, novelizations, and crossover series stories. They have published six special crossover or continuing story series, and more are planned. Many of the novels have been issued in audio book form, and there are several audio book–only novels. In 1997, Pocket introduced *Star Trek: New Frontier,* an entirely new Star Trek series that is solely novel-based and will never see film, but which nevertheless captures all the best qualities of the four televised series. Recently, Pocket sponsored two short-story writing contests for new writers to explore strange new worlds with the Star Trek characters and published the best entries in the *Strange New Worlds* anthologies. Star Trek adventures were published for the Young Adult market, including the *TOS, TNG,* and *Voyager Starfleet Academy* books and the *DS9* Jake and Nog stories.

This is a lot of books. Over a twenty-year period, Pocket has produced enough Star Trek fiction to keep fans in Star Trek adventures during all the future empty times when there is no Star Trek in television production, and will keep publishing more. That there is such a strong market for Star Trek fiction while television episodes and regularly spaced feature films are in production attests to the enduring role Star Trek plays in our culture. The novels will be there when *DS9* and *Voyager* end; there will never again be a dark ages with no Star Trek.

Not only do the novels provide Star Trek when there otherwise would be no Star Trek, the novels can tell stories that episodic television and films cannot. Novels can explore characters' backgrounds and biographies with a depth that would be impossible in the television episode format with ensemble casts. They can bring back beloved guest characters, aliens, and crew members. They can go where no Star Trek series is able to go in exploring strange new worlds and seeking out new life and new civilizations. Writers are not limited by network or studio budgets for special effects; the only limit to special effects is the imagination of the writer, and the authors in the Star Trek universe have taken advantage of this freedom in incredible ways. In the pages of Star Trek books readers can find Hortas on the bridges of starships or munching at space stations, sentient insectoid species living in space-going hives, planets with multiple sentient, non-humanoid races who live in symbiosis, non-corporeal cybernetic life forms who are not certain that physical life is real, and intelligent felines with the temperament of Earth-bound house cats.

*Star Trek: Adventures in Time and Space* is a celebration of twenty years of Star Trek fiction. It is a "clip show" for the novels. It is my tribute and thanks to Pocket and Paramount for bringing these wonderful writers together and encouraging them to share their stories with us. Included in this book are excerpts from novels that represent the best of the characters, species, and stories in Star Trek. Unfortunately, many more-than-worthy books have been excluded simply because there is not enough space in a trade paperback to include selections from all the deserving Star Trek novels or even from all of my favorites. I hope that you will enjoy my selections. I do, however, expect to hear from a reader or two who feels that I made the wrong choices. Going into this project, I was 100 percent certain of only one thing, that no matter which books I chose, I would be overlooking someone's favorite or including an excerpt from a book someone else hated. Star Trek readers are a passionate lot! But then, I knew the job was dangerous when I took it, and I look forward to the ensuing debate.

Star Trek truly lives again, and it always will. Pocket Books will continue to provide adventures in time and space for the crews and the readers, and perhaps in another twenty years, there will be an *Adventures II.* . . .

I owe a special debt of gratitude to David Bowling, Johan G. Ciamaglia, Ryan J. Cornelius, James R. McCain, Jr., Alex Rosenzweig, Paul T. Semones, and Corey W. Tacker, who prepared *The*

*Pocket Books Star Trek Timeline* included in this book. This is a complete timeline to the Pocket Books Star Trek novels, short stories, original audio recordings, and young adult books published through November 1998. Events of the books have been combined with events of the series and films. The timeline was prepared with a meticulous and loving attention to events in the Star Trek film and print universe. Fans have long awaited and often requested such a timeline, and I think that you will agree that this one was worth the effort and the wait.

# PART I

# The Crew

If you met someone who had lived in a cave for the last thirty-three years and had never experienced Star Trek, how would you explain it to him? You could say that Star Trek is about space aliens, fantastic adventures, starship battle scenes, phasers, and futuristic technology. Or you could explain that Star Trek is about the exploration of ideas and issues in a science fiction and futuristic setting. You would not be wrong if you gave either of these answers, but neither would your response be complete. Star Trek is about all these things, but more importantly, it is about *people* having fantastic adventures, exploring strange new worlds, seeking out new life and new civilizations, and fighting space battles. Without these people we have come to love, the technology, adventures, science fiction and space battles would be lifeless; they could not sustain the cultural phenomenon that is Star Trek. The television series' themes reverberate through the novels, and as such, this book starts with the people, the crews, and the first captain, James T. Kirk.

# CHAPTER 1

# The Captain's Captain—
# James Tiberius Kirk

JAMES TIBERIUS KIRK WAS THE FIRST CAPTAIN OF THE *ENTERPRISE* NCC 1701 introduced to viewers in the original series, although he was the third *Enterprise* captain after April (introduced in the animated Star Trek series) and Pike (introduced in the original series episode "The Menagerie"). Kirk, played so unforgettably by William Shatner, set the standard by which all the other Star Trek captains are judged. Yet who was this, this captain among captains who led so ably, capturing the imaginations of so many? James T. Kirk above all else was a natural leader. An adventurer and explorer, he was a strong captain willing to display that strength whenever necessary. He often acted first and asked questions later. He was a galactic cowboy, a lover of women, and a passionate fighter. Captain Kirk was brave, intelligent, resourceful, clever, and impulsive. He was a nice Iowa farmboy who worked in outer space.

Captain Kirk was a friend willing to risk everything, ultimately suffering the loss of his son for others dear to his heart. Kirk was a man wed to his ship but who, nevertheless, destroyed her in order to cheat death—yet again—for himself and his friends. He was a man willing to sacrifice the woman he loved to save the future of humanity. He was introspective but decisive. He cared about doing the right thing.

When I think of Kirk, I see a man in action, constantly moving, restless to make a difference in his world. Kirk has been likened to C. S. Forester's Horatio Hornblower, and the resemblance is tangible. James T. Kirk was a cowboy captain when the galactic community was still a frontier to Earth and when the United Federation of

Planets needed starship captains who could operate independently of home and authority. Kirk and his crew were often required to provide justice and civilization to a sometimes outlaw and always dangerous frontier. In so doing, they encountered civilizations both advanced and primitive, malicious and benign. They sometimes interfered with developing civilizations in ways that arguably violated Starfleet's Prime Directive but invariably had their best interests at heart.

Ultimately, Captain James T. Kirk was human; he was fallible, and he knew it, but he was always willing to learn from his mistakes, to grow and to change. He was a hero in the truest and most classic sense. Kirk is the main character in most of the original series novels, although several stand out as providing special moments that capture Kirk's spirit and character at their best.

## *Star Trek: The Motion Picture,* a novelization by Gene Roddenberry

Told as an historic and biographical tale, the *TMP* novelization is the first of Pocket's Star Trek adventures and includes a preface by then-Admiral James T. Kirk. In his preface, Admiral Kirk provided a brief commentary on his command of the *Enterprise* in the original five-year mission. I admire Kirk's willing self-assessment. It says much for the strength of his character that instead of crowing about his accomplishment in bringing so many of his crew home, he reminded the reader of those who lost their lives during the mission. Despite Kirk's self-criticism and soul-searching, bringing home his ship and most of his original crew was no mean accomplishment. His willingness to consider his flaws and possible mistakes and to put the needs of his crew before his own, though, speaks well of his character. It therefore seems appropriate that the first book excerpted in *Star Trek: Adventures in Time and Space* describes this captain's captain in his own words.

### Admiral Kirk's Preface

My name is James Tiberius Kirk. *Kirk* because my father and his male forebears followed the old custom of passing along a family identity name. I received *James* because it was both the name of my father's beloved brother as well as that of my mother's first love

4

instructor. *Tiberius,* as I am forever tired of explaining, was the Roman emperor whose life for some unfathomable reason fascinated my grandfather Samuel.

This is not trivial information. For example, the fact that I use an old-fashioned male surname says a lot about both me and the service to which I belong. Although the male-surname custom has become rare among humans elsewhere, it remains a fairly common thing among those of us in Starfleet. We are a highly conservative and strongly individualistic group. The old customs die hard with us. We submit ourselves to starship discipline because we know it is made necessary by the realities of deep-space exploration. We are proud that each of us has accepted this discipline voluntarily—and doubly proud when neither temptation nor jeopardy is able to shake our obedience to the oath we have taken.

Some critics have characterized us of Starfleet as "primitives," and with some justification. In some ways, we do resemble our forebears of a couple of centuries ago more than we do most people today. We are not part of those increasingly large numbers of humans who seem willing to submerge their own identities into the groups to which they belong. I am prepared to accept the possibility that these so-called *new humans* represent a more highly evolved breed, capable of finding rewards in group consciousness that we more primitive individuals will never know. For the present, however, this new breed of human makes a poor space traveler, and Starfleet must depend on us "primitives" for deep-space exploration.

It seems an almost absurd claim that we "primitives" make better space travelers than the highly evolved, superbly intelligent and adaptable *new humans.* The reason for this paradox is best explained in a Vulcan study of Starfleet's early years during which vessel disappearances, crew defections, and mutinies had brought deep-space exploration to a near halt.* This once controversial report diagnosed those mysterious losses as being caused directly by the fact that Starfleet's recruitment standards were dangerously *high.* That is, Starfleet Academy cadets were then being selected from applicants having the highest possible test scores on all categories of intelligence and adaptability. Understandably, it was believed that such qualities would be helpful in dealing with the unusually varied life patterns which starship crews encounter during deep-space exploration.

---

*See STF 7997B.

5

Something of the opposite turned out to be true. The problem was that sooner or later starship crew members must inevitably deal with life forms more evolved and advanced than their own. The result was that these superbly intelligent and flexible minds being sent out by Starfleet could not help but be seduced eventually by the higher philosophies, aspirations, and consciousness levels being encountered.

I have always found it amusing that my Academy class was the first group selected by Starfleet on the basis of somewhat more limited intellectual agility.* It is made doubly amusing, of course, by the fact that our five-year mission was so well documented, due to an ill-conceived notion by Starfleet that the return of the *U.S.S. Enterprise* merited public notice. Unfortunately, Starfleet's enthusiasm affected even those who chronicled our adventures, and we were all painted somewhat larger than life, especially myself.

Eventually, I found that I had been fictionalized into some sort of "modern Ulysses" and it has been painful to see my command decisions of those years so widely applauded, whereas the plain facts are that ninety-four of our crew met violent deaths during those years—and many of them would still be alive if I had acted either more quickly or more wisely. Nor have I been as foolishly courageous as depicted. I have never happily invited injury; I have disliked in the extreme every duty circumstance which has required me to risk my life. But there appears to be something in the nature of depicters of popular events which leads them into the habit of exaggeration. As a result, I became determined that if I ever again found myself involved in an affair attracting public attention, I would insist that some way be found to tell the story more accurately.

As some of you will know, I did become involved in such an affair—in fact, an event which threatened the very existence of Earth. Unfortunately, this has again brought me to the attention of those who record such happenings. Accordingly, although there may be many other ways in which this story is told or depicted, I have insisted that it also be set down in a written manuscript which would be subject to my correction and my final approval. This is that manuscript, presented to you here as an old-style printed book. While I cannot control other depictions of these events that you may see,

---

*Editors' Note:* We doubt that "limited intellectual agility" will stand up in the face of the fact that Kirk commanded the *U.S.S. Enterprise* on its historic five-year voyage and became the first starship captain in history to bring back both his vessel and his crew relatively intact after such a mission.

hear, and feel, I can promise that every description, idea, and word on these pages is the exact and true story of Vejur and Earth as it was seen, heard, and felt by . . .

*James T Kirk*

## *Best Destiny,* by Diane Carey

The television series provided only a few details about Kirk's early life: he was from Iowa, he had a brother named Sam, and he took Starfleet Academy very seriously, so seriously in fact that he was an annoyance to other students. We learned in "The Conscience of the King" that Kirk was witness to and scarred by tragic events at Tarsus Four, when Kodos the Executioner exterminated thousands in a test of his eugenics theories. Because these facts about Kirk are mere tidbits from his life before his command, fans and writers hungered for answers to other questions, particularly concerning what led Kirk to a life in Starfleet.

*Best Destiny,* by Diane Carey, answered the critical question of why Kirk was driven to Starfleet and how he learned that his first, best, and only viable destiny was as a starship captain. Ms. Carey clearly loves James T. Kirk. She has written some extraordinary stories for him, and she seems to understand this man's psyche with a depth that is unmatched. In *Best Destiny,* she captured his soul. *Best Destiny* is not quite a biography, but it is the story of the key events that changed Kirk's life. It is the story of an adolescent in pain, traumatized by his horrific experience on Tarsus Four and estranged from and resentful of his absentee father, Starfleet officer George Kirk. The biographical story is framed by a mission set shortly after the events of *Star Trek VI: The Undiscovered Country.* As the crew struggled with the emotional consequences of decommissioning, Kirk encountered an enemy from his past, and while the *Enterprise* raced to the rescue of a starship in danger, the captain's past unfolded before him.

Young Jimmy Kirk was a natural leader yet a rebel without a cause who led other youngsters into danger for no clear purpose. This natural but misdirected leader seemed likely to lead criminals rather than a starship crew, and his resentment of his father and traumatic experience at Tarsus Four colored every decision he made. There are times when the reader longs to slap Jimmy; in many ways, he was an obnoxious little thug. Gradually, though, the reader starts to see the glimmerings of the man he would become. In *Best Destiny,* Jimmy was tempered by the fire of life-threatening danger. He was greatly affected by the example of courage and self-sacrifice provided not only by Captain Robert April, but by his father as well. Ultimately, Jimmy became a hero who understood his father and Starfleet in ways he could not have imagined before. Jimmy Kirk learned that he had a destiny and chose to follow it. In the framing story, Captain James Kirk learned that even after his long career in Starfleet, he had more to give and a continuing destiny to follow.

In this passage from *Best Destiny,* Jimmy Kirk, a young punk with no wisdom and even less judgment, led a group of children into danger, using some of the leadership qualities that would eventually serve him as a starship captain.

### A rope footbridge over the swollen North Skunk River, Mahaska County, Iowa

"STICK WITH ME AND YOU'LL GET THE RIDE OF YOUR LIVES."

A surly clutch of teenagers clung to those words as tightly as they clung to the tatters of the ages-old jute footbridge. Beneath them, the swollen Skunk River lazily whispered *dare you, dare you, dare you* and suggested they fall on in.

"Don't look down! Nobody look down."

Immediately the grunts and complaints went silent. Nobody wanted to get chewed out by the stocky boy with the sawdust-colored curls and the stingers in his eyes.

"Keep moving," he added. "No looking down."

"It'll be our luck a tourist tram floats by and sees us," Zack Malkin said. He wanted to scratch his neck, but he didn't dare let go. "We're on the Tramway's historical trail, you know."

"They won't."

"What if they do?" Lucy Pogue spat. Her soggy, bloodshot eyes were wide and her hands twitched on the prickly ropes. "You didn't think of that did you, genius?"

"We'll wave at 'em, all right?" their leader snapped, scowling from under the brim of his grandfather's touring cap. With a shift of his shoulders he rearranged his high school jacket to free his arms a little. "Shut up and keep moving. One step at a time. And don't look down."

"I don't like this, Jimmy," said a brittle, fragile boy who had trouble breathing. He didn't look down, but he did glance back over the third of the walkway they'd already crossed. "Nobody told us we'd have to cross something like this."

8

"There's going to be a lot out there that nobody tells us about. We've got to find out for ourselves," their leader said, "before it's too late."

Tom Beauvais squinted into the sun and cracked, "You mean before we get caught."

"We could just sit at home," Jimmy shot back. "Be real safe that way."

The only person ahead of him was a girl whose powdery complexion barely picked up the light of the western sun. Her small eyes were like clear gelatin—hardly any color but lots of shine—and they were tightened with fear. Her cheeks were large, the shape and color of eggshells, and on a less swanlike creature might have been ghastly.

Shivering, she murmured, "Jimmy . . ."

"Keep moving," he told her softly. "Don't try to hurry. We're not going to move any faster than you can go. That's why I had you go first. I'm right here next to you, Emily. Nothing can possibly happen."

Their muscular leader curled his fingers around the jute and packtwine ropes and willed the sixty-foot-long footbridge to hold up.

It stretched from one cliff to another, east to west over the river. It had two sides for handholds and a walkway on the bottom that once had been tight and safe—a *long* time ago. Now it was rotting. An adventure, or a death wish.

Jimmy gritted his teeth at it. It'd been there for two decades, so it could just stay there another ten minutes. He'd argued them down about how this was the best way to cross the Skunk without getting caught, and how the authorities would be after them by now, and anything else he could tell them to keep them in line. He tried to make this look easy, to pretend the old ropes weren't scratching his palms and to act light on his feet.

Giving the others his voice to concentrate on, he kept talking.

"Always think four or five moves ahead. That's the trick."

"If it's such a good trick," Tom countered, "why didn't you think of one of us going across this wreck first to see if it would hold up?"

His brow in a permanent furrow, Jimmy tightened his eyes and tried to slip around the truth. "Better this way. Even distribution of weight."

He held his breath, hoping nobody would notice how little sense that made. He squinted into the west and ignored the sun's glow off his own peach-fuzzed cheeks.

Peach fuzz. That was his father's phrase. Peach fuzz, baby face, greenhorn. Damn his cheeks for fitting that description. Deliberately he looked away from the sunlight.

"We're pioneers," he said. "We're going straight up the Oregon Trail, just like the people who settled this country and put in the railroads and the towns like Riverside across this part of Iowa. Only instead of horses or steel, we're hopping the Stampede."

Though he had played for team spirit, his only reward was a nasty grunt from Tom. "Sure. We're going to hop onto the fastest train in North America while it's doing nine hundred kpm five centimeters above the ground, *in* a tube. That'll be a whole new definition of 'friction.'"

"Glad you're paying attention, Beauvais."

"Glad you can fly, Kirk."

Jimmy shot a glare at him. Warning.

"Even the Stampede stops once in a while," he said. "All we have to do is make Omaha at loading time and we're aboard. Next stop, Oregon, and next after that . . . South America."

"What're we gonna do when we get to South America?" Quentin Monroe asked.

"Anything we damned well please." Jimmy glanced past Lucy and Zack again to see how Quentin was doing, and hoped Beauvais would look after the little guy.

Quentin's brown face was ink-spotted with big black freckles, enhanced by his spongy black hair and perpetually worried eyes, which in this light looked like two more inkspots. Jimmy hadn't wanted to bring him along. Quentin was only fourteen and everybody else in the gang was sixteen, he'd never held his own in a fight, and he hadn't even been to the city, but there was something about the frail black boy that said I'm okay, I'll grow, I'll learn.

So here he was, on the great adventure with the big kids, and Jimmy had to live with the decision. There was no turning back now.

"Maybe we'll become archaeologists," he said. He tightened his brow and nodded in agreement with himself. Inch by inch he urged them toward the middle of the rope walk. "Hack through rain forests looking for the ancient Mayan city-states. Find out why they went extinct after a thousand years of—"

"They found those."

Jimmy stopped. So did everybody else. The bridge shuddered.

"What?" he snapped. "What'd you say?"

Quentin clung to the ropes and blinked. "They found them. The Mayan palaces. A long time ago. You know . . . how the twentieth-century archaeologists found lance heads in the walls, and later they proved that the city was under siege, and how the siege forced them to do all their farming behind the walls, and how the crop yields fell off, and how—"

"Where'd you hear all this?"

"It was . . . in our history of science book."

"Books!" Jimmy spat out. "You're going to believe what you read in some book? Why waste your time with a book when you can get out and live!"

Quentin fell silent, ashamed that he had wasted his time.

Jimmy shook his head and barked, "Keep moving."

Suddenly an arm of wind swept downriver, pushing the bridge with its enormous hand. The ropes started whining and the whole footbridge began to sway.

"Damn, I almost dropped my pack!" Zack complained, and tried to rearrange his load.

"Don't do that," Jimmy said. "You've got the fake IDs."

"How'd you get those, Zack?" Quentin asked.

"Tapped into the voting records for people who hadn't voted in five years. Figured they were long gone, so we took the IDs of any children they had who were the right age five years ago to be eighteen now. Took their numbers, and *bing*—we're legal."

"Damn. Good idea."

"It was Jimmy's idea. I just did the hardware."

"Told you," Jimmy said. "You don't have to worry about anything. I've got it all stitched up."

Lucy grimaced. "These ropes stink! What if they're rotten? What if they break? We'll die here like some goddamned trout in that rolling throw-up down there."

"We're only thirty feet over the water."

"Water can break your neck if you hit it at the wrong angle," Zack provided.

Lucy let her lips peel back and broke the looking-down rule. "My astrologer *told* me not to do anything dangerous this week. I *knew* I should've paid attention to the signs—now look where I am."

With a stern scowl Jimmy said, "Don't believe in it."

Zack nudged Lucy another sidestep west and called to Jimmy over the wind as it howled between them. "You don't believe in destiny?"

"Didn't say that," Jimmy called. "Said I don't believe in *predestiny*."

"Why not?"

"Because somebody else has to tell me what mine is. That means somebody else is in charge. Means somebody else knows more about me than I do. Malkin, see this main line?" He put his hand on the only braided line on the side of the rope bridge. "That's the one you hang on to. No, the other one. Look at me. *This* one."

Lucy's voice sounded a little steadier when she spoke again. "I know there's something about the stars and when you're born and all. I've *seen* enough. I've had crazy things happen that can't be coincidence. Like when they advised me to start packing a knife, and the next week I had to use it."

Glad he had managed to distract her, Jimmy said, "The stars care whether Lucy Pogue carries a knife? We know what stars are. We know that's one." He spared a hand and poked a forefinger at the bright golden sky. "Am I supposed to believe some arrangement of things in the sky makes life just a package deal? A frame-up all set before we're born? What if your mother trips on a pig like mine did and you're born a month early? Which date sets destiny—my birthday, or a month later? Which stars should I look at? A batch of hot atoms a billion light-years away has some influence on my future?" He snorted.

Some of the gang nodded. Others didn't. So he continued talking as long as they were moving.

"Destiny and predestiny are two different things. Predestiny is pointless. If it's true, we might as well turn around right now, go back to Riverside, and sit on our bulkheads, because whatever's going to happen's gonna happen anyway."

"How's destiny any different?" Tom Beauvais challenged.

A crooked grin danced on Jimmy's face as he leered back at them.

"That's the one *I'm* in charge of."

From the west, the sun buttered his apricot curls and sweat glittered on his brow. To the others, he looked like a demon with a license to smile. If anyone in the group wondered how he had talked them into running away, a moment like this snuffed the thought. Something in the ballistics of Jimmy Kirk was tough enough and vivid enough to keep them going across the shabby old rope bridge, stepping one by one over their better judgments.

Zack coughed as the wind filled his lungs, and he forced himself to move along the ropes, to stay distracted, and not to look down. "Sounds like plain luck to me."

"It sounds like that, but it's not," Jimmy said. He held out one hand, fingers spread, as though gripping the imaginary brick with which he would lay his foundation. "Luck is blind chance. Destiny . . . *that* you *build.*"

He eyed them, one by one, even Beauvais, until the belief returned to each face.

Then he said, "Move along. Twenty more feet and we're there."

The river whispered below. They moved slowly toward the west bank, a few inches at a time, each burdened with a backpack of survival supplies and foodstuffs.

Lucy's voice showed she was trying to keep control as she asked, "How are we going to find our way to Omaha?"

Jimmy helped Emily find a handhold. "Dead reckoning."

"Dead what?"

"Basic sail training."

"Who's gonna sail?" Tom cracked. "We're going on a cargo carrier!"

"It's basic seamanship, Beauvais. Get used to it. The captain's going to expect us to know this stuff. The STD formula. Speed, time, distance. If you know your constant speed and distance, like how far you'll go and how fast, you can figure how long it'll take. If you know your time and speed, you can figure how far—"

"Maybe we should go to space instead," Zack suggested.

"Space? Cold and empty. We got it all right here."

He dismissed the subject with his tone and twisted forward, watching Emily's tiny feet custodially. He moved his own feet carefully after hers, along the miserable knots and fraying lines that once had been sturdy enough to carry teams of Girl Scouts and Boy Scouts across the Skunk River. Long abandoned, the sixty-foot ropewalk had been left up for sentimental value as part of the Tramview of the Oregon Trail. He and Zack had worked for almost an hour breaking through the protective grating that kept hikers off the old footbridge. Zack could break into anything. That's how they'd gotten the food in the backpacks—it was how they'd gotten the backpacks. That's how they'd finagled tickets for the Stampede Tubetrain.

All they had to do was get to Omaha without being spotted for runaways, and they'd never be seen again.

Jimmy shook his head and forced himself to stop thinking about what they'd stolen. What choice did they have? They hadn't been given anything, so they just had to take somebody else's. That was fair.

*Snap*

"Ah—ah—Jimmyyyyy!"

The shriek cracked across the ravine at the same moment as the rope bridge waggled hideously to the snap of parting jute—and Quentin went over backward. His hand clawed uselessly at a broken line, then at open air.

Lucy screamed, driving the needle of terror under all their skin.

Jimmy cranked around in time to see Quentin bounce against the ropes on the other side of the bridge and bend them almost all the way down to the level of the walkway. Part of the braided walkway caught the small of Quentin's back and bounced him stiffly, but finally held. And there he was, hanging.

The boy was arched backward over the outermost strands, his upper body in midair, hanging halfway out over the greedy water. His loaded pack yanked at his shoulders and held his arms straight out sideways. The whole bridge wobbled back and forth, back and forth, in a sickening bounce.

None of them did any more than freeze in place, clinging to their own ropes.

"Nobody move!" Jimmy bellowed. "I'll do it!"

"Goddammit!" Beauvais shouted. His face twisted. "This was your stupid idea! We could've just taken the long way, over ground, but no! We had to do it Kirk's way! Why does anybody listen to a blowfish like you!"

"Cram it, bulkhead. I'm busy." Jimmy unkinked his fingers from the scratchy ropes and forced himself to move back toward Lucy.

"Please, Jimmy," Emily murmured, "don't let him fall . . ."

Jimmy pressed her hand just before she was out of reach. "I'm not going to let him fall. Nobody else move. Quentin, hold still."

They were only a couple of stories up, but Jimmy knew it was enough to kill. Below, the muddy water chewed and gurgled.

Jimmy maneuvered around Lucy, then around Zack, careful not to dislodge either of them from their hold. The ropes shivered, but no more parted or frayed.

"It'll be all right," he said steadily. "Everybody stay calm. He just put his foot on the wrong braid. Nothing else is breaking."

"Tell the ropes," Beauvais snarled.

Jimmy's face flamed, and he stopped moving toward Quentin. "I'm telling the damn ropes!" he bellowed. "Leave me alone and let me do this."

Beauvais rearranged his grip and muttered, "Okay, okay . . . just get him."

Below them Quentin dangled backward, his hips tangled in the old ropes, and gasped as though he couldn't remember how to breathe. "J-J-Jimmy—"

14

"I'm almost there. Don't whine."

Jimmy reached Quentin and lowered himself to the braided cordage, his own breath coming in rags. Old tendons wobbled and grated against the cross-braids, threatening to open beneath him. By the time he got above the dangling boy, his palms were bleeding.

Quentin's left foot was caught between two braids that had twisted as went backward. If he turned his foot now, it would slip through and he would be tossed out like a circus performer on a springboard. No one wanted to point that out; they all saw it.

A finger, a limb, a joint at a time, Jimmy lowered himself to his hands and knees onto the walkway of the bridge. The old jute cut into the flesh of his kneecaps right through his clothing. He bit his lip, ignored the pain, and searched for a secure position over Quentin's entangled legs.

There wasn't one.

The ropes quivered defiantly under him, refusing to cooperate. Ultimately he arranged himself on his stomach across the braids, right beside Quentin's leg. He shoved an arm through the side ropes of the bridge.

"Monroe, give me your hand."

Nothing happened. Spread halfway out in open air, the younger boy was muttering unintelligible sounds.

"Monroe, what are you doing?"

"P-p-praying."

"Well, do that later, will you? Give me your hand."

"I can't—move—"

Jimmy lowered his voice, literally made it darker, grittier, meaner. "This is one of those times when you've got two possible destinies, right?"

"Mmmm . . ."

"Pick the best one."

No one else breathed, no matter how the rising wind pushed air between their clenched teeth.

"Now!" Jimmy ordered.

A brown hand arched upward toward the sky. Jimmy caught it, and hauled.

"My arm! My arm!" Quentin bellowed as his body cranked sideways, upward.

Jimmy twisted his fingers into the boy's shirt collar. "Beauvais, take his backpack. The rest of you, keep moving. Zack, you're in charge."

"What? I don't want to be in charge."

15

"You don't have any choice, do you?"

"This was your idea."

"Fine. Lucy can be in charge."

The bridge waggled.

"I don't want it either!" Lucy protested.

"We're more than halfway across!" Jimmy shouted. "All you have to do is go twenty more feet! How many decisions do you have to make?"

"I'll be in charge," Tom said as he slung the extra backpack over his shoulder.

Jimmy cranked upward the other way. "I didn't pick you!"

"We didn't 'pick' you either."

"Yes, you did. This was all *my* plan."

"Some plan! We're not even out of Iowa and we're already in trouble. You're all gas, Kirk."

"Look, any time you're ready to turn back—"

"Jimmy . . ."

The soft beck from above drifted down and silenced the disharmony.

Jimmy twisted back toward the others. "What is it, Emily?"

The girl stood with each narrow white hand on a side of the bridge, unable to push back her hair as the wind blew it forward over her cheeks and into her eyes. "Quentin," she murmured.

"I know, I've got him," he grumbled, and returned his attention to where it should have been.

Quentin's brown face had gone to clay by the time Jimmy hauled him up and pulled his legs out of the ropes he'd gotten tangled in. He had both eyes knotted shut and refused to open them until Jimmy threatened to leave him in the middle of the bridge.

Then Jimmy took him by the shoulders and almost broke his shoulder blades. "Quentin, this is how it is," he said. "We're going on. It's just rope. We're not going to be beaten by rope. Are you with me?"

He didn't wait for an answer. He straightened, placed Quentin's hands on the side support lines, nodded toward the bank, and started picking his way westward again. He didn't look back. Quentin would follow, or be left out there.

But through his boots he felt the pressure on the braided rope behind him, and knew he would win that bet.

On the bank Tom Beauvais was the last to jump onto solid ground. They turned to watch Jimmy bring Quentin all the way in.

Jimmy jumped onto the hard, rocky ground, pulled Quentin up

behind him, then stepped aside as Zack and Lucy came forward to help Quentin stumble onto the grass.

When he turned and looked up at Tom Beauvais, there was mercury in his eyes. He took two steps forward, and *boom*—

A roundhouse right pitched Tom's head backward, and he staggered but didn't go down. He gathered himself and let fly a rabbit punch to Jimmy's midriff, but Jimmy saw the punch coming in time to tighten up. He had the advantage of *not* being too lean.

His buff curls flickered, his brow drew in, his eyes turned to arrowheads, and the heels of his hands struck Tom in the shoulder hollows. Another flash spun Tom around, and Jimmy had his challenger's wrist forced halfway up his spine.

Tom ground out a senseless protest and arched his back, then bellowed in pain.

Forcing the arm upward another inch, Jimmy asked, "Your way or my way?"

"Okay, okay, your way! Don't break it!"

Jimmy shoved him off and dropped back a pace, satisfied. Holding his arm and swearing, Tom stumbled away.

"I'll break it next time," Jimmy said.

The others looked away from both boys, embarrassed and unsure about their adventure.

He pushed through the others to Quentin, and his entire demeanor changed as he took Quentin by the shoulder and said, "Take a deep breath. Now take another one . . . you did it. You beat it."

Quentin managed a nod.

Jimmy turned him to look at the shaggy rope bridge as it waved in the wind as though to say good-bye. "There it is . . . everything you were afraid of. You went one step at a time and you trusted somebody. Now it's all behind you. Understand?"

As Quentin looked at the rope bridge, at how far it was back to the other cliff, and at how far he had come, his trembling slowly faded away.

It *was* behind him. He never had to cross it again. He'd done it.

He cleared his throat and said, "You're stronger than you look."

Jimmy smiled. "All right, everybody, mount up. Get your packs on and let's get moving. We've got a schedule to keep."

He strode cockily away from Quentin, leaving most of the group to stare at the back of his head, closed almost his whole hand around Emily's upper arm, and started walking her west.

"I," he said, "will take care of you. You don't need anybody. You don't need your teachers, you don't need your parents, you don't need your sisters . . . you need only me. By morning we'll be in Omaha. Then, four hours on the Stampede, and *zam*—we're in Bremerton, Oregon, signing on as deckhands of dynacarrier *Sir Christopher Cockerell."*

## The Ashes of Eden, by William Shatner, with Judith and Garfield Reeves-Stevens

*The Ashes of Eden* is the first in a series of extremely successful collaborations between William Shatner and Judith and Garfield Reeves-Stevens. Following *The Ashes of Eden, The Return* told the story of James T. Kirk's rebirth after his death on Veridian III in *Star Trek Generations. Avenger* followed with Kirk's continuing twenty-fourth-century adventures and a reunion with Spock, as the two joined together to save the galaxy from an environmental menace, and in the process confronted Captain Jean-Luc Picard. Finally, in *Spectre,* Kirk joined an alternate universe Kathryn Janeway in an adventure. *Spectre* ended on a cliffhanger, leaving James T. Kirk's adventures to be continued in *Star Trek: Dark Victory.* The Kirk series has been so popular that *The Ashes Of Eden, The Return,* and *Avenger* have been republished in an omnibus trade paperback edition entitled *Odyssey.*

The *Ashes of Eden* is set shortly before the events of *Star Trek Generations* and Kirk's apparent death aboard the *Enterprise* 1701-B. No longer an active starship commander, Kirk felt useless and depressed. As he faced life without the *Enterprise,* Kirk received a mysterious and seductive invitation from the beautiful and young Romulan–Klingon hybrid, Teilani, beckoning him with the promise of eternal youth and the chance to protect the secret world of Chal from destruction. Always striving to make a difference, Kirk was seduced not only by Teilani, but also by the notion of recapturing his youth through usefulness. When he decided to help Teilani and Chal, an old enemy accused him of treason and plotting to start a war between the Federation and the Klingon Empire. His loyal crew were puzzled by his actions but determined to prove that he was no traitor. They set out with Captain Sulu and the *Excelsior* to discover the truth and save Kirk. Eventually, Kirk accepted that nothing lasts forever, including his destiny as a starship captain. Allowing himself to be open to whatever destiny the stars led him to finally brought him the understanding that he was truly forever young.

I have enjoyed the Kirk-back-from-the-dead books. They bring Kirk, Spock, and McCoy back together for continuing adventures involving the *TNG, DS9,* and *Voyager* crew members. Because they are non-canon and contradict events of the films and the televised series, I tend to think of them as Star Trek fiction, if you will (oxymoron notwithstanding). Regardless, they are fun reads.

In this excerpt from *The Ashes of Eden,* Kirk was at a crossroads, the decision point that took him to Teilani and the promise of a fountain of youth. He felt alone and out of touch with his friends. Spock and McCoy, who believed that Teilani was using Kirk, attempted to dissuade him from abandoning his life.

LEONARD MCCOY WAS IMMUNE TO THE PARISIAN CITYSCAPE SPREAD OUT before him. It was aglow with entire galaxies of lights, drawing the eye unerringly to the floodlights bathing the newly restored Eiffel Tower. But the beauty of the ancient city held no charm for him tonight. He scowled over his mint julep.

"Our ancestors had a descriptive medical term for what you're going through, Jim."

"Did they?" Kirk asked, without enthusiasm. He had just finished telling his two closest friends about his intention to resign from Starfleet and accompany Teilani to Chal. But the evening was not progressing as smoothly as he had hoped. He should have realized. Things seldom did when both Spock and McCoy were involved.

The doctor sourly regarded his drink. "They called it 'middle-aged crazy.'"

By the kitchen alcove, Spock raised an eyebrow. "Indeed. A most fitting description."

Kirk slumped in his chair. An uncomfortable position because it was Vulcan, and most Vulcan chairs were not meant for anything other than ramrod-straight posture. "Spock, not you, too."

"What did you expect?" McCoy's exasperation was evident. It gave his voice an edgy tenseness that flattened the friendly warmth of his Southern drawl. Even to Kirk it was unsettling to hear strong emotions being voiced in the serene sanctuary of Spock's quarters in the Vulcan Embassy.

"I don't know what I expected," Kirk said. "But what I had hoped was that . . . you'd wish me well."

Spock handed Kirk a thimble-sized glass filled with a yellow liquid. Kirk looked at it skeptically. It smelled like licorice. "You keep the makings for McCoy's *mint julep* here, but no scotch?"

"The doctor is a frequent visitor," Spock said. "He maintains his own supply of refreshments."

Kirk looked at his two friends. McCoy was a *frequent* visitor? *Here?* He felt out of touch, as if he had ignored the people closest to him. After a few moments' thought, he realized he had. And regretted it. But it was still time to move on.

"As you must know," Spock continued, "we, of course, do support you in any decision you make and indeed wish you well."

"Even if we also think you're a horse's ass," McCoy grumbled.

Kirk couldn't take it anymore. "Didn't you hear a word I said?" He jumped to his feet, began to pace. "I *love* her, Bones."

McCoy was not impressed. "Didn't you hear a word *I* said? You're crazy!"

Spock stepped between the two men as a mediator. "Captain, if I may, you say you are 'in love.' How are we to expect that this time is different from any of the others?"

Kirk stared at Spock, surprised by the bluntness of his question. "The point is, *I'm* different. Don't you see . . ." Kirk looked around at the plain gray walls of the Vulcan-designed room. They were the same walls that confined his existence, pressing in on him from all sides, restricting movement and freedom and life itself. "Spock, I'm dying here."

McCoy couldn't let that go. "Speaking as your doctor. No, you're not."

Kirk ignored him. "That's not what I mean, and you know it. My time's running out. *Your* time. Spock's time. This past year it's been as if everyone expects me to sit in my rocker and stare at the sunset and wait for night to bring an end to everything. But now, Teilani's showing me . . . a new horizon."

"She's blinding you, is more like it," McCoy said.

Kirk had no argument with that. "Yes, she is. And I love it. I can't stop thinking about her, Bones. I can't stop remembering what it's like to be with her."

"Your hormone levels would probably short out my tricorder."

Kirk grinned. "Exactly. Can you know what it's like to feel that way again? Bones, she's . . . incredible. Beyond incredible. I mean, when she—"

McCoy turned away. "Spare me the details."

But Kirk wouldn't let himself be ignored. He couldn't keep Teilani bottled up inside him. "I feel like I'm twenty again. That thrill, that expectation, it's all come back to me. Each morning. Each day. Each *night*. Everything is new again. Everything, Bones."

20

"The only thing that's new is the *Enterprise*-B."

That stopped Kirk.

McCoy was visibly working to hold in his anger, now. "Almost finished. Up in spacedock. Going to be launched within the year. And she's already been assigned to Captain Harriman—*not* James T. Kirk."

Kirk angrily rejected the diagnosis. It was too simplistic. He felt his temper spiraling upward to match McCoy's. "You're not listening to me. This is *not* about the *Enterprise*. This is about me. My feelings. My needs." He turned to Spock. "Spock, you know, don't you? We spoke of passion. You said that's what I needed. And Teilani has made me feel that again."

"Of that, I have no doubt, Captain. But that same passion has adversely affected your judgment."

Kirk was astounded by Spock's blanket assessment. "Exactly how has my judgment been affected?"

"Have you stopped to consider what Teilani's motives in this matter may be?"

"Spock, what does it matter?"

McCoy stepped to Spock's side.

"It matters because she's using you, Jim."

Kirk spread his arms wide. "Then let her use me. My God, Bones. Do you know what it means to be useful again? You've got medicine. Spock's got diplomacy. But what do I have? What *did* I have until Teilani came to me and said her world needs me?"

McCoy shot Spock a sideways glance. "Well, I suppose it is a more original line than, 'Come here often, sailor.'"

Kirk didn't know how much more of this he wanted to hear. "Bones, Spock himself confirmed everything Teilani told me. The failed Klingon-Romulan colony. How neither side claimed it. How it declared independence."

"So she read the same handful of paragraphs in a Starfleet almanac that Spock did," McCoy said dismissively. "Ha. No one even knows the exact location of this Chal place."

Spock steepled his fingers in a meditative pose. "To be fair, Captain, the drastic nature of your intentions does not seem to coincide with the apparent threat faced by Chal. I therefore suspect you have not told us everything Teilani has revealed to you about her world and its predicament."

Kirk wore his best poker face, though he knew it had long since stopped working on Spock and McCoy. "I've told you everything that's pertinent. Some things, minor things, she did tell me in confidence. There's no need to repeat them."

He still found it difficult to believe in the amazing medical properties Teilani claimed for her world.

But if he dared tell anyone, even his friends, what Teilani had told him about . . . being young forever, they'd lock him up. The galaxy was littered with false fountains of youth. Not to mention the con artists who fleeced those desperate enough to believe in them. He had no intention of looking more foolish to his friends than he apparently already did.

"In confidence," McCoy sputtered in the midst of a sip. "Pillow talk is more like it."

"Bones, don't."

McCoy slammed down his glass, as if he'd lost his taste for his favorite drink. "And if I don't, who will? Face it, Jim, you've got all the symptoms of someone escaping reality at warp nine. We all know you need something to do. But to go off, you'll excuse the expression, half-cocked with this *child—"*

Kirk faced McCoy as if facing an accuser, shouted back at him, surprising himself as much as his friend. "She's an adult, Bones. She knows what she's doing. Her planet has no defense system, no military history. They need me . . . someone of my experience to . . . set up a police force, show them how to defend themselves, secure their world and their future."

"And you think there aren't a thousand consulting companies on a hundred worlds that are better equipped to do that than you? You don't think that the Federation would jump at a chance to set up a joint peacekeeping operation with the Klingons and the Romulans to improve relations?"

"There are other considerations," Kirk insisted.

"I'm sure there are. *Her* considerations!" McCoy held up his fingers as he counted them out. *"Your* reputation. *Your* prestige. *Your* instant access to virtually any level of government and industry in the Federation and almost anyplace else you'd care to mention." McCoy's eyes were wide with indignation. "How long do you think it's going to be before your little playmate snuggles up to you in bed some night and asks if you could set up a teeny-tiny meeting between her and some planetary official? Or some industrialist that she couldn't get to in ten years of negotiations?"

"What's wrong with *any* of that?" Kirk demanded.

McCoy shook his head in pity. "She's a third your age."

"Which is how she makes *me* feel!" Kirk took a deep breath. He hadn't wanted any of this to happen. "Bones, even if everything you say is true, what's *wrong* with it?" Kirk reached out to his friend, anger turning to a plea for understanding. "Teilani and I are *both* adults. We're *both* going into this with our eyes wide open. If I can take five steps with her, and then drop dead on the sixth, at least I will have had those first five."

Kirk turned to Spock. His Vulcan friend revealed no trace of what he was thinking. "Spock, you understand what I'm saying."

"I do," Spock said.

At last Kirk felt hope. Perhaps there was a way back from this emotional precipice after all. "Then help me here. Help Bones see that what I'm doing isn't wrong."

But Spock shook his head. "I cannot. For in this instance, I find myself in the unique position of agreeing with everything Dr. McCoy has said."

Those simple words, spoken so calmly, were more of a shock to Kirk than if McCoy had come right out and punched him.

"Spock . . . no."

"If you have been forthcoming with us, Captain, then I must say your actions involving this woman are uncharacteristic, unsuitable, and ill-serving your past reputation and accomplishments."

Kirk stared at Spock. Mortified. In his own Vulcan way, Spock was shouting at him, too.

"To abandon Starfleet and your career in order to become little more than a mercenary, apparently paid by the sexual favors of a young woman about whom you know little or nothing, is not an act of passion."

"Then just what is it?" Kirk demanded hotly.

"It is an act of desperation. And desperation is also an emotion with which I am familiar."

The silence in the room was physical, like a jungle to be hacked through.

"Spock," Kirk said quietly, "you once asked me if we had grown so old that we had outlived our usefulness. . . ."

"The times have changed, Captain. As have our abilities. Our functions and our goals must change with them. To refuse to accept the inevitable is the first step toward obsolescence, and extinction."

Suddenly, Kirk felt empty. There was no need to control his emotions. He no longer felt anything. "What if I don't want to change?" His voice sounded flat to him. As if it came from a great distance.

"Then that would be . . . unfortunate."

23

"Unfortunate . . ." Kirk said. Three decades of friendship dissolving in that one spoken word.

That one verdict.

Kirk faced Spock, and then McCoy, and it was as if he looked at strangers. Had they ever known him well? Had he ever understood them so little?

After almost thirty years, Kirk could think of nothing more to say to Spock or McCoy.

"It's late," Kirk said. He stared at them both, fixing them in his memory. In case he might never see them again. "I have to . . . take care of some loose ends."

Spock and McCoy let him go. In silence. As if they, too, could think of nothing more to say to him.

Times had changed.

Kirk continued on his journey.

Alone.

## *Invasion! Book One: First Strike,* by Diane Carey

One of Kirk's most endearing traits is his tendency to rush in where angels fear to tread when one of his crewmates is in danger. The next selection shows this aspect of Kirk's personality, as he challenged an inferno of demons to save Dr. McCoy. Diane Carey's *First Strike* is Book One of a special 1996 four-book series developed by her and John Ordover. *Invasion!* is the story of invaders, called Furies, who were archetypes of terror for humans, Klingons, Vulcans and the other species in the Alpha Quadrant. The Furies believed that the Alpha Quadrant was stolen from them millennia ago, and they were determined to regain it from its twenty-third-century inhabitants. Kirk's rescue of McCoy in *First Strike,* excerpted here, is classic Kirk in action.

"VERY DANGEROUS FOR YOU TO BE HERE NOW. IF THERE IS REACTION, I cannot protect you."

"I'll take my chances. Where's my chief surgeon?"

"Come with me. Prepare yourself."

Not very reassuring, as phrases went.

The tour through Zennor's ship was skin-chilling. Like wandering through a cave behind a suddenly agile bat. Zennor, who had moved with such cautious reserve down the broad, bright, open corridors of the *Enterprise,* now skirted down shoulder-wide passages coated with dark velvety moss and overhung with some kind of web.

Kirk stumbled several times until his eyes adjusted, then stumbled a little less, but the deck was nearly invisible in the dimness. He felt he was stepping foot by foot through the chambers of a hornet's nest. Somehow they had beamed directly into these veins and now were moving through them.

There was something beneath his feet, not carpet or deck, but a litter of crunchy and mushy matter, all different sizes, different textures, as if he were treading over a dumping ground. Fungus gave under his weight and puffballs popped as he stepped on them. Other things cracked. The air was thick and musky with smells both plant and animal.

When he thought he couldn't stand another meter of the cloying dimness and moss that grasped at his hair and arms, Zennor led him out into a broader cavern, though still coated with growing plant life—and a sense, if not a visible presence, of other life, of eyes watching him. To all outward senses, he and Zennor were alone here.

But Kirk had spent his life being looked at. He knew when it was happening. There were beasts in the walls.

No, the walls didn't have eyes, but they did have punctures, dark recesses from which more of those skulls peered out, many skulls, but not humanlike skulls. There were many kinds, some belonging to creatures he hadn't seen yet but now assumed were here. Unless they were dragging along the skulls of aliens they met on their voyages, Zennor's amalgamated crew was even more amalgamated than Kirk had first guessed. These were most likely the skulls of fallen comrades.

So they kept the skulls of some, and the "souls" of others. And who could tell what else? Foreign cultures could be very complicated.

Suddenly he wanted the chance to get to know them better, and felt that chance slipping away as he dodged behind Zennor up their icy slope.

He forced himself to ignore the skull niches as he hurried behind Zennor, also forcing himself not to bellow an order to move even faster.

All at once they burst out into a blinding brightness, creased with the noise of hundreds of voices making disorganized, wild cheers and chants. Kirk shaded his eyes and paused until they adjusted, then tried to look.

The chamber was enormous, as big as a stadium and half again taller, lit with green and yellow artificial light, and twisting with a white haze created by vents clearly spewing the stuff near the ceiling. From the configuration of the *Rath,* he guessed they were near the aft end. So the propulsion units weren't back here, but somehow arranged elsewhere. He'd have to remember that—

But thoughts of hardware and strategy fled his mind as he looked up, and farther up.

In the center of the huge foggy chamber stood—yes, *stood*—a giant mannequin in humanoid form, with a head, two arms, two legs, like a vast version of one of those poppets, except that this mannequin was a good six stories tall and made entirely of slats of wood and raw tree branches, and veined with braided straw or some kind of thatch. Its arms stood straight out like a rag doll's, bound at the wrists with some kind of twine; its legs ended at the ankles, with only stumps of chopped matter for hands and feet.

Bisecting the hollow arms, legs, and torso of the wickerwork giant were narrow platforms—scarcely more than slats themselves, but enough to stand upon—and there, in the middle of the straw giant's see-through right thigh, Leonard McCoy hovered twenty-five feet above the deck.

The doctor clung pitifully to the twisted veins of thatch, looking down upon a gaggle of cavorting beings, all types of misshapen vagabond demons, from the snake-headed beings to the horned ones to those more squidlike than anything else, and the others who looked as if they had wings.

Evidently this was Zennor's crew, dancing around the straw legs of the monster, laying more straw and twigs in heaps around the giant's ankles, and chanting while they did this.

*The Furies.* Even if it wasn't them, it described them now.

Kirk stared, measuring the critical elements; consumed for a moment with astonishment and a bad chill. He knew a preparation for a bonfire when he saw one.

Stepping forward from the entranceway, he felt the green-tinted light reflect off the topaz fabric of his uniform shirt and sensed how bizarre his facial features must look with that light cast from below, like something boys would see playing with flashlights in a pup tent.

"Jim!" McCoy knelt on the slats and called down, pushing his face between the veins of thatch.

Kirk turned to Zennor. "What is *this?*"

Zennor gazed at him with ferrous eyes that held no apology. "Punishment."

The crew of the *Rath,* at least the off-duty crew presumably, jumped and rushed, chanting all the way, around the giant straw mannequin in a gangly kind of organization, each going his own way at his own pace, but all going in the same direction. They deposited bundles of straw, branches, and even whole trees at the ankles of the giant. Their metal wristbands, chains, medallions, bracelets, and belts bounced and rang, creating a fiendish jangling in the huge hall. On their metal belts, many of them had those linen poppets, each in the rough image of the wearer, doing another kind of dance.

As Zennor stood before him in his dominating and statuesque manner, Kirk was careful to stand still, not attract any more attention than necessary until he could size things up.

A sundry train of beings broke off from the dancing circle and hurried toward him and Zennor. It took all of Kirk's inner resolve to stand still and let Zennor handle his own crew.

The horrendous gaggle descended upon them in a rush until the last four feet, when they skidded to a stop and made Kirk glad he was still wearing his portable translator, because they were all speaking at once.

"We're home!" a winged thing said to Zennor.

"The Dana told us the news!" crowed an elongated creature that seemed to have no bodily mass other than bones thinly veiled with rubbery brown skin. It would've looked like a Halloween skeleton, appropriately enough, except that it had four arms.

A tentacle-head repeated, "The Dana told us the good news!"

"This is our place!" someone else trilled in a high voice, clearly meant to congratulate their leader.

"The Dana had no authority, Morien," Zennor said. His voice had a tenor of bottled rage. "You should be at your posts."

"But we have a criminal, Vergozen," the tentacled person said, and looked at Kirk. "Is this another one?"

The "it" gestured at Kirk.

"He is here for the final visitation," Zennor snarled, and Kirk couldn't tell whether it was sarcasm or not. Then Zennor motioned for Kirk to move past them. "Fetch me the Dana."

Morien quickly said "Yes, Vergozen!" and skittered off into the crowd.

Kirk took his cue and moved toward the wicker colossus. Other creatures seemed uninterested in him, though many glanced up in mild curiosity. They were involved in their work and looking forward to what they were about to do. They didn't seem to care about visitors who walked in with their captain.

He came to the bottom of one straw leg, as big around as a warp engine, close enough to speak to McCoy in a normalish voice, without attracting attention.

"Bones," he began tentatively, "you all right up there?"

"So far." The doctor gripped the reedy filaments of the colossus. "Did they hurt Spock?"

"They knocked him off his bunk. Chapel's taking care of him. I've never seen her so happy."

"Are the Klingons here yet?"

"Just popped onto our long-range. We were about to make a border run when you turned up missing. Now I'll settle for anything I can get away with."

Frustrated, McCoy glanced around, then reached down with a toe and found a lower slat, and climbed down through the wooden webbing until he could stand inside the giant's right leg, just above the knee. He could only make it about another seven feet down before the straw webbing stopped him.

"Jim . . . they're going to set fire to this."

Caught with empathy, Kirk nodded and tried to be clinical. "Yes, I know. I'm working on it."

"I broke their laws with that damn doll. You might not be able to do anything about it."

"Don't make any bets."

"I don't want to," the doctor said. "Jim, listen—when they put me in here, they shoved in a lot of other things. They put my medical tricorder in with me, and all this other stuff." He maneuvered with difficulty, having to stand on slats of bowing straw twisted to provide a foothold that was obviously temporary, and scoop up bits of material from around him. "There are thigh and hand bones here . . . and hanks of hair, skin scrapings . . . and this bony plate is the back part of a cranium."

"The place is full of skulls."

"Yes, I know. But this skull is Andorian!"

"That's not possible," Kirk said, but it came out with a terrible resignation that surprised even him.

McCoy raised a long gray bone, scored with cracks. "And this thighbone . . . it's human. From Earth. It's a perfect DNA match." He leaned on the slat with one knee and held up his medical tricorder with his other hand.

"Could they have acquired it here in the past twenty-four hours?"

"They could've. Except that they'd have had to raid an archeology lab for this. It's old as a bristlecone pine!"

"How old is that?"

"As nearly as I can estimate, it's over four thousand years old. A human bone!"

"Bones, are you sure about this?"

"I've had nothing else to do in here."

"They put those in there with you just now?"

"Just a half hour ago. I think they're raiding their own coffers and placing things in here that look physiologically like me. At least to their minds. Some kind of symbolic connection—who knows?"

"Can you explain the DNA link?"

The doctor scowled. "I'm not saying that humans or Klingons went out into space and met these people, but I'm wondering if somehow these people ended up on our planets a long time ago and affected our beliefs. If a shipload of Vulcans showed up on Earth in the fourteen-hundreds, they'd sure be taken for devils."

"And life has been around the galaxy for millions of years. Is it really any surprise if Earth, Vulcan, the Klingon homeworld, and a lot of other planets might've had visitations?"

"Given the numbers, I'd be surprised if they hadn't." McCoy squirmed for a better grip.

Kirk gripped the straw spokes too, as if to make a connection. "The dangerous bottom line is that it's beginning to look like this *was* their space."

"Then we'd all better get used to carrying pitchforks," McCoy said, "because I think that's the conclusion." He held up the human thighbone and shook it. "Unless they killed a human in the past twelve hours and somehow made this bone appear to my readouts as if it were four to six thousand years old. I think we got that mythological stuff from our Greeks and Egyptians and druids, but I think the Greeks and Egyptians and druids got it from *them.*"

He swept the medical tricorder to indicate the circle of aliens, then reached out between the wood and straw and tossed the tricorder to Kirk.

"If I don't make it, you've got to take that to Spock," he said urgently. "I don't mind being right, but this time I was even more right than I had the sense to know. It's not just a coincidence that these people look like our legends and myths of evil. They *are* our legends and myths of evil!"

A sight within a sight.
Furies and fire.

29

In the center of the great hall, twisted with manufactured fog and looming nearly to the ceiling, the straw giant had no face and no hands, only the bound strands of thatch to make up the most base form of intelligent life. On the walls, carved forms of animal heads and double-headed statues flared down in carnal images of the beings dancing below.

"Have you got your phaser with you?"

McCoy's question was subdued.

"Yes," Kirk said. "They didn't take it away. I don't know if that's courtesy or they're just not afraid of it. It's not because they're stupid, I'll bet."

Around them a drumbeat began, low and not very steady, timpani made of skin stretched over some kind of iron cauldron. Horned beings like Zennor were pounding them with thighbones the same as the one McCoy had shown him.

"Jim," the doctor began.

Kirk turned. "What?"

"If you can't get me out of here and they light this up," McCoy said with great struggle, "use the phaser on me."

Anguish pushed at the backs of Kirk's eyes as he looked up and saw McCoy for the fullness of his character at that instant. McCoy hadn't asked him to open up on these creatures in order to get him out of here, to incinerate them in order to spare him incineration, never mind that a single phaser could easily do that. Hundreds could be killed in a single sweep, much more painlessly than the death they were offering the doctor now.

McCoy didn't want that. He'd take the death, but he wanted to make sure that his life was the only sacrifice and that, if there was still a chance for peace, he should die to smooth that path of possibility.

"Understood," Kirk accepted. Sympathy tightened his throat. "I promise."

Each knew a heavy price was being asked here, and a terrible guilt to be risked. The space between them was a cursed thing.

He stepped back, through the chanting circle of aliens, to where Zennor stood waiting, colossal in his own way, perhaps vile in the same way.

"You know I won't let them do this to him," Kirk said.

"Nor would I, were he mine," Zennor said. "There are customs."

Abruptly petulant, Kirk squared off in front of him. "Where I come from we have laws instead of customs to rule us. We have trials before we have punishment. What about that?"

30

## *The Patrian Transgression,* by Simon Hawke

One of my favorite Kirk scenes is from *The Patrian Transgression,* by Simon Hawke. The *Enterprise,* ordered to Patria to discuss possible Federation membership, discovered the apparent use of Klingon weaponry by rebels against the government in power. The *Enterprise* crew quickly learned that not all was as it seemed, and the Patrians had concealed the fact that their law was enforced by a telepathic police force who had the power to execute criminals—or potential criminals—without arrest, trial, or due process of law. They were at once investigators, judges, juries, and executioners.

In the following excerpt, Kirk risked death by accepting a challenge from a Patrian gladiator, and in so doing, learned some critical information about Patria. When I first read this passage, I could only think, "now, *this* is James T. Kirk." It is enormous fun.

IT WAS EASY TO GET CAUGHT UP IN THE EXCITEMENT OF THE MATCH, KIRK realized, but they were playing another, more dangerous game of their own. He could not afford to allow himself to be distracted. Anyone in the crowd could be a rebel terrorist. And in a place like this, an attack could come from anywhere, without warning.

Suddenly, in a bold move, Yalu parried a thrust from Barg and leaped toward the centrally positioned white tower. Barg, positioned once more on his own illuminated tower, turned to the center as Yalu leaped, but at the same time, Kalo executed a leap in the same direction, timing his jump perfectly so that he landed on the white tower at the same time as Yalu. Before Yalu could fully recover his balance, Kalo threw a hard body block into the startled challenger, knocking him backward off the tower, and in almost the same motion, he hurled his fighting staff, stunner tip first, at Barg. Caught completely by surprise, Barg was struck squarely in the chest by Kalo's thrown staff and there was a crackling discharge as the stunner tip made contact. Barg cried out and spasmed wildly, then lost his footing and toppled back into the crowd. The audience roared as the champion raised his arms over his head in victory.

"Fascinating," Spock said.

"Fascinating?" McCoy repeated. "You call that *fascinating?* If you ask me, it's barbaric!"

"Nevertheless, Doctor, it is a contest that involves speed, strength, agility, coordination, and quick thinking," Spock replied. "And no small degree of fighting skill. As such, I find it fascinating."

"It does get the blood up to watch such a competition," Chekov said.

"I believe it does at that, Mr. Chekov," Kirk admitted. "Lieutenant, I . . ." His voice trailed off as he saw the faces of the crowd all turning toward him, and he suddenly realized that the victorious champion, Kalo, was pointing at him and holding out his staff. "What's going on?" he asked.

"Interesting," Iano said. "I do believe you're being challenged, Captain."

*"What?"* McCoy said.

The spotlight struck their table. Kalo was looking straight at Kirk and beckoning to him. The crowd grew even more excited.

"Is this your doing?" McCoy asked Iano angrily.

Iano shook his head. "No. But you must admit it is an interesting development."

"Well, I've never been one to turn down a challenge," Kirk said, getting up.

"Jim! You're not seriously thinking of accepting?" McCoy said with alarm.

"Why not?" Kirk replied. "We came here to be noticed. And what better way to be noticed than to become the center of attention?"

"That man is a professional!" McCoy said. "A champion!"

Kirk smiled. "Oh, I don't think he'll hurt me, Bones. He's just making a gesture. And we are here to establish diplomatic relations, after all." He turned toward the champion, held up his hands in acknowledgment, and bowed slightly. "How do I get down there?"

As if in answer to his question, an attendant suddenly appeared at his side, beckoning him to follow.

"I think I had better go with you," Iano said, gazing at the crowd uneasily.

"No, Lieutenant, you stay here and keep an eye out," Kirk replied. "Mr. Spock will accompany me."

"Watch yourself," Iano said.

Kirk nodded. "I intend to."

Spock got up and they accompanied the attendant to the basement, where they were led to the bases of the towers and Kirk was given a fighting staff. He hefted it experimentally. It was a relatively simple device, weighted for balance. There were no controls of any sort. The stunner device at the tip was automatic, working on contact. The attendant beckoned him toward the entrance at the base of one of the towers. Kirk turned to Spock.

"As soon as I'm up there, get back up with the others," he said. "Keep your eyes open."

Spock nodded. "Be careful, Captain."

Kirk smiled. "I'll be all right. This will be a good opportunity to make some points for the Federation, show them we're good sports. But don't watch me. Keep your eyes on that crowd. I'm going to make a good target up there."

"I am aware of that, Captain," Spock replied.

"Right. Well . . . here goes."

He stepped into the tower, holding the staff upright by his side. The attendant pointed up. Kirk glanced up and suddenly felt himself launched through the hollow tube with a loud hiss of compressed air. A second later he came up through the open hatchway at the top, rising several feet above the tower as the crowd roared all around him. He looked down quickly and saw the hatch slide shut, then his momentum stopped and he began to drop. He landed lightly on top of the tower and looked around.

All the towers were now illuminated, though only he and the challenger stood upon them. The noise of the crowd was deafening. This was going to be a special treat for them. Their champion was going to fight a human, something they had never seen before. He glanced at Kalo.

The Patrian looked much bigger up close than he had from a distance. He was taller than Kirk by almost a foot, and powerfully built. He stood on his tower a short distance away, facing him, and held his staff out straight in front of him, across his body and parallel to the ground. Kirk took up the same position.

*"Ladies and gentlemen,"* the announcer said, *"in an unprecedented event, we are proud to present a special exhibition match! Captain Kirk, of the United Federation of Planets, commander of the* Starship Enterprise, *which is currently visiting our world for the purpose of establishing diplomatic relations with the Patrian Republics, versus the undisputed, undefeated champion of the arena games, the one and only, Zor Kalo!"*

The crowd went wild.

*"For the purpose of this special exhibition match, all the towers will remain illuminated,"* the announcer said. *"And out of deference to the Federation challenger, who is a stranger to our games, there will be a special time limit of three minutes. At the end of the elapsed time, the tone will sound, signaling the conclusion of the match. Are the competitors prepared to start?"*

33

Kirk turned toward the announcer's booth and nodded. Kalo simply held up his staff and shook it. Kirk smiled at the champion. Then the electronic tone sounded to signal the start of the match.

Kirk immediately crouched into a fighting stance. The champion attacked at once. He thrust his staff at Kirk, ball end first, and Kirk parried the thrust. Kalo immediately brought the staff around, twirling it impressively, and swept the stunner tip toward Kirk's body. Kirk executed a sideways parry, blocking it with his own staff. The crowd roared in appreciation.

Then the champion made a feint and suddenly vaulted from his tower to Kirk's, landing right in front of him. Startled, Kirk brought up his staff to block. Kalo locked staffs with him, bearing him down. The Patrian was astonishingly strong. The crowd shouted encouragement as the champion tried to force Kirk down. Their faces were only inches apart as Kirk strained against his opponent's strength.

"You are being lied to, human!" Kalo said. "Can you understand me?"

"What?" Kirk said, taken aback.

Kalo suddenly swept his feet out from under him and Kirk went down. Kalo raised his staff, stunner tip aimed at Kirk, and brought it down. Kirk rolled out of the way in the nick of time, coming close to the edge of the tower. He quickly shifted his grip on his staff and swung it hard, sweeping Kalo's feet out from under him with the ball end. Kalo went down and the crowd could not believe it. The champion had almost fallen! Kirk quickly scrambled to his feet and launched himself at Kalo.

The champion got up to his knees and brought up his staff to block Kirk's blow. Kirk pressed against his staff, trying to keep him from rising. "What did you say?"

"I said, you are being lied to," Kalo replied. No one could hear them above the roar of the crowd. Kirk could barely hear what the champion was saying. "Do not trust the police!"

Kalo suddenly twisted his staff, hooking Kirk's and throwing him off balance. Kirk staggered toward the edge of the tower. Then he felt Kalo's mace strike him in the back from behind. He grunted with the shock of the impact. The champion had not pulled his blow. Kirk found himself propelled toward the lip of the tower. Instead of fighting the momentum, he used it and leaped.

He landed on the green tower, recovered, and quickly turned to face the champion. Kalo was taking this thing seriously! Or was he? The Patrian was immensely strong, and it occurred to Kirk that he probably could have struck much harder. He could easily have

34

knocked him right into the crowd. Instead he had impelled him toward the other tower. And what did he mean about being lied to and not trusting the police?

As Kalo swung at him again, Kirk blocked the blow and struck one of his own. They stood near the edges of their towers, striking and parrying, to the immense enjoyment of the crowd, then Kalo vaulted to the purple tower. Kirk leaped at the same time he did, landing on the same tower and driving into him. They both went down, falling dangerously close to the edge.

"What do you mean, don't trust the police?" Kirk asked. "Who are you? Are you with the rebels?"

"You are being used!" Kalo said. "They are lying to you about the energy weapons! The underground is not to blame!"

Kalo brought his knee up hard into Kirk's stomach. The breath whooshed out of him as he doubled over, and Kalo regained his feet. He came at Kirk again, and Kirk just barely got his staff up in time to block the blow.

"Iano is a telepath!" Kalo said, his face inches from his. "He can read your thoughts! Be careful!"

"A telepath!" Kirk said. And then Kalo butted him with his head. Kirk staggered back, and Kalo reached out and caught him just as he was about to fall off the tower into the crowd below. He pulled Kirk toward him sharply.

"We have no quarrel with the Federation," he said. "You are our only hope!"

"But what about the disruptors?" Kirk asked. He drove his fist into Kalo's stomach. Kalo doubled over and pulled Kirk down with him. They both went down together.

"We have no such weapons!" Kalo gasped as he struggled to catch his breath.

"And the Klingons?"

"We have had no contact with them!"

"How do I know you're telling me the truth?" Kirk asked, breathing heavily.

"How do you know that Iano is?"

Kalo struck Kirk in the face and broke away from him. They both came up to their feet.

"We have to talk!" Kirk said.

"Too dangerous," Kalo replied.

"I can protect you!"

"And who shall protect you?"

Kalo feinted a jab, and when Kirk moved to block it, he reversed his staff and lightly tapped Kirk on the shoulder with its stunner tip. There was a crackling discharge and Kirk cried out as the shock went through him. Stunned, he dropped his staff and went down to his knees, clutching his shoulder.

Back at their table, the officers of the *Enterprise* tensed as they saw their captain go down. Spock noticed that Iano was staring at the two competitors intently. Suddenly, he spun around, rose to his feet quickly and, in one smooth motion, drew his weapon and fired. There was a loud, popping report, followed by a high-pitched whine as the projectile left the barrel of Iano's massive pistol. A man near the bar cried out as the shot took him in the chest, exploding and throwing him backward. People immediately started screaming and scrambling to get out of the way, in case there should be any further shooting. Immediately, Iano turned back toward the arena, but Kalo was nowhere in sight. Neither was Kirk.

McCoy was the first to react. "My God!" he said, and moved quickly to the side of the Patrian Iano had shot. He had not noticed that Kirk and Kalo had disappeared from the towers, but Spock was already out of his chair and running back toward the stairs leading to the basement. He had paused only long enough to tell Chekov to stay with McCoy, and then he was moving fast. He plunged down the stairs, unclipping his phaser from his belt as he pushed past one of the attendants and ran toward the entrance to the towers. Kirk was there, having his shoulder looked at by an attendant. Kalo was nowhere in sight.

"Captain!" Spock said with concern. "Are you all right?"

"I'm okay, Spock," Kirk replied. "I heard what sounded like a shot, and then the hatch opened up beneath me and I fell through. What happened?"

"Lieutenant Iano shot someone by the bar," Spock said. "Dr. McCoy is with him. What happened to Zor Kalo?"

"I don't know," Kirk said. "That was a pretty nasty shock. I couldn't see straight for a moment or two, and by the time I came around, Kalo was already gone. I'll be all right, but we'd better get back up there on the double."

They hurried back to the lounge area, where McCoy was crouching over the Patrian Iano had shot. He was putting away his medical kit. It was obvious that there was nothing he could do. The Patrian's chest was a mass of blood. Eyes bulging, McCoy got up and turned to Iano. "What did this man *do?*" McCoy demanded with disbelief.

"Take it easy, Bones," Kirk said, taking McCoy by the arm.

36

"Take it easy?" McCoy said. "Take it *easy?* He just shot this man down in cold blood!" He glared at Iano. "What kind of police officer *are* you? This man didn't *do* anything!"

"He was thinking about it, Doctor," Iano replied flatly.

McCoy simply stared at him with amazement. *"What?"*

Kirk alone understood Iano's reply, but he could scarcely believe it. Turning to the Patrian lawman, he repeated Iano's words, as if uncertain he had heard them correctly. "He was *thinking* about it?"

"That's right, Captain," Iano said. "He was thinking about committing murder."

"Murder?" McCoy replied with astonishment. "How could you possibly know that?"

"Lieutenant Iano knew because he is a telepath," said Spock.

*"What?"* McCoy said.

Iano's gaze met Spock's. "Yes, that is correct, Mr. Spock," he said. "As you had already surmised some time ago."

"You *knew* this?" Kirk asked him with surprise.

"I was not completely certain, Captain," Spock replied, "but I had strongly suspected it."

"You mean . . . the Patrians are *all* telepaths?" Chekov asked with astonishment.

"No, Mr. Chekov," Iano replied. "Not all of us. Only a few."

"A few who comprise an elite force of telepathic law enforcement agents," Spock said.

"A deduction based on intuition, Mr. Spock?" Iano said.

"Merely a logical inference, Lieutenant," Spock replied. "I am correct, am I not?"

"Yes," Iano said. "You are correct."

"Telepathic law enforcement agents?" McCoy said. *"Thought police?"*

"Telepath or no telepath, that doesn't give you the right to act as judge, jury, and executioner," Kirk said grimly.

"Quite the contrary, Captain," Iano replied. "I have precisely that right. The law specifically grants me that authority."

McCoy stared at Iano with disbelief. "You mean to tell me the law here allows you to *execute* a man simply because of what he's *thinking?"*

"According to Patrian law," Iano said, "intent constitutes transgression." He looked down at the body. "This man intended to commit murder."

"Whose murder?" Kirk demanded.

"Mine," Iano replied as he bent over and removed a pistol similar to his from the corpse's body. "I believe this is what you would call 'acting in self-defense.' What happened to Zor Kalo?"

"I don't know," Kirk replied.

Iano merely stared at him for a moment, then he said, "No, I see you don't. I think that I had best take you back to the legation. There is nothing more we can accomplish here tonight."

"I'd like some answers," Kirk said.

"To what?" Iano asked. "To the ludicrous claims of a fanatic? They are not worth discussing. The rebels were more clever than we thought, Captain. They used you for a distraction while they made an attempt on my life. It was not the first, and it shall not be last. And if I had died, then rest assured, you would have been next."

# CHAPTER 2

# Most Logical—Spock of Vulcan

MR. SPOCK, MY FAVORITE CHARACTER IN *STAR TREK*, WAS JAMES T. Kirk's best friend and one of the most interesting characters ever written for television. Spock was a Vulcan–human hybrid who struggled for many years with his dual heritage before he finally found peace through acceptance of both parts of his heritage. Leonard Nimoy showed us Spock's struggle and made Spock real through his elegantly understated performances.

Spock was a more mysterious character than James Kirk. His Vulcan reserve was hard to penetrate; he was cerebral and appeared to be emotionally distant. He analyzed every situation dispassionately, through logic. As a result, he occasionally appeared monstrously "inhuman" to his shipmates, particularly when he remained cool and logically analytical when someone had been brutally killed. His battles with Dr. McCoy were legendary, and if one listened only to the dialogue, one might have believed that they shared only dislike and disdain. Observant viewers, though, saw through both Spock's reserve and the war of words between him and McCoy, paying attention to body language and tone of voice. Such viewers saw the true depth of emotion Spock felt and the complexity of his friendships. Fans realized many years ago that Vulcans, including Spock, have emotions but seek to control them.

Although Spock was logical and reserved, he also was compassionate and caring. He respected life and avoided destroying living beings whenever possible. He had enormous respect for McCoy and absolute loyalty to Kirk. His journey toward fulfillment and self-acceptance was carried through the original three-year mission, into the films and up through *TNG.* Vejur's loneliness in *TMP* taught Spock the value of his contacts with his friends, and in *Star Trek II: The Wrath of Khan,* Spock made the ultimate sacrifice to save them. It was the logical thing to do, but it was also the most "human" thing to do. In the *TNG* episode "Unification," Spock risked his life to bring the teachings of Surak to Romulans, after respected careers as a Starfleet officer and an ambassador. Spock's story is not over yet.

One of the empty spaces calling to be filled by novelists was Spock's life after Star Trek VI, particularly his decision to enter the diplomatic service and eventually go to Romulus. Spock gave up so much to build his Starfleet career, including nearly destroying his relationship with his father. The ultimate question, then, was what led Spock to his Romulan journey? What prompted him to give up his life in the Federation and undertake the mission to bring the teachings of Surak to Romulans? *Vulcan's Forge,* by Josepha Sherman and Susan Shwartz, answered many of these questions.

## *Vulcan's Forge,* by Josepha Sherman & Susan Shwartz

I was privileged to be the first fan reader of *Vulcan's Forge,* and what a privilege it was! *Vulcan's Forge,* the quintessential Spock story, is my favorite Star Trek novel. I love this book! The love the authors have for Spock comes through on every page. They understand Spock and Sarek, the difficult relationship between son and father, and how Amanda felt about both of them. They appreciate how difficult it was for Sarek to reject Spock for his choice of careers and the impact it had on the entire family. They understand the pain endured by the young Spock from being of two worlds yet not comfortable in either.

*Vulcan's Forge* tells two stories, each with galactic implications. Each is the story of Spock's desert trek with a human, David Rabin, who became Spock's first human friend. In the later story, set about a year after Kirk's reported death on the *Enterprise* B, Spock served as captain of the science vessel *Intrepid II* on its shakedown cruise. Commander Uhura was Spock's first officer, and McCoy his chief medical officer. Many former *Enterprise* crewmembers served on *Intrepid II,* and all still grieved from the loss of Kirk. Spock handled his captaincy well, although he was still searching to find his own style.

*Intrepid II* was called to the planet Obsidian by Starfleet Captain David Rabin, head of the Starfleet mission on Obsidian, where mysterious events and sabotage were interfering with the outpost's attempts to make life better for the planet's inhabitants. Obsidian, a protectorate of the Federation near Romulan space, was a harsh desert planet with an erratic sun, and its people were dying. Spock knew and trusted Rabin from his boyhood on Vulcan, when he and Rabin became friends during a difficult trek across the fierce Vulcan desert. Shortly after arrival on Obsidian, Spock, McCoy, and Rabin took a party in a shuttlecraft to investigate the sabotage and became victims of a sandstorm. Spock and Rabin then set out across the Obsidian desert to search for water and assistance, and they found adventure, Romulans, and the answers to their questions.

Spock's experiences in the attack on Vulcan and what he learned on his youthful journey across Vulcan's Forge with David Rabin led to his decision to enter Starfleet. Similarly, the struggle on Obsidian against the Romulan incursion and its relationship to the Romulan attack on Vulcan many years before prompted Spock to reconsider his life's path. What he learned in his second desert journey with David Rabin led to his decision to leave Starfleet to walk the path of his father and eventually work for reunification with the Romulans. *Vulcan's Forge* is nothing less than Spock's personal journey toward his own best destiny.

Romulans are the primary villains of *Vulcan's Forge,* and these Romulans were written in the tradition of the Romulan commanders, from "Balance of Terror" and "The *Enterprise* Incident." These Romulans, like Mark Lenard's Commander in "Balance of Terror" had an agenda antagonistic to the Federation, but most acted with an honor of their own based on their own warrior code.

The following passage from *Vulcan's Forge* shows the first meeting of Spock and David Rabin as boys, really, young men, at a ceremony honoring Vulcan boys who have survived the difficult *kahs-wan* ordeal. (I was much amused by David Rabin's pointed and audacious questions about Vulcan girls and how they are honored, having wondered the same thing myself!) A treacherous Romulan attack interrupted the ceremony, and in its aftermath, David and Spock found themselves on their difficult journey across Vulcan's Forge.

*Vulcan, Mount Seleya*
*Day 6, Seventh Week of Tasmeen, Year 2247*

DAWN HOVERED OVER MOUNT SELEYA. A HUGE *SHAVOKH* GLIDED DOWN on a thermal from the peak, balanced on a wingtip, then soared out toward the desert. Spock heard its hunting call.

*Where it stoops, one may find ground water or a soak not too deeply buried,* Spock recalled from his survival training. He had no need of such information now. Nevertheless, his gaze followed the creature's effortless flight.

The stairs that swept upward to the narrow bridge still lay in shadow. Faint mist rose about the mountain, perhaps from the snow that capped it, alone of Vulcan's peaks, or perhaps from the lava that bubbled sullenly a thousand meters below. Soon, 40 Eridani A would rise, and the ritual honoring Spock and his agemates would begin.

It was illogical, Spock told himself, for him to assume that all eyes were upon him as he followed his parents. Instead, he concentrated on his parents' progress. Sustained only by the light touch of Sarek's fingers upon hers, veiled against the coming sunrise, Amanda crossed the narrow span as if she had not conquered her fear of the unrailed bridge only after long meditation.

Few of the many participants from the outworld scientific, diplomatic, and military enclaves on Vulcan could equal her grace. Some had actually arranged to be flown to the amphitheater just to allow them to bypass the bridge that had served as a final defense for the warband that had ruled here in ancient days. Others of the guests crossed unsteadily or too quickly for dignity.

Vertigo might be a reasonable assumption, Spock thought, for beings acclimating themselves to Vulcan's thin air or the altitude of the bridge.

"The air is the air," one of his agemates remarked in the tone of one quoting his elders. "I have heard these *humans* take drugs to help them breathe."

All of the boys eyed the representatives from the Federation as if they were xenobiological specimens in a laboratory. Especially, they surveyed the officials' sons and daughters, who might, one day, be people with whom they would study and work.

"They look sickly," the same boy spoke. His name, Spock recalled, was Stonn. Not only was he a distant kinsman to Sered, he was one of the youths who also eyed Spock as if he expected Spock's human blood to make him fall wheezing to his knees, preferably just when he was supposed to lead his agemates up to the platform where T'Lar and T'Pau would present them with the hereditary—and now symbolic—weapons of their Great Houses. By slipping out early into the desert to undergo his *kahs-wan* ordeal before the others, Spock had made himself forever Eldest among the boys of his year. It was not logical that some, like Stonn, would not forgive him for his presumption, or his survival; but it was so.

A woman's voice provided a welcome interruption. "Let's assume your tricorder is broken or missing—*David, don't lean over like that or you'll give me a heart attack!* Your tricorder's crashed, and you have to calculate how long it'll take you to hit the lava down there and turn into shish kebab. Say it's a thousand-meter drop."

*One thousand point five nine,* Spock corrected automatically, but in silence.

"Remember, you'll have to account for less air resistance; the air's thinner. Get *back,* no, you're not stretching out flat on the bridge, and you can't see the lava from here! I gave you an assignment, David!"

From the corner of his eye, Spock could see a woman in the glittering uniform of a Starfleet captain tug a boy who resembled her back from the edge of the bridge. Allowing for variations in species and body type, the human youth seemed close to his own age—perhaps a little old for such brusque treatment, although he seemed amused rather than annoyed. He had courage, if not judgment, Spock decided. If it were not that emotion was impermissible at any time and completely unacceptable this morning so close to the Shrine, Spock might have envied the boy his excited grin and that eager gaze darting from Mount Seleya's peak to the bridge and the desert.

He might also, were emotion not unacceptable, have envied the way the Starfleet officer, clearly his mother, did not rebuke her son with a politeness that would be worse than any human rage, but instead distracted him with mathematics.

Almost absently, Spock solved the simple equation, then estimated how long it would take the Terran boy to produce a reasonably correct solution. The answer came within the parameters he had set: a sign of quick intelligence in the human.

"That's better," said the Starfleet captain. "Believe me, David, if you don't settle down, I've got more snap quizzes where that one came from. I know you're excited about seeing Vulcan—"

"Aren't you?" the boy countered. "I mean, look at that *desert!* It makes Sinai National Preserve look like a sandbox!"

Fascinating. Even Spock's mother did not speak of the deserts that occupied much of her adopted world with such admiration.

"David, I swear, someone spiked your tri-ox with adrenaline."

The tri-ox compound did, Spock mused, sometimes have such an effect on some already excitable humans. But he was too intrigued by this show of blatant emotion to comment.

"Calm down!" the woman was ordering. "Before we return to Earth, I may be able to arrange a field trip. But not if you create an interstellar incident."

That sparked a wry grin from the boy but no repentance, and his mother sighed and continued, "Once you actually start at the Academy, you'll learn how important diplomacy is for a Starfleet officer—even one who plans to be an explorer."

"Yes, ma'am." The boy subsided, tugging at his close-fitting formal tunic, so much less suitable for Vulcan's heat than Spock's loose, dark robe with its embossed metallic heir's sigils.

Lecturing offspring seemed to be a constant among all sentient beings, Spock observed.

Then he had to force himself not to start. Not fifty meters away stood Sered, in a more formal version of the austere brown robe he had worn for his visit to Sarek's house. The robe bore the bronze symbols that denoted Head of House, but he had chosen the most archaic forms of the complex glyphs. Intriguing.

"We shall pause here, my wife," murmured Sarek to Amanda. He added, "Captain Rabin." The ambassador had not raised his impeccably modulated voice, but the captain turned and came to . . . *military attention,* Spock knew from his studies, although he had never actually seen the posture before.

"Ambassador Sarek."

"Do you find your stay on Vulcan instructive?"

The Starfleet officer's face was impassive. "My highest function is to strengthen the figurative bridge—like the literal one we just crossed—between your world and mine. My assignment honors me."

Remarkable. Her son had achieved stillness, if not her military bearing.

"You do your service justice, Captain. My wife, may I present Starfleet Captain Nechama Rabin, from the planet of your birth? Captain, this is the Lady Amanda, my wife."

Amanda, who had courteously raised her light veil, somehow managed to seem taller and more stately than the woman who snipped roses in a wet-planet conservatory and admitted to worrying about the son whom she lectured. "Shalom, Captain," she said, hand raised in the Vulcan greeting.

"Live long and prosper, Lady Amanda." The two human women studied each other for an instant, then smiled.

"Peace and prosperity," said Lady Amanda. "Could we have better greetings between compatriots on such a fine morning?"

"Let us hope," Sarek took up her words, "that such greetings extend as well to . . . friends."

With a raised eyebrow, he acknowledged the captain's son. Sered,

Spock noted, stood all this while as if paralyzed by *le-matya* venom, watching. *My father delivers an object lesson,* Spock realized.

"May I present my son, David?" asked the captain. "He enters Starfleet Academy next year."

"Another generation of service?" Sarek said. "Highly commendable."

Spock knew that Sarek, like most Vulcans, held the military in low esteem. Did diplomacy require the speaking of lies? No, Sarek had said that "service" was laudable; he had said nothing of its type. And his approval drove home his "lesson" to Sered: Sarek favored both today's ceremony and the invitation of Federation representatives.

The boy stepped forward fearlessly (*Of course,* Spock thought), looking up into Sarek's keen eyes, then raised his hand in the proper salute. "I am honored, sir." His Old High Vulcan formal greeting was hesitant, but correctly phrased; he had even mastered the glottal stop. "I also thank you for the opportunity to witness this ceremony."

Sarek managed without the slightest change in expression or posture to register his approval. "It has its parallels in the customs of your own people, does it not?"

His father was being positively expansive to this stranger! *Jealousy,* Spock reminded himself, *is an emotion. A perilous one. Why should he not be polite to a visitor?*

Spock wasn't the only one who had noticed. He saw Sered's expression alter in a way that would have been imperceptible to a human, but to a Vulcan looked as blatant as a grimace of revulsion. *Contempt is an emotion as well,* Spock thought. Then the tall, austere Vulcan vanished into the crowd.

"Yes, sir," David was continuing. "Boys undergo a ritual that confirms them as adults. But not just boys. What about . . ."

Captain Rabin's hand came down firmly upon her son's shoulder, cutting off what Spock was certain would have been a most revealing question. "My son has completed advanced desert survival training, Ambassador Sarek. All morning, he has told me how magnificent he finds the view. He is hoping for an opportunity to visit the Forge."

It seemed that humans knew the art of using words as a diversion as well.

Sarek dipped his head a polite fraction. "A most feasible ambition, David. Captain Rabin, with your permission, I shall have one of my aides arrange an excursion."

No mention was made of including Spock. Again he warned himself against emotion. Against jealousy. And almost succeeded.

David visibly *glowed*. He glanced over at Spock, who kept his face impassive.

"We have presumed upon your time, sir," said Captain Rabin. "I know you must be eager to see . . . your son?" She raised an eyebrow inquiringly at the ambassador. ". . . welcomed into the ranks of adult Vulcan males."

"Spock," Sarek introduced him briefly. Spock bowed in silence.

Was Captain Rabin disconcerted by the brusqueness? "Lady Amanda, my congratulations," she said carefully.

"We are very proud of Spock," Amanda replied, just as carefully.

With a noncommittal smile, the captain withdrew, towing a reluctant David as though he were a much younger child. He, giving up the struggle for dignity, left trailing questions. "Do you think they'd let him go with me? I'd love to talk with a Vulcan my age. Who else would come? You know, everyone's talking about Vulcan boys. What about *girls?*"

Lady Amanda's shoulders shook almost imperceptibly. Captain Rabin stopped in her tracks. "I tell you what, David. Ask that question, which probably breaks every privacy code the Vulcans have—and they've got *plenty*—create your interplanetary scandal, and you can forget seeing the Forge. In fact, it would be a wonder if we weren't kicked off Vulcan."

"But what *about* girls?" he whispered, clearly forgetting about keen Vulcan hearing. "It's not as though they were secondary citizens. I mean, what about T'Pau? She's important enough, isn't she? Yes, and what about T'Lar of—of Gol?"

The captain's expression changed to what Spock's mother called her "give me strength" face, used when her patience was severely tried. "Will you please stop thinking about Vulcan girls? They probably all have dates for Saturday night anyway."

David flushed. "Mother, please. You know I wasn't talking about that. And you mean you approve—"

"Look, son," said Nechama Rabin. "As you just lectured me, T'Lar of Gol and T'Pau will be honoring these boys. Is it logical to assume that they, as women, would slight girls—who one day may grow up to be Elders themselves?"

"But we don't know—"

"And aren't likely to. Before you ask, I am *not* about to try to find out. And neither are you. Now, *quiet* or you go back to Base. This is not, incidentally, your mother speaking. This is the captain. Understood, mister?"

"Aye-aye," said the boy. Spock suspected he would behave appropriately now—until his next attack of "why." But surely there was nothing improper about an inquiring mind! It would be interesting to speak with this Terran who shared a trait with him that—

But Sarek would probably not allow his son to risk exposure to human emotionalism by learning more about this boy or any of the others.

A deferential three paces behind his parents and two to the side of Sarek, Spock strode past a series of deeply incised pits—the result of laser cannon fire two millennia back—and up to the entrance of the amphitheater. Two masked guards bearing ceremonial *lirpa* presented arms before his father, then saluted Spock for the first time as an adult. For all his attempts at total control, he felt a little shiver race through him as he returned the salutes as an adult for the first time. The clublike weights that formed the *lirpa* bases shone, a luster of dark metal. The dawn light flashed red on the blades that the guards carried over their shoulders. At the guards' hips, they wore stone-hilted daggers, but no energy weapons—*phasers*—such as a Starfleet officer might wear on duty. Of course, no such weapons might be brought here.

Lady Amanda removed her fingers from her husband's and smiled faintly. "I shall join the other ladies of our House now, my husband, while you bring our son before the Elders. Spock, I shall be watching for you. And I am indeed *very* proud."

*As,* her gaze told him, *is your father.*

She glided away, a grace note among the taller Vulcans.

Spock fell into step with his father, head high, as if his blood bore no human admixture. *As it was in the beginning* . . . Silently, he reviewed the beginning of the Chant of Generations as he glided down the stairs.

Long ago, some cataclysm or some unspeakable weapon had peeled half the face of the mountain away, leaving only a ridge above the crater that had been shaped into a natural amphitheater. Beneath this roof was a platform from which two pillars reared up. Centered between the pillars stood an altar of dark stone on which rested the greatest treasures of each Great House on Vulcan: ceremonial swords, of which Spock and his agemates would receive replicas.

*We are trained to abhor violence. Yet, we are taught combat and, to honor us, we are awarded archaic weapons. This is not logical.*

None of the other boys accompanying their fathers seemed to have such reservations. The Federation guests simply watched, the adults clearly impressed, the youngsters honestly openmouthed. Sered,

Spock thought, would no doubt think that awe was a highly appropriate reaction.

Behind the pillars glistened a pool, ruddy with 40 Eridani A's dawn. To either side of the pillars, dark-robed students of the disciplines of Gol stepped forward to shake frameworks of bells. Another, whose robes bore the sigil of a third-degree adept, swung a great mallet at a hexagonal gong so ancient that its precious iron central boss had turned deep red. Again, the bells rang, dying into a whisper and a rustle.

Everyone in the amphitheater rose. T'Lar, adept and First Student, walked onto the platform. Then, two guards, their *lirpa* set aside for the purpose, entered with a curtained carrying chair. From it, robed in black, but with all the crimsons of the dawn in her brocaded overrobe, stepped T'Pau. She leaned on an intricately carved stick.

Spock's father stepped forward as if to help her.

"Thee is kind, Sarek," said the Elder of their House, "but thee is premature. When I can no longer preside unassisted over this rite, it will be time to release my *katra.*"

Sarek bowed. "I ask pardon for my presumption."

"Courtesy," T'Pau held up a thin, imperious hand, "is never presumptuous." Her long eyes moved over the people in the amphitheater as if delivering some lesson of her own—but to whom? Carefully, she approached the altar and bowed to T'Lar. "Eldest of All, I beg leave to assist thee."

"You honor me," replied T'Lar.

"I live to serve," said T'Pau, an observation that would have left Spock gasping had he not been getting sufficient oxygen.

Both women bowed, this time to the youths who stood waiting their presentation.

Again, the adept struck the gong.

T'Lar raised both arms, the white and silver of her sleeves falling like great wings. *"As it was in the beginning, so shall it always be. These sons of our House have shown their worthiness . . ."*

"I protest!" came a shout from the amphitheater.

Even the Vulcans murmured what would have been astonishment in any other people as Sered, his heavy robes swinging about him, strode down the center aisle to stand before the altar.

"I protest," he declared, "the profanation of these rites. I protest the way they have been stripped of their meaning, contaminated as one might pollute a well in the desert. I protest the way our deepest mysteries have been revealed to *outsiders.*"

48

T'Pau's eyebrows rose at that last word, which was in the seldom-used invective mode.

"Has thee finished?" asked T'Lar. Adept of *Kolinahr,* she would remain serene if Mount Seleya split along its many fissures and this entire amphitheater crumbled into the pit below.

"No!" Sered cried, his voice sharp as the cry of a *shavokh.* "Above all, I protest the inclusion of an outsider in our rites—yes, as leader of the men to be honored today—when other and worthier men, our exiled cousins, go unhonored and unrecognized."

Sarek drew deep, measured breaths. *He prepares for combat,* Spock realized, and was astonished to feel his own body tensing, alert, aware as he had only been during his *kahs-wan,* when he had faced a full-grown *le-matya* in the deep desert and knew, logically, he could not survive such an encounter. *Fight or flight,* his mother had once called it. That too was a constant across species. *But not here. There must not be combat here.*

"Thee speaks of those who exiled themselves, Sered." Not the slightest trace of emotion tinged T'Pau's voice. "Return lies in their power, not in ours."

"So it does!" Sered shouted. "And so they do!"

He tore off his austere robe. Gasps of astonishment and hisses of outrage sounded as he stood forth in the garb of a Captain of the Hosts from the ancient days. Sunlight picked out the metal of his harness in violent red and exploded into rainbow fire where it touched the gem forming the grip of the ancient energy weapon Sered held—a weapon he had brought, against all law, into Mount Seleya's amphitheater.

"Welcome our lost kindred!" he commanded and gestured as if leading a charge.

A rainbow shimmer rose about the stage. *Transporter effect,* Spock thought even as it died, leaving behind six tall figures in black and silver. At first glance they were as much like Sered as brothers in their mother's womb. But where Sered wore his rage like a cloak of ceremony, these seemed accustomed to emotion and casual violence.

For an instant no one moved, the Vulcans too stunned by this glaring breach of custom, the Federation guests not sure what they were permitted to do. Then, as the intruders raised their weapons, the amphitheater erupted into shouts and motion. From all sides, the guards advanced, holding their *lirpa* at a deadly angle. But *lirpa* were futile against laser rifles.

As the ceremonial guard was cut down, Sarek whispered quick, urgent words to other Vulcans. They nodded. Spock sensed power summoned and joined:

"Now!" whispered the ambassador.

In a phalanx, the Vulcans rushed the dais. They swept across it, bearing T'Pau and T'Lar with them. They, at least, were safe. Only one remained behind. Green blood puddled from his ruined skull, seeping into the dark stone where no blood had flowed for countless generations.

"You dare rise up against me?" Sered shrilled. "One sacrifice is not enough to show the lesser worlds!" He waved his weapon at the boys, at the gorgeously dressed Federation guests. "Take them! We shall make these folk of lesser spirit *crawl.*"

Spock darted forward, not sure what he could do, knowing only that it was not logical to wait meekly for death. And these intruders were not mindless *le-matyas!* They were kindred, of Vulcan stock; surely they could be reasoned with—

As Sered could not. Spock faltered at the sight of the drawn features, the too-bright eyes staring beyond this chaos to a vision only Sered could see: Few Vulcans ever went insane, but here was true madness. Surely his followers, though, clearly Vulcan's long-lost cousins, would not ally themselves with such insanity!

Desperately calm, Spock raised his hand in formal greeting. Surak had been slain trying to bring peace: if Spock fell thus, at least his father would have final proof that he was worthy to be the ambassador's son.

They suddenly seemed to be in a tense little circle of calm. One of the "cousins" pointed at him, while a second nodded, then gestured out into the chaos around them. The language had greatly changed in the sundered years, but Spock understood:

*"This one."*

*"Him."*

*It may work. They may listen to me. They—*

"Get back, son!" a Starfleet officer shouted, racing forward, phaser in outstretched hand, straight at Sered. "Drop that weapon!"

Sered threw back his head. He actually laughed. Then, firing at point-blank range, reflexes swifter than human, he shot the man. The human flared up into flame so fierce that the heat scorched Spock's face and the veils slipped across his eyes, blurring his sight. He blinked, blinked again to clear it, and saw the conflagration that had been a man flash out of existence.

*Dead. He's dead. A moment ago alive, and now—*Spock stared at

Sered across the small space that had held a man, his mind refusing to process what he'd just seen. "Half-blood," muttered Sered. "Weakling shoot of Surak's house. But you will serve—"

"Got him!" came a shout. David Rabin hurled himself into Sered, bringing them both down. The weapon flew from Sered's hand, and Captain Rabin and Sered both scrambled for it. The woman touched it, Sered knocked her hand aside—

And the weapon slid right to Spock. He snatched it up, heart racing faster than a proper Vulcan should permit, and pointed it at Sered.

"Can you kill a brother Vulcan?" Sered hissed, unafraid, from where he lay. "Can you?"

Could he? For an endless moment, Spock froze, seeing Sered's fearless stare, feeling the weapon in his hand. Dimly he was aware of the struggle all around him as the invaders grabbed hostages, but all he could think was that all he need do was one tiny move, only the smallest tightening of a finger—

*Can you kill a brother Vulcan?*

He'd hesitated too long. What felt like half of Mount Seleya fell on him. Spock thought he heard his father saying, *Exaggeration. Remember your control.*

Then the fierce dawn went black.

## *Time for Yesterday,* by Ann Crispin

Perhaps it was because Spock was so emotionally unapproachable that he became a romantic figure; episodes in which he succumbed to relationships with women were especially popular. "All Our Yesterdays" remains a fan favorite largely because of Spock's passionate involvement with the lovely Zarabeth. Because Spock and McCoy had been transported 100,000 years in the past, to a time when Vulcans were primitive and barbaric, Spock lost his normal control and reacted quite emotionally to Zarabeth. Years later, in *Yesterday's Son,* by Ann Crispin, Spock learned that he and Zarabeth had a son, Zar, as a result of that tempestuous union. *Yesterday's Son* was very popular and was followed by another story involving Zar, *Time for Yesterday.*

In *Time for Yesterday,* Kirk, Spock, and McCoy were forced to seek Zar in the distant past for his help in communicating with the Guardian of Forever to save the galaxy and perhaps the entire universe. After the universe was saved and Zar had returned to his own time, Spock followed him back into the past to save his life, a move that was highly emotional and, of course, highly logical as well, as seen here.

SPOCK MATERIALIZED OUT OF NOTHINGNESS ON A ROCKY, BRUSH-COVERED slope between two gigantic gray boulders. The Vulcan glanced around him, then gave a short, satisfied nod—the Guardian had, as requested, deposited him in the foothills bordering Moorgate Plain. He wanted to survey the battlefield from a higher elevation, in an attempt to locate Zar's position. He knew where his son *ought* to be—but that was no guarantee that he was there. The Sovren had planned to personally lead the first wave of reinforcement troops, so he could be anywhere along the front lines.

Spock had no difficulty locating the battle itself, even though he could not see it.

In the first place, he could hear it—the clang of weapons, the shrieks of wounded people and animals, war-cries filled with terror or triumph—even from some distance away, it was an appalling din, and the closer he drew, the more ear-shattering it became.

But the sound, horrible as it was, was as nothing compared to the smell—the mingled stench of blood, excrement, vomit, and death. The Vulcan nearly gagged the first time he rounded a boulder and almost stambled over the sprawled body of a soldier, guts trailing behind him for meters, who was covered in a living curtain of insects that rose, buzzing angrily, from their feast.

He swallowed hard, clenching his teeth. Clamping down iron control, Spock stepped around the body and moved on, holding his *lirpa* at the ready.

He emerged from the foothills at the lower edge of the plain, not far from the Redbank, and for a moment stood staring in horror at the battleground before him. Moorgate Plain was a roiled sea of mud, smashed chariots, and bodies—animal and human, living and dead.

Spock had seen war and its results; had picked his way through colonies devastated by Klingon or Romulan attack, had ministered to dull-eyed refugees who were literally more dead than alive. But war in his time was usually cleaner. Phasers and disruptors killed instantly, neatly vaporizing the bodies.

The main fighting was still some distance ahead of him, near the mountain pass leading to New Araen. Storm clouds shouldered their way over the peak of Big Snowy as Spock began trotting toward the conflict, constantly scanning the horizon for a certain hillock, one forever fixed in his memory.

Often, he had to slow to a walk, trying to pick a way through the maze of caved-in pits, spilled entrails, gutted bodies, and weapons, some still clutched in severed hands or arms.

Whenever possible, he detoured around the bodies, but in places they were piled waist- and even shoulder-high, and he was forced to use the buffeting end of the *lirpa* to roll enough of them out of the way so he could step over them.

And the worst of it was, not all of them were dead.

"I'm sorry," he murmured, the first time an armored figure clawed at his boot, begging for water. Her shoulder was a hacked ruin. "I'm sorry, but I don't have any."

He moved on, trying not to hear them. But it was impossible. *"Water,"* they pleaded or demanded, mostly, and sometimes, *"help me,"* or *"kill me."* Some spoke in languages he did not know, but he understood their meaning anyway.

One wounded man, maddened by pain, lunged at the Vulcan with a halberd, and Spock had to use the *lirpa* to knock him aside.

He was getting closer to the battle; the clang of weapons was louder, mixed now with the gathering rumble of thunder. And still he had not identified the little rise where Zar would fall.

Or had fallen.

Or was even now falling.

The Vulcan tried to go faster, slipping and skidding in the greasy muck that seemed to be composed of equal parts mud and spilled blood. It didn't help that the blood was almost the color of his own.

He found that he had to check some of the little hills from several different angles, which slowed him down further. *I may be too late . . . even now, I may be too late . . .*

He was on the fringes of the fighting now, and several times had to defend himself for a moment before he could run. But he was not wearing armor, and offered no challenge, so most of the combatants simply ignored him.

*Which hill? There are so many. I'm on the side of the field where Zar was supposed to be directing the Lakreo forces, but suppose he crossed over to the other side? Am I too late?*

Spock could tell that Zar's forces were being driven back, but the retreat was controlled, orderly. *The Lakreo and Danreg forces are inflicting heavy damage. If they can hold out long enough, they stand a chance of winning.*

He staggered and slid in the muck, catching himself with the *lirpa. Which hill? They all look the same!*

As he stared, a voice echoed in his mind: *Straight ahead. Hurry.*

Such was the ring of authority in those warm, ringing tones that the Vulcan began to obey, even before he recognized the identity of the mind touch.

*The Guardian! But how can it know?*

Still, he had no other guide, so he forged straight ahead, running hard now.

*Which way, Guardian?* he thought, as he passed another hillock, his breath catching fire in his chest.

*To your left. Hurry. Hurry.*

Spock bore left, trying to pick up his pace despite the rocks underfoot. He was in the midst of the front lines, but, strangely, many of the troops in this portion of the field were not fighting. Instead, knots of soldiers from both sides huddled in small groups with their comrades, staring up at one of the little hills. Spock zig-zagged around them, anxiously scanning the ground to his left—*nothing . . . nothing, am I too late?*

*There! The one they're all staring at! That's the one!*

Unwrapping the *ahn-woon* from around his waist, Spock dropped the *lirpa* and raced toward the hillock he'd recognized, putting on a burst of speed that made his heart feel as if it were about to explode. He could hear shouts of encouragement and the sounds of a struggle as he reached its foot, then, as he began to climb, all sounds abruptly ceased.

Gasping, the Vulcan scrambled the last few meters, finding himself on the edge of a circle of warriors. An armed figure stood in the middle of that circle, dripping sword up and ready, clutching a small, battered shield. Spock could not see the man's face, but from his stance and his chain mail, the Vulcan recognized Zar. A blood-drenched body lay sprawled at his feet. Spock heard his son call out a phrase in a language he did not recognize, then the Sovren pivoted slowly around.

As Zar's back appeared, Spock glimpsed a flash of movement to his own left—one of the Asyri warriors leaped forward, axe raised high, his movement the same as the one the Vulcan had witnessed on the screen of his tricorder.

"No!" The Vulcan knocked startled enemy soldiers aside as though they were straw men, and lunged after the Asyri. With every bit of skill he had in him, Spock lashed out with the *ahn-woon,* his target the warrior's raised weapon—and *missed.*

The *ahn-woon* whipped around the man's neck, instead, and even as the Vulcan jerked back on it, the flat of the axehead impacted with the Sovren's red-plumed helmet. The blow echoed in Spock's mind, as he saw Zar half whirled around with its force, glimpsed his son's bloody face, heard him grunt as the breath went out of him.

Zar's knees buckled . . . he fell forward . . . to lie, unmoving.

A dreadful calm settled over Spock. *I've failed. To come this close and fail . . .*

Absently, he looked down at the man he had pulled down, seeing that he was dead. The body was still twitching, but the Asyri's neck was obviously broken.

*I did not intend to kill him* . . . Spock thought, dully, but he could not summon any remorse for his action.

The handle of the *ahn-woon* slid out of his numb fingers, and he left it where it fell. Blindly, the Vulcan pushed his way through the Lakreo troops that were suddenly milling about, crowding the top of the little hillock.

As he reached the sprawled figure, Spock saw the dent in the right side of the battered steel helmet. He dropped to his knees beside his son's still body, and, gently but hopelessly, rolled him over onto his back. The face that came into view was a gory greenish mask, the right eye puffed nearly shut, the mouth split, the nose swollen and canted. Blood trickled from one nostril in a thin, steady stream . . .

Blood trickled . . .

Blood *trickled* . . .

Spock stared unbelievingly at the blood, watching it well, then drip—

*If he's bleeding, he's still alive!*

Hastily, he slipped a finger beneath the edge of Zar's helmet and touched his temple. He sensed the low-level mental activity even as he felt the pulse—weak and thready, but there! He put a hand over his son's mouth and nose, and after a moment, warm breath brushed his palm.

A gauntleted hand seized his wrist and yanked it away, even as a voice snapped, "What the hell do you think you're—"

Spock looked up, seeing that it was Cletas who had grabbed him. The Second stared at him, then let go. "I'm sorry, sir. I didn't realize who you were."

"He's alive," Spock said, reaching for his tricorder.

"Yes, I see," Cletas agreed, crouching on his heels beside the Vulcan. "Dead men don't bleed."

"We have to take him to safety." Spock glanced up, to find Voba kneeling across from them. He studied the tricorder's readings. "Concussion . . . possibly serious. He could go into shock, especially with the ground this cold and damp. We'll need a stretcher."

Voba snapped out an order to one of the Lakreo guards, and the woman saluted, then raced off.

*I had better get that armor off so he can breathe,* the Vulcan thought. He began fumblingly to unfasten Zar's helmet, but the red-haired aide-de-camp gently pushed his hand away. "I'll do that, sir. I'm used to it."

"So much for the prophecy," Cletas muttered, glancing at the troops milling around them. "Damn it all, we were holding them . . ." he began swearing, a profane litany in a language Spock didn't understand.

"What prophecy?" the Vulcan asked.

Cletas busied himself helping Voba unlace the sides of the Sovren's byrnie. "Wynn's oracle," he said, distractedly. "She pronounced it to the enemy troops the afternoon before we captured her—'if he who is halt walks healed, if he who is death-struck in battle rises whole, then Ashmara will turn her face from us'—meaning that, unless he wakes up and walks out there, we've had it. If our troops think he's dead—and the word that he's fallen will be spreading like wildfire, it always does—that's going to take the spirit right out of them. The invaders will run over us like the Redbank in flood."

"'If he who is halt . . .'" Spock repeated, slowly. "But half the prophecy has already been fulfilled. Zar is no longer lame."

"Right enough," Voba said, "but now he's got to stand up and walk out there, where they can all see him . . . and there's no way that's going to happen—even if he lives, he'll not be on his feet for days."

Spock, his mind racing, thought of the silently staring faces, defender and invader alike, and an idea came to him. The Vulcan met Cletas's gaze squarely. "Suppose he *does* stand up and walk out there?"

"But he—" The Second's eyes widened as sudden understanding flowed between them like a current. *"Yes!* By Ashmara, it could work!" He turned his head and shouted, "Guards! Guards! Stand close, here, shoulder to shoulder. On the double! I want a complete circle."

Quickly, they were surrounded, walled in, by soldiers. Cletas snatched up the blood-smeared helm. "Here, put this on. No—wait, you'll need mail first. Nobody will notice the breeches, but the mail—"

With frantic haste, he began ripping at the lacings of his own byrnie. "Voba, where's his red cloak?"

"I have it," the little aide said, calmly.

The Second dragged his byrnie, then his padded undergarment, over his head. Cletas shivered as fat raindrops spattered onto his bare shoulders. "Put this on. Don't bother lacing, you'll have the cloak to cover it. Here." He thrust the mail shirt and the quilted leather at the Vulcan.

Spock pulled the shirt, followed by the byrnie, over his head. He rose to his feet, feeling the unaccustomed weight of the armor settle onto his shoulders. "How should I do this?"

"Just stand there on the hillside and let them notice you," Cletas said, pointing, holding out the battered helmet. "Then take off the helm and let them see your face. The cloak, Voba."

The aide swung the red folds around Spock's shoulders. "You're thinner," Cletas fussed, pulling the mail into place.

"From a distance, nobody will notice that," Voba said, sounding positive. "Here's the sword, sir."

As Spock eased the scarlet-plumed helmet over his head, the aide hastily buckled Zar's swordbelt around him.

Cletas growled a soft order at the surrounding guards, and they all snapped to attention, saluting, as Spock stepped between two of them, out from behind the screen of armored bodies.

Several of the Asyri captives gasped when they saw him.

Trying to imitate Zar's walk, Spock strode boldly over to the side of the hill and stood there, silhouetted against the livid, dark-clouded sky, the scarlet cloak whipping behind him in the gusty wind. Thunder rumbled ominously.

He had been there only a few seconds when somebody noticed him and pointed, then an uncertain cheer began rising from the Lakreo forces. Spock waited another beat, then pulled off the helmet, tucking it under his left arm.

The cheer strengthened as more and more of the troops turned to look up, until it flowed up to him in waves of deafening jubilation. The Vulcan could see the Asyri and Kerren forces hesitate, then begin pointing up at him, obviously frightened. *They're almost ready to flee,* he thought. *But I need something else . . . Jim has a flair for the dramatic. What would he do?*

The answer came to him immediately, and he grasped the sticky hilt of the sword at his left hip, then drew it, holding the stained blade high in salute.

*"Victory!"* Spock shouted, so loudly his throat hurt.

A white crack of jagged lightning split the sky above him, followed a moment later by a deafening clap of thunder.

The enemy troops broke and ran.

57

# *The Pandora Principle,* by Carolyn Clowes

*ST:TWOK* introduced Saavik, Spock's protégé, who appeared to be Vulcan but who was quite, well, emotional, something that was not explained in the theatrical release. The televised version of the film and the novelization by Vonda McIntyre, however, included dialogue between Spock and Kirk that explained that Saavik was half-Vulcan and half-Romulan. Considering her origin, it was understandable that her emotional control was less than perfect. As with other unanswered questions in Star Trek, Saavik's story was ideal for a novel, and in *The Pandora Principle,* Carolyn Clowes provided the answers. In the film novelization, Ms. McIntyre explained that Saavik was born on a world called Hellguard; *The Pandora Principle* expanded this background and described horrific experiments on unwilling Vulcan subjects forcibly mated with Romulans. These experiments resulted in Saavik and other children.

Spock found the wild young Saavik on Hellguard and shamed other Vulcans, including Sarek, into taking responsibility for the abandoned children. Touched by the wild young child's tenacity and courage to survive, Spock raised Saavik and sponsored her for Starfleet Academy. Eventually, vicious doomsday weapons developed in the Hellguard experiments threatened the Federation, and Spock and Saavik returned to Hellguard to attempt to destroy them.

The following excerpt shows Spock's eloquent argument in support of the Hellguard children and his first meeting with Saavik.

SPOCK SAT BY HIMSELF IN THE SHADOWS THAT FLICKERED AGAINST THE walls of the main tent. Around the flame of a single lamp, twelve more Vulcans gathered, sat down together and waited. Somewhere outside a tent flap came loose and whipped and rattled in the wind. The recording device looked incongruous lying there on the mat-covered ground, a gleaming metallic piece of technology, out of time with lamplight, men in robes, and the keening wind that blew through this treacherous, alien night.

Spock watched his father switch on the recorder. The only change in Sarek's composed, expressionless face came when the lamplight caught his eyes; for an instant they burned like flames. Then Sarek began to speak. And Spock was grateful for the shadows, grateful for the dark, grateful that his part in this was done. Tonight his elders met to testify to tragedy; he had only been a messenger, bearing news from beyond the grave.

58

Vulcan's fleet had lost four ships in the past fifteen years: *Criterion, Perceptor, Constant,* and *Diversity,* all science survey vessels, all Vulcan crews, all gone missing in space. One by one they simply vanished—the last, *Diversity,* six years ago. In every case transmissions were routine, from sectors bordering the Neutral Zone but within the Federation. Then silence. No signals, no log buoys, no debris. Nothing. Until three months ago.

*Enterprise* was crossing Gamma Hydra sector, patrolling up the uneasy perimeter of the Romulan Neutral Zone, when the bridge heard a faint, frantic Mayday in obsolete Federation code. It originated from a Romulan cargo craft fleeing toward Federation space, with a warship of the Empire in pursuit and gaining. As *Enterprise* breached the Line and drew within transporter range, the warbird unleashed a bolt of fire enveloping its prey. The only occupant, a Vulcan woman, was beamed aboard unconscious and too badly burned to live. Spock reached her side in sickbay just before the end, touched gentle fingers to her charred face and joined her fading mind so she would not die alone. His log of the incident read "Explanation: None." But when *Enterprise* docked at starbase he requested leave and hired transport home to Vulcan.

That all took precious time. Vulcan's Council took even more with private inquiries to the Empire and lengthy discussions of Federation law, which Vulcan was about to break. In the end the Federation was not informed. *Symmetry* carried no complement of weapons; Vulcan's survey vessels never did. Crossing the Neutral Zone and penetrating the sovereign space of the Romulan Star Empire were tasks better left to long-range sensors, secrecy, and speed. Even a starship, a *Constitution* or an *Enterprise,* would stand no chance in the Empire's front yard. A single ship of Vulcan registry would be doomed, but a single ship it had to be.

For this mission flew only on the last thought of a dying Vulcan in the final mindtouch of her life, a thought that sent shock waves through Council and families alike: On an abandoned world called Hellguard—the fifth planet of 872 Trianguli—there were children, Vulcan children, dying on a burning rock in space.

". . . but no trace at all of our science ships or their small crews," Sarek said, speaking for the record. "Five hundred and fifty-six citizens of Vulcan, our sisters and brothers, daughters and sons, are lost to us. If they are alive," and the deafening thought of thirteen minds was a prayer that they were not, "they are beyond our reach. In memory I speak their names . . ."

The Empire had denied everything. No, it knew nothing of Vulcan ships! What evidence did Vulcan have to make such charges? . . . Children? How could there be *children?* It was biologically impossible; their scientists had said so; regrettable these ships had gone astray, but did Vulcan have some *proof?* . . .

Now they had proof, living proof. And Vulcans would keep no more secrets tonight, at least not from each other. Sarek spoke the last of the names. Lamplight flickered in the dusk. Shadows danced up the walls of the tent; the air hung heavy, and time seemed to be standing still. The recorder went on blinking.

"The remaining inhabitants range in approximate ages from five to fourteen. Life-scans confirm what we were told. They are indeed half-Vulcan." He switched off the recorder to allow a moment of grief. Heads bowed in silence and in pain. There was no need to state what every Vulcan knew, no witness to reconstruct events. Only the shattering, irrefutable truth: a band of starving children who should not exist at all.

Vulcan males and joined females are subject to a season as primitive and unrelenting as their planet's windswept sands. At other times mating (or not) is a matter of personal choice; but every seventh year it becomes a matter of life or death, a matter of being Vulcan. *Pon Farr:* eternal paradox of the Vulcan nature, its private pain, its illogical, secret soul. When their times approached, Vulcans would never choose to venture off-world in survey ships. Vulcans would never choose to mate far from home. And Vulcans would never choose to mate with Romulans. Somehow on this remote, decaying world, internal chemistries had been tampered with. Vulcan minds had been broken. The sacred personal cycles had been disturbed.

Vulcans had been raped.

Sarek lifted his head and reached for the recorder once more. The flames in his eyes came not entirely from the lamplight, and his quiet voice filled the tent like a tolling bell—or a peal of distant, dangerous thunder. "I conclude the statement of fact. Now Salok will speak of the survivors and what is to be done."

Salok was old even by Vulcan reckoning, a healer with a very special skill: he was extraordinary with children. When Salok told them not to be afraid they weren't. When Salok told them that it wouldn't hurt it didn't. And whatever else he said, they neither questioned nor explained. Salok always healed them, and he always understood. But not tonight. Tonight he looked worn and frail. His hands trembled. His eyes clouded. Here were things he did not understand and had never encountered before. He mourned with Vulcan for the lost, but the pain he felt was for the found.

"As Sarek has spoken," he began, "we meet to consider the children. Spock's information was correct: they were left here to die. Many have. Survivors hide in the empty buildings and rubble of the abandoned colony. It is a vicious life, a wonder that they live at all. Malnutrition is their immediate problem, but not the most serious. That is their minds, their savagery and ignorance. I observed no system of values, not even a primitive code of behavior. They kill without thought or regret over a morsel of food. They even kill each other—the youngest, weakest ones. The bodies," his voice became carefully remote, "are used for food."

Thirteen pairs of eyes closed briefly. Vulcans killed no living creature for food, and cannibalism was beyond their imagining.

"This planet is dying. We cannot help them here. I suggest our research station at Gamma Eri, a protected environment where they can be healed and taught. I shall go with them, and we must send them our finest, our most adept physicians and teachers. When the children have attained some measure of civilization and rational thought, they can be relocated on worlds for which their progress and their gifts are best suited. This will take . . . a very long time." He paused, exhausted. Consenting silence, nodding heads, and a vast unspoken relief answered his words. "Then it shall be done. Tomorrow the ship returns. At dawn we must begin the—"

"I ask forgiveness." Spock was standing, hands clasped behind his back. "I regret that I cannot concur."

Heads turned. Spock felt the disapproval at his impertinence; it could not be helped. He took a deep breath and went on.

"Someday these children will seek to know their origins, their identities, their places in the universe. Gamma Eri is an orbital science station, not a world, not a home—"

"We save their lives, Spock!" The thunder in Sarek's voice was not so distant. "We seek to repair their minds. What more would you have us do?"

"Treat them as we would our own," Spock said quietly, "for in fact they are. To uproot them from their birthworld as we must, to tend them on a station that does not even orbit Vulcan's sun, to instill in them a 'measure' of Vulcan thought and then to send them on their way—is that the sum of our debt to those we named tonight? These are their children. They deserve a home."

Sarek's face was stone. The others averted their gaze, allowing a father to deal with his wayward son, who was behaving so incorrectly. "These children, Spock," Sarek explained, "are the products of coercion. Rape. Living reminders of Vulcan nature torn apart and shamed. Our kindred were violated. They did not choose their fate."

"Nor did their children." Spock looked at his father across the tent, across a lifetime. "Our world is their birthright. It is for *them* to decide what measure of Vulcan shall be theirs."

"Now, now, Spock," old Salok intervened, "we mean to help them, and we will. We do not blame them for the poverty of their natures, but we must recognize it. Adapting to life on Vulcan would be painful and difficult—for *them,* as well as for us. We must seek to do the greatest good for the greatest number."

"Forgive me, Salok, but that equation fails to balance when the greatest good is merely the avoidance of difficulty, and when it is purchased at the expense of a helpless few. We say we value diversity in its infinite combinations. Are we to abandon that principle simply because it becomes inconvenient?"

"Do not presume to speak to us of our principles, Spock!" Sarek's voice cut like a knife through the shocked, uncomfortable gathering. "This decision was never yours to make. It is not now. Your . . . dissent . . . has been noted."

Spock regretted it had come to this. "I am constrained to point out," he said into the chilly silence, "that the Federation Council would agree with my concern. A homeworld is considered mandatory for displaced populations, and displaced populations are a matter for the Federation."

Simple blackmail. They all stared at him in disbelief; Sarek closed his eyes in shame.

"You would speak to *outworlders* of this?" S'tvan, philosopher and physicist, was on his feet, his voice unsteady with the effort at control; his only daughter and his youngest son had been aboard the *Constant.* "You would threaten disclosure? Public humiliation? How dare you! This is *not* a Federation matter—this is a *Vulcan* problem! We will care for these half-breeds in our *own* way!"

Spock let that pass. "I am an officer of Starfleet, S'tvan, sworn to uphold a Federation law that Vulcan itself helped to draft. Violation of the Treaty on this mission would result only in our own deaths, since we come unarmed, and the loss of yet another ship. We do not provoke war, so my silence, like my life and my commission, was my own. But now we speak of others. I could not keep silent. They are children—and they are Vulcans."

"They are *not!*" Sickened, S'tvan sat down again, and one by one the others turned away. Spock thought he saw a glimmer of respect in the old healer's eyes, but then he stood alone.

"You are dismissed from our proceedings, Spock!" said Sarek.

Spock nodded. It was just as well; the thing was done. He picked up his tricorder and walked to the tent's only exit. As he unfastened the flap, his father spoke sadly at his shoulder.

"You would betray all of Vulcan, Spock?"

"If I must." The tent flap caught in the wind, tugged at his hand. "I did not believe it would be required. Or that all of Vulcan would be so fragile."

"Before you do, Spock, consider this: You did not speak from logic here. Perhaps your human nature betrays *you* . . . once again."

"Perhaps. It sometimes does. I am what I am, Father." Spock let go of the flap and stepped outside. When he turned to fasten it behind him, he found it was already closed.

He left the circle of the camp and walked out on the plain, so absorbed in thought that he was unaware of a shadow, not his own, moving after him in the dark.

What happened in the tent came as no surprise, even Sarek's reminder of his human failings. Spock hardly needed reminding.

Only months ago he had knelt upon the plain of Gol to leave behind the things of Earth, to belong at last to Vulcan in the peace and freedom of *Kolinahr.* But the Time of Truth was not within his reach. And his teacher watched him fail. *Your answer lies elsewhere, Spock* . . . not on Vulcan. Spock walked away from Gol that day, knowing that he would never be free, knowing that some things could not be left behind.

Now he stood on another plain, watched the skies, and knew his father was correct: his human nature did betray him, then and now. But he'd known all that before. It changed nothing. Tonight he spoke *because* of what he was, because of what he'd seen.

Spock had seen their faces. Darting, fearful, wasting faces. Starving bones and starving minds. Dull, empty eyes that held no promise, that watched and waited for the dark. Half-children and half-dead, half-animal . . . and half-Vulcan. He walked upon their world well-fed, nourished by millennia of civilization, by blessings and aspirations, by all it meant to be a Vulcan. And except for a fortunate circumstance of birth, any one of those savage, starving creatures might as easily have been himself.

No, he could not keep silent. *I do what I must,* he thought, *but the children's fate is not the only question here.*

There were far too many questions here. He must find answers, or other ships and other lives might never see their homes. If it happened to Vulcans, it could happen to anyone.

But why had it happened at all?

Spock turned his back against the wind, set his tricorder on the ground, and shielded it from blowing dust as he monitored its readings. They confirmed his earlier data and told him nothing new: seismic instability. Recurrent planetquakes would have made mining too hazardous, which could account for the Romulans' departure, but so could many things on this inhospitable world.

Why had they been here in the first place? And what had they been mining? He'd found no resources of scientific or military value. At the excavation sites his scans showed only common iron ores: hematite, pyrite, a few more useful minerals that could be mined anywhere else with far less trouble. Investigations of two mine shafts revealed both blocked by cave-ins; the expedition had no time to explore further. But Spock knew he must.

Because neither *Symmetry's* instruments nor their own surface scans could penetrate the damping field emanating from those rocky cliffs. A natural phenomenon? Or something of value buried there? That might explain the mining colony; it did not account for missing Vulcan ships. If there were answers here they lay beneath those mountains, and he had until dawn to find them.

As Spock reached for his tricorder he felt a pricking at the edges of his mind—and at the back of his neck. A new awareness intruded on his thoughts, sent a warning ripple down his spine.

He was not alone. Something was watching him.

With every appearance of unconcern he keyed the bioscan, rose to his feet and began a sweep of the horizon. Halfway around, it registered. Life-form: small, Vulcanoid; distance: 30.2 meters—between himself and the camp. He stared into the windy dark, saw no one, then continued scanning and considered what to do. He perceived no danger, no hostile intent, only the palpable sensation of being observed. So this watcher was allowing him to study and to think undisturbed. For the moment he decided to do likewise. Shouldering his tricorder he set out across the plain and did not glance back. He knew he was being followed.

A long-ago rockfall from the mountains created a natural barrier, partially separating the colony from the plains. Spock should have gone around it. It yielded no new information, provided no shortcuts, and came to an impassable dead end. He retraced his path through the maze of boulders, and in sight of open ground again resigned himself to taking the longer—

A split instant's warning wasn't enough. The attacker dropped from the rocks above, slamming him down against jagged stone. The sickening crack he heard was the impact of his skull, and to Spock's profound annoyance the world began to fade. He fought to remain conscious, aware of his right arm pinned beneath him, his left arm flung back over the rock, and the glint of starlight on a sharp piece of scrap metal pressing into his throat.

A ferocious face with teeth bared in a snarl belonged to a young boy, a surprisingly strong young boy. Too late Spock knew he'd underestimated the danger here, but he'd been so certain—

The boy growled a warning, jammed a knee into his chest.

Spock's vision swam. His left hand seemed far away, but free; if he could distract this youth for a moment . . . the point of the metal jabbed into his flesh just below the angle of his jaw, and Spock felt blood trickle down his neck. Any movement at all would drive it deeper. A groping hand found his ration pack, ripped it from his belt. After some hurried scrabbling Spock heard it hit the ground. That ration pack was empty, and the grim purpose in the face looming closer was unmistakable. Spock knew then that there would be no distracting him. There was no more time.

Suddenly the boy jerked upward, stiffened. His mouth opened in a scream that never came. The light went out of his eyes, and he toppled backward to the ground, then lay still.

Spock pushed himself off the rocks to kneel beside the body, searching the shadows, steeling himself for another attack. None came. But if the boy was alone, what had killed him? The body lay sprawled on the ground, the mouth a silent scream, the eyes still open, staring up at a sky they would never see again. He had been young. Gently Spock closed the eyes and turned the body over.

Then he saw the knife.

It pierced the rib cage neatly on the lower right side, where the heart would be, if this half-Vulcan's anatomy were similar to his own. Someone out there was efficient—and so far, invisible.

He found his tricorder, shut it off, and tried to ignore the throbbing in his head. His mysterious watcher seemed to want him alive—or intended to kill him next. Then his ears caught the faintest of sounds: a pebble pinging against rock, scattering to the ground. Mindful of the risk, he sat down in a patch of dim starlight and waited. So did his silent sentinel. Just when he was ready to concede defeat, a shadow moved soundlessly from behind one rock to another. It moved again. Finally, from between large boulders, the shadow separated itself from the blackness. It crept toward him and stepped into the light. At last his elusive watcher stood revealed—and an eyebrow lifted in the dark.

Fascinating. It was a little girl.

She was starving. Naked, except for some rags tied about her waist, she was a walking skeleton. Every rib, every bone in her body stood out in stark relief, covered only by skin and layers of dirt. The child was filthy. Dark hair hung down her shoulders in shaggy, matted tangles. Sores blistered her feet and legs, and a lifetime of dust crusted between her fingers and toes. With wary eyes on Spock, she circled until the corpse was between them, jerked her knife free, then prodded and shoved to turn the body over. She seized his empty ration pack and searched it with a practiced hand. Never glancing at the boy's face, she pried the sliver of metal from his grasp, examined it and stuck it in the rags at her waist. Then holding her knife ready, she advanced.

Spock sat very still. A sudden feeling of disquiet grew as he watched her approach, and the reason for it was impossible.

She peered at him under her dusty snarls of hair with bright, hollow eyes. Intelligent, crafty, curious eyes. *How old?* he wondered. *Nine? Ten? And how often has she killed?* She stopped out of reach, leveled her knife at his face and sighted along its blade. They studied each other in silence. What was in Spock's mind simply could not be: it was absurd, but . . . he felt he *knew* her. Nonsense. He was obviously concussed and must alert himself to further symptoms. She sidled closer, inspecting him inch by inch. His face, hands, clothing, and shoes were all gone over with acquisitive interest. Eyes lit on his tricorder. She pointed with her knife. Reluctantly, Spock pushed it toward her on the ground.

"What?" she hissed, displeased that it contained no food. Her language was Romulan, and Spock answered her in kind.

"It . . . tells me things," he said. Her eyes went wide. She snatched it up and held it to her ear, listening, then scowled.

*"Tells!"* she ordered, shaking it soundly. When it refused she bashed it with a bony fist. "Stupid sonabastard!" she swore, and flung it back to him: *"You tells!"*

"Certainly. What do you wish to know?"

"Stars!" She pointed up at them, and Spock stared. *She spoke that word in Vulcan. When—and how—did she learn it?*

"You know what they are?" . . . *and what else do you know?*

She swept a scrawny arm across the sky. *"My* stars!" she said fiercely, aiming her knife at his heart lest he disagree.

"Yes, I see that." This encounter was becoming stranger by the minute, and Spock thought it wise to reassure her. "I mean you no harm. I go that way." He nodded to the mountains beyond. "If you wish you may—" A look of sheer terror crossed her face. She turned where he pointed, then whirled around in fury.

"Not!"

"But why? What about those—"

"Not *not!"* She stamped her foot; eyes flashed, nostrils flared, and she brandished the knife for emphasis. She backed up to a rock in sight of the open plain, shoved the boy's piece of metal under it, and sat down to watch. The knife never wavered. With her free hand, she shook his empty ration pack and began picking crumbs out of the dust. The wind whistled around them, and she shivered in the cold.

Spock's head throbbed. He sought to identify that disturbing impression, which he could neither understand nor dispel: she still seemed *familiar.* Or reminded him of . . . whom? The Vulcan woman beamed aboard the *Enterprise* had been T'Pren, but T'Pren was on board *Diversity,* gone missing only six years ago. This child could not be T'Pren's daughter, she was far too old. No, he could *not* know her . . . yet he did. Explanations eluded him, and time was slipping away. When he tried to shift his legs into a more comfortable position, she menaced him with her knife.

"As you wish, but I must go now," he said, starting to rise.

*"Not!"* The knife sang past his face, missing him by inches, to lodge in a crevice in the rock beyond. She darted over, yanked it out—and hadn't missed at all. Something small wriggled on her blade: A species of rock-dweller about three inches long writhed on the sharp point that impaled it. She thrust it out by way of example. *"Not*go!" she hissed, and seemed very firm about it.

Spock concluded that he was overmatched and might do well to keep it in mind. The child retreated to her rock and unstuck her prey, whose muscles went on twitching even after she sliced off the head, popped it into her mouth and began to chew. Resolutely he concentrated on the open plain where lights still burned in the Vulcans' tents, but he couldn't shut out the sounds of crunching bone and sharp teeth gnawing through tough, leathery skin. He felt quite ill. No doubt that blow to his head . . .

"You eats," she ordered him, holding out the last piece of meat. A precious gift indeed . . . but it ended in three claws, and dark blood dripped between grimy fingers onto the ground.

"No," he said, hoping she wouldn't insist. "It is yours."

Frowning, she crammed it into her mouth. Blood ran down her chin. She licked it away, licked all her fingers and bent over the drops of blood on the ground. She scraped them up with the dirt and ate that too; all the while, she guarded him relentlessly.

Spock looked up at the sky, trying to judge the hour by the movement of the stars. They burned near and bright and beautiful against a faint glimmer of the dawn. *Dawn*—no time to reach those mountains now. Out across the plain the Vulcans were emerging from their tents, beginning to break camp. Today would see the success or failure of their mission. *Symmetry* would be making its rescue run across the Zone—a calculated risk, marginally safer than remaining in orbit without defenses or a cloaking screen. But if it failed to elude patrols and never arrived at all, they would be stranded here, along with the children of Hellguard.

With a start he realized the child had moved so stealthily he never noticed. Now she stood at the far edge of the rock where he was sitting, watching him watch the stars. After a moment she climbed onto it and sat with him looking up at the sky, so intense and quiet that Spock felt he was witnessing some private ceremony. Her knife dangled forgotten in her hand.

"Stars," she whispered, her face solemn and expectant. She searched the sky as if she were waiting for something to happen—or trying to remember something. *Where did she learn that word? Why did she save my life? And why,* Spock questioned his own rationality again, *why should this all seem so . . . important?*

"I am going there," he murmured, "to see your stars. And you shall come with me." She stared at him transfixed, eyes huge and wondering. "My people come to take us there. They bring you food. You will eat. And then we go—"

*"Not!"* She scrambled off the rock and backed away, clutching the knife and ration pack in her hands, shaking her head in fear, looking from him to the approaching Vulcans and to the mountains behind her. Then she pointed at the sky. *"Run!"* she cried, and to Spock's utter consternation, she vanished into the dark.

The incident left him profoundly disturbed. Her last word was also Vulcan, meaning *flee,* run for one's life. Whatever his words meant to her, the attempt to win her trust had failed. But she was hungry, she would come with the others to be fed. Of course she would. If she didn't, her face would haunt him all his days.

He lifted the body and carried it out onto the plain, the body that so nearly was his own. He lived because this boy died, because an intelligent, dangerous child had saved his life for reasons known only to herself. Spock vowed under Hellguard's blazing stars that today he would return the favor. And he began to build a cairn of stones.

## *Mind Meld,* by John Vornholt

In *Mind Meld,* Spock also assumed guardianship of a child, but under very different circumstances from those in *The Pandora Principle.* Here, Sarek arranged for a young female relative raised on Earth, Teska, to become betrothed to a Romulan boy as part of the quest for reunification. Teska was a likely candidate to test the success of such a union because she had a talent for mind-melds and was familiar and comfortable with emotional non-Vulcans. En route to the betrothal ceremony, Teska and Spock became trapped on Rigel V following an inadvertent mind-meld between Teska and a dying Rigelian. They were pursued by a criminal organization bent upon their deaths, and Spock was horribly wounded while protecting Teska in their escape. Teska saved both their lives, and Spock was nursed back to health by a Rigelian woman determined to add him to her marriage group.

In this passage from *Mind Meld,* Teska pondered her future and made an unusual request of Spock. Spock's dialogue with Teska is fascinating because it revealed his understanding and respect for Teska. Although she was merely a child, Spock was willing to subject both himself and Dr. McCoy to the mind-meld so that Teska could learn to control her abilities.

TESKA LIFTED HER CHIN OFF THE DESK WITH A START, NOT REALIZING UNTIL then that she had fallen asleep while studying the wisdom of T'Pau. Oh, what would her *pele-ut-la* think of her? She looked around the room, expecting him to be standing there, gazing at her with disapproval. When she realized she was alone, she calmed quickly. She knew that she wasn't the only one who found the stoic Captain Spock intimidating—she had seen the young crew of the *Enterprise* regard him with awe. And why not? The places he had gone, the things he had seen—they were enough to fill the logs of a dozen Starfleet officers. Spock was arguably the best-known Vulcan in the Federation, after his accomplished father.

These were her kinsmen, she reminded herself, but they existed more in reports and histories than in reality. She had not seen much of them in the flesh. Sopeg's old apartment in the Tenderloin district, her playmates at school, the crashing of the waves on the Embarcadero—these things seemed real to her. The idea of getting married on Vulcan, when the day before she had been playing hopscotch on Haight Street, was such a strange juxtaposition that it didn't seem possible. But Teska knew it was more than possible, it was going to happen.

*In a matter of days, she would be married to a Romulan.* The seven-year-old rose from her desk and paced the confines of her quarters. She was Vulcan, Teska told herself, even if her homeworld was nothing but a blurry memory. The *koon-ut-la* would have been her fate no matter what her circumstances, even if her parents had lived.

A chime came at the door, startling the girl from her reverie. Teska straightened her tunic, which was rumpled from sleeping, then called out, "Come in!"

The door slid open, and Spock entered, followed by Hanua from the Heart Clan. Teska bowed to them. "Uncle, I must report that I fell asleep while studying."

"Hanua predicted you would be asleep," said Spock. "I have been reconsidering my advice, and I believe you can best prepare for the ceremony by relaxing. Instead of studying, we will engage in recreational activities."

Hanua nodded. "My daughter, Falona, said she would like to play with you tomorrow. Shall we make a date, say, ten-hundred hours?"

Teska glanced at Spock, and he nodded in approval. "That would be acceptable," said the girl.

"Good," replied Hanua. "Well, I'll see you both tomorrow. I enjoyed our games of chess, Captain Spock. I'm sure it was just beginner's luck."

"No," insisted Spock. "You are an excellent player, and you beat me fairly. Your play was most unpredictable."

"Your play was a little *too* predictable," said Hanua with a smile. She backed out the doorway. "Good night." The door slid shut after her.

"You found a worthy opponent," said Teska.

"It would appear so," said Spock with a thoughtful nod. "Which activity would you prefer? Shall we take a tour of the ship or visit the exercise room?"

"I wish to practice the mind-meld."

Spock frowned. "That is not required for the *koon-ut-la*. You will have High Priestess T'Lar to guide you."

"I know," said Teska, working up her courage. "You asked me what I preferred to do, and I have told you. I wish to practice the mind-meld."

She turned away from Spock's stern gaze, but she never hesitated in her explanation. "I am Vulcan—I know this—but I have lived among humans for so long that sometimes I sense I am somehow disconnected. Perhaps if I mastered the mind-meld, I would feel more at peace with our rituals. Sopeg said I had a talent for it. On Vulcan, children my age practice the mind-meld."

Spock held up his hand. "That is true. However, it is also true that the mind-meld is mentally and physically exhausting. There can be unknown repercussions, especially if you perform it on non-Vulcans."

"I do not ask this lightly," said Teska. "I need to know what it means to be Vulcan."

Spock looked away from her and then finally spoke once again. "I can see the logic in your position—the path to freedom from emotion is too arduous without seeing the benefits. We will perform the mind-meld, if you wish."

Teska resisted any outward show of emotion over this decision. What she really wanted was to tap into Spock's solid beliefs in the Vulcan way, although maybe those convictions weren't as solid as they seemed. It was impossible to look at him and think he was half human. But now, slumped wearily on the edge of the bed, Captain Spock seemed more human than Vulcan. His face was still expressionless, but Teska sensed genuine empathy coming from him. He *cared* about her, and he *understood* what she was going through.

Spock suddenly reached out and grabbed her right hand. He spread her fingers and studied each one, as if inspecting fine machinery. Teska held perfectly still.

"The *katra* is a stream," said Spock as if in a trance, "and it flows from one mind to another. Your fingers are channels to direct the flow, and your mind is a pool to be filled. Envision your hand reaching into my mind and drinking from the pool."

He lifted her hand to his face and positioned her fingertips at his nose, sinuses, and temple, and her thumb on his chin. Instantly, Teska felt a burning in her hand, which flowed like a surge of electricity along her arm until it reached her brain. She almost lost consciousness, but Spock grabbed her shoulder with his hand and held her upright. His touch seemed to complete a circuit, and the being that was Spock flowed into her mind.

The tears came unbidden to her eyes; she could do nothing to fight them, because they were not her tears. She realized Spock was more torn and incomplete than she would ever be. She saw his mother, his death, his father, his crewmates, bursts of laughter and joy, abject fear and horror—all at once!

Then the iron will asserted itself, and Teska saw the man pulling his disparate parts together into an amazing whole. Not a perfect whole; he had to work harder than most Vulcans. But Spock had found contentment. The bridge of the *Enterprise* was a constant in his life, even when he spent years away from it, and so was his friendship with Jim, Bones, and the others. His sense of righteousness and duty was as solid as the deck under her feet.

Spock pulled away, breaking the contact between them. Teska started to faint again, but she managed to catch herself on the bed and shake off the dizzying effects. She focused her eyes to find Spock staring numbly at her.

"Sopeg was right," he said hoarsely. "You have a natural ability. Of course, you will need to gain greater control of the initial impulses— they can be overwhelming. Unlike most children of your age, your training will focus on controlling your abilities, not developing them. You must *not,* I repeat, *not,* send your thoughts into someone else's mind, until you receive much more training."

Teska thought about the morass of conflicting desires and emotions she had seen within her uncle, a glimpse that was rare for a child. Spock knew far better than she what it felt like to be drawn toward humanity.

"Thank you, Uncle. I will not forget this."

He rose wearily to his feet. "However much you may admire other races, Teska, you are a Vulcan. Nothing will change that. We believe that wisdom flows from generation to generation, never to be lost but only expanded. Let my experiences guide you in the difficult years ahead of you. We are not dissimilar."

"Thank you, *Pele-ut-la,* I will."

The older Vulcan nodded curtly and headed for the door. "It is time for both of us to get some sleep."

"Can we continue to practice the mind-meld?" asked Teska hopefully.

Spock stopped at the door to consider the question. "We need a suitable subject, but I might know one. I will awaken you early."

"Thank you, Uncle."

72

"Until then, sleep well." Captain Spock stepped out the door, and it shut after him.

*I will sleep well,* thought Teska, *knowing that you are watching after me,* Pele-ut-la.

Dr. McCoy gaped at the two Vulcans. "You want to do *what?*"

The girl looked down, and McCoy wasn't sure but he thought he saw her smile. Even though she was a Vulcan, she had an impish quality about her that he liked. Still, he didn't really want her poking around inside his mind.

Spock merely regarded him with his usual obstinacy. "Doctor, I assure you, it won't be harmful. Teska is very accomplished for her age, and the meld will be unidirectional. This is my only opportunity to work with her, and I must see how accomplished she is before I recommend a teacher. There are no other Vulcans on the ship, and I know from firsthand experience that your mind is receptive to a mind-meld."

"Now you're trying to insult me," McCoy grumbled. One of his young medical technicians grinned with amusement, but McCoy's glower chased him out of the room.

"I would not allow this if there were any danger," said Spock.

"I know, I know. It's not dangerous," grumbled McCoy, "but it's also not my idea of a good time."

"Come," said Spock to Teska, "we can search the computer for a suitable subject."

Spock headed for the door, but the seven-year-old hesitated. "Perhaps we need to offer him a deal."

"A deal?" asked McCoy and Spock at the same time.

"Yes. I have found that humans favor a quid pro quo arrangement. If you want them to do something for you, you must do something for them."

McCoy grinned, thinking that he definitely liked this little girl. Anyone who stood up to Spock was okay with him. "Yeah, Spock, listen to Teska. Humans aren't all that hard to figure out."

"I am well aware that humans are often motivated by greed," said Spock. Was that a glimmer of amusement he saw in Spock's eyes, McCoy wondered.

"Not greed," offered Teska, "just fairness. What can I do for you in exchange, Doctor?"

McCoy scratched his chin. "Well, I don't know. We don't have any patients at the moment. If there was an emergency, I could think of all kinds of things I would ask you to do."

"I am very good at filing and organizing," said Teska. "Do you have anything that needs to be catalogued and filed?"

The doctor snapped his fingers. "We've picked up a lot of new supplies, like bandages and hyposprays. I haven't really counted them yet, so maybe you could go through the supply cabinet and do a quick inventory."

"I will start at fourteen-hundred hours after my play date," promised Teska. "Do we have a deal?"

"Sure," said McCoy, shaking her small but cool hand. He tapped a comm panel on the wall. "Hendricksen, you're in charge of sickbay for a few minutes. I'll be in Examination Room One, doing some, uh . . . therapy."

"Yes, sir."

McCoy led his visitors to the examination room with its clear windows all around. As he approached the door, it opened, and lights came on inside the room. The doctor entered and found himself twisting his sweaty palms together. He tapped a panel which turned the windows opaque, so they would have more privacy, but it didn't help relax him. Besides, he had just thought of something.

"I've got to admit I'm a little nervous," said McCoy. "And I just realized—you're a little girl. I'm a grown man, and there are things in my head that are for grown people."

"I have studied human mating practices," said Teska neutrally.

Spock nodded in agreement. "We mind-melded last night, and she has shared all of my experiences as well. Of course, it will take her many years to understand them. Teska will obey the oath of confidentiality."

McCoy took a deep breath and let out a groan. "Okay, I agreed, so let's do it before I change my mind. I should have my head examined." He groaned. That was exactly what was going to happen to him!

Spock pressed a panel and turned the examination table into a reclining chair. After it clicked into shape, the Vulcan guided the doctor into it. The metal seat felt cold against his back, which only aggravated his fear. *Damn it,* thought McCoy, sometimes it would be nice to be a Vulcan and avoid those rushes of terror to which humans were prone. Then again, sometimes terror was only your common sense telling you that you were doing something crazy!

Teska moved her tiny fingers toward him, and he wondered if she would be able to reach the important nerve synapses that Spock had told him about. But as soon as her fingers touched his cheekbone, he felt as if an immense claw had ripped into his face, and he jerked involuntarily. McCoy felt himself surging forward, like flood waters breaking through a dam. Then he rushed into a place of calmness, like an ocean. His muscles went numb, leaving him conscious but unable to move or react.

It could have been an eternity or a second before the claw disengaged from his face and he felt control over his body and mind returning to him. He touched his cheek and found to his surprise that he wasn't bleeding—his face wasn't ripped away. Then he saw the angelic pixie gazing at him, and he remembered that he wasn't in a nightmare.

"Doctor?" cut in a stern voice. "Are you all right, Dr. McCoy?"

McCoy jumped to his feet, filled with energy for no good reason. "Not bad!" he said in astonishment. "I think she's better at that mumbo-jumbo than you are, Spock."

"I am sure that is not the case," said Teska with a polite bow. "Thank you, Dr. McCoy. I believe it was a success."

He shrugged. "Maybe I should rent myself out to Vulcans for this type of thing on a regular basis. What do you think?"

"This is the doctor's idea of humor," added Spock.

"Well, at least I *have* an idea of humor." McCoy suddenly felt like scheduling the new crew members for physical exams, so it was time to usher these two out of his workplace. "I'm going to have lots of bandages for you to count later, Teska."

"Agreed," said Teska. She didn't smile, but she did bounce on her toes.

Spock turned to the girl. "Would you leave us alone for a moment?"

"Certainly, Uncle." Teska walked briskly out the door.

Spock turned and cocked an eyebrow at McCoy. "Doctor, it is highly irregular not to take inventory of a shipment of supplies."

McCoy scowled. "Oh, I know how many hyposprays we have, but I had to give her something to do. You won't tell her, will you?"

"No. In fact, I will make certain that she returns to work off her debt. She is gifted for such an early age—there is a chance that I could enroll her for training as a priestess. Perhaps even a healer."

"Yes, a healer," agreed McCoy. "She's got the touch—it just makes you feel better."

"Thank you for helping me."

"Helping *you?* I was helping *her!*" grumbled McCoy. "If the only mind she ever looked into was *yours,* heaven help the poor girl."

"My thoughts exactly," said Spock. He headed for the door and stopped. "When we deliver our passengers to Rigel V, we are beaming down for a courtesy call. Are you going with us?"

McCoy grinned. "Wouldn't miss it. I *love* the Rigel solar system. Did I ever tell you about these two dancers I met on Rigel II?"

Spock nodded. "Many times. Rigel V has a precious-metal economy, so if you would like a refreshment, I could bring enough local currency."

"Why, Spock," said McCoy in amazement, "are you—in some roundabout way—offering to buy me a drink?"

"Yes."

"As long as you let me pick the place."

"Agreed."

Spock started out the door, but McCoy called after him, "Before you leave, could I speak to Teska for a moment? In private."

"Certainly." The Vulcan went out of the room, and Teska entered. McCoy waited for the door to shut behind her.

"Yes, Dr. McCoy?"

He paced a few steps. "Teska, when you were inside my mind, did you, uh, find out anything about Spock?"

"I know you hold him in high regard and consider him a friend, as well as a loyal shipmate."

"Well," said McCoy, "I'd appreciate it if you didn't tell him any of that. I don't want him to get a big head."

Teska cocked her head. "As you wish. Thank you again, Dr. McCoy. I'll see you at fourteen-hundred hours."

"Good, I've got lots of inventory for you to count."

# CHAPTER 3

# "I'm a Doctor, Not an Excerpt"—
# Leonard H. "Bones" McCoy

IT IS IMPOSSIBLE TO THINK OF CAPTAIN KIRK AND MR. SPOCK WITHOUT also thinking of Dr. Leonard H. "Bones" McCoy. McCoy was gentle, kind, compassionate, and loving. Commentators often have observed that McCoy and Spock stood for opposing aspects of Kirk's personality, with Spock the intellect and McCoy the emotional side, the "human" side. I have always been puzzled by the separation of the intellect from the "human" side, as though intellect is somehow foreign to someone who is truly human, while only emotions symbolize a person's humanity. This is especially puzzling because McCoy was no intellectual slouch. Although he often described himself as "an old country doctor," there was never any doubt that he was a brilliant physician, surgeon, and space psychiatrist. The intellect and emotions were both well represented in him. Even so, he often acted as Kirk's conscience, while Spock was the voice of cold reason, and in this, they were emotion and intellect in conflict.

Despite his tender soul, McCoy also had an acerbic, biting wit and a grouchy temperament. He was not afraid to make use of both, generally against Spock and his analysis of whatever situation they encountered. Their sparring matches often made it seem as though the two despised each other, but as time passed, it became clear that the bickering masked a deep and abiding friendship.

McCoy also had some of the best and most humorous lines in *TOS*. At Star Trek conventions, De Kelley has often led fans in an enthusiastic chorus of "he's dead, Jim!" Dr. McCoy's infamous "I'm a doctor, not a" whatever lines also have been used to great effect in *TNG, DS9,* and *Voyager* in tribute to *TOS*. My favorites are "I'm a doctor, not a bricklayer," from "The Devil in the Dark," and "I'm a doctor, not an escalator," from "Friday's Child."


## *Dreams of the Raven,* by Carmen Carter

Two of my favorite Dr. McCoy novels explored the effect on McCoy of the most painful event in his past, his divorce from his wife, the mother of his daughter, Joanna. The first is *Dreams of the Raven,* by Carmen Carter. In the scene excerpted here, just after an utterly exhausted McCoy learned that his ex-wife has remarried, a "gravity adjustment" rocked the ship and caused McCoy to strike his head, resulting in a severe head injury and traumatic amnesia. He forgot everything about his life for the past twenty-five years, including the divorce that drove him into space, his friendships with Kirk and Spock, and his lifetime of medical knowledge. Retreating from the reality of his life, Bones rejected his friends and his position aboard the *Enterprise.* What was most interesting was McCoy's total refusal to even try to recover his memories; he had decided that he simply did not like the life of "Bones" McCoy and would simply eliminate it. *Dreams of the Raven* is his journey back to himself.


MCCOY PULLED AWKWARDLY AT HIS SURGICAL GOWN, THE TABS AND CLIPS eluding his tumbling fingers. Only minutes ago his hands had been sure and steady, nimbly weaving a tangle of severed nerves into a functioning spinal cord. Now surgery was over after fifteen grueling hours of human cut and paste, tedious and dangerous work even with the aid of the best medical technology Starfleet could offer. Freed from the demands of operating he felt exhaustion overtake him with numbing rapidity. The loose gown dangled in his hands, then dropped to the floor. How many times had he, as chief surgeon, lambasted any doctor or nurse for just such a lapse?

*There's no excuse for messy medical practice. Messy habits have a way of staying with you.*

He still made no move to pick the garment up. Instead he slumped down onto an equipment locker. If it hadn't been there he would probably have collapsed to the floor, next to his discarded gown.

The surgical washroom was a peaceful eye between the two storms which had buffeted him relentlessly for nearly two days. Behind him, for the moment, the operating room was empty, while the sounds of the recovery ward ahead were muted by closed doors. The only voices were those of the ship's intercom droning an interminable list of damage reports and status updates. Scotty was busy with his own particular surgery.

"Doctor." Nurse Chapel was standing by his side. He realized that she had been standing there for a while, but the fact of her presence had barely registered.

"Who's next?" he asked automatically. He had started receiving patients within minutes of the first impact against the hull. Now, over a day later, he was still at work treating the lesser injuries that had lost priority to those courting death. Two crewmen were in bio-stasis, so badly injured that only a starbase, a very modern starbase, could put them back together in a form resembling the human body. Sixteen others would never wake up. The ship had not suffered such heavy casualties in a long time.

"That's all, Doctor. Your shift is over for the day." Chapel began to rattle off the duty roster for the medical personnel in a no-nonsense tone that implied that any objection on his part would be a professional insult to the capabilities of his department. Four names were missing from the list; a team of paramedics had been killed on the hangar deck. He had hand-picked each of its members . . .

McCoy listened wearily, half admitting to himself that his supervision would be useless even if he stayed. His head was throbbing, his eyes were unfocused, and his response time was barely beyond catatonia. Then he stopped short, mentally stifling a groan of irritation. "I can't leave yet." He leaned forward with effort. "There's Benson, the chest injury from Engineering. Those lacerations were only stapled together until he stabilized."

Chapel hesitated, then reluctantly spoke. "That won't be necessary."

McCoy's head snapped up. "Dammit, Christine, don't coddle me! What's happened to Benson?"

She turned coldly matter-of-fact. "He's dead. Vital signs were low but stable when he entered op-prep, but then . . ."

A burst of fury propelled the surgeon to his feet. "Why wasn't I called? Where is he now?" *Enough death, dear God. Please, no more.*

Chapel blocked his steps bodily, forcing him to a halt. "Doctor McCoy, Crewman Benson is dead. You know as well as I do that our staff took every possible action to save his life, but it simply wasn't possible."

The spurt of adrenaline gave out, leaving him drained. "Of course. I'm sorry, I didn't mean . . . I just . . ." He trailed off in confusion.

What had he thought he could do—catch the Angel of Death on his way and wrestle him to the ground? "Thank you, Nurse Chapel." He looked into her face and saw the fatigue that blurred the strong lines of her features. "I guess it's time for me to go away."

"Yes, it is." She still looked stern, but her voice had regained an edge of tolerance.

"How the hell do you put up with me?" he muttered as he stumbled out of the room.

Walking down the corridor revived McCoy somewhat, at least sufficiently to enable him to dodge the scurrying work crews and skirt the obstacle course of conduits, uncrated spare parts, and the occasional body half submerged in the floor or ceiling or wall. Though it was early morning by ship's time, the corridors were lit at daylight intensity to accommodate repairs. The concept of morning and evening in space was wholly artificial, but he hated such a blatant reminder of that fact.

*"Gravity crews t'Deck Seven . . . gravity crews t'Deck Seven. Prepare for adjustment procedures in 4.5 hours, Repeat . . ."* Scotty's voice sounded hoarse even through the filtered intercom.

McCoy idly wondered just how much damage the *Enterprise* had sustained. As a doctor he was most concerned with the human wreckage, yet he had been unusually alarmed by the gyrations of the deck during the attack. With what little attention he could spare from his medical duties, he had gathered that the identity of their assailants was still to be determined. Pieces of the Frenni ship were stored in the shuttle bay; pieces of strange bodies, salvaged from amidst that space debris, were in stasis next to Ellison and Takeoka. With luck, the latter might defrost in slightly better condition than the aliens. McCoy shook his head as if to dislodge the relentless stream of sickbay concerns that trailed after him. There wasn't much sense in dwelling on their chances now—the ship wouldn't reach a sizable starbase for several weeks.

Uhura's voice rang out of the intercom. *"Captain Kirk, to the bridge."* Then Scotty's voice sounded out. *"Captain Kirk, come to phaser control."*

*"Kirk here. I'll be there when I get there."*

McCoy chuckled over the conflicting demands and wondered how soon it would be before Kirk headed for sickbay. The frustration in the captain's voice was the first step to a tension headache.

These musings kept the morbid ghosts at bay until McCoy reached his cabin. Once inside he headed straight for the sonic shower, stripping off his soiled clothes along the way. *Sweat feels like blood,* he thought and shuddered at the persistence of dark thoughts. Even the blast of cleansing vibrations failed to clear his mind.

Out of the shower, McCoy caught sight of his face in the mirror. It was the same face he stared at unthinkingly, every morning. This time he studied it carefully. The broad, regular features implied a stockiness that he did not possess. Fatigue accentuated the lines around his mouth and forehead. The blue of his eyes was dulled to gray, the whites veined with red. Above them his brown hair had not thinned, but it was lightly flecked with white.

*I look more like my father every day.*

Pushing away from the mirror, he wrapped himself in a robe and turned to survey a room littered with crumpled clothes and towels which he hadn't bothered to stuff in the cycle bin. His plants looked wilted. Unread medical tapes lay scattered over his desk, along with a pile of printouts from the last batch of correspondence that had come with sub-space communications from Starfleet. Uhura had a way of wheedling personal mail deliveries onto every official communications exchange. He hadn't had time to read any of it yet, but a few more hours' delay would hardly matter, since the messages had probably taken several weeks to work their way across space channels. The doctor also resisted the impulse to start cleaning up. He needed sleep desperately, yet had reached that stage of nervous exhaustion that left him restless and slightly nauseous. It was a familiar sensation, first encountered during the grueling routine of a first-year resident.

*I'm too old for this.*

He threw himself down on the bed and tried unsuccessfully to empty his mind. Twice he sprang up to call sickbay as one question after another invaded his thoughts. Had he actually entered the new dosages on Vergalen's chart or only made a mental note that it had to be done? Then he had a sudden sick feeling that he had failed to alert Dr. Cortejo about the need for follow-up surgery on Galloway's abdominal wound. No, Chapel would have passed that information on to the other surgeon anyway. Dammit, he trusted her wits more than his own at times. Oddly reassured by this, he finally drifted into sleep.

The shrill whistle of shipboard communications dragged McCoy out of unconsciousness. He awoke slowly, the tendrils of a nightmare blending with reality, drowning out the meaning of the words blaring out through the room. His fingers were actually twitching in response to the dream, in which he had been knitting together yards of nerves that lay scattered about the command deck.

*". . . commences in approximately 30 minutes."*

Blast Montgomery Scott. Couldn't he fix this ship without creating such a public ruckus? A glance at the chronometer showed the passage of only four hours, but McCoy felt no desire to fall asleep again. A return to nightmares wasn't all that inviting. As long as he was awake he might as well get some work done. Jim had asked for a report on the alien tissue fragments as soon as possible, and while the autopsy had been handled by Frazer, the xenobiologist, it wouldn't hurt to translate the man's obsessive technical jargon into a language somewhat more accessible to the captain. Besides, McCoy was curious to see just what kind of life form had wreaked such havoc in sickbay.

He pulled himself out of bed, donned his last batch of fresh clothes, then stumbled to his desk. Rubbing bleary eyes into focus, he logged on to the computer system and called up the autopsy file.

The report opened with photos of the fragments—a gory beginning but useful for a sense of the aliens' morphology. The first two shots were practically meaningless, just chunks of orange pulp that could as easily have been anything from vegetable matter to foam insulation. They were followed by a startling close-up of a massive head covered with steel-blue skin, its round red eyes open and staring with a look of almost human malevolence. A blue-black crest of brushy hair ran from the forehead back over the skull; a chitinous beak gaped open at the center of its face.

McCoy felt the hairs on the back of his neck stand on end. What the hell . . . He stared at the image in surprise. Though somewhat grotesque in its decapitated state, there was nothing inherently frightening about the alien's appearance, certainly nothing to justify the tingle of apprehension that was tickling his spine. Yet, he sensed a shroud of menace in the features of this unidentified being. He continued to stare at the head for several minutes, but no further chills developed, and Frazer's technical discourse failed to loose any more impressions.

*". . . morphological structures evidence no congruency with established configurations . . . DNA molecular sequences of amino acids reveal origins considerably divergent from biochemical evolution of known alien species."*

McCoy snorted. "In other words, you've never seen anything like it and you don't know what it is." Picking his way through a few of the most convoluted of the xenobiologist's sentences, McCoy amended a less abstruse version to the explanatory text. He made no mention of his own reaction to the alien; Spock would flaunt an intolerable condescension if McCoy reported "vague terror" with no apparent basis to support his uneasiness. The association, if indeed there was one, would come in its own time.

Still restless, McCoy snapped off the terminal and turned to rifle through the printouts. Despite Spock's disapproval, the doctor's professional correspondence was automatically printed by the computer system. McCoy liked the feel of paper and the rustle of pages: a flat screen filled with type was not a proper manuscript.

The first few packets were journal reprints and an unpublished report from the ship's surgeon of the *U.S.S. Welborne.* These were tossed aside for more careful perusal in the future; a long, limping voyage home had certain advantages. Then, unexpectedly, he saw the single page of a letter. Most of his personal correspondence came on tape, from a small circle of people who were willing to pay the extra cost of transmission. Here was an exception.

Puzzled, he glanced down at the signature. The name unleashed a sudden flood of memories that left him weak with the pain of their return. After the memories, he absorbed the meaning of the words written in the terse, brief paragraph.

He crumpled the sheet convulsively. After all this time, it shouldn't matter so much. Hell, it shouldn't matter at all. Yet his hands trembled. One corner of his mind retained a clinical detachment, noting that he had entered into a mild state of shock. The rest of him just felt sick. For a moment, he considered calling Jim Kirk. But no, that would mean talking, explaining, more remembering. And to what purpose? He had talked himself out years ago and failed to . . . Well, he had just failed.

McCoy stared at the wad of paper resting in his palm and fought against a tide of bitterness.

*God, I'm too old and too tired to start this battle again.*

Pulling himself upright, he carried the letter into his bedroom and placed it in the center of a decorated metal tray that lay on his dresser. From the drawer beneath, he pulled out a worn travel pouch. His fingers withdrew a small probe and deftly flicked a switch that lighted the tip with a pinprick glow. At its touch, a small spot on the paper began to darken, then smoke. In seconds the paper was engulfed in flames.

*"Alert, alert! There is fire in this room."*

"That, my dear shipboard computer, is the smoke of a funeral pyre. It is definitely against regulations." However, the brief burst on the tray was over and the computer fell silent.

Sleep was out of the question now, but McCoy was too shaken to do anything else. If he stayed awake, the recriminations would start creeping in, a litany of anger and regrets that were almost like old friends. With unsteady steps the doctor made his way to a small cabinet and opened its door. Riskelian mescal should do the trick just fine. Using both hands to steady the shaking bottle, he soon filled a squat glass to its rim with a pale red liquid.

"To the waters of Lethe!" Half the drink was quaffed in one gulp. His body convulsed for a second at the jolt of hot fire that ran down his throat. The Red Nova brand-label wasn't kidding. Before the remaining contents could be downed, the door buzzer announced a visitor. Good, the more distractions the better. "Come in."

Spock entered the room. The first officer's hands were full of memory chip packs and data tablets. He was wearing the look of self-absorbed concentration that accompanied every ship refitting. He launched into a stream of technical jargon without any preamble; at times like these he tended to forget human social conventions.

"Hold on there," interrupted McCoy with a wave of his hand. With effort, he could keep his voice steady. "I didn't hear, much less understand, a word you said. I was prepared for a 'Good morning, how are you?' or at least a simple 'Hello, Doctor.'"

Spock did not argue the issue. "Hello, Doctor," he said flatly and began to repeat his statements. "The electromagnetic pulse dampeners failed to fully protect the circuit backup for the MedQuiz PF-3500 internal systems file . . ."

"And I don't want to understand a word," McCoy said emphatically. He took another, tidier, swallow of his drink. "I'm off duty."

The first officer still could not be sidetracked. "I require your permission for a systems adjustment to the medical department computers. It will in no way interfere with patient care."

"Well, why didn't you say so in the first place. I thought you were in a hurry to get these things done." McCoy grinned maliciously as the Vulcan's mouth tightened. Baiting Spock was the best restorative to be found on board the ship.

"Sign here." A data tablet was stiffly proferred.

McCoy drained the last of the Red Nova before putting his glass down. His hand was still shaking as he reached for the tablet, a fact which did not escape Spock's notice. "Don't look so disapproving,

Mr. Spock." The doctor scrawled a hasty initial on the form and returned it. "I'm not drunk. At least not yet. Care to join me for a drink before you disappear into your computerized briar-patch?"

An arched eyebrow flew up. "Your species' preoccupation with ingesting large quantities of alcohol-based compounds . . ."

*Gotcha,* McCoy exulted and poured himself another glassful.

". . . is a constant source of puzzlement. Despite its known poisonous qualities, you persist in this custom."

"Not despite, Mr. Spock. *Because* of its poisonous qualities." He swallowed another mouthful of the fiery liquid.

The first officer frowned, suddenly aware that once again he had been maneuvered into an argument that he couldn't win because his logic wasn't part of the game. "I must attend to my duties." He ignored the smirk on McCoy's face and turned to leave.

*"All hands alert. Gravity adjustment in 10 seconds."*

"Oh, Spock," called out McCoy, reluctant to let his prey escape so soon. "I've been meaning to talk to you about that little transaction you botched for Jim at the trading post . . ."

When the deck tremors began, the first officer was already braced for the movement but McCoy immediately lost his balance. Above the whine of the ship's engines came the shatter of glass hitting a far wall and the crack of bone against metal.

"McCoy!" Spock fell to his hands and knees to crawl across the floor as it heaved and buckled. By the time he reached the crumpled form there was already a small pool of blood forming under the head.

*"Gravity adjustment complete. Repeat, gravity adjustment complete."*

## *Shadows on the Sun,* by Michael Jan Friedman

In *Shadows on the Sun,* set shortly after the events of *Star Trek VI: The Undiscovered Country,* the *Enterprise* was sent to Ssan, a world struggling to end a centuries-long tradition of ritual assassination. They were assigned to aid a diplomatic team, McCoy's ex-wife, Jocelyn, and her husband. In an example of Murphy's Law in action, McCoy was the only person with previous experience with the Ssana, and thus he was forced to work with them. When McCoy was a young physician in Starfleet Academy, he was part of a medical team assigned to Ssan to aid victims of the Ssana civil war against the assassins, and he came to know one of the assassins personally as he saved the man's life. In a horrible twist of fate, that man had been responsible for the death of a close friend of McCoy's and later became the Ssana high assassin. In *Shadows on the Sun,* McCoy relived his prior experiences on Ssan, and those experiences had much to do with the person McCoy eventually became.

McCoy was forced to confront his long-buried emotions when Jocelyn was kidnaped by the Ssani assassins, who were led by the man whose life he had saved years before. In this excerpt, McCoy reconciled with Jocelyn as he faced losing her forever. At the same time, he strove to save the life of the master assassin responsible for Jocelyn's plight. In typical McCoy fashion, he could neither kill the man nor let him die, although many others would have. The passage sums up everything McCoy was and believed in. *Shadows on the Sun* is a must-read for McCoy fans who want to know more about how that man came to be.

"DROP YOUR WEAPONS," ONE OF THE ASSASSINS REPEATED, IN THE VOICE that had spoken to them from the darkness. "I will not say it again."

He stood in front of all the others, an older Ssana whose face spoke of dignity and purpose—whose robe bore an emblem of a red cross inside a red circle just below his left collarbone. Instantly McCoy recognized the symbol.

This was the High Assassin, he realized. This was Shil Andrachis.

But that wasn't all the doctor recognized. As he stared at the dignified visage of the High Assassin, he realized that he had seen it before.

Amid the ruins of a government tower in Pitur. And later, in a Federation biobed. And still later, in nightmares where Merlin Carver lost his life over and over again to the blast from a killer's bomb.

It was the young Ssana whose life McCoy had saved all those years ago. *He* was the High Assassin. *He* was Shil Andrachis, the one behind the latest wave of killing and death.

Suddenly, McCoy's fear was gone, replaced by a boiling, blistering malice. Without thinking about it, he stepped forward, ignoring Jocelyn's attempt to hold him back, ignoring the prospect of death at the hands of the assembled assassins.

"You bastard!" he bellowed. "You coldhearted, murdering bastard!"

The High Assassin leveled a molten look at the human. But recognition must have dawned in him too, because his eyes narrowed and his mouth shaped the doctor's name.

"McCoy?" he muttered. The word carried in the vastness of the cavern.

Behind him, the white-robed assassins looked at one another. Obviously they didn't know what to make of this.

*"You're* still kicking," the doctor spat, eyeing his adversary. "Why shouldn't I be kicking too?"

At some point the captain had come up beside him. "Bones . . . you *know* this man?"

McCoy nodded. "Remember that friend I started to tell you about? *He* killed him in cold blood, when the wars were almost over."

Overhearing them, the Ssana shook his head. "I killed no offworlders. There is no honor in such a deed."

"I couldn't agree more," the doctor growled. Raising his voice accusingly, he said, "But another of my comrades saw you. It was at a public house. You were with four others. One of you threw a bomb . . . and my friend died in the explosion."

Andrachis's brow creased as if he were trying to remember. "I was young then," he replied at last. "And angry. It is difficult to remember some of the things that happened in those days." He dismissed the subject with a quick sweep of his hand. "But we are no longer living in the days of Li Moboron's wars."

Suddenly McCoy saw an opportunity and, stifling his anger, grasped at it.

"Part of me," argued McCoy, "will always live in those days. I can't forget all that took place back then, High Assassin. Can *you?"*

Of everyone assembled there, only Andrachis would understand what he meant by that. Only Andrachis would recall the way the human had saved his life, bringing him the sort of dishonor that time and accomplishment couldn't erase.

That gave McCoy a certain amount of power over him. Because if he told the other assassins that tale, the master would be disgraced, and they would have to seek another leader.

On the other hand, a well-thrown knife would eliminate that threat. After all, the Ssana had helped to kill Merlin Carver forty years ago; why not kill McCoy now?

If it were only Shil Andrachis he was dealing with, he could predict the ultimate outcome—and it wouldn't be a good one. But the man was no longer merely Shil Andrachis. He was the High Assassin, sworn to uphold his predecessor's principles. And Li Moboron had stated plainly that his kind did not kill offworlders.

That was why they hadn't simply been cut down in the darkness, wasn't it? Because Andrachis couldn't kill a bunch of offworlders and still call himself a master in the mold of Li Moboron.

"In the spirit of those days," McCoy said, loudly and clearly, "I ask you to let us go. We have no quarrel with you. We came only to see if we could resolve your conflict with the city-states."

"Silence," hissed another of the Ssana, a younger man. "We do not care why you came. Your methods and objectives are of no interest to us."

"You hurt us simply by being here," bellowed another. "By exposing Ssan to your alien notions of life and death."

The doctor ignored them. After all, Andrachis was the one who wielded the power. His word was the only one that really mattered.

"But surely," McCoy went on, "among civilized people—and I *know* you are civilized people—there's no just cause for imprisonment. No reason to keep people in cages as if they were animals. That brings no more honor to the jailer than the jailed."

The other assassins turned to Andrachis to see what he would say. For a time he mulled the human's words. Then he opened his mouth to answer them.

But before he could get a word out, one of his followers provided another kind of answer. There was a whisper of metal on the air and a glimmer of reflected candlelight and a single, angry cry:

"Marn, no!"

Fortunately the knife missed them, clattering against the lip of the crevasse at McCoy's feet. With such a clear shot, a veteran assassin wouldn't have missed—so it had to have been a youngster who'd thrown the thing.

Which meant there was still a chance to contain the potential for violence. As long as they stayed in control and no one fired back . . .

But someone did. Clay's phaser erupted with bloodred fury before anyone could move to stop him. As the doctor watched, horrified, the beam crossed the crevasse and struck Andrachis himself, sending him spinning out of control at the very brink of the pit.

One of the assassins at his side reached for the master, but it was too late. With a roar of pain and anger, Andrachis plunged into the yawning fissure.

But not before he gained a measure of retribution. For even as he fell, the High Assassin produced a knife from his robes and pitched it in his assailant's direction.

Unfortunately the Ssana's aim was spoiled by his fall. Missing Clay, the blade came whirling at McCoy instead. The doctor had no time to avoid it, only to brace himself for its lethal impact.

But somehow it found another target en route—another body with the speed and agility to slip in front of Bones and absorb the knife's breastbone-shattering force. It was a moment before McCoy realized which of his companions had saved his life.

And by then, Jocelyn was already teetering over the edge, clutching at the blade that protruded from the base of her throat. Eyes wide, knuckles white with her effort to pull out the weapon, she plummeted into the crevasse just as the High Assassin had a moment before.

"Jocelyn!" he cried, as the realization of what had happened sank in. Like a madman, he tried to leap in after her.

"Bones, no!" bellowed the captain. He took hold of the doctor's right arm even as Spock grabbed the sleeve of his left. "You don't know what's down there!"

It was true, he didn't. But he didn't care. Tearing free of both Kirk and the Vulcan, he jumped away from the edge of the fissure and felt a cold breath of air engulf him as he dropped into nothingness.

Abruptly, much sooner than he had expected, something hard and unyielding rushed up to meet him. It jarred him, awoke spasms of agony in the arm he'd injured earlier.

As he recovered, he could hear a moaning in the darkness. Assassins didn't moan, even in mortal pain. It had to be Jocelyn.

As Kirk watched McCoy vanish into the sea of darkness that stretched between himself and the assassins, his first impulse was to jump in after him. But he resisted, reminding himself that he had more immediate concerns.

Paramount among them was to make sure there was no more violence—no more phasers, no more knives. To that end, but with a certain amount of satisfaction as well, he belted Clay Treadway square in the jaw.

The diplomat staggered backward with the force of the blow, right into Spock's waiting arms. The Vulcan caught Treadway with one hand and grabbed his weapon with the other. Then, before the human could even think about getting it back, Spock placed him at arm's length.

Instantly the diplomat rounded on the captain, hands balled into fists, eyes burning with the desire to pound Kirk into the ground. But to his credit, he held himself back.

"That's right," said the captain. "You don't want to hit me. You don't want to do anything that will tempt our friends to send a shower of knives our way."

Treadway glowered at him, but that was the extent of it. Little by little, he unclenched his fists and came out of his hostile crouch.

Finally he tore his gaze away from Kirk and peered into the blackness at their feet.

"My god," he whispered hoarsely. "Jocelyn . . ."

The captain turned to the assassins gathered on the other side of the fissure. They were watching the intruders, poised for any eventuality. But they weren't flinging any of their weapons this way. Not yet, anyway.

That in itself was something to be grateful for. Obviously there were some cooler heads among the white-robed killers, despite their reputation to the contrary. Or was it just that they were confused without Andrachis to guide them?

After all, the High Assassin might still be alive. And if he was, it was still his right to determine the offworlders' lot.

Either way, Kirk couldn't trust fate alone, he had to establish a dialogue. And he had to do it before one of the assassins decided to change his mind.

"My comrade made a mistake in firing at your master," he called across the crevasse. "He will *not* fire at you again. None of us will."

The Ssana eyed him warily. Finally one of them came forward to answer him. He was young, but his voice had a ring of authority to it.

"I hope you are right," he said. "For your sake. We have practiced forbearance because that is the High Assassin's way. But if we find out you are trying to deceive us—"

"We're not," the captain assured him. "All we want now is to find out what happened to our people—and your master. If you could shed some of your candlelight into the depths of this crack . . ."

The Ssana regarded him for a moment or two. Then he turned to the nearest candle-holding assassin and nodded.

Following the sound of her moaning, McCoy felt along the floor of the crevasse for Jocelyn. Before long, he came up against something soft, something that trembled with fear and sadness. It was her hand, turned palm up as if in supplication.

Immediately her fingers closed around his, albeit weakly. With his free hand he groped for the knife that had lodged so hideously at the top of her sternum. It was still there, still hard and unspeakably ugly to his touch.

His first inclination was to pull it out, to rid her of the evil that had invaded her. But he didn't, because the resulting torrent of blood would only hasten her death.

Swallowing against the ache in his throat, he could hear the sound of urgent voices above, the hiss of protests and the crack of commands. But that was none of his concern. All he cared about was the woman who lay dying on the cold rock floor, the woman who had borne his child and broken his heart and, at long last, restored it to him.

"Leonard?" Her voice was little more than a burbling whisper.

"Hush," he told her, gritting his teeth lest he break down and become useless to her.

Slipping his tricorder out of his jacket, he worked the controls by rote. As the tiny monitor lit up, automatically compensating for the darkness, he played the device along Jocelyn's body. Numbers flashed on the screen, which to a layman would have meant nothing. But to him they meant a great deal.

It confirmed his initial fears. Jocelyn was dying, quickly and painfully, and it was beyond his power to save her. All he could do was ease her suffering.

McCoy set his tricorder down on the ground. By the light of its monitor, and little light it was, he removed a hypospray from another pocket. Working quickly, for he didn't know how many more breaths she had in her, he punched in the formula for a painkiller that would mitigate the torment but still leave Jocelyn lucid. Then he injected her with it.

It took effect immediately. In the blue light from the tricorder screen, his ex-wife's eyes met his. They looked as clear and beautiful as the evening he'd met her, when he was too young to guess what life might have in store for them. Now, as then, he would have done anything for her—but unfortunately, he'd already done all it was possible for him to do.

"Leonard," she said, even more softly than before. She seemed to take pleasure in saying it, as if it were an incantation against the darkness.

"I'm here," he told her, grasping her hand more tightly. He didn't know what else to say.

She took in a ragged breath. "I'm sorry," she said. "For everything."

McCoy shook his head. "There's nothing to be sorry about. Not anymore."

Jocelyn smiled at that, or at least tried to. "I don't want to leave you," she sobbed. "Not now. Not after we—"

Suddenly her eyes opened wide, as if she were seeing some truth she had never seen before. And they simply didn't close again.

"Jocelyn?" he ventured. And then again: "Jocelyn?"

But there was no answer. No answer at all.

Heaving with emotion, McCoy buried his face in her still-fragrant cheek and, shamelessly, he bawled like a newborn baby.

Sometime later he remembered they weren't alone at the bottom of the crevasse. There was another presence there, another living being, who hadn't uttered a word.

Andrachis.

The man who had killed not only Merlin Carver but now Jocelyn as well. The single individual who had caused McCoy more grief than any other.

Through his pain, McCoy listened, and he heard a shallow wheezing in the otherwise perfect silence. He crept toward it and the sound grew louder. Finally, his eyes better adjusted to the lightlessness, he made out a vague outline that could only be Andrachis.

"Come no closer!" the Ssana snapped. But his voice didn't have the strength it should have. There was something wrong with him.

Knowing better than to ignore the High Assassin's warning, the doctor stopped just shy of Andrachis's reach. Then, ignoring the ache in his throat, he ran his tricorder the length of the Ssana's body and read the results.

It was as he had suspected. Andrachis had broken several ribs. One of them had punctured a lung. The assassin's pain must be incredible.

"You're bleeding to death," McCoy said aloud, eyeing Andrachis's silhouette where he figured the Ssana's face was.

"I know that," Andrachis rasped. "It is my time, Doctor. Let me die."

"Your *time?*" Suddenly McCoy was furious. "Like it was *hers?*" he demanded. "Like it was Merlin's?"

Andrachis gasped in pain, and rolled away from the doctor. On his tricorder, McCoy saw the assassin's vital signs dip even lower.

"Leave me now," the High Assassin said. "As you should have left me then."

The words struck McCoy like a physical blow. He *should* have left Andrachis to die in the wreckage of the Pitur council chamber long ago, or let Bando kill the Ssana that night in the infirmary. He should have. If he had, Merlin would still be alive.

And so would Jocelyn.

And now, he could make up for that. He could even the scales. All he had to do was let the Ssana perish. It was so simple. How many Ssani lives would he save that way? A hundred? A thousand? Without

92

its leader, the assassins' movement might even die out completely. At the very least, it would be severely weakened.

All he had to do was let Andrachis die.

Next to him, the assassin cried out involuntarily.

And McCoy felt tears well up in his eyes.

"Damn it," he said hoarsely. He looked over at Jocelyn. "Damn it, I'm a doctor, not a blasted politician."

If Andrachis wanted, he could take his own life later on. Right now, right here, McCoy wasn't going to let him perish.

Punching new instructions into his hypospray, he drew closer to the assassin. Despite his infirmity, Andrachis lashed out at him, catching his wrist in a steely grip.

"Let me die!" the assassin repeated.

"You can go to hell," McCoy told him, "on your own time." With his free hand, he injected a stabilizing agent into Andrachis's arm.

It was significantly more effective than the drugs he'd used on the Ssana the last time: Federation medicine had come a long way in forty years. Andrachis's hold on his other hand grew stronger as the medication took effect.

"No!" the Ssana gasped. "You must let me—"

"Shut up!" snarled McCoy, sounding more like an animal than a man. "Break my wrist if you want, but you're not going to keep me from doing my work."

Abruptly, the darkness lurched and parted, as he and Andrachis were caught in a wave of flickering candlelight from above. Looking up for a moment, he saw faces peering down at him from either side of the abyss.

Jim Kirk, Spock, and Clay Treadway were arrayed along one edge, the assembled assassins along the other. Their expressions contained varying proportions of surprise, horror, relief, and repugnance.

"Jocelyn!" cried the diplomat. "Jocelyn, answer me!"

"Bones, are you all right?" called the captain.

"I'm fine," the doctor snapped, forcing himself to concentrate on the task at hand. Resetting his hypo, he injected the Ssana with an antibacterial compound.

"What are you doing?" bellowed one of the assassins.

"I'm *trying* to keep him alive!" McCoy barked.

"Jocelyn!" Clay called again, refusing to believe the evidence of his own eyes. "She's not dead, she *can't* be dead!"

"Stop," insisted Andrachis, too weak to enforce the directive. "It is wrong for you to save my life. You know that."

"I know no such thing," countered the doctor. He saw the Ssana's cursed visage through the prism of his own tears. "Life is precious. I won't be a party to your wasting it."

The assassin grimaced at the indignity being heaped on him. "I will cut your heart out," he threatened, "and feed it to you on a stick. I will shred your flesh and grind your bones to dust."

"No," said McCoy just as venomously. "You won't. Because that would bring you dishonor too, wouldn't it? I'm an offworlder, remember?"

"The human is attempting to heal Andrachis!"

"He cannot! It is sacrilege for such as he to preserve the master's life!"

The hell with them, McCoy thought, setting the hypospray a third time. What's the worst they can do? Kill me?

I feel dead already, he told himself. When he'd obtained the medication he was looking for, he injected the Ssana yet again.

"Damn it, what is he doing down there?"

Clay again, noted the doctor, through a haze of misery.

"That's the one who killed my wife. Doesn't he know that? Why is he helping the bastard when he murdered Jocelyn?"

*Because I'm a doctor,* McCoy thought, *swallowing back his sorrow. Because that's what a doctor's supposed to do.*

"Stop it!" blared the diplomat. "Let him die for what he did, you fool!"

But McCoy didn't. Not for Clay, not for the assassins. Not even for Jocelyn. Instead, he reached for his communicator to arrange an emergency transport.

## *Doctor's Orders,* by Diane Duane

*Doctor's Orders* is a complete change of pace from *Shadows on the Sun* and *Dreams of the Raven.* Watching *TOS,* I often wondered what would happen if Kirk ever responded to Bones's endless grousing and second guessing about command decisions by saying, "If you don't like it, Doctor, why don't you try to do a better job?" In this passage from *Doctor's Orders,* that is precisely what happened. When Kirk handed over command to Bones, he intended it to last only a short time, but fate had other plans. Just after McCoy assumed command, Kirk disappeared, Klingons arrived, and trouble ensued. At first, McCoy seemed out of his depth, but he managed to keep the ship together despite the battles with the Klingons. This book is a terrific read, filled with humor, space battles, and clever tactical decisions by Dr. McCoy, who made better command decisions than any might have thought.

In this excerpt from *Doctor's Orders,* Kirk surprised an unsuspecting Dr. McCoy by turning command over to him.

MCCOY BURST INTO THE BRIDGE SO TORN BETWEEN DELIGHT AND WILD annoyance that he didn't know which to let go with first. For the first moments, at least, the need to choose was aborted. Kirk was sitting there in the center seat, facing the elevator doors.

"You made it," he said, "just."

"Jim," McCoy said, "we've got a breakthrough on our hands here. It's the ;At."

"Are you catching cold?" Kirk said, looking suddenly concerned.

"No, I am *not* catching cold! Jim, I think we're concentrating on the wrong species here. I was just talking to one of the ;At, and—" He paused for a moment and looked around the bridge. It was surprisingly empty for the time of day: The only ones there besides Kirk were a Communications officer and someone from Navigation, sitting in Sulu's spot. "Where is everybody?"

"Down on the planet, most of them, or coordinating data. Or off shift. Sulu had just done two back to back, and I remember what I'm told about shift relief."

"Oh. Well, good. Jim, the ;At translation algorithm seems to be okay, they have idiom and everything, and this one said to me that it was—"

*"Doctor,"* Kirk said, "you have been overworking yourself just a bit. I think it's time you got some rest. But not even your own staff seems able to get you to slow down. Nurse Burke has been complaining to me."

*I'll kill her,* McCoy thought.

"You say a word to her and I'll dock your pay," Kirk said, wagging a finger at him. "I want you to sit down here and write me a decent report, not like that whitewash you did for Starfleet a little earlier today. They may be suckered in by all your long words, but you can't hand *me* that stuff and expect to get away with it. I want an analysis of what's going on down there."

"But I can't do that without more data—"

"Give me what you've got, and make sense of it. If you just sit still and think for a while, you're bound to come up with something that will do me some good. And you stay out of sickbay to do it, too. You go down there, you'll just start treating someone for something.

Sickbay is off limits to you except for legitimate medical emergencies, until further notice. That's a direct order. Understood?"

McCoy glowered. It was best to humor Jim when he got in these moods. They passed quickly enough. "Understood," he said.

"Good. And just to keep you out of trouble—" He got up from the center seat and stretched. "Here. Sit down."

McCoy stared at him.

"Come on," Kirk said. "Have a seat. It's nice and comfortable, you can sit here and dictate your report. But anyway, I'm leaving you the conn."

McCoy was outraged. "You can't do that," he said. *"I* can't do that!"

"Of course I can," Kirk said, "and of course *you* can. You've had line officer's training. Not the full Command course, naturally, but enough to know what to say at the right times. Not that you'll need to. And I can leave anybody with the conn that I please, most especially a department head and a fellow officer. There's no need to be in the direct chain of command at all—that's a common misconception. I could leave an ensign third-class with the conn if I liked, and the situation seemed to call for it. Well, at the moment, it seems to call for captain's discretion."

"Uh—"

"So sit down," Kirk said.

"Uh, Jim—"

"I am *leaving the bridge,* Bones. Then I am going to get something to eat. And then I am going to go down to the planet and have a chat with Spock, who is also overworking, and who I've also got to yell at; and then I'm going to meet some of these people we're supposed to be talking to. I've stood it up here about as long as I can. And *you,* Doctor, are going to sit in this comfy chair, and have a nice relaxing time, and coordinate data, which you are better equipped to do at the moment than *I* am, and then you're going to call me on the planet's surface and give me sage advice. You got that?"

McCoy nodded.

"Then get down here."

Slowly, McCoy walked down to the center seat, and very slowly, very gingerly, lowered himself into it. It was indeed very comfortable.

"You have the conn," Kirk said. "I'll be back at the end of the shift. Have fun."

"Mmf," McCoy said as Kirk walked away, and the bridge doors closed on him.

Leonard McCoy sat in the command seat of the *Starship Enterprise* and thought, *I'm going to get him for this.*

Kirk had a sandwich and a cup of coffee, grudging the time for anything more complicated. He then took himself straight off to the transporter room, and down to the clearing on the surface of Flyspeck. The sweet taste of the fresh air made the hair stand right up on his neck, as usual. It was one of the small, secret delights that he had never really managed to tell anyone about—the scent of a new world's air, for the first time, with its particular compendium of strange new aromas. This one smelled as if there had been rain recently; and there was an odd edge of spice to the air too, as if the growing things here were mostly aromatics.

He glanced around him at the business of the clearing—all the Ornae and Lahit rolling or trundling or wading around through the ground—and at his crew, doing their jobs, talking, examining, collecting data. *Spock must be around here somewhere,* he thought, and looked around for him, but couldn't see him anywhere.

"Morning, Captain," someone said behind him; he turned and saw that it was Don Hetsko, one of McCoy's people. "Looking for anyone in particular?"

"Oh, Spock, if you've seen him."

"Not for a while. The doctor went off that way just a few minutes ago, though," Don said, pointing toward one of the paths that led out of the clearing. "You ought to be able to catch him."

"Thank you, Mr. Hetsko," Kirk said, and went off that way, smiling slightly.

His businesslike stride slowed to a stroll as he got into the forest proper. The quality of the light here was unusual, somehow: more intense than he had been expecting. It was as if some photographer had purposely lit the place to look both warm and coolly enticing; a curious effect, caused by the brassy gold of the planet's sun, probably, and the extreme greenness, almost blue-greenness, of its plants' dominant chlorophyll. The science of the situation aside, it was a very pleasant effect, restful, and he was in no mood to get out of it in a hurry.

The path gave onto another clearing, bigger than the first one. Kirk paused on the fringes of it, looking at the great stone shape in the middle. He remembered the pictures of the ;At from the briefing; he remembered McCoy's insistence that the ;At were the people he wanted to talk to. But at the same time an odd reluctance came over him, almost a shyness. There was a sense of remoteness about this creature, somehow, a feeling that it knew things that might make it wiser not to disturb it . . .

Odd feelings, and baseless, of course. Kirk shook off the slight case of nerves and stepped out into the bright sunshine of the clearing.

The ;At saw him coming, Kirk knew, though it had no eyes that showed, and seemingly no other sense organs. *I wonder if Bones managed to get a scan on it,* he thought. *Have to ask him about that later.* Some feet away from it, Kirk slowed down, and stopped.

"I beg your pardon," he said.

There was a long silence before the ;At said to him, "I am not aware of your having done anything that requires pardon."

The voice was astonishing: It rumbled like a landslide. But there was nothing threatening about it. Rather, its tone of voice was so grave, and at the same time so humorous, even through the Translator, that Kirk smiled. "That's good," he said. "The phrase is an idiom of my culture, often used when one person interrupts another. I didn't want to take the chance that I might have been interrupting you in the middle of something important."

"You have not interrupted me, Captain," said the ;At.

"I'm glad." He paused and said, "You must have been the one with whom the doctor was talking."

"We did speak," said the ;At.

Kirk hesitated. "I hope you'll excuse my ignorance," he said, "but I have no name to call you by. Not even a gender designation, if you use such things."

"The doctor would have called me Sir," said the ;At.

Kirk nodded. "If I may, then. Did the doctor speak much to you of why we are here?"

"He began to," said the ;At, "and I said to him that the matter was one of some philosophical complexity. He then disappeared."

"He went back to our ship," Kirk said. "The vessel in which we travel, and by which we came here."

*"Enterprise,"* the ;At said.

"That's right."

"I see it," said the ;At. "All silver, but it shines gold where the sunlight touches it. And it has lights of its own, for the dark."

"Yes," Kirk said, while thinking with some excitement, *These creatures must have a sensorium that we've never seen the like of. I know the sound of a direct perception when I hear one. Anything that can see a starship, somehow, from the surface of a planet—what else can it see?* "Sir," he said, "did he speak to you at all of why we came?"

"No," said the ;At. "No more than did the first party who arrived here, though they asked us many a question. They were cautious. But we knew well from the sight of them that they did not come of this world, and had traveled from some other."

Kirk shook his head, thinking. *There has to be a better way to get these initial surveys done. Dammit, these are intelligent species we're dealing with, not idiots. They figure out what's going on quickly enough. How does it make us look?*

He glanced up. The ;At had not moved, but the sensation that it was looking closely at him grew quite strong—in fact Kirk was finding it a little difficult to breathe normally, with the closeness of that regard acting almost like a physical pressure on him. There was nothing angry or threatening about it. It was merely a level of interest so intense that it was actually affecting his body.

"Sir," he said, "that ship up there, and the people who are here with your people and the Ornae and the Lahit, are under my command. We have all come here to see how much we can discover about your people, and how much we can tell you about us. Once that is done, we have some questions we would like to ask all three species as a whole—if that is even possible. That is one of the things we need to discover."

"Many questions," said the ;At. "And what questions do *we* get to ask?"

"Any you like," said Kirk, just a bit nervously.

"So we shall," said the ;At, and fell silent.

Kirk stood in that silence and felt the hairs rising on the back of his neck again, but this time for no reason that had anything to do with the sweetness of the morning air. That intense interest was bent on him, and on his ship, and all his people. He could feel it on his skin, like sunlight, but it was not a warming or calming feeling at all.

"When will we start?" he said at last, when the silence became too much for him.

"We have started," said the ;At.

McCoy sat in the center seat and yawned.

He was tired, and annoyed, but at the same time he felt a certain smug satisfaction. Kirk had counted on his being terrified by this experience. Unfortunately he had not reckoned with McCoy's great talent for learning to cope at high speed. It was probably the first important thing a doctor or nurse learned—how to turn the sudden surprising or annoying situation into a commonplace.

He had been playing with the buttons on the center seat's arms. There was quite an assortment of links into the library computer, so that even without a Science officer at his or her station, you could display all kinds of information on the main bridge screen, and even do things like voicewrite reports. McCoy had finished the report that Kirk had asked him for, and then had gone back to playing with the machinery, pulling various information up out of the library computer and annotating his report with it.

The bridge intercom whistled, and McCoy glanced over to the communications officer on post, Lieutenant DeLeon, to say that he would take it himself. He pushed the appropriate button on the seat console and said, "Bridge. McCoy."

*"Heaven help us, Doctor, what're ye doing up there?"* Scotty's shocked voice said.

"Blame the captain, Scotty," McCoy said. "He stuck me with the conn two and a half hours ago."

Scotty chuckled a little at that. *"Well, it'll do you no harm, I suppose. Himself is downplanet, I take it."*

"You take it right. Anything I can help you with?"

*"Not a thing. He had asked me to do a reset on the warp engines, and I have the figures for him on how long it would take and how much antimatter we would need. It can wait till he gets back up."*

"Why did he want a reset?"

*"Ah, I talked him into it. It's a matter of maximizing our fuel consumption, is all. He was looking to save some power by resetting the fusion timing. I found a better way, but I shan't trouble you with the details."*

"Thanks, don't," McCoy said. "I'll let him know you've got the figures for him."

*"Right you are,"* Scotty said. *"Engineering out."*

McCoy pushed the button with satisfaction, and sat back in the center seat. "DeLeon," he said, "would you get me the landing party? I want to see what they're up to down there."

"Yes, sir," said DeLeon. A moment later the screen was showing the main clearing down on Flyspeck and crewpeople all over the place, busily doing their work.

McCoy saw Spock, and Lia, and various other people he knew; but there was no sign of Kirk.

"Off gallivanting again," he said. "Pinpoint the captain, would you, Lieutenant?"

"Sure, Doctor." DeLeon touched a few controls, then peered at his board. It was a curious look.

"What's the matter? Did he turn his communicator off? Just like him," McCoy said, grumbling.

"No, Doctor," said DeLeon. "I can't find him."

McCoy got up and stepped up to the Communications station, looked at the scanner screen, and frowned. No trace of the captain was showing at all. Even if Jim had dropped his communicator, the scanners would still clearly indicate where it had fallen.

But there was no trace of it at all.

McCoy swallowed hard and called Spock.

## *Spock's World,* by Diane Duane

*Spock's World* is a saga of Vulcan's past and the evolution of its people framed in a story of Vulcan secession from the Federation. *Spock's World* is discussed and excerpted later in this book, but it is included here because McCoy was its true hero. To prevent Vulcan secession, he investigated the underlying causes of the movement, and he discovered that not only was the situation not what it appeared to be, but that some parties involved were acting from personal grudges and greed rather than logical political motivations. In a climactic moment in the secession debate, McCoy delivered a moving speech against secession and demonstrated unequivocally his love and respect for the Vulcan people. This speech is my single favorite passage from all the Star Trek books.

"NUMBER SIX," SAID SHATH.

McCoy stepped up there with great calm. Considering that those who spoke before him had been vehemently anti-Federation, and the audience was (if Jim judged the mood correctly) in a very satisfied mood, Jim thought he was being even calmer than he needed to be. McCoy stood in the shafts of downpouring sunlight, glanced up at them for a moment, and then looked once right around the room, as if taking the measure of it. His stance was remarkably erect for a man who habitually slouched a bit. But Jim looked at this and wondered if he was not seeing Vulcan body language, rather than Terran. Bones was shrewder than people usually thought.

"My name is Leonard Edward McCoy," he said, and the focusing field caught his voice and threw it out to the back of the room, all around: but there was still something about the tenor of the voice itself that hinted that the focusing field might be doing slightly less work than usual. "I hold the rank of commander in the Starfleet of the United Federation of Planets: my position is chief medical officer of the *Starship Enterprise.* And as regards the question of the secession of Vulcan, my position is, hell no!"

There were chuckles from some of the humans present, a bemused stirring from some of the Vulcans. "I hope you will pardon me the momentary excursion into my mother idiom," McCoy said: "perhaps I should more correctly say, with Surak, *ekhwe'na meh kroykah tevesh."* This time there were murmurs from the Vulcans, and they were of approval. The translator did not render the words—Jim assumed they were in classical or "Old" Vulcan, which the translator was not equipped to handle.

When the crowd settled a bit, McCoy went on in very precise Vulcan, and this caused a minor stir as well, which died down eventually. "I want to keep this on a friendly basis," he said, "despite the fact that some of you are feeling decidedly unfriendly toward Terrans. Nor am I here to lecture you. Others here have been doing that a lot better than I could." There was a dry sound to his voice for a moment. "I am here to ask you, as a planet, not to pull out of what has been a very old and successful affiliation for everyone involved."

He paused for a moment, looking around. "It's kind of sobering to be looked at by an entire planet," he said. "You people have hidden the cameras perfectly: I appreciate the effect. Anyway. Some people here have spoken about the mode of their comments—scientific or ethical or whatever. Well, for my own part I'm not sure there's a difference, or should be. Science is barren without ethics, and ethics has very little to use itself on without science. But I'll speak of what I know, if I may. The medical mode, I suppose we might as well call it. I understand that Surak valued the healer's art highly, so I suspect there's some precedent."

Bones walked around the stage for a moment, his hands clasped behind him. Jim had to smile: he had seen this particular pacing mannerism many times, while McCoy tried to figure out the best way to deliver some piece of good or bad news. "The first thing I would want to say to you," he said, "is that it is illogical to re-wound what is already healing. Or as my mother used to say, 'If you don't stop picking at it, it'll never get better.'" A soft sound of amusement ran around the hall.

"Most of the agreements going these days between Terrans, or the Federation, and Vulcan, are in the nature of Band-Aids. One of our species hurt the other, somewhere: the other said, 'Sorry,' and put a bandage on it. It's the usual thing you see when you see two children playing together. At first they hurt one another a lot—"

"Our species is hardly a child compared with yours," said someone in the audience, a sharp angry voice.

"Well," McCoy said, turning that way and searching the audience with his eyes, "that depends on how you reckon it. Certainly your species was making bombs and guns and missiles and such while ours was still mostly playing with sharpened sticks and stone knives, or in a few favored areas, bronze. But I'm not sure that any particular virtue accrues to that distinction. And even if we *have* been kicking one another's shins for less time than you, it's still true that era for era, Terra's people have kicked a lot fewer shins per capita than Vulcan has. You have several times almost reduced your population to below the viability level: it took a miracle to save you. We may be a bloody, barbaric lot of savages, but we never went *that* far. Even when we first came up with atomics." He chuckled softly at the slight silence that fell. "Yes," he said, "you saw that article in the data nets last night, too, some of you. Where *is* Selv?" he said, peering amiably around the audience. "You in here?"

"Here," said the sharp voice.

"Aha," McCoy said, looking out in that direction and shading his eyes. "Long life and prosperity to you—though I doubt you'll attract much prosperity with that kind of worldview. Still, maybe wishes count. But it might help if you went to Earth some day and checked out what you talked about so blithely—"

"The data about Earth speaks for itself—" Selv's thin, angry voice came back.

*"No* data speaks for itself," McCoy said, forceful. "Data just lies there. *People* speak. The idiom 'speaks for itself' almost *always* translates as 'If I don't say something about this, no one will notice it.' Sloppy thinking, Selv! You are dealing with second- and third-hand data. You have never been to Earth, you don't understand our language—and this is made especially clear by some of the material you claim to be 'translating' from Earth publications: an Andorian spirit-dancer with a Ouija board and a Scrabble set could do a better job. Though I must admit I really liked the article on the evolution of the blood sacrifice in Terran culture. That is *not* what major-league football is for. . . ."

McCoy let the laugh die down, and then said, "Anyway, where was I? Agreements as bandages. *Every* species in this galaxy that bumps into another one, bruises it a little. Some of them back off in terror and never come out to play again. Some of them run home to their mommies and cry, and never come out again without someone else to protect them. That's their problem. I for one would like them to come out and play—"

"And be exploited? The Federation's record of violations of the Prime Directive has been well documented—"

"Selv, I love you. How many violations of the Prime Directive have there been?"

A brief, frantic silence. "Well documented," McCoy said, good-humored, "but not well enough for you to have seen it. Too busy reading about football? Anyway, don't bother looking it up," McCoy said, "I'll tell you myself. In the last one hundred and eighty years, there have been twenty-nine violations. It sounds like a lot . . . except when you consider that those took place during the exploration of twenty-three *thousand* planets by the various branches of Starfleet. And don't start with me about the *Enterprise,"* he added, "and her purported record. There have been five violations . . . out of six hundred thirty-three planets visited and physically surveyed over the last five years."

"And all those violations have taken place under a Terran's captaincy—"

"Oh, my," McCoy said, and it came out almost in a purr, "can it be that Vulcan is leaving the Federation because someone here *doesn't like James T. Kirk?* What an amazing idea! Though it would go nicely with some rumors I've been hearing." Bones strolled calmly around the stage for a moment, while Jim and Spock looked at one another, slightly startled. "Well, no matter for that. Still, Selv, your contact with the facts about things seems to be sporadic at best. If I were the people who've been reading your material in the nets—and a busy little beaver you've been of late—I would start wondering about how much of what I was reading was for real. That is, if I were logical—" McCoy lifted his head to look up over the audience's heads, and Spock glanced meaningfully at Jim. McCoy knew perfectly well where the cameras were.

"You may say what you like," Selv said, "but even five violations are too many! And your use of your data is subjective—"

"Of course they're too many!" McCoy said. "Do you think I would disagree on that? And as for my data, of course it's subjective! So is yours! We are each of us locked up in our own skull, or maybe skulls, if you're a Vulcan and lucky enough to be successfully bonded. If you start going on about objective reality, I swear *I'll* come down and bite you in the leg!" There was some chuckling at that.

"Though I hope you've had your shots," McCoy added. "If not, I

104

can always give them to you afterward. I've become pretty fair at taking care of Vulcans over the past few years. At any rate, I was talking about bandages—"

"The doctor is tenacious," Spock said softly.

"The doctor is a damn good shrink," Jim whispered back, "and knows damn well when someone's trying to give him the runaround."

"—There's no arguing the fact that Vulcans and Terrans, or the Terran-influenced functions of the Federation, have had a lot of bumps into one another over the course of time," McCoy said. "There have been arguments about trade, and weapons policy, and exploration, and exploitation of natural resources, and the protocol of running a Vulcan space service, and everything else you can think of. And every one of those arguments is a bandage over one of the other species' hurts. Now," he said, "you would destroy all that hard-built cooperation at one blow: rip off all the bandages at once, yours and ours together—"

"We can bind up our own wounds," Selv said angrily. "And when two species are no longer going to be cooperating, what does it really matter about the other's?"

McCoy gazed up at him. "'The spear in the other's heart is the spear in your own,'" he said: "'you are he.'"

A great silence fell.

"So much for the man who claims, in the net media, to speak for a majority of all right-thinking Vulcans," McCoy said, glancing up over the audience's heads again. "You see that there is at least one Vulcan he does *not* speak for. Surak."

Jim and Spock looked at each other in utter satisfaction.

McCoy strolled about calmly on the stage for a moment, as if waiting to see whether Selv would come up with anything further. "Can't have Vulcan without Surak," he said: "most irregular. At least, that seems to be most people's attitude here. But a few of you seem quite ready to throw him out along with us." He kept strolling, his hands clasped behind him again, and he gazed absently at the floor as he walked. Then suddenly he looked up.

*"We* are what he was preparing you for," McCoy said. "Don't you see that? Along with everything else in the universe, of course. *Infinite diversity in infinite combinations!* That means people who breathe methane, and people who hang upside down from the ceiling, and people who look like pan pizzas, and people who speak no language we will ever understand and want only to be left alone. And it means *us!* A particularly hard case. An aggressive, nasty, brutish little species . . . one that nonetheless managed to get out into space and

begin its first couple of friendships with other species without consulting *you* first for advice. A species that maybe reminds you a little too much of yourselves, a while ago—confused and angry and afraid. A hard case. Probably the hardest case! . . . the challenge that you have been practicing on with other species for a while now! And you met us, and welcomed us, though you had understandable reservations. And since then there have been arguments, but generally things have been working out all right. We are proud to be in partnership with you.

"But now . . . now comes the inevitable reaction. There's always a reaction to daring to do the difficult thing, day after day. Every action has an equal and opposite reaction: this is its reaction. The temptation is arising to chicken out. It would be easier, some people are saying. Cleaner, nicer, tidier, without the messy Federation and the problems it raises just by being there. And you are backing off, you are panicking, you are saying, No, we can't cope, Surak can't have meant *everything* when he taught the philosophy of IDIC: he actually meant everything *but* the third planet out from Sol.

"COWARDS!!"

McCoy paced. The Hall of the Voice was utterly still.

"Pride." he said finally, more quietly. "I keep hearing about Vulcan pride. An emotion, of course. One you were supposed to have mastered, those of you who practice *cthia:* or something you were supposed to have gotten rid of, those of you who went in for *Kolinahr.* Well, I have news for you. The stuff I've been seeing in the nets lately, that is *pride.* Not to be confused with admiration, which is something else, or pleasure in integrity, which is something else entirely. This is good old-fashioned pride, and it goes with fear, fear of the Other: and pride and fear together have gone with all your falls before, and the one you're about to take now, if you're not very careful." McCoy's voice softened. "I would very much like to see you not take it. I am rather fond of you people. You scare the hell out of *me* sometimes, but it would be a poor universe without you. But unless you move through your fear, which is the emotion Surak was the most concerned about—and rightly—and come out the other side, the fall is waiting for you: and you will bring it about yourselves, without any help from our species or any other. This," he gestured around him, "all this concern about humans, and indirectly about the Federation—this is a symptom of something else, something deeper. Trust me. I'm good with symptoms."

He took one more silent turn around the stage. "If you throw us out—for what you're really doing here is throwing the Federation out of Vulcan, not the other way around—beware that you don't thereby take the first step in throwing out Surak as well. We are, after all, just a different kind of alien from the sort you are from one another: the first fear he taught you to move through was the fear of one another. Unlearn that lesson, and, well, the result is predictable. Ignore the past, and repeat your old mistakes in the future."

McCoy gazed up over the audience's heads one last time. "Surak would be *very* disappointed in you if you blew up the planet," he said. He bowed his head, then, regretfully.

"And so would we."

McCoy straightened after a moment and lifted the parted hand. *"Mene sakkhet ur-seveh,"* he said, and walked off the stage.

There was a long pause, and then the applause. It was thunderous.

McCoy found his way back to his seat between Jim and Spock and wiped his forehead.

"I take it the deep breathing worked," Spock said quietly.

McCoy laughed out loud, then looked at Spock a little challengingly. "That," he said, "was just about every argument I've ever had with you, rolled into one package."

"Then I would say you won," said Spock.

McCoy shot a glance at him and grinned. "Thanks."

"Pity you weren't on last," Jim said softly. "You would have brought the house down."

"I would have preferred that placement," McCoy said, looking up.

"Number seven," Shath said from the stage.

Sarek stepped up.

# CHAPTER 4

# Second to None—Scotty, Uhura, Sulu, and Chekov

NO COMPILATION OF ORIGINAL STAR TREK NOVELS COULD BE COMPLETE without Scotty, Uhura, Sulu, and Chekov. Although the original series did not develop any of these crew members as fully as Kirk, Spock, or McCoy, each is well loved by fans, as are the actors who play them, James Doohan, Nichelle Nichols, George Takei, and Walter Koenig. Because novels do not have the same limitations as episodic television, writers have been able to explore their backgrounds and develop these characters in ways that could not have been possible on the NBC television series.

## Scotty and *The Kobayashi Maru*

Chief Engineer Montgomery Scott was third in command of the original *Enterprise,* but he was never so happy as when he was working miracles and changing the laws of physics with his beloved "bairns," the warp engines. Even so, Scotty had his moments in the sun in the original series, for example, in "Wolf in the Fold" and "Who Mourns for Adonis." Likewise, he was a key player in a number of the novels, including *Memory Prime,* by Garfield and Judith Reeves-Stevens, discussed later in this book, and *The Kobayashi Maru,* by Julia Ecklar.

In these flashback scenes from *The Kobayashi Maru,* Starfleet Academy Cadet Scott found himself on the command track but desperately wanted to be an engineer instead. His novel approach to the no-win scenario was not only typically Scotty, it got him out of command school and back with his beloved engines. In his own way, Scotty defeated the no-win scenario.

AMUSING. I NEEDN'T WORRY ABOUT CURFEW. BUT YOU SHOULD—IT'S AFTER 03:00. WHY RISK SO MANY DEMERITS FOR SUCH A SILLY PROJECT?

Labeling Cheryl's coupler "silly" wounded Scott's pride. He'd promised Cheryl a finished design before he left; he was delivering nearly three months late, but he was confident enough in his abilities to believe she'd think the wait well worth it. He wasn't about to try and explain his affection for design to some peeper whose very hobby made clear that he didn't give a damn about the pride people took in their systems. "Who are you?"

PERHAPS I'M YOUR FAIRY GODMOTHER. I AM WILLING TO GRANT YOU ONE WISH.

*Send me home!* Scott thought, all unbidden. He shook his head to scatter such dreams, afraid to even mention them, much less wish for them.

YOU ARE A FINE ENGINEER, BUT AN UNHAPPY CAPTAIN. IF YOUR FAIRY GODMOTHER WERE TO OFFER YOU A CHANCE TO LEAVE COMMAND SCHOOL AND RETURN TO ENGINEERING—WITHOUT SHAMING YOUR FAMILY OR REQUIRING YOU TO BE REMISS IN YOUR DUTIES—WOULD YOU ACCEPT?

Scott touched the screen with wondering fingers. The coupler design sprang up beneath them, rotating a slow, silent waltz.

YES OR NO, MISTER SCOTT? the peeper pressed impatiently. THE ANSWER IS THAT SIMPLE.

"Yes."

It was done. He couldn't take the word back now, no matter what happened. The genie was out of the bottle and promising his fealty.

VERY WELL. SIMPLY BE YOURSELF, SCOTTY. LEAVE THE REST TO ME.

The coupler vanished, along with the glowing words, leaving Scott all alone in an empty computer lab. He thumbed the power switch with one numb hand, then sat for a long time after the faint hum of the machinery faded.

Early the next morning, as Scott pulled on his boots in a crowded, brightly lit barracks, he realized it all must have been a dream. You just didn't get second chances of such magnitude—Cheryl would get her coupler design, Scott would get his captain's stripes, and all these silly wishes would be left far behind. Unknown peepers just didn't come in and fix everything without being asked. That just wasn't how the real world worked.

He tried not to let the incident bother him anymore.

\* \* \*

"Tell me again—*how* did I get to be in command of this scenario?"

"Computer selection. I always thought the computer picked the best commander for any scenario based on student records." The other cadet glanced Scott quickly up and down, shrugging more to himself than to his companion. "I guess it's just random draw, though."

Scott was inclined to agree. In a previous scenario, he'd been assigned the position of chief engineer, and the annoyance of having to tell a half-dozen other cadets what to do (as if engineers couldn't think of enough duties for themselves) nearly killed him. Now the computer was saying that Montgomery Scott was the best it could do for a starship commander from this class; if that were the case, Scott was heartily concerned about the rest of Starfleet.

The simulation chamber—so startlingly like a real starship's bridge that Scott kept expecting the *real* captain to chase him out of the command chair—rumbled shut like a monstrous clam. How could they lock him in here like this, responsible for so many people? It was only make-believe, true, so any decisions he made couldn't *really* affect the whole Federation. Still, no one had even *asked* Scott if he wanted to be the captain, and he most emphatically *didn't!* Oh, Admiral Howell had asked, "Are you ready?" just before steering Scott off for the bridge, but Scott knew that was only a polite question, not a real question wanting a real answer. So Scott had replied, "I'm ready," in a voice whose steadiness lied about his trembling hands. Smiling a little sadly, Howell had clapped him manfully on the back and sent him on his way. Scott would rather the admiral had banished him to the outer Pleiades.

The first part of the scenario passed in a haze. The *U.S.S. Saratoga* didn't appear to be doing anything important in this simulation—just a routine training cruise to Gamma Hydra, without even supplies to drop off or passengers to coddle. Scott mouthed meaningless course changes, responded woodenly to questions and comments. He couldn't completely divorce knowledge of the simulation's falseness from everything that happened, so he tried to convince himself that nothing impressive would be expected from him. When asked about rescuing a damaged neutronic fuel carrier, Scott responded with an automatic affirmative, then turned back to the discussion he'd been conducting with *Saratoga's* nonexistent engineering staff.

The red alert siren startled him out of a dissertation on circuit rerouting and energy dispersal. "What's the matter?" he asked, realizing belatedly that he probably should have directed that question to his exec.

110

"Three Klingon cruisers, dead ahead," the science officer reported, just as helm exclaimed, "They're readying their weapons!"

Scott's stomach turned to hot water and started to crawl about his insides. "Communications," he summoned evenly, "try to explain to these . . ." Mindful of the monitoring officers, he tempered the label he'd intended to employ. ". . . *people* that we're here on a rescue—"

*"Incoming!"*

"Full power to screens!" The command had barely cleared Scott's lips when the first barrage of disruptor fire expended itself against *Saratoga's* deflectors. Scott's teeth clacked together as he was flung back into his seat by the impact.

"Screens four, seven, and eight are down," the executive officer, bent over his viewer, reported stonily. "Screens three and sixteen are damaged. They won't last another round, sir."

Scott stared at the exec in stunned disappointment. "Were our deflectors *up?*" he sputtered. Intellectually, he knew they were; instinctively, he just couldn't believe a simple disruptor could wreak that much havoc, even through only partial shielding.

"We've also got premature detonation in four of our six torpedo tubes," the exec continued.

"What?!"

"And a complete loss of power in the starboard warp nacelle." The young officer raised his head from his viewer like a doctor pulling away from a dying patient. "We're just about done, sir."

Scott would have been less confused if the man had started speaking in tongues. *"That* much damage . . . ?"

The exec nodded. "That's the whole tally, sir."

*"How?"*

"Disruptors, sir," the helmsman sighed, a bit irritably. "They can do a lot of damage to a ship."

"Is that so?" Scott grated softly, feeling the blood rise hot and angry into his cheeks. He lifted his chin to the Klingons who closed on the viewscreen, suddenly not caring that this was just a damn scenario. "Well, not to *my* ship, they don't—not with a single damn barrage!" Any computer that thought otherwise deserved whatever Scott could throw at it. He slammed his fist onto the command chair's intercom button. "Phaser bay!"

"Aye, captain?"

"Yes, sir?"

"Sir?"

Another blast rocked the ship. Scott felt each rumble like fire in his blood. "Number three screen, down!" the exec called. Scott ignored him.

"I want all phaser bays to fire on my command, each of you aimed at one of those bedeviled crafts," Scott instructed the phaser chiefs grimly. "Continuous fire—start at your lowest possible frequency—"

Another disrupter hit. And another.

"Number three screen is *down,* sir!" the exec repeated loudly.

Scott wished the beggar would quit interrupting his thinking.

"—range upward until you match their interference pattern and cut through those shields like butter!"

"Aye, aye!" all three bays responded in unison. Scott smiled the smile of a satisfied hunter.

The navigator was already plotting an escape course as the *Saratoga*'s bays opened fire with a chilling. climbing wail. "I can't signal Starfleet," the communications officer interjected from behind Scott. "The Klingons are jamming my signal."

Golden-red light burst across the viewscreen like a nova, burning Scott's eyes with its brilliance as *Saratoga*'s phasers finally reduced the Klingons to atoms. "Not anymore, they aren't," Scott told communications. "Contact Starfleet. Helm—get us out of here."

"Working on it, sir." The helmsman swore suddenly, punching at his panel "But we've got company again!"

The five blue-gray cruisers hove into view even as the helmsman reported.

"That's it for the phaser banks, sir," the science officer reported as the *Saratoga* began her limping retreat. "Bay crews report all cells exhausted beyond our ability to recharge."

Scott waved off the report, dropping back into his chair. He wanted to feel weak and wasted after that first adrenaline surge. All he felt was sere and angry—angry at the monitoring officers for making him captain in a scenario he patently had no business commanding, angry at whoever had programmed this fatalistic computer in the first place. "Don't worry about the phaser bays. We aren't going to need them again, anyhow."

"Klingons closing!"

"Cut all rear shields," Scott ordered. His brain raced about like light in a mirrored box, searching his memory for any ideas at all. "I want everything we've got up front." *Especially with a computer that so overestimates Klingon firepower.*

"Transporter room to bridge!" The call came immediately upon the torpedo bay's sign-off. "We've got that antimatter canister, sir. What now?"

Scott held the channel open, turning to the helmsman. "Pull us back. *Keep* pulling us back as fast as impulse drive will allow."

"Aye, aye, sir."

"Navigator?"

"Sir?"

"Start a continuous reading on the crux ship's position, and transmit your data down to the transporter room." He bent to the intercom again. "Prepare to receive coordinates."

"Incoming," the helmsman announced, with somewhat less concern than before. Scott nodded his acknowledgment, already working equations in his head for the next fleet of ships he knew the computer would send.

"Coordinates received, bridge," the transporter room responded after a moment. Then: "Uh, sir? Which should we use?"

Scott grinned. "Give me less than two kilometers in front of the crux ship—"

The second barrage hit with considerably more force than the first. Scott clung to the command chair while half his bridge crew was thrown to the floor, the lighting dimmed sharply before climbing again on emergency power.

"—less than two kilometers," Scott picked up again when the systems had stabilized, "from whatever its coordinates are when you energize. Then I want you to *immediately* beam back the canister."

"But—"

"*Just* the canister," Scott stressed. When would these bairns learn to shut up and just *listen?* "Leave the antimatter behind."

"Holy cow. . . ."

Scott listened while transporter techs scurried about like busy ants. The distance was too great for the bridge crew to see when the antimatter was delivered, but everyone knew when the crux ship struck the antimatter's area of affect: all five cruisers flew apart into white noise and molecular wind just as they leashed another assault. Scott was grinning like a fool when the ship bucked him out of the chair and onto the deck.

"Screens are *down,* Captain!" sounded on top of someone else's frantic, "Hull breach! We've got a hull breach in section six hundred!"

Scott climbed back into the command chair without bothering to ask the science officer if any trace of the enemy ships remained (the velvet emptiness beyond the viewscreen rendered such questions extraneous). "Navigator! Are we out of the Neutral Zone yet?"

"We *have* been!" the navigator replied. "They're *following* us!"

"Ah, hell . . . !"

"Nine!"

Everyone on the bridge jerked about at the science officer's broken squeak. "What?" Scott demanded, irrationally annoyed at the man's interruption.

*"Nine!"* the officer replied, still looking shocked. "We've got *nine* Klingon ships closing on our port. bow!"

"Coming around!" helm announced even as Scott stabbed at the intercom to call, "Transporter room!"

"We've got them!" the main transporter room proclaimed. "Six torpedoes in every room. Orders, Captain!"

*It won't work,* Scott realized suddenly. He checked the equations in his head again, and wondered if a computer would let mathematics outprove experimentation. Shaking his head, he admitted that he had nothing to lose. "Take your coordinates from navigations again—" The navigator nodded understanding and started to scan. "—and from the science station." The science officer whirled to face her panel. "Lock on the juncture points in the Klingon screen system and beam six torpedoes to each juncture point on my command."

Scott studied the sleek ships on the viewscreen as he awaited the transporter rooms' readiness. The monitors would stop the scenario, he was sure of it. Someone would blast open the screen and rail at him for dishonesty—for cheating! His career would end in ruin!

"Transporter room, here." The voice at his elbow made him jump. "All rooms ready for beaming."

Scott licked dry lips and nodded at the approaching ships. "Transport at will."

The resultant explosion was beyond deafening; Scott's ears rang in painful symphony with his aching heart as atomic fire consumed the nine Klingon war dragons less than a thousand kilometers beyond his bow. He ducked his head against it, hearing the navigator bark a startled curse. He was still staring at the floor as the world faded from white, to ephemeral pastels, to gray-speckled normalcy again. *They're going to kill me,* he thought with sick resignation.

*"Fifteen* war dragons, on the way." The helmsman began to laugh a little manically. "Jesus Christ! *Fifteen* . . . !"

Scott couldn't make himself look up to watch the ships close. The knowledge that this was not reality—and that he could pay dearly for taking advantage of that fact—had been driven home again with gale force when those nine ships cleared the screen. Suddenly, he'd lost interest in defending the honor of a ship that wasn't even really there. He would do his best until this travesty was all over, but he knew better than anyone else at this Academy just how pitiful his best would be. "Engine room, unlock the warp drive main control. You'll need somebody from weapons, but . . ."

## Lieutenant Uhura: *The Tears of the Singers* and *Uhura's Song*

Lieutenant Uhura was a television first on a show that had a lot of firsts, and she was a role model not so much for what she said or did, but for the fact that she was there, doing an important job on an important ship. She was a black woman in a position of authority on a military vessel, and she helped round out a multi-racial, multi-ethnic, and multi-species crew. Although Uhura's dialogue all too often was limited to opening hailing frequencies, she was present on the bridge, on camera and visible. She was a capable officer who knew her job. She was a graduate of Starfleet Academy, and she demonstrated her capabilities not only in her own position but by staffing other bridge positions in crises. As LeVar Burton, Whoopi Goldberg and even astronaut Mae Jemison have said, Uhura's presence on the bridge as an officer showed that black people made it out into space at a time when the future was not at all clear for many minorities. That was a powerful message in 1966.

Several novels gave Uhura the chance to expand her range beyond hailing frequencies, particularly *Uhura's Song,* by Janet Kagan, and *The Tears of the Singers,* by Melinda Snodgrass. To hold the bridge position of chief communications officer, Uhura had to have extensive language knowledge, competence with the universal translator, and first contact skills. The communications officer would necessarily be the officer responsible, literally, for first contact with aliens, particularly alien vessels. These talents were critical to the success of the missions in *Uhura's Song* and *The Tears of the Singers.*

## *Uhura's Song,* by Janet Kagan

*Uhura's Song,* by Janet Kagan, is the fascinating tale of a felinoid species divided for millennia by painful events in the past, as well as the resulting pride and fear that prevented reestablishment of relations. One branch of the species, the Eeiauoans, were dying of a plague that threatened humans as well, and Uhura's facility with languages and music led her to the discovery that the other branch, the Sivaoans, very likely had the cure. However, to obtain the cure from the Sivaoans, the *Enterprise* crew had to engage in some very basic communications with them and gain their trust. *Uhura's Song* essentially was a quest by the *Enterprise* landing party for acceptance by the felinoids and a cure for the disease. The excerpt is from the initial contact between the humans and the Sivaoans, aided by Uhura's command of the language of the their relatives, the Eeiauoans. Can you imagine a race of giant sentient house cats? This story's visual imagery alone is a delight.

THE TRANSPORTER ROOM VANISHED AND, IN ITS PLACE, THE LANDING PARTY found a small clearing. All around them ancient trees rose to heights she had seen only in wilderness preserves, but—Uhura blinked back tears of relief—they were familiar. She laid her hand on the trunk before her and its very solidity warmed her: she *knew* this place. CloudShape to-Ennien had once cloaked herself in mist and climbed a tree like this one . . . to where the storm clouds had been at play with their lightnings. Fooled by the mist, the storm clouds invited CloudShape to join their game. They tossed a lightning to her—and CloudShape caught it with her tail and scurried down as fast as she could climb, leaving the storm clouds to boom their anger.

Once Sunfall had burst into laughter at the sight of a barbecue. When Uhura had asked her why, Sunfall said, "To see a cooking fire is to see the singe marks on CloudShape's tail."

"Mr. Spock?" Captain Kirk's puzzled voice broke into her thoughts and drew her back to the business at hand.

Spock took a reading from his tricorder and said, "The inhabited area is about three hundred yards in that direction, Captain. As these people have, in all probability, seen neither a human nor a Vulcan, I did not wish to add to their surprise with a materialization."

"Good thinking, Mr. Spock." Kirk gestured. "Let's go then. . . . Set phasers on stun and stay alert, people." With him in the lead, the party began to move warily through the forest.

Before her, Mr. Chekov took quick suspicious steps, matching his pace to Captain Kirk's. Slightly to her right, Evan Wilson crept swiftly along; the rapt concentration on her face made Uhura think of a child at play but her steps made no sound. Behind her, she could sense Spock's reassuring presence.

The captain stopped, raised his hand to motion them forward. They approached cautiously. "We hev found a trail, Mr. Spock," said Chekov, somewhat unnecessarily; he kept his voice low.

The trail was not broad—two might walk abreast—but it was hardpacked from frequent use. Kirk looked inquiringly at Spock, who said quietly, "We do not come as enemies, Captain. A straightforward approach would seem most appropriate."

"My thought exactly." Captain Kirk spoke in a normal tone of voice.

A single shriek of wordless anger stabbed through the forest.

"Down!" shouted Kirk, diving for cover himself, as the branches high above them came alive with furious movement and a chorus of chilling cries.

Uhura found herself sheltering beneath a partially fallen tree trunk as a hail of small round objects struck and bounced. She lifted her phaser and scanned the trees. At first, all she could make out were flapping branches, then she caught a glimpse of one of the creatures: it was small and brightly furred. Its feet and long tail were definitely prehensile. Another bounced suddenly into view; it too was screaming, but Uhura could see that the teeth it bared so threateningly were the flat teeth of leaf-eaters.

"Nuts!" said Evan Wilson from just beneath Uhura's left elbow. "They're throwing nuts at us!" The announcement brought a second hail down on them.

That stirred the memory of one of Sunfall's songs. Uhura twisted to look at Evan, but found herself face to face with Captain Kirk. Evan was wedged beneath the two of them, staring down at her tricorder. "They're *welcome-homes,* Captain," Uhura said. "That's all they do—make noise, wave branches and throw things."

Kirk nodded at her and emerged cautiously from cover. Spock followed suit. The welcome-homes kept to the safety of their perches; farther up the trail, another group took up the raucous cries. "All bark and no bite," he said to Spock and winced as a shower of pellets bounced off his head.

"If I understand your meaning, sir, yes. These creatures would be herbivorous. Shall we go on?"

"Yes, Mr. Spock. The Sivaoans can hardly have failed to notice our presence. I suggest we go meet them before they come looking for us." A mischievous expression touched the corners of his mouth as he watched Evan crawl from cover and dust twigs from her trousers. "You can stop sneaking, Dr. Wilson."

117

"Begging the captain's pardon, but I wasn't sneaking."

"What would you call it?"

Evan straightened and, as if surprised he should ask, said, "Pussyfooting, sir."

Captain Kirk laughed. "All right. Don't."

The party set off down the trail to ever louder squawks and rustlings as the welcome-homes leapt from branch to branch to keep pace with them. The path veered abruptly to the left and down and spilled into a wide opening between the ancient trees. In the clearing beyond, gigantic flowers of a dozen shapes and colors bloomed in the sudden sunlight.

Kirk spread a hand, silently commanding a halt. Spock took a single pace more. His action was perhaps deliberate, for it gave Uhura an unobstructed view; what she had thought flowers were brightly colored tents.

Emerging from doorways, tending cooking fires, rising from open-air looms, startled Eeiauoans—*no,* Uhura thought, correcting herself immediately, *Sivaoansi*—froze and stared at the *Enterprise* crew members.

There were about three dozen of them that she could see, but she had the uncanny feeling the number was considerably larger. This was confirmed by Chekov, who said in a whisper, "They're in the trees, too, sair."

The captain nodded and said, "Keep still and make no threatening gestures." With exaggerated slowness, he holstered his phaser, spread his empty hands out at waist level and took two cautious steps forward. "We come in peace," he said. "On behalf of the United Federation of Planets, my people greet your people."

Uhura could tell the universal translator was doing its job. The Sivaoans' ears pricked forward to listen. Half a dozen children of varying ages drew close to adults for security, but they did not take their eyes off Captain Kirk.

"I am Captain Kirk of the *U.S.S. Enterprise,* a Federation starship currently orbiting your world. These are members of my crew." He introduced each in turn and each stepped forward slowly and calmly, to the same unblinking scrutiny. Spock, for once, got no second look. That didn't surprise Uhura—Sunfall would have considered Spock well within the range of human variation.

When he was finished, Kirk stepped back and waited. Save for the continued stares, there was no response. "Suggestions, Spock?" he said, at last, sotto voce.

118

"Perhaps Lieutenant Uhura might be of some assistance."

"Yes. Lieutenant?"

"I'll try, sir."

"Lieutenant," said Spock, "may I suggest you try the oldest form of the language you know well?"

Uhura was puzzled. "That would be like speaking Latin, Mr. Spock."

"Indeed," he said, "and another scholar might well be able to converse with you, despite the fact that neither of you knew the other's contemporary tongue. In two thousand years, this people's language has surely diverged from a common root."

"I see," she said.

However much she might remind herself that these were Sivaoans and should not be judged on Eeiauoan terms, she had little else to go on. So, as she stepped forward, she focused on the one that seemed to her most friendly—a Sivaoan that, in all but coloring and youth, might have been Sunfall's twin sister.

The Sivaoan's tail and legs were longer than average. Her fur was short; a beautiful silver gray on back, ears, and tail; a striking white down her chest and belly. Her face bore a triangle of white reaching from between the eyes, over the nose, and down across the lower half of the cheeks and muzzle, giving her the appearance of wearing a silver gray mask over her copper eyes.

As Uhura advanced toward her, the two youngest children started to back away. Uhura stopped. Very slowly, she knelt . . . and the two little ones stopped backing and instantly regained their curiosity.

Scholarly language wouldn't mean much to someone that young, but she knew something they might understand. She rather hoped the captain would understand as well; she couldn't leave children frightened by their first sight of humans and Vulcans. She began to sing an old, old lullaby she'd learned from Sunfall.

If they did not understand the words of the song, the Sivaoans clearly understood her intention. All around her, eyes widened, whiskers and ears quivered.

Uhura let the last note of her song trail away and bowed her head slightly to each of the little ones, then slowly she rose. This time, the two children did not move away.

Once more, Uhura turned her attention to the masked Sivaoan. She stretched out her arms, her hands just slightly above shoulder height, one hand extended an inch or two beyond the other, and curved her fingers as if displaying claws; then, without lowering her arms, she relaxed her hands, as if drawing in those same claws. It was a formal greeting described in ballad after ballad.

The Sivaoan, after a moment's consideration, returned the gesture. Uhura saw the gleam of real claws displayed then withdrawn into silky gray fingers.

Drawing her words from the same old ballads, Uhura asked, "Can you understand me if I speak this tongue?"

The Sivaoan's ears flicked back in surprise. "Yes," she said, "your accent is a bit odd but I understand you." She turned briefly and seemed to received agreement from several others—*at least,* thought Uhura, *that would be agreement from a Eeiauoan.* "Most of us are able to understand you—do you understand me?"

Uhura nodded. "With some difficulty," she admitted. "If you would speak more slowly, I think it would be easier; and I would be pleased if you would correct any errors I might make."

"If you wish it," she said. The delight in her eyes warred with the formality of the Old Tongue words and for a brief moment she reminded Uhura so much of Sunfall that, quite without meaning to, Uhura asked, "Are you of Ennien?"

*"To*-Ennien. Forgive me, you may call me Jinx to-Ennien. You are called StarFreedom to-Enterprise? Is that correct?"

This took a moment's interpretation on Uhura's part. The universal translator must have rendered "Nyota Uhura" as "StarFreedom" and Jinx added "to-Enterprise" to conform to local custom. *"To*-Ennien" was obviously a language correction; Captain Kirk had been right to question the different versions of CloudShape's name.

"Essentially correct," she said, "Jinx *to*-Ennien." Uhura took a deep breath and went on, choosing her words with care, "I bring sad news of kin of yours on a distant world. . . ."

Jinx's whiskers quivered with excitement. "Kin of mine? On another world?—Please try again, StarFreedom, perhaps I misunderstand you!"

Very slowly, Uhura began again, "Your distant relatives, your kin on another world, are in great danger. I believe—I pray—your people may be able to help them." She got no further.

A second Sivaoan, gray-striped of fur and somewhat older and larger than Jinx, stepped aggressively between the two of them. He said a few terse words to Jinx, who bristled and began what seemed to be an explanation, for it involved pointing to Uhura with her tail.

With no warning, he struck Jinx a stunning blow to the side of the head; she rocked with the force of it, but made no attempt to strike

120

back. Then he said something more, this time with the air of an adult jollying a child, but Jinx made no reply. Her tail drooped perceptibly and she backed away.

The striped Sivaoan turned to Uhura. She tensed, ready to duck a blow, but instead he said something. Again, it was in the contemporary language and she did not understand. She told him so in the Old Tongue.

He made a gesture of greeting and replied in kind. "I am Winding Path to-Srallansre. You do not understand, StarFreedom, yet your companion spoke our language well."

"Captain Kirk used the universal translator, sir. It would make it easier. May I?" Uhura turned on her universal translator again.

"Do you understand me now?" he said.

"Yes," said Uhura. "As I tried to tell Jinx, we believe your people may be able to help your relatives—"

Winding Path flicked one ear back—in Sunfall it would have been a gesture of disdain—then he said, "Have you walked far?"

Puzzled by his change of subject, Uhura said, "No. As Captain Kirk told you, we come from the *Enterprise*, which is now orbiting your world. . . ."

"You and your friends are welcome to stay under our protection until someone comes for you. You will speak to Stiff Tail," he said firmly before she could repeat her plea for help. "I will tell her how it happened."

There was nothing further to say for the moment. "Thank you," said Uhura, searching her memory for something more formal. But before she found it, Winding Path had already walked away. All her urgent questions would have to await Stiff Tail. Dismayed as she was by her failure, she had only duty to fall back on. She returned to Captain Kirk and Mr. Spock to make a full report of what little she had learned.

## *The Tears of the Singers,* by Melinda Snodgrass

*The Tears of the Singers,* by Melinda Snodgrass, is one of my favorite books. It is a lovely story, richly textured and written with an almost lyrical style. The very survival of the galaxy was threatened by hunting of the inhabitants of a planet called Taygeta, semi-aquatic creatures reminiscent of baby harp seals. The creatures were killed because at the moment of their deaths, they excreted valuable and highly prized crystal "tears." Uhura's talent for music and skill with languages were necessary to communicate with the Taygetians and solve the problem threatening them and the galaxy. Drafted into service by Captain Kirk, a famous musician named Guy Maslin worked with Uhura, and the two fell in love. This passage from *The Tears of the Singers* describes the communications problem they were working on and the difficulty Uhura was having making decisions about her future.

"I BROUGHT YOU SOME LUNCH," UHURA SAID TO MASLIN'S HUNCHED BACK. He didn't respond. Instead his long, slender fingers continued to play across the synthesizer's double keyboard. She moved to his side and tried again. "Guy, I said—"

"I heard you the first time," he said, not looking at her. His eyes were locked on the long, narrow screen where two lines of indecipherable dots and dashes marched monotonously past.

"You have to eat. Otherwise you're going to end up in the sickbay, and be of no use to any of us."

"Never mind all that. I'm finally on to something."

"What?" she asked. She set aside the plate, both food and her concern over Maslin forgotten in the excitement that they might at last be on the verge of a breakthrough.

"Come on." He slid off the bench and, grabbing her hand, began pelting down the beach. "If I'm right," he panted as they slogged through the deep sand, "an entire group of Singers up there," he gestured at a section of the cliff face, "will drop out of the song, and I want to be there when they do."

"Why?"

"Because it finally started making sense."

"I'm glad it does for someone," she said with some acerbity.

"I'm sorry, I'm being cryptic. Remember when Chou and Donovan reported the strange fish behavior?"

"Yes."

"Well, I went back and checked the recordings the synthesizer had made at that time. I keep a recorder on at all times because I keep hoping that the more passages the machine hears and compares the easier it will be to decipher the language. Anyway, at approximately the time that Donovan and Chou observed the fish, the cubs began a very rigid and coherent song. It's totally unlike their usual random hoots and tweets. Moments later a group of voices in the adult song dropped out. Since then I've been watching for it, and it happens with clockwork regularity every twelve hours."

"So what do you think it means?"

"I've got a theory, but I'd like to see if I can find any evidence to support it before I go out on a limb." He paused and stared up the cliff face. "This ought to be just about the place. Feel like a climb?"

"I do, but how do you feel?" Uhura asked, studying his drawn face.

"I can make it. Just knowing I may finally be on to something is enough to totally rejuvenate me."

She questioned that statement, but prudently kept her doubts to herself. She didn't want to fight with Guy, and since she had begun to nag him about rest and food, fighting seemed to have become their major form of communication. She began searching the base of the cliff for a way up to the grottos, and found a place where the rock had slipped and shifted, forming a series of natural steps and handholds. It wasn't going to be an easy climb, but they wouldn't need special equipment.

She went first, carefully testing each foot- and handhold for stability. She was glad Guy was small and light for there were several points where she doubted that the rock would have held under a man of Spock's or Kirk's weight. After fifteen minutes of steady climbing she reached the first grotto. She gripped the lip of the ledge, and pulled herself up.

And found herself face-to-face with a Taygetian adult who lay placidly feeding in the midst of a mound of fish. The blue green scales still gleamed wetly, and sea water puddled about the bodies of the quivering fish. She had become so accustomed to being ignored by the adults that she was startled, and almost lost her grip on the ledge when the creature stopped chewing and lifted its head to regard her out of deep blue eyes.

"Uhura, could you go up or come down, but please don't just stay there. My arms are about to break."

She quickly boosted herself onto the ledge and, rolling over, reached back for Guy. He accepted her hand, and she could feel his arm shivering with strain as she helped him onto the ledge. His face was bone white except for two hectic spots of color that burned high on his thin cheeks, and a spasm of coughing seized him as he collapsed face down in the grotto. After a few moments the spasm passed, and his breathing eased. The Taygetian continued to watch them until Guy pushed up into a sitting position, then it went placidly back to its meal.

"Is this what you expected to find?" Uhura asked with a gesture to the fish.

"Yes."

She sat back on her heels, and wrapped her arms around her knees, thoughtfully watching the Taygetian. "Donovan's been going nuts trying to figure out how the adults maintained themselves when they never left their grottos."

"And he really isn't going to be happy when he hears about this."

"You must have some idea how this happens. After all, you made the connection between the cubs' song and the fish."

"I have ideas, but none of them makes any sense. If only the great song weren't so ragged. It's like trying to learn a language when only half the words and none of the grammar are available." He stared silently out at the ocean for several minutes, then nodded. "But this is going to help. At least now I have a direct action that flows out of a song. I'll just start cross checking to see if any of the phrases and passages in this song reoccur in others."

"Do you want to start back down?"

Maslin peered over the ledge and shivered. "We climbed *that?"* he said, pointing down the cliff.

"'Fraid so. It did look easier coming up, didn't it?"

"Do you suppose if we sit here long enough the action of wind and weather will lower this cliff by two or three hundred feet?"

Uhura chuckled and reached out for his hand. "We could always call the ship and have them beam us back to camp."

"Maybe that's how the Taygetians get the fish up here, they have transporters hidden beneath the crust of the planet."

"You've been reading too much fantasy. Our sensors would have picked up that kind of activity."

"Must you always be so literal," he complained, sliding over to her, and lying back with his head in her lap.

"It's in my job description," she said, softly running her fingers through his heavy hair.

"What would it take to give you a new job description?"

"I don't know. How much clout do you have with Starfleet?"

"Not near enough, I'm sure." He paused, and picked up her free hand, twining her fingers through his. "So maybe we ought to find you a new position outside of Starfleet."

An aching lump seemed to settle into the pit of her stomach, and she cast wildly about for some way out of this situation. She wasn't ready for this conversation. She had no idea what she felt or really wanted, and she didn't want to be forced to make a choice. They had never spoken of love, and her commitment to Starfleet was so strong that it would take a very powerful and driving need to pull her away from her chosen career.

She wanted a ship and a command of her own, and she thought she had a good chance of getting them—but it was going to cost. The price of a starship was ceaseless devotion to work and career. She had seen it with Captain Kirk. However much he might yearn there was only one lady in his life and her name was *Enterprise*.

*But do I want to become a lesbian?* she thought rebelliously. *Devoting my life to a mass of circuits and metal that by some ironic quirk of phraseology has been designated a she?*

Or did she want the comfort of home, husband and children? And was it possible she could have both? Or was that a foolish dream placed forever beyond the reach of a woman in Starfleet?

She looked down into Guy's face and found him intently watching her. She touched his lips with the tips of her fingers, and he pressed a soft kiss against the sensitive skin. She realized she was probably reading too much into his statement. Guy was a man who could have—did have—any number of women on a dozen different worlds. He couldn't possibly be offering her anything more than a casual affair. She had been foolish to immediately begin thinking of long-term commitments and agonizing over career decisions.

She smiled, and leaned over to kiss him. He reached back to clasp his hands behind her neck and pull her into a far deeper embrace than she had planned. She closed her eyes, savoring the taste and touch of him. Finally he released her.

"Frankly, my darling, I wouldn't trust you to find me a new position," she teased.

"And why not?"

"You won't even take care of yourself. How can I be sure you'd do any better looking out for me?"

"I don't need to take care of myself. I have more than enough people nagging me at any given moment," he grumbled, his face thunderous. He sat up and scooped up a handful of loose crystal flakes, and allowed them to trickle through his fingers.

"And I'm going to start nagging just as soon as we get back to camp," she replied placidly. "Dr. McCoy wanted you to rest," she continued, pulling out her communicator. "I'm sure climbing cliffs was not what he had in mind."

"What are you doing?"

"Calling the ship so they can transport us back to camp."

"I am perfectly capable of walking back to camp," he said stiffly.

"I'm sure you are, but *I* don't want to go back down that cliff."

"Why didn't you have the ship transport us up here in the first place?" he asked suspiciously.

"Because we had no coordinates. Now they can pick us up on their scanners, and send us back to camp. Those coordinates they have."

"Then you're really not doing this just to baby me?"

She sighed and shut her communicator before it could signal the ship. She then rested her hands on his shoulders and looked seriously into his face. "Of course I am. You're not well, Guy, that's a fact." She hesitated. "I care for you, that's another fact. Anything I can do to protect and care for you I'm going to do." She dropped her hands, and turned away. "Now go ahead and jump down my throat."

"Ah, Madam Starfleet." He sighed as he wrapped his arms around her body and rested his cheek against her back. "You constantly force me to rise above my own naturally unpleasant nature. Call the ship. And I promise I'll go to bed like the very best of boys when we get back to camp." He glanced over his shoulder at the Taygetian who was just finishing its meal. "Are the females of your race as difficult to handle as ours are?" The creature eyed him serenely and, drawing in a great breath, resumed the song. "Clearly they are," he said to Uhura. "He is forced to take refuge in art."

She flipped open her communicator and gave him a disgusted look. "I'm sure if I compared notes with Kali, and ever managed to communicate with a Taygetian female, we would all agree that it's the males of *any* species who cause the problems."

## Mr. Sulu and *The Captain's Daughter*

The original series probably told viewers more about Hikaru Sulu than it did about Uhura, Scotty, and Chekov. Several episodes mentioned his love of plants as well as his secret passion for fencing, romantic swashbuckling, and derring-do. At his helm position, Mr. Sulu frequently had the first on-camera reaction to an alien menace or friend. He occasionally led landing parties, and he was a skilled helmsman. He acquired an official first name, Hikaru, in *Star Trek VI: The Undiscovered Country,* which originally had been bestowed by Vonda McIntyre in previous novels. Sulu had prominent parts in all of McIntyre's film novelizations and in *The Entropy Effect,* discussed later in this book. My favorite Sulu novel is, however, *The Captain's Daughter,* by Peter David.

## *The Captain's Daughter,* by Peter David

Hikaru Sulu's daughter, Ensign Demora Sulu, was introduced in *Star Trek: Generations* as a member of the crew of the *Enterprise* B. *The Captain's Daughter* is the story of how she came to be; it is Sulu's story about his adventures on shore leave. It is a story of great tragedy and great joy. In this passage, Sulu awakened from a frightening dream about his daughter and learned of her alleged death at the hands of Captain Harriman of the *Enterprise* B.

CAPTAIN HIKARU SULU WOKE UP TREMBLING AND COVERED WITH SWEAT.

"Demora," he murmured.

He sat in the darkened quarters for a moment, and then said, "Lights." They came on in prompt response.

He felt an absurd sense of relief. He was, naturally, still within the confines of the *Excelsior*. No reason he wouldn't be; that was, after all, where he'd gone to sleep at the end of his shift.

But for a moment it had all seemed so real.

Demora had been dead.

The dream could not have been any more clear, or any more frightening. She had been lying there, unmoving, on the surface of a dark and frightening world. Phaser burns covered her broken body. And Sulu had been there, shouting her name, unable to make himself heard over the steady roar of the wind. It had seemed to blow the name back into his face.

He had tried to reach her, to get to her somehow so that he could help her. But he'd been unable to move. Indeed, he had seemed intangible, incapable of physically interacting with the world in any way. So he'd stood there, an impotent and frustrated ghost, shaking fists that no one could see and shouting names with a voice no one could hear. He was so close to her, so close, and yet unable to help her.

"Demora," he said again. He checked the time and discovered that he had awoken an hour before he was supposed to. He tried lying back down, but it did him no good. He simply lay there and stared at the ceiling until he couldn't stand it anymore and roused himself out of bed.

As he showered and dressed, he thought of Demora. He also thought of the dream about her. He'd read any number of cases wherein a relative—mother, father, sibling—had a sort of psychic "flash" at a time of a loved one's crisis. It didn't matter how much distance separated the two. There was somehow, in some way, a connection that no one really professed to be able to understand. It happened without rhyme or reason. Many people who reported such instances made no claim to psychic ability. They'd had no similar experiences before, and could go (and probably happily would go) the rest of their lives without having such a thing recur.

Some scientists tended to dismiss such notions out of hand. There were some, though, who gave it credence and greater study. It was their position that the human mind was capable of far more than it was generally given credit for.

*Demora,* he thought again, and he did not like one bit the tremendous discomfiture he was feeling every time Demora's name crossed his mind now.

He had hardly been in touch with her since her assignment to the *Enterprise.* Something had happened between the two of them, and he wasn't entirely sure of what it was. Ever since she had gotten into Starfleet Academy there had been a change in her. She was still polite to him. That much was unfailing. But it had come across as very . . . formal, somehow. The warmth wasn't quite there the way it used to be. Or at least so he thought.

"Velcome to reality," Chekov had said to him. Chekov and Sulu had spoken of it, right around the time that Sulu had been given command of the *Excelsior.*

"What are you talking about?" Sulu had asked.

"Eesn't it obvious? A child always rejects her father. All part of growing up, Meester Sulu."

Sulu had smiled in amusement. "The wifeless, childless Pavel Chekov is the world expert on what children do and don't do, eh?"

"Of course I am the expert," Chekov had said sagely. "Only an expert in children vould be intelligent enough not to have any."

"Well, that's tough to argue with, I suppose. Although that is an alarming attitude for my daughter's godparent to have."

Chekov had shrugged and then gestured expansively. "Vat can I say?"

Sulu had been unwilling to accept Chekov's easy answer, in any event. Sulu had never "rejected" either of his parents, and he had done just fine. . . .

*Demora . . .*

His mind had drifted, and was once more pulled back to his feeling of unease. If he tried to contact her on the *Enterprise* out of the blue, what would he say? "Honey, I dreamed you were dead; how are you doing?" That wouldn't sound particularly good.

Besides which, they were probably nowhere near enough to the *Enterprise* to have a real-time conversation anyway. He'd probably have to settle for a letter. Yes. That was definitely the way to go. A letter.

He sat down at his workstation and said, "Activate messaging service."

"Service activated," the computer informed him.

"To Demora Sulu. Ensign, helmswoman"—the latter he added somewhat unnecessarily, but with distinct pride—"*U.S.S. Enterprise.* Demora . . ."

He stopped a moment, unsure of what to say, and came to the surprising realization that he'd never composed a letter to her that was merely for the purpose of chatting.

Oh, he'd sent communications to her, of course. Many a time, in fact. But there was always a specific reason for it that was based in conveying information: promotions, extended stays, unexpected events that could have an effect on her. That sort of thing. For all his hobbies, for all his interests, simple "Hi, how are you" gabbing over subspace was not something in which he indulged.

Which was why he was struggling now. The "information" to be conveyed was that he'd had a bad dream about her. But he couldn't call her and tell her that, because either he'd make himself look foolish or else he'd worry her needlessly. Needlessly because he didn't *really* think anything was going to happen to her. He was just trying to quell his admittedly irrational concerns.

Left to her own devices, Demora might very well get around to contacting him on her own. Then again, she had acquired Sulu's knack for being unable to turn out anything except the most perfunctory of missives. Unless something genuinely major happened to her, it might be ages before he heard from her. The only way to speed up the process was to write to her himself.

And maybe it was about time he did that.

"Waiting," prompted the computer, just in case Sulu had forgotten he'd left the function on.

Sulu looked into the screen, trying to appear relaxed, since it was a video message and his image was naturally going to be recorded. "Honey . . . I'm just writing to say hi," he started, using the term "writing" in its traditional sense—as so many still did—even though he was, of course, not really writing anything. "I was thinking about you . . . thinking about all the things you're experiencing and . . ."

Might as well be blindingly obvious about it.

". . . I'd like to hear from you. Things that seem trivial to you will very likely be interesting to me. Think of it as me being selfish, wanting to see early days aboard the *Enterprise* through your eyes so that I can relive my own early career just a little. As I said, selfish. I hope you can forgive me the indulgence. Of course, since I outrank you, I can order you to forgive me." He flashed a smile and hoped that the joke seemed remotely funny. Ah, well . . . if it didn't, well, to paraphrase Leonard McCoy, he was a captain, not a comedian.

"I hope all is well, and that you'll inform me soon of how things are going. Very truly yours . . . your father." The closing line seemed a bit hokey, considering that she would have to be both deaf and blind not to know who was sending her the letter. But it was traditional, and besides, there was something about the way the words "your father" rolled off his tongue.

"Computer, end transmission and send."

"Sending."

Sulu nodded with satisfaction. It was on its way. Now it would just be a matter of time before he received a response from Demora. It would be one of her usual pleasant, straightforward letters, perhaps with a touch of mild surprise that her father had initiated the contact. But why shouldn't he have done so? He was her father, after all. They weren't estranged. Sure, there was that distant way she acted sometimes, but hell, she had a lot on her mind. Starfleet Academy, as Sulu well knew, was enough to change anyone's behavior patterns. Why should Demora be any exception?

She'd respond, the sheer normality of her reply helping to ground him once more. And that would be that.

He headed for the door of his quarters, only to discover Lieutenant Commander Janice Rand, the communications officer, standing outside his door about to push the door chime.

"Janice," he said, somewhat in surprise. "Is something wrong?" It was a natural question to ask. As far back as the two of them went, nevertheless it was unusual for Rand to simply drop by, particularly at such an early hour.

She looked down. "Captain . . ."

"Captain?" He made no effort to hide his amusement.

"Getting somewhat formal on me, aren't you, Jan—"

Then his voice trailed off because he knew, he *knew.*

He backed up, his legs suddenly feeling weak, and when he bumped into a chair it took no effort at all to release the muscles in them so that he dropped heavily into it.

"Demora," he said.

Rand blinked in surprise. But her wonder vanished immediately as the gravity of the situation reasserted itself. "Yes" was all she could bring herself to say.

There was a long moment of silence. Then, sounding about a thousand years older, he said, "How?"

She paused a moment.

"How?" he asked again. "In combat? An accident? Ambush? What?" It was amazing—truthfully, he himself was amazed—how calm and even he was keeping his voice. Actually, it took no effort. He was simply numb.

She looked down, and could barely get out the words: "Friendly fire."

It was a term that had survived centuries. Terms that have such remarkably self-contradictory perversity often do.

All the color drained from his face. "What?" he said, the word thudding from him. "One of the crew shot her?"

"Captain . . . maybe you should just read the report. . . ."

He looked at her oddly. "The report . . . would have been marked 'Personal.' You read something directed to me that was indicated to be personal."

She looked down guiltily. "Yes, sir. It was from the *Enterprise* . . . but from the chief medical officer. I . . . put two and two together. I am aware that my actions could be considered cause for severe penalties . . . even court-martial, if you choose to pursue it . . ."

"Oh, be quiet, Janice," he said, but there was no heat in his voice. Indeed, just for a moment, he sounded like the Sulu of old. The one who, back when she was a yeoman and he was a helmsman, she would bring sandwiches to while he messed around with whatever his latest hobby might be. Back when they were both young, and the galaxy was an infinity of possibilities.

And in the spirit of those long-gone days, the ranks fell away for a moment. She stomped her foot in irritation. "Well, dammit, Sulu, what did you expect me to do? I mean, this message comes in, and I can pretty much guess what it says. And I'm supposed to just forward it down to you without comment?"

He walked to her and rested a hand on her shoulder. "If you wanted me to read the report, you'd simply have sent it down to me. Obviously you wanted to cushion the . . . the blow." And now it was an effort to keep his voice level, the initial numbness having worn off. "I can handle it. Tell me."

"It's . . . I don't pretend to understand it, sir. It . . ." She gathered her strength and then it all came out in a rush. "The report is that she began attacking other crewmen while on a landing party. Assaulted the science officer, nearly killed the captain. He was compelled to shoot and ki . . . to use terminal force against her."

He stared at her as if she'd grown antennae. "The . . . captain shot her? Are you serious?"

"Yes, sir. The report was very specific."

Sulu looked as if he'd been sucker-punched. "And . . . and what caused it? Caused her to attack her own people?"

"They don't know. They haven't been able to determine any . . ."

"There must be an answer," Sulu said, his efforts to rein in his frustration stretched to their limits. "It's insane. Demora wouldn't just . . . something must have caused it. Some virus, some animal that bit her . . . something. What sort of subsequent investigations is Harriman performing?"

"Reading between the lines: none. The CMO made mention that the planet's been placed under quarantine. No one in or out."

"That's a reasonable precaution," he admitted slowly. "But my daughter's life ended there. I see no reason that the investigation should end as well. Are we close enough to *Enterprise* for a direct subspace link?"

"No, sir."

He nodded. "That's . . . probably fortunate. I don't think I'd . . . trust myself to speak with Harriman right now. I need time to . . . deal with this, so that I can act in an appropriate manner."

"Meaning a manner more appropriate to the decorum of a Starfleet captain than to a grieving father."

Rand took a step toward him and said softly, "I know how you feel."

"I know. No one knows better than me how close you and Demora . . ."

"It's not just that. I mean, that's part of it, sure. But . . ." She looked down. "There's something I never told you."

He looked at her, waiting. He didn't feel like he had the strength to say anything.

With a sigh that sounded heavy with exhaustion, Rand said, "It was years ago. Years and years. Didn't you wonder why I took a leave of absence from Starfleet for a time?"

"Your record cited personal reasons. I never felt it was my business to ask."

"Yes, well . . . that was the personal reason. Her name was Annie. She lived until the ripe old age of two, and then she got sick and died. Because for all our medical knowledge, sometimes people—even young people, even very young people—still die. And after she was

132

gone, I was at loose ends for a time before I was able to bring myself to return to Starfleet. End of my life as a mother."

He put a hand on hers. "Janice . . . I'm so sorry . . ."

"This is not the time for you to be comforting me. I just . . . I wanted you to know how much I feel for you."

"Do you still think about her?"

Rand smiled thinly. "Only on days ending in the letter *y.*"

Sulu stared straight ahead. Rand reached over and touched his back. Every muscle under his jacket was knotted. It was like touching rock. There seemed to be nothing more to say, so she headed for the door.

"Rand . . ."

She stopped, turned, and looked at him questioningly.

"The father," Sulu asked. "Do you mind my asking . . . who it was."

She sighed. "It doesn't matter," she said. "He's dead now, too."

"Did you ever tell him?"

"I didn't want to risk sidetracking his career. You see . . . I suspected that he was headed for a great destiny, and I didn't want to do anything to distract him from it."

"And did he fulfill his great destiny, Janice?"

With a sad look she said, "We all do, Sulu. We all do." And she walked out of his quarters.

Sulu sat there for quite some time. He waited for the tears to come . . . but none did. There was a slight stinging in his eyes, but overall it was like the sensation of a sneeze that's puttering around one's nose but doesn't quite escape.

He was still numb. That was it. Still overcome by the shock.

Demora was dead. His little girl, whom he had known for so brief a time, was gone. Never to laugh with him or at him again, or to puncture any of his pretensions with her musical laugh or her mischievous wit.

Never again to look into Demora's face, or into her eyes, and see *her* staring back at him.

*Her* . . . Demora's mother.

The lunatic. The madwoman. The exotic nut, straight out of those old adventure stories that Sulu had read when he was so young, a lifetime ago . . .

*You know the old Russian saying . . . be care—*

Sulu shook it off. He didn't want to think about those times now. Didn't want to dredge up the old memories of that period in his life. Of that insane time, with *her,* and the mysterious enemies, dangerous cities with threats hiding within every shadow, a roller-coaster ride which, for all that he had experienced in his very full life, remained for him the pinnacle of loopy, non-sequitur bizarreness . . .

And the tears still weren't coming.

He wanted that release. Wanted to get the anger and rage and hurt out of his system, but it wouldn't go. What the hell was the matter with him? Had he become so closed up, so out of touch with his emotions, that he couldn't even properly grieve his daughter?

Or was it that with this loss, coming so hard on the heels of the demise of James Kirk, had simply overloaded him. Robbed him of his ability to deal with any more grief.

He thought of Demora, and he thought of Ling . . . and couldn't deal with thinking of either of them.

He informed the bridge that he would be indisposed for a short time and would be late in arrival. And then he lay back on his bed and, even though he had just awoken from a full night's sleep . . . he closed his eyes.

The words echoed once more . . . *You know the old Russian saying . . . be careful vat you vish for . . .*

. . . and then, mercifully, the darkness claimed him before the memories could return.

## Pavel Chekov and *The Disinherited*

Pavel Chekov was added to the crew during the second season of the original series to appeal to young female viewers. His endless claims of Russian superiority in nearly everything provided moments of humor and levity, and his presence on the bridge as an officer demonstrated inclusion and diversity at a time when the United States and the Soviet Union were fighting a dangerous cold war. Chekov was important in both *The Wrath of Khan* and *Star Trek IV: The Voyage Home.*

Chekov's Academy experiences were depicted in *The Kobayashi Maru,* and he and Spock worked and were kidnaped together in *Deep Domain,* by Howard Weinstein, both included in this book. Chekov's story in *The Disinherited,* by Peter David, Michael Jan Friedman, and Robert Greenberger, showed a very young officer striving to be perfect for his hero Captain Kirk while continuing to make mistakes that mortified him. The following excerpt from *The Disinherited* describes the experience of the young ensign on a landing party investigating the deaths of people who had been brutally murdered by attackers from space. Distressed by the horrible deaths, Chekov made a serious mistake and was called on it by Kirk. One cannot help but be sympathetic to the youth he was, but by the end of the story, Chekov showed significant growth and was helpful in solving the mystery of the brutal attacks from space.

STALKING THROUGH ONE OF THE COLONY'S BURNED-OUT BUILDINGS, CHEKOV scanned the place with his tricorder. The air was thick with smoke and dust, and a number of small fires added to the black haze that hid the sky. As he approached a cabinet, his tricorder showed him something unusual and he stopped suddenly. Crouching, he reached for the cabinet door, grabbed the handle, and swung it open.

Despite the tricorder reading that had tipped him off, he was shocked to find a boy inside—a boy who had sought refuge in the cabinet. The grimace on his face told Chekov that the youth had been asphyxiated.

Chekov took a ragged breath and lifted the body out of its hiding place. After gently stretching it out on the floor, he turned away and bit back the tears.

*Damn.* So much destruction, so much waste. Images of what they'd found at the other colonies flooded his mind unbidden. He shook his head.

None of his training missions had prepared him for anything like this. In fact, the only scenes of devastation he had seen were in historical briefings on the old Federation-Romulan wars or the classic Russian Revolution of 1917. It had just never occurred to him that this would be a part of his Starfleet experience.

He wanted to travel among the stars, sure enough—but there was definitely a downside to exploration, and this was it. Stepping cautiously around the rubble, he couldn't help but glance back at the boy.

People weren't supposed to be blasted by beings from space—that was the stuff of old Earth stories. Who would want to make that gruesome fiction a reality? Part of him wanted to grasp a phaser, just to feel secure that this kind of attack would not happen to him.

Instead, Chekov raised his tricorder, forcing himself to recalibrate its sensor pickup to find more examples of the radiation Spock had detected earlier. The best samples were to be gathered and beamed up to the *Enterprise* for forensic inspection. His fingers, slick with sweat, slipped twice before he finally got the adjustments right.

Bending low, Chekov waved the tricorder in front of a burned-out gray street lamp. The reading was too low to be useful. This is good, he thought. *This is making me concentrate.* Chekov liked puzzles, and this kind of work was good for him; it kept him interested in minutiae and how everything formed a larger picture.

He walked several meters away and then bent again, this time aiming the tricorder at a small storage building. The radiation and spectrographic readings were within the range specified by Spock. The source of the radiation was a small portable computer that had apparently been near a direct hit. *Perhaps the memory was still intact,* Chekov mused.

The ensign knelt to study the device more closely and gave some thought to the kind of beings who would slaughter an entire population so far inside Federation boundaries. Surely they must have realized this would bring about some sort of Starfleet action. What could the stakes be? So far no one, not even Captain Kirk, had a theory.

Unfortunately the computer's memory had been wiped clean. Chekov rose and started back toward the beaming site.

As he walked among the blackened shells of buildings, his mind turned back a few months to his graduation from Starfleet Academy. With his high grades in just about everything, it had been a certainty he'd find a berth aboard a starship, but he had not known which one.

He would have settled for any one of the twelve Constitution-class vessels currently commissioned, although his preference was definitely the *Enterprise.* It had a unique legacy, stretching back through the heroic captaincy of Christopher Pike to the command of the legendary Captain Robert April.

Even more impressive, however—at least to Chekov—was the ship's current captain, James T. Kirk. Skippers like Commodore Decker on the *Constellation* and Bob Wesley on the *Lexington* were older men with great accomplishments in their record. But it was the young Captain James T. Kirk who had fired Chekov's imagination.

At thirty-four, Kirk had done more and seen more than Chekov imagined possible. It was Kirk who had helped draw up the Organian Peace Treaty, Kirk again who had gone head-to-head with the Romulans and actually returned unscathed.

The *Enterprise* was the first ship to discover the First Federation and to make that critical first contact with the heretofore unknown Gorn, who were near this system. So much adventure. Chekov had been so certain he wanted to be a part of it.

But now there was a nagging doubt in the back of his mind. Was he really up to serving on this ship? He was no longer sure he had what it took to serve under Kirk.

He recalled vividly how, during his first shift on the bridge, he'd nearly navigated the ship in the wrong direction. Sulu had helped cover up the mistake, and the two had become friends, but Chekov kept comparing himself to those other navigators who were paired with the always cheerful lieutenant.

Chekov started when he heard a noise coming from within a collapsed building—but it turned out to be some lab rats scurrying with newfound freedom.

Chekov's thoughts settled again. He sighed. Even when he beamed down as part of a landing party, he never quite felt he was giving it his best. It always seemed to him he could do something more or something better, despite the fact that most of the time the landing parties were surveying lifeless worlds.

It was doubly distressing to know that Captain Kirk was taking note of his every shortcoming. Kirk was his idol, his standard. The man was a living legend, even though he never acted like one—not even the time they were on Beta Damoron V and found themselves in the middle of a revolution.

Trying to measure up to someone of Kirk's stature was a discouraging task at best—one that made him nervous on some occasions and depressed on others. On the other hand, if he was going to become a captain himself one day, he'd *have* to measure up.

All this thinking had Chekov walking blindly, not even listening for warning sounds from the tricorder. He trudged through the debris, glancing now and again at his tricorder for signs of something that might be of value.

At one point he rounded a corner of a burned husk of a building and tripped on a chunk of plastisteel. When he tried to get up, he found himself face-to-face with another corpse.

This time he wasn't sure if it was a man or a woman because the skin had been charred and all traces of hair were gone. The face was a mask of terror, the mouth forever caught in a rictus of a scream. Chekov could almost hear the corpse's voice crying out as death staked its claim.

Breath came raggedly to the Russian as he scrambled to his feet. The sweat that had begun to bead on his forehead now seemed like a torrent; his shirt stuck uncomfortably to his back.

Swallowing hard, Chekov began to walk away from his close encounter. He gulped air a few times, trying to steady himself as he resumed his search.

What brought him back to attention was a resounding crunch. Looking down, Chekov saw a pile of data tapes under his boot. He stopped to look around and realized he was in a research center that had been pretty much leveled. Husks that might have been dead scientists lay under desks or in metal closets.

After bending to wave his tricorder over the debris, Chekov tried to see if any of the data on the tapes could be retrieved. No way, he concluded after a moment or two. He'd destroyed them when he stepped on them. They were now as useless as the computer he'd found earlier. He prepared to redouble his efforts at being vigilant—

He sensed the presence of someone behind him. Whirling, he was startled to see that he was right.

But it was only Captain Kirk, standing there with his hands on his hips, looking none too pleased.

The ensign's hands fumbled with the tricorder, which would have hit the ground had it not been for the safety strap slung over his shoulder. As he quickly scrambled to attention, a fresh torrent of sweat covered his body, and Chekov cringed at what he knew was to come.

"Ensign, have you any idea what just happened?"

"Yes, sir. I accidentally stepped on these computer tapes, ruining the information encoded on them."

Kirk stepped closer to Chekov, narrowing his gaze. The ensign, for his part, actually thought he could feel his pores opening up, letting sweat roll over his body.

"Those tapes may have contained information recorded during the attack."

"Aye, sir. I know, sir."

"In fact, we may have lost a chance to discover who the raiders are . . . thanks to this haphazard approach you have decided to take on a landing-party assignment. Just what are they teaching cadets these days?"

"I don't know, sir."

"No, I suppose you don't. You're not a cadet anymore, mister, and I expect my crewmen to perform better than cadets. Better than any other crew members in the fleet, in fact. Am I making myself clear?"

"Yes, sir. It von't happen again, sir." Chekov felt his accent growing thicker as his brain threatened to freeze up on him.

There was a long pause, and then Kirk seemed to change tactics. "Of course, we don't know what was on those tapes. They may have contained something as useless as fuel-consumption reports.

"But"—and now Kirk began to circle the ensign—"now we'll never know. I dislike not knowing things, Ensign. I do not want any more mistakes on this mission. You understand that?"

"Yes, Keptin. Perfectly."

"Good. Now let's salvage what we can. Dismissed."

Ensign Chekov did as he was told. For the rest of the day he tried not to allow himself to become distracted. When Spock informed him it was time to return to the ship, he glumly joined the rest of the landing party. His last thought before beaming up was an idle one: How did one *avoid* beaming back aboard a starship?

# CHAPTER 5

# The Shakespearean Captain—
# Jean-Luc Picard

STAR TREK: THE NEXT GENERATION DEBUTED IN 1987 WITH A NEW SHIP, the *U.S.S. Enterprise* 1701-D and a new captain, Jean-Luc Picard. Played by Patrick Stewart, Captain Picard seemed cast in a different mold than Captain Kirk, and there have been endless fannish discussions about who was the better captain. Where Kirk occasionally seemed impulsive and prone to fisticuffs rather than diplomacy, Picard seemed more thoughtful and inclined to diplomacy and discussion. To an extent, this comparison is accurate. Both captains were men of their times, and both represented the best of their times. Kirk was captain during the 1960s—and in the twenty-third century—when Westerns ruled action television and the galaxy was more of an unexplored frontier. Picard came on the scene during the late 1980s—and the twenty-fourth century—when Westerns and other action-packed "shoot-'em-ups" were no longer popular and the galaxy was a more settled place. In Picard's time, negotiation was often more productive than phasers.

The two captains were more alike than is often thought, however. Both understood that there is a time to make war and a time to make peace. Picard did not hesitate to fight when it was time to make war, and Kirk did not balk when it was time to make peace. He took more than one chance in an effort to make peace, declaring that all that is necessary is the decision that "we will not kill today." Of course, that decision was often made at the point of a phaser.

Picard, though, is my favorite captain. He was thoughtful, articulate, courageous, powerful, yet capable of flexibility. He was willing to say, "I surrender" if it could buy his people a fighting chance of survival. Kirk, though, made the same choice in *STVI,* when his ship fired on Chancellor Gorkon's battle cruiser. Although Picard trusted his people and often asked for their advice, he was always the captain, and he was the one who made the call. He was a master of diplomacy, but he was also a master battle tactician. His "Picard Maneuver," after all, was legendary in Starfleet.

As with Kirk and the original series, Picard is the main character in most of the *TNG* books. Included here are several that best showcase different aspects of Picard's command abilities and personality.

## *The Devil's Heart,* by Carmen Carter

*The Devil's Heart* is one of my favorite novels. Carmen Carter has woven an intricate tale that crossed the eons, the story of a small piece of forever that traveled the stars, seeking to journey ever onward. Whenever the Heart found a new holder, it granted awesome and dangerous powers. Empires stood or fell based upon the gift, or curse, of those powers. Eventually, the artifact always chose to move on, and the holders who kept it too long or refused to relinquish it were destroyed. Picard found the Heart at the site of the mysterious deaths of a Vulcan archaeological team. When the Heart came into his possession, Picard began to dream its history. The dreams took him on the Heart's journey through the millennia, and the reader journeyed with him. As the Devil's Heart's power over Picard increased, the crew worried about whether he would be able to give it up or whether it would destroy him—and them—before he did.

In the first passage from *The Devil's Heart,* Picard was awakened by new orders from Starfleet to render medical assistance to a Vulcan archaeological team and tried to soften the news to Dr. Beverly Crusher over breakfast. In the second scene, Picard was beginning to lose control of the Heart and its influence on him, raising serious concerns in Picard's officers.

CAPTAIN JEAN-LUC PICARD SLEPT WITH THE SAME AIR OF AUTHORITY HE carried with him on the bridge of the *Enterprise.* Even in the privacy of his darkened cabin and the haven of unconsciousness, he maintained a commander's demeanor. The silken blue pajamas he wore only emphasized the hard contours of his body: he lay flat on his back, his lean frame held at attention except for one arm flung above his head; his lips were set in a firm, unyielding line.

It was not a comfortable pose, but then Picard was not a comfortable man.

A spacious cabin with generous furnishings, their smooth wash of pastel colors, a lush plant gracing the table by his bed—none of these luxuries had softened his sense of responsibility, or his conviction that danger could be held at bay only by unceasing vigilance.

As if to vindicate his subconscious wariness, the trill of a communications call marred the silence that had surrounded him. The captain was awake and alert before the second ring of the summons had sounded. Quickly rolling to a half-sitting position, he cleared his throat to erase any trace of sleep from his voice.

"Picard here."

*"Incoming message from Starbase 193, Priority Two."*

"Thank you, Ensign Ro. I'll take it here in my quarters." Knowing the commander of the starbase in question, Picard automatically scaled down the urgency of the call by at least one degree; Miyakawa had a tendency to overdramatize, an occupational hazard for officers mired in the mundane activities of an administrative post. He allowed himself the indulgence of a leisurely stretch before slipping out of bed to activate the transmission.

At his touch, the viewscreen on the wall flickered to life. The first part of the communiqué was brief and to the point, but then Vulcans were not given to circumlocution. Miyakawa's subsequent request for aid was brusque, even imperious, as if she suspected the captain of the *Enterprise* might balk at such an insignificant task.

Perhaps there were some captains who would resent the diversion of a Galaxy-class starship on a small errand of mercy, but Picard was not one of them.

Besides, he wanted this particular mission.

A combination of natural reticence and Starfleet training stripped Picard's voice of emotion as he activated the intercom and issued orders to the bridge crew. His excitement was strictly personal and had no place in the execution of duty.

*"Course change initiated."*

Data's voice betrayed no reaction to the new coordinates, but Picard could swear he heard Ro Laren's muffled curse in the background.

*Merde.* The captain belatedly remembered the consequences of this diversion on the crew's own affairs. "Increase speed to warp six." That was faster than the assignment warranted, but a more moderate pace might tax everyone's patience.

142

In the time it took him to step out of his pajamas and into a clean pair of uniform pants, Picard was hailed over the intercom yet again.

*"Riker to Captain Picard."*

"It's a routine diversion, Number One," said Picard, aiming his reply at the ceiling intercom. "At warp six, we'll only experience a short delay." He slipped the tunic jacket over his head, confident that the heavy cloth could not drown out his first officer's emphatic response.

*"With all due respect, sir, routine missions aren't rated Priority Two. If this takes more than a few extra days . . . well, it's damn inconvenient for Geordi's maintenance agenda at spacedock."*

"Ah, yes, the new magnetic constrictor coils," said Picard, careful to keep the smile on his face from seeping into his voice. Reaching for his boots, the captain did his best to allay Riker's anxiety. "In my opinion, the urgency of the situation was slightly overstated, so we should be able to make up the lost time without too much difficulty. Schedule a briefing this morning for all senior officers so we can ensure a swift completion of this mission."

*"Aye, sir."*

The soft hum of the open channel cut off.

Now that the immediate demands of duty had been fulfilled, Picard walked out into his living room and turned his attention to breakfast. As was his custom, he ordered a light menu for two from the food synthesizer. However, reflecting over Riker's strained reaction to the change of plans, the captain considered the probable effect on his guest's more volatile temper.

"Computer," he said quickly. "Extra butter and cream."

He had added two different fruit juices and a jar of orange marmalade to the spread on the table when his chief medical officer arrived. Some mornings, Beverly Crusher appeared with the slightly rumpled look of a doctor just coming off duty, her eyes darkened by fatigue, but the previous night must have been free of medical emergencies because her face was free of stress; the lines of her blue medical coat were sharp and crisp, and her long red hair was neatly coiled at the nape of her neck.

"What's the special occasion?" Crusher asked, surveying the offerings.

"Nothing beyond the pleasure of your company."

"Hah!" She spooned a large helping of eggs onto her plate. "If I weren't so hungry, I'd seriously question your motives."

"I'm wounded by your suspicion, Doctor."

Fortunately, her mouth was too full for her to press the issue, even in jest.

Judging from her animated spirits, Beverly seemed to have missed the news working its way through the ship's grapevine; he would be able to inform her of the diversion himself. Later. He sought safer ground by asking about the progress of her latest theatrical production. Unfortunately, his mind was too preoccupied with their new destination to actually absorb much of her answer.

Picard had started on the French toast when she turned their conversation to the ship's next port of call.

"There's a restaurant on Luxor IV," said Crusher, her blue eyes bright from the recollection, "that serves the best pancakes in the entire Federation. It would make a great place to celebrate—" she caught herself just in time, "shore leave."

"I'm afraid there will be a slight delay, just a day or two, in our arrival to Luxor IV. We've been diverted to a fringe-territory star system on a medical assistance mission." Picard assumed a look of nonchalance in the face of Beverly's sharpened attention. "In fact, the *Enterprise* was chosen specifically for this mission because of your expertise in handling Bendii's syndrome."

"What?" she stopped mid-bite into a scone lathered with butter. "I'm not an expert in Bendii's syndrome! I've only seen one case in my entire medical career."

"Yes, well, it seems that even one is one more than any other doctor outside of the Vulcan Medical Academy."

"And Ambassador Sarek wasn't even my patient," she said, shaking the scone at him for emphasis. "I didn't treat him, I just diagnosed the condition."

"Think of this as an opportunity to expand your medical experience."

"Thank you, Captain, but I prefer to do that on my own time and not at the expense of my patients."

Picard poured her a fresh cup of tea with a generous measure of cream. "We're also the only Federation starship within easy reach of the system. Under the circumstances, there is no other option for you or for your new patient."

The doctor sighed in reluctant agreement. "So just who is this Vulcan with Bendii's syndrome?" She hastily popped the last bit of bread into her mouth, then accepted the cup he offered her.

"A scientist. T'Sara."

Beverly frowned. "You say that name as if I should know her."

"Forgive me," Picard said. "Just because I've followed her work for years, I expect others to be aware of her as well." He nodded in the direction of his bookshelves. "She began her career as a preeminent folklorist renowned for her work in comparative mythology, then moved on to archaeology."

"Ah, so that's why she's out in the back of beyond."

"Yes," said the captain. "For the past ten years, T'Sara has been the expedition leader for an archaeological excavation on Atropos. Her assistant radioed for medical assistance, claiming that her erratic and irrational behavior appeared to be symptomatic of early stage Bendii's."

"She was diagnosed by an *archaeologist?*" Crusher rolled her eyes in exaggerated despair. "Save me from amateurs."

"I'm sure Sorren will welcome your professional assessment."

"I'm sure he's very welcome."

Despite her sarcasm, she seemed resigned to the necessity of the mission. Picard smiled with satisfaction as he offered the doctor another scone. . . .

Beverly Crusher was the last of the senior officers to slip into place around the conference table but the first to be fixed with Picard's intense questioning gaze.

"Doctor?"

Although she had brought a medical padd with her, the report it contained was still fresh in her mind. She recited the statistics to a somber audience.

"Reports of minor injuries are still filtering in from all decks, but the current count of notable casualties is thirty-five. Intensive care has two crewmen who are in critical condition and another five in serious condition; twelve patients are in the general sickbay ward; the rest have been released after treatment." Fighting against a feeling of defeat, she finished with, "There were three fatalities."

This last statement keyed the tension in the captain's shoulders even tighter, but he made no comment beyond a curt nod of acknowledgment. Picard turned to Geordi La Forge next.

"Maintenance teams have repaired the hull breach," said the engineer, "and Deck 38 is already repressurized, but we've uncovered serious damage to several starboard deflector shield amplifiers and at least two gravity field generators."

Crusher half-listened to Geordi's unfolding report, but her attention was focused mainly on Picard. Troi's concern had been well-founded; it was difficult to assess the captain's condition from across the length of the conference table, but what she could see from here was disturbing.

At first glance, even as she had entered the room, Crusher had been struck by the haggard look of his face. Picard was a lean man at the best of times, but now the bones of his skull were far too prominent, and the skin that covered them was pale and stretched taut. From previous experience, the doctor knew that prolonged stress had a tendency to melt flesh off his frame, but she had never seen him develop a nervous tic before. Yet she noted that Picard's hands were in constant subtle motion, with fingers twitching or tracing patterns on the surface of the table.

Crusher waited until the round of reports had concluded and the other officers were filing out of the room before she approached the captain. Picard was still sitting at the head of the table, fingers drumming a repetitive rhythm, but he had turned to face the window. His eyes were flitting from side to side as he scanned the vista of stars. She wondered what he was looking for.

"Captain."

His head jerked up, as if pulled against his will. "Yes, Doctor?" His query was clipped with impatience.

One look at the stubborn set of his jaw, and Crusher realized that gentle persuasion would only waste her breath. "You look like death warmed over. My medical recommendation is that you get some rest, immediately."

As she expected, he shook his head. "In light of Mr. La Forge's damage reports, Doctor, I don't have the luxury of abandoning my duties to satisfy your whims. Please direct your excess medical passion to the patients in intensive care."

Crusher drew a sharp breath, stung by the cutting remark. Yet she also recognized that Picard's bristling anger was probably just another symptom of his exhaustion. Before she could frame a tactful reply, the doctor felt someone brush against her arm; Riker had stepped back from the doorway to stand beside her.

"Captain," said the first officer with an affable grin. "I don't think a quick nap could be construed as abandoning your duties. In fact, this would be a good opportunity to take a break so you'll be refreshed by the time Geordi has a new status report."

Crusher rushed in before Picard could debate this point. "And if you've been having trouble sleeping, I can prescribe appropriate medication." This was the obvious recommendation under the circumstances, yet she knew that Picard would perceive this sugges-tion as a veiled threat.

The captain shifted his glance from her over to Riker, then back again to her. Rising from his chair, Picard said, "No drugs will be necessary, Doctor. I will go to my cabin without further protest."

"Very sensible," she said, with what she hoped was a lighter tone, but Picard's stoic reserve did not soften. He stalked from the room without uttering another word.

Crusher turned to the first officer. The grin on his face had faded away. "How long has he been this way, Will?"

"He's grown noticeably worse in the last day," said Riker. "But I think the trouble started when he took possession of the Heart."

Crusher sighed. "I was afraid you'd say that. Unfortunately, this is one condition I don't know how to treat."

Picard stripped off his uniform jacket and tossed it aside. This would be his one concession to comfort for tonight. Doctor Crusher could order him to his cabin, but now that he was in the privacy of his own quarters, he had no intention of following her instructions any further.

Sleep was out of the question. Even closing his eyes was asking too much when reminders of disaster continued to mock him at every turn. After leaving the conference room, he had walked through smoke-filled corridors and listened to the crackling exchanges of repair crews on the intercom; the deck had lurched several times as a gravity stabilizer weakened, then failed; and now, Picard could see the blackened hulk of the Romulan warbird drifting in space just outside his cabin window.

Perhaps Counselor Troi would argue that it was symbolic of his success in defeating an enemy. She would remind him that not all conflicts could be resolved peacefully and that sometimes even the right decisions could not lead to triumph against overwhelming odds. To him, however, the wreckage was a reminder of his failure to protect his own ship.

The *Enterprise* was crippled, stranded far outside Federation territory, and he alone was responsible for this situation.

His glance dropped down to the Heart, a crude centerpiece for the elegant glass-topped table that held it.

What if this quest for the Heart's destination was a fantasy created within his own mind? If that was the case, the entire starship crew would pay the price for his self-delusion. On the other hand, what if the Heart could help pull the *Enterprise* out of this predicament?

*You have waited too long . . .*

T'Sara had advised him to give up the stone, or at least to stop making use of its powers. Yet, so far he had only taken part in the dreams. Surely there was no harm in that? And perhaps the dreams could show him the way to safety.

He stooped to pick up the Heart, his hands eagerly closing around its familiar shape. If there was even a chance of that being true, he must take the risk.

With measured steps and grim determination, Picard carried the stone into his bedroom. He placed it at the head of his bed, then slipped beneath the covers without bothering to undress.

Closing his eyes, he waited impatiently for that night's dream to claim him . . .

The morning sun was still low in the Delula sky, but he could feel sweat beading on the back of his neck. He shivered, chilled by a cool breeze brushing over damp skin, and rubbed his hands dry on the front of his thin shirt. There was nothing he could do to quell the fluttering emptiness in his stomach. He told himself the ache was hunger, but the very thought of food brought a rush of bile up his throat. He swallowed it down and fought against the impulse to gag.

"Nervous, Picard?" Chiang's inquiry sounded sympathetic, but his mouth curled ever so slightly at one corner. His body was solid, thicker than Picard's wiry form; his blue shorts and shirt were crisp and dry.

"No, I'm not nervous." The hoarseness of his reply betrayed the raw burn in the back of his throat.

"No, of course not. After all, you're going to win this race." Chiang's smile deepened into a sneer as he tossed a white towel into the air. "Here, before you flood the field."

Picard lunged forward to catch the towel before it could fall to the ground, a certain offense for a lowly first-year cadet. By the time he straightened up again, Chiang was walking back to a tight knot of upperclassmen gathered by the field house.

"Damn you," Picard muttered softly under his breath, but he took no pleasure in the curse. He cast a furtive glance at the cadets around him, wondering how many had noticed the exchange and understood its significance. They seemed intent on their own business: Drager and T'Soron were on the grass, arms and legs waving gracefully back and forth as they stretched hamstrings and triceps; Miyakawa was knotting her hair into an intricate braid that would keep her long black tresses out of her face; and Gareth was fastening and refastening his shoes for the perfect fit that always eluded him.

"Too tight this time?"

The young Andorian looked up from his task. "Too loose," he corrected and cast his gaze quickly downward again. It was the shortest conversation they had ever had; usually Gareth was tediously chatty.

Picard felt himself flush with shame, and the wave of warmth drove more beads of sweat out of his skin. So, Gareth had heard.

Everyone at the Academy had probably heard.

He mopped his face and neck with Chiang's towel and raked back a wayward curl of hair. Well, there was no help for it now. The boast had been made and was beyond recall.

He heard the crunching tread of boots on grass coming up behind him, and his muscles tensed and tightened, counteracting the effects of his recent warm-up.

"Jean-Luc."

"Oh, hello, Walker." He continued to dry himself off, rubbing first at one arm then another, careful not to turn and look his friend in the face. Walker Keel lacked flair, some cadets even implied he lacked the fire necessary for command, but at this moment Picard would gladly trade all of his own brash bravado for just an ounce of Walker's quiet dignity.

"We'll be waiting for you at the finish line."

His hands clenched and twisted the soft cloth into a knot. "Jack's here, too?"

He caught Walker's nod out of the corner of his eye. "The crowd is already pretty thick, so we're taking turns holding our space."

"Actually, I'd rather . . . it would be easier . . ." Picard couldn't finish, couldn't find the words to tell them both to go away. Neither of them had reproached him for his arrogance, for the absolute lunacy of his drunken outburst, yet facing them at the end of this race would be as great a trial as suffering the scorn of the entire Academy for the remainder of the term. "You know something, Walker? I talk too much."

"Yes, I've noticed that," said Walker with a slow smile. He thumped Picard's back with an open hand, a gesture of both exasperation and affection, then strolled away, melting into the stream of spectators rushing to take their places along the path.

"Starters up!"

Blue-clad figures all across the field froze in mid-motion at the announcement, then responded to the call with a leisurely approach to the broad white line that marked the beginning of the 40k marathon. Picard mimicked their nonchalance, but his gait felt stiff and unnatural. He longed for another stretching session, but there was no time left.

As fifty-three pairs of feet stepped up to the starting line, he had one last stabbing thought: What if Boothby had heard?

The sharp crack of the starting gun caught him unprepared. He pushed off last, almost immediately trailing behind the throng of runners who jostled for position and pace. He was a front-runner—he'd always been a front-runner—but his concentration had flagged during that critical instant when reflexes triggered muscles into a first burst of speed. Faced with an unexpected wall of pumping legs and flailing arms, he faltered again, then braced himself for a collision with any runners moving up behind him. He risked a darting backward glance.

There were no other runners. He was last.

*No freshman has ever won the Academy Marathon . . . until now!*

Those echoing words—his own foolish words—set fire to his lagging feet. Enough of this self-pitying indulgence; he had a long race to run. Shoving aside despair, he narrowed his mind to the demands of the moment. The track surface beneath his thin-soled shoes was firm with a slight texture that provided traction without gripping for too long. He barely registered the towering forest trees that lined the first portion of the winding path, but he welcomed their cool shade as exertion warmed his body.

For the first two kilometers he worked at loosening his tight muscles and setting a rhythm to his breathing. In the process, he passed six runners out of the fifty-three, counting them off one by one. By the fifth kilometer he was sufficiently centered to ignore such petty distractions and his weaving progress around slower runners was unconscious, the automatic avoidance of obstacles.

When he broke out of the forest into bright sunlight and baking heat, he spied the quarter-marker of the Delula course. The air was filled with the sounds of cheers from the waiting crowds, and he had only to reach out his arm to have a cup of cool water eagerly thrust into his hand. He drank greedily of the first offering and reached out again for some more. A fresh burst of cheers, then another, signaled the appearance of more runners from the forest track.

*At least I'm not last.*

The memory of his late start propelled him ahead even faster, but his breathing remained steady. Another cup was thrust into his hand, and he poured its contents over his head before he succumbed to the temptation to drink too much.

He began to run for the sheer joy of it.

By the time Picard reached the halfway marker, he had finally passed Gareth and seen Miyakawa crumple to the ground with a cramp in her calf. All the other freshmen cadets were running behind him on the course.

At the three-quarter mark, he approached a tight knot of five upperclassmen that blocked his way. He could hear the sound of their breathing, ragged with the effort of keeping pace with each other. They were all pushing themselves a little too hard and a little too fast by their determination to break free from the pack. Picard swung left and drove himself forward through a narrow gap on the edge of the path. He caught a glimpse of faces twisted with annoyance at the sudden increase in congestion. An elbow knocked against his side as one of the less generous runners moved to keep him back in place. The unwarranted jostling fueled his next burst of speed.

He was running alone now.

The level path gave way to the rise and swell of gentle hills. In his training runs he had fought to keep a steady pace as he worked the slopes, but now he used the pull of gravity to gather another sliver of speed as he sped downward, then pushed to maintain the new pace on his climb up the next rise. Sweat poured off him, stinging his eyes with its salty flavor; the soft cloth of his clothes chafed against damp skin. The slight tingle in his thigh and calf muscles would turn to a tremble if he misjudged his endurance and pushed too hard. He tossed his head, slinging back the hair plastered to his forehead, and then threw off the intrusion of physical discomfort with an equivalent mental shrug. It was important to feel his body at work, and that included the pain, but that knowledge must not distract him from the run.

He crested another hill and spotted a string of four runners just ahead. Chiang was leading them, but even as Picard watched, the others were challenging his position. Telegar, the fastest of the Andorians, must be the woman in second place. The other two cadets were probably Dorgath and Stemon, both favored to win the race and both pushing the front-runners to exhaust themselves on the final stretch.

As he sped steadily onward, driving one foot after the next, his breath heaving in and out of his chest, a dull background roar sorted itself into the sound of a cheering crowd, and he realized that there were throngs of people lining the path up the next slope.

No, not just the next slope. He was approaching Mount Bonnell, the last hill of the marathon.

*No freshman has ever won the Academy Marathon . . . until now!*

Perhaps it hadn't been such an empty boast after all. Reaching deep inside himself for the last of his reserves, Picard propelled himself faster down the slope. The ground leveled beneath his pumping feet. He passed Dorgath just as the ground began to rise again. Chiang was ahead, having fallen back to third place.

Momentum carried him up the first few meters of the hill without effort. When the weight of the climb finally hit him, he expected to slow down, but he was locked into a rhythm and grace of movement that remained steady and controlled.

Then the terror struck.

*It happens here, soon.*

It was as if his mind were detaching from his body, pulling back to observe and comment on the scene.

*I've done this before. This run, this dream.*

Chiang had been flagging for the past few minutes. He was easily overtaken.

*Oh, god, it's a very bad dream.*

Telegar and Stemon remained ahead. As Picard pulled even with the Andorian, the dread deepened and clarified.

*I stumble. Any step now, I stumble.*

He willed himself to wake up, to stop from reliving the humiliation of that one false step. The last few minutes of the race stretched out before him like a rack. How many times had he tortured himself with these memories?

*All the false sympathy, all the pity. But they were relieved to see me fail. I came too close to winning.*

Now only Stemon remained. He had a Vulcan's superior muscular strength and stamina, but the humidity of the Delula atmosphere clogged his lungs and reduced their efficiency. If his keen hearing picked up the sound of Picard's approach, he was still unable to summon more speed. The gap between them narrowed.

*Now? Two steps from now?*

Picard tried to brace himself for the sharp jolt that would signal his loss of footing, but he could no longer control his body, could hardly even feel it, and thus he could not avert the disaster about to happen.

The scenario varied. Sometimes the jarring fall landed him at Chiang's feet, at other times he actually took the lead before dropping to the ground, breath knocked out of his air-starved lungs, as the four upperclassmen thundered past him. The countless variations had plagued his sleep so many times and for so many years that he couldn't remember when the real fall had actually taken place.

Doubtless any number of his classmates at the Academy would remember the true accounting of events.

*Even fifth place would have been a cause for celebration . . . if not for my boast.*

That was the true misstep. Perhaps his subconscious had searched for a metaphor to frame his arrogance. Certainly this was no less plausible an explanation for tripping on a smooth path than the imaginary pebble he had conjured afterward to explain his sudden failure.

His body passed Stemon.

*Now. It must come now. I've never gone beyond this point.*

But he crested over the hill and began the descent at a breakneck speed that would have tangled his feet if this hadn't been a dream. Physical sensation returned, and the rush of air against his outstretched arms felt like the lift of wind on the wings of a hawk flying through the sky.

The cheering that had sent him up Mount Bonnell to overtake the other runners was nothing compared to what met him on this side. He was buffeted by the clamoring sound of massed voices.

The white ribbon over the finish line rippled and waved a greeting to him, waiting for his embrace.

He closed his eyes, too sick with dread to watch any longer.

*No. This is more than I can bear. To lose when I'm this close . . .*

Then the ribbon cut across his chest.

# *The Children of Hamlin,* by Carmen Carter

In *The Children of Hamlin,* also by Carmen Carter, the *Enterprise* was ordered to negotiate with the Choraii for the return of humans captured as children during a Choraii attack upon the Hamlin colony. The Choraii lived in space in bubbles filled with liquid air, and they communicated through music. They did not consider humans to be sentient and thus had no difficulty in wiping out human settlements, but they agreed to negotiate because they wanted to trade for certain metals.

The story left me curious about the Choraii and wanting to know more about who they were, about their motivations and why they refused to communicate. They remained something of a mystery, and that alone was fascinating. It is as though neither the *Enterprise* crew nor the reader had a frame of reference for understanding a people so alien. I like science fiction that keeps me wondering.

This scene shows Picard's frustration at his inability to engage in a productive exchange with the Choraii. Ruthe, a human captured by the Choraii as a child, had beamed over to the Choraii ship and refused to return. She volunteered to remain to make the Choraii understand that humans were worthwhile because they also had music. She wanted to stay so that she could stop the killing. Picard was unwilling to allow her to make such a sacrifice; he was ready to fight the Choraii to enforce her right to live with humans if that was her choice. Only when Picard believed that she truly wished to stay with the Choraii did he allow them to leave with her. Until that point, he was prepared to go to battle to get her back.

THE *ENTERPRISE* HAD REACHED A PATCH OF SPACE NO DIFFERENT FROM ANY other within a distance of several light-years. No different at that moment, reflected Andrew Deelor. If the Choraii followed their usual habits, the situation was subject to change without any prior notice.

"This is the place," announced Geordi. "I've double-checked the navigation settings."

"Sensors do not detect any traces of organic particles," reported Data. "Either our coordinates are incorrect or the Choraii have not yet arrived."

"We are at the right place and they will come," said Ruthe without rising from the deck. "The song is a long one."

"Not that long," Lieutenant Yar exclaimed. "I'm picking up a faint radio transmission. Boosting reception to the maximum." She released a thrumming sound into the air.

The bridge crew stopped in mid-motion, entranced by what they heard. The throaty chorus was far deeper than that of the *B Flat* singers; it possessed the broad resonance of a cathedral organ and a wide range of voices which rose and fell in complex harmony. Deelor waited for Ruthe's reaction; she displayed none that he could observe. Either she was indifferent to the character of the sound or she already knew what to expect.

"Not a single note," said Picard with surprise as he listened to the undulating music. "More like a chord."

"A D major chord, to be precise," noted Deelor. He stepped up to the captain's chair. "We're in trouble."

The quiet statement snapped Picard's attention away from the Choraii song. "Explain."

"Pitch is an indication of a ship's age. In addition, listen to the number of voices," Deelor instructed. "Only five different tones are present, but I suspect many of the parts are doubled or even tripled. A conservative estimate indicates eleven singers, which means the ship is very old and therefore very powerful. More than a match for the *Enterprise.*"

Ruthe's answering song caught him by surprise. She had mounted the aft bridge and played as if from a stage. The tripping notes from her flute hovered several registers above the drone of the Choraii D major chorus as she wove an intricate counterpoint to their melodic line.

"Captain, shall I broadcast her response?" asked Yar, lowering the growing volume of the Choraii transmission.

Picard hesitated. "Is something wrong, Ambassador?"

"What?" Then Deelor realized he had been frowning as he listened. "No, nothing's wrong."

The captain waved an assent to Lieutenant Yar. Ruthe played on and the tempo of the intertwined sounds quickened.

"They've heard her." Deelor's own heart began to beat more rapidly, as if striving to match the pulse of the music.

"And here they come," announced Geordi from the helm. His energy-sensitive visor had picked out the first glimmer of the approaching vessel on the battle-bridge viewer, but by the time his warning drew the crew's attention to the screen, the image of the Choraii ship had tripled in size.

Deelor caught his breath at the sight. Even without any reference point in space, he could sense how massive the ship must be. Whereas the *B Flat* had been composed of some two dozen neatly packed bubbles, the *D Major* was a jumbled conglomeration of over a hundred spheres. An elongated stream of large bubbles formed the central mass, with smaller ones tucked into crevices and dotted here and there over the outer edges. Deelor had never faced a ship of this complexity before.

"Reduce magnification," ordered Picard as the *D Major* filled the frame, then spilled beyond its borders. His brow furrowed. "So these are the destroyers of New Oregon."

The approaching cluster tumbled in space. As a new side rolled into view, Deelor spotted several purple spheres nestled in the exterior layer. "Captain . . ."

"Yes, I see them," said Picard tersely. "Data, prepare your neutralizing probe for launch. Just in case we end up inside another energy net."

"Neutralization efforts would be ineffective," said Data. He fur-

155

ther reduced the screen magnification as the Choraii ship threatened to outgrow the frame once again. "The net draws power from the mother ship and the *D Major* can release a far greater energy surge than can be siphoned off by the probe."

"Which means their net would crush us faster as well."

"Captain, we would still have time to drill through the spheres with our phasers," said Worf.

"Yes," agreed Data. "But my calculations indicate a seventy-eight point five percent chance that such a scenario would end in mutual destruction."

"That's enough talk of battle," said Deelor impatiently. "This is going to remain a peaceful encounter."

"So far, the peaceful intentions have remained ours and ours alone," said Picard bitterly. "The Choraii loot and destroy and then we pay them for their ill-gotten gains."

The flight of the *D Major* came to an abrupt halt. The glowing orange spheres quivered with the strong currents of their liquid interior.

"Ambassador . . ."

Deelor hushed the captain with a wave of his hand. "Listen." The journey song had ended, but Ruthe continued playing with the Choraii, modulating without a break into a new melody. "They're singing the greeting."

Shifting his weight in the captain's chair, Picard leaned closer to Deelor and spoke more softly. "The exchange sounds friendly."

"Yes, it is." So even the captain could detect the joy of the meeting. "Once Ruthe establishes our good intentions, we can—" Deelor broke off.

"What's happened?"

"Ruthe has begun a third melody," explained Deelor. She hadn't looked to him once for a sign of what to do, yet apparently she was moving beyond the ritual preliminaries. In what direction? Deelor tried to make sense of her exchange with the Choraii, to untangle the mix of high flute and booming organ voices, but the scales they used were unfamiliar and his understanding of the exchange faltered.

Dr. Crusher edged up behind him. "Do they have the child?"

"Yes, I think so," answered Deelor, less certain than he sounded. He had lost track of the melodic line and could grasp only scattered phrases of meaning.

"So how do we get her back?" Picard's voice rang out over the bridge. All singing had stopped abruptly, replaced by an unvarying bass hum emanating from the *D Major.*

Snapping off a section of her flute, Ruthe answered the captain. "Arrangements have already been made for the girl's return." The translator rapidly disassembled the remainder of her instrument and tucked the pieces inside her cloak. "Emily was found when they plundered New Oregon for silver. She isn't a bonding gift, so they are willing to let her go for the proper price."

The palms of Deelor's hands grew moist. He rubbed them dry against his uniform. "What price is that?"

"Three pounds of gold, some few ounces of zinc and platinum." Ruthe stepped down from the aft deck. "I'll beam over while the metal is gathered."

Deelor was too shaken to reply. He had trusted Ruthe with his life over and over again; he would do so now. Yet he knew her well enough to sense a lie in what she told him. A lie to what purpose?

Picard stepped down from his chair to confront Ruthe. "I don't like the appearance of this transaction. They've agreed too easily."

"Would you rather fight the Choraii?" asked Ruthe, arching one brow. "I'm not so certain you would win."

A full beat passed before the captain spoke again. "Lieutenant Yar, Dr. Crusher, please accompany Ruthe to the transporter chamber." Picard fell back and the translator swept past him.

Deelor stared after her until the doors of the turbo cut her off from his sight. "I trust Ruthe's judgment." Then he wondered if he had jumped too quickly to her defense and betrayed his growing unease to the captain. "She knows what she's doing."

Picard settled back into place, his feet braced firmly on the dais, his hands gripping the armrests. He focused his attention on the viewer. "You may trust Ruthe, but I don't trust the Choraii."

Tasha Yar felt uneasy about opening a window in the ship's shield for the critical seconds when Ruthe would transport over to the Choraii ship. Her tension eased very little even after the deflectors snapped back into place; she couldn't relax while the massive vessel loomed so near to the *Enterprise.*

"I hate this part," admitted Yar leaning against the console. "Last time we waited for nearly three hours before Ruthe's contact signal."

Crusher sighed heavily. "If the ritual swim through the *B Flat* took hours, how long will she take to go through the *D Major?*"

"Days, weeks . . ." A high-pitched tone jerked the security chief back to the controls. "The beam signal," Yar announced, swiftly reversing the procedure that had sent Ruthe out of the ship only minutes before.

"It's too early! Something must have gone wrong." Crusher rushed to the dais as white light flooded the chamber once again. When the blinding beam died away, the doctor found a young girl standing on the platform. And only the girl. Around her neck she wore the chain with Ruthe's com insignia.

"Get her out of the way," cried Yar as she hastened to broaden the reception beam around the coordinates. Each second she spent adjusting the controls increased the ship's risk.

Crusher swept the child off the platform, drawing the small body to her chest with a fierce hug, rejoicing in the recovery of at least one life from the devastation on New Oregon. The face that had peered out from behind water-soaked brown tresses bore a strong resemblance to Dnnys. "Emily!"

"I was having fun," answered the girl happily when the doctor loosened her embrace. Emily had made the transition to breathing air without assistance. "Can I go back to play soon?"

"No, honey. You're going home," said Crusher, trying to smile back. Had the Hamlin children been this untouched by their parents' deaths?

"Is that nice lady coming, too?"

Ruthe. The doctor looked across the room. Yar's hands were on the transporter controls, but they weren't in motion any longer. "Tasha, where is she?"

"I couldn't lock on to her," said the security chief. Her face was wooden, her eyes downcast. "Shields are raised."

"The entire ship registers as a life-form," boomed Worf across the smaller bridge. "Sensor readings are garbled. I can't pinpoint her exact position in the interior." He checked another section of the tactical console. "Still no answer on hailing frequencies."

"What can have happened over there?" Picard had doubted the Choraii's intentions from the start, but he mustn't let his suspicions override judgment. A misreading of the alien motives could embroil both ships in unnecessary combat. "Would the Choraii send over the child without receiving payment first?"

"It's possible, I suppose. Perhaps as a statement of extreme arrogance."

Another thought increased Picard's concern. "Or would she have snatched the child away without the Choraii's knowledge?"

"No," said Deelor firmly. "She's not that foolish."

"We're blind to what's happening over there, but unless they make a hostile—"

"Captain," broke in Data. "The *D Major* is moving away."

"Helm, full speed pursuit!" ordered Picard. He followed quickly with a shipwide announcement. "All hands to battlestations."

The *Enterprise* surged forward after the Choraii bubbles. The wide gap between the two vessels began to narrow, but very slowly.

"Ambassador, we can't force Ruthe's return," said Picard. "Not without placing her in grave danger."

Deelor nodded. His face was pale but composed. "Just get their attention and buy me some time, Captain."

"Understood." Picard took a deep breath and issued his next order. "Worf, lock tractor beams as soon as the Choraii are in range."

Worf's clawed hand hovered above the tactical console like a raptor, then swooped downward. Contact. Deck tremors racked the starship as a half-dozen tractor beams latched onto the spheres of the *D Major*. White bridge lights guttered out; bloodred emergency lights flickered to life. On the viewer, the Choraii ship shuddered to a slow halt.

*"Humans, release us!"* Deep, slurring voices thundered like an angry Greek chorus.

"You still carry one of our people within your ship," shouted Deelor, but his solo tenor was weak in comparison. "Return her to us."

*"You mean the lost one? We were forced to give her up many years ago, but now she's come back."*

"Damn her," cursed Deelor under his breath.

Picard signaled Worf to cut off communications. Silence blanketed the bridge. "Ambassador, what do they mean by 'the lost one'?"

"I suspected this earlier. There are only a few ships in the local cluster that are large enough to land on a planet, but I thought sure Ruthe would tell me . . ." He trailed off distractedly.

"Tell you what?" demanded Picard.

"The *D Major* is Ruthe's homeship. She was born and raised there." Deelor raked his fingers through his hair, leaving a wake of angry spikes on the top of his head. "She must have known as soon as she heard their song, but she didn't tell me."

"Why not?"

"Because I would never have let her beam over." Deelor waved urgently to Worf and raised his voice to resume his exchange with the Choraii. "We'll give you any metal you want. Just let Ruthe return here."

*"No, Wild One. This is her home. She agreed to stay if we gave you the young one in her place."*

159

Rising from the captain's chair, Picard brought his deeper voice to the ambassador's service. "We will not accept her sacrifice."

*"But it's not a sacrifice, Captain."* Ruthe's words quavered and echoed, distorted by the liquid that filled her lungs. *"I'm here of my own free will."*

"No, I don't believe you!" cried out Deelor. "You've struck a bargain for the girl and this is the price."

*"A small price."* Her laugh rippled through the waters.

"An unacceptable price," countered Picard angrily. "The Choraii have brought death to so many people without thought, without remorse. How can we abandon you to live with them?"

*"But I can stop the killings. I will sing them your songs! Songs of Mozart, and Beethoven, and all the others! I will show the Choraii that even beasts can make music. Once they recognize your worth, they will learn to ask for what they need."*

"This action is too drastic, too final. There are other ways to—"

*"You still don't understand. I have always wanted to return here, to my real home. I've betrayed many of my kind in the search for this ship, but only the children, because they are young, and can forget. I was too old to forget and too young to die for the memories."*

"Is she telling the truth?" demanded Picard of the man standing frozen beside him. "Can this be what she really wants?"

"Yes," whispered Deelor hoarsely. "Damn her, yes."

Ruthe's voice sang out again, more insistent than before. *"Let us go, Wild Ones. We have many songs to sing."*

"Lieutenant Worf," said Picard in a low voice. "Let them go."

The Klingon quickly obeyed, releasing the *D Major* from the tractor beam hold. The bright lights and chattering sounds of the battle bridge, muted by a lack of power, sprang back to full intensity.

"They're not leaving," observed La Forge of the alien craft. He lowered his hands closer to the helm controls.

A deep humming sound reverberated from the communications link with the *D Major*. Resonant Choraii voices swelled into a dirgelike song, flooding the bridge with their music. One high soprano echoed the somber melody.

The oppressive sound raised a prickle of apprehension in the captain. "What's happening?"

Deelor didn't answer. Instead, Data turned from the helm. "I believe that is their way of saying good-bye."

# *The Captain's Table, Book Two: Dujonian's Hoard,* by Michael Jan Friedman

*Dujonian's Hoard* is an action tale told in the first person by Captain Picard and the *TNG* entry in *The Captain's Table* book series. To find a missing archaeologist and a legendary treasure trove, including priceless and powerful *glor'ya* gems, Picard and Worf traveled underground and joined a mercenary ship captained by a woman known as "Red Abby." In their search, they fought Romulans, Cardassians and the tyrannical Abinarri race on the other side of Hel's Gate, a beautiful but deadly celestial phenomenon. In this excerpt, Picard fought his way out of a Cardassian brig with his mercenary companions and led the battle to rescue Red Abby from their captors. This jail break scene would have been at home in the original series; Kirk would have fought alongside Picard at every step.

## The Tale

As soon as the Cardassians left us alone, Astellanax knelt by my side. "Are you all right?" he asked.

I nodded. The numbness in my arm and my side was already beginning to wear off, leaving a dull ache in its place.

"I'll live," I told him. I glanced at the door, which had closed in the Cardassians' wake. "But I'm not so sure about your captain. She'll die before she gives Ecor what he wants."

The first officer nodded. "Agreed."

"We can't just let them kill her," protested Thadoc, who was standing behind Astellanax. "We must do something."

"This is a Cardassian warship," Dunwoody reminded him, "full of trained soldiers. It won't be easy."

"No," said another voice. "It won't."

I turned and saw it belonged to Corbis. He looked around the cargo bay at his fellow prisoners, captivating them by virtue of his size.

"I don't know about the rest of you," he went on, "but I signed on to find treasure—not to risk my skin for a captain I hardly know."

"She is not just our captain," Thadoc countered. "She is one of us."

"And if I don't do something to help her," said Astellanax, "what right have I got to expect help when they take *me* away?

"Well said," I declared, getting to my feet—no easy task, I might

161

add, but one I deemed necessary. "However, Mr. Dunwoody has a point. As I told Red Abby herself, there is no easy way out of here."

"Oh, no?" asked a broad, dark-haired Tellarite named Gob. His tiny eyes squinted at me expectantly.

Corbis grunted, picking up on the Tellarite's meaning. "Not even when we've got a high-and-mighty Starfleet captain among us?" He turned to Worf. "And his Klingon lapdog?"

I eyed my lieutenant, counseling patience with my glance. Somehow, he found the wherewithal to embrace it.

"Not even then," I told the Pandrilite reasonably. "Certainly, I have a working knowledge of Cardassian vessels and the technologies that drive them. But before I can use that knowledge to advantage, we've got to get out of this cargo bay."

"Then, let's do it," Astellanax said. He looked around. "There's got to be a way out of here. It's just a matter of finding it."

I frowned. The Orion was long on enthusiasm but short on suggestions. And as it happened, I'd been racking my brain for a way out since the Cardassians threw us in there.

Assad pointed to a narrow, raised section of ceiling running from one bulkhead to another. If you've ever seen the schematics for a Cardassian vessel, you know it contained power-distribution circuitry.

"If we could get up there," he said, "maybe we could short out the ship's energy grid." He looked around at his fellow prisoners. "It's worth a try, isn't it?"

Worf scowled. "Even if there was a way for us to reach it, we would be risking an explosion that would rip this bay apart."

Astellanax started to suggest it might not be so bad a risk after all. I emphasize the word "started," because at that moment we heard the shrill complaint of a half-dozen Klaxons.

Clearly, something had gone wrong on the warship. Something *serious,* I told myself, with a certainty that depended on instinct more than logic.

I looked at Worf, wondering what it could be. An accident in the engine room? Or perhaps the approach of an enemy?

Either way, it represented a danger to us—one we were helpless to do anything about. If something was amiss, the Cardassians would likely worry about themselves first and about us not at all.

Then something else happened. We felt a jolt, right through the deckplates. The lights went out at the same time, leaving us nothing to see by except the ghostly glow of blue-green emergency strips.

Corbis moved to the doors and pounded on them with the flat of his big, blue hand. "Let us out!" he cried.

I knew he'd get no satisfactory response. As it happened, he got no response at all.

But that was good—the best outcome we could have hoped for, in fact. It meant our guards had abandoned us to attend to an emergency elsewhere on the ship—and with the power that maintained the force field down, the only thing that stood between ourselves and our freedom was the doors themselves.

Standing beside the Pandrilite, I tried to dig my fingers into the tiny crevice between the rhodinium surfaces.

"What are you doing?" asked Thadoc.

"Trying to pry the doors open," I explained. "And if it's all the same to you, I could use some help."

Even before I spoke, Worf had come over to join me. As he and Thadoc dug their fingers into the opening, Corbis lent his efforts, as well.

"Heave!" I cried.

We heaved. The doors parted ever so slightly.

"Heave!" I cried again.

This time, with a little better grip, we made more progress. A space the width of two of my fingers opened between the doors.

"Heave!" I cried a third time.

We put our shoulders and our backs into it, tugging as hard as we could. I felt some unseen restraint give way and the doors slid back into their wall-pockets, clearing the way for our escape.

The corridor outside our cell was dark as well, only the lighting strips providing illumination. With a cheer, the other prisoners pushed us into it, unmindful of what we might find there. Fortunately, there wasn't a single Cardassian in sight—but that didn't mean it would stay that way.

Even if all other systems were down, internal sensors from other parts of the ship might pick up the movements of so many beings. It would only be a moment or two before the Cardassians realized what had happened, and less than a minute before they responded.

Two things were clear to me. First, we had to go on the offensive. Second, if we didn't recover Red Abby immediately, we might never get another chance to do so.

And there was only one place they would keep her.

"This way," I shouted over the tumult of voices, and started down the corridor toward the nearest lift.

"Where are you going?" asked Astellanax.

"The gul's quarters," I told him.

"Why there?" asked Thadoc.

"Because," I said, "that's where we'll find your captain, assuming she's still alive."

"Wait a minute!" someone bellowed.

The Oord—Corbis's friend from the melee in the mess hall—stepped forward with a belligerence characteristic of his species. He made an exaggerated gesture of dismissal with his arms.

"I don't give a *damn* about the captain," he rumbled. "I want to know where the escape craft are."

More than a dozen voices went up in support of the Oord's demand. With the casualties we had sustained on the *Daring* and the loss of Sturgis, that represented almost half our number.

But there was no time to argue. "Very well," I said, pointing past them. "They're over there. Two decks down."

The Oord looked at me with narrowed eyes, no doubt wondering if I had any reason to lie to him. Then he took off in the direction I'd indicated, with the green-splotched Thelurian and several others on his heels.

To my surprise, Corbis wasn't one of them. The Pandrilite watched his friends go for a second, then turned to me. He seemed ready to follow where I led—at least for the moment.

Suddenly, the deck rocked beneath our feet, forcing us to grab the bulkheads for support. I was no longer willing to accept the accident theory. More and more, it was becoming clear to me that the ship was under attack—though I couldn't divine by whom and for what reason.

"The captain!" Astellanax cried, even before we'd recovered.

Thrusting myself away from the bulkhead, I made my way toward the lift. Ideally, I'd have proceeded with the kind of caution we had employed on the *Daring,* but there simply wasn't time for that.

So when we came around a corner and met our first squad of Cardassians, we were almost nose to nose with them before either party knew it.

As we were unarmed, the close quarters worked to our advantage. I drove an uppercut into the jaw of one Cardassian while Worf decked a second with an open backhand. Corbis lifted a third soldier and sent him flying into his comrades, just as Thadoc used a Romulan lightning jab to crush the windpipe of a fourth man.

The fighting was savage and unrestrained, but mercifully quick. And when the proverbial dust cleared, our side had emerged victorious. In fact, we hadn't lost a single combatant. Knowing how lucky we'd been, we grabbed whatever arms we could and surged down the corridor.

Reaching the lift, we jammed in and Worf programmed it for the main deck. I half-expected the compartment to halt in midtransit, interdicted by a command from the bridge. But it did nothing of the kind.

While we were in the lift, the ship lurched twice. The second time was the worst one yet. All the more reason to move quickly, I mused.

When the doors opened, I took a quick look around in the darkened corridor. Seeing no evidence of an ambush, I tightened my grasp on my Cardassian pistol and led the way to Gul Ecor's suite.

Our goal was almost in view, I told myself. There was a chance we would make it—an outcome on which I wouldn't have wagered a strip of latinum just a few minutes earlier.

We came to the end of the corridor, turned right and then right again. And there before us, not more than fifty meters away, was the entrance to the gul's quarters. Unguarded, no less.

It seemed too easy. And it was.

Someone cried out and we whirled. A moment later, the Cardassians' energy beams exploded in the darkness. All but one of them missed.

In the eerie half-light of the emergency strips, Astellanax glanced just once at the blackened, oozing mess that had been his stomach. His eyes grew round and wide. Raising his weapon, he fired off a blast. Then he toppled forward, dead before he hit the ground.

The rest of us fired as well, sobered by the Orion's destruction. I regret to say he was not the only casualty we suffered in that encounter. One of the humans among us cried out and crumpled, followed by a Bajoran and a squat, light-haired Tellarite.

Still, we created equal havoc in the ranks of the Cardassians. Before long, we had forced them to retreat to the joining of corridors behind them.

"The gul's quarters!" I rasped, ducking another flash of deadly energy. "Move if you value your lives!"

I didn't dare check to see who had responded to my command. I was too busy laying down cover fire for them, with Lieutenant Worf on one side of me and Corbis on the other.

"Picard!" a voice said, crackling in the darkness. "Quickly!"

It was a woman who had called me—and not just any woman. The summons had come from the throat of Red Abby.

"Dammit, Picard, get in here!" she cried.

165

As if to emphasize the urgency of her summons, a whole new flood of Cardassians filled the corridor, stepping over the bodies of their fallen comrades. Worf and Corbis and I retreated as one, continuing to provide cover for the other prisoners.

Then we ducked into the gul's quarters, and the door irised closed in our wake. It cut off any possibility of our being hit by enemy fire— temporarily, at least.

In the muted blue-green glow of the emergency lighting, I turned to Red Abby. She was hefting a Cardassian energy rifle, scanning the ranks of those who had retreated into the room with me.

Abruptly, she turned to me. "Astellanax?" she asked, her brow creased deeply with concern.

I shook my head. "He didn't make it."

## *The Dominion War, Book Three: Tunnel Through the Stars,* by John Vornholt

Many fans have wondered what the *Enterprise* crew were doing during the Dominion War that was so much a part of the *DS9* storyline for its last season. John Vornholt answered these questions in two original novels of the *TNG* crew's exploits during the war. *Behind Enemy Lines* is Book One in the *Dominion War* series, and *Tunnel Through the Stars* is Book Three. In *Behind Enemy Lines,* Picard learned that the Dominion was building an artificial wormhole to bring troops into the Alpha Quadrant. His mission in *Tunnel Through the Stars* was to destroy that wormhole, and he joined former Lieutenant Ro Laren and what was left of her Maquis crew to lead the mission. Picard's strength and leadership skills convinced exhausted former slaves of the Dominion to march back into hell for him to destroy the wormhole.

SAM LAVELLE STRODE ONTO THE BRIDGE OF THE *ORB OF PEACE,* HARDLY able to believe that he had given up a spacious Cardassian antimatter tanker for this austere Bajoran transport. He was sure he had gotten the worst of the deal, especially considering that he *thought* he was going to be rescued and sent home. His last voyage had been a perfect example of Murphy's Law, and this one promised to send him from the frying pan into the fire.

The cramped bridge had a strange viewscreen with Bajoran writing all around it. He was able to translate two phrases: "The devout will enter the Celestial Temple," and "The Kai holds the lantern of Bajor." Even without the platitudes, the stars glimmered enticingly on the screen, making him wish that he were going home.

But Sam knew there was no escape from this war—not until the Dominion was driven back to their part of the galaxy.

He spotted the slim Bajoran, Ro Laren, seated at the conn. Both Captain Picard and Geordi La Forge looked Bajoran—with nose ridges and earrings—but Ro was the real thing. Sam remembered hearing stories about her on the *Enterprise,* but he had only seen her once, in Ten-Forward, just before her ill-fated mission to infiltrate the Maquis. Now she was captain of this Bajoran vessel.

"I'm your relief, Captain," he said, keeping his voice low in the dimly lit bridge.

"Thank you." Ro Laren rose from her seat and stretched like a willowy lioness, shaking her short-cropped mane of dark brown hair. She was wearing a Bajoran uniform which hugged the lanky contours of her body, and Sam looked longer and harder than he should have. Ro caught him staring at her, and her eyes drilled into his. Sam knew he should look away, but it had been a long time since he had gazed lustfully at a woman, and he wasn't anxious to stop.

"I'm sorry," he said, managing a shy smile. "I don't know what got into me. It's funny what even a small taste of freedom will do to a man."

Her face softened, and she looked sympathetic if still annoyed. "How long were you a prisoner of the Dominion?"

"About two months, I guess," answered Sam. "It's hard to say, because we were never allowed to see any chronometers, except when we were on work detail, building that damn collider. And then, we only saw shift timers. We were kept segregated from the women. I saw them every now and then on the worker transports, but that was it."

"I know the Cardassians—it must have been bad."

He nodded slowly. "Yes, it was, and a lot of good people are still there. I wish we could do something to help them."

"There's no chance for a mass escape?"

"I don't see how," Sam answered glumly. "The complex where the prisoners are housed is near the collider, but each pod of prisoners is isolated. There's no way to get hold of a ship like we did—that was a fluke. No matter when you do this, thousands of prisoners will be working. If your mission is to destroy the artificial wormhole, your mission is to destroy them, too."

Ro crossed her arms and wrinkled her ridged nose. "You know, that's exactly what I've been telling Captain Picard. And it sounds even worse coming from you, because you've been there."

"Yes, I've been there, and I can't believe I'm thinking about going back. This isn't exactly the way I envisioned my escape—going back to that place, on purpose." Shivering, Sam sunk into the chair at the conn and studied the unfamiliar instruments.

"I'm sure Captain Picard would offer you a chance not to go, if he could," said Ro. "But we only have this craft, and no way to split up."

Sam snorted a laugh. "Yeah, if you don't mind me saying so, your demolition squad is a little short-handed."

"We had a whole crew and more than one torpedo. But we lost five torpedoes fighting our way through the Dominion border patrol, then we got shanghaied by pirates in the Badlands, and hijacked by Romulans—"

"Pirates and Romulans?" asked Sam with boyish curiosity. The smile faded from his lips when he saw how upset Ro was about these incidents. "Hey, I'm sorry if we lost more good people, but I'm sort of burned-out on death. I can't even think about it, if you know what I mean."

"I know what you mean," admitted Ro, staring down at the deck. "The *Enterprise* is supposed to take us home, but only if we alert them with a subspace beacon."

"But how quickly could they get here?"

"That's a good question." The Bajoran hovered over Sam's shoulder and pointed at his console. "You'll want to watch the hull pressure—right there."

"Okay, thanks." Sam took some time to scan all the readouts, finding them fairly easy to understand. It wasn't nearly as complex as the antimatter tanker. He tried to concentrate on his duties, but the Bajoran's presence was bringing back memories and emotions he had tried to push away, without much success.

"I had a good friend who was Bajoran, Ensign Sito Jaxa," he said with a wistful smile. "Her death was the first casualty I really experienced in Starfleet, and it hit me pretty hard. She was killed by the Cardassians, and that act started the war for me a couple of years early. I was gung-ho to get at them."

"I followed Sito's career," said Ro, "but I never got a chance to meet her. I think I was away at Tactical Training while you and your friends were serving aboard the *Enterprise.*"

Sam chuckled. "You couldn't help but to follow Sito's career—she was full of zip. She got into a lot of trouble at the Academy."

"Along with Wesley Crusher," said Ro with a smile.

While they shared an unexpected moment of nostalgia, Sam glanced at the striking Bajoran. It was too bad that his life expectancy was so short, or he would have been tempted to pursue the former Starfleet officer. Of course it was wartime, and anything could happen.

Returning his mind to his duty, Sam adjusted the viewscreen, and a brown-magenta cloud coalesced into view, still some distance away. Pulses of light blinked on and off within its murky depths, which gave it an oddly cheerful glow, like a surreal Christmas wreath.

"The Badlands," he mused. "Is it all that bad?"

"Worse," muttered Ro. "I wouldn't go back there, except there's no other place to hide."

"Well, if it's any consolation, you're within striking distance of the artificial wormhole from here. It's just that there's a fleet guarding it, and it's ten kilometers long."

"So I gather," replied Ro solemnly.

They heard footsteps, and Sam turned to see Captain Picard come striding onto the cramped bridge. He looked odd with his Bajoran earring, nose ridges, and tufts of white hair; but his voice, bearing, and stern demeanor left no doubt who was in charge. Immediately, Sam stiffened in his seat and studied his readouts until he was caught up.

"Status?" asked Picard as he consulted the small padd in his hands.

"Estimated arrival time at the Badlands: one hour," reported Sam. "No sign of enemy craft."

"Thank you, Lieutenant. I haven't had an opportunity to say how good it is to see you again, although I wish it were under better circumstances."

"Me, too, sir."

The captain looked somber. "I've talked to your crew. I realize that we ruined your escape attempt. I'm sorry. I'm sure you expected to get farther away than the Badlands—"

"I wasn't really expecting to escape," replied Sam honestly. "I just wanted to die like a Starfleet officer, not a slave. I don't want to go back to that place—and I doubt if this mission will work—but it's still a good chance to die as a Starfleet officer."

The captain's lips thinned. "I wish there was an alternative, but there isn't. We can't allow the Dominion to ever use that artificial wormhole."

"I know, sir," admitted Sam. "I thought the same thing every day, even while I was building it."

Picard consulted his padd and looked around to make sure they were alone. "I need an honest evaluation of every member of your crew. You know what we have ahead of us—a major sabotage mission with a high degree of risk."

Sam frowned thoughtfully. "The only member of the crew I really know is Taurik, and I would trust him with my life. As for Woil, Shonsui, Horik, and Maserelli—they're all career Starfleet officers, who ought to be fine in a crisis. But they've been through some rough times lately, and they may be close to cracking. I'm sure you could say that about all of us, except for Taurik, of course. Many times during our imprisonment, I wished I were a Vulcan."

"I've often wished that I were a certain android," said Picard with a wistful smile. "What about the scientist, Enrak Grof?"

Sam winced, trying not to show his doubts. "Until today, I would've said he was a traitor and a collaborator—and an unpleasant one at that. He could've stopped us but didn't, so I guess he's on our side. As I'm sure he'll tell you, he's basically in it for the science and the glory. Grof knows that artificial wormhole backwards and forwards—he helped design it."

"So he told me," said Picard. "None of the rest of you have any in-depth knowledge of its workings?"

"No," answered Sam. "Taurik knows some of the theory, but we were grunt labor, only told what was needed. Grof was right in there with the Vorta engineers, on a buddy-buddy basis with our resident changeling."

"You saw a changeling?" asked Picard with interest.

"Only once, when they put me in charge of the tanker." Sam smiled nostalgically. "To tell you the truth, Captain, I remember more about the food than anything else. It was the first decent food I'd had in weeks."

Captain Picard allowed him a slight smile. "I know this has been difficult for you, Lieutenant, and I wish I could relieve you of further burden. But you know our situation."

"Not really," answered Sam. "Taurik and I were captured early on, defending the outer colonies. We volunteered for that service, if you can believe it. I've heard rumors—if this ship is any indication of what Starfleet can spare, I guess we're in a lot of trouble."

The captain looked grave as he explained, "If the Dominion manages to bring through reinforcements from the Gamma Quadrant—either by clearing the mines from the Bajoran wormhole or through their new artificial wormhole—the situation will be desperate. We didn't even know about the artificial wormhole until we encountered Ro and her passengers. There wasn't enough time to do anything but gather intelligence, which is why we're using this ship. We've done that, we know it exists, and now it's time to take the next step."

The way Picard said it almost convinced Sam that they could pull it off. He tried not to think about what few resources they had at their disposal, even if the *Enterprise* was out there somewhere. *These people have no idea what they're up against.*

After a few moments of uneasy silence, during which no one voiced their obvious concerns, the captain turned off his padd and set it on an empty console. "It appears we have to depend upon this makeshift crew, despite our doubts. Now I have to go talk to the Romulan."

Sam blinked at him. "*Romulan?* There's a Romulan on board?"

"A wounded Romulan," answered Picard. "He lost an arm when we recaptured the ship, and he's in the captain's quarters, recuperating. Had I known we would have all these casualties to deal with, I would've brought Dr. Crusher along."

Hesitantly Sam asked, "Is Alyssa Ogawa still serving on the *Enterprise?*"

Picard smiled. "Yes, we've managed to hold on to Ogawa. She's now chief nurse in sickbay, and that's quite a job in wartime. Do you feel confident with the Bajoran conn, Lieutenant?"

"Yes, sir. I'll contact you if I have any questions."

"Good. Ro, will you please accompany me?"

"Yes, sir."

Sam couldn't help but watch Ro and Picard walk off the bridge— they were two of a kind, calm and controlled on the surface and wild-eyed gamblers underneath. *My life is now in the hands of those two.* He would have disobeyed anybody else in the universe who ordered him to go back to that monstrous collider and the slave pens, but he had to follow Captain Picard. If anybody could get them through this insane war alive, it would be him.

# CHAPTER 6

# We Are Family—A Study in Our Humanity

THE STAR TREK NOVELS PROVIDE ENDLESS OPPORTUNITIES FOR WRITERS TO delve into the characters' pasts and futures in real depth, to tell us more about their lives and careers and explain what influenced and guided them on their paths to the stars. The novels included here are among the very best.

## *Imzadi,* by Peter David

*Imzadi,* by Peter David, is a beautiful story. I have always liked Counselor Deanna Troi and Commander William Riker of the *Enterprise*-D, and the undertones of romance and hints about their past history together always gave the show a more human touch. *Imzadi* is both their love story and an exciting time travel adventure; it is the story of lost love and failed chances, and it is the story of the premature death of Deanna Troi that an older and embittered Riker traveled back in time to prevent.

My favorite passage from *Imzadi* is a love scene between Will and Deanna. Brought together when the young Lt. Riker was assigned to Betazed, Will and Deanna were overwhelmed by their feelings for each other when he rescued her from a kidnapper. Although they were later torn apart by misunderstandings and different goals for their lives, their love story is one for the ages. I was quite happy to see them decide to explore their feelings and recapture what they once had in *Star Trek: Insurrection.*

172

RIKER WENT TO DEANNA AND SAW HOW SHE WAS STARING AT THE CENTER of the mud pit. In a low whisper, she said, "He won. He was never caught."

"Are you all right?" asked Riker, taking her by the shoulders. "Did he hurt you?"

"I'm fine." She got to her feet, pausing only to nurse the dull ache in her stomach. "I'm fine. I want to get out of here."

"All right. Let's just wait a few minutes until—"

"No. Now." There was an urgency in her voice, a desperation to try to distance herself as much as possible from the site of these events.

"Okay. Let me just get my equipment together."

She nodded, her gaze never wavering from the mud pit.

Riker quickly got his jacket and belt and retrieved his phaser from where he'd tossed it. Then he tapped a small button on one of the belt compartments, and Deanna blinked in surprise as two small diamond-shaped objects shot past her. "What are those?"

"Target-practice devices. Standard issue for ground-based security personnel. They're what I used to distract Maror."

"Oh." She nodded, and her voice sounded very distant. "That was quite clever, Will. Quite clever."

He stared at her. "Are you sure you're all right?"

"Positive. Let's go."

Riker didn't say anything further, but simply guided her gently away from the mud pit site. He studied her bedraggled condition and, insanely, still couldn't help but think how good she looked despite her ordeal. She seemed to have an endless reserve of inner strength.

Once they began walking, Riker contacted Tang. Maror had indeed been correct in his guess. Riker and the various members of the security crew had split up, the better to cover the vast distances of the jungle. It had been Riker who was fortunate enough, after several days of searching, to detect the life readings of Deanna and Maror using his tricorder.

He informed Tang that Deanna had indeed been recovered (he avoided using the word *rescued* . . . it sounded melodramatic somehow) and that they would now be heading toward the rendezvous point. It would take a few days to get there, but Riker was still well stocked with provisions, and no abnormal delays were anticipated.

Riker had been preoccupied with his mission throughout the past few days and had not paid all that much attention to the jungle, other than to avoid its pitfalls or obstructions. His judicious use of a phaser to carve himself a path now served him in good stead, making it that much easier for him to make his way back . . . even if the tricorder wasn't capable of enabling him to retrace his steps.

With the pressure off, he was really able to take notice of the true beauty of the Jalara Jungle. He realized now that the flowers and vines that had decorated the interior of the wedding chapel must have been taken from the jungle. The flowers and growths were exotic combinations of colors. The air was warm, even steamy, without being irritatingly humid. It was filled with a scented mist that was invigorating, or perhaps simply smelled all the sweeter with Deanna's freedom now a reality.

He turned and looked to Deanna, who had been extremely silent for the past half hour.

She was shivering. Her arms were wrapped around herself, and there, in the midst of a warm jungle, she was shivering. Her teeth were chattering.

Immediately he knew what was happening. All during the time when she was in danger, she had managed to keep everything bottled up. She had detached herself from the fear and uncertainty, from the terror that must have accompanied every moment. Such feelings could be repressed or ignored for the duration of a crisis. But sooner or later they would come roaring back and would have to be dealt with.

He went to her and put his arms around her, settling her into a seated position. "Shh. It's okay. Let it out, Deanna. That's all right."

She trembled more violently, staring not at Riker but straight ahead, as if she expected someone or something to come at her from the underbrush. Her hand clamped onto his upper arm, her finger-nails digging into the skin with such fierceness that Riker had to stifle the impulse to push her hand away. As it was, he kept his mouth shut, not letting on that it hurt like hell.

He stroked her face, continuing to make soft, comforting noises. Letting her know that it was okay to be frightened. Reminding her that she wasn't alone. Telling her that everything was going to be all right, that she was out of danger and soon all of this would just be a distant, bad dream.

As he spoke, she drew herself closer to him, pressing against him and readjusting his arms so that he completely enveloped her. The quaking still convulsed her body, and her lower lip trembled. Tears rolled down her face, but she did not cry out loud. Her complete silence was almost eerie.

He didn't say anything further. He merely rocked with her, back and forth, gently, letting his mere presence be something from which

174

she could draw reassurance. And slowly, ever so slowly, the trembling diminished and eventually stopped. The tears ceased, and then she brought her hand up and wiped away the remainder of the moisture.

Then she looked up at Riker. He smiled down at her and, wondering if she was prepared to move on, said, "Ready?"

She nodded. "Yes. Yes, I am." She reached up, wrapped her hand around the back of his head, and drew his face to hers.

The kiss was very long and very sweet and filled with promise. Their lips parted and he looked at her, the jungle air making him feel giddy. There was an unreality to it all. *Going native* was the old phrase.

"Deanna," he said, his voice low. "This . . . this isn't right. This isn't the time. You aren't thinking straight, you've been through a lot, you—"

"Let me"—she held his face in her hands—"let me put this to you in a way that I know you'll understand."

He waited. With her eyes wide, her lips mere inches from his, she whispered, "Shut up and kiss me, Riker."

He did.

Moments later, all the perfectly logical reasons why this was wrong, inappropriate, completely incorrect behavior for a Starfleet officer . . . all those blessed reasons flew completely out of Riker's mind. Instead all there was was *her,* was the moistness of the jungle combined with the sweat of her. The rustling of trees mixed with the rustling of clothes, and this time when their nude bodies pressed against each other, there was no intellectualizing, no deep discussions that required anything beyond soft, whispered words, punctuated by faint, occasional gasps.

In that moment they knew all there was to know of each other . . . body and soul, flesh and spirit, all combined and permeating every inch of both of them. Instead of moving away from each other, instead of resisting the pull, they gave in to it completely. They complemented each other, became each other, filling out each other's needs and rejoicing as pressures built in them. Throughout the Jalara Jungle it seemed that all noise had ceased. That there was nothing in the jungle, nothing in the planet, nothing in the universe except the two of them and their discovery, their admission, of their mutual need and hunger.

The pressure built beyond their ability to contain and they released, clutching each other, as if hoping they could meld their bodies into one as seamlessly as they had with their souls. And somewhere, somewhere deep within Riker's mind, merged with his spirit, a word echoed. A word that he had never heard before. A word filled with mystery and promise and a future . . .

And the word was *Imzadi.*

They lay next to each other, Deanna's head against his shoulder. She ran her fingers idly across his chest hair.

"I hear that's for traction." It was the longest sentence she had uttered in half an hour . . . the first sentence since their lovemaking. Their most recent lovemaking, to be precise, although how many times they had engaged in their mutual sexual calisthenics was a bit of a mystery to both of them. Things had blurred one into the other, had just finished and begun again with hardly a word passing between them. It was as if, having decided upon a course of action, they were both afraid to speak after that for fear of botching it up somehow.

They had not moved from the spot where it had all first begun untold hours ago, and Riker had a feeling that impressions had been dug into the ground that would probably mystify future geologists.

"You heard about that, did you?" he asked.

She nodded. "Chandra's father told her. She told me."

"Oh. Well . . . yes. Traction." Riker paused, trying to find something to say.

She said it for him. "So where do we go from here?"

"To the rendezvous point. But I have a feeling we're going to be pretty late."

"That's not what I meant."

"I know." He turned over, propping himself up on his elbow, and ran his fingers through her hair. He picked out a length of vine that had become tangled up in it and was about to toss it aside. But she took it from him.

"No. I want to keep that. As a souvenir."

"A piece of vine?" he asked incredulously.

She shrugged.

"In answer to your question . . . I don't know. I know how you make me feel. I think I know how I make you feel. But I . . . I don't have any answers. I'm still getting this all sorted out. I mean . . . you're the expert on feelings. What do *you* think?"

She sighed. She felt slightly chilled, even in the warm jungle air, and she drew her naked body tightly against his. "I don't know. That's . . . that's what I find appealing about you, Will. When I'm with you I don't think."

He raised an amused eyebrow. "I'm not sure how to take that."

"When I'm with you . . . when I think about you . . . all my training, all my . . . my overintellectualizing, as you put it . . . just vanishes. I've never felt this way about anyone and I . . . I finally decided I wanted to give in to it. To fully experience it. How can I be any sort of complete person if I'm not willing to go where my . . . where my spirit wants to take me."

He brushed back a lock of her hair. "I think you have a very beautiful spirit."

"Why thank you, Lieutenant. It's nice of you to notice it. And so do you."

He paused. "This is going to sound so . . . so trite, but believe me when I say . . . I've never felt like this with anyone. More than just the physical part . . . which was great, don't get me wrong," he added hurriedly. "But there was . . ." He felt tongue-tied. "I really don't have words to express it."

"There are none. There don't have to be."

"There was . . . when we were . . ." He cleared his throat. "There was a word. You thought it at me . . . at least, I presume it was you. I don't think there was anyone else rattling around in there. 'Imzi' or something?"

Now she propped herself up as well and faced him fully.

"Imzadi," she said softly. When she said it, there was a musical, loving tone to her voice such as he had never heard.

"That's it. Imzadi. What does that mean?"

"Well . . . it has several meanings. The surface level is simply 'beloved' or 'dear one.' But when used with certain people, under certain circumstances . . . well, you need to know the further nuance to it to understand its full meaning."

"So what is its full meaning?"

She smiled shyly, which was a direct contrast to the casualness of her nudity. "It means . . . the first."

"The . . . the first?" He wasn't sure he had heard correctly, or perhaps didn't want to.

"Yes. No matter what happens from here on . . . we will always be true Imzadi. We will forever be each other's 'first.' "

She looked up at him with those large, dark eyes, and he felt like a total cretin.

"You mean . . . you mean I'm the first man that you . . . that you ever . . ."

She nodded.

"Had sex with?" he managed to finish.

She nodded again.

"Oh, my God."

"You seem surprised," she said, looking quite amused. "Is it so difficult to believe?"

"Well, I mean . . ." He couldn't remember when he'd felt quite this embarrassed. "I mean, you're such an open society and all . . . and you're so gorgeous . . ."

"Thank you," she said demurely.

"That I'm . . . I mean, it never occurred to me that no man had ever . . ."

"Bagged me?" she asked, her eyes twinkling slightly.

He winced. "That's one term that's occasionally used . . . although not by me."

"Oh, of course not. Never by you."

"And . . . um . . . look. Deanna. I . . . I don't know if I said or did anything to give you the impression otherwise, but . . . but you're not my first. I mean . . . I've been with other women."

"No, you haven't," she said serenely.

"Yes, I have. I mean, I was there. I think I'd know."

"Oh, *I* understand. You mean you've had sex before."

"Well . . . well, yes. I thought that's what we were talking about."

"You still don't understand, Will. The physical part, as pleasurable as it was . . . and as exciting as it was for me, I must admit . . ." She hesitated and suddenly looked vulnerable. "Did I do all right?"

"Oh, yes! Yes. You did . . . you did great. I'd never have known if you hadn't told me that . . ." He gestured, trying to sum up his conflicting feelings.

"All right, then. But you see . . . the concept of Imzadi goes beyond the physical. You've had other women physically. I know that. And even though I haven't had other men before you, that's almost incidental. To be Imzadi is to go far deeper than that. Don't you understand, Will? Other women may have had your body"—she smiled—"but I'm the first who's ever touched your soul."

And he realized, with a dim astonishment, that she was right. Sex for him had always been directed toward the pleasurable aspects. Even when he had thought he was in love, it had turned out to be purely superficial . . . an excuse to add some additional excitement to the physical gratification.

Was he in love now? Thoughts were tumbling around far too fiercely for him to assimilate fully. It was the kind of sensation that he had always wanted to avoid. He liked knowing precisely what he was doing at all times. He liked being in control. But to be in love was to surrender some degree of that control, and he had never been willing or able to do that.

And now, here with Deanna Troi, he still wasn't sure if he was able. But for the first time in his life, he realized that he was genuinely willing.

"Imzadi," he said, and smiled.

She returned the smile and nodded. "I understand."

He sat up and saw that the sun was setting. It hung low, streaks of pink and orange dancing like liquid fingers across the Betazed sky.

"You know," he said slowly, "I've been looking at stars in space for so long . . . that I completely forgot how utterly beautiful a star can be when it's setting. And you know what else? Those clouds right there"—he pointed—"the way they're coming together . . . they look like two dragons battling."

"You see conflict in the sky. That's understandable. When you launch yourself into space, then to a very large degree, it's you against the vacuum."

"It's like the painting, isn't it."

"To some degree," she acknowledged. "When you look at any sort of tableaux, be it hanging on a wall or hanging in the sky . . . you see in it a reflection of your innermost wants and desires. That is, if you look at it in the right frame of mind."

"You want to watch the sunset and wax philosophical?"

"By all means."

She drew her body next to his and they sat there, staring up at the setting sun and seeing in it all sorts of aspects of their souls that they had never before examined.

Riker was thoroughly enraptured.

But after about thirty seconds, Deanna turned to him and said, "Right, then. That's enough of that. Come here, Imzadi." She pressed against him and bore him tenderly to the ground. The sun set the rest of the way without them.

## Triangle: Imzadi II, by Peter David

During the closing seasons of TNG, there were hints at a developing relationship between Worf and Deanna Troi. Indeed, "All Good Things . . . ," the series finale, more than hinted at such a relationship; there was a strong implication that Riker's interference may have brought about Deanna's early death. At the end of the episode, it seemed as though Riker was going to step back and allow Worf and Deanna to pursue a relationship. However, the Worf–Deanna pairing never felt right to me; I always thought of Deanna and Will as true

Imzadi. Worf and Deanna seemed far too different from each other to be able to be truly happy together. Worf's involvement with Jadzia Dax made more sense to me, but it was hard to reconcile with his supposed relationship with Deanna. In *Triangle: Imzadi II,* Peter David resolved these issues in a most satisfactory manner.

In the opening pages of *Triangle: Imzadi II,* Worf's bitterness at his loss of Jadzia Dax was poisoning him. He blamed everyone, including Will and Deanna, because he felt that if he had been married to Deanna, he would not be suffering from the loss of Jadzia. His thoughts journeyed back to his relationship with Deanna. *Imzadi II* is that story.

The turning point for Worf's relationship with Deanna occurred when Alexander and Deanna were kidnaped by Commander Sela and used as leverage to attempt to blackmail Worf and Will Riker into poisoning Gowron and destroying the Klingon homeworld. Worf was forced to work with Riker to rescue them and stop Sela's plan, but they were captured. In the first scene quoted here, each realized what Deanna meant to the other and to himself, and their jealousy over Deanna and their frustration over their capture drove them to blows. The novel closed with Worf's tragic and poignant realization that Jadzia Dax was *his* Imzadi, and his life was richer for having known her, despite her tragic death as quoted here.

"YOU CALL YOURSELF A STARFLEET OFFICER!" WORF SHOUTED.

Will and Worf had been tossed into a room together, apparently to wait while the Romulans scrounged up, somehow, a Starfleet uniform for him. There was nothing of particular interest in the room to look at. Will had found a door on one side against the wall, but when he had slid it open all he found was a closet with some uniforms stashed in it. Riker considered trying to don the uniforms and sneak out in disguise. But he didn't think he would pass for Romulan, and he was sure as hell positive that Worf didn't have a prayer of doing so.

So Riker leaned against a wall, trying to sort through his thoughts, and he didn't even bother glancing at Worf. "Not now, Worf."

"How could you agree to their demands!"

"I said not now, Lieutenant Commander," Will said with a far sharper tone.

"Not this time," Worf said hotly. "This time . . . no ranks . . . if you have the stomach for that."

Will's face grew flushed as he turned to face Worf. "All right," he said, in a slow, deliberate voice. "No ranks. Man to man . . . you watch yourself."

"What you did back there was wrong. Admit it."

"I had no choice."

"I see. You're going to say that this . . . empathic bond you've developed with Deanna forced you to do it."

But Will shook his head. "That bond, Worf . . . it was just a sort of . . . of locator device in my head. Emotionally it didn't make me any different . . . and it didn't cloud my judgment, I assure you."

"Then why . . . ?"

"I told you. I didn't have a choice."

"Meaning I did. Meaning you think I was wrong."

"You did what was right for you. I had to do what was right for me."

"What you should have done," snarled Worf, "was what was right for Starfleet! For the oath you took as an officer—!"

"Don't lecture me, Worf!" thundered Will. "I don't have to put up with it! I don't have to prove anything to you!"

"No. But you had to prove something to her."

"I wasn't trying to prove anything, Worf, I was trying to save her life. And in case it escaped your notice, I saved your son's life, as well."

"And do you expect his gratitude?" Worf demanded. "To die with honor is—"

"The Klingon way, yes, I know, believe me, I know. But did it occur to you that maybe, just maybe, there was an off chance that he wasn't ready to die simply because you had decided it was time for him to go."

*"Do you think I did not want to save my own son!"*

"I don't know, Worf! I've known you for almost half my adult life, and you're still as much of a mystery to me as you were when I first met you! I don't know what you want! I don't know what was going through your mind!"

"I wanted to save them," Worf said tightly. "But what is more important than life is the way that life is lived."

"And I wanted them to keep on living it, any way they could. And if you didn't, fine. I took the decision out of your hands, all right?" He spread his arms wide in a gesture indicating that he was fed up with the conversation. "If there's any dishonor here, it's on my head. The bottom line is, I bought us some time. Obviously I don't want to poison Gowron . . . but we needed time to think, time to—"

"You showed them that Starfleet officers can be pressured into turning against their oaths. Can be blackmailed. Do you think that it will end here? Even if they do let us go, which I very much doubt, they will know that they can make similar demands on others, endeavor to make other officers bend to their desires. And perhaps those other officers will not cave in as you did. In which case, you have doomed their innocent loved ones."

"I didn't . . . cave in . . ." Will said with forced calm. "I made a reasoned decision that—"

"You . . . caved . . . in . . ."

"Would you have had me watch them die? Would you?"

"I was prepared to."

"Well, maybe they weren't prepared, Worf! Despite all your training of Alexander in the Klingon way, maybe he wasn't ready to throw his life away just to satisfy his father's definitions of honor. Did you consider that?"

Worf stepped in close to him. "I know why you did this."

"Enlighten me."

"You did this to make certain that you would always be between us. Between Deanna and me."

"That's ridiculous . . ."

"You never stopped loving her. Admit it."

"Worf, now is not the ti—"

*"There will not be another time!* This will be said now! No more niceties! No more politeness dictated by rank! No more indecision on your part! I knew what I wanted with Deanna, I got it, and that sickens you, doesn't it. And when we announced our engagement, you were angry! Angry at yourself for years of wavering! Angry at me for stepping in when you would not do anything about it!"

"I did what was right for Deanna and me at the time, Worf! I can't fabricate emotions that weren't there and wish they were present when it was convenient for me!"

"They were always there, and that was the inconvenience," Worf shot back. "You could not muster yourself to take Deanna when she was yours, but you could not stand the thought of her being mine."

"If I couldn't stand the thought, then why didn't I say something at the time you two got together?"

"Because then you would have had to commit to her. And you are too selfish, too self-absorbed, to commit to anything except yourself. But I am not. I commit to the Klingon code of honor, to Deanna, and to our life together."

"Interesting order that you put those things in, Worf," Riker noted. He was moving now, unconsciously plotting a course like a matador guiding a bull. He and Worf were circling each other, their body language mirroring the pent-up anger of their words. "If you knew anything about love, you'd know that she comes first, always. Always."

"If you knew anything about honor, you would know that there are things more important than love. But then, you knew that. Except to you the things more important than love are your career and your own interests."

"If that's the case, then why am I putting my life on the line to save her?"

"I already told you: to make me look bad. To make certain that you are always uppermost in her thoughts. Admit it, that is what you want."

"You have no idea what I want."

"I know you fully—"

*"You have no idea!"* and suddenly it all burst out of him, a gushing torrent of emotion. "You had no idea what it was like, Worf! To see the two of you together, to see her in your arms! To see a true love light in her eyes, the kind that she once had for me, except she was looking at you! Every time, every damned time I saw you with her, it was like a knife in my heart. I never stopped loving her! Is that what you want to hear? I was coming to Betazed to tell her that. If it meant breaking you up, I was prepared for that, providing she still felt something for me! If she didn't, I wouldn't have blamed her. I made a command decision for years that we wouldn't be together. It was me, Worf, all me. You saw how quickly she got together with Tom, with only the slightest urging. She never stopped loving me, never. But me, I was second-in-command of the *Enterprise!* I had no time for distractions, for some sort of ongoing relationship! I couldn't give in to the emotions she stirred in me! And what if we did pursue it and, for whatever reason, it didn't work out? After all the years apart, who knew what kind of people we had become. So I forced myself to believe those emotions weren't there. And I did it so well that I convinced not only myself, but the woman who knows me better than anyone else. The one who is the better part of everything I am. I did it for her own good, for the good of both of us. And having made that decision, how could I stand in your way? How could I deny her happiness with you? It would have been wrong. It was what she wanted, it would have been wrong . . ."

"And am I supposed to feel sympathy for you?" Worf's fists were shaking with barely pent-up emotion.

"We're Imzadi, Worf. It means—"

"I know what it means. Lwaxana told me."

"Knowing it intellectually isn't enough. I don't expect you to understand."

"Because you believe I am stupid?"

"No!" shouted Riker, fed up with Worf's defensiveness. "Because you've never felt about anyone in your life the way I feel about Deanna! Not if you were willing to let her die! No matter how much I tried to force myself to think it was over because I wanted it to be so, the fact is that we are, now and forever, Imzadi."

"How dare you," Worf snapped. "How dare you tell me how I have and have not felt." He came in very close to Riker, barely inches away. "Do you think I did not know what the two of you meant to each other? Do you think I did not sense your ghost hovering between us whenever I was with her? That I did not feel as if I was constantly being measured up to you? That nothing I did was good enough? When we spoke, I always sensed that she was comparing my sentiments to yours. When we made love, I was always positive that she was thinking of you! Here I was willing to pursue the relationship that you were unwilling to give her. Afraid to give her—"

"I wasn't afraid—"

"You were! Afraid to share your life! Afraid to risk your precious career! Afraid to love someone more than you loved yourself! Do you think I was unafraid when I approached her, courted her? The risk of rejection, humiliation . . . it was overwhelming! But I pushed past that, went through it, because I believed that the prize was worth the risk! Yet still she remained attached to you, you who were unwilling to take any risk for her." Worf's voice escalated in volume until it was almost deafening. "Laying your life on the line now, that is easy for you! Entrap her love forever and then go off to die a hero's death, and leave me behind, painted as the one unwilling to sacrifice himself! When the fact is that you were too much the coward to be there for Deanna when she needed you, and too much the coward to be there for your duty when the Federation needed you!"

Riker hit him.

It was not one of the smarter moves Riker had ever made.

He hit him bone on bone, which was never a good move to begin with. His fist caught Worf squarely on the chin, promptly breaking one of Riker's knuckles. It landed with enough impact to knock Worf to the floor, and the combination of surprise and power behind the punch was enough to keep Worf down for a whole three seconds.

At which point Worf came up swinging.

Will backed up quickly, as Worf's first two roundhouses—driven more by fury than technique—missed him clean. While Worf was off-balance on the second one, Riker drove a knee up into Worf's gut. It doubled the Klingon over long enough for Riker to bring his hands together and double-slam a blow to the thick set of muscles in the base of Worf's neck. It was a move that Riker had used before, when he had been assigned to a Klingon vessel as part of an exchange program. It had worked rather well at the time against that particular opponent.

In this case, it didn't slow Worf down at all. It did succeed, however, in ticking him off.

Will Riker was suddenly airborne. Worf had grabbed his leg in one hand and his arm in the other, and when he straightened up, Riker was over his head and helpless. For one hideous moment Riker thought that Worf was going to make a wish and use Riker as the wishbone. Instead Worf pivoted and threw Riker. Riker meteored across the room and slammed into the far wall with the sound of a wet sack of potatoes. He slid to the ground, momentarily stunned, and then saw Worf charging toward him. He tried to muster the strength to get out of his way, but all he could manage was to try and crawl away, and then Worf had hauled him off his feet, his arm across Riker's throat, snarling in fury into his ear.

Riker dug his nails into Worf's hand. It was the only part of him that he could get close to, and the only tactic that he could think of.

Worf didn't let out a sound, other than a grunt. He tried to pull his hand free of Riker's but Riker held on as if his life depended on it—which it might very well have. Blood began to trickle from the point of penetration and finally Worf shoved Riker furiously away. Riker stumbled around but stayed on his feet.

Worf came at him and what followed was a dazzlingly fast flurry of blows. Riker stood his ground as Worf delivered one rapid-fire shot after another. Will blocked, moving entirely on instinct, faster than he ever had in his life. Worf growled in annoyance and then, for a moment, Worf got too close and his snarling face was near Riker's.

Riker tried to head-butt him, slamming his skull against Worf's.

If there was any move that Riker could have made that was less wise than having swung in the first place, it was that one.

The impact was audibile from nearly three rooms away. Worf didn't give in the slightest, but Will stood there for a moment, the world swirling around him. And then, without Worf having to do another thing, Riker fell backward, crashing to the floor.

To his credit, Riker began to get back up again, even though he was starting to turn rather pale. Worf watched him, shaking his head.

Riker suddenly kicked him in the crotch.

Worf had been sure that Riker was virtually out for the count. The speed and ferocity of Riker's move caught Worf completely off-guard. The shot landed squarely and Worf sank to his knees. It was everything he could do not to moan.

Will staggered in place for a moment, about to try and press his advantage. Unfortunately he didn't have the opportunity, because suddenly he completely lost his ability to remain on his feet as a wave of nausea swept over him, courtesy of a delayed effect of the head-butting. Riker sank to the floor a few feet away from Worf, propping himself up with one hand and clearly trying not to vomit.

"H . . . had . . . enough . . ." he managed to get out.

"Was that . . . a question to me . . . or a . . . description of your-self . . ." Worf said between lungfuls of air.

At that moment, a squad of Romulans entered. They surveyed the damage that the two of them had done to each other, and Dr. Tok—who was carrying what appeared to be a medical kit—shook his head in annoyance. "Take this one," he pointed at Worf, "and stick him with his son and fiancée."

The Romulans did as they were told, while Tok knelt down opposite Riker. He pulled instruments from his kit and started working on Riker's face. "Hold still please," he said as the tools began to stimulate cellular growth in Will's skin.

"What are you doing?"

"Getting you fixed up. In case you're unaware of it, you came in here looking rather in bad shape to begin with. Your little brawl with the Klingon didn't do much for your complexion on top of that. Sela reasoned that sending you to the Klingon homeworld looking like you've been in a series of fights is hardly going to facilitate your passing yourself off as William Riker."

"Believe me," said Will, "that's the last person I'd want to be right now."

Worf awoke with a start . . . and looked for Jadzia.

She wasn't there. Her scent remained in the chair, but she was gone. It took a moment for that fact to sink in, and when it did, he felt more empty than ever.

Nothing. It had all been for nothing.

He rummaged around their . . .

. . . his . . .

. . . quarters a bit more . . . and then he found a picture. A picture

186

of the two of them from their wedding day. Worf and Jadzia, smiling toward the camera. Happy. So happy.

For nothing.

It had made no difference at all.

He ran his fingers across her portrait . . .

And the portrait was wet.

He didn't realize the origin at first . . . and then he did. It was liquid, coming from his own eyes, dripping onto the picture.

And his mind suddenly went to the world of Soukara. The world where they were to meet the Cardassian informer, Lasaran . . . and Jadzia had become injured. Had he left her, had he completed the mission . . . she would have died, there on Soukara. Instead he had come back for her, abandoned the mission, tossed aside everything that he had ever learned about duty . . .

. . . for her.

. . . for Jadzia.

Because of what he had felt for her. Feelings that were beyond anything, he realized, that he had ever felt for Deanna.

More tears fell from his eyes and he moved the picture so it wouldn't become wet.

He was still Klingon. Honor was as important to him as ever. That had never lessened in him . . . and yet . . .

. . . and yet . . .

. . . his first duty had been to her. To them. To his wife, to his beloved.

And he knew, beyond any question, perhaps with greater clarity than he had ever known before, that he would have done anything for her. That had been the plan, that they were to be together, forever and ever. Nothing could ever separate them. But she had gone away, and he had not expected it. And his first impulse had been to close off everything, to retreat once more, to look back on their life together and say it had made no difference. No difference . . .

. . . but he was wrong.

It had made a difference. For he felt things now, depth of emotion, passion, and the ability to covet a loving relationship beyond anything that he would once have thought possible. The death of their union did not end that. Those feelings, once tapped, could not be denied. He could try, of course. He could try and push it away . . .

. . . but that would be wrong. Wrong for the legacy that she had left him, wrong for the man that he had always wanted to be and—thanks to her—now was.

He held the picture tight to him and allowed the tears to cascade down his cheeks. He did not sob out loud; that would have been too much. Instead the tears flowed in eerie silence, but it didn't matter.

It hurt . . . but he didn't mind. It was a good hurt, the kind that one can grow from and learn from if one chooses to.

If he loved again, it could never be as it was with her. Never.

For she had been his first.

The first to get into his heart and soul. He realized that now. The first that he would sacrifice anything for. He would have died for her. Now he had to live for her.

And love with another . . . would be different, not necessarily better or worse. Even though he had once said it to Alexander, only now did he truly understand. It was just different, and should be celebrated as such. And it would never diminish what they had. He would keep it close to his heart, tucked away, and even as he made his way through life, that first love would still always be there. Nothing could end that love . . . even the end of the lover herself.

For he would always have in his head that first time they saw each other . . . the first time they held hands, the first time they kissed, the first time that their bodies pressed against each other, flesh to flesh, and they joined in a perfect union that neither time, nor distance, nor even death itself could ever take away.

He could move on without her, but in a way, she would always be with him. A fragrant flower, gone, yet he still had the sense of her within him.

And it would not be for nothing as long as he remembered that.

He kissed the picture gently, and she smiled back at him. And a word came to him through the years . . . a word that belonged to neither his race, nor hers . . . and yet, somehow, it was a part of the heart and soul of all races.

He pressed the picture against his chest, and in a voice that was deep and resonant and filled with hope for the future, he said . . .

"Good journey . . . Imzadi . . ."

## *Warchild*, by Esther Friesner

Dr. Julian Bashir, chief medical officer of DS9, was extremely wet behind the ears during *DS9*'s first season, and his overeager, puppy-dog behavior was fairly annoying to his co-workers. He was a good doctor, though, and his medical skills and compassion for others were his saving grace. I always liked Dr. Bashir; Alexander Siddig, then known as Siddig el Fadil, made Bashir appealing even when Bashir was at his most enthusiastic. By the second season of *DS9*, Bashir seemed to have changed. He was more subdued and settled down than he had been the first season, but the series did not really explain the change.

*Warchild*, by Esther Friesner, describes Dr. Bashir's experiences between the first and second seasons and how he was affected by them. In *Warchild*, Bashir was sent to Bajor to bring a plague under control when the badly equipped and understaffed Bajoran medical people could not. At the same time, the Bajorans searched for a child called the Nekor, a child who prophecy predicted would unite Bajorans.

I like the Dr. Bashir shown in this book. He was a good doctor, and he truly cared for his patients, like Dr. McCoy before him. Like all the other heroes in Star Trek, Dr. Bashir was willing to risk everything to help people. In the passage from *Warchild* included here, Bashir objected to his orders to return to the station when he finished development of a vaccine; he felt that he was still needed and decided to stay.

DR. BASHIR LOOKED UP FROM HIS MICROSCANNER. "OH, HULLO, KAHRI-manis," he said. "I didn't hear you at the door. I've been studying samples of the drinking water. There appears to be a bacterium in some samples and not in others. I think it might have a connection with the intestinal problems some of the children have been experiencing. Odd thing: I've sampled the well water and found nothing, but it's not universally present in all the rainwater samples. I think it may have something to do with how the rainwater barrels are—" He caught himself running on and laughed sheepishly. "Listen to me babble! You didn't come here to listen to a disquisition on water supply. What can I do for you?"

"I've just come to secure a few things, sir. Don't worry; I won't be in your way." Ensign Kahrimanis walked past Dr. Bashir to where the supply chests were stacked. He took down the top one and began packing.

Dr. Bashir's face turned pale. "What are you doing? Don't tell me we've been ordered to leave already?"

Kahrimanis paused and turned around to face him. "No, sir, we haven't been ordered back; not yet. But it's only a matter of time. Lieutenant Dax told me to begin preparations. Our mission here's done."

"But it can't be!" Dr. Bashir protested. "Granted, we've stopped the fever cold, but that's not the sum total of the health problems these people—these *children* still have to face!"

Kahrimanis rested one hand on the lab table. "That's the truth, sir. Physical and mental health, both. I've been meaning to tell you, I think it's wonderful the way you've been helping the kids. Having someone give a damn about them—" He glanced guiltily at Cedra. Sullen-faced, the boy was polishing some glassware for the doctor. "Uh, Cedra?" the ensign called. "Sorry about how I spoke to you before."

Cedra looked up and gave him a half-smile.

"This is impossible," Dr. Bashir went on, shaking his head. "If we leave now, how can we assess the long-term effectiveness of Lieutenant Dax's antibody injection? And if it *is* effective, we have to implement an inoculation program in every refugee camp in the Kaladrys Valley. Word must be gotten to the hill fighters, too. They're a dangerous vector, they could take the infection out of the valley altogether, and then where would it—?"

"Sir, calm down," Ensign Kahrimanis urged. "There's three medical aides from the Federation ship *Keppler* and one nurse from the *Shining Blade* waiting to replace us here. They'll look after things."

"The *Shining Blade* . . . a Klingon nurse . . . wonderful," Dr. Bashir muttered. "If she doesn't scare the children to death first."

"He," Kahrimanis corrected him.

"Even better." Dr. Bashir sounded ironic enough to pass for Odo.

"I wouldn't worry about how the kids react to a Klingon nurse if I were you, sir." Kahrimanis grinned. "They've seen worse."

Dr. Bashir bent over his microscanner. "When do we leave?" he asked dully, not looking at the ensign.

"Whenever the orders come, I suppose." Kahrimanis waited for the doctor to comment; there was only silence. He might as well have been invisible. He shrugged and went back to packing.

He had only secured a few items when Dr. Bashir's voice rang out, sharp and commanding: "Leave that for now, Ensign. I may need some of that equipment."

"But sir, I—"

Julian's eyes blazed. "That's an order, Ensign."

Kahrimanis gave him an odd look, but replied, "Yes, sir," and left the laboratory.

As soon as the ensign left, Dr. Bashir declared, "Thank you for your help, Cedra. You can go now. You must have lots of preparations to make for your departure."

The boy gave Bashir a sideways look that seemed to measure the doctor, inside and out. However, all he said was "All right." He set down the polishing cloth and the glassware and went without an argument.

Alone in the laboratory, Bashir leaned back against the table wearily. *Leaving . . . we can't be leaving! Not with so much left here—*

He thought of the children, sick and well. He would never forget the change he saw in their faces when those still fit enough to work the fields came back to camp to find their fever-stricken playmates on the road to full recovery.

*They thought their friends would die. They had no reason to hope for anything better. Their lives were stripped of hope, and then I—we gave it back to them! We let them see that there's still a chance for something good to happen. They can go on now.* He pressed his fist to his mouth. *They can, but what of the others? The children in the camps on Cedra's map, what about them? Are their eyes dead? Do they still have the strength to dream? I can't go back yet. I was sent here to do a job. I'm not done. My work isn't done. I—I was ordered to Bajor to help the children, but—but—*Realization hit him so hard he had to voice it aloud:

"But I haven't received orders to return. Not direct orders. Not yet."

There was little time. If Dax had sent Ensign Kahrimanis to start packing, the orders must be coming soon. How soon? He couldn't lose a moment. He dashed to the laboratory door and glanced outside. There was no sign of Kahrimanis or Dax. If he avoided his crewmates, he avoided the chance of receiving the departure orders through them.

*I can't hear the orders. I* must not *hear the orders. Once I do, I'll have no choice but to obey.*

He slammed the door behind him and rested against it, eyes closed, making a swift mental listing of the bare minimum of supplies he would need to carry on his work where he was going. It was the task of moments for him to secure an array of hypodermics, all loaded with Dax's miracle-working antibody vaccine. A physician's basic field kit followed, assembled with a degree of efficiency that would have made his old teacher Selok nod approval. There were no theatrical flourishes, there was no fuss at all in Julian's preparations. He no longer acted for an unseen audience of potential admirers; he acted for a purpose, a cause that claimed his heart.

It took him a while to find a comfortable way of carrying the Klingon biosample replicator. He had no idea of how many patients in the valley camps were awaiting inoculation; with this device, he was relatively certain he could manufacture enough vaccine for all. He slipped the thick carrying strap over one shoulder and his head. It felt somewhat awkward, but he had no choice; it was necessary.

Outside the lab, the paths of the camp were largely deserted. At this hour, the refugees were finishing their day's labor in the fields, the monks were supervising rounds in the infirmary, and anyone left over was lending a hand with dinner preparations in the square. Quickly and quietly Dr. Bashir ran through the camp and sought the privacy of his own tent. He saw no one, and reasoned no one could see him. Once safely inside, he selected only the most essential personal items and stowed them in a crude bedroll.

"Where are you going, healer?"

Bashir whirled around. Talis Cedra stood just inside the tent flap. "What are you doing here?" he snapped.

"What are *you* doing?" the boy replied. He strolled over to examine Julian's preparations. "Won't you get in trouble for defying orders?"

"Defying—?" Dr. Bashir tried to turn the whole thing into a joke. "I knew this day would come, Cedra; you've been eavesdropping and for once you've gotten the story dead wrong."

The boy's mouth twisted into a skeptical knot. "Am I hearing wrong or are you pretending not to hear?" The words made Julian startle. Cedra's eyes were not dead, but they were older than his years, their stare piercing to the bone. "You like to teach us your people's games. Teach me how to play hide-and-find with the truth, healer."

"I'm doing nothing of the sort," Dr. Bashir said, strongly on the defensive. Then, more gently: "Cedra, do you know what it means to be a healer?"

"What d'you mean?" the boy asked cautiously. "I know *I'd* be a good one. There wouldn't be any more fevers on Bajor, or any more gut-cramp, or—When Dejana goes to live in the Temple, I'm going to join Brother Gis's order and become the best healer on Bajor!"

"Being a healer means more than how good you are," Julian said, wistfully hearing much of himself in Cedra. "When I was at Starfleet Medical, the first thing they taught us was that a doctor's prime directive is never to betray his trust. There are people depending on healers for health, for life, for a *future,* Cedra. Every healing is a part of that trust. You can't walk away from a task half-done. I came here with orders to cure the camp fever. It's gone now, but only gone from *this* camp. I can't leave it at that and still be true to my trust. Do you understand?"

The boy nodded. "You don't disobey orders that you don't want to hear; you just make sure you're too far away to hear 'em when they come." He ducked out of the tent without another word, leaving Julian puzzled and perturbed.

*What if he's run off to tell Lieutenant Dax?* Dr. Bashir threw himself back into the work of tying up the bedroll with even more haste. He had to be gone before they returned.

He stepped out of the tent just in time for Cedra to come barreling into him. The doctor staggered back. "What—?" he gasped, catching his breath.

"Here." The boy shoved a package, a flask, and a paper into his hands. "You're right: Just 'cause Dejana and I can get away safe doesn't mean the job's done. Good luck." He gave Dr. Bashir a fierce, gawky hug and darted away.

Julian stared at Cedra's offerings: food and drink for the journey, right enough, but what was that paper? He unfolded it and saw the map of the other refugee camps that was Cedra's pride. Smiling broadly, he stowed it all.

The day was fading, but there were still a few good hours of light left. Dr. Bashir consulted the map and noted where the closest camp was, then selected another, farther away. He had no illusions: they would search for him as soon as they discovered he was gone. They might not miss him at dinner, but his absence would not go unnoticed for long after that. Better a few nights' roughing it in the hills than taking the short march toward comfort and inevitable capture. He made his choice and headed out of the camp.

"Healer?"

As Dr. Bashir stood on a rocky rise to the west of the camp, a whisper from the shadows behind him brought him up short. He turned and saw Cedra leading a small, stocky creature that looked like a cross between a horse and an ostrich. "You'll go faster if you ride." The boy extended the loops of the reins. The *verdanis* snorted and tossed its head.

Dr. Bashir took the reins and regarded the beast thoughtfully. "I can't take this, Cedra," he said. "It would be stealing a valuable animal that they need here."

"Tossi's not valuable." Cedra spoke as one who knew. "Not here. He's too small to pull any carts and he's too wild to turn the millstone or the thresher. They're keeping him here only until he grows big enough to earn his keep, but he never will. You'll be doing them a favor by taking him off their hands and saving his fodder for a *verdanis* that'll give something back. Tossi's got too much racing blood in him; all he's good for is riding. My father taught me how to tell a good *verdanis* from a bad 'un, so you can take my word."

"I can, can I?" Bashir asked. He stroked the beast's pointed muzzle, and it tried to take a bite out of his hand.

"You will," Cedra replied confidently. "It's what you want to hear." He scampered back into the camp.

Julian studied his new mount. Tossi glowered at him but made no further moves to bite. The *verdanis* wore no saddle, just a folded blanket slung across its back. Grudgingly it deigned to allow Julian to pat its neck.

"I used to be a pretty fair rider," Julian remarked to the beast. "Of course, that was horses. Well, let's see." Clutching the reins, the doctor rested his hands on the animal's back and vaulted up and over to land heavily astride. Tossi did a little sideways dance but did not bolt. There was a giddy moment when it looked as if the unwieldy burden of Dr. Bashir's many packs was about to overbalance him. But he held the reins tight with one hand while steadying himself on Tossi's rump with the other.

"Ugh," he said, adjusting across his chest the set of the heavy leather strap from which the biosample replicator hung. "Nearly choked myself." The thick edge hooked itself under the tip of his comm badge, nearly tearing the insignia from his chest. "I'd better—" he began, preparing to hang the replicator at a different angle. Then he touched the badge and froze.

*Orders to leave . . .*

"I have my orders," he told the horizon. He left the replicator strap as it was and clapped his heels to the barrel of the *verdanis*. It launched itself into a land-devouring gait cousin to a fast canter. Dr. Bashir held on with his knees and concentrated on interpreting the landmarks they passed. The replicator strap worked its way further and further under his comm badge with every lurching step of the *verdanis*.

*I really ought to do something about that,* he told himself, knowing he would do nothing. *Accidents happen; they're no one's fault. I can't worry about that now. I have a job to do.*

He left the fields behind and took to the rocky upslopes of the hills.

# *Mosaic,* by Jeri Taylor

Jeri Taylor, co-creator and former executive producer for *Star Trek: Voyager,* wrote this excellent novel of the life of Captain Kathryn

Janeway of the Federation *Starship Voyager. Mosaic* is not a complete biography, but more a collection of vignettes from Janeway's life set amidst a ship in danger plot that provided Janeway the impetus for recollections about her life. The events in her life shaped the Captain Janeway we know and the complexity of her character, the many facets that created the mosaic that is her personality. *Mosaic* is not the story of a perfect person; it is the story of someone who learned from her mistakes, and who changed and grew as she faced the impact of her behavior on other people. She learned to be a leader, and in this regard, *Mosaic* reminds me of *Best Destiny.* Jimmy Kirk was an obnoxious punk; he was mouthy, unpleasant, spoiled, pushed his friends into doing things they did not want to do, and he was very angry at his absentee Starfleet father. Similarly, Janeway was unhappy throughout her childhood with her absentee father, and like Jimmy Kirk, she eventually learned that he was absent with very good cause that had nothing to do with rejection of her.

In this selection from *Mosaic,* Kathryn Janeway cajoled and bullied her friends into a cave diving expedition on Mars. When she found herself in trouble, she admitted her responsibility and refused to allow her friend Hobbes to take the blame. This passage showed her growth as a person on the road to becoming Captain Kathryn Janeway.

"HELLO, LADIES. GOING SWIMMING?" THE VOICE WAS FAMILIAR BUT WAS definitely not her father's. Kathryn rose and as the figure moved closer, he turned and his face was illuminated.

Hobbes Johnson.

Relief and dismay struggled for supremacy inside Kathryn: that it wasn't her father was a vast comfort, but the sight of Hobbes Johnson, lanky and dull, was about the final dismal touch in a day that had been rapidly going downhill.

"Hobbes, what are you doing here?"

"I could ask you the same thing. Aren't the quarries off-limits to you?"

"At least there are three of us. You came by yourself. That's foolish."

"No, it wasn't. I saw you leaving. I figured you were going to the quarries."

Kathryn felt a rush of annoyance, which, on top of her frustrations with Emma and Mary, pushed her from irritation to anger. "Don't you think if we'd wanted your company, we'd have asked you?"

Hobbes paled at the attack, and Kathryn was immediately sorry.

She didn't mean to hurt his feelings, she was just irked. But she saw Mary and Emma looking at her in shocked surprise, and realized she'd gone too far.

"I'm sorry, Hobbes. I didn't mean it . . . it's just been a frustrating day. I really want to go swimming, and I can't seem to get any enthusiasm from these two."

Mary's dander was still up. "I *was* enthusiastic—until I realized how reckless and dangerous this is. Kathryn wants to *climb* down the face of the quarry. That's ridiculous."

"Only way to get there," said Hobbes mildly.

"Well, I'm not doing it. I'm going back."

"Me, too," chimed in Emma, and both rose to their feet. Kathryn stared at them. Were they abandoning her? Leaving her here with *Hobbes Johnson?* She glared in disbelief.

"Fine," she heard herself saying. "Go on back. If you're not brave enough to do it, I don't want you around." Again, she immediately regretted her words. It was as though her mouth were an organism unto itself, acting without her permission. She saw Mary draw herself up, hurt and angry.

"If you have any sense at all, you'll come back with us. Face it, Kathryn—this was a terrible idea."

"If I decide to do something, I'm not going to back out just because it gets a little difficult. But you do whatever you want." Kathryn's face felt hot, and she realized she was just being stubborn, but the more the conversation went on, the more she felt herself dig in.

"Come on, Mary. Let's go." Emma looked eager to leave the quarry and the unpleasantness. Mary gave Kathryn one more somber look. "Kathryn?"

Kathryn merely shook her head, obstinate. The two other girls shrugged, lifted their bags, and headed for the maze of rocks that would lead them away from the quarry and back toward the colony. Kathryn watched them leave, suddenly feeling alone and friendless.

And worst of all, now she was stuck with Hobbes Johnson. She gave him an awkward glance. He was watching the retreating girls, face impassive. What should she do? Wait a decent interval and then follow them? She couldn't imagine spending another two minutes with Hobbes.

She looked down at the water below, remembering her determination to make it down there, to swim in the clear waters of the quarry, to practice her diving techniques. She felt Hobbes's eyes on her and looked up at him.

He wasn't quite as vulky-looking as he used to be, but no one would ever call him attractive. He no longer wore braces, but a few red pimples dotted his face; apparently even dermal-regeneration treatments didn't work on his acne. Kathryn thought it looked disgusting.

And he was as thin as ever, a long, reedy boy with a skinny neck and hair that tufted in unruly patches on his head. And there they were, alone together at the top of the quarry. Now what?

"Want to give it a try?" Hobbes's voice was as neutral as ever. It was as though he were suggesting they take a walk through the cornfields.

Kathryn hesitated, options warring within her. She really, really wanted to swim in that quarry. She really, really didn't want to do it with Hobbes Johnson. She glanced down again, saw the clear water below, beckoning to her.

She shrugged, feigning tedium. "Might as well." She hefted her bag, rearranged the straps to carry it on her back, and edged toward the cliff wall to search for the best starting place.

"It's over here," said Hobbes, walking to a small crevasse a few meters away. He stepped easily into it, swinging his body around and deftly grasping handholds. He began climbing confidently down the quarry face, hands and feet finding their way with ease and efficiency.

Kathryn was impressed. She'd done her share of rock climbing— credit The Meadows with that, for including this ancient sport in their physical curriculum—and had always enjoyed the challenge, but she lacked ease and style. She moved to the crevasse, immediately saw the places where Hobbes had found purchase, and began to follow him down the steep wall of the quarry.

Ten minutes later, they stood on a stone shelf that protruded over the water, a natural diving platform. Hobbes had already opened his bag and was removing his breathing gill and thermal tripolymer suit. Kathryn looked at him in surprise.

"You're going to dive?"

He glanced up at her as he calibrated his breathing gill. "That's why I come here. I'm looking for an opening into the Olympus Mons cave system."

She thought maybe she hadn't heard him correctly. "You? You're looking for the Olympus system?"

His gray eyes sought hers. "Why? Do you know about it?"

She nodded. "Some day I'm going to explore the caves. I'd like to map the system."

"How did you know about the caves?"

"Someone from Starfleet once told me. How did you?"

"I read about them. Some obscure story I found in a historical database at the library."

It figured. Hobbes always had his nose in a padd—and never one anyone else would be caught dead reading.

"So," he continued, "my dad and I have been diving the quarries since last year, looking for an entrance. We've covered about seven of them. We were here a few days ago but my gill started malfunctioning and we had to leave."

"Your dad lets you dive the quarries?"

"Sure."

No wonder Hobbes was so strange—he came from a strange family. *No one* let their children go to the quarries. What could his father have been thinking?

"Well, I hope you have enough sense not to dive alone."

"Of course not. Usually I'm with dad. Today I have you."

Something about the placid ease of his presumption rankled Kathryn. She almost said she didn't want to dive, just to punish him for jumping to the conclusion that she'd dive with him, but in time she remembered that it was exactly what she wanted to do, and there was no point in spoiling her day. For once, she managed to squelch herself before she said something she regretted.

Quickly, she pulled on her thermal suit, an intricate web of nichrome filaments that would keep her body comfortably warm even in near-freezing water. They both had equipment they'd used in school, where diving had been taught along with rock climbing, tennis, and swimming. Lightweight tripolymer body suits, vented fins, and the breathing gills, which constantly extracted breathable oxygen from the surrounding water, much like the gills of a fish. Long ago, humans had used bulky oxygen tanks, and then rebreathers, which processed exhaled air, removing the carbon dioxide by mixing it with alkaline hydroxide, and then injecting the resultant oxygen with helium. These tanks would allow divers to stay underwater for up to twenty-four hours at a time.

Now, of course, they could be under for as long as they wanted, just like fish.

They checked each other's buddy lights, readjusted their gills, and then lowered themselves off the platform and into the water.

The first thing she noticed was the cold. The suits they wore were light as cotton, but chemically treated to keep them warm at temperatures as low as two degrees C. Even so, Kathryn felt cool immediately.

The second thing to strike her was the pristine clarity of the water.

She felt she could see for a hundred meters—if there had been anything to see. No flora graced this chilly lake, no fauna inhabited its depths. There was nothing except rock and water.

The silence soothed her, as it always did when she was underwater. A sense of tranquillity enveloped her, and she swam effortlessly through the clear water, keeping her eye on the two green buddy lights on Hobbes's back, signaling that he was doing fine.

He was stroking steadily downward, moving toward the periphery of the quarry, searching for an opening in the wall—a crack, a dark spot—something that might indicate the presence of a cave system beyond.

They swam like that for some forty minutes, methodically searching the quarry walls, but finding nothing except impenetrable stone. They had circumnavigated the quarry twice, the second time at a significantly lower depth. Then Hobbes signaled her to surface, and gradually they floated their way to the top.

Kathryn was grateful. She was unpleasantly cold, and thirsty; she wanted to get out for a while, warm up, and have a piece of fruit. But Hobbes had other ideas.

"I think I saw something."

"Where?" Kathryn had been looking as carefully as he had, she was sure, and had detected nothing that resembled an opening in the stone walls.

"It's quite a bit lower than we were. I'd like to go back one more time, leave you at about twenty-five meters while I go check it out."

"That's pretty deep."

"But not past our safety limits. Remember, with Mars's lower gravity, water pressure isn't as intense as on Earth." He eyed her as they trod chilly water. She really wanted to get out and dry off, but she wasn't about to admit that to Hobbes Johnson, of all people. So she nodded and refit her breathing gill. He did the same, and they sank underwater once more.

She followed him down to twenty-five meters, then saw his hand signal for her to hold there. She watched as he stroked deeper into dark waters; she could barely see the flutter of his fins as he moved steadily down into the gloomy depths where sunlight could not penetrate.

Then he disappeared completely.

Kathryn felt a coldness in her stomach which was icier than the quarry water. How would she know if anything happened to him? How deep did he plan to go? How long would it take?

She forced her mind to quiet, breathing steadily, focusing on the sight of her hands floating in front of her, pale and ghostly. Gradually the panic faded, and she peered once more down into the depths of the dark water. She hadn't brought an aquadyne torch, never figuring to be this deep, never thinking she'd have a reason to go where there was no light.

She saw nothing.

Ten minutes passed, and she knew it was time to act. Gradually, she moved herself deeper, breathing regularly, pulling herself down through the water.

As far as she could see below her, there was only darkness. She scanned the wall of the quarry, hoping to discover whatever aberration it was that had drawn Hobbes to these deep waters.

And then she saw it—another five meters below her.

A dark gash in the side of the wall, barely visible in the gloom, no more than a faint shadow. Was that what had caught Hobbes's eye? As she got closer, she could see that the shadow was in fact an opening—a black trench in the rock face some ten meters wide and five meters tall. She pulled steadily toward it.

And then she realized *it* was pulling *her.*

A current was flowing into the opening. She realized that meant it was the ingress to an underground river, perhaps even a network of subterranean caves extending deep into the planet's crust.

She let the current pull her toward the mouth that was now yawning just below her.

And realized, too late, that as soon as she was on a level with the opening, the current became immeasurably stronger, and then she was sucked into the dark hole, out of control.

Desperately, she struggled against the pull, quickly realized it was too strong for her, and lunged for the wall of the cave mouth.

Incredibly, her hands found purchase. An upward-thrusting shard of rock allowed her to grip it firmly, stopping her inexorable drag back into—into what?

Fear paralyzed her for a moment. She thought of her father, how she had been so afraid it was his footsteps they'd heard climbing toward the quarry, wishing now that it had been him and that she were safely back in the colony with him—chastised, to be sure, even restricted. But alive.

Where was Hobbes? Had he been sucked into this channel as well? Clenching the rock with all her might, she gradually turned her head and looked behind her.

She saw the two green buddy lights another five meters in, glowing dully through the pitch black water, not moving, but flickering in and out of her view as the currents of the water struck them. Hobbes must have found something to grab on to, also. For the first time, she realized she could see absolutely nothing; no light penetrated here, and only the flittering green lights interrupted the terrifying darkness.

She'd have to inch her way back to him. She carefully let go with one hand, the other scrabbling along the wall, feeling for a handhold.

She found one. Releasing her other hand, she clutched at the new hold, body pressed as close to the wall of the channel as she could get it. The sucking current was less pronounced there.

Then she repeated the process, minute after agonizing minute, creeping backward centimeters at a time through the darkness and the relentless tug of the icy water. Why, she wondered, wasn't Hobbes doing the same? Pulling himself forward, little by little?

By the time she reached the two lights, she realized why. He wasn't on the cave wall, but out toward the center of the channel. He must have found an obstruction to hold to, but he couldn't reach the wall. He was stranded.

How was she going to reach him? Did he even know she was there? He must—if she could see his buddy lights, he could see hers. Clamping her hands around a small rock outcropping, she gradually extended her legs into the center of the channel, guiding them toward the buddy lights.

And felt them touch a body. Then rubbed them on that body, trying to communicate, trying to get him to realize that he had to grab her legs.

It didn't take long. She felt a hand around her ankle, then another, and suddenly the pressure on her was twice as strong, as Hobbes's body weight was pulling against her. Would this work? Could she possibly pull both of them out of this underwater tomb?

She had to get him toward the wall, where he could grab hold and help pull. She let the force of the current help her sweep her legs toward the wall, felt his body pulling on her legs, pulling so hard she wasn't sure she could hang on, felt one hand begin to slip—

And then the pressure on her legs was released. She turned around and saw the buddy lights behind her, against the wall. He had managed to find a hold.

And then the real struggle began. Pulling even herself against the flow of water was almost impossible. Her fingers were cold, nearly numb; they slipped against the wet rock. Desperately she scrabbled the wall to find a grip.

Slowly, impossibly, she pulled herself toward the mouth of the channel, imagining that it was slightly lighter there, that the water was gray, not black, and that the opening was only a few meters away and soon she'd be out of this hellhole, looking toward sunlight filtering down into the water, moving toward the surface and warmth.

But before she ever reached the gray, her hands found a corner. An edge.

She was at the mouth. If she could turn the corner, she was out.

She reached her right hand around the edge of the cave, pawing for a grip. She found nothing but sheer rockface.

She felt panic rise, felt her heart begin to pound, forced the feelings down. There had to be a way. She felt Hobbes behind her, bumping her feet, and knew they were very close to making it.

Holding her grip with her right hand, she twisted her body in the water so that she was pressed face-first against the wall. This way, she could extend her left arm higher than she'd been able to reach with her right, though it was in a more awkward position.

But with her left hand, she felt a blessed indentation, not much, but enough to dig her fingers into. Would it give her enough leverage to swing her body around and outside the cave?

She paused for a few breaths before trying it. Gripping the indentation as hard as she could, she knifed forward in the water and pushed her body so it twisted out of the opening, staying flat against the wall on the outside. The current was weak there, and she could actually swim along the wall, away from the opening. She turned to see if Hobbes would follow.

What seemed like minutes passed. She was numb from cold, and still faced a slow rise to the surface. *Come on, Hobbes,* she thought intensely, *I did it, you can do it.* She peered toward the dark gash from which she had safely emanated, willing him to appear.

And he did, rolling around the corner in much the same fashion she had, flattening himself against the wall until he had risen high enough to where the current was no longer a danger to them. They eyed each other in the murky gloom, making gestures of joy and victory, rising only as quickly as they could safely ascend.

In ten minutes, they were on the surface, then onto the platform, toweling vigorously to restore warmth to their bodies, eating and drinking and laughing with a giddiness that belied the trauma they were processing.

When they had rested, warm and full, they climbed the quarry face again, giggling at how easy it seemed compared to what they'd been through. On the top, they looked back down at the water that had so recently tried to destroy them both.

Hobbes eyes sought her face. "You saved my life, Kath," he said simply. "I'll never forget that."

She shrugged, embarrassed. "You'd do the same for me."

"Yes, I would," he said, and there was something in his voice that made her look sharply at him, but she saw nothing in his face.

"Well, we better get back," she said, feeling suddenly awkward.

"I'd say that's a very good idea," said a voice from behind them, cold and potent.

They whirled, and Kathryn saw her father standing there. "What were you two thinking? You know the quarries are off-limits."

"It's my fault, sir," Hobbes said instantly. "I've been here with my father, and I asked Kathryn to come swimming with me."

Her father's eyes shifted to her. "Kathryn?" he said simply, and while every part of her wanted to let Hobbes's gallant statement stand, she knew she couldn't lie to her father.

"Hobbes is being a gentleman, Dad. I was here with Emma and Mary. I talked them into it. Hobbes came later." She glanced at Hobbes. "Thanks anyway."

Vice-Admiral Janeway tapped his commbadge and then took each of them by an arm. "Janeway to Ops Center. Three to beam in."

And in an instant they were standing inside Ops, where curious officers looked at them, smiling at the incongruity of two young people in swim gear standing in the pristine room.

Kathryn's father ushered them into an adjacent corridor. "Is there anything else you have to say about this little escapade?"

"It just seemed like fun. We swam and we dived some." Kathryn held her father's gaze firmly. She wouldn't lie to him, but choosing to omit some of the details seemed perfectly justifiable. There was no way she was going to tell him about their near-miss in the cave opening.

"But you knew you weren't supposed to be there?"

"Yes, Dad."

"You're grounded for the next week, Kathryn. And no holodeck privileges, either. Hobbes, I expect you to tell your parents about this. What they decide to do is up to them."

"Yes, sir."

"Dad . . ." Kathryn was trying to keep the despair out of her voice. "We're only going to *be* here another week. I made plans, and there's a party next Saturday—"

"You should have thought of that before you headed for the quarries. Now go back to quarters and be prepared to spend the week there."

She felt tears begin to form, and quickly blinked them back. There was no way she was going to cry in front of him, no way she'd let him know this unfair punishment meant anything to her. She lifted her chin and looked him right in the eye.

"Yes, *sir*," she snapped, and turned on her heel and stalked out. As she left, she heard Hobbes talking softly with her father, apologizing, trying to take more responsibility for the incident, hoping to spare Kathryn. She hated him for it.

Indignation mounted in her. How could her father treat her like this? He was never around anymore, always off conferring with Starfleet officials—what right did he have descending on her just to mete out punishment? The unjustness of it enveloped her like a noxious fog.

But those thoughts didn't suppress the one that had tickled her mind ever since they had climbed up the rockface from the quarry: some day, she would go back there. She would be prepared. She would dive into the quarry, enter the cave opening, and explore the Olympus Mons system. No matter what her father had to say about it.

## *Pathways,* by Jeri Taylor

What she did for Captain Janeway in *Mosaic*, Jeri Taylor repeated for the other *Voyager* crew members in *Pathways*. At the story's opening, Janeway's command crew have been captured and imprisoned in an alien death camp from which escape seems hopeless. In an effort to keep themselves alive, they told each other about the paths and critical turning points that led them to *Voyager* and the Delta Quadrant. As the crew shared the stories of their lives, the bond between them strengthened and they found the courage to endure and plan their escape. Their stories are compelling, thought provoking and moving. More than once, I found myself in or near tears.

*Pathways* is much like a collection of novellas. As I read each story, I savored it for a day or so before I turned to the next. By the time I reached the end of *Pathways*, I felt as though I knew Chakotay, Tuvok, B'Elanna Torres, Tom Paris, Harry Kim, Neelix, and the departed Kes in ways I had not known them before. Reading *Pathways* has enriched the experience of watching *Voyager*.

*Pathways* has one of the most exciting openings I have ever read in a book. As the story begins, Tom Paris was engaged in practicing shuttlecraft maneuvers in atmosphere and extreme daredevil flying. The excerpt ends with the beginning of Chakotay's story.

TOM PARIS WAS WELL AWARE THAT BRINGING A SHUTTLE INTO A PLANET'S atmosphere was easy if you followed procedure; it only became challenging—and interesting—if you deviated from Starfleet's carefully regulated system.

He had developed a number of ways to cheat the routine, but the only one that consistently provided what Tom wanted—the ineffable thrill that accompanied danger—was what he had termed the Yeager maneuver, after an ancient but renowned pilot of the twentieth century. Now he had the chance to try it again.

Captain Janeway had deposited an away team, including the ship's senior officers, on an unoccupied M-class planet that promised abundant foodstuffs as well as time off their starship, *Voyager.* She then took the ship on a diplomatic mission to a nearby system where she hoped to secure safe passage through a part of space rumored to be rife with danger.

Tom had requested shuttle time during the away mission, not an unusual request. Logging shuttle time was required duty for every pilot, a necessary means of keeping one's skills honed. First Officer Chakotay hadn't hesitated when Tom suggested he use this downtime to log a few hours on his file.

The request was legitimate, of course, and Tom had no pangs about making it, even if he did have an agenda that had gone unspoken. The two functions weren't mutually exclusive, and he saw nothing wrong with combining them.

Now, at the controls of the *Starship Voyager's* shuttle *Harris,* he saw the planet looming before him. It was a watery sphere, much like Earth, and the marbled blue-and-white orb gave him a few pangs of nostalgia—a fact which surprised him, for he usually found himself far happier in the Delta Quadrant than he had been at home. He shoved the feelings aside and made the necessary preparations for entering the atmosphere, which, his instruments told him, would first be encountered some thirty thousand meters above the surface.

First would come the mesosphere, where molecular structure was thin and porous, bleeding into the stratosphere, where atmospheric pressure heightened and friction became a genuine concern; finally, the descent into the full oxygen-nitrogen atmosphere and the landing.

The Yeager maneuver was accomplished just at the transition from mesosphere to stratosphere.

Atmospheric flight was always done under thruster power, and as such was accomplished much as it had been with pre-warp vehicles. There were safety mechanisms in place now, of course, that hadn't been available to earlier craft, but safety systems could always be taken off-line. That was the first thing Tom did as the image of the planet filled the window of his ship, growing larger by the minute.

At the point where gravity began to exert a substantial pull on the shuttle, Tom tilted up the nose of the vessel and cut the thrusters, so that the ship began sinking toward the surface tail first, without power.

And that's when his body went into an autonomic response: pulse rate increased, blood pressure heightened, and adrenaline was released. These systemic reactions were biochemical and as old as man's earliest ancestors, but to Tom Paris they provided a state of crystalline awareness that was almost hallowed. All his senses sharpened as endorphins flowed into the brain, creating a mix of fear and pleasure that were mysteriously and inextricably linked.

He stared only briefly into the black sky, which, he knew, would soon begin to change color, becoming more blue as the atmosphere thickened. From now on he had to keep his eyes down, locked on the control panel. Because very soon the shuttle would be pulled into a violent spin, and a glimpse out the window would produce instant and disabling vertigo. Then he'd be doomed.

The only way to restart the thrusters now was to get the ship into a dive, nose-down, so that air was forced through the intake manifolds, which would start the magnaturbines spinning and build up the RPMs. Atmospheric oxygen would then combine with fuel from the shuttle's tanks in a supersonic combustion chamber, providing power for the thrusters.

The ship snapped into a flat spin, whirling right over its center of gravity, like an ancient pinwheel. The force of the spin drove Tom back against the seat, his head on the outer edge of the circle.

This was the moment he'd waited for.

He could pull out of this if he functioned perfectly. He needed every sense, every instinct keen and chiseled, responding with diamondlike clarity. And that's what the fear gave him—intensified awareness that would allow him to make the moves to save himself.

The trick now was timing. He had to gauge—through a combination of skill, experience, and luck—just the right time to maneuver the nose of the ship down. Too soon and it would throw him into an end-over-end tumble from which it was almost impossible to escape. Too late and the atmosphere would be dense enough to keep the shuttle nose-up and he would continue to spin out of control, screaming into the atmosphere at a speed that would incinerate him.

His body was being slammed against the seat with increasing pressure, his head filling with blood from the centrifugal force of the spin. He forced his eyes to bore into the control panel, watching as the altitude was displayed. He was falling about fifty meters a second, three thousand meters a minute. He estimated he'd have to engage his emergency drogue field at an altitude of about thirty thousand meters, and that was coming up fast.

At thirty-one thousand meters, he realized he was in trouble. His vision was darkening and his head throbbed as blood sloshed through it. He'd better engage the field now . . . but he knew it was too soon. He'd go tumbling into an endless somersault until he and the craft became a hellish fireball.

He had to wait . . . until it felt right. But how would he know when it felt right? Maybe his judgment was becoming impaired by the unnatural rearrangement of his bodily fluids. *Go ahead,* something told him, *the altitude's close enough . . . engage the drogue field.* His fingers slid with practiced ease to the controls.

But *no!* screamed through his mind, and his fingers responded, poised over the panel, refusing to enter the command. The ship was now under thirty thousand meters. Was he heading for dangerously turbulent atmospheric levels?

Wait . . . wait . . . wait . . .

Darkness was overtaking him, and the panel was nothing more than a dim arrangement of lights that swam in his field of vision. Much longer and he wouldn't be conscious to enter the field engagement command. *Hang on, Tom . . . hang on . . .*

Suddenly, the startling image of the incident from long ago— another time when he had told himself to wait . . . wait . . . wait— ripped through his mind like a phaser, and he cried out involuntarily. He thought he was over that, had long ago purged himself of those awful sights, but there they were in his mind's eye, brilliant and indelible, shot through with colors . . . colors of fire, colors of death . . .

The shock of the memory cleared his vision briefly and he saw that he was under twenty-nine thousand meters above the surface.

Now.

His fingers danced on the controls and the drogue field engaged . . . within seconds he would feel the tug as the ship nosed down and fell out of its spin. He drew great gasps of air because now he felt light-headed and dizzy—had his eyes flicked for a half second to the window? He was sure they hadn't, and yet he was unaccountably queasy . . . why wasn't the nose pitching down? Had he entered the wrong command? The beginnings of panic crackled in his mind like arcing plasma.

That wouldn't do. Can't panic. Think. Nose down . . . why not happening . . . think . . .

He had just promised himself that if he got out of this, he'd never flirt with danger again—when the long-awaited tug pulled at him and he felt the shuttle pitch downward. In a flash, he realized that nothing had been wrong, after all, except his perception of time, distorted by his biological responses. Everything was going as it should.

Air flooded the intake ducts and the thrusters began to respond. Tom regained control and drew the shuttle into a vectored descent, then looked out to see the ripe blue sky of the alien planet, familiar and welcoming. Soon he was dropping to the surface, searching for a landing spot, telling himself that his promise not to try things like this anymore should be nullified because nothing had really been wrong, after all.

Beneath him, he saw the figures of the *Voyager* crew, tiny as dust motes at first, then gradually increasing in size as he descended.

He wasn't sure when he realized that something was wrong—maybe when he saw that several people seemed to be running in unnatural patterns, as though they were driven by some urgent need but couldn't quite figure out what they were supposed to be doing. Then he saw that a great number of them were lying on the ground, motionless.

"Paris to away team. What's happening down there?"

There was no answer. For the first time since he began his descent, Tom checked his sensors and realized the *Voyager* crew wasn't alone on the planet. There were alien life signs, dozens of them. Where had they come from?

He quickly put down the shuttle and opened the hatch, hurrying to reach his friends and find out what was happening and where those aliens were. But as soon as he stepped outside he became dizzy, and found himself lurching, staggering as though drunk. Vaguely he noted a certain sick sweetness in the air and knew it was responsible for his rubbery legs. Ahead of him, most of the away team was now slumped on the ground, though whether dead or just unconscious he couldn't tell. He saw Chakotay, the last person standing, sink to his knees, and then Tom, too, succumbed, wondering for an instant if he had survived the dangerous descent through the atmosphere only to die in this cloying poison.

When Chakotay regained consciousness, he didn't know exactly where he was. Inside a structure of some kind, for he could see walls and a low ceiling by virtue of a few lights spotted on the walls of the room; they emitted a dim yellowish light that cast small pools of illumination before being absorbed by a foreboding darkness. He raised up to a sitting position and realized the rest of the away team was in the room as well, some still lying unconscious, others sitting in a kind of groggy stupor.

His head throbbed and his mouth was parched. He couldn't seem to produce saliva. Where were they? What had happened to them?

He spotted B'Elanna Torres nearby, sitting perfectly still and staring at nothing, dark hair a matted mass and dirt smudging the Klingon ridges on her forehead. Chakotay struggled toward her on hands and knees.

"B'Elanna?"

She turned to him and stared dully. She seemed remote and uncomprehending. "Do you know where we are?" he asked.

Several seconds passed before her eyes flickered in understanding. "Chakotay . . ." she whispered hoarsely, her throat as dry as his. "What happened to us?"

Only when she'd asked the question did he realize he didn't know. The last memory he possessed was of being on the bridge of *Voyager*—and then he woke up in this strange, dark room. "I don't know," he answered.

"I was on *Voyager* . . . and then suddenly I was here."

Around them, others were beginning to stir, moving out of their curious sleep like drowsy bears emerging from hibernation, ponderous and heavy. It occurred to Chakotay that he should get up and search the room, but his legs felt unequal to the task. He turned back to B'Elanna and saw that the Vulcan tactical officer, Lieutenant Commander Tuvok, had crawled to join them, looking as stuporous as everyone else.

"Where are we?" rasped Tuvok, and Chakotay had a moment's amusement at the thought of the disciplined, controlled Vulcan reduced to the same confused state as everyone else.

"We're trying to figure that out. What's the last thing you remember?"

Tuvok's upswept eyebrows rose and his dark forehead knotted in concentration. "Being on *Voyager.* At my station on the bridge. But I have no idea how we got here."

Chakotay felt as though his head was beginning to clear slightly, though it still ached. There were things they had to do. "We have to count heads—see who's here. Ask them if they remember anything about what happened to us."

The three struggled to their feet and moved off through the languorous bodies, each in a separate direction, exhorting their crewmates to wake, to sit up, to try to remember anything they could about their strange predicament.

A few minutes later a head count had been taken, revealing that fourteen members of the crew were present. Presumably the others were still on *Voyager,* wherever the ship might be now.

Suddenly Neelix spoke up. The orange-tufted Talaxian was wearing one of his typically garish outfits, but it looked unusually subdued in the darkened room. "A picnic," he said tentatively.

Everyone turned to him. "Picnic?" echoed Chakotay. He sensed this was important. "Are you saying we were on a picnic?"

Neelix looked momentarily confused. "I think so . . . I can almost remember the captain telling me I should pack food for . . ." He trailed off vaguely, unable to come up with anything more.

But it had triggered others' thinking. "On a planet," called out Harry Kim, the black-haired operations officer. "We all went to the surface of a planet."

"He's right," chimed in Seven, the beautiful blond human woman who had lived most of her life as a member of a Borg collective, and who had been on *Voyager* for less than a year. "The captain said we all needed to get out and stretch our legs. I remember thinking that was an odd thing to do."

Several people smiled at that. Seven had made remarkable strides in her return to humanity, but some of the nuances still escaped her. Her memory, however, fueled that of several more people, and as they all began tossing out the bits and pieces they recalled, the story began to emerge.

It was Tom Paris who remembered the sickly-sweet smell in the air, as soon as he'd opened the hatch of the shuttle, and when he mentioned it, many of the group added their similar recollections.

"It started suddenly," said B'Elanna pensively. "One second it wasn't there, and then it was overpowering."

"It must've been a gas of some kind," speculated Chakotay, "but did it occur naturally? Or were we purposely attacked?"

"The fact that we're here—wherever here is—tells me someone did it to us," offered Tom. "We were gassed and then dumped into this room."

They had found no evidence of any entrance or exit to the room—no doors, no windows, no control pad. Nothing but the bare walls and the few weak lights, nothing to give them any clue as to their location. They could be anywhere.

It was Tom, through his pilot's feel for such things, who correctly surmised where they were, although his guess wouldn't be verified for many hours, when they were finally released. "We're on a spaceship," he announced, "I'd bet anything on it. It just *feels* like a ship flying at warp speed."

This was disheartening. If they were being taken away from the planet where they had succumbed, then they were probably being taken away from *Voyager*. They had no ship and no captain, and didn't know the fate of the crew who had remained with the ship. They were boxed into a cramped, dark room with no apparent way in or out, and at the mercy of whoever had attacked them.

And they were all wildly thirsty. The gas had left them with aching heads and parched mouths, and every one of them craved a cooling drink of water, but they all sensed that was unlikely.

What none of them knew was that this was the most comfortable they were to be for a long time.

Chakotay was having a vivid and frightening dream involving a forest fire from which he was trying to escape, when a sudden lurch jolted him awake. He sat up and saw that Tom had felt it, too. "We've entered an atmosphere," said Tom. They both felt the sensation of a descending ship.

At almost the same moment, a disembodied voice filled the room, rasping and harsh. "Prepare to disembark," it announced, and then was silent.

They weren't sure how long they had been on this mysterious ship. The effect of the gas they had inhaled was enervating, and soon after the head count, most of them had fallen asleep, though for how long they couldn't be sure. Chakotay hoped that some of the mysteries were soon to be solved.

The vessel seemed to slow, and soon after there was a heavy impact which they could feel in their bones. Then nothing.

They waited, disciplined and alert, for whatever was to come next. Most felt anxiety to one degree or another, but were experienced enough not to manifest it. They stood poised, wary, ready to do whatever was expected of them when that time came.

Chakotay heard a grating noise, soft at first, but rising in volume and intensity; then one wall of their enclosure separated at the ceiling and began to lower. Intense sunlight immediately flooded in, assaulting their dilated pupils, and they all squinted or threw up a shielding hand.

Finally the top of the wall lay on the ground, providing a ramp into the hot glare of that ferocious light, so bright they couldn't yet make out what awaited them.

"Exit slowly," said the same voice as before.

Chakotay led the way, followed in an orderly fashion by the others. Gradually his pupils were contracting in the light, and he lowered his hand to see what environment, what terrain, they were walking into.

What he saw astonished him.

A vast meadow stretched before them, filled with what looked like thousands of the most miserable beings he had ever seen. Many alien species were represented, all of them emaciated and filthy, most wearing nothing but rags. Small fires burned here and there, creating an acrid, smoky haze that didn't quite serve to mask the unbelievable stench of the place.

Three hours later, spirits somewhat restored by the slaking of their thirst, the group had found a reasonably bare patch of ground, which they chose as a campsite. Soon after that an alarm sounded, numerous doors in the walls opened, and hover vehicles emerged from them. The prisoners all rose and stood alongside the paths that crisscrossed the meadow, and the vehicles moved among them, dispensing rations.

Taking their cue from the others, *Voyager*'s crew did the same, and were each handed a crumbling cake of something resembling baked grains, shot through with dirt and small bits of rock. They stared at it, dismayed. Chakotay once again led the way, breaking off a small portion, putting it in his mouth and chewing carefully to locate the stones.

"Eat up," he said as cheerfully as he could, and the group sat down and had their first meal as Subu prisoners. The torturous sun finally went down, and as night came on, the temperature cooled, bringing blessed relief. Tomorrow they would see about shelter, which might require bartering for materials, and about fuel for a fire. And they would reconnoiter the camp even more carefully, assessing the possible escape routes and methods, in preparation for what they now believed was a perfectly plausible effort. Food and water, no matter how unappetizing, had restored their optimism, and made them think that all things were possible.

"Commander," said Harry after they'd eaten and stretched out on the ground, weary after the events of the last two days. "How'd you get along with Commander Nimembeh?"

"Get along with him? Fine, I guess. I only had him during prep squad, before my freshman year started. He was tough, but everyone respected him."

Harry looked a little sheepish. "I had quite an experience with him," he said. "It wasn't a lot of fun."

"No one would ever call Nimembeh fun," agreed Chakotay. A silence fell on them, but Harry seemed to be pondering something. After a few moments, he turned again to Chakotay.

"Sir . . . if I'm prying or anything, you don't have to answer. But how was it . . . that you quit Starfleet, and joined the Maquis? I mean, to go through the Academy, and be a Starfleet officer . . . and then to give it all up—well, I just wondered how that happened."

Chakotay drew a breath. It was something he had spent a great deal of time contemplating, and he wasn't entirely sure he had an easy answer. "To tell you that, I'd practically have to tell you the story of my life."

"If you're willing to tell it, I'd sure like to hear it."

Chakotay looked around at his group. Several people were listening to the conversation, and seemed intrigued by the prospect of learning more about their first officer. It occurred to him that this might be as good a way as any to pass some time. "All right. If anybody gets bored you can go to sleep. I won't be offended."

He paused a moment to think how to start, and looked up at the night sky, dotted with stars. Suddenly an image shot into his mind, one he hadn't thought about for some twenty years, and he knew that was the beginning of his tale. "When I was fifteen, my father and I took a trip together, and it was a turning point in my life."

## *Seven of Nine,* by Christie Golden

Christie Golden has written several excellent *Voyager* novels, including *The Murdered Sun* and *Marooned.* She has captured the characters' personalities and brought them to life with every novel, and

*Seven of Nine* is her best. In this story, Ms. Golden explored the effect on Seven of her assimilation of countless sentient beings even before the series dealt with the issue in the episode "Infinite Regress." In this novel, *Voyager* agreed to transport the Skedans, the last survivors of a race that was assimilated by the Borg, to the seat of the empire that had failed to protect them. Unknown to the *Voyager* crew, the Skedans planned to destroy the tyrannical emperor and were distracting them by using telepathic suggestion and control. They constantly influenced the minds of the crew, and they tortured Seven of Nine with her memories of the lives of those she had assimilated. The following passage from *Seven of Nine* describes Seven's experiences with those memories.

SEVEN COULD HEAR THEM TALKING. THEIR VOICES WERE DISTANT, MUFFLED, but she could catch words now and then. They penetrated her hallucinations, this living of other lives, like a gentle fragrance wafting toward her nostrils. But the voices went away again almost immediately. There was no place for them, no time. One doesn't concentrate on the smell of roses or the softness of their petals when one is about to die.

*The skorrak bird had eluded her. Seven felt anger and frustration swell inside her and emitted a low growl. Her tail twitched.*

*"You stalked well, my little sweet Keela," her mother reassured her. The words were a comfort but the voice was vague and distracted. Seven glanced back and saw her mother staring up at the sky. She had been distantly aware of the cloud that had fallen over them, but now realized that it was no cloud at all. It was a ship, huge, square, floating in front of the life-giving sun and blocking its rays.*

*Seven knew fear. She had never seen anything like this vessel before. None of the people with whom they traded had that kind of ship. Who were they? What did they want? She padded back to her mother's side, the skorrak bird and her failure to catch it forgotten.*

*"Keela." Her mother's voice was calm. "Go inside. Now. Put through a message to the Council. Tell them—"*

*A blast of light burst from the ships. It reached clear to the ground and began to slice up chunks of Seven's world. The ground trembled and Seven fell hard. She splayed out her legs and dug her claws in an attempt to hold on as the earth bucked beneath her.*

*Buildings collapsed about her. Mammoth trees, centuries old, toppled and fell. How long this went on, Seven didn't know, but when she finally lifted her head she saw devastation beyond her ability to fully comprehend.*

*These intruders had not only shattered her world, they had taken it. From this vantage point, Seven could look down into the heart of the city. Except that the city was now completely gone. It had been scooped out like a cub might scoop a pawful of sand, and all that remained of a city that housed ten thousand souls was a huge, gaping tear in the good earth.*

*They came out of the shadowy jungle like walking nightmares. Bipedal, like the Graa, but unlike them in all other ways. Part pale flesh with no muzzles or fur, part black and frightening-looking machine, they charged forward, utterly unafraid. Seven yelped in terror. Her mother recovered and launched herself at the intruders, teeth and claws bare.*

*"Run, Keela! RUN!"*

*Seven froze, unable to obey. The intruders fired a strange weapon at her mother and the mighty huntress dropped like a stone. The intruder who slew her mother now lifted its eyes and fastened them on Seven. A single blue eye—the second had been replaced with a red light—stared at the small, cowering kitten. She—for it was female—parted full, gray lips and uttered a sentence:*

*"We are the Borg. Your biological and technological distinctiveness will be added to our own. Resistance is futile."*

Without warning, Seven erupted into motion. She jerked in a series of violent convulsions, arching her chest up and slamming her head down hard. Paris and the doctor leaped into action.

Tom fumbled for the right hypospray, his heart in his mouth. His fingers betrayed him and the instrument toppled off the tray to the floor. Before he retrieved it, cursing his clumsiness, Seven's flailing had ceased.

Cardiac arrest.

Seven of Nine was dying. . . .

*Darkness. Silence. And out of the silence, a voice . . .*

*"Mother." A gentle shake. "Mother, wake up!"*

*"Kalti Druana? Honored Kalti, please . . ."*

*Seven shook off her sleep and sat up in her bed. Old bones and ancient muscles protested, but she ignored them. She had lived with the aches and pains of old age long enough so that they had become friends to the great artist. They were proof positive that she was still alive, that she had made it successfully through another day and had not slipped into the eternal darkness and silence that eventually waited to embrace her.*

*The children, her daughter Oplik and her daughter's mate Rel, had woken her. "What is it?" Seven asked sleepily. "What is wrong?"*

*"We are under attack," Rel replied somberly. "Orders have been given to the populace to congregate at certain areas. From there, they will try to transport us to more easily defensible ground."*

*Seven permitted herself a humorless smile. If her planet full of peaceful artists were indeed under attack, there was no place that was "defensible." They might run, frightened, but in the end, if a conqueror wished to take the planet, taken it would be. For millennia the Lennli had been undisturbed save for trading vessels. The planet held no strategic position, brought forth no unique minerals. Its treasure was its people and their talents, nothing more but certainly nothing less.*

*But she had to keep pretending, for the sake of the children. They stared at her with frightened eyes, pleading for her to say something that would somehow make everything all right.*

*She reached to stroke her daughter's cheek with a bright-red, seven-fingered hand. "Let us go," was all Seven could find to say.*

*The world she had known was no more. The thriving urban center near her home in the hills was under attack, and even as the three of them watched, the entire city was dug up with the conqueror's weapons and rose high in the air above them, floating with an incongruous grace toward the gaping maw of the waiting alien vessel.*

*They hadn't even made it to the transport vessel when the attack came. Dozens, perhaps hundreds of the enemy came out of the night to descend on the fleeing populace. Rel, no warrior born, nonetheless fought to the death, taking one of the black-bodied, white-headed machine-beings with him. Oplik shrieked in horror at the sight of her mate's broken, bloody body lying on the purple grass. She was easy prey, gathered up into the arms of one of the obscenely evil intruders as if she weighed nothing at all.*

*Through it all, Seven remained oddly calm. She grieved, bitterly and with all her sculptor's sensitive soul, for her people, for her children, but for herself, she could find little to lament. She had had a full life, with a loving mate and children who were a daily joy. She had sculpted all her life, and the only thing that caused her a moment's pain was the knowledge that her hands would never again caress* simmik *stone.*

*The one who claimed her was female, although only just. Young, still. And monstrous. As the woman-machine advanced purposefully on her, Druana demanded, "Who are you?"*

216

*"We are Borg." Arrogant, the voice and the eyes.*

*"No!" demanded Druana, turning the tables if only for a few seconds. "Who are you? What is your name?"*

*The abomination slowed, halted. "We are Borg," she repeated. "My designation is irrelevant." The Borg woman's eye—she had only one, bright blue and full of contempt—narrowed. She reached out for Druana and—*

"She can't take much more of this."

"You've got to stop it. You said the part of the brain that was overstimulated was the, what, the—"

"Hippocampus, among other areas. Lieutenant, don't you think if I could stop this I would?"

Someone could. Dimly, Seven knew it. The image of nine black birds flying in a circle plucked at her mind. Someone could stop this. *When the pie was opened, the birds began to sing—*

*They had her strapped down, the harsh metal casing crumpling her beautiful feathers. She wasn't supposed to be awake, Seven knew that much, but she was, though her voice died in her throat. She couldn't move her head, but her eyes darted about wildly. In the . . . pod? . . . beside her, she caught a glimpse of her beloved. Fresh terror flooded her. His left arm was gone, replaced by a black metal substitute. He had only one eye; the other socket was crammed with a twisted piece of machinery out of which a red light gleamed.*

*Sulmi!*

*Her heart ached for him, but he was no longer Sulmi, really, was he? He had become—what did the Destroyers call themselves—become Borg. She had heard the whispered tales, knew what the machine-things did to those they captured, or, as they coldly referred to it, "assimilated." It had been done to Sulmi, and now, it was being done to her, Amari, First of Six in her household.*

*She felt a sharp prick of pain as something was jabbed into her arm. Then, as she watched, one of the Borg—a female—stepped forward and cut off her arm.*

"Seven? It's Neelix. They tell me you've been having a pretty rough time of it." A pause. The sound of fidgeting. An image: a short, rather stout being with puffs of whiskers and a friendly countenance. Talaxian; Species 218. A man whose duties on the ship were many and varied.

"I thought I'd just pop in and tell you to hang on. Nobody knows what's going on inside that pretty head of yours but let me tell you, we miss you. We do! Why, did you know that you are the only one on the ship who actually likes my roast jak'ra? I promise I'll make you a special batch if—when you pull out of this."

A touch on her hand—warm, strong. "You're one of the toughest people I've ever met. You've got to pull through this, Seven." The voice grew husky. "You brought me back, you darn well better come back yourself. Please."

*Seven chuckled to herself as her two little ones chased each other around her ankles. They had not yet mastered telepathy, so the warm spring air was filled with their happy chirps and trills. She glanced up at the sky, as she had done every day since word came that the Borg were heading toward their verdant planet. But her mate was the elected One of the continent of Ioh and the selected leader of the entire Circle of Seven, and he had reassured her that reinforcements would soon be arriving.*

*Still. The atrocities the Borg committed on those unfortunate enough to be assimilated were well known, and the thought of the monsters approaching their planet made Seven shiver. But surely the Emperor would honor the pact, would send his mighty battleships to protect the planet. Surely, there was a reason for the delay. Besides, the attack was not due for another six—*

*"What's that?" asked her youngest. Seven craned her long neck and followed his gaze.*

*Large cubical shapes were penetrating the atmosphere. And there was a voice—or rather hundreds, millions of voices—shattering the silence of the spring morning:*

*"We are the Borg. Prepare to be assimilated. Your biological and technological distinctiveness will be added to our own. Resistance is futile."*

*Tamaak! thought Rhiv. Tamaak, they are early!*

Seven of Nine, lying prone on the diagnostic bed safely in sickbay, began to scream. She kept her eyes closed and opened her mouth in a large *O* and screamed from her very gut. She kept screaming, as Rhiv of Skeda was assimilated and her children placed in stasis tanks. As To-Do-Ka and Zarmuk and Shrri underwent the same ordeal. As one after the other of innocents were ripped from their lives and transformed into Borg. She felt the deaths of their personalities, sometimes the deaths of their physical bodies as well. They marched on in a merciless line, hundreds—no, thousands—of them. Their

218

faces, their histories, their loves and losses and dreams were inextricably part of her and her body and mind writhed in agony as she died again and again.

Through the pain she heard voices, felt the warm press of hands, even of lips on her sweat-slicked forehead. She was told that she, Seven of Nine, was cared about, was safe, had value.

She didn't even recognize the name.

She was no one, and everyone. Designations meant nothing, and everything. She screamed until her voice was gone and even after that silent, heaving gasps erupted from her belly.

# CHAPTER 7

# Friendship Bonds in Classic Star Trek

ONE OF STAR TREK'S MOST ENDURING THEMES IS THE IMPORTANCE OF friendship. The Star Trek crew members were more than co-workers; they were each other's friends and family, and they were closer to each other than to blood family members. More than a few Star Trek novels have explored the depth and breadth of these friendship bonds, but some stories are exceptional.

## *The Lost Years,* by J. M. Dillard

*The Lost Years,* by J. M. Dillard, is one of those exceptional stories. It filled part of the empty years between the end of the first five-year mission of the *Enterprise* under Captain Kirk and *TMP* and told what happened to Kirk, Spock, and McCoy. It was the first of a four-book continuing story of the crew's experiences during those years. *The Lost Years* was followed by *A Flag Full of Stars,* by Brad Ferguson, *Traitor Winds,* by L. A. Graf, and *Recovery,* by J. M. Dillard. *The Lost Years* began upon the return of the *Enterprise* from its five-year mission. Shortly thereafter, Kirk accepted promotion to admiral, McCoy departed for Yonada to visit Natira, and Spock began a teaching assignment at the Vulcan Science Academy. McCoy later went to Vulcan when his plans with Natira did not work out and became involved in an incident that could have destroyed the Federation. Although McCoy and Spock prevailed against the enemy that threatened Vulcan and the Federation, victory came at a high cost and the loss of an innocent life. Devastated by that loss, Spock turned to the *Kolinahr,* Kirk returned to life in the admiralty, and McCoy decided to research the Fabrini medical data for its practical applications. At the story's poignant end, the three were separated, and Spock was estranged from Kirk. Spock's good-bye to McCoy was heartbreaking.

In this excerpt from *The Lost Years,* Spock tried to make Kirk understand that he did not want a captaincy of his own and believed that Kirk would be pressured into accepting promotion to admiral; Spock thereafter took his leave from Kirk and McCoy.

AUSTERELY ELEGANT IN HIS BLUE DRESS TUNIC, SPOCK STEPPED ONTO THE turbolift with the captain. The others, as if picking up on the fact that the captain might have a few things to discuss with his first officer, remained on the bridge to shut down their stations.

Kirk spoke the instant the lift doors closed. "Spock, I want you to know that I've sponsored your promotion to captain. It should come through in a matter of days."

Spock opened his mouth and drew in a breath as if to reply, but Jim didn't give him a chance. He'd expected a protest—the Vulcan had often enough voiced his lack of desire to command. "Look, Spock, there's no need to repeat that business about not wanting a ship of your own. You *deserve* it—you've earned it—and a newly commissioned research vessel, the *Grissom,* is in need of a captain. I've recommended you for the job."

Spock stared ahead at the turbolift doors for a few seconds, apparently weighing his answer. At last he turned his head to regard Kirk with sober dark eyes. "I appreciate the gesture, Captain."

Jim waited for more; when it did not come, he frowned. "You appreciate the gesture . . . but *what,* Spock? Don't you have any opinion on the matter?"

Spock blinked and looked back at the lift doors. His long, angular face was composed in an entirely inscrutable, unemotional expression, but Kirk got a fleeting impression of mulish stubbornness. Spock was not in the mood to discuss it because he'd already made up his mind, and that was that. "I shall . . . consider it, along with another offer."

Kirk felt a surge of surprised irritation. Was *everything* at Scheduling being done behind his back? "What offer? No one at Starfleet mentioned the possibility of your receiving another assignment."

Spock's coal-black brows rose slightly as he half-turned his head to glance at the captain. "An assignment as an instructor at Starfleet

Academy. The information is available from the Detailer's office."
He hesitated. "Did you ask?"

"No, but—" Kirk broke off and tried to return to the topic the
Vulcan had so successfully led him away from. "Look, Spock, the
point is that it makes no sense to stagnate where you are. Command
is a challenge—but you've learned a lot over the past five years. You'd
make a damn fine captain, whether you'll admit it or not. It's the best
thing for your career—"

"Captain." There was the faintest tinge of irritation in the first
officer's voice as he turned to face Kirk, but it disappeared before
Kirk could be certain he'd really detected it. "My desire to remain at
my present rank has nothing whatsoever to do with a lack of
confidence as to my fitness for command. And while I appreciate
your concern for my career, I remain somewhat puzzled by your
insistence on my promotion. I respectfully point out that *you* are in
the same position as I at the moment—under pressure to accept a
promotion you do not want. I am frankly at a loss to understand your
reasoning, as you yourself have requested a lateral career move, to the
captaincy of the *Victorious.*"

Kirk felt a flush of warmth in his neck and face. "I haven't told
anyone except the Detailer about that. How did you find out?"

"I asked," Spock replied simply. "Such things are public record."
The turbolift began to slow. "May I speak openly, Captain?"

Kirk reached out for the control and brought the lift to a halt. "I
wouldn't have it otherwise. You know that, Spock."

"Then may I know why you have not requested me as first officer
aboard the *Victorious?*" Spock's deep-set eyes narrowed slightly as he
studied Kirk's reaction to the question.

*I'll be damned,* Kirk realized with amazement. *He's angry about it.*
"I already told you, Spock—it wouldn't be fair for me to hold your
career back. If I requested you as my first officer, it would be a purely
selfish move on my part. And I was afraid your sense of loyalty
wouldn't let you put what's best for you foremost."

A shallow crease appeared between Spock's upward-slanting
brows. "You are making the assumption, Captain, that what is best
for my career is also best for me. However, you do not make the same
misguided assumption in your own case. Why did *you* refuse promotion?"

Kirk didn't have to consider the answer for even a second.
"Because I'm doing what I love best. I want to be in the middle of the
action, not stuck behind some desk as an administrator—"

"And *I,*" Spock countered, "am a scientist. As science officer aboard a starship, I am constantly exposed to new life-forms, new scientific discoveries—it is an opportunity for field research which is unparalleled. I therefore submit that my request to continue to serve as your first officer and science officer is quite reasonable."

"I understand that. But the *Grissom* is a research vessel—" Jim began, but he knew his line of attack was doomed to failure.

"If I were science officer aboard her, the scientific opportunity would be an excellent one. However, a captain's duties do not permit the luxury of research."

"Mr. Spock, I can't withdraw my recommendation—"

"I quite understand, Captain. But I wanted you to understand why I shall most likely refuse it . . . if Starfleet decides to permit me, which I believe it shall, considering the other option it provided me with."

Kirk acknowledged defeat with a sigh. "Understood, Spock—and no hard feelings." He smiled grimly. "Actually, after arguing with Fortenberry and Admiral Morrow the past few weeks, it's refreshing to talk to someone who shares my point of view about a promotion to the admiralty." He paused. "That is, assuming you feel I'm justified in refusing one."

"You would be foolish," the Vulcan said deliberately, "to accept it. Your temperament ill suits you for an administrative assignment."

"You make it sound like a personal failure, but I'll take it as a backhanded compliment. And I'll remember that when I talk to Fortenberry. I was just on my way to talk to him. Since you've obviously been in touch with him, then you also know I still haven't received my orders."

Spock gave a nod.

"Opinion. What are they trying to pull by delaying my orders?"

"My best hypothesis is that they intend to pressure you into accepting the promotion—but as to what precise action they intend to take in order to do so, I am at a loss."

Kirk touched the control. So . . . he wasn't being paranoid after all. A very small relief compared to the greater worry of being right. The lift began to move again, very slowly, then eased to a halt. "My thoughts exactly. Not that pressure will do them any good—I can play that game as well as they can."

Spock tilted his head, puzzled. "I scarcely see what pressure you could bring to bear on Starfleet Command—with the sole exception of threatening them with your resignation."

"If necessary, that is exactly what I intend to do."

The lift doors opened. "Then by all means, Captain," Spock

223

replied slowly, "I suggest you prepare yourself for the possibility of having to carry out your threat." He stepped out into the corridor.

Startled, Kirk watched him go. "It won't come to that," Jim said, more to himself than to Spock. He stepped from the lift before the doors closed over him.

He caught up to the Vulcan. "It won't come to that," he repeated, more loudly this time.

Spock glanced sideways at him with hooded eyes. "Perhaps not," he said, but his tone was noncommittal. He did not speak again until he arrived at the door to his quarters, where he stopped and turned to face Kirk. "I have . . . deeply appreciated the opportunity to serve under you, Captain. It is my hope to do so again."

"I guarantee it," Kirk said emphatically, but as the Vulcan disappeared behind the door to his quarters, Jim found himself wondering whether he would be able to keep that promise.

The doctor was in the middle of a dead sleep when the buzzer woke him. "What the devil . . . ?"

He struggled to a sitting position and waited, gasping, for the mental fog to lift enough for him to understand where he was and what had just happened. He and Jim had stayed up late the night before, drinking—an entirely morose experience, given the captain's mood; the more cognac Jim had, the more vehemently he swore never to give up the captaincy—and although McCoy had had the good sense to take a pill before retiring, to diminish the effects of the alcohol, he still felt hungover, as if his tongue and brain were swaddled in cotton. It had been a rough night; he'd awakened several times from anxious dreams of Natira . . . and at least once, bolted upright in bed, pulse racing, fully alert a split second after waking, a single thought circling his brain:

*Am I doing the right thing?*

Of course he was. He'd always known he'd return to Natira someday, and that she'd be waiting for him. There had never been any doubt in his mind.

At least, none that he'd known about. He hadn't been able to go to sleep after that, not for hours; finally, when it was almost morning, he'd drifted off, exhausted.

Now the buzzer sounded a second time. McCoy rose grumbling, found his pants, and for decorum's sake pulled them over his underwear, then gave his black T-shirt a couple of mindless tucks so that it hung half-in, half-out of his pants. He staggered toward the door.

"Now, who in Hades would have the nerve to wake people up at this ungodly hour—" McCoy pressed the lock release without thinking to ask who was there. The doors slid open.

Spock stood in the doorway. McCoy scowled and rubbed his burning eyes with a fist.

"Good Lord, Spock." It came out a low growl; McCoy coughed in an effort to get his voice working again. "What are you doing up?"

"It is ten o'clock in the morning," Spock said evenly. There was something inexplicably odd in hearing him say *ten o'clock in the morning* and not *ten hundred hours.* McCoy blinked and realized that the Vulcan was dressed in civilian clothes, a sight which made the doctor's mind, if not his tired body, do a double take.

"Ten o'clock in the morning," McCoy repeated. For a moment, he was too confused to make sense of it.

Spock prompted patiently, "I have come to say good-bye."

It struck him then; like Jim, Spock was taking six months' leave before returning to duty. There was a very real chance that McCoy would never see the Vulcan again. He felt a painful and—because it was Spock—embarrassing tightening of his throat. "Oh. Well," he said. "Guess we won't be seeing each other for a long time, will we?"

Spock gazed at him steadily without answering. If the Vulcan felt any discomfort at the potential emotionality of the moment, he did not show it.

McCoy shifted his bare feet awkwardly and cleared his throat. "Look, Spock, I know I've teased you a lot over the years, and maybe we've had a few serious arguments, but I want you to know that in spite of it all . . . Well, hell." He thrust out his hand thoughtlessly, from sheer instinct. When he realized what he had done, he tried to pull it back.

If Spock's Vulcan sensibilities were offended by the doctor's bad manners, he did not show it. He took the proffered hand briefly, then let it go. His grip was strong, warm to the point of feeling feverish. "In spite of our philosophical disagreements, Doctor, I have a great deal of respect for you."

That did it. McCoy felt himself choking up, and was angry at himself for doing so. He cleared his throat a few more times and hoped Spock wouldn't notice the film of tears in his eyes. He did not speak until he was absolutely certain he had control.

"Good-bye, Spock," he said quietly, and then, unable to contain his exasperation: "Dammit all to hell, I think that of everyone, I'm going to miss you most."

225

Spock smiled without smiling—something McCoy had seen him do once or twice before, and damned if he knew how the Vulcan did it; something with the eyes, maybe—and nodded ever so slightly in acknowledgment. "Live long and prosper, Doctor."

He turned and walked away down the corridor. McCoy watched him for a while and then withdrew to his quarters to wipe an errant tear and swear at himself for sniffling. He couldn't really help it; he had the strangest feeling he would never see the Vulcan again.

The atmosphere aboard the *Enterprise* was one of muted sadness in comparison to the previous day's gaiety. Most of the crew were gone now, so that the ship began to take on an empty, deserted feel. Those still aboard struggled with suitcases as they murmured good-byes, some of them in civilian clothing, headed at a leisurely pace for shore leave, others still in uniform, dashing to make the shuttle to their next assignment.

Jim Kirk stepped, suitcase in hand, from his quarters into the corridor and very nearly collided with his first officer.

"Spock." Jim stepped back. "I thought you had already gone." He had made his farewells the night before, and this morning had hoped to slip out unseen. Last night had drained him, and he had slept little after the confrontation with Nogura, a scene he replayed in his mind a thousand times, each time trying to figure out what he should have said, *could* have said to the admiral that would have changed the outcome, that would have guaranteed him the *Victorious* . . . and each time, failing.

"I was just leaving." The Vulcan wore a dark blue tunic of Vulcan style and cut; he paused, his expression guarded as he apparently considered the best phrasing for what he had come to say. "But I must admit, Captain, that I am curious."

Jim did not smile, but his tone lightened. "That does seem to be a characteristic of yours, Mr. Spock. Let me guess. You came to ask about Nogura."

"Yes. I understand he came aboard for a brief time yesterday afternoon."

The lightness vanished. "He did," Jim said. "They're putting pressure on me to accept the admiralty—nothing you and I didn't talk about yesterday, really. Nogura asked me why I didn't want a promotion to flag rank, and I told him. When he told me why he wanted to promote me, I threatened to quit; he asked me to reconsider. Told me to take time and think it over while I'm on leave." Jim saw that he was still clutching the suitcase, and set it down.

"Will you?" Spock asked.

He frowned, not following. "Will I what?"

"Think it over. Reconsider."

"No." Jim shook his head firmly, his lips thinning at the very thought. "I stand by what I said to you yesterday, Spock. If I have to resign my commission—"

Spock was gazing implacably at him; Jim averted his eyes. He'd almost said, *and join the border patrol, or become a commercial captain,* but both alternatives were impossible to voice, much less seriously consider. Jim couldn't really believe Nogura would push him that far. Was he being conceited, deluding himself to think that Starfleet would never risk losing him, that Starfleet needed him so badly—in whatever capacity—that they would let him call the shots? He forced himself to look Spock in the eye.

"—then, dammit, I will. And my answer will be the same six months from now."

"I see," Spock said.

"And what about you, Spock?" After last night, Jim was tired of fielding questions about his uncertain future, eager to let someone else do the talking. Besides, in the Vulcan's case, he was honestly curious. "Have you made up your mind yet?"

"No. However, six months is more than sufficient time in which to reach a decision."

"It is indeed," Kirk said. "And I hope you'll consider what I said about the *Grissom.*"

"I will. And if that is all, Captain, then I will again wish you farewell."

"Not exactly 'farewell,' Spock. 'Good-bye,' maybe, or 'till we meet again.' We'll be seeing each other in six months or so." He did not let himself say, *God willing.* Jim smiled, a grim little smile. "Give my regards to your parents."

"I shall. Good-bye, Jim."

"Take care, Spock."

They did not, as they had done last night, shake hands, nor speak formally of the privilege it had been for each to serve with the other. Spock nodded briefly and turned to go back toward his quarters.

Jim did not watch him go. He picked up his suitcase and headed briskly in the opposite direction. He did not, he told himself firmly, feel at all sad to be leaving his first officer, or the *Enterprise.*

After all, it wasn't really good-bye.

227

# *Crossover,* by Michael Jan Friedman

*Crossover* is a terrific story in which the old gang, minus Kirk, have one last grand adventure. Spock and his Romulan students were betrayed by a spy in their midst and arrested by Romulan authorities. Although at first the Romulans were not aware that their captive was Spock, Starfleet knew immediately and was concerned that Spock's knowledge of Federation secrets would fall into the hands of the Romulans. Captain Picard was ordered to resolve the situation, and Starfleet assigned Admiral Dr. McCoy to the *Enterprise* as advisor. In the meantime, Captain Montgomery Scott learned of Spock's capture and, in a gesture worthy of James T. Kirk, stole a starship to ride to Spock's rescue. In their efforts to play galactic cowboy to rescue Spock, both McCoy and Scotty found that old tricks no longer worked as well as they once had. However, when their old tricks did not achieve the expected results, both listened to the *TNG Enterprise* crew and proved that old dogs can learn new tricks.

In this selection from *Crossover,* McCoy and Scotty each received word of Spock's capture and jumped into action to try to save him.

A LIGHT TAP WAS ALL THAT WAS REQUIRED TO ROUSE THE ADMIRAL FROM his nap. When he opened his eyes, he saw Captain Drake's slightly embarrassed face hovering over him.

McCoy was used to the look, but didn't feel any embarrassment himself. If he needed or wanted to sleep, he'd damned well do it. At his age, he had learned to listen carefully to his body's whims.

"Admiral," said Drake, "there's a Priority One message for you from Starfleet Command."

McCoy felt a chill. *Someone's died,* he thought.

"You can take it in my ready room," Drake offered.

"Thanks," McCoy grunted automatically.

As he got up, he noticed for the first time how painfully silent the room had become. No one was talking—they were too busy looking at him.

"As you were," he told them. "Don't stop on my account."

Exiting the conference room, the admiral couldn't shake his sense of dread. One of the few regrets he had on reaching 145 was that he'd lived to see so many friends kick the bucket.

Through the years, he'd received "the call" more times than he wanted to remember. He had developed a peculiar sixth sense about it—an ability to recognize it with uncanny accuracy.

Now, as he crossed the bridge escorted by Captain Drake, he didn't permit himself to think about who it might be. Still, the feeling of horror was stronger than it had been in the past.

Whatever the message was about, he didn't want to hear it. Yet, at the same time, he couldn't turn away.

Entering the captain's ready room, he allowed himself to be guided around Drake's desk.

"Please sit down, Admiral," the captain said softly.

"No," McCoy said simply. "Thanks," he added as an afterthought. "If it's all the same to you, I'll stand."

Drake nodded. "If you need me, I'll be on the bridge," he said. Then he left the room.

McCoy paused only for a moment to put his hands down on the desk in front of him. He could feel the familiar tremor in his arms as they helped to support his weight.

"Computer," he said, "please relay message for McCoy, Leonard H., Admiral, to this station."

Without delay, the small screen in front of him produced an image of Admiral Keaton. Keaton was highly placed in Starfleet security and posted to Command headquarters on Earth. The fact that she was relaying the information personally told McCoy that whatever the message was, it was important.

"Admiral McCoy," she said curtly.

McCoy responded with a nod. "Admiral Keaton."

Her expression changed. "I have some bad news," she told him. "It relates to Federation security, but it's of direct interest to you personally." A pause. "It appears your former colleague and friend, Ambassador Spock—"

"Has been killed," McCoy finished for her, realizing he'd been right all along. Ice water trickled down his pine. "How?" he asked.

The admiral shot him a quizzical look before she spoke again. "No, Admiral McCoy. You misunderstand. To the best of our knowledge, Ambassador Spock is still alive. That is why we have a security problem."

Keaton gave him a second, even more quizzical look.

"Why did you think he was dead?" she asked.

McCoy could feel the tightness in his chest release a notch. He took a breath, let it out.

"Doctor's intuition," he replied. "So . . . what's Spock done to make himself a security problem?"

She frowned. "What I'm about to tell you is highly classified,

Admiral. Only people with Priority One clearance are privy to this information, and even then it's released strictly on a need-to-know basis."

"I understand," McCoy replied.

But he was thinking: *I was wrong about "the call."* That had never happened before.

It figured that Spock would give him a scare like that over nothing. Despite his annoyance with his old comrade, he couldn't help but feel a tide of relief wash over him.

Apparently, that pig-headed Vulcan had gotten himself into some kind of hot water. That was all right. McCoy had seen Spock overcome the odds before.

Too stubborn to die, the admiral thought. Like *me.*

"Ambassador Spock," Keaton explained, "has been involved in a private, covert operation on the planet Romulus for the last few years. He's working with a small group of Romulan insurgents called unificationists, who—"

"—are seeking a reconciliation and reunification with the planet Vulcan," McCoy remarked. "I've heard of them. But I'm surprised that Spock would get himself mixed up with a bunch of pie-in-the-sky idealists."

McCoy made a note to put that question to Spock when next he saw the Vulcan.

"I will assume he had a logical reason," Keaton responded. "In any case, Spock was among a group of unificationists who were recently taken prisoner on one of the Romulan Empire's outer worlds. A place called Constanthus."

McCoy leaned forward. "Taken prisoner?"

*Damn that Spock.* His feeling of relief died aborning.

"Do the Romulans know who they've got?" he asked.

Keaton shook her head. "No. The communications we've been able to intercept show they're so far unaware of it. However, if and when they *do* find out, we're facing a security breach that could be a most serious threat to the Federation."

The implications of Spock's capture were very clear to McCoy. As an admiral, he had learned more about Federation security than he had wanted to know.

He knew that if the wrong person fell into hostile hands it could be disastrous. Unfortunately, Spock was very *much* the wrong person. His Vulcan mind was like a steel trap, full of secrets the Federation couldn't afford to see exposed.

"What's the plan to get him out?" McCoy asked.

Though he would later decide that he must have been mistaken, for a moment McCoy was sure that Keaton had squirmed at the question. And he had never seen her squirm before.

"We're dispatching a Galaxy-class vessel to the Romulan Neutral Zone," she told him. "We would like you to join them, as an expert on Ambassador Spock. No one alive knows him better than you do."

McCoy was surprised. But the more he thought about it, the more sense it made. After all, he *did* know Spock better than anyone.

"Of course," he responded. "I'll be glad to help however I can."

She nodded. "Good. The coordinates have already been forwarded to Captain Drake. You will rendezvous with the Galaxy-class ship I spoke of. Only you and the senior officers on board will know that Spock is in the custody of the Romulan Empire. This briefing and the one being given to those officers are being sent with the most sophisticated coding available to Starfleet today. I expect everyone involved to take all possible precautions."

Admiral Keaton eyed McCoy intensely.

"Let me remind you once again that secrecy is our greatest weapon here, Admiral. It must be maintained at all costs."

McCoy bristled at that. He hadn't reached his rank and age without a clear understanding of security.

"Thank you," he told her. "I know what a Priority One classification means. After all, I had that rating when you were still a plebe at the Academy."

McCoy made no effort to soften his tone, letting his displeasure show. Technically speaking, he didn't outrank Keaton, but he had certainly lived a damned sight longer than she had.

His words and tone had their desired effect. Keaton looked contrite. Or anyway, as contrite as McCoy expected she had ever looked.

"Of course," she said. "I didn't mean to suggest—"

"Fine, fine," McCoy cut her off. "Now, what's the name of the ship that I'm meeting?"

Keaton paused for a moment, as if she were delivering important news.

"It's the *U.S.S. Enterprise.*"

Montgomery Scott was sleeping when the call came, and he was still groggy when he reached the computer console. He had spent a long night reconfiguring the warp engines of his shuttlecraft.

The net result of his work was only a minimal increase in engine efficiency. Still, he had taken pleasure in getting any increase at all, after the computer had told him the system could not be improved even marginally—and definitely not, the computer pointed out, using the configuration Scotty had planned for it.

He activated the computer screen with a tap of his controls—and straightened when he saw why the computer had flagged him. It was a Priority One communication, heavily encrypted. Holding his breath, the engineer waited to see if the computer would be able to decode it.

It had been a simple matter to program his computer to scan subspace messages and news services for information that interested him. Among the subjects it was programmed to flag were a select group of names.

Doctor—nay, Admiral—McCoy was on that list. So was Captain Spock—or Ambassador Spock, as he was known these days. Of course, most of the information Scotty's computer scanned was on open public and Starfleet channels.

Coded messages were more difficult—he was no Uhura when it came to deciphering such things. However, Scotty knew that a number of the codes Starfleet used were based on engineering protocols.

As a result, he'd designed and added circuits to the communications system that looked for codes based on these same principles and then interpreted them based on Scotty's personal data base. The Priority One code that contained this particular message was based on the shifting harmonics of warp field physics.

After a long moment, the message finally came through, allowing him to eavesdrop on it. He smiled at the sight of Doctor McCoy, though he didn't know the woman on the other end.

Then Scotty heard the news Keaton was bringing, and his smile faded. He leaned back heavily into his padded chair.

Spock was in danger. Grave danger.

Even if the Romulans never found out the Vulcan's true identity, Romulan justice was swift and sure. And in the Romulan Empire, there was only one punishment for treason.

Scotty knew that the Federation was in a difficult position. It couldn't launch a full-scale attack to retrieve one man.

And even if such a thing were possible, it wouldn't work. Spock would be tried, convicted, and punished long before forces could be mobilized.

A smaller-scale rescue would have a little better chance, but a Starfleet vessel would never get very far into the Romulan Empire. This time, it seemed to Scotty, Spock would not escape death or have anyone there to help him cheat it.

The thought left him cold. Scotty felt he was listening to the death knell of someone he'd once believed was indestructible.

That, of course, was at a time when he was young—when they all were young. When they firmly believed their adventures would go on forever.

In those days, Scotty had been known as a miracle worker—though in truth, the engineer and his friends had accomplished their miracles together. Still, he'd believed that anything was possible.

Maybe in those days something could have been done for Spock. But Montgomery Scott had lived too long and seen too much to believe that anymore. In any case, he was alone now, and there was certainly nothing he could do by himself.

Scotty shook his head sadly. This time, there was no hope. None at all.

Unless . . .

No.

It would never work. . . .

Absolutely not.

. . . even if there was time.

And then Scotty felt that rush of ideas that never seemed to come on call, but always managed to appear when absolutely necessary.

Checking the navigational computer, he saw that he could cover the distance in a reasonable time—possibly even quickly enough to save Spock.

But there were too many variables. Too many things the engineer didn't know and couldn't plan for.

Scotty quit that line of thinking, deeming it unproductive. He wouldn't bother to calculate the odds; he could guess that they would be very high. And, in any case, the decision was already made.

He reset the shuttle's course. Starbase 178 and what he needed were twelve hours away, and he had a lot of work to do before he arrived.

Captain Jean-Luc Picard sat down behind the sleek, dark desk in his ready room and tapped the padd on his control panel.

The monitor in front of him displayed the long, weather-worn face of a Starfleet commodore. Picard didn't normally hear from such a person unless the circumstances were grim.

233

"There's no easy way to say this, Captain." Commodore Edrich frowned, emphasizing the deep lines already in his face. "It's Ambassador Spock. He's been captured with a group of unification-ists on one of the Romulan Empire's outer worlds. A place called Constanthus—literally, *Crossover*, for its position halfway between Romulus and the Neutral Zone."

Picard's mouth went dry. Spock . . .

"Do they know who he is?" he asked.

Edrich shook his head. "Not yet—so time is of the essence. That's why we're dispatching a consultant to help you. Someone who knows Spock like the back of his hand."

Picard shifted uneasily in his chair. "A consultant," he echoed.

The commodore nodded. "His name is McCoy. Admiral Leonard McCoy. He and Spock—"

"I know who he is," Picard interrupted. "And I know his relation-ship to Spock." Better than anyone could possibly guess, Picard mused.

"Then our business is finished. I am forwarding the rendezvous coordinates and formal orders to your ship," Edrich said. "Good luck, Captain."

Picard nodded. "Thank you," he replied.

With that, Edrich disappeared from the monitor.

The captain turned away from the blank screen to consider the stars outside his ready-room windows.

*Time is a path from the past to the future and back again. The present is the crossroads of both.* He wondered at the simplicity and wisdom of Surak's words.

In the past, he had traveled into the Romulan Empire to find Spock and to determine the ambassador's reason for being there. Then, as now, Federation security had been at stake. Picard's orders had been to determine whether Ambassador Spock had turned to the Romulan side.

Undercover on Romulus, Picard had found Spock and discovered the Vulcan's work in the reunification movement. In the course of events, Picard had been able to help Spock—though truthfully, they had helped each other.

But that was in the past, when the Vulcan was living freely, if secretly, on the Romulan homeworlds. Now the ambassador was a prisoner of the Empire—a different matter entirely.

Picard felt his past and future with Spock merging into the same moment—the crossroads that Surak had identified as the present. In

234

his mind, Picard despaired for the future of Ambassador Spock, the man who had helped shape the Federation's destiny and who had touched Picard's mind as well as his life.

Knowing that his options and the time to act would be severely limited, Picard could only resolve to honor the man and—whatever happened—to do his duty.

# CHAPTER 8

# Heroes Under Fire

STAR TREK AT ITS BEST IS A HERO'S STORY. STAR TREK IS ABOUT PEOPLE OF courage and conviction who are willing to sacrifice everything, including their very lives, to achieve a greater good. Our crews are people who strive against impossible odds to save their friends, their crewmates, and the lives and freedom of countless billions. Our heroes share the nobility of every hero in human history who has sacrificed his or her life to save another or who has risked everything to achieve something greater than himself. These are people who do what they have to do in the face of imminent death.

In *TWOK,* Spock gave up his life to save the lives of his friends. In *Star Trek III: The Search for Spock,* to save his friend, Kirk risked his entire career and his life, and he sacrificed his beloved ship. Again and again, the original crew risked everything to save the universe as they knew it. The *TNG* crew followed in their footsteps, even ultimately chasing the Borg into Earth's past to save human history. Sisko and his crew fought the Dominion to save everything they knew. Janeway destroyed the Caretaker's array and stranded her crew in the Delta Quadrant to save the Ocampa from the Kazon, even though she could have used the array to get back home. Starfleet captains and crews see beyond themselves and understand that some things are worth the ultimate sacrifice.

The theme of courage under fire resonates through the Star Trek novels. Among the best stories of heroes under fire are *Invasion! Book Three: Time's Enemy,* by L. A. Graf, *Fallen Heroes,* by Daffyd ab Hugh, and *The Rings of Tautee,* by Dean Wesley Smith and Kristine Kathryn Rusch.

# Invasion! Book Three: Time's Enemy, by L. A. Graf

*Time's Enemy* begins with the *Defiant* being found encased in ice in the far reaches of our solar system, apparently having been there for five thousand years. The *Defiant* appeared to have been caught in a battle that threw it into the past, and most of the crew died in the battle. Others lived but were trapped in the far distant past. Dr. Bashir kept the Dax symbiont alive in a stasis tank and forced himself to stay alive through many lonely years to keep the symbiont company. The symbiont remained alive through five thousand empty years because it had to survive to tell the story and prevent disaster for the Alpha Quadrant.

The threat of disaster drove the story, which moved relentlessly onward from the opening pages. This is a true "can't put it down" sort of book, and the reader's growing feeling of horror and inevitability increases as the pace of the story advances. *Time's Enemy* is the story of how the Furies were driven out of the Alpha Quadrant. The new threat to the Quadrant was more frightening even than the Dominion. The alien mass consumed all life it encountered in a relentless quest for new DNA, and the sentient minds eaten by it remained conscious within the mass. At the novel's climax, the reader is struck by the realization of the incredible sacrifice made by Jadzia, the Dax symbiont, and all the other sentient minds still conscious within the alien life-form. The *Defiant* crew gave their lives heroically in the final battle in the past, and Jadzia Dax gave up the freedom of true death, to save everyone in the Alpha Quadrant from the threat of the Furies' enemies. I read the ultimate scenes through a veil of tears, but I could not pull myself away, nor did I want to.

*Time's Enemy* is a genuine story of heroes under fire. The passages I have selected include first, the opening pages, and second, the scene that revealed the true nature of the sacrifice of Jadzia and her symbiont Dax.

OUT HERE WHERE SUNLIGHT WAS A FARAWAY GLIMMER IN THE BLACKNESS OF *space, ice lasted a long time. Dark masses of it littered a wide orbital ring, all that remained of the spinning nebula that had birthed this planet-rich system. The cold outer dark sheltered each fragment in safety, unless some chance grazing of neighbors ejected one of them into the unyielding pull of solar gravity. Then the mass of dirty ice would begin its long journey toward the distant sun, past the captured ninth planet, past the four gas giants, past the ring of rocky fragments that memorialized a planet never born. By that point it would have begun to glow, brushed into brilliance by the gathering heat of the sun's nuclear furnace. When it passed the cold red desert planet and approached the cloud-feathered planet that harbored life, it would be brighter than any star. Its flare would pierce that planet's blue sky, stirring brief wonder from the primitive tribes who hunted and gathered and scratched at the earth with sticks to grow their food. In a few days, the comet's borrowed light would fade, and the tumbling ice would start its long journey back to the outer dark.*

*One fragment had escaped that fate, although it shouldn't have. It carried a burden of steel and empty space, buried just deep enough in its icy heart to send it spinning back into the cloud of fellow comets after its near-collision with another. For centuries afterward, it danced an erratic path through the ice-littered darkness before it settled into a stable orbit in the shadow of the tiny ninth planet. More centuries passed while dim fires glowed on the night side of the bluish globe that harbored life. The fires slowly brightened and spread, leaping across its vast oceans. They brightened faster after that, merging to form huge networks of light that outlined every coast and lake and river. Then the fires leaped into the ocean of space. Out to the planet's single moon at first, then later to its cold, red neighbor, then to the moons of the gas giants, and finally out beyond all of them to the stars. In all those long centuries, nothing disturbed the comet and its anomalous burden. No one saw the tiny, wavering light that lived inside.*

*Until a fierce blast of phaser fire ripped the icy shroud open, and exposed what lay within.*

"It looks like they're preparing for an invasion," Jadzia Dax said.

Sisko grunted, gazing out at the expanse of dark-crusted cometary ice that formed the natural hull of Starbase One. Above the curving ice horizon, the blackness of Earth's Oort cloud should have glittered with bright stars and the barely brighter glow of the distant sun. Instead, what it glittered with were the docking lights of a dozen short-range attack ships—older and more angular versions of the *Defiant*—as well as the looming bulk of two Galaxy-class starships, the *Mukaikubo* and the *Breedlove*. One glance had told Sisko that such a gathering of force couldn't have been the random result of ship refittings and shore leaves. Starfleet was preparing for a major encounter with someone. He just wished he knew who.

"I thought we came here to deal with a *non*military emergency." In the sweep of transparent aluminum windows, Sisko could see Julian Bashir's dark reflection glance up from the chair he'd sprawled in after a glance at the view. Beyond the doctor, the huge conference room was as empty as it had been ten minutes ago when they'd first been escorted into it. "Otherwise, wouldn't Admiral Hayman have asked us to come in the *Defiant* instead of a high-speed courier?"

Sisko snorted. "Admirals never *ask* anything, Doctor. And they never tell you any more than you need to know to carry out their orders efficiently."

"Especially this admiral," Dax added, an unexpected note of humor creeping into her voice. Sisko raised an eyebrow at her, then heard a gravelly snort and the simultaneous hiss of the conference-room door opening. He swung around to see a rangy, long-boned figure in ordinary Starfleet coveralls crossing the room toward them. Dax surprised her by promptly stepping forward, hands outstretched in welcome.

"How have you been, Judith?"

"Promoted." The silver-haired woman's angular face lit with something approaching a sparkle. "It almost makes up for getting this old." She clasped Dax's hands warmly for a moment, then turned her attention to Sisko. "So this is the Benjamin Sisko Curzon told me so much about. It's a pleasure to finally meet you, Captain."

Sisko slanted a wary glance at his science officer. "Um—likewise, I'm sure. Dax?"

The Trill cleared her throat. "Benjamin, allow me to introduce you to Rear Admiral Judith Hayman. She and I—well, she and Curzon, actually—got to know each other on Vulcan during the Klingon peace negotiations several years ago. Judith, this is Captain Benjamin Sisko of *Deep Space Nine,* and our station's chief medical officer, Dr. Julian Bashir."

"Admiral." Bashir nodded crisply.

"Our orders said this was a Priority One Emergency," Sisko said. "I assume that means whatever you brought us here to do is urgent."

Hayman's strong face lost its smile. "Possibly," she said. "Although perhaps not urgent in the way we usually think of it."

Sisko scowled. "Forgive my bluntness, Admiral, but I've been dragged from my command station without explanation, ordered not to use my own ship under any circumstances, brought to the oldest and least useful starbase in the Federation—" He made a gesture of reined-in impatience at the bleak cometary landscape outside the windows. "—and you're telling me you're not sure how *urgent* this problem is?"

"No one is sure, Captain. That's part of the reason we brought you here." The admiral's voice chilled into something between grimness and exasperation. "What we *are* sure of is that we could be facing potential disaster." She reached into the front pocket of her coveralls and tossed two ordinary-looking data chips onto the conference table. "The first thing I need you and your medical officer to do is review these data records."

"Data records," Sisko repeated, trying for the noncommittal tone he'd perfected over years of trying to deal with the equally high-handed and inexplicable behavior of Kai Winn.

"Admiral, forgive us, but we assumed this actually *was* an emergency." Julian Bashir broke in with such polite bafflement that Sisko guessed he must be emulating Garak's unctous demeanor. "If so, we could have reviewed your data records ten hours ago. All you had to do was send them to *Deep Space Nine* through subspace channels."

"Too dangerous, even using our most secure codes." The bleak certainty in Hayman's voice made Sisko blink in surprise. "And if you were listening, young man, you'd have noticed that I said this was the *first* thing I needed you to do. Now, would you please sit down, Captain?"

Sisko took the place she indicated at one of the conference table's inset data stations, then waited while she settled Bashir at the station on the opposite side. He noticed she made no attempt to seat Dax, although there were other empty stations available.

"This review procedure is not a standard one," Hayman said, without further preliminaries. "As a control on the validity of some data we've recently received, we're going to ask you to examine ship's logs and medical records without knowing their origin. We'd like your analysis of them. Computer, start data-review programs Sisko-One and Bashir-One."

Sisko's monitor flashed to life, not with pictures but with a thick ribbon of multilayered symbols and abbreviated words, slowly scrolling from left to right. He stared at it for a long, blank moment before a whisper of memory turned it familiar instead of alien. One of the things Starfleet Academy asked cadets to do was determine the last three days of a starship's voyage when its main computer memory had failed. The solution was to reconstruct computer records from each of the ship's individual system buffers—records that looked exactly like these.

"These are multiple logs of buffer output from individual ship systems, written in standard Starfleet machine code," he said. Dax made an interested noise and came to stand behind him. "It looks like someone downloaded the last commands given to life-support, shields, helm, and phaser-bank control. There's another system here, too, but I can't identify it."

"Photon-torpedo control?" Dax suggested, leaning over his shoulder to scrutinize it.

"I don't think so. It might be a sensor buffer." Sisko scanned the lines of code intently while they scrolled by. He could recognize more of the symbols now, although most of the abbreviations on the fifth line still baffled him. "There's no sign of navigations, either—the command buffers in those systems may have been destroyed by whatever took out the ship's main computer." Sisko grunted as four of the five logs recorded wild fluctuations and then degenerated into solid black lines. "And there goes everything else. Whatever hit this ship crippled it beyond repair."

Dax nodded. "It looks like some kind of EM pulse took out all of the ship's circuits—everything lost power except for life-support, and that had to switch to auxiliary circuits." She glanced up at the admiral. "Is that all the record we have, Admiral? Just those few minutes?"

"It's all the record we *trust,*" Hayman said enigmatically. "There are some visual bridge logs that I'll show you in a minute, but those could have been tampered with. We're fairly sure the buffer outputs weren't." She glanced up at Bashir, whose usual restless energy had focused down to a silent intensity of concentration on his own data screen. "The medical logs we found were much more extensive. You have time to review the buffer outputs again, if you'd like."

"Please," Sisko and Dax said in unison.

"Computer, repeat data program Sisko-One."

Machine code crawled across the screen again, and this time Sisko stopped trying to identify the individual symbols in it. He vaguely remembered one of his Academy professors saying that reconstructing a starship's movements from the individual buffer outputs of its systems was a lot like reading a symphony score. The trick was not to analyze each line individually, but to get a sense of how all of them were functioning in tandem.

"This ship was in a battle," he said at last. "But I think it was trying to escape, not fight. The phaser banks all show discharge immediately after power fluctuations are recorded for the shields."

"Defensive action," Dax agreed, and pointed at the screen. "And look at how much power they had to divert from life-support to keep the shields going. Whatever was after them was big."

"They're trying some evasive actions now—" Sisko broke off,

seeing something he'd missed the first time in that mysterious fifth line of code. Something that froze his stomach. It was the same Romulan symbol that appeared on his command board every time the cloaking device was engaged on the *Defiant.*

"This was a cloaked Starfleet vessel!" He swung around to fix the admiral with a fierce look. "My understanding was that only the *Defiant* had been sanctioned to carry a Romulan cloaking device!"

Hayman met his stare without a ripple showing in her calm competence. "I can assure you that Starfleet isn't running any unauthorized cloaking devices. Watch the log again, Captain Sisko."

He swung back to his monitor. "Computer, rerun data program Sisko-One at one-quarter speed," he said. The five concurrent logs crawled across the screen in slow motion, and this time Sisko focused on the coordinated interactions between the helm and the phaser banks. If he had any hope of identifying the class and generation of this starship, it would be from the tactical maneuvers it could perform.

"Time the helm changes versus the phaser bursts," Dax suggested from behind him in an unusually quiet voice. Sisko wondered if she was beginning to harbor the same ominous suspicion he was.

"I know." For the past hundred years, the speed of helm shift versus the speed of phaser refocus had been the basic determining factor of battle tactics. Sisko's gaze flickered from top line to third, counting off milliseconds by the ticks along the edge of the data record. The phaser refocus rates he found were startlingly fast, but far more chilling was the almost instantaneous response of this starship's helm in its tactical runs. There was only one ship he knew of that had the kind of overpowered warp engines needed to bring it so danger-ously close to the edge of survivable maneuvers. And there was only one commander who had used his spare time to perfect the art of skimming along the edge of that envelope, the way the logs told him this ship's commander had done.

This time when Sisko swung around to confront Judith Hayman, his concern had condensed into cold, sure knowledge. "Where did you find these records, Admiral?"

She shook her head. "Your analysis first, Captain. I need your unbiased opinion before I answer any questions or show you the visual logs. Otherwise, we'll never know for sure if this data can be trusted."

Sisko blew out a breath, trying to find words for conclusions he wasn't even sure he believed. "This ship—it wasn't just cloaked like the *Defiant.* It actually *was* the *Defiant.*" He heard Dax's indrawn breath. "And when it was destroyed in battle, the man commanding it was me."

*Rehk'resen.*

The alien word glowed like a spangle of light in the darkness, warmed Dax like a shivering flush of color melting its way through coils of translucent gel. In this floating state of barely liminal consciousness, it was all Dax knew, without even knowing what it meant. But remembering it was crucial. *Rehk'resen. Rehk'resen.*

Something tugged at Dax's awareness, in the vague nerveless way things happened in fever dreams. *Maybe I'm sleeping,* Dax thought. *Maybe I'm sick.* With an effort, Dax tried to crawl free of the floating numbness, and only succeeded in making the surrounding nothingness feel more like a tight, strangling shroud than the warm blanket it had been a moment before. *Maybe I've been drugged.*

The mental tugging came again, this time sharper and more electric, as if tiny circuits were plugging themselves directly in. Dax tried to focus on that feeling, tried to pin down what was happening. There was a familiar funneling rush, eerily similar to the rush that happened when a symbiont first connected to a brand-new host and began pouring itself in to share their brain. Except this time, what Dax's blind, encapsulated consciousness poured itself into wasn't a Trill brain trained and disciplined to receive it. It was utter chaos.

Mental links stretched out in all directions, linking to five thousand moving appendages, five hundred digestive systems, a thousand light-sensing organs all transmitting shared images like the faceted eyes of a bee, except that each of them saw something different. A warp exhaust, a portion of breached hull, a curve of duranium carapace . . . too many disparate images to make sense of. And hearing was no better. From every direction came the roar of hundreds of overlapping mental voices, some speaking, some screaming, some making only mindless animal grunts. Dax reeled under the cascade of random sensory input, choked on the wild schizophrenic explosion of voices. This was insane! What kind of host was this?

*Rehk'resen,* said an urgent internal voice, closer to Dax than all the rest. The alien word stirred a ghost of memory, like ashes floated by a vagrant breath of air. This was no host. This was an alien life-form, and Dax was here to do something to it, with it—but could not remember what!

". . . can't lower her isoboromine any more than that . . ."

". . . have to know whether the infiltration is working . . ."

Now, there was something different about *those* voices. Unlike the surrounding crash and babble of sound, those came from a more distant place, through the soothing swash and ripple of familiar Trill host-mind. Dax pulled back from the chaos of sight and sound that was the newly formed neural connections, and concentrated instead on the internal channel that seemed to link with someplace else.

". . . old man, can you hear me? Do you know where the symbiont is now?"

"Benjamin?"

With enormous effort, Dax opened what seemed to be someone else's eyes, and had a dizzying moment of seeing the clean lines of the *Defiant*'s bridge overlaid on jigsaw-puzzle insanity. The sight of the breached Jem'Hadar station on the viewscreen above her brought memory crashing back, cold and heavy as an avalanche. Her twinned symbiont had just been linked into the alien neural core on that station. Now it had to learn how to bend that group mind to her will and use the Jem'Hadar self-destruct code before it was too late.

*"Rehk'resen,"* she murmured, only vaguely aware of her own real voice above the fitful clamor around the symbiont. "That's the Jem'Hadar code for self-destruction."

"You with us again, old man?" A strong hand slid behind her head and turned it so she could blink muzzily up at Sisko's face. "What's happening on the station?"

"Symbiont is linked in . . ." She swallowed past an odd dryness in her throat, hoping it was just a side effect of all the medication Yevlin had been injecting her with and not a precursor of systemic host-symbiont shock. "How much time . . . ?"

Sisko's voice turned bleak. "Twelve minutes, maximum. The station's accelerated to point-oh-five of light."

"Can't tell time in there," Dax warned him. "You'd better keep us posted. . . ."

"Us?" Sisko demanded.

She nodded and closed her eyes. "The symbiont can't do this all by itself. I'm going back to help. . . ."

It was easier sliding back into the chaos of the alien group mind, now that she knew her own name and self and purpose. Dax felt herself merge into the familiar Trill symbiont-mind that was her ancient counterpart, feeling again its fierce millennia-old determination to stop the wormhole from rifting. She grounded herself in that shared emotion, then stretched her mind—their minds—out along the newly grown nerve pathways that bound her to the other mental entities trapped in this strangest of alien prisons.

244

"I am Dax of Starfleet! Who will join with me?" She launched the demand in Standard English like a quantum torpedo, using the mental force of three joined brains to power it through the babble of voices. It made a surprisingly loud explosion in the chaos, followed by a short, startled silence. Just as the random chatter began to rise again, she repeated the words in her own native language. The musical rise and fall of the Trill speak/song echoed down the neural network, and this time the silence lasted a little longer. Dax identified herself over and over again, first in Vulcan, then in Ferengi, then in Klingon—

"Dax of Starfleet!" It was a Ferengi voice, not far away, sounding half insane with frustration. Dax felt an electric crackle of power rush through her as another mind added its control of the network to hers. "I'll join with you, I'll do anything you want. Just get me out of here!"

"Dax of Starfleet!" A half-familiar Vulcan voice, echoed by others a little farther away. This time, the power surge was enormous but far more controlled, connecting to her through what felt like miles of precisely calibrated computer circuits. "If you're here to rescue the wormhole, the crew of the *Sreba* will join with you. We have already formed a network around the navigations controls. Tell us what we can do!"

"Dax of Starfleet!" It was a distant thunder of Klingon voices, their accent the archaic growl of a previous millennium but their lust for battle undiminished by their time inside the group mind. Dax felt the power of their joining roll through her like the shock wave of an earthquake. "Dax of Starfleet, wherever that kingdom is, you speak our language. We hold the territory near where the fires of hell burn brightest. Share with us your battle plans."

"Dax." The faint, tired whisper barely reached her, from somewhere very deep inside the alien core. A jolt of recognition and disbelief shivered through Dax as the familiar mind-pattern overlapped hers. "This is . . . Jadzia. I've been waiting for you, for so long . . . tell me what we have to do to save the ship."

## *Fallen Heroes*, by Daffyd ab Hugh

*Fallen Heroes* is an ultimate hero's story. Like *Time's Enemy*, it is set on *DS9*, and like *Time's Enemy*, everybody dies nobly, setting up conditions that buy time for others to escape or find a way to defeat the invaders. In *Fallen Heroes*, invaders from the Gamma Quadrant

245

systematically killed everyone on the station who could not tell them what they wanted to know. These invaders, called Bekkir, could not be defeated through ordinary means; their armor was impenetrable by energy weapons, and they carried a device that transported them about a day into the future, escaping immediate threats. The sacrifices of those who died and those who lived allowed the handful of survivors, Quark, Odo, and Jake (with Molly) to implement the solution that saved everyone and kept the Bekkir threat from the Alpha Quadrant.

Choosing a passage from *Fallen Heroes* was not easy; each person's sacrifice is worthy of inclusion. The passage I have chosen ties together all of the crew members' sacrifices and achievements and finishes with Odo's heroic effort.

JAKE FINISHED HIS TALE. ODO MADE A SLOW, STEADY TRICORDER SWEEP OF the fiery furnace they found themselves in.

"Rest easy, Jake," said the constable; "you are in no danger of radiation poisoning. The radiation released by Commander Sisko's action was electromagnetic, not nuclear, and if it had actually struck you, you would have died instantly."

"But it's so hot!" wailed Molly, squatting on her haunches. She had tried sitting down, but the burning floor hurt her fanny. For some reason, the silly grownups had turned the heat up way too high.

"It's heat-hot," explained Odo, "not radioactive-hot. Whatever the commander did, it must have blown down the force containment shield on the fusion reactors. This would have created a single, electromagnetic pulse wave that would have killed any normal, biological creature within a certain radius not shielded against EMP.

"Then the reactors would have *immediately* shut down."

"Why?" asked Jake.

"Much as Chief O'Brien hates to admit it—sorry, used to hate to admit it—Cardassian technology is not primitive. They know enough to install fail-safes to protect the station in the event of a fusion catastrophe. If the force containment shield disappears, the laser stops. No laser, no laser-induced fusion."

"Then why is it so hot?"

Odo squirmed. This was the tricky part. "Jake, are you sure you want to hear this?"

"No. Tell me anyway."

"For a single moment, there were two exposed, *uncontained* fusion reactions occurring in the chamber directly below us. Each contained a magnetic platform, upon which was a single pellet of carbon that

246

the laser had just flash-heated to several million degrees. There were also beds of superheated silicon and sodium, but my understanding is that they were only a few tens of thousands of degrees, therefore negligible."

Jake stood, backed away. The image began to form in his head even before Odo described it.

The constable continued. "For an instant, Jake, just before they fused, the two carbon pellets were exposed to the air.

"They superheated the air . . . not to the core temperature, or the entire station would have vaporized; but far hotter than humans or Ferengi can tolerate.

"The metal walls reflect and contain the heat, which means the reactor well below us is still radiating heat at eight thousand K, according to my tricorder."

"No!" insisted Jake, putting his hands over his eyes. "Stop it!"

Odo wished he could just stop; but he decided the boy had to face the truth. "If there was anything left of Commander Sisko before the containment shield broke, Jake, there is nothing left now. His body melted into constituent molecules and immediately evaporated into superheated gases—carbon, hydrogen, oxygen—and perhaps some trace amounts of heavy ash."

He paused; the good news seemed limpid indeed compared to the bad. "Fortunately, I think it would take more than eight thousand K to melt the Bekkir armor; so if the EMP knocked out their incendiary devices, we might still recover an intact time key."

For a solid minute, Jake clenched his teeth, balled his fists as if he were about to attack the constable. Odo fretted; in his present condition, he was too weak to fend off the boy.

Then at once, Jake relaxed. His muscles softened, his eyes mellowed; he lost the "haunted, hunted" look he had worn since they first found him nearly two hours ago.

"I still don't understand how *we* survived," he said, putting his arm around Molly.

"I don't know," said Odo.

"I do," interjected Quark, wheezing full-time now. "You—you went up—to the upper weapons sail?"

Jake nodded. "But we couldn't get in."

Quark looked at Jake. "You have the luck—of a Ferengi," he said. "If you had—gone down—instead, you would have died."

"But we weren't shielded! How come the pulse didn't get us, too?"

The Ferengi shook his head. *"Were* shielded."

"By what?"

"By the *lower* weapons sail. It sat—between you and—and the reactor. You were—sitting in its shadow."

For a long moment, Jake stared out the window. Then he smiled. "The luck of the Ferengi," he said, and coughed.

"Why didn't you just go to Ops?" asked Odo, too tired to cause any facial expressions. "Ops is the most heavily shielded point on *DS9.* Quark, you saw that some of the systems in Ops were still functional."

Jake shrugged. "I—well, *I* didn't know that. Molly said the weapons sail. And how would I have gotten there anyway?"

"Good thing he didn't," added Quark, who had regained some breath by sitting still. "Remember the bullet—holes, Odo? Might have met—Bekkir on the way."

Jake smiled, finally accepting his father's death and finding in it some meaning. The other senior members of the crew had died bravely, but the commanding officer of *Deep Space Nine* had died the most bravely of all.

Odo pondered Commander Sisko's death. *So at least one triumph came from the tragedy.*

*No, that's not fair,* he argued with himself. Each *did* triumph in his or her own way:

Lieutenant Dax discovered that the Bekkir were not invulnerable. She proved they could be killed by killing one. And it was her act that allowed Quark and Odo to finally understand what had happened, who had attacked the station, and how the attack might still be averted.

Major Kira performed her duty as a warrior, killing more of the Bekkir than anyone else and leading the rescue mission to the runabout. It was her special tragedy that this triumph was trumped by the inability of the pilot to navigate the ship safely away from the station.

Dr. Julian Bashir kept the Bekkir talking while his medical log recorded the interrogation. From that recording Odo and Quark could reason out the timetable and infer that there still might be a chance to return and stop the attack from ever happening.

Keiko tackled a Bekkir, saving Jake, Nog, and Molly; then her husband, Chief O'Brien, threw the grenades that allowed the children to escape.

Nog sacrificed himself to allow Jake and Molly to live—and it was Jake's special knowledge of what his father did that brought Odo and Quark to the lowest pit of *DS9,* the inferno where they might still find the tools to set everything aright.

And last, Commander Benjamin Sisko had killed all the remaining Bekkir, who otherwise would have simply killed Odo and Quark as soon as they reappeared—and who might have left behind the keys to returning to their original timeline.

*Every single death* materially contributed to the one chance they had to prevent all the terror, the anguish, the death and destruction . . . to avert the tragedy.

Each brave death was actually a small triumph; and together, the triumphs added up to a possibility, a fifty-fifty shot.

It was all they could hope for; they had been given a chance to undo what had been done.

Odo stood shakily. He would not allow this magic moment to be lost by his own weakness. Despite the fact that he could barely even hold his shape, he knew what he had to do.

"I'm going down," he announced succinctly.

Quark turned from the window, a curious look on his face—almost like *concern.* "Odo, that's insane. Not even you could walk into an eight-thousand-degree blast furnace and walk out alive!"

"Am I insane? I don't know that I am." Odo smiled. "I don't know what I *am,* remember? Maybe I *can* withstand heat equivalent to the surface temperature of a large star; I don't know.

"But I do know that I'm the only one here who *might* be able to endure. Could you? Could Jake?"

"The keys are probably melted," said Quark, his voice soft and pleading; he desperately wanted to be contradicted. "And if they aren't, then the EMP wave destroyed them!"

"We do not know that. We don't know how tough the Bekkir armor is, or how they shield their emergency beacons." Odo forced himself to stand tall, cross his arms. "Quark, I am resolved. I'm going down: be prepared to help me out, even if it means you burn yourself."

The Ferengi muttered to himself something that sounded suspiciously like "you're *dissolved,* not resolved," but he moved into position near the final ladderway leading down to Level Thirty-four, where the still-open trapdoor to the reactor well awaited. He turned his face away from the terrific heat.

Odo stepped forward briskly, his indomitable will belying the enervating exhaustion he actually felt. He was scant minutes from collapsing into his liquid state, heat or no heat. He removed everything in his pockets and handed it all to Quark, who tucked the flash and data clip into his boot and dropped the rest on the deck. Then Odo allowed one last shapeshift, eliminating all protruding edges, digits, clothing—anything unnecessary to the final task. He stepped to the ladder, wading through the energy swamp, and descended smartly into Hell.

## *The Rings of Tautee,* by Dean Wesley Smith & Kristine Kathryn Rusch

Many, perhaps most, of the original series novels are stories of heroic self-sacrifice and risk. *The Rings of Tautee,* though, appealed to me because it had all the elements of good Star Trek: a fascinating alien society in danger, the future of the entire galaxy at risk, menace from an alien enemy who ultimately cooperated to help save the galaxy, and Kirk and company risking everything to save people they did not know.

In *The Rings of Tautee,* scientists from a pre-warp alien society tapped into an energy source without knowing what they were doing. Their mistake spelled disaster for their entire solar system and death for their species. Because of their presumption in dealing with energies they did not understand, their solar system exploded into cosmic rubble in waves that continued to spread outward from the source and endangered the entire galaxy. When the *Enterprise* investigated, they discovered that several thousand Tauteeans remained alive in pockets of rubble throughout the system. Risking their own lives by playing dodgeball with meteoric debris, they rescued as many Tauteeans as they could, straining the resources of the ship to do so. Kirk also convinced a reluctant Klingon commander and a by-the-book Federation starship captain to help with the rescue. Finally, Kirk risked all to attempt to close the rift, in the scene excerpted here.

THE ENVIRONMENTAL CONTROLS *WERE* STRAINED. SPOCK'S ESTIMATE HAD been off. Instead of nine hundred and eighty survivors on the surface below, there had been nine hundred and eighty on the first level. Another five hundred had been on the level below.

The *Enterprise* had beamed them all aboard, and Scotty said they were crammed like breeding gophers under an island green, something Kirk hadn't understood. Sulu had said Scotty was using a golf metaphor, and Kirk didn't ask any more.

He had tried golf once, in Iowa as a boy.

He preferred chess.

Or basketball. Either all cerebral activity or none.

And here he was, in the middle of a crisis, pondering a golf analogy.

"Captain"—Scotty's voice sounded harried over the comm—"I do think we should move some of these poor folks to the bridge."

"No, Mister Scott." Kirk sat on his chair, then winced and stood abruptly. The pad was completely gone now. "They stay below-decks."

Kirk still needed the thinking room. Even if the survivors were packed below. He was glad Bogle had taken the rest. The *Enterprise* was strained almost beyond her capacity, and they weren't done yet.

"Captain," Prescott said. "Do you think we have time to find one more group?"

And one more, and one more. She would keep asking, and they would miss their opportunity. Kirk looked into her exhausted, bruised face. This was the face that even the good tightass Captain Kelly Bogle couldn't refuse.

But Kirk had to.

"We're out of time, Prescott," he said. "I'm sorry." Then he turned to Sulu. "Take us to the rendezvous point near the rift."

"Aye, sir," Sulu said. His fingers moved across the board. "Course laid in. We're on our way."

He sounded almost relieved. Maybe he was. The sooner they got to the rendezvous point, the sooner this would all be over.

He hit the comm button. "Mister Scott. Return to engineering. We'll need you there."

"Aye, sir," Scotty said. He sounded relieved too.

Kirk sat down despite the ruined pad. "Are the other ships in position?" he asked.

"The *Farragut* and the Klingon ship *QuaQa* carrying KerDaq are in position," Spock said. "The Klingon ship *SorDaq* is headed in that direction and will arrive in one minute."

"Good," Kirk said, leaning back and watching as the *Enterprise* moved above the plane of the destroyed solar system and headed for the debris field of the ninth planet. "What's our estimated arrival time, Mister Sulu?"

"We'll be there in two minutes, sir," Sulu said.

"So fast," a voice said from behind Kirk.

He swiveled his chair. Prescott was standing at the rail, her arms resting on it, staring at the screen. She was so short that she looked like a little girl peering over a fence. Her face had that look of awe and wonder that he had seen on others, and felt a few times himself.

"What took us weeks to travel you do in minutes," Prescott said.

"And you travel between the stars? Not one of my people dared dream of such a thing. We always just assumed it was impossible."

"Sometimes dreaming is the only way to find ways to do the impossible," Kirk said.

Prescott pulled her gaze from the screen and met his. Here, he knew, was a woman who would continue to lead her people. She had nearly destroyed them, but she had also helped rescue them. Sometimes that culpability, that guilt, made survivors try even harder.

They all had a long road ahead of them.

"I see now that you are right, Captain. Our problem was that we were too cautious, our dreams too small," she said.

"It seems to me," Spock said, "that the dream of unlimited energy for your people is not small."

"Yes it is," she said, "when we could have had the stars." And then she smiled.

"Captain," Spock said. "We have reached the designated point. All four ships are in place. The third Klingon ship, *Suqlaw,* is waiting outside the system."

"Understood," Kirk said. "Lieutenant Uhura, patch me in to the other three ship captains. Make sure they can also see each other."

"Yes, sir," she said. The picture of the other ships on the main screen dissolved and was replaced by a divided screen showing three faces, one human and two Klingon. Captain Bogle, a streak of dirt across his chin, nodded to Kirk.

KerDaq glowered. Kirk could see survivors behind him.

The unknown Klingon captain squinted at Kirk. Kirk squinted back.

"I am Commander Kutpon," the new Klingon said, in what was obviously the most menacing tone he could manage.

"Captain Kirk," Kirk said, deciding not to play that game. KerDaq could explain to Kutpon that relations with the Federation were cordial, for the moment. "I hope the hunting went well for everyone."

"We have gathered over two hundred survivors," Kutpon said.

"We also have two hundred crammed aboard," KerDaq said.

"The Tauteean people will hold you in great honor for your bravery," Kirk said before Bogle could say anything. There was no point in getting into a useless numbers game over who rescued the most.

Bogle clearly understood. "You crammed us full, Jim. And I see you made another stop on the way."

Kirk shrugged. "We found we had the room."

Bogle just shook his head in obvious disgust. Kirk wasn't sure if Kelly was mad at him, or himself. "And how are your environmental controls?"

"Strained to the breaking point," Kirk said, and suppressed a grin.

Bogle nodded. "I suspect you're right. If we hadn't had our rendezvous, you would have lost your environmental controls. Funny how that works, isn't it? Too many bodies in too small a space."

Kirk shrugged. "Just planning ahead, Kelly."

"Obviously," Bogle said.

"We have two minutes, Captain," Spock said.

Kirk took a deep breath and felt his grin fade. The serious work had begun. He faced the other three captains. "Are we all clear on what we're going to attempt?"

KerDaq snorted. "Of course we are, Captain. A single blast from each ship timed together will close the hole."

Kirk could see the other captains nodding in unison. It seemed that everyone had been briefed. "Mister Spock will count down to the firing time. The moment after you have fired your full burst, jump to warp. You will have only thirty seconds to get out of the subspace wave's path."

All three captains nodded again.

The Klingons and the Federation might be enemies, but that didn't stop them from respecting each other. KerDaq was an excellent captain. Kirk had no doubt that Kutpon was the same. They knew the risks they would place their ships under, the possible damage that could occur.

Of course, if this didn't work, the damage wouldn't matter. This rift in space would destroy this entire sector of the galaxy and no one would live through it.

"The nearest starbase, Starbase Eleven, is only a half day away," Bogle said. "We can dock there. With the survivors." He said the last with a touch of sarcasm.

"Understood," KerDaq said. "We will be there."

His third of the screen went blank.

"And so will we," Kutpon said.

His section of the screen went dark as well.

Bogle said. "And good luck. We'll talk when we reach the starbase."

"I am looking forward to it," Kirk said. "And good luck to you, too. We're all going to need it. Kirk out."

The screen went back to showing the four ships spaced in a square formation above the debris field of the ninth planet.

"We have one minute, Captain," Spock said.

Kirk glanced around. Uhura was still monitoring communications. Sulu was staring at the screen. Chekov was double-checking the coordinates.

Prescott leaned against the railing, her feet barely touching the ground. Her slender face was lined with tension. Spock was bent over his scope, looking as unruffled as ever. Only the ensigns sitting off to the sides seemed frightened. And even they were working.

They were the only sign that this moment was different from any other, that they faced more danger than they ever had.

Kirk's crew was the best in the galaxy.

He only hoped they would be good enough.

"Course laid in for Starbase Eleven," Sulu said.

"Lasers armed and ready, sir," Chekov said.

"Good," Kirk said. "On Mister Spock's mark."

"Thirty seconds," Spock said.

"Are all four ships' weapons powered up?" Kirk asked.

"They are, sir," Chekov said.

Thirty seconds seemed like an eternity. Kirk resisted the urge to stand and pace. He needed to focus all his concentration on that shot.

Because it was the only one they would ever have. The only one, or the last one, depending on whether they hit their target or not.

"Ten seconds," Spock said.

Kirk gripped the armrest.

"Nine."

Another countdown. Someday he would have to count down how many countdowns he'd been in.

"Eight."

He watched the other ships get into position.

"Seven."

Chekov checked the coordinates again.

"Six."

Prescott braced herself against the rail.

"Five."

Uhura swiveled so that she could see the screen.

"Four."

Kirk leaned forward, his stomach in knots.

"Three."

The ensigns stopped working and watched, their expressions guarded.

"Two."

Spock raised his head out of the scope.

"One."

Kirk clenched his fist.

"Fire!" Spock said.

On the screen Kirk could see the other three ships firing and the beam from the *Enterprise* joining theirs at a point below in the destruction.

A long red line grew wide and powerful, like a stream of water poured from a pitcher. Kirk felt that if he tilted the *Enterprise* slightly, he could see through the debris hole into the next universe.

Then, as a unit, all four beams from the ships cut off.

"We hit our target," Spock said with an amazing lack of excitement. Sometimes Kirk wondered how he managed that flat tone in life-threatening situations. "The feedback loop is building as planned."

"Get us out of here, Mister Sulu," Kirk snapped. "Warp four."

"Aye, sir," Sulu said. He ran his hand up the board as he said, "Engaging."

Nothing.

Absolutely nothing happened.

The screen remained focused on the asteroids below. None of the other three ships remained. All had jumped to warp. Kirk couldn't see the huge destructive subspace wave building up below, but he knew it was coming.

"Mister Sulu!" Kirk said.

"The warp drive is off-line!" Sulu said, his voice suddenly on the edge and rising.

Kirk punched the comm button. "Mister Scott, we lost warp."

"I know, sir," the voice came right back. "All this shaking and rattling knocked the coils out of alignment. I warned you this might happen."

"The wave will hit in twenty seconds," Spock said with annoying calm.

"Oh, no," Prescott said behind Kirk. "This can't be happening."

"Fix it, Scotty. Now!"

"I canna fix her in twenty seconds, sir," Scotty said.

"I can't hold off that wave."

"I know, sir. If we had a minute, maybe. But a minute might as well be forever."

Forever. Way too long. They had less than twenty seconds to figure out a way to survive.

Twenty very short seconds.

\* \* \*

Less than twenty seconds.

They had to do something.

Kirk opened his eyes. All he saw was Prescott, her hands pressed to her face.

He saved her people only to lose them again.

"Scotty!" Kirk shouted into the comm line. "Get those warp drives up! And put any extra power you can to the shields. Now."

"Aye, sir," Scott said.

"The rift is closing," Spock said. "We have fifteen seconds until the subspace wave reaches this location."

Kirk couldn't believe this was happening. There had been no warning.

Of course, there might have been, but he had assigned Scotty to the transporter room. Scotty usually always babied that warp engine. He'd have noticed if anything was going wrong.

But he hadn't been there.

Kirk had thought he needed Scotty to supervise the tricky transports.

And he had.

He needed a dozen Scotties.

Right now.

"Mister Sulu," he snapped. "Take us directly away from that rift at full impulse!"

"Aye, sir," Sulu said.

The screen showed the destroyed system angling away out of view, then a starfield.

"At this speed," Spock said, "the subspace wave will reach and overtake us in fifty-one seconds."

He had bought some time.

*Scotty, do your magic.*

*Now.*

Kirk turned to Spock. "What are the odds we can surf this one out and survive?"

Spock shook his head. "There are too many factors. I could not give you an accurate estimation."

"Guess, Spock," Kirk said, his hands doubled into fists.

Spock leaned back. "I believe there is a less than zero-point-one-percent chance shields will hold and the hull will not breach."

"Nice guess," Kirk said.

"I do my best," Spock said.

"Are we going to die?" Prescott asked.

"Not if I can help it," Kirk said. "But I'd hang on to something real tight in the meantime."

He punched the comm link. "Scotty? Warp?"

"The engine's on-line, Captain, but she's not responding."

"I thought you said we had a minute, Scotty. You should have had plenty of time."

"A minute to get her back on-line, Captain. But I didna say she was going to work."

"Well, keep trying." Kirk punched the intercom off.

Spock stood and clasped his hands behind his back, as if he were going to make an important pronouncement. "The rift has closed."

They had succeeded, but they could not celebrate. The first time, he had saved the galaxy by sacrificing Edith. This time, he was saving the galaxy by sacrificing himself and his crew.

And fourteen hundred and eighty Tauteean survivors.

He would not lose to the galaxy twice.

He.

Would.

Not.

He turned to Spock. "Is there any way to get any more impulse power?"

"No," Spock said. "Not *enough* power, anyway. But I do have an idea."

"Make it quick," Kirk said.

Spock bowed his head once. Then he stepped forward, and all the repressed emotion, the excitement and the fear, was in his eyes. But not his voice. "We must apply Dr. McCoy's theory again. We cannot defeat the entire wave. But we can modify a small section of it."

"How, Spock?"

"At the precise moment that the wave overtakes us, we use a photon-torpedo blast to cut down the intensity of that small section of the wave."

Kirk frowned. "Like cutting a hole through it for us to ride in?"

"Precisely," Spock said.

"Would ten photon torpedoes be better?"

"If they are concentrated," Spock said, "at the exact point and time that the wave would hit us."

"Spock, you're brilliant," Kirk said. He leapt out of his chair. "Chekov, arm ten photon torpedoes and wait for Mister Spock's mark."

"Armed and ready, sir," Chekov said.

Spock had returned to his chair. He was peering into the scope again, his fingers flying over the keys in front of him. "We have twenty seconds," he said.

Kirk paced the area behind the helm. Twenty seconds suddenly felt like an eternity. A moment ago they had seemed like nothing. He stopped beside his chair and punched the intercom.

"Scotty?"

"She's a stubborn wee beastie, Captain."

"I'll take that as a no." He had hoped the warp would come back, but now that it wasn't, he had to do something else.

He hit the shipwide comm button. "This is the captain speaking. Brace yourselves. This last wave will be greater than anything we've experienced. Hold on tight and do not move until the bumping ends. Captain out."

"The wave will hit in ten seconds," Spock said.

Prescott slid under the nearest console. Uhura wrapped her boots around the base of her chair. Chekov gripped the sides of his console.

"Scotty?" Kirk said into his intercom.

"I'm sorry, sir," Scotty said, the exasperation clear in his voice, "but I canna do it. She's taken too great a beating."

"Five seconds," Spock said. His chair was all the way against the console. But he hadn't grabbed anything yet.

Neither had Kirk.

Kirk returned to his chair and gripped the arms. He would rather have joined Prescott under the console, but he had to stay here to monitor everything.

"On my mark, Mister Chekov," Spock said.

Some crewmen had also crawled under the consoles. Kirk almost reprimanded them, but then decided against it. He didn't really need them at the moment anyway. Sulu followed Uhura's example, and wrapped his legs around his chair.

"Fire!" Spock said.

The ship rocked as the photon torpedoes fired.

Then the wave hit.

It felt as if the *Enterprise* had slammed into an interstellar wall. The ship rocked forward, then stopped, before propelling backward and bouncing along the surface of something Kirk couldn't see.

The lights went off, the computer began reciting damage statistics, and the screen went dead. Sparks flew from the consoles and someone screamed.

Kirk hung on to the chair as hard as he could, but he didn't stand much of a chance of staying in it.

Chekov flew past him, twirling in the air like a top.

The ship felt like a bucking horse. Kirk rode his chair for the first few major jolts and then it moved down when he was moving up.

He lost his grip on the arms and soared through the air, as he had done as a boy on his second riding lesson.

Time seemed to stop, yet the bridge was a blur of noise and darkness and sparks around him.

He slammed into the navigation console, and felt a pain so deep that his body couldn't encompass it all.

Something was wrong.

His mind wanted to leave.

But it couldn't.

He'd fallen before and remained conscious.

He reached for the console, in an attempt to stand up.

Then everything went black.

# PART II

# Aliens, Allies & Enemies

Before Star Trek, most aliens in televised and movie science fiction were demons of one kind or another and threatened the very survival of humanity. Star Trek presented aliens who were sympathetic and who had good qualities and a valid point of view. Many aliens were friends, and the humans of Earth had joined with them in creating the United Federation of Planets. Other aliens were in conflict with Earth and its allies, but more often were seen as misunderstood and as having valid, although different, points of view. This part of *Adventures in Time and Space* examines the treatment of aliens in Star Trek fiction, including allies, enemies, and entirely new life and new civilizations.

# CHAPTER 9

# The Vulcan Chronicles

OF ALL THE ALIENS IN STAR TREK, THE VULCANS ARE MY FAVORITES, AND, I think, the most interesting and complex. Spock and Sarek, the Vulcans we know best, are beloved by many fans. Despite the hints about their lives and the history of their planet provided by the motion pictures and televised episodes, Sarek, Spock, and their fellow Vulcans remain somewhat mysterious, and the mystery left by the movies and episodes affords opportunities for novelists to develop answers. Novels that explore Vulcan and the lives of our favorite Vulcans continue to capture the imagination of the writers as well as the readers. Thus, *Spock's World,* by Diane Duane, *Sarek,* by Ann Crispin, and *Vulcan's Forge,* by Josepha Sherman and Susan Shwartz are logical additions to any collection of Star Trek books and stories. Each of these books weaves new threads into the Vulcan tapestry begun by Star Trek episodes and films and tells us more about Vulcan society and families.

Vulcans are hard characters to draw. A writer who believes their protestations about having no emotions could fall into the trap of painting a picture of a mechanized robot or society of robots. Few viewers, though, ever believed Spock or Sarek when they insisted that they had no emotions. Viewers always realized that, to the contrary, Vulcans learned to control very powerful emotions. This belief was confirmed in the *TNG* episode "Sarek." Even before that episode, Sarek's powerfully leashed grief at his son's death, witnessed in *Star Trek III,* told the truth about Vulcan emotions. Diane Duane, Ann Crispin, Jo Sherman, and Susan Shwartz clearly understand both the strength of Vulcan emotions and the absolute necessity for Vulcans of maintaining their famed control. They also understand that Vulcans are an ancient and honorable people who love their families and make mistakes with them just as humans do with theirs.

The books excerpted in The Vulcan Chronicles fit together as an epic saga, each giving the reader insight into the culture and the planet that created Spock and Sarek. While aspects of *Spock's World* and *Sarek* are somewhat inconsistent with the Star Trek canon that has been established in aired episodes and films, the major events and significant revelations about Spock, Sarek, and the woman who loved them both, Amanda Grayson, endure uncontradicted. Moreover, descriptions and characteristics of Vulcan itself from *Spock's World* have been substantiated through Tuvok's story in Jeri Taylor's novel, *Pathways,* quoted elsewhere in this book.

As with other aspects of the novels which have not yet been validated as Star Trek canon through the films and television episodes, I choose to accept the events of *Spock's World, Sarek* and *Vulcan's Forge* as valid Vulcan history and as the back-stories of the people I love the most in Star Trek. The recently published *Vulcan's Heart,* also by Josepha Sherman and Susan Shwartz, similarly fits into the epic.

## *Spock's World,* by Diane Duane

Less a story about Spock than about Vulcan itself, *Spock's World* provides the ultimate Vulcan history and back-story. Ms. Duane carries the reader back to the beginning, to before Vulcan pre-history, to the formation of the planet itself. *Spock's World* is the tale of the sort of planet that produces people like Vulcans, who are strong, brilliant, and capable, and who have psi powers that are capable of rejoining mind and body after death.

Ms. Duane described to her readers the arduous environment in which survival was a constant struggle and only the strongest and most capable lived to pass on their genetic traits. She explored the violent heritage Spock and Sarek only allude to, and she related the story of Surak, Vulcan's savior figure. Perhaps most intriguing of all, Ms. Duane elaborated on the connection between Vulcans referred to by Spock in "The Immunity Syndrome," as well as the Vulcan certainty of a soul that survives their deaths. She revealed that Vulcans have a direct and living connection with and consciousness of a supreme being, a creator of all.

*Spock's World* is more than an epic of Vulcan's past. In the twenty-third century, the Federation faced a crisis between Vulcan and the Federation, more specifically, Earth. Not all Vulcans were open-minded explorers, and not all Vulcans were of the same mind following the IDIC philosophy ("infinite diversity in infinite combinations"). Some Vulcans were rabid xenophobes. It was up to Spock, Sarek, Kirk, and McCoy to discover what was driving the Vulcan movement to secede from the Federation and to persuade them to stay.

The excerpt from *Spock's World* is from Vulcan's early and violent history and tells a story of the Vulcan experience with powers of the mind and the resulting rudimentary genetics programs practiced by these ruthless and determined people.

WHEN T'THELAIH HEARD OF IT, HER FIRST RESPONSE WAS TO RAGE, AND then to weep. But she dared do nothing else. Her father, who had made the match, she saw perhaps once a month, when his leisure allowed it, and then rarely for more than a few minutes. At such times she often wanted to cry out to him. *It's not my fault!* But there was no hope of his understanding, and no use in making trouble.

She was a murderess.

It wasn't her fault.

T'Thelaih had most of her family's traits: the fair or light brown hair, the light bones and short stature, good looks that tended to be blunt rather than finely drawn. There the obvious assets of the Old House ended in her, for she did not have the psi-communications gift: she was mindblind, like her father, and that had been hard enough to bear in a house where almost no one ever had to speak— the slightest intention to communicate with another person was always heard.

One gift she did have, though, that the house had acquired long before and striven hard to be rid of. They had never succeeded: every six or seven generations it would pop up again, and there would be curses and fear. It was associated with the communications gift, but independent of it. When angry, the person with this pernicious gift could kill with the mind.

She had not known until she was betrothed for the first time. She was frightened: she had not yet suffered the Rapture, and though her body was ready, her mind was not. Her first husband, a son of rich House Kehlevt, and one who thought well of himself, had taken her to the room set aside for their binding and had simply begun to rape her.

She killed him. Without touching him, without laying a hand to a weapon—though she would have liked to—suddenly she was inside his head: suddenly the connection that had never been complete before was complete: and her rage and terror burst out through it and froze his heart and stripped the receptor chemicals out of his brain and deadened the life-fire in his nerves. He was dead before he rolled off her. No healer had been able to do anything.

There had been the expected uproar. But the bruises on her body spoke clearly enough about what had been going on, and the matter was hushed up, and money changed hands to keep the quiet well in place. So much she had heard later. She had been very afraid that that would be the end of her—that some evening, someone would slip something deadly into her cup; or that some day before dawn, someone would come in over the sweet white flowers on her window-sill and put a knife in her. Such things had been heard of. But no one troubled her. T'Thelaih went about the house keeping small and still. It took her some time to realize that other people were now keeping small and still around *her.* No one had ever cared a *jah* before whether she was angry. But now, the people of the house were not sure that *any* anger of hers was something to cause, or to be near.

She tried to ignore the changed status of things and went about her studies and work as usual. Everybody in the house worked, whether they were marriage-fodder or not. T'Thelaih was very clear that that was just what she was—a gaming piece. She was not an own-child, but a "right-line child"—that was a euphemism that said she had some relationship to the head of the house, but not one confirmed by binding or other legal instrument. She was a by-blow, destined to be married off to some other house in return for some political favor or potential alliance. Now she went about her accounting work as usual and wondered whether the business with her first husband would put her out of the marriage market. That could be bad: she could wind up disowned, or sold as a servant. But things quieted down after a while, and another offer was made, this time from House Galsh. It was a good enough match, and the young man was very nice, and T'Thelaih wondered whether or not the first time might have been a quirk or an accident. In any case, she looked forward to the wedding. She felt the slow burn of the Rapture coming over her as the days till the binding grew closer, and she welcomed it. The binding fell in the middle of it: her blood fever kindled her new husband's, and the night was wild and memorable.

But in the morning he was dead.

There were no more matches made. T'Thelaih had leisure to work with the house's accounts, now: all the leisure she liked. Everyone, the servants, her half sisters, her mothers, looked at her with terror. Sometimes it relaxed a little, but never for long. No one dared tease her or say something that might make her laugh . . . because it might make her angry, too.

The time that followed was long and lonely.

But now she stood in front of her father, listening incredulously to the news that she was being bound again. To a young man of House Velekh, of the "High House." She stared at her father.

"But they are great," she said. "What do they want with us?"

"Alliance," he said.

T'Thelaih had her own ideas about that. She handled the accounts, after all. "Noble father," she said, "surely there are other houses they might more profitably ally with."

He glared at her. Yes, he knew perfectly well that he was being condescended to.

"Noble father," she said, "how can this match be made? Do they not know about the—the other bindings?"

"The Eldest of the House knows. Yes." Her father breathed out. "You have nothing to fear from them if there is an accident." He paused. "They will adopt you."

*You are giving me away,* she thought, *and relieved you are to do it. Foul, ah, foul!* "But noble father," she said, desperate, "the young man—"

"I care nothing for the young man," he said angrily. "No more do they. And I'll spare no tear if you make an end of him: it will rather please me if you kill something of theirs, than otherwise. So do your pleasure, girl. The match will be made when T'Khut is full. The young man comes to meet you tomorrow."

And that was that. She bowed her father reverence, and left, and sat long by her window that night, smelling the sweet white flowers, and contemplating the knife in her hand. It was very sharp.

The crescent set late: watching it, she thought that there was time yet. There was no harm in seeing the young man, at least. The knife would not be any less sharp for a couple days' delay.

Then she saw him.

They were left alone for the meeting, in the great hall of the house's lower level. It was all barren, there being no great dinner or festival there, no reason to adorn or garnish the place with the old banners and the riches garnered from long years of trade. And indeed many of the rich ornaments had been sold, over time, or were the worse for wear. Some kindly person among the servants had brought out two couches, of the antique style, and each of them sat on one and looked at the other.

T'Thelaih liked what she saw. The young man had a frank, calm look about him, and his eyes rested on her in a friendly way. "Well," he said, "they say we're going to be bound. I hope it's something you desired."

"It's not," she said.

He colored. "I'm sorry I don't please you."

"Oh, but you do!" she said.

They both fell silent for a moment: he was surprised at the remark, and she was surprised that it had slipped out, and equally surprised at how seriously she meant it. "I simply did not desire to be bound," she said. "I have been bound before. I killed my husbands."

He looked at her with even more surprise. "Not that way," she said, rather desperately. "It was the killing gift. You know—from the stories." She bowed her head. "I have it. No one survives the binding."

He gazed at her a long time, and finally she had to turn her head away.

"I think I would take the chance even if the choice were mine," he said, very slowly, as if just discovering this for himself.

T'Thelaih looked up in shock. "You must not!" she said. "You must flee! There's still time for you to get away!"

He shook his head. "You do not know my grandam," he said. "She would have me hunted down and brought back. And besides, why would I want to disgrace our house? She is our Eldest. It is my duty to obey her."

"She sent you here to kill you! She *knew!*"

He actually shrugged.

"You are an *idiot,*" T'Thelaih said in wonder.

He shrugged again. "That's as may be. There's no escaping, in any case, so I shall not try."

The argument went on for nearly an hour. T'Thelaih wondered what the eavesdroppers must be thinking of it all . . . for certainly, there *were* eavesdroppers: she might be mindblind, but she was not so stupid as to think that every mind in the house was not bent in this direction at the moment. And once the thought crossed her mind, *Why am I trying to talk him out of it? No worse blame will fall on me this time than has before. My father has practically given me leave to kill him. Why am I arguing the point?*

She could think of no reason.

Finally the argument trailed off, and she found herself staring at her hands. "Come again tomorrow," she said.

"I will," he said. And he paused and colored again. "I hate to say this," he said. "They announced it when I came in, but I've forgotten your name."

"T'Thelaih."

"Mahak," he said, and got up and bowed her reverence and left.

She sat there shaking her head for a long time, and then went back to the accounts.

He came back the next day, and the next, and the day after that, and they argued. The arguments always started about the binding itself, but then they began to stray out into more interesting topics—the relationships and interrelationships in their families, the politics that went on, and the doings of the kingdoms and lordships of the world; and finally, about themselves, or rather, each other. The arguments started early and ended late: it was *almost* improper.

After about three days of this, T'Thelaih realized that she was going to *have* to be bound to this man, just to have the leisure to argue properly with him.

On the fourth day she realized, with a start, that she was in love with him, and he with her. He realized it, for his part, the next day. The argument that day was particularly noisy.

Two days later, T'Khut was full.

The public part of the binding was held with great splendor in the hall of the High House. Mahak had decided to take his grandam at her word: tables actually bent under the weight of the food, and drink ran more freely than water. Petty-kings and great lords and Eldest Mothers filled the galleries to look down on the formal touching, as the priest of the god of bindings took the hands of the two to be bound, put them each to the other's face, and saw that the minds were properly locked together. Not even he saw how each pair of eyes, resting in the other's gaze, told the other that the locking had already happened, perhaps a hand of days ago, while both parties were shouting at one another at the tops of their voices. Neither of them cared a whit for one of the things they had argued about, the exchange of mind-technicians taking place, just about then, elsewhere in the house. Neither of them paid the slightest mind to the cold, interested glance bent down on them from another of the high galleries, as Lady Suvin looked down satisfied on her handiwork.

They completed the binding and spent the afternoon and the early part of the night celebrating it with the assembled dignitaries, not caring in the slightest who had just declared war on whom, or what border skirmish was taking place because of an insult or a strayed *sehlat.*

They lay together that night and found that there was at least one thing about which they had no argument whatsoever: though afterward, there was some sleepy discussion as to who had a right to the most of the sleeping silks.

T'Thelaih was the first to awaken. Without looking to the side where her husband lay, she reached over to the little table by the head of the couch and picked up the knife. It was as sharp as it had been when the moon was thin. She knew what she was going to see: she knew what she was going to do about it.

She turned over and saw him sleeping quietly and breathing.

And quite alive.

The knife fell with a clatter to the floor and awoke him.

They began to quarrel. It did not last long. . . .

"I am with child," she said to him, quite shortly thereafter. He was so surprised that he forgot to start an argument about it.

"All the good Gods be praised," he said, taking her hands, "and bless the bad ones for staying out of it!"

"Sit down, beloved," she said, "and be calm a little. We need to think."

"About what?"

"The child, for one thing." T'Thelaih sat down on the couch in their chambers in the High House and looked at him keenly. "This child could be something that our houses have been waiting for for a long time."

"There are lots of children," Mahak said, somewhat confused.

"But none of both our houses. Mahak, listen to me. My father has as good as sold me to Suvin. I'm not bothered by that. Something like it was always bound to happen someday. But this child, depending on how and where it is raised, could be mistress of both my old House and my new one."

"Mistress—"

"A girl, yes."

"My grandam is not going to like that," Mahak said.

T'Thelaih was silent for a moment. "We are going to have to find some way to stop her not liking it," she said, "or to see to it that it does not matter. This child can be a bond, an end to the old warfare between our houses. Or the opportunity can die with us."

"Have you any idea how we are going to bring this to pass?" he said.

"Have you?"

He shook his head.

"Nor have I. But we must start thinking . . . whom we can cultivate, and how, to see that the child is brought up between the houses, not wholly of one or the other. Otherwise the child will be one more gaming piece, nothing more. . . ."

They sat quietly together for a moment.

"We must be very careful," Mahak said. "Otherwise this may be the death of us."

T'Thelaih nodded. "As you say."

He drew her close. "And in the meantime . . ."

And they discussed at some length the subject on which there were no arguments.


T'Thelaih woke up cold and alone. "Mahak?" she said, confused, and sat up on the couch, looking around for him. There was something wrong at the other end of their bond: he was upset—then she froze.

Sitting at the end of the couch was the Lady Suvin. She looked at T'Thelaih, and the look was cold and terribly pleased.

"You are a foolish child," Suvin said, "but it does not matter. I have what I want of you."

"Madam," T'Thelaih said, holding on to her manners, "what do you mean?"

"The child," said Suvin. "This will be your home now: you need fear no interference from your own house, poor thing though it be. I much regret that Mahak may not join you again until your confinement is done. But you will be given every care . . . so long as you take proper care of the child."

T'Thelaih felt her head beginning to pound. "What good can our child do you?" she said.

Suvin leaned closer, looking even more pleased. "Fool. You have the killing gift. Imperfect, at best: you did not kill my grandson, for some reason. I suspect it is the usual problem, that one must feel her life to somehow be threatened. But did you not know? His great-grandmother had it as well. When two with the gift in their blood, so close in degree, engender a child, it will have the gift as well."

271

T'Thelaih shook her head, numbed. "A weapon," she said at last.

"Such a weapon as none will be able to defend against," said Suvin. "Trained with the Last Thought technique, raised under my hand, obedient to me—those who resist me will simply die, and no one will know the cause. How much simpler life will become. I have much to thank you for."

She saw T'Thelaih's glance at the table. "Forget your little bodkin," she said. "You'll not lay hands on yourself: if you try, Mahak will suffer for it. I shall see to that. Resign yourself to your confinement. It need not be uncomfortable."

"Bring me my husband," T'Thelaih said. "Now."

Suvin's eyes glittered. "Do not presume to order me, my girl. You are too valuable to kill out of hand, but there are ways to punish you that will not harm the child."

The pounding was getting worse. "My husband," T'Thelaih said.

"Folly," said Suvin, and got up to go. "I will talk to you when you are in your right mind."

And from the courtyard below came the sound of swords, and the scream.

*"T'Thelaih!!"*

And nothing else . . . except, in T'Thelaih's mind, the feeling of the bond, the connection, as it snapped, and the other end went empty and cold.

"My husband," she said. Suvin turned in shock, realizing what had happened. An unfortunate accident—

She realized too late.

T'Thelaih was getting up from the bed. The pounding in her head she had felt before, at her first binding, and remotely, in the heat of *plak tow,* at the second. Now she knew it for what it was, and she encouraged it. *Yes. Oh, my husband, yes*—

"Old woman," she said to Suvin, getting out of the bed and advancing slowly on her, "beg me for your life." Suvin backed up, slowly, a step at a time, coming against the wall by the door. "Beg me," T'Thelaih said, stepping slowly closer. "Bow yourself double, old *le-matya,* let me see the back of your neck." Her teeth gleamed. Suvin trembled, and slowly, slowly, began to bow.

She didn't finish the gesture: she came up with the knife, poised, threw it. T'Thelaih sidestepped it neatly and replied with the weapon that could not miss: slid into the hateful mind, cold as stone, reached down all its pathways and set them on fire, reached down through every nerve and ran agony down it, reached down into the laboring

272

heart and squeezed it until it burst itself, reached down into the throat and froze it so there should not even be the relief of a scream. From Suvin she turned, and her mind rode her gift down into the courtyard, and wrought death there, death—left minds screaming as a weight of rage like the whole universe collapsed onto them, in burning heat, pain, blood, the end of everything. Her mind fled through the house, finding life, ending it, without thought, everywhere.

Finally the rage left her, and she picked up the little knife that Suvin had taken, thought about it . . . then changed her mind. "No," she said aloud, very softly: "no, *he* is down there."

She went to the window. "Child," she said, "I am sorry."

The fall was too swift for there to be time to start an argument, even with a ghost.


The extermination of the High House set back the first manned landing on T'Khut by some fifty standard years. Much of the psi-communications technology had to be rediscovered, and the gift bred for again, in the centuries that followed: it is still the least developed of the Vulcan arts of the mind, though the most broadly disseminated.

T'Khut was mined later, of course, and colonized, and thereafter the Vulcans set off for the outer planets. Several small wars broke out on Vulcan at the first successful landing, in token of the shifting of balances, which are always feared. But other balances were shifting as well: love became increasingly less of a reason for a binding than eugenics. Lives were sacrificed, long wars begun, for the sake of some marriage which might or might not produce a talent of one sort or another. And the terrible example of the attempted union of the High House and the Old House dissuaded many another house from trying such a solution to its problems. Houses grew away from one another, as nations did: grew in enmity and pride, forgot working together for the joys of conquering separately. *Fear the other,* was the message of that time: *keep to your own. Beware the different. Those too different should not seek union. Alone is best.*

Alone, T'Khut, her face now scarred with mines, took her way around the planet, and as the centuries passed, the fires that began to kindle on Vulcan's surface mirrored her own. She had no clouds so strangely shaped as Vulcan came to have in later years: but the fires burned on and on. . . .

# *Sarek,* by Ann Crispin

What fan, when thinking of Sarek and Amanda, Spock's parents, cannot remember them from "Journey to Babel," touching fingertips only, but expressing a loving intimacy not expected of Vulcans and seen with few human couples? No one who witnessed the open affection Sarek bore for Amanda could come away believing that he did not love her. Where *Spock's World* gave the reader a history of Vulcan and its culture, *Sarek,* by Ann Crispin, provided a more intimate portrait of Spock's parents and their life together. Their story is told against a backdrop of Romulan intrigue and a Klingon adventure and romance enjoyed by Captain Kirk's nephew, Peter. At the center of the story is the death of Amanda and the resulting estrangement between Spock and Sarek. At the novel's resolution, the Romulan plot to destroy the Khitomer accords was defeated, and father and son reconciled.

*Sarek* provides a good example of how the authors and editors of the Star Trek novels deftly combine different story lines to please multiple audiences. The back-story and romance of Sarek and Amanda, the tension between Spock and Sarek, and the pathos of Sarek's mission taking him from Amanda's deathbed, appeal to the reader primarily interested in character-based stories. In contrast, Peter Kirk's Klingon adventure, as well as the adventures of Kirk, Spock, and McCoy, appeal to the action-adventure enthusiast. The blend of the two into an integrated whole is a delight.

*Sarek* is a beautifully told tale of love, sacrifice and loss, made all the more poignant by the loss several years ago of Mark Lenard, who brought Sarek to such vibrant life. Mr. Lenard knew of this novel and spoke with Ms. Crispin during its writing. Ms. Crispin understands Sarek so well that I can hear Mr. Lenard's voice in Sarek's dialogue in the story. In this excerpt, Sarek, called away on a mission that no one else could handle, said good-bye to Amanda, both knowing that she would not survive until his return.

"AMANDA." THE VOICE REACHED HER IN THE DARKNESS, PULLING HER BACK to light and awareness. The voice was familiar, known, beloved. An authoritative, precise voice with a faint resonance. Pleasantly deep, extremely cultured. The voice of her husband.

Amanda opened her eyes. Strong fingers grasped her hand gently but firmly. Sarek's fingers.

"Sarek," she murmured, gazing up into the face she had known and loved for so many years. "Have I been asleep long?"

"Several hours. My wife, I regret having to wake you, but I must speak with you . . . before I take my leave."

Amanda's eyes opened wider. "Leave?" she asked faintly, too weak to conceal the dismay his words caused her. "Why? Where are you going?"

"There is an emergency on the planet Kadura," Sarek said. "I just finished speaking to President Ra-ghoratrei. He asked me to negotiate the release of a Federation colony that has been seized by Klingon renegades. There are thousands of colonists whose lives are in jeopardy. I must go, Amanda. It is my duty."

Her heart contracted at his words. "How . . . how long will it take?" she asked, her words scarcely audible above the faint hum of the medical monitors. "Must you go?"

"Yes. I must take ship for Deneb Four within the hour. It is difficult to say how long I will be gone. Ten days, at the minimum. If the negotiations proceed slowly . . ." He trailed off and his fingers tightened slightly on hers.

"I see," Amanda whispered. "Very well, Sarek. I understand."

Her husband regarded her, his dark eyes shadowed with grief. Gently, he reached out and touched her hair, her cheek. "Amanda . . . if I could, I would stay here with you. You know that, do you not?"

Silently, she nodded, fighting to hold back tears. His dear, familiar face began to swim in her vision. *No!* she thought, blinking fiercely. *I will not cry. I will not let tears steal my last sight of you. I will not let weeping mar our last farewell.*

"Sarek . . ." she whispered, turning her fingers so her hand grasped his, returning the pressure. "I will miss you, my husband. I wish you did not have to go."

"I will return as soon as possible, Amanda," he promised, his eyes never leaving hers. "The instant Kadura is free, I will come home."

*But you will almost certainly be too late, and we both know it,* Amanda thought, her eyes never leaving his face for a moment. She hated even to blink. In a few minutes her husband would be gone, and she would never see him again . . . at least, not in this life.

"I want you to remember something," she said, struggling to keep her voice even.

"What, Amanda?"

"Never forget that I love you, my husband. Always." She gazed at

275

him intently, holding his eyes with her own. "You will need to remember that, Sarek, very soon now. Promise me you won't forget."

"My memory is typical for a Vulcan," he said, quietly. "I forget very little, my wife."

"I know. But remembering my words in your head, and remembering them here," freeing her hand, she gently laid it on his side, where his heart lay, "are two different things. Promise me."

"You have my word, Amanda," he said, his dark eyes filled with profound sorrow.

*I know that you love me,* she thought, gazing up at him. *But I will not embarrass you by telling you so. . . .*

"Spock will be here with you," Sarek said. "Do not forget that, my wife."

"His presence will be a great comfort," she said, softly. Her gaze moved over his face, tracing the angular lines. Putting her hand up, she touched his cheek, his eyes, his lips, thinking of the many times she had kissed him there. "Sarek, hold me. I want to feel your arms around me. Hold me."

Gently, he reached forward, scooped her up, and cradled her against him. Amanda slid her arms around him and laid her head on his chest with a long sigh. Briefly, she abandoned herself to the moment . . . her soul was content. Finally she raised her head. "Sarek, I want you to promise me one more thing."

He had difficulty meeting her eyes . . . Amanda could tell through their bond that he was profoundly moved. "What is it, Amanda?"

"I want you to read my journals . . . afterward. Take the first one with you now, my husband. Promise me you'll read all of them. Please?"

Sarek nodded; then, with infinite gentleness, he helped settle her back onto the bed. Going into her sitting room, he returned with a slim, red-covered volume. On the spine was affixed the number 1. "This one?" he asked, holding it up.

"Yes, that one," Amanda said, regarding him steadily as she lay propped up on her pillows. "Read it. And when you've finished that one, go on and read the next . . . until you've read them all."

"I will do so, Amanda."

"I know you will," she said, and holding out her hand, two fingers extended, she smiled at him. Somewhere deep inside herself, she was crying, but she refused to let him see. *Let him remember me smiling,* she thought.

Her husband held out his hand, brushed two fingers against hers, and they remained that way for many seconds. Then, with a last, grave nod, Sarek walked away, pushing through the pressure curtain without looking back.

Spock saw the pressure curtain move; then his father appeared. The ambassador's eyes widened slightly as he realized that his son must have been listening to him as he bade farewell to his wife; then they narrowed with anger. Before his father could speak, the first officer signaled curtly for silence and beckoned the ambassador out into the hall.

Only when the *tekla* wood door was firmly closed did Spock turn to regard his father.

"Eavesdropping is discourteous, my son," Sarek said, and Spock could tell he was irritated, though his voice was carefully neutral.

Spock ignored the mild rebuke. He held his father's eyes with his own, and his own voice was cold. "Soran told me that the president called, and why. He also told me that you have ordered your transport prepared. You intend to go to Deneb Four?"

"Yes," Sarek said, eyeing his son with a touch of wariness. "I have just taken my leave of your mother."

"So I heard." Spock's voice cut like a shard of obsidian. "I must admit that I found it difficult to believe. You actually intend to *leave* her? In her present condition?"

"I must," Sarek said, quietly. "The needs of the many outweigh the needs—"

"To quote an appropriate human phrase, 'To hell with that,'" Spock broke in, his voice rough with anger and grief. "You cannot leave her like this."

"I recall a time," Sarek said, "when you chose to remain at your post, when only you could save *my* life."

Spock paused. "Yes," he said, after a moment, "but *I* have grown since then. It is a pity that you have not."

Sarek's eyebrow rose at his son's words and the unconcealed emotion. "Spock, we all have our duties to consider. The situation at Kadura is critical."

"So is my mother," the first officer said flatly. "She will not survive long enough for you to return, and you know it. Your leaving in itself will very likely hasten her end." He regarded his father unwaveringly.

The ambassador paused, and Spock knew that the thought of his leaving actually harming Amanda had not occurred to him until now. "You will be here with her," he said, finally. "She will not be alone."

"She needs her *family* with her," Spock said obdurately. "You are her bondmate—her husband. Your loyalty should be to her. There are other diplomats on Vulcan. Senkar has handled situations of this nature before. Let him negotiate for Kadura's release."

"The president requested that I handle the negotiations personally," Sarek said.

"He cannot order you." Spock's gaze never wavered as he held his father's eyes. "Refuse . . . under the circumstances, no one will question your actions."

Sarek straightened his shoulders. "Spock, I have no more time to discuss this. I must leave now."

"You mean that you *wish* to leave," Spock said, his voice cold and flat. "You do not have the courage to stay and see her through this."

Answering anger sparked in Sarek's eyes. "I will not remain to hear such acrimonious—and illogical—outpourings, Spock. I suggest that you meditate and attempt to regain your control." He drew a deep breath, and added, in a tone that was intended to be conciliatory, "Remember, my son, you are Vulcan."

"At the moment, if you are any example, being Vulcan is hardly a condition to be desired," Spock snapped. Without another word, he brushed past his father and headed down the corridor. Behind him he could hear the ambassador's footsteps receding.

When Spock regained control, he gently opened the door to his mother's room, and entered, parting the pressure curtain with both hands.

Amanda was awake. Spock noted the unmistakable signs that she had been crying, but there were no tears present when she smiled at him wanly and held out her hand. "I was just about to eat my lunch," she said, nodding at a tray placed across her lap by the healer's aide. "Would you like to join me, Spock?"

The Vulcan nodded and drew a chair up beside her bed. Amanda was making a valiant effort, he could tell, but she had to force herself to swallow several small mouthfuls. She smiled at him. "Do you know what I dreamt of last night?" she asked. "It was so strange . . . after all these years on Vulcan, being a vegetarian . . ."

"What, Mother?"

"I dreamt that I was eating an old-fashioned hamburger. It tasted wonderful—nice and rare, with cheese and lettuce and tomato. . . ." She smiled, shaking her head.

"If you would like one," her son said, "I will contact my ship and ask them to beam one down immediately."

278

"Oh, no, don't," Amanda said. "I'm sure that eating meat after all these years would make me quite ill. And the real thing could never match how good it tasted in my dream. . . ." She chuckled slightly. "But it was odd to dream about that after what . . . sixty years?"

"Indeed," Spock said, cautiously. He sensed that his mother was chattering on as a way of working herself up to what was really on her mind. Sarek, he thought, was probably aboard his transport and leaving orbit by now.

"Spock," Amanda said, softly, putting down her spoon and gazing at him directly, "what is death like?"

Spock stared at her for a long moment. How many times had he been asked this same question in the past three and a half years? Never before had he attempted an answer, but this time . . . he cleared his throat. "Mother, I cannot tell you what death is like. In a way, since my *katra* departed to reside in Dr. McCoy when my physical body expired, I was not truly dead, as humans understand the term."

"Oh," she murmured, disappointed. "I'm sorry if that question was . . . disquieting. My curiosity got the better of me . . . under the circumstances."

Spock forbore to comment on her reference to her "circumstances." Instead he said, gently, "I cannot tell you what death is . . . but I remember dying. I know what it is to die."

Amanda sat up a little straighter against her pillows, pushing her tray aside. Her blue eyes never left his. "Really? Tell me if you can, Spock."

"It was painful," Spock admitted, and if he had been human, he would have shuddered. "I had been exposed to enough radiation to literally burn me. In addition, my mind, while clear in some ways, was affected, and thus I could not control the pain. I suffered, but I knew before I even entered the chamber that I would not survive, so I also knew that I would not have to endure for long. . . ."

Amanda's eyes filled with tears. Spock knew that imagining her son burned, poisoned, and dying of massive radiation exposure was upsetting her. He hesitated, watching her. "Mother . . . if this is too painful for you, I will . . ."

"No," she said, fiercely. "It's a relief to talk about death, Spock. I couldn't, not with your father. It would have . . . distressed him too much. But you . . . you, of all people, you can understand."

"I do," he said, quietly. His hand slid across the coverlet and grasped hers, holding it tightly, reassuringly. "As my body shut down, the pain stopped, and I experienced relief when that happened. All the while I knew that I was dying, but as soon as the pain ceased, I realized with some surprise that I was not frightened, or distressed. It was more as if what was occurring was simply a further, entirely natural step in the order of things. I found myself at peace . . . such peace as I have never felt."

"Peace," Amanda whispered. "No fear?"

"Fear," Spock reminded her, "is a human emotion. No, Mother, there was neither fear nor pain. Do not forget that I had established a link between myself and McCoy, so I knew that my *katra* would . . . continue."

"No fear, no pain . . ." she mused, plainly attempting to envision such a state. "What was there, then?"

"For a moment, I had a sense that knowledge was waiting for me, infinite knowledge. It was a heady sensation, and lasted only for a moment—then my consciousness blanked out, and I did not return to awareness until I awakened on that pallet with T'Lar standing over me."

"Did you have a sense of an afterlife?"

"No, there was none of that. However, my *katra* was residing within Dr. McCoy, so I cannot categorically state that there is no afterlife."

"Do you believe in an afterlife?" his mother asked slowly.

"I do not know. I have no objective data to allow me to draw a conclusion."

Amanda smiled dryly. "Spoken like a true Vulcan, Spock."

Attempting to lighten the moment, the first officer bowed slightly. "Mother . . . you honor me."

"Oh, stop it," she said, chuckling despite everything. "You and your father . . . when you do that, I want to throw something at you!" She grasped one of the pillows, but her strength was not sufficient for her to make good on the implied threat . . . instead she sank back against her pillows, gasping.

Amanda's mention of his father caused all of Spock's anger to return full force. His mother did not miss the change in his expression, slight as it was. "Spock," she said, putting out a hand toward him, "try not to be angry with your father. Sarek is simply doing what he has to do, being who and what he is." Pride surfaced for a moment on her features. "And he *is* the best, Spock. Never forget that. Those people on Kadura could not have a better champion than your father."

"Senkar is also an experienced diplomat who has handled situations of this kind before. My father could have allowed him to negotiate with this Klingon renegade."

"You're really angry with him, aren't you?" Amanda's eyes were huge and full of distress. "Oh, Spock . . . long ago I begged Sarek to try and understand you, instead of simply judging you and finding you wanting. Now I ask you the same thing . . . try to understand your father! Forgive him . . . I know I do."

"Mother, I cannot," Spock said flatly. "You are his wife. His place is by your side."

Visibly upset, his mother closed her eyes, shaking her head as she lay limply against her pillows. "Oh, Spock . . . don't be so hard on him. We all make mistakes."

The Vulcan regarded her with concern, realizing that she was fighting back tears. He'd never meant to distress her. . . .

Spock put out a hand, closed it comfortingly over his mother's. "Very well, Mother. I will attempt to be more . . . understanding."

Amanda nodded weakly, her eyelids drooping. "Thank you, Spock. . . ."

The healer's aide suddenly appeared from out of the shadows in the sitting room, where the monitor screens were placed. Motioning to Spock to go, she whispered, "She will sleep now, Captain Spock. I suggest you leave and return later."

The Vulcan nodded quietly, and left the chill room and the slight, silent form of his mother.

## *Vulcan's Forge,* by Josepha Sherman & Susan Shwartz

Although an excerpt from *Vulcan's Forge* is included in Spock's chapter, *Vulcan's Forge* is an integral part of the Vulcan Chronicles because it continues the epic story of Vulcan that began in *Spock's World*. Ms. Sherman and Ms. Shwartz proved their understanding of Vulcan, its harshness and beauty, and how it formed the character of the people who evolved there as they took Spock and David Rabin on a journey that formed their characters. The related tales of Spock at two critical turning points that shaped his life told us as much about Vulcan as it did about Spock. Everything the authors described about Vulcans and Spock flowed logically and consistently from the histories presented in "Amok Time," *Star Trek III*, *Spock's World*, and

*Sarek.* What Ms. Sherman and Ms. Shwartz established of Spock's story in *Vulcan's Forge* might not be official Star Trek canon, but it ought to be.

This passage from *Vulcan's Forge* told the story of a difficult journey across the Vulcan desert by two boys of different worlds. In this journey, Spock and David Rabin learned to appreciate the best in each other and their home worlds.

*Vulcan, Deep Desert*
*Day 6, Eighth Week of Tasmeen, Year 2247*

SPOCK AND DAVID STOPPED TO GET THEIR BEARINGS, BOTH BOYS STARING at the far horizon, where a jagged mass of blackened rock hunched up from the reddish desert floor.

"No easy way to get around that," David said.

"No need to get around it. We must, instead, get over it."

"That . . . wasn't a joke, is it?"

"A play on words, I believe you call it? No. I only mean that we must climb over it, quite literally."

"Oh, now you've *got* to be joking!"

"The ascent is not as difficult as it seems. Others have climbed the ridge, and indeed the al-Stakna Mountains beyond, without mountaineering gear." That those others had been scientists trained in mountaineering was a fact he saw no reason to mention to David. "And once we have crossed it, we will be on the edge of the Womb of Fire."

"Now, that really makes me feel cheerful." David shaded his eyes with a hand. "I know distances in the desert are deceiving, but it looks like we could reach that thing in about an hour or so of quick hiking. How far away do you think it really is?"

"If my calculations are correct . . ." Spock began.

"If they're not correct, I'm dead and so are the rest of the hostages. I'm assuming that if I stick my head into the hypotenuse of this navigational triangle of yours, we won't both hang."

Spock flicked the human a sharp glance, letting him know what he thought of people who punned on mathematics. David's grin made his lips crack. "Once we cross the ridge," the human continued, giving them a perfunctory swipe with his tongue, "will we be able to see where Sered's got the hostages?"

"We should." Spock studied the rugged landscape, trying to pick out the easiest route: impossible at this range, even for sharp Vulcan vision. "As to your first question, barring unforeseen storms or other hazards, we should reach the ridge in time to rest overnight and start our ascent at first light."

"You think there's water up there?" David asked. "Not that I'm worried or anything, but we're pretty low on liquid supplies."

Spock glanced up. A *shavokh* circled high overhead, but it was clearly watching something other than the boys, and hunting other than dead prey. "The *shavokh* senses water," Spock said, then looked directly at David. "So will every other creature in the range."

"All of which are likely to be fanged, taloned, or toxic. Warning taken."

They started forward, heads down against a sudden sand-laden gust. Ahead, a shower of phantom rain quickly formed, tantalized them for a few moments, then just as swiftly disappeared. David stopped, blinking.

"Spock, what does a Vulcan mirage look like?"

"First I must know what mirages look like on your world."

"Oh . . . pools of water, swaying palm trees, happy camels, that sort of thing. Even buildings, sometimes. On Vulcan, a mirage wouldn't look like a dried-up streambed, would it?"

"Not unless you assume that the planet has turned malicious. Vulcan already possesses significant hazards without such fanciful concepts. And that," he added, following David's glance, "is hardly a mirage."

"Water?"

"Possibly just below the surface. Come, we shall see."

It was a long, shallow channel, faintly darker than the surrounding land, its smoothness broken by a rumble of rocks that had clearly been swept down from higher ground. It was even remotely possible, Spock thought, that this seemingly dried-up watercourse was part of the aquifer that supplied Sered's fortress. He cautiously studied the sky, then gestured to David to fan out some distance to the left.

"We may find water below the surface, but we must be wary."

"Gotcha. Whatever the odds are against a cloudburst anywhere in the vicinity—ha, or even miles away—I don't want to be anywhere near a water channel in a flash flood."

There was mud below the dried surface, and yet more mud below that, and after a time of fruitless digging, both boys gave up.

"Not worth it," David gasped.

"The energy expended in digging would far exceed the energy replaced by whatever water we reached," Spock agreed.

"But there's got to be water somewhere nearby if there's mud under this."

"The *shavokh* would not be hunting if there was not. Come, David, we shall follow its lead."

"And," David said, glaring up at the bird and rubbing his thorn-wounded arm reminiscently, "hope it's not going to be hunting us."

The land grew steadily rougher as the boys hiked toward the ridge, forcing them to pick their way among larger and larger chunks of basalt. By the time Vulcan's fierce sun had slipped behind the horizon, they had reached the sharp slope that was the true base of the ridge.

"You were right about how long it would take," David said, plopping down on a convenient rock, then added a wry, "Not going to say 'I told you so'?"

Spock glanced at him in genuine surprise. "Why? I did tell you so."

"Agh. Save me from literal-minded Vulcans."

"That, I take it, is a rhetorical remark." Recognizing one of the thorny plants clinging to the rough ground, Spock carefully broke off two stalks. "This contains sufficient moisture to keep us at least relatively comfortable."

"Food." David ironically held up one of the nearly inedible ration bars in one hand. "Moisture." He held up the stalk in the other. "And a nice, firm bed. Servants, wake me when it's morning."

"Before morning," Spock corrected. "We cannot waste the precious hours before the day's heat."

"Before," David agreed with a groan, and went flat.

By the time the sun had risen, the boys had been climbing for several hours.

"You're right," David panted. "Don't need special gear. Climbed worse at home. Climbing into a whole new set of hazards, though," he added, stopping to catch his breath. "Who'd have guessed there'd be so many blasted *crystals* in the rocks?"

"It is an unusual formation," Spock agreed.

"Why do I not feel privileged? And yes, that was another rhetorical question."

As the sun continued to rise, its rays beat down on boulders and rock spurs with ever-increasing force, the flare of sunlight on the crystals dazzling the boys despite David's protective visor and the veils of Spock's eyes. The narrow trail they were following blazed as though filled with melted stone, and they climbed slowly, afraid of pitfalls they might not see in time.

"If our path were easy," Spock said, trying to reassure the human and himself both, "predators native to this range would find it so as well."

"Gee, now that's comforting."

This low in the foothills, the temperature was not appreciably cooler. Nevertheless, the smallest increase in humidity brought Spock's head up; he could almost feel the skin of his face, taut against his planet's dryness, relax in proximity to . . .

He sniffed deliberately. The powdery, alkaline scent of a recent rockfall, but something else . . . He sniffed again. Yes! Unmistakably water! There was also the spoor of some animal, acrid enough to be a carnivore, vaguely familiar, but possible threats were overpowered by his survival instincts clamoring at him that *here was water, here was life, he must hurry!*

No. Haste was fatal in the desert, particularly when something had its lair nearby. David had scented it, too, reaching for the sling at his belt and checking his sidepouch for suitable ammunition.

*Let David hunt. Fresh meat will keep him healthy.*

As for himself, Spock thought, where there was water, there would surely be edible plants. That would extend how long they could survive out here—

*Until David runs out of tri-ox compound. If that happens, what then?*

Spock had already worked it out. To save David's life, he would have to be turned over to Sered, even if that put Spock's own chances at risk. He would have to be careful that David, jumping to one of his intuitive conclusions, did not anticipate this line of reasoning.

"Spock," David called softly, "there's something around here. I've spotted tufts of something that looks like fur, camouflaged against the rocks."

"Be careful."

"I will. But I don't see anything around."

*Neither do I. A predator prefers not to be seen. Until it springs.*

David was already scrambling up over a heap of rocks, and Spock hurried after. Yes, there was the pool, tiny, a deep indigo amid the black rocks, and infinitely welcome to his sight. Beyond the water lay a jumble of immense basalt boulders. Some long-ago earthquake must have sent them tumbling down to end up slanting against each other, forming a wilderness of caves.

How very curious: Although birds circled overhead, no animals came to drink.

"Something's wrong," David whispered. "Think the water's bad?"

Spock shook his head, pointing at animal tracks in the mud at the water's edge; creatures clearly used this pool regularly. "Our presence could be frightening them away."

"Or it could be some nasty predator lurking about."

"Exactly," Spock said softly. "I will stand guard while you fill the water bottles."

The human warily knelt at the water's edge. "Hey," he whispered, "here's another tuft of that fur. Not too pretty: orange with greenish tinges."

Spock stiffened as memory belatedly processed and returned data, all at once knowing exactly what he had smelled, what had left that fur.

"*Le-matya,*" he murmured.

"Heh?"

"It is a felinoid predator, a deadly mountain hunter. I did not think we had reached its range."

David shrugged. "Predators don't read the guidebooks. Now what?"

But Spock held up a warning hand, listening. He heard a faint mewling coming from the shadow of a rocky overhang. That was hardly the scream of a *le-matya.* Was something injured? Warily, he stalked forward, David following to guard his back.

So. Here were more tufts of fur, orange with green markings, teased by the wind. The mewling grew louder as the boys approached. Moving with exaggerated care, Spock peered into the darkness. Inside was a nest of dried plants and more fur. And within it squirmed six tiny *le-matya*s.

Full memory flashed to life:

*A scream of feral rage, a scrabble in the rock dust, and the* le-matya *all but cornering him until I-Chaya rose up, growling, the* sehlat*'s shabby coat fluffing upward in a feeble threat display as he showed his broken fangs. I-Chaya hurled himself between the* le-matya *and the child Spock, clearly demanding that his Vulcan "cub" take himself off and hide. Spock heard I-Chaya's yelp of agony as the* le-matya *swiped at him with those poisoned claws, knew his* sehlat *had just given him life at I-Chaya's own expense—*

These babies, so young that the poison sacs at the base of jaws and claws had not had time to fill, would grow into predators such as had killed I-Chaya. His hand clenching around a rock, Spock bent over the nest.

But then he hesitated. Warily, hardly understanding the urge, he reached out to touch one small creature, hearing it hiss in childish defiance. Why, *le-matya* fur was soft, softer than he would have imagined! How tiny the babies were—and how foolishly, marvelously brave, all but helpless yet trying to defend themselves, raising plump little paws that were only a fraction of the size they would one day be. The needle-thin talons that tipped them were more of a promise than a menace. One baby opened its mouth and yowled, showing what would one day be formidable fangs but were now little more than milk teeth. How could he—

"Spock, *look out!*"

With a shriek, the outraged adult *le-matya* lunged toward its nest—her nest—to protect her young. Spock flung himself away from the nest, falling, rolling, scrambling into the cover of a projecting rock, staring at the sheer size of the predator. The ones around Shikahr were big, but this was a creature of the Womb of Fire, perhaps even a successful mutation. He swung up onto the rock, fighting for the advantage of height.

But the creature had clearly caught his scent—and the smell of fear. Once again, Spock was seven years old and paralyzed at the approach of a deadly enemy. Once again, his control slipped as the *le-matya* screamed, exposing discolored fangs that were lethal enough of themselves but that carried a deadly nerve poison.

*David!* The thought stabbed through his paralysis. *If he moves, the* le-matya *will turn on him!*

Spock's hand fell to a sharp rock. He was no longer a child; he had most of the strength that an adult Vulcan male was supposed to have, and if he hit the *le-matya* just right, he would crush its skull.

But if he killed the creature, what happened to the kits? Ridiculous, illogical, maybe even fatal to hesitate, and yet—

"Move it, Spock!"

Spock had an instant's confused thought that David's shouts put him at risk. Then a rock bounced off the *le-matya*'s head. The creature howled and whirled, just in time for another to hit it on a sensitive ear, drawing green blood. A third rock struck near its eye. The *le-matya* screamed with rage and charged. But David was nowhere in sight.

*Oh, clever!* Spock thought, and threw a stone at the *le-matya*. The creature whirled, shrieking, and David launched a fusillade of tiny stones from his sling, peppering the *le-matya*'s tawny hide. As the predator spun and spun again, trying to find this enemy that could attack from all sides, Spock saw David gesture frantically, *Let's get out of here!*

*Indeed!*

287

He leaped from rock to rock, jumping down as David came running up, water bottles sloshing at his side. The two boys ran together until Spock brought them to a stop, listening.

"We are safe. She will have returned to her nest by now."

"Are you all right?" David was grabbing at him, wildly looking for wounds. "Did that thing claw you? And what in hell *was* it?"

The contact was not unpleasant, but it was a breach of control. As tactfully as he might, Spock freed himself. "That," he said, "was a *le-matya.*"

"The top predator? Well, it looks like about the top of the food chain to me, and I bet it thinks so too. Still," the human added, "to be fair, if I had a litter to protect, I guess I'd be furious, too."

"All *le-matya*s are like that," Spock corrected. "Perpetually raging. Alone of Vulcan's predators, they kill more than they need."

David's eyes widened. "Then why didn't you kill it? Or the kits? Those cute little critters are only going to grow up into monsters like that thing."

"It is wrong to kill an entire litter of even these babies. And killing their mother would bring about their deaths as well."

"Well, yes, but . . . well . . ."

"Besides, this is her land, not ours; and she was merely defending her young."

"Well," David said again, "at least we got the water. Let's put some distance between us and Mrs. *Le-matya.*"

He appointed himself—and his sling—as rear guard. Moving as quickly as they dared while keeping a watch for more *le-matyas,* they clambered up to the crest of the ridge. Spock pointed, not sure if he was satisfied with his navigational skills or—most illogical to feel this—alarmed at their accuracy.

"That," he said, "is the Womb of Fire."

Before them lay a twisted wilderness of black rock and gray cinder. Steam swirled up from fumaroles and pools of superheated water or boiling mud. Crusts of yellow sulfur and patches of blazingly green lichen were the only color in all that vast, tormented landscape, and the air shimmered with heat.

"Oh my God," David said with genuine reverence. "And we're going to cross *that?*"

"It can be done."

"You don't sound too sure about that."

"It can be done," Spock repeated. "We must merely be careful where we step."

"And breathe. Hey, no problem!"

"That, I assume, is sarcasm?"

"It most certainly is." David sank to his haunches with a sigh. "But we're on the right track, right? We're almost at Sered's hideout."

"We are."

"God. Never thought I'd be glad to see anything that looks like a burned-out hell," David said, then straightened, looking out over the waste. "Or maybe not burned-out at that. Still smoking down there somewhere. I just hope whatever's brewing doesn't boil up at us."

"It is illogical to worry about what cannot be helped."

"That's me, good old illogical human that I am." David produced a water bottle and held it out to Spock. "How long since you've had a drink?"

"Twenty-four point eight three six of your hours," Spock replied. He took the bottle and drank, then added, "You must surely know by now that it is a mistake to ask a Vulcan a 'rhetorical question.'"

"As long as you're alive to answer," David said. He looked out at the Womb of Fire. "That thing looks like it really is going to give birth."

"There," Spock said, suddenly realizing where he was and pointing. "We do not need to cross the entire Womb of Fire after all, merely one corner. That is what we seek, at the right edge of the Womb of Fire."

"That mountain? No . . . not a mountain. Bet it's what's left of a caldera all fallen in on itself."

"It is. And Sered's fortress lies within it. I recognize the rock formations."

David shuddered. "They're all in there. My mother, the students in the compound, half the diplomatic community resident on Vulcan. I . . . just hope they're all alive."

A human, Spock suspected, would have put his hand on David's shoulder, trying to reassure him by touch. He raised a hand, let it fall. For a Vulcan, touch provided no reassurance; and the simple need for contact was a breach of control.

David opened his pouch, looking inside. "I've got three tri-ox shots left," he told Spock. "Maybe I should space them further apart?"

"On the contrary," Spock said, "I would suggest that you inject yourself all the more regularly because of the sulfur fumes we will encounter as we proceed. Anoxia leads to bad judgment."

"Do *they* have tri-ox?" David demanded. "Do you think that Sered even cares if their hearts or lungs give out?"

"They have us," Spock said. "Such as we are. And such plans as we can contrive."

David settled himself more comfortably, clearly battling with himself for calmness. "We need a communicator. Once we get one, we can signal my mother's ship, Shikahr, oh, anything . . ."

"Including search teams. The authorities have surely been conducting overflights."

"Oh, right. With all this desert to be searched, I don't think we can count on the cavalry to come riding to the rescue."

Spock looked at him blankly. Cavalry? Was that not an archaic form of—ah. Another of David's movie references. One he had made before, equally illogically. "Perhaps not," Spock agreed. "But one of them might be able to provide reinforcements."

"First, we need that communicator. But . . . Spock, who were those people with Sered? Not Vulcans, and yet . . . I heard Sered speak of 'sundered cousins.' "

Spock met David's eyes unflinchingly. He owed the human his life, but privacy guarded the story of the "sundered cousins," one of the most tragic chapters of the calamitous time just before Surak's teachings and the saving transformation of Vulcan society.

David was the first to glance away. "I get it. 'I could tell you, but then I'd have to kill you.' "

Spock stared at him in startled horror. "I would never—"

"No, no, it was just an idiom! You meant it's classified stuff, right? Well, then we can assume a news blackout on material going out of this system. Time enough to worry about that when we get back." He whistled softly. "What a mess security's going to be!"

"As you say, time enough to worry when we are back."

"Still," David mused, "it's obvious those guys are Vulcanoid, so we know that what affects Vulcans affects them. I wish they didn't have all the Vulcan strengths."

Spock shook his head. "They may not," he said softly. "I have not heard that they preserved all of our ancient arts. This much I may tell you: Of the kindred who left Vulcan, not one came from Mount Seleya. Not one was an Adept of Gol."

"And wouldn't Psyops love that information! Never mind, never mind. Spock, we've survived on a wing and a prayer this long—yeah, another movie quote—so here's my plan. We get down there as quickly and safely as we can, and we seize any opportunity we get, just like we did when we escaped. We're bound to find time to set up a rockfall or something, or signal someone."

"You make it sound very simple."

"Well, yes, but remember that we'll have help. I know that the Starfleet folks will be doing everything they can to escape."

"And if they are too ill for that?"

"Oh. Well. We'll just have to . . . well . . ."

"Create a distraction?"

"Yes!"

"One strong enough to confuse an entire troop of armed and well-trained warriors?"

"We'll think of something," David said with a bold sweep of an arm. "After all, it's up to us."

Granted, Spock thought, his experience with humans was limited. But from what he had seen so far, it seemed that when humans made such sweeping statements, they usually did "think of something." Yes, and David was living proof of human resourcefulness—and the sheer will to survive. It might be only logical to trust both one more time.

In any event, Spock thought, looking out on the deadly waste before them, there was hardly a choice. Human wit and Vulcan logic were just about all that they had.

*Will it be enough?*

*As David would say,* he answered himself, *it will. It has to be.*

# CHAPTER 10

# The Noble Enemy, Part 1—Klingons

WHEN FIRST INTRODUCED ON THE ORIGINAL *STAR TREK*, THE KLINGONS were analogous to the Soviets, and the Federation–Klingon relationship was comparable to the dangerous cold war between the United States and the Soviet Union. The Klingons were seen as ruthless, dangerous, violent, and perhaps even evil. Their system of government was anathema to that of the Federation, and the Klingons and the Federation fought for influence over newly discovered planets and their people. However, the analogy was not precise; sometimes, the Klingons were seen not as irremediably evil, but as different, with a different point of view that might be as legitimate for them as ours is to us. In "Errand of Mercy" and "Day of the Dove," the *Enterprise* crew and the Klingons learned that they were not all that different from each other. Both species were rather violent and wedded to their own point of view. Far too frequently, each misunderstood the other, and both were prone to shoot first and ask questions later.

Despite the legendary Klingon bloodthirstiness, fans have always embraced Klingons and their warrior code. Klingons may even be the most popular aliens in Star Trek; fans dress as Klingons at Star Trek conventions and the premieres of the Star Trek films, fans attend Klingon language camps during the summer, and Pocket is publishing a Klingon version of *Hamlet* later this year. Worf, the sole Klingon in Starfleet, is a popular *TNG* and *DS9* character.

Klingons are adversarial in numerous Star Trek novels. They are Kirk's primary enemies, although Kirk frequently convinced them to fight against a common foe or toward a common goal. Although earlier Klingon adventures painted Klingons in a more negative light, most Klingon stories show them to be honorable warriors, with a code of their own and a workable system of values. Each of the books excerpted here examines Klingon honor and society.

# *The Final Reflection,* by John M. Ford

Many details about Klingon society presented in *The Final Reflection* have been contradicted by official Star Trek sources, including series episodes and films, but the tone and character of the Klingon people as established in *The Final Reflection* have never been questioned. *The Final Reflection* presented a complex and fascinating Klingon warrior culture and society in which the warrior code prevailed over all other concerns. There was a rigid class and family structure, but worthy individuals could advance within that structure. The story opened with a game of *klin zha,* a sort of live chess where the players fought each other and lived or died based on their skill and cunning, like gladiators of ancient Rome. Vrenn, a youth without a family, was a player who defeated his opponents and was adopted into a prominent Klingon House. When the House was disgraced and every member of it killed, he changed his name to Krenn. This book is his story.

*The Final Reflection* is a novel within a novel. On the surface, it is the story of *Enterprise* crew members reading a novel about Klingons, the story of Krenn's life and adventures. However, many of the events in Krenn's life actually occurred in the twenty-third-century Star Trek world. The book was popular but controversial fiction in the Federation, and it raised eyebrows on the *Enterprise,* particularly because it described brief encounters between Krenn and Spock, and Krenn and Dr. McCoy's grandfather. The following excerpt describes a chess game between Krenn and a very young Spock as they tested their wits against each other. This scene is intriguing, and, for the most part, consistent with Spock's character. However, I am not persuaded that Amanda would react to a Klingon with such unveiled hostility.

THE ONLY GOOD THING ABOUT THE EMBASSY RECEPTION, KRENN THOUGHT, was that it was not also a dinner. Those present were free to wander around a large building, starting or avoiding conversations as desired.

It was now common knowledge that the two Klingons understood the Federation language without translators, and discussions tended to sputter and shift as Krenn approached. This made little sense to him. Not only did half the beings present carry translating machines (or have servitors to carry them) but Krenn could not even hear very well. Akhil said it was the thinness of the air.

The air seemed thick enough to Krenn, but not pleasantly so. The Federation beings preferred talking around him than to him, but when he was asked questions, they were the same. Yes, he had been a privateer. No, he had never taken Federation prizes. Yes, he had killed with his hands. *And* his teeth. Krenn thought he should have a tape recorded.

In one of the larger rooms, the Vulcan Ambassador to Earth stood near a fireplace, speaking to a moderately large circle of guests of a dozen miscellaneous races. A human female, even-featured and light-haired, stood near the Ambassador: Krenn recalled from the first day's shock wave of introductions that she was the Vulcan's sole consort. Interested, Krenn went that way, not quite joining the group; no one turned to notice him as the tall Vulcan talked on.

Krenn could not understand any complete sentence of the lecture. The Ambassador's Federation Standard was Vulcan-flawless, of course, but there was no machine program that could make a Vulcan's technical conversation intelligible. Krenn supposed the other listeners must all be Thought Masters, or one of the equivalent Federation degrees. Or perhaps they had other reasons for standing in the barrage of words.

Krenn watched the human female. There seemed to be a tightness in her expression; if it was humor, it was not any sort he had seen. It looked more like distress, but at what? Krenn? No, she was not looking at him. She was not, Krenn saw, looking at anything.

A few of the Vulcan's words registered on Krenn: something about *chromosomes* and *intersplicing.*

Krenn withdrew, and wandered from room to room until he found Akhil, who was amusing himself with an electronic pattern-matching toy.

"Where did you get that?" Krenn said.

"There's a games room upstairs. Want to try this? It helps if you drink something strong."

"How does that help?"

"You don't mind losing. Here."

"Not now. Come with me. I need a Specialist to listen to something."

They went back to watch the Vulcan Ambassador, and listened

until the two Klingons together began to attract the attention Krenn alone had avoided.

"What was he talking about?" Krenn asked Akhil.

"I'm an astronomer, not a geneticist." There was a hesitation in his voice.

"That still tells me more than I knew. What was he talking about, even generally?"

"Oh, I know more than generally. He's discussing genetic fusion. Don't you remember, when we were meeting half the Federation, that son of theirs—seven or eight years old? He's a fusion, and the Ambassador was describing the process."

"With his consort present?" Krenn said, astonished and disgusted.

"What? Was she there?" Akhil said, distracted. "He said something really interesting, in with all the technical detail."

Krenn said, carefully, "Interesting?" He had heard Akhil call off incoming fire as if it concerned him not at all; he had heard the exec tear a slacking junior officer into raw protein with his voice. But only very rarely had he heard Akhil angry. It was not a loud effect. The sharpest knives are the quietest. And 'Khil was angry now.

"He was saying that the fusion techniques were 'only recently perfected by Vulcan scientists.' *Recently perfected?* If that gets back to the Imperial Institutes of Research, there are going to be some *tharavul* headed back to Vulcan, warp four. Without a ship around them."

"How can he say that? If he lies—" Krenn thought that, if it should be found that a Vulcan could lie, the *tharavul* would soon be more than just deaf telepathically.

"Lies?" Akhil said, and stopped short; the anger slipped out of his voice. "No. He doesn't lie. He reports scientific results." Akhil laughed. "Scientists know some tricks Imperial Intelligence will never master."

Krenn asked Akhil the way to the Embassy game room, and they separated again. Krenn climbed a curving white staircase, carpeted in black velvet with tiny crystal stars, and turned down the corridor Akhil had indicated. He passed a door, and despite that it was closed and his hearing diminished, he could clearly hear a human voice within, saying, ". . . not whether Tagore's a competent negotiator, we're not even that far along in the argument. First I want to know if the bastard's *sane.*"

There was an unintelligible reply.

"I'll *grant* you that . . . volunteering for this should be grounds for confinement. But you know his record . . . all right, sure, but would you send Gandhi to argue Hitler out of . . . How do we *know* he won't?"

The rest was lost in a sound of plumbing. Krenn moved on to the room he wanted.

It was dim within, pleasantly so after the Earth-level lighting of the main rooms. Spotlights shone on tables set for several different games; Krenn examined the unfamiliar ones, and sat down at a chessboard with pieces lathe-turned from bright and dark metal.

"Would you wish an opponent, sir?" said a voice behind Krenn. He turned, hand dropping to his weapon. There was a small being a few meters from him, in a spotlit alcove of the room; it had been reading a book. It came forward.

It was only a child, Krenn saw at once. The hair was cut in the Vulcan style, and the ears were unmistakable.

"My parents are downstairs," the young Vulcan said. "I did not wish to be an annoyance. I will leave."

This must be the ambassador's son, Krenn thought, the fusion. "You do not annoy me," he said, as the boy moved toward the door. "And I would welcome a chance to play this game."

Krenn won the chess game, but he did not win it easily. "A pleasant game," he said. "My compliments to a worthy opponent."

The child nodded.

Krenn said, "That is a phrase we use at the conclusion of our game, *klin zha.* In my language it is *'Zha riest'n, teskas tal'tai-kleon.'*"

*"Zha riest'n,"* the boy said, carefully copying Krenn's pronunciation, *"teskas tal . . . la . . ."*

*"Tal'tai-kleon."*

*"Tal'tai-kleon."*

*"Kai,"* Krenn said, and laughed.

"Are you the Klingon captain, sir, or the science officer?"

"I am the captain . . . of the cruiser *Fencer,*" Krenn said. He had been about to give his full name and honorific, but it had suddenly seemed unnecessary. *Rather silly.* And he was tired of introductions. "Have you ever thought of being a starship captain?"

The boy's lips compressed. Then he said, "I plan to be a scientist. But perhaps I will join the Starfleet."

"The sciences are a good path. I'm sorry my specialist isn't here to talk to you."

"No insult was meant, sir—"

"None was assumed."

"There will be a logical choice."

296

"Sometimes there is," Krenn said. "Another game?"

They talked as they played. It did not affect the boy's play, but Krenn let a bishop get away from him, and lost. The boy gave him the whole *klingonaase* phrase, perfectly accented.

*"Sa tel'ren?"* Krenn said.

"What does that mean, Captain sir?"

"Two out of three."

Krenn wondered what Vulcan children said to a fusion in their midst. The two races were similar to start with, and this one's physical characteristics leaned to the Vulcan. The ears especially. Krenn tried to think what would have happened, in his House Gensa, to one with Vulcan ears. He seemed to feel the blood on his fingers. Would it be green, he wondered.

The boy moved a knight, taking one of Krenn's rooks. He waited.

Krenn slid a pawn forward.

"Given the established balance of our skills, Captain, and other factors being equal, you cannot defeat me with the odds of a rook. It would be logical for you to resign."

"Klingons do not resign," Krenn said. Seven or eight years old, Akhil had said. Krenn had killed his first intelligent being when he was this one's age. A human starship crewman, a prize, in the Year Games.

"The sequence of moves is predictable, and barring suboptimal strategies, inevitable. The time consumed—"

"If I go to the Black Fleet, what matter that I go a little slowly?" Krenn thought of the human, who had shouted challenge into Krenn's face even as he died. It was an honorable death, and a glorious kill.

"What is the Black Fleet?" the Vulcan asked.

Krenn was pulled back from his memory. "One who serves his ship well, in the life we see, will serve on a ship of the Fleet when this life ends." Krenn's Federation vocabulary was not right for this; the words would not fit together as Dr. Tagore could make them to fit. "In the Fleet there is the death that is not death, because not the end; there is the enemy to be killed a thousand times, and each time return; and there is the laughter."

"Laughter?" the boy said. "And enemies?" His eyes were calm, and yet almost painfully intense to Krenn who struggled to make the languages meet, and wondered why he so badly needed to.

"Fed, Rom . . . others," Krenn said. "Without *kleoni,* what would be the purpose?"

"My mother says that the spirit is eternal," the boy said. "My father says this is true in a purely figurative sense, as the wisdom of Surak is not forgotten, though Surak is become unstructured."

"We have one who is not forgotten," Krenn said. "His name was Kahless. When his ship was dying, he had his hand bound to his Chair, that no one could say he left it, or that another had been in the Chair at the ship's death. Then all his crew could escape without suspicion, because Kahless had taken on all the ship's destiny.

"*Kahlesste kaase,* we say. Kahless's Hand."

"This would seem a supremely logical act."

"*Logical?*" Krenn said, and then he understood. The boy was raised in his father's culture. It was the highest praise he knew. "I think you are right," Krenn said. "I had not perceived the logic of the situation."

"My father says that this is his task: to communicate logic by example."

Is that why you were caused to exist? Krenn was thinking. As an example? He could see that the boy was proud of what he had just done—communicated to a Klingon! Was that not the victory? And yet he could not shout it. Vulcans did not shout.

"My mother is a teacher," the boy said. "She also communicates. My parents are—" He looked away.

"My mother," Krenn said, "was not of my father's race."

The boy turned his eyes on Krenn once more. It could not be called a stare, it was absolutely polite, but it did pierce, and the arched eyebrows cut.

"It is a custom on Earth," the Vulcan said, "on concluding a chess game, to shake hands."

Krenn's liver pinched. That was not a Vulcan custom, he knew well enough. Touching a Vulcan's hand opened the path for the touch of their minds. And *that* touch could pull out thoughts that the agonizer or the Examiner's tools could never reach. It was said by some that it could burn the brain; Krenn did not believe this, but . . .

*The touch,* Krenn thought, *the touch.* And he raised his right hand, slowly held it out over the chessboard, palm up.

The boy extended his own hand, above Krenn's, palm down. A drop of water fell into Krenn's palm.

*A Vulcan sweating. And I am drenched already.*

There was a choked cry from the doorway, a scream stopped at the last instant. Krenn and the boy turned together, and saw the ambassador's consort standing there, her whole body rigid, her knuckles bone-white against the sides of her face.

*"What is this?"* the human said.

The boy said, "We were playing a game—"

"Game!" It was half a gasp. The female looked at Krenn, and the hatred in her look was like a blow against his body.

Then she said, very calmly, without looking away from Krenn, "Your father's looking for you. Go to him now."

"Yes, Mother." At the door, the boy stopped, turned, held up his hand with fingers at an angle. "Live long and prosper, Captain."

Krenn nodded. He could still feel the hate and fear radiating from the human. He raised his hand and saluted the boy, who bowed and went out.

"I don't . . ." said the ambassador's consort, still angry and frightened, but now with the tension of confusion as well.

"You would fight for your line," Krenn said. "That is a good thing. I think that is the best honor I know. That one is . . ." He tried to think of a praise the human could not misinterpret. ". . . worthy of the stars." He was, now, a little relieved that events had ended when they had.

The woman's face had softened, though her stance was still rigid. "Perhaps I misunderstood," she said. "I am sorry. It can be hard to . . . protect a child, on Vulcan."

"You fear the Klingon," Krenn said. "In this is no need for apology."

## *Day of Honor, Book One: Ancient Blood,* by Diane Carey

*Ancient Blood* is Book One and the *TNG* entry in the *Day of Honor* series about a joint Klingon-human holiday. As established in the original series Day of Honor book, *Treaty's Law,* by Dean Wesley Smith and Kristine Kathryn Rusch, the Day of Honor holiday originated from an alliance between Kirk and Kor in the defense of a Klingon colony against an alien threat. On the Day of Honor, Klingons pay homage to what it means to be Klingon, reflecting on their lives and the meaning of honor. In *Ancient Blood,* Worf's honor was sorely tested during an undercover mission on the planet Sindikash, a human colony that was an unusual mix of the American Old West and the Middle East. Worf was assigned to investigate the criminal activities of the government and prevent its secession from the Federation. Everything Worf believed about honor was tested by his mission on Sindikash, and his relationship with his son was endangered because Alexander questioned the decisions Worf made in the name of honor.

Because the mission took Worf away on the Day of Honor, he requested Captain Picard to take his place and observe the holiday with Alexander. Picard gave the boy his choice of activities, and Alexander chose to reflect on the concept of honor as followed by his human relatives and ancestors from the United States Revolutionary War. Picard and Alexander learned much about honor from their adventure on the holodeck as crew members of a British ship in that war.

The excerpt from *Ancient Blood* describes Worf's first encounter with the evil Odette Khanty and her rogue Klingon guards, Klingons with no honor.

HE FELT THE EYES OF ODETTE KHANTY AND HER GUARDS. THE CAFE D'Atraq was in the middle of the city square, and he knew she would not notice him as long as he and Grant did not get up. All the natives were clearing a path, tightening into the sides of the square to allow her and her elite team of Klingon guards to pass through.

This place, this planet and its townships, was a tapestry woven of the Oriental Express and the American Old West. With a transplanted populace of Greeks, Turks, Lebanese, Armenians, Assyrians, Tuscans, and Moors, Sindikash bore a decidedly Gothic atmosphere. The planet's buildings were frontierish, its prevailing spirit exotic, and Worf and Grant were two outworlders in a place that knew its identity.

Watching Mrs. Khanty and her hooded guards move toward them under the tiled arches of the mosquelike square, Worf and Grant were now alone in a deserted cafe, while dozens of people eyed them from the sides of the square. All others had moved politely aside.

The woman touched the front of her pink suit to make sure it was perfectly presentable, then fingered the silk Paisley scarf neatly pinned at her neck. Her dark blond hair had been put perfectly in place, though it appeared to be casual; straight but thick, curved under slightly at the bottom, just above her shoulders. Just right. Feminine, yet efficient. Worf knew about her—she was not born to the place with which she had become so unbreakably associated. She saw herself as having earned her position.

Anger bled into Worf's heart as the eyes of the guards, the Rogues, fixed upon him and he felt their animosity.

Klingons. They really were Klingons! Every one of them was a *Klingon!*

Khanty nodded to her vanguard to keep moving forward in spite of Worf blocking their path.

Klingons. Klingons in service to a human. A human woman. A woman criminal.

What kind of Klingons . . .

He knew Commissioner Toledano wasn't lying, and Worf had expected Klingons, yet until this moment he had been hoping that the perpetrators of such atrocities were not *just* Klingons. Perhaps dregs had been dug up from all sorts of cultures across space, and Starfleet Intelligence had mentioned only the Klingons because Klingons were so visibly different from most humanoids. Perhaps that.

But now, as he looked at Mrs. Khanty's Rogues, as they were known on Sindikash, he saw that this was a pack of Klingons and only Klingons, a pack who had simply rejected anything Klingons are supposed to think about right and wrong, not here because of any sense of honorable conquest, duty, family loyalty, or anything else Klingons might be motivated by. These had just thrown all that away, cast off centuries of attachment to the things that held a culture together. These Klingons were destructively pursuing personal power, rather than acting in some way that would hold society, even Klingon society, together. Profit and gain could be pursued in a way that strengthened culture, but these Klingons wanted to go around those rules and achieve through the basest acts of brutality and opportunism.

Scum. Nothing. He was looking at empty hoods. Empty!

"Ugulan." Mrs. Khanty's voice sounded in the quiet square as she spoke quietly to the sergeant of her guard. "The Klingon."

"Yes, Mrs. Khanty." As if he didn't notice that he himself was Klingon and so were all his men, Ugulan motioned for his men to halt, but they remained in formation around her.

Then Ugulan himself stepped forward, his face deeply shaded by the purple hood. He moved through the empty tables to the one where Worf sat defiantly. With his purple hood and the dagger at his belt, he was effectively threatening.

"You will stand aside for Mrs. Odette Khanty to pass through," he said.

Grant looked at Worf, but said nothing.

Worf sipped his drink, took a long, considered swallow, then said, "I will not be moved."

"All citizens must stand aside when a public official comes through," Ugulan insisted. His tone implied this would be the last polite suggestion.

Worf looked up at him. "I am not a Seniard. Therefore I do not move."

"Therefore," Ugulan responded, pulling his dagger, "your friend is arrested."

Springing to his feet, Grant gasped, "What? Hey! I'm just visiting!"

The dagger swung upward as if to be its own exclamation point, and was on the downward arc when Worf came to life. Ah! At last! His move was extremely simple and not particularly inspired, a basic block of Ugulan's arm, but Worf imagined he had Ugulan nearly figured out already and could afford to not be creative.

He was right. Ugulan was thrown off, and clattered into a stand of empty iron chairs. The chairs went over, clanging like gongs against the brickwork street, and Ugulan went down among them. By the time he had scrambled to one knee, Worf was squared off between Ugulan and Grant, standing ground like a living portcullis.

One of the other Rogues clasped Mrs. Khanty's arm to draw her away from the developing trouble, but she resisted.

Worf didn't wait for Ugulan to get entirely to his feet, but freely charged the guard and drove him into a parqueted wall, knocking a stenciled sign from its hook. Ugulan's hood fell from his head, revealing his spinelike brow ridge and showing clearly that he, too, was a Klingon, as if there had been a bit of doubt.

Worf had clung to that silly doubt, but now his rage drove down his illogic.

Angry now, Ugulan reached into his jacket and drew his government phaser.

Worf didn't back off. "So," he said, "the Rogue Force of Sindikash uses women's weapons."

Evidently one of the universe's classic simpletons, Ugulan allowed himself to be goaded. He thrust himself to his feet and accommodated his opponent by holstering the phaser and bringing the dagger forward again.

Guarding Mrs. Khanty, the other Rogues were furious, too. Any guard who had his phaser out now put it away.

"You're so predictable, boys," the woman commented.

"Let us!" one demanded.

Would they make no move without her permission? Were Klingons not Klingons?

"Go, Genzsha," she said.

Two of the Rogues stayed with her, but the forward four rushed to Ugulan's side, and all squared off against Worf.

The big contenders circled slowly against the square's buildings. By appearance, Klingons fit well among the medieval dye colors of Sindikash—earthy, moody, deep and stirring colors that gave an impression of permanent autumn, flickering with gilded designs crafted from the planet's micalike ores. Even the brickwork imitated the woven texture of the Persian-style carpets the colony was famous for.

It also made a mean surface to knock against. Hitting a wall on Sindikash was entirely different from hitting a wall anywhere else. The walls here had exposed dentils of brick to smash against, and the newcomer made good use of that. Careful not to let Ugulan get a grip on him, Worf shoved Ugulan and two other Rogues into the same wall so hard that the impact set a stained glass window rattling. They all came up again, but came up bruised and gashed from the ragged brickwork. If only all planets cooperated so well.

Holographers who had been following Mrs. Khanty and the Rogues sprang forward now and began recording the moment. Some even dared skirt the onlookers or dodge through the grappling Klingons so they could get images of Mrs. Khanty standing there, watching calmly.

A silk wall covering shivered as Worf blew past, with two Rogues in his grip. The cafe became a blur of kicks, spins, elbows, and grunts. Stacks of etched clay urns dissolved and skittered across the brick, matched instantly by the audible crack of a limb. Worf almost stopped to make sure the limb wasn't his—then decided a broken arm would only make him angrier and that might help.

An instant later, though, one of the Rogues went down groaning. Genzsha moved forward to drag his fallen comrade from the arena, but did not join the fight himself.

Worf decided he would have to do without a broken arm, and therefore crammed his elbow into the face of a second Rogue and knocked him silly. Two down.

He knew he might be giving himself away—certainly, if they paid any attention they would see the Starfleet training involved in his movements. Not just the systematic moves of a schooled Klingon, but uneven elements of surprise, attack, feint, never letting his timing or style be mapped. Just when he was expected to block a punch, he would let it through, but dodge it, ripping every tendon in his attacker's arm. The two remaining Rogues were still fighting, but they were also dizzy and grunting.

Driven by the personal insult these men were to him, Worf took on both at once, not allowing them to divide the attack as they attempted. He took a vicious blow from one, but, instead of swinging back, he reached out to the other and dragged them together before him.

Then, with physical control that surprised even himself, Worf lowered his arms and stood very still. His shoulders went slack. His stance changed. He stopped fighting.

Since he had stopped, the two remaining Rogues could no longer be justified in attacking him again. Like wolves twitching around a stag who refused to run, they blinked, gaped, shifted, and glanced back at Mrs. Khanty, but they didn't know what to do. Boiling with frustration, Ugulan burped a command in Klingon, and then the Rogues grappled the newcomer.

Their eyes rolled with contempt, for he had humiliated them by stopping. Clearly, they knew, Worf hadn't had to let himself be arrested.

His plan was a success. Odette Khanty was intrigued.

She moved between her battered guards and stood before the only Klingon in the square who didn't work for her.

"Why did you let yourself be taken?" she asked.

Worf controlled his breathing enough to imply that he wasn't even winded. He could breathe later.

"Because you have to maintain order," he said, too quietly for the people watching to hear. "If your men are not feared, you will not have order."

"Then why did you fight in the first place?"

"To demonstrate that I did not have to be moved if I did not want to be."

"If you had just let yourself be stunned, you'd have just woken up later on the street. Now they're going to have to beat you."

"Fine."

"And after making your point, you'll let yourself be beaten?"

"That's right."

"You'd have done very well during the Middle Ages. On Earth, I mean. Where did you learn to fight?"

He felt his dark face flush bronze. "I tried to join Starfleet."

"Why?"

"Some Klingons claimed that Starfleet is the place to be. That they were trying to get in. I spit on them all."

"On Starfleet?"

"Daily."

"Why do you spit on a force you tried to join?"

"I spit on their insistence that lessers should be able to tell me what

304

to do. That I should be subservient to people I knew were not my equals. They do not allow men who disagree to settle it like men."

"So what happened? They kicked you out? Why?"

"I disciplined my commanding officer."

Odette Khanty grinned. She seemed to find that idea appealing, considering Starfleet's buttoned-up manners.

"Well, you're going to be taken into custody for a while for disturbing the peace. What's your name?"

Worf said nothing.

The woman continued to gaze at him, refusing to ask again.

Finally he shifted and answered, "My name is Worf."

"All right, Worf. I'll probably speak to you later."

Odette Khanty looked through the groaning guards to Ugulan, who was glaring through his own wounded ego at Worf.

"Detain him in the capitol prison. Hold his friend, too."

"On what charge?" Ugulan asked.

"The same. And check out his story about Starfleet."

"Yes, Mrs. Khanty."

"Well, here we are. In jail."

Grant seemed untroubled by their predicament, Worf thought.

"Obviously." Stating the obvious was another of Grant's habits that Worf found hard to bear. Then again, what was obvious to Grant might not be obvious to others. An observation Grant had made on Gariath IV had saved ten people's lives.

"Not bad, as jails go. I mean, they got carpets, y'know?"

As vital as Grant's observations might be, Worf could not force himself to listen. Grant's voice faded into the background as he reflected on what his oath to Starfleet and his own honor had forced him into: He had lost a battle on purpose, which was difficult enough. But to lose it to warriors who had forsaken their code of honor!

But by his action, Worf had gotten this powerful woman's personal attention. For good or otherwise? Worf refused to judge yet but clung to the statement the woman had made about talking to him later. He knew he had managed to tickle her interest in him, and that she preferred using Klingons as her personal security team. She had shown definite curiosity about him when he'd proven that he was more clever, if not stronger, than any of her current Rogues.

How the other Rogues would feel if he joined them—he would deal with that when the time came.

"Somebody's coming!" Grant said suddenly.

Worf sat up, listened to the faint thud of several footsteps on the stone outside this dugout holding area, then carefully eased back and tried to look as if he didn't care about much.

Under the soft lights of the cellblock corridor, Ugulan and two of his guards strode in, with Odette Khanty in their midst. She was a poised woman who struck Worf as efficient but cold, colder in person than her carefully crafted public image. She approached the cell bars as if they weren't even there.

She looked directly at Worf, ignoring Grant entirely. "It's even worse than you said. You broke your commanding officer's jaw and three ribs."

Worf offered only a limited shrug. "It is not my fault if he had weak bones."

"Why did you come to Sindikash?"

"I like the architecture."

Mrs. Khanty's mouth pursed a bit, rounding her cheeks. "You came because Starfleet has so little authority here at the moment. You came because we're in a state of flux between Federation membership and autonomy. You weren't kicked out of Starfleet. You're absent without leave. There's a pending assault charge."

"How interesting."

"Why didn't you go back to Qo'noS?"

Sudden silence fell between them. They looked at each other, dueling.

"Same problems there, hm?" Mrs. Khanty eventually said.

Worf scowled. "Many Klingons no longer understand the need for authority. They made a treaty with the Federation."

"I understand that sort of feeling."

"It is not a feeling. It is fact."

"Yes, of course." She watched him for a moment. "You beat my Rogues. How did you do that?"

Worf clenched his fists to keep from spitting on her. Here was a woman who had found a way to make Klingons turn from their honor. They were nothing but low-life murderers, souring the reputation of Klingons all around. Could he pretend to be a Klingon with no honor?

"Klingons are ethnocentric," he said. "They have a tendency, more than most, to think they are superior in every way. They do not see the strength in others. That is why we could not, for so long, beat back the Federation. But I have grown beyond such constraints. I see the strength of rigorous rationality in Vulcans. I see the stubbornness of humans. There is strength in patience. There is strength in calmness.

I remained calm and stubborn in the face of your Rogues, and I beat them."

"By understanding those who would be your enemies, yes," she said. "I see that. Very good. I like that. You beat Klingons by understanding the weakness of Klingons."

Stung by this woman's approval, Worf forced a nod of thanks. He saw in her eyes an incredible coldness that seemed to compensate for her inability to wield a weapon. Oh—it burned to be admired by such a person! He was embarrassed for himself because he had to gain her approval at all, but embarrassed also for the Rogues, who were for some reason ruled by this person.

"I have an offer for you. As you noticed, I have a special security team of Klingons. They call themselves the Rogues. That's their own name for themselves. I need them, because I can't trust anyone else. Not until my husband recovers and can take his governorship again. My husband wants us to establish our independence. I stand by that."

"Sindikash is a Federation colony."

"Was. Was a colony. We stand on our own now. We're frontiersmen, we Seniards. We're all expatriates from Earth, mostly from middle and eastern Europe. We're very tough people; we want our own identity. The lieutenant governor doesn't want us to have that chance. With the governor ill, I have to stand alone against those who would destroy my husband's dream."

"You think the lieutenant governor arranged the assassination attempt on your husband?"

The woman paused. "You're very blunt, aren't you?"

"Yes."

"I appreciate that. Within the next two hours, you should decide whether you might like to be part of the Rogue Force. If so, I can offer you protection from Starfleet."

"Can I have this human as my assistant?"

"Why would you want a human assistant?"

"He saved my life once. I owe him."

Khanty seemed to appreciate that on some level or other. "I guess you can have whatever you want. The Rogues are very independent. We appreciate independence here. But be clear on this: I need loyalty. Things happen to those who betray me or don't keep their agreements. The rewards of loyalty are equally bountiful."

Worf eyed her. "And what if you fail to keep your part of the agreement?"

The woman looked at him, and she was suddenly as cool as the wall.

"Then you may kill me," she said. "That's the deal."

# *Kahless,* by Michael Jan Friedman

Kahless the Unforgettable was an iconic figure in Klingon society, an icon brought back to life by genetic cloning technology in the *TNG* episode "Rightful Heir." In *Kahless,* the novel by Michael Jan Friedman, the alliance between Gowron, Kahless and the Klingon High Council was threatened by a military coup and assassination plot against Gowron. The threat was compounded by a threat to Klingon society itself from the discovery of a scroll purporting to contain the actual history of the original Kahless. This scroll, found on the road to *Sto-Vo-Kor* traveled by Kahless at the very end of his life, told a very different story of Kahless's battles against the tyrant Molar than the legends passed down through the eons. Those legends had formed the basis of everything Klingons believe.

Worf faced a severe crisis of faith caused by the discovery of the ancient scroll because of his literal belief in the ancient legends. He decided to replay the ancient stories on the holodeck to test his beliefs, but his quest for understanding merely raised more questions. He searched for answers as he, Picard, and the current Emperor Kahless worked together to combat the threat to the Empire.

THE VOLCANO SHOT GLORIOUS RED STREAMERS OF MOLTEN ROCK HIGH INTO the ponderous gray heavens. But that was just the first sign of its intentions, the first indication of its fury.

A moment later, in an angry spasm of disdain for the yellow and green plant life that grew along its black, fissured flanks, a tide of hissing, red lava came bubbling over the rim of the volcano's crater. The tide separated into rivers, the rivers into a webwork of narrow streams—each one radiating a horrible heat, each one intensely eager to consume all in its path.

In the distance, thunder rumbled. At least, it appeared to be thunder. In fact, it was the volcano itself, preparing to heave another load of lava out of the scorched and tormented earth.

The name of this severe and lonely place was Kri'stak. It was the first time the volcano had erupted in nearly a hundred years.

A Klingon warrior was making his way up the volcano's northern slope, down where the rivers of spitting, bubbling lava were still few and far between.

The warrior wore a dark leather tunic, belted at the waist and embossed with sigils of Klingon virtues. The shoulders of the garment were decorated with bright silver circlets. On his feet, he wore heavy leather boots that reached to midthigh; on his hands, leather gloves reinforced with an iron alloy.

The warrior's enterprise seemed insane, suicidal. This was a volcano in full eruption, with death streaming from its every fissure. But that didn't seem to dissuade him in the least.

Picking his way carefully over the pitted slope, remaining faithful to the higher ridges the lava couldn't reach, he continued his progress. When he reached a dead end, he simply leaped over the molten rock to find a more promising route elsewhere.

At times, the figure vanished behind a curtain of smoke and cinders, or lost his footing and slipped behind some outcropping. Yet, over and over, he emerged from the setback unscathed, a look of renewed determination on his face. Sweat pouring from his bright red brow, he pushed himself from path to treacherous path, undaunted.

Unfortunately, his choices were narrowing radically as he approached the lip of the crater. There was only one ridge that looked to give him a chance of making it to the top—and that was guarded by a hellishly wide channel.

It wasn't impossible for him to make the leap across. However, as drained as he must have been by this point, and as burdened by his heavy leather tunic, it was highly unlikely he'd survive the attempt.

Spreading his feet apart to steady himself, the warrior raised his arms above his head and unfastened the straps that held his tunic in place. Then he tore it from him and flung it into the river of lava below, as if tendering a sacrifice to some dark and ravenous demon.

In moments, the tunic was consumed, leaving little more than a thin, greasy trail of smoke. Nor would the Klingon leave the world much more than that, if he failed.

But he hadn't come this far to be turned away now. Taking a few steps back until his back was to yet another brink, the warrior put his head down and got his legs churning beneath him. It was difficult for his boots to find purchase on the slick, steamy rock, but the Klingon worked up more speed than appeared possible.

At the last possible moment, he planted his right foot and launched himself out over the channel. There was a point in time, the size and span of a long, deep breath, when the warrior seemed to hover over the crackling lava flow, his legs bicycling beneath him.

Until he completed his flight by smashing into the sharp, craggy surface of the opposite ridge. For a moment, it looked as if he had safely avoided the lava, as if he had come away with the victory.

Then he began sliding backward into the river of fire. Desperately, frantically, the warrior dug for purchase with fingers and knees and whatever else he could bring to bear—even his cheek. Yet still he slid.

The rocky surface tore at the warrior's chest and his face, but he wouldn't give into it. Slowly, inexorably, by dint of blood and bone, he stopped himself. Then he began to pull himself up from the edge of death's domain.

Finally, when he felt he was past the danger, he lay on the ground—gulping down breath after breath, until he found the strength to go on. Dragging himself to his feet, too drained even to sweat, he stumbled the rest of the way up the ridge like a man drunk with too much bloodwine.

At the brink of the crater, the Klingon fell to his knees, paused, and pulled a knife from the inside of his boot. It was a *d'k tahg,* a ceremonial dagger. Lifting a thick lock of hair from his head, he held it out taut and brought the edge of his blade across it. Strand by severed strand, it came free in his hand.

For a long moment, he stared at the lock of hair. Then he dropped it into the molten chaos inside the volcano, where it vanished instantly.

But only for a moment or two. Then it shot up again on a geyser of hot, sulfurous air. Except now it was coated with molten, flaming rock, an object of unearthly beauty, no longer recognizable as a part of him.

Mesmerized, the warrior extended his hand, as if to grasp the thing. Incredibly, it tumbled toward him, end over end. And as if by magic, it fell right into the palm of his gauntleted hand.

Bringing it closer to him, the Klingon gazed at it with narrowed eyes, as if unable to believe what had happened. Then, his glove smoking as it cradled the lava-dipped lock, he smiled a hollow-cheeked smile—and started his journey down the mountain.

Worf, son of Mogh, hung in the sky high above it all, a spectator swathed in moist, dark cloud-vapors, his eyes and nose stinging from the hot flakes of ash that swirled like tiny twisters through the air.

He hovered like some ancient god, defying gravity, hair streaming in the wind like a banner. But no god ever felt so troubled, so unsettled—so pierced to the heart.

For a moment, all too brief, he had been drawn to the spectacle, to its mysticism and its majesty. Then the moment passed, and he was left as troubled as before.

"Mister Worf?"

The Klingon turned—and found himself facing Captain Picard,

who was walking toward him through the clouds as if there were an invisible floor beneath him.

The captain had come from the corridor outside the holodeck, which was still partially visible as the oddly shaped doors of the facility slid shut behind him. It wasn't until they were completely closed that Picard became subject to the same winds that buffeted Worf.

The captain smiled politely and tilted his head toward the volcano. "I hope I'm not interrupting anything important," he said.

Inwardly, the Klingon winced at the suggestion. Certainly, it had *seemed* important when he entered the holodeck half an hour ago. There had been the possibility of solace, of affirmation. But the experience had fallen far short of his expectations.

"No," he lied. "Nothing important. I am merely reenacting the myth of Kahless's labors at the Kri'stak Volcano."

Picard nodded. "Yes, of course . . . the one in which he dips a strand of his hair into the lava." His brow wrinkled as he tried to remember. "After that, he plunged the flaming lock into Lake Lusor—and twisted it into a revolutionary new form of blade, which no Klingon had ever seen before."

Worf had to return the human's smile. Without a doubt, Picard knew his Klingon lore—perhaps as well as the average Klingon. And in this case even better, because this particular legend had been nurtured by a select few until just a few years ago.

"That is correct," he confirmed.

Pointing to the northern slope of the volcano, he showed the captain Kahless's position. The emperor-to-be had hurled himself across the deep channel again—this time with a bit less effort, perhaps, thanks to the improvement in the terrain he was leaping from—and was descending the mountainside, his trophy still in hand.

It was only after much hardship that he would come to the lake called Lusor. There, he would fashion from his trophy the efficient and graceful weapon known as the *bat'telh.*

Picard made an appreciative sound. "Hard to believe he could ever have made such a climb in fact."

Worf felt a pang at the captain's remark. He must not have concealed it very well this time, because Picard's brow furrowed.

"I didn't mean to question your beliefs," the human told him. "Only to make an observation. If I've offended you—"

The Klingon waved away the suggestion. "No, sir. I am not

offended." He paused. "It was only that I was thinking the same thing."

Picard regarded him more closely. Obviously, he was concerned. "Are you . . . having a crisis of faith, Lieutenant? Along the lines of what you experienced before Kahless's return?"

Worf sighed. "A crisis of faith?" He shook his head. "No, it is more than that. Considerably more." He watched the distant figure of Kahless descend from the mountain, making improbable choices to defy impossible odds. "A few years ago," he explained, "it was a personal problem. Now . . ."

He allowed his voice to trail off, reluctant to give the matter substance by acknowledging it. However, he couldn't avoid it forever. As captain of the *Enterprise,* Picard would find out about it sooner or later.

"You see," he told the human, "these myths—" He gestured to the terrain below them, which included not only the volcano but the lake as well. "—they are sacred to us. They are the essence of our faith. When we speak of Kahless's creation of the *bat'telh* from a lock of his hair, we are not speaking figuratively. We truly believe he did such a thing."

Worf turned his gaze westward, toward the plains that formed the bulk of this continent. He couldn't see them for the smoke and fumes emerging from the volcano, but he knew they were there nonetheless.

"It was out there," he continued, "that Kahless is said to have wrestled with his brother Morath for twelve days and twelve nights, after his brother lied and shamed their clan. It was out there that Kahless used the *bat'telh* he created to slay the tyrant Molor—and it was out there that the emperor united all Klingons under a banner of duty and honor."

"Not just stories," Picard replied, demonstrating his understanding. "Each one a truth, no matter how impossible it might seem in the cold light of logic."

"Yes," said Worf. "Each one a truth." He turned back to his captain. "Or at least, they *were.*" He frowned, despite himself.

"Were?" Picard prodded. He hung there in the shifting winds, clouds writhing behind him like a monstrous serpent in terrible torment. "What's happened to change things?"

The Klingon took his time gathering his thoughts. Still, it was not an easy matter to talk about.

"I have heard from the emperor," he began.

The captain looked at him with unconcealed interest. "Kahless, you mean? I trust he's in good health."

Worf nodded. "You need not worry on that count. Physically, he is in fine health."

In other words, no one had tried to assassinate him. In the corridors of Klingon government, that was a very real concern—though to Worf's knowledge, Kahless hadn't prompted anyone to want to kill him. Quite the contrary. He was as widely loved as any Klingon could be.

"The problem," the lieutenant went on, "is of a different nature. You see, a scroll was unearthed alongside the road to *Sto-Vo-Kor.*"

Picard's eyes narrowed. "The road the historical Kahless followed when he took his leave of the Klingon people. That was . . . what? Fifteen hundred years ago?"

"Even more," Worf told him. "In any case, this scroll—supposedly written by Kahless himself—appears to discredit all the stories that concern him. It is as if Kahless himself has given the lie to his own history."

The captain mulled the statement over. When he responded, his tone was sober and sympathetic.

"I see," he said. "So, in effect, this scroll reduces Klingon faith to a series of tall tales. And the emperor—"

"To a charlatan," the lieutenant remarked. "It was one thing for the modern Kahless to be revealed as a clone of the original. My people were so eager for a light to guide them, they were happy to embrace him despite all that."

"However," Picard went on, picking up the thread, "it is quite another thing for the historical Kahless to be nothing *like* the legend."

"And if the scroll is authentic," Worf added, "that is exactly the message it will convey."

Below them, the volcano rumbled. The wind howled and moaned.

"Not a pretty picture," the captain conceded. "Neither for Kahless himself nor for his people."

"That is an understatement," the Klingon replied. "A scandal like this one could shake the empire to its foundations. Klingons everywhere would be forced to reconsider the meaning of what it is to be Klingon."

Picard's brow furrowed. "We're speaking of social upheavals?"

"Without a doubt," Worf answered. "Kahless revived my people's dedication to the ancient virtues. If he were to fall from grace . . ."

"I understand," said the captain. His nostrils flared as he considered the implications. "For a while there, Kahless seemed to be all that kept Gowron in his council seat. If that were to change, the entire diplomatic landscape might change with it. It could spell the end of the Federation–Klingon alliance."

"It could indeed," the lieutenant admitted.

He saw Picard gaze at the volcano again. Down below, Kahless had reached its lowermost slopes, though it looked to have cost him the last of his strength. Still, according to the legends, he would make it to the lake somehow.

"So that is why you constructed this program," the captain remarked out loud. "To play out the myths before your eyes. To test your faith in the face of this scroll's revelations."

Worf confirmed it. "Yes. Unfortunately, it has only served to deepen my doubts—to make me wonder if I have been fooling myself all along."

Still gazing at Kahless, Picard took a breath and expelled it. "I suppose that brings me to the reason I barged in on you like this." He turned to the Klingon again. "A subspace packet has arrived from the Klingon homeworld. It seems to be a transcript of some sort. I would have notified you via ship's intercom. . . ."

"But you were concerned," the Klingon acknowledged, "about the possible political implications."

"Yes," the captain confirmed. "Anything from Qo'noS makes me wary—perhaps unnecessarily so." He paused. "Any idea what it might be?"

Worf nodded. "I believe it contains the contents of the scroll," he rumbled. "As I requested."

"I see," said Picard.

At that point, he didn't ask anything of his officer. Nonetheless, the Klingon sensed what the captain wanted.

"After I have read it," he said, "I will make it available to you."

Picard inclined his head. "Thank you," he replied. "And please, continue what you were doing. I won't disturb you any further."

Worf grunted by way of acknowledgment and turned to watch Kahless begin his trek toward the lake. Out of the corner of his eye, he saw the captain make his way through the clouds and exit from the holodeck.

The Klingon sighed. He would read what was written in the cursed scroll soon enough. For now, he would track the emperor's progress from his place in the sky, and try again to stir in himself some feeling of piety.

# CHAPTER 11

# The Noble Enemy, Part 2—Romulans

FIRST INTRODUCED IN "BALANCE OF TERROR," THE ROMULANS WERE THE second major nemesis from the original *Star Trek* series. The example of the Romulan commander in "Balance of Terror" proved that Romulans, like Klingons, lived by a warrior code of honor, although they also were capable of treachery and cruelty toward humans. Imagine Vulcans without logic and a sense of ethics: powerful, brilliant, clever, but ruthless and relentless. The result would be a Romulan. Even so, the Romulan commanders from the *TOS* episodes "Balance of Terror" and "The Enterprise Incident" were strong, charismatic, fascinating and honorable.

## *My Enemy, My Ally,* by Diane Duane

Writers of early Star Trek novels about Romulans, particularly Diane Duane, in *My Enemy, My Ally,* and Diane Duane and Peter Morwood in *The Romulan Way,* gave Romulans a name for themselves, the Rihannsu, and an entire culture and civilization. Fans will be pleased to learn that Pocket will publish new adventures by Diane Duane featuring the Rihannsu.

In *My Enemy, My Ally,* a Romulan commander named Ael learned of a secret research laboratory being maintained by the Romulans with captive Vulcans, including the crew of *Intrepid,* as research subjects. Romulan scientists were experimenting with Vulcan genetic material in an effort to induce Vulcan mind powers in Romulans, including mind control. As part of that experiment, they extracted

315

brain tissue from Vulcans and cloned it for implantation into Romulans. Because Ael realized that this experiment placed the entire galaxy in jeopardy, she forged an alliance with Kirk and the *Enterprise* to stop the experiments and free the Vulcan captives.

This passage from *My Enemy, My Ally* shows Ael's tortured thoughts as she contemplated an act of treason against her empire.

ACCORDING TO A WIDELY-HELD RIHANNSU MILITARY TRADITION, THE BEST commanders were also often cranky ones. Normally Ael avoided such behavior. The showy, towering rages she had seen some of her own commanders periodically throw at their crews had only convinced Ael that she never wanted to serve under such a person in a crisis. Pretended excitability could too easily turn into the real thing.

Now, however, she saw a chance to turn that old tradition to good advantage. She came back from her tour of her fleet not positively angry, but looking rather discommoded and out of sorts when she reentered her bridge. T'Liun noticed it instantly, and became most solicitous of Ael, asking her what sort of condition the other ships were in. Ael—hearing perfectly well t'Liun's intention to find out the cause of the mood and exploit it somehow—told t'Liun what she thought of the other ships, and the Klingons who had built them, and the Rihannsu crews who were mishandling them, at great length. It was a most satisfying tirade, giving Ael the opportunity to make a great deal of noise and relieve some of her own tension, while leaving t'Liun suspecting her of doing exactly that—though for all the wrong reasons.

Then off Ael stormed, and went on a cold-voiced rampage through the ship, upbraiding the junior officers for the poor repair of equipment that was generally in good condition. Late into the ship's night she prowled the corridors, terrorizing the offshift, peering into everything. The effect produced was perfect. Slitted eyes gazed after her in bitter annoyance, and in eavesdropping on ship's 'com, after she had theoretically retired for the night, Ael heard many suggestions made about her ancestry and habits that revised slightly upward her opinion of her crew's inventiveness. Ael felt much amused, and much relieved by the discharge of energy. But far more important, no one had noticed or thought anything in particular of a small interval she spent peering up a circuitry-conduit—an inspection from which she had come away frowning on the outside, but inside quite pleased. Ael fell asleep late, her cabin dark to everything but starlight—thanking her ancestors that the most immediate of them, her father, had once made her spend almost three months taking his own old warbird apart, system by system, and putting it back together again.

In the morning she took things a step further. She called together t'Liun and tr'Khaell and the other senior officers and instructed them that they were to begin a complete check of all ship's systems. Her officers, not caring for the prospect of trying to do several weeks' work in the several days she was ordering, did their best to reassure Ael that the systems were in perfect working condition. Ael allowed herself, very briefly, to be mollified—thus setting up for a rage that even her worst old commanders would have approved of, when a message came in from Command later that day, and t'Liun's communications board overloaded and blew up.

Ael had been restraining herself the day before. Now she let loose, resurrecting some of the savagely elegant old idioms for incompetence that her father had used on her the day she forgot to fasten one of the gates of the farm, and three hundred of the *hlai* got out into the croplands. She raged, she flushed dark green-bronze (an inadvertent effect; she still blushed at the memory of that long-ago scolding, but the effect was fortuitous—it made the rage look better). She ordered the whole lot of them into the brig, then changed her mind; that was too good for them. They would all work their own shifts, as well as extra shifts doing the system analysis she had ordered in the first place. But none of them would touch the Elements-be-blessed communications board, which had probably been utterly destroyed by t'Liun's fumblings. Who knew what orders Command had had for them, and must they now send messages back saying, "Sorry, we missed that one"? She would let t'Liun have that dubious pleasure, and served her right; but in the meantime someone had best bring her a toolkit, and the rest of them had best stay out of her sight and make themselves busy lest she space them all in their underwear, *now get out!*

Afterward, when the bridge was quiet except for one poor Antecenturion too cowed to look up or speak a word, Ael lay on her back under the overhang of the comm station and called silently on her father's fourth name, laughing inside like a madwoman. *Possibly I am mad, trying to make this work,* she thought, first killing all power to the board so that none of the circuit-monitoring devices t'Liun had installed in it would work. *But how then—should I lie here and do nothing? No, the thrai has a few bites left in her yet. . . .* Ael gently teased one particular logic solid out of its crystal-grip, holding it as lovingly as a jewel. The equipment she had been brought naturally included a portable power source; this she attached both to the solid and to the board, bringing up only its programming functions.

Reprogramming the logic solid, which held the ship's ID, was delicate work, but not too difficult; and she thought kindly of her father all through it. *Ael,* he had said again, *times will come when you won't have time to run the program and see if it works. It must be right the first time, or lives will be lost, and the responsibility will be on your head when you face the Elements at last—probably long before that, too. Do it again. Get it right the first time. Or it's the stables for you tomorrow. . . .*

She sat up with the little keypad in her lap, touching numbers and words into it, and thinking about responsibility . . . of lives not merely lost, but about to be thrown away. *Bitter, it is bitter, I am no killer. . . . Yet Command sent me here to be a prisoner; to rot, or preferably to die. What duty do I owe these fools? They've pledged me no loyalty; nor would they ever. They are my jailers, not my crew. Surely there's nothing wrong in escaping from jail.*

*Yet I swore the Oath, once upon a time, by the Elements and my honor, to be good mistress to my crews, and to lead them safely and well. Does that mean I must keep faith with them even if they do me villainy? . . .*

The thought of the Elements brought Ael no clear counsel. There was little surprise in that, out here in the cold of space, where earth was far away, and water and air both frozen as hard as any stone. The only Element she commonly dealt with was fire—in starfire and the matter-antimatter conflagration of her ship's engines. Ael had always found that peculiarly agreeable, for she knew her own Element to be fire's companion, air, and her realm what pierced it: weapons, words, wings. But even the thought of that old reassuring symmetry did nothing for her now. *Loyalty, the best part of the ruling Passion, that's of fire: if any spark of that fire were alive in them, I would serve it gladly. I would save them if I could. But there is none.*

*Besides . . . there's a larger question.* She sat still on the floor of her bridge for a moment, seeing beyond it. There was the matter of the many lives that would be lost, both in the Empire and outside it, should the horrible thing a-birthing at Levaeri V research station come to term. Thousands of lives, millions; rebellion and war and devastation lashing through the Empire itself, then out among the Federation and the Klingons as well. For the Klingons, she cared little; for the Federation she cared less—though that might be a function of having been at armed truce with them for all these years. Still—theirs were lives too.

And beyond mere war and horror lay an issue even deeper. When honor dies—when trust is a useless thing—what use is life? And that

318

was what threatened the spaces around, and the Empire itself, where honor had once been a virtue . . . but would be no more. Tasting the lack of it for herself, here and now, in this place where no one could be trusted or respected, Ael knew the bitterness of such a lack right down to its dregs. Even the knowledge of faith kept elsewhere, of Tafv on his way and her old crew coming for her, could not assuage it. She had led a sheltered life until now, despite wounds and desperate battles; this desolate tour of duty had dealt her a wound from which she would never recover. She could only make sure that others did not have to suffer it.

She could only do so by sacrificing the crew of *Cuirass* to her stratagem. There was too much chance that they would somehow get word back to Command of what was toward, if she left them alive. But by killing them, Ael would make herself guilty of the same treachery she so despised in them; and with far less excuse (if excuse existed), for she knew the old way of life, knew honor and upright dealing. There was no justifying the spilling of all her crew's lives, despite their treachery to her. Ael would bear the weight of murder, and sooner or later pay their bloodprice in the most intimate possible coinage: her own pain. That was the way things worked, in the Elements' world; fire well used, warmed; ill used, burned. All that remained was the question of whether she would accept the blame for their deaths willingly, or reject it, blind herself to her responsibility, and prolong the Elements' retaliation.

She remembered her father, standing unhappily over one of the *hlai* that Ael had not been able to catch. It had gotten into the woods, and there it lay on the leafmold, limp and torn; a *hnoiyika* had gotten it, torn its breast out and left the *hlai* there to bleed out its life, as *hnoiyikar* will. Ael had stared at the *hlai* in mixed fascination and horror as it lay there with insects crawling in and out of the torn places, out of mouth and eyes. She had never seen a dead thing before. "This is why one must be careful with life," her father had said, in very controlled wrath. "Death is the most hateful thing. Don't allow the destruction of what you can never restore." And he had made her bury the *hlai.*

She looked up and sighed, thinking what strange words those had seemed, coming from a warrior of her father's stature. Now, at this late date, they started to make sense . . . and she laughed again, at herself this time, a silent, bitter breath. Standing on the threshold of many murders, she was finally beginning to understand. . . .

*Evidently I am already beginning to pay the price,* she thought. *Very well. I accept the burden.* And she turned her mind back to her work, burying her wretched crew in her heart while instructing the logic solid in its own treachery. First, she pulled another logic solid out of her pocket, connected to the first one and then to the little power-pack. It was a second's work to copy the first solid's contents onto the blank. Then, after the duplicate was pocketed again, some more work on the original solid. A touch here, a touch there, a program that would loop back on itself in this spot, refuse to respond in that one, do several different things at once over here, when *Cuirass*'s screens perceived the appropriate stimulus. And finally the whole adjustment locked away under a coded retrieval signal, so that t'Liun would notice nothing amiss, and analysis (if attempted) would reveal nothing.

Done. She went back under the panel again, locked the logic solid back into its grip, and closed up the panel again, tidying up after herself with a light heart. No further orders would reach this panel from Command. It would receive them, automatically acknowledge them, and then dump them, without alerting the communications officer. It would do other things too—as her crew would discover, to its ruin.

Ael got up and left the toolkit lying where it was for someone else to clean up—that would be in character for her present role, though it went against her instincts for tidiness. She swung on the poor terrified Antecenturion minding the center seat, and instructed him to call t'Lium to the bridge; she herself was going to her quarters, and was not to be disturbed on peril of her extreme displeasure. Then out Ael stalked, making her way to her cabin. In the halls, the crewpeople she met avoided her eyes. Ael did not mind that at all.

She settled down to wait.

She did not have to wait long. She had rather been hoping that Tafv would for once discard honor and attack by ship's night. But it was broad afternoon, the middle of dayshift, when her personal computer with the copied logic-solid attached to it began to read out a ship's ID, over and over. She ripped the solid free of the computer and pocketed it, glanced once around her bare dark cabin. There was nothing here she needed. Slowly, not hurrying, she headed in the general direction of Engineering. The engine room itself had the usual duty personnel, no more; she waved an uncaring salute at them and went on through to where *Hsaaja* stood. As the doors of the secondary deck closed behind her, the alarm sirens began their terrible screeching; someone on the bridge had visual contact with a ship in the area. Calmly, without looking back, Ael got into *Hsaaja,* sealed him up, brought up the power. It would be about now that they realized, up in the bridge, that their own screens were not working.

*"Khre'Riov t'Rllaillieu urru Oira!"* the ship's annunciator system cried in t'Liun's voice, again and again. But Ael would never set foot on *Cuirass'*s bridge again; and the cry grew fainter and fainter, vanishing at last with the last of the landing bay's exhausted air. Ael lifted *Hsaaja* up on his underjets, nudged him toward the opening doors of the bay, the doors that no bridge override could affect now. Then out into space, hard downward and to the rear, where an unmodified warbird could not fire. *Cuirass* shuddered above Ael to light phaser fire against which the ship could not protect herself. Space writhed and rippled around *Cuirass;* she submerged into otherspace, went into warp, fled away.

Ael looked up with angry joy at the second warbird homing in on her, its landing bay open for her. She kicked *Hsaaja'*s ion-drivers in, arrowing toward home, and security, and war.

## *The Romulan Prize,* by Simon Hawke

In the *TNG* story *The Romulan Prize,* by Simon Hawke, the Romulans are again shown to be clever, treacherous and ruthless in pursuit of their goals. Commander Valak of the Romulan warbird *Syrinx* had a dangerous but brilliant plan to capture Captain Picard's *Enterprise* by faking the deaths of his entire crew complement. When the *Enterprise* answered a distress call, it found the *Syrinx* drifting in Federation space, its entire crew apparently dead. Shortly after the *Enterprise* sent boarding parties to investigate, the Romulan crew awakened from death and took over the *Enterprise* in a flawlessly executed plan.

The passage from *The Romulan Prize* shows Picard's confrontation with the Romulan commander upon the resurrection of the dead Romulans and the takeover of the *Enterprise.*

"PERHAPS IT ISN'T SO CURIOUS, MR. DATA," SAID PICARD. "ROMULAN captains are trained as warriors, not as engineers. It follows that their systems would have been designed to be easily accessible to any of the bridge crew. The possibility of a Romulan warbird falling into enemy hands was probably unthinkable to them. They would destroy their ships before surrendering them."

"That would seem wasteful and illogical," said Data.

"Not to a Romulan, Mr. Data," replied Picard. "To a Romulan warrior, surrender means dishonor and disgrace. On Earth there is an old military saying, 'Death before dishonor.' The Romulans have their own version: 'Death before defeat.'"

He turned and glanced around at the bridge of the warbird again. In this case, he thought, it was the Romulans' own ship that had defeated them. He heard a faint, unintelligible sound, rather like a moan, and turned back to Data with a frown.

"What was that, Mr. Data?"

The android looked up at him, "I said nothing, Captain."

"I thought I heard—"

And then he heard it once again, this time accompanied by a rustling sound of movement. This time Data heard it too, and he glanced up from the screen, looking for the source of it. Picard's first thought was that it might be someone from the away team, but as he looked up toward the warbird's communications station, he distinctly saw the arm of the communications officer move.

At once he reached for his phaser, but even as his fingers closed around it, a voice behind him said, "If you draw that phaser, Captain, it will be the last thing you ever do."

Picard spun around, eyes wide, to see the Romulan captain standing behind him with his disruptor drawn and aimed squarely at his chest. Data reached quickly for his phaser, but the "corpse" of the Romulan science officer suddenly rose from the deck beside him and pressed the emitting cone of his disruptor against the android's head.

"Lieutenant Commander Data, is it not?" said Valak. "I would advise against resistance. It would be a shame to destroy Starfleet's only android officer."

Picard stared with utter disbelief as the bodies of the Romulan bridge crew suddenly came to life around him. "But . . . this is *impossible!*" he said, his senses reeling in the face of the unacceptable reality. *"You were dead!"*

"In the words of your human philosopher, Mark Twain," said Valak with a smile, "'The reports of my death are greatly exaggerated.' Korak, relieve Captain Picard of his phaser before he succumbs to temptation and does something foolish."

As the Romulan first officer stepped up to Picard and took his weapon, Picard twisted away from him and slapped his communicator. "Picard to *Enterprise:* red alert! Battle stations—"

Korak clubbed him down with the butt of his disruptor, and Picard fell to the deck, stunned.

"That was admirable, Captain," Valak said, "but pointless and not entirely unexpected. Even as we speak, my warriors are transporting to your ship. Korak, open a channel to the *Enterprise.*"

The Romulan first officer quickly moved to the communications console. "Hailing frequency is open, Commander," he said.

"This is Commander Valak of the Romulan warbird, *Syrinx.* Your ship has been boarded, and your captain is my prisoner. I wish to speak with First Officer William Riker."

As Picard slowly got to his feet, his head still aching from the blow, he heard Riker reply to the Romulan commander. "This is Commander William Riker of the *Starship Enterprise.*"

Valak glanced at Picard and smiled. "Put him on the viewer, Korak."

As Picard stared at the viewscreen on the warbird's bridge, he saw an image that made his heart sink. Riker stood on the bridge of the *Enterprise* flanked by two Romulan warriors, their disruptors drawn. Other warriors were covering the remainder of the *Enterprise* bridge crew, and Riker's face bore a taut and grim expression.

"Captain," he said tensely, "are you all right?"

"For the moment, Number One," Picard replied, rubbing his head. He glanced at Valak. "May I ask my first officer for a report?"

"As you wish," Valak replied.

"Status report, Number One."

Riker took a deep breath. "The ship has been boarded, sir. The bridge and the engineering section have been seized." He moistened his lips. "Our scanners detected power surges aboard the warbird, but I assumed it was La Forge getting the ship powered up. Instead, it must have been their transporter activating and beaming their boarding parties to our ship. I'm sorry, sir."

Riker looked shaken. He's blaming himself for this, Picard thought. "You couldn't possibly have known, Number One," he said. "Considering the circumstances, I would undoubtedly have made the same mistake. What about the crew? Damage report? Casualties?"

He could see Riker's jaw muscles clench as he replied. "I have been prevented from communicating with the away teams aboard the warbird or with other sections of our ship, sir, but it seems there have been casualties. I have also been informed that hostages have been taken on Decks Five, Seven, Twelve, Fourteen, and Thirty-six." He swallowed hard and continued. "They moved very fast, sir, and they knew exactly what they were doing."

They did indeed, Picard thought grimly. The Romulans must have simultaneously beamed boarding parties to the bridge, the engineering section, and the family housing decks. The whole thing had been an elaborate trap, flawlessly planned and executed. His eyes were hard as he gazed at Valak. "You seem quite well informed about the layout of my ship, Commander."

"I have studied the construction of Federation starships in great detail, Captain," Valak replied smoothly. "To quote one of your Earth sayings, I know your ship 'like the back of my hand.' I have also made a study of key Starfleet personnel, and I might add that it is both a pleasure and a privilege to meet face-to-face with the famous Captain Jean-Luc Picard of the *Starship Enterprise.*"

"I am sorry to say I cannot share your sentiment," Picard replied, a hard edge to his voice. "My compliments, Commander Valak. You have executed your plan brilliantly. However, if you expect to use your hostages to force my unconditional surrender—"

Valak held up his hand. "I would never expect *you* to surrender, Captain. Quite the contrary. I fully expect you to resist to the utmost of your ability. However, you will see that I have taken steps to ensure that your ability to resist has effectively been neutralized." He signaled his first officer to close the channel to the *Enterprise,* then activated his communicator. "This is Commander Valak. All units, report."

Picard listened with a sinking feeling to the litany of Romulan boarding parties reporting in. The Romulans were in control of the battle bridge, the shuttle bays, and key environmental systems in addition to the family housing decks, the bridge, and the engineering sections. He would not have thought it possible to execute so complex an operation with such incredible speed and efficiency.

There was, he realized, only one way it could have been done. The entire warbird, in a sense, had been a loaded gun, a booby trap set to go off and trigger the ambush the moment the ship was powered back up. The Romulan commander must have had his boarding parties distributed throughout the warbird, with their coordinates fixed and locked in to the transporter. He also must have had his transporter programmed with the coordinates of the assault points aboard the *Enterprise*—but Picard could not see how on earth Valak could have done that. It seemed utterly impossible.

His train of thought was interrupted when Data spoke to Valak. "Commander," Data said, gazing curiously at the Romulan commander, "a question, if I may be permitted?"

Valak turned to face him. "Ask."

"In order to beam your boarding parties so quickly to key positions on the *Enterprise,* your transporter would have to have been preprogrammed with the appropriate coordinates. I am puzzled as to how you anticipated the position of the *Enterprise* in relation to that of your own ship at the time of your assault."

Valak smiled. "An excellent question, Mr. Data, and an astute observation. Let us see if your reasoning capabilities are equally as excellent. You already possess all the information you need to allow you to deduce the answer, if you consider that there is only one way we could have accomplished that goal."

Data frowned slightly. "You have already demonstrated your familiarity with the layout of Federation ships," he replied. "And since your entire assault plan depended on programmed coordinates and settings on your transporter, sequenced for automatic engagement the moment the ship was powered up, the only unknown variable would have been the position of the *Enterprise* in relation to that of your ship." He cocked his head in a curiously birdlike movement.

Valak was watching him intently, confident that Picard was covered by his other officers. He actually seems to be enjoying this, Picard thought. This was a very different sort of Romulan from those he had encountered in the past.

"There is no way you could have determined the position of the *Enterprise* when we arrived," Data continued, "for you were, to all appearances, quite dead. The logical assumption is that you employed some sort of drug to induce a state of suspended animation so deep that tricorder readings would detect no life functions. In that state you could not possibly have ascertained the position of the *Enterprise* in relation to that of your own ship. Therefore you must have devised some method for your scanners to automatically compute our ship's position and communicate it to your ship's computer, which would initiate the preprogrammed transporter functions." Data frowned again. "However, that still does not explain how so many varied coordinates could have been anticipated and plotted so quickly and so accurately. There would not have been adequate time for you to—" Data stopped suddenly and cocked his head in the opposite direction, raising his chin slightly.

Valak watched him almost as if he were a teacher listening to the recitation of a gifted student, or a scientist observing the object of his research.

"Of course," said Data. "You programmed your scanners ahead of time to fix on the emissions of our dilithium crystals. Once your scanners had ascertained the precise position of our matter-antimatter reaction chamber, your ship's computer initiated a preprogrammed sequence that allowed it to rapidly compute the necessary transport coordinates aboard our ship, based on your knowledge of the layout of Federation vessels. It was all planned and carefully programmed in advance, for automatic initiation once your ship was powered back up." Data nodded. "Most impressive, Commander. A brilliant and audacious scheme."

"Thank you, Mr. Data," Valak replied. He turned to Picard. "Your android is every bit as sophisticated as I had expected, Captain. It must be quite an asset to your command."

"We prefer to think of Lieutenant Commander Data as a 'he,' rather than an 'it,'" Picard replied dryly.

Valak gave him a slight bow. "I stand corrected. No offense intended, Mr. Data."

"None taken, Commander," Data replied.

Picard's mind was racing. The Romulan was toying with them, confident that he had the upper hand. Unfortunately, so far as Picard could see, he *did* have the upper hand. There had to be some way to get out of this desperate situation, but for the moment, Picard could only stall for time and await an opportunity—assuming Valak would allow them one.

The doors to the turbolift slid open, and Picard heard a roar of rage as five Romulans dragged a struggling Worf onto the bridge. His arms were bound behind him, but it still took all five of them to hold him. They threw him down onto the deck and stood over him, breathing heavily.

"Commander, this Klingon filth killed five of our warriors before we could subdue him," one of the Romulans said through gritted teeth.

"He did no less than his duty," Valak replied evenly. "You were warned to expect severe physical resistance from the Klingon, were you not?"

"Yes, Commander, but—"

"Then the men who died paid the penalty for not having properly prepared themselves. Lieutenant Commander Worf is now our prisoner, and he will be treated with the respect due to a Federation officer of his rank."

"But, Commander, surely you do not intend to allow this Klingon filth to live!"

Valak turned a steely gaze on his subordinate. "Do you question my authority?"

The Romulan warrior quickly averted his gaze. "No, Commander, of course not."

Picard watched this interchange with interest. In battle, Romulans were always merciless and utterly ruthless. This Romulan, however, was different. This Romulan has studied us, he thought, and studied not only our behavior but also our social and military customs. This was a Romulan who believed in knowing his enemy, a Romulan who *respected* his enemy. Valak was a Romulan who believed in exhaustive preparation and who took nothing for granted. And that, Picard thought, made him exceedingly dangerous.

"Forgive me, Captain," Worf said heavily, as he got up from the deck. "I have failed you."

"You did not fail me, Mr. Worf," Picard replied. "The fault is mine. I fear I was simply out-generaled."

"That is high praise indeed, considering the source," said Valak, inclining his head toward Picard.

"It was said as a statement of fact, not praise," Picard said. "You have seized my ship, Commander, and that constitutes an open act of war."

"Quite the contrary, Captain," countered Valak. "You had boarded my ship and were attempting to pirate classified information from our data banks. I have acted entirely in self-defense."

"Nonsense," said Picard. "Your ship was in Federation space, and you had gone to considerable trouble to disguise it as a derelict. We merely responded to your distress beacon."

"Which was operating on a Romulan frequency," said Valak.

"Let us dispense with this pointless charade, Commander Valak," said Picard. "We both know what has occurred here. You set a trap to capture a Federation starship, and for the present, you appear to have succeeded. Now precisely what do you intend?"

"Refreshingly direct, as I expected," Valak replied. "Very well, Captain, I shall tell you what I intend. I intend to hold your ship and your crew. Resistance will be dealt with harshly, but as I expect you to resist. I have made preparations for it. I control your engineering sections, your bridge, and all of your ship's vital functions. Any attempt at resistance will result in the execution of hostages. And I shall start with the children."

"And to think I was just beginning to respect you," Picard said with disgust.

"I do not require your respect, Captain Picard," Valak said flatly, "merely your compliance. Personally I find the prospect of executing children loathsome, even if they are merely human children. However, I can think of no better threat to compel your cooperation. And if you hope to engage your emergency autodestruct sequence, let me assure you that my engineers will have deactivated it by now, as that was their first priority once they had seized your main engineering section."

Picard compressed his lips into a tight grimace. It seemed the bastard had anticipated everything. But no plan, no matter how carefully conceived or brilliantly executed, was without a flaw. Somewhere the Romulan had overlooked something. The trick was to find out what it was.

## *The Romulan Stratagem,* by Robert Greenberger

*The Romulan Stratagem* is somewhat reminiscent of *TOS* episodes in which Kirk and various Klingon commanders competed for alliances with developing planets. Here, Captain Picard challenged Romulans led by Commander Sela for an alliance with the Elohsians, inhabitants of a planet near the Romulan-Klingon border. The Elohsians needed a strong alliance to help rebuild their world and stabilize a newly unified planetary government after many years of war. Sela, Picard, and their respective diplomatic teams demonstrated the best each had to offer the Elohsians. Their efforts were complicated by terrorist attacks which cast suspicion on first the *Enterprise,* and then on Sela's crew.

The excerpt is from a dinner party early in the competition. Sela's officers engaged in verbal sparring matches with *Enterprise* officers, and Sela made a serious misstep in her diplomatic mission. Ultimately, though, in a surprise ending, the Elohsians chose membership in the Romulan Empire because of its strength and stability. They wanted unity, even if enforced at gunpoint.

TROI GAZED AT THE VARIOUS DELICACIES, ALLOWING LARKIN THE PRIVILEGE of explaining each dish to her despite the small blue placards next to each setting. With her plate amply loaded, she moved off toward the far table and took a seat. Politely, she awaited company but carefully eyed the foods before her. As she waited, a small, dark-paneled trolley was wheeled into the room and a serving woman with hair in yet another elaborate design went directly toward the counselor.

"May I offer you a beverage?"

Troi smiled in surprise. "I didn't think you were allowed to speak."

The woman nodded solemnly and said, "We speak when we have something to offer. Our role here is to fully support the diners and staff, not become a part of the event itself."

"Do these banquets happen often?"

"No. The parliament has a meal like this at the beginning of each assembly. We had the largest one when the peace was declared. Now, would you like something hot or cold?"

The Betazoid selected a frothy hot drink that had some spices sprinkled on top. The hostess indicated that given Troi's choices for dessert, this would be the most complementary drink. One whiff and Troi beamed in agreement. She strode off, inspecting one of the murals, when Plactus stepped toward her.

"Counselor Troi, I believe," he said, in a smooth tone.

"Yes, Subcommander. What do you think of the painting style?"

He merely glanced at the wall for a moment and admitted, "I know so little about art, it does not pay to ask me. But, may I ask you something?"

"Of course," she nodded, wondering at Plactus's sudden interest in her.

"We have not seen much of you on this world and wonder why the ship's counselor is not attending more of the informational sessions?"

Troi sipped at her drink and considered. "Actually, I have been part of the away teams studying the planet."

"I am surprised that you did not attend the parliamentary session yet. I would imagine a good captain would want a counselor's interpretation of the people."

Troi studied Plactus, who remained unmoving, hands clasped behind him. He had declined all manner of dessert and seemed intent on talking with her. "You seem to know a good deal about how we should do things."

"We study the Federation quite carefully, Counselor. We watch who is near our borders because they might pose a threat to our security. Did you know, for example, that we have had troubles of late with Corvallens?"

The mention of the Corvallens made Troi stiffen. Did Plactus know she was involved with the recent incidents involving the defection of Vice Counsel M'ret? The deception had involved Troi disguising herself as a Romulan. Plactus must be toying with her. Or was he? Troi could read nothing from the Romulan.

"Oh, yes, we had one near us that seemed engaged in piracy," Plactus continued. "We may be many things, but not pirates. Am I right, Counselor?"

"'Pirate' is certainly not a name I would associate with a Romulan," was all she managed to say.

Plactus beamed. "True. In fact, we blew up such a pirate ship recently. If I'm not mistaken, the *Enterprise* was nearby at the time."

He knew! Troi forced a curious expression to her features. "If we had been nearby, I certainly don't recall being there when it occurred. You're not saying we had anything to do with piracy."

"No, no," Plactus said reassuringly. "Pirate is certainly not a name I would associate with the Federation. Instead, I just find it interesting how often we actually manage to blur the lines between our peoples. Comings and goings across the border in both directions. You'd almost think we were friendly neighbors."

Troi recalled the days she spent as an imperious Romulan, summoning those feelings of discipline. She wanted very much to redirect the conversation. Plactus obviously enjoyed baiting members of the *Enterprise* crew for the Elohsians' benefit, but she was not going to submit.

"We are not friendly neighbors, Plactus," she said. "The goings-on you mention involve spying and deceptions that are forced by the hostile state of affairs between us. They will remain hostile, too, until you recognize the galaxy *is* big enough for the both of us."

"Of course, Counselor," he said. "Your bluntness surprises me. If you were Romulan, I'd say you were capable of command . . . of, say, even one of our warbirds. Perhaps the *N'ventnar* or the *Khazara.*"

Oh yes, he knew and he was having fun taunting her with the information. The Romulans might not be pirates but they were sadists. "Both seem to be fine representatives of the Romulan Empire," Troi replied in as hard a voice as possible. "Both ships' captains—Sela and Toreth—far better exemplify the Empire than their underlings."

"Well said, Counselor."

Troi decided to take the offensive. "It's even more interesting to note that the Romulans must use subterfuge to get what they want. It must be difficult to spend every waking moment looking for the next way to take advantage of your opponents."

Plactus rose to the bait, acting annoyed at Troi's turnabout. "Our methods have worked for a millennium and we remain a force to be reckoned with. On the other hand, you sound like your precious Federation is above subterfuge of its own. Using unidentified Betazoids during negotiations, hiding Vulcans on our homeworld, probing our borders with every passing sensor sweep. . . ."

"I think the continuation of this conversation serves little purpose, Plactus," Troi snapped, cutting him off. She had heard enough.

"I don't think so, things are getting interesting," he said with a sly smile.

"I believe I said the conversation was over, Subcommander," Troi stated firmly. He continued to step closer.

"You heard the counselor," thundered Worf, striding over and catching their attention. Both looked at the imposing Klingon, who seemed to get larger by the second.

"Thank you for the interesting chat." And as suddenly as he approached her, the subcommander wandered off, immediately engaging Waln in some new conversation.

"Thank you, Worf," Deanna said as the Romulan left hearing range. She let out a deep breath and leaned against the wall, suddenly feeling drained.

"The captain did say we should not cause any incidents," Worf said matter-of-factly. Troi could not tell if he was teasing or being dead serious.

"My hero," she said with a grin and then grew serious as she mentally reviewed the confrontation.

Troi and Worf were quickly joined by Riker.

"Plactus knows I posed as Major Rakal," Troi said, "He knows I was on the *Khazara*. How could he possibly know, and why bring it up here?"

Riker thought a moment before answering. "Plactus was testing us, Deanna. He tried to provoke Beverly just as that centurion tried to provoke Worf. They want us to look bad but we haven't risen to their bait."

"But, Will, how could he know?"

"I don't know, Deanna, but it could mean trouble. We'd better tell the captain."

The room quickly filled as people took small desserts, reflecting the amount of food consumed prior to this final stop. In a break from previous arrangements, Elohsians were clustered together while Romulans stayed near a corner, having taken the smallest portions possible while still remaining polite.

Picard listened to Troi's report, his face growing dark with concern and anger. "Toreth, of course, reported the deception to the senate and now it's one more piece of information for their files. So be it. It won't have any bearing on us this mission. We won't let it."

"Of course, Captain," Troi said.

"I believe that if we convened our group right now, each and every one of us would report a confrontation with a Romulan. This is a deliberate gambit on their part." Picard returned his attention to Troi. "I hope it didn't ruin your dessert. The pastries look delicious."

"They were, Captain, but I've lost my appetite," she answered. "We'd better not stay in a cluster, it's counterproductive to the spirit of the evening and might let Plactus think he won some victory."

"I agree," he said. Mug in one hand, he purposefully walked toward Commander Sela, who was near her countrymen but not part of a grouping.

"Our earlier conversation was certainly not dinner talk," he began. "I was not trying to irritate you."

Sela stared at Picard with no discernible expression on her face. She merely looked down at her nearly finished plate and contemplated it.

"We each have a job to do, and parading our philosophies so nakedly before Daithin is not how I intend to win this world."

"So, you expect to win it, Captain?"

"Of course, Commander. Starfleet has entrusted this mission to me and I would be something less than officer material if I didn't approach each assignment expecting to complete it satisfactorily."

Sela seemed to consider his words, the soft tone, and the force of character Picard radiated, even standing before her, drinking something smelling sickly sweet.

"I, too, expect to come out of this victorious. Only one of us will be satisfied."

Now it was Picard's turn to consider this woman. Her cold confidence continued to fascinate him because he recognized that beneath the icy exterior was a woman of tortured emotions. She was half-human and half-Romulan—very few such hybrids were known to exist in the universe. Just as other interspecies offspring had trouble adjusting to their dual natures, he could only imagine what Sela was going through, committed to one culture while still holding on to vestiges of her past. Surely something of Tasha Yar survived within her.

"Commander, I must compliment you and your officers on the way you have comported yourselves. I know this is difficult given our past . . . differences."

"I act as the situation demands, Captain. In fact, the way I act now is directly because of you."

Picard looked at her in astonishment but said nothing.

"Yes, Captain. After all, coming to convince the Elohsians to willingly join the Romulan Empire is not exactly a choice assignment. In fact, some might see it as a form of punishment." Her glare grew even more intense.

"You've cost me, Picard. Cost me in ways you've never imagined. I fought my way to the top and was given command of key operations. With each success I was given more authority and more power. I was feared and my very word meant life or death. In a short time, I conceived two very unique plans. Had they worked, I would have challenged the powers that be for a seat of power. The praetor himself would have feared my success.

"Instead, both plans failed. *You* spoiled them both, Picard. First, you ruined years of planning and work that would have left the Klingon Empire ripe for the taking. Just payback for the abuses we suffered at their hands decades ago. You and your Klingon servant—Worf—spoiled that.

"And there was, of course, your miraculous mission on my homeworld. We're still hunting down Spock and his paltry underground. Mark my words, Picard, they will be found and their insurrectionist movement will be stopped before much longer."

Picard calmly took the verbal lashing and just watched the officer. Emotions foreign to most Romulans—or their Vulcan cousins—were on display, and he remained captivated.

"You may think what you will, Sela, but from my brief visit to your people, they seem ready for something . . . different. The way of life I saw was not at all the way of life of a strong people. They may be better off if they follow Spock's way."

Sela listened to Picard's words and remained silent for a moment. For just an instant, Picard thought he might have reached something within her, made her reconsider her course of action.

She shook her head.

"You cost me," she continued. "Two defeats that turned out to waste untold man-hours and resources that I'm now told could have been used successfully elsewhere. The Romulans are a very unforgiving people, Captain. I was duly punished for my failures, and this is the result." She gestured toward her colleagues, who by now were at least mingling a bit with members of the Elohsian party. Picard noted his own officers were also fully engaged in mingling.

"I have been reduced to command of an old, failing starship peopled by a crew of officers that no one in the fleet wanted. This diplomatic mission is the best assignment I've had since the demotion. They said this was to see if I had learned my lesson." Her eyes grew wide and she looked directly at Picard. If possible, her face hardened all the more.

"I will win this world, Picard. And I will do it following my orders and by playing within the Elohsian rules. I shall bring this world's flag to the praetor and then see how I fare against the senate. You're very good with words, Captain, but to win a world you need more than that."

With that said, she turned away from him and walked off toward Plactus, who was speaking with Dona. Picard watched her stalk off and pondered her words. He resolved that he would keep a closer eye on her, if such a thing was possible. His thoughts, though, were interrupted when Simave and Larkin wandered by, each finishing a steaming mug of something strongly sweet.

"All in all, I think this turned out wonderfully," Simave offered when they paused by Picard.

The captain nodded and smiled. "Indeed. The food on this world is quite a treat. People may come here just for that, should things work out in the Federation's favor."

Larkin looked down at Picard with a touch of surprise. He placed his mug on the nearest table and asked, "Do you really think Federation tourists would come to this world just to eat?"

"There are those who line up to be first to visit any new Federation member world. Being this far out, there would be trade ships and diplomatic missions and, of course, Starfleet vessels patrolling the new borders."

"And just how much protection would Starfleet offer?" Simave asked.

"This is neither the time nor the place to get into such specifics, sir, but all worlds are offered protection by patrolling vessels, and if this were to be the new border, then it would be monitored and protected by a starship assigned to this sector. We would be able to answer a distress call, more often than not, within hours."

Larkin nodded silently, storing away the information. Like Dai-thin, he seemed an information sponge, and continued to allow those around him to probe and inquire. Picard had seen his like on many other worlds and noted, with mild interest, that world leaders always seem to need someone just like him.

"And now, Captain, the hour is beginning to draw late. Would you do us the honor of going first?"

"First? I don't understand, Larkin."

"It is our custom, at the end of such an event, to have our guests of honor conclude the evening with a short speech. Something to signify the importance of the event and give the guests words to remember."

"I had not been so informed and have not prepared anything."

Larkin merely nodded and said, "That was a mistake from my office, then. My apologies. Could you say something anyway?"

"Of course. Give me a moment to prepare." With that, Picard stepped away from his hosts and moved slowly toward his crew. Deep down, he suspected that Larkin did not tell him on purpose, and this was another little test to see how the differing worlds handled unprepared scenarios. No doubt, though, his years of experience in diplomacy would enable him to best Sela in a match of words. He hoped.

No more than five minutes later, Daithin stood before the exit door with serving women flanking him on both sides. The Elohsians assembled recognized the formation and quickly grew silent. They had placed their plates and mugs on tables and stood in rapt attention. Federation and Romulan officers quickly matched movements, although a look of confusion was found on more than one face.

"My people, my guests, this has been a truly marvelous evening, truly marvelous. But we grow tired and rest is required for tomorrow's challenges. We have asked Captain Picard from the Federation to honor us with the first closing approbation. Captain?"

For a moment Picard thought he was about to testify before a court—something he also had experience with. But he banished those stray thoughts, plucked his uniform straight, and stepped up by Daithin. The premier sidestepped to the left and created a space for the Starfleet officer.

"Premier Daithin, on behalf of the United Federation of Planets, and most immediately my crew and myself, I thank you and the people of Eloh for your kind and generous hospitality this evening.

"Our very credo is to explore, seek out new civilizations, and study the wonders of the universe. During my years of such exploration, I have helped discover new worlds and explanations for what has become of older civilizations. I have seen new life and far too much death.

"I have also seen, in my lifetime, peace settle in between peoples that never imagined such things happening. Just as Eloh itself has healed divisions that many probably considered irreparable. We share your joy in such unity. As you leave a better world for your children, it is our intention to leave the universe a better place after we have left it. We do that in the form of help. Our ships and personnel can help disaster victims or teach the latest planting techniques to worlds in need. We've kept the corridors of space safe for merchants, visitors, and newly discovered peoples.

"Recently, the Federation has helped discover, and now protects, a marvelous new doorway to the other side of the galaxy. With our help and protection, scientists are now beginning to learn what's out there. Something people have only dreamed about.

"We do not set these goals because we feel they are the only way to ensure our point of view prevails. Instead, we have established the United Federation of Planets to preserve each world's identity and let people grow and evolve as they choose. But each world knows that it can expect help from a neighbor, not exploitation. They can grow safe in the knowledge that they can take a risk and learn from the experience. And should disaster fall, that help is not far off.

"We bring this same set of assurances to Eloh and the Elohsian people. Our experience here has been short, but I would say that this is a young world, having grown up in a terribly short amount of time. Such survival against the odds is impressive. It's that independent spirit I have felt here on Eloh, and bask in it.

"I have no doubt that tonight symbolizes a great step forward in a friendship between peoples, Romulans included, that can even be a turning point in our galaxy. It's an honor to be here and participate in such a moment. I thank you for the invitation and the opportunity to come and know you and your families."

Picard smiled warmly toward Dona and the others. All had stood rapt while Picard spoke. The captain's love for performing Shakespeare certainly stood him in good stead here. Mentally reviewing the just-completed speech compared with comments he had heard during his stay, Picard was satisfied that he said enough to be substantive but kept it short enough so as not to bore. All in all, a good performance. The assessment was confirmed by the big grin from Deanna Troi and the happy look in Will Riker's eyes. Even Dr. Crusher offered him a discreetly placed thumbs-up. Worf remained stoically silent, but when Picard caught his eye the captain received a knowing, albeit short, nod of the head.

Across the room, Sela, Plactus, and the others stood still; no emotion was visible from any of them. The commander's arms were crossed, holding her form tight, not allowing Picard even to guess how his words were received by the Romulans.

Daithin stepped before Picard, all smiles. "Marvelous, Captain, marvelous. We've recorded those words and will broadcast them on tonight's news feed. No doubt they will be much discussed at tomorrow's school sessions. And now, would you join us up here, Commander Sela?"

The Romulan leader purposefully moved through the parting crowd, her arms hidden under the cloak and her expression unchanged. When Daithin once again sidestepped to make way for her, she took her place at military attention, adding a smile for the benefit of her audience.

"The Romulan government also thanks Eloh for its kind invitation to visit and get to know your world and your people. This is something new for us and a sign that the galaxy is changing. Old rules and old ways do not always work in new circumstances. We have learned this and have acted accordingly. Your world, as you know, lies directly between border spots between the Klingon–Federation and Romulan governments. Yesterday it could easily have been a spoil of war, but not today. No, today brings about a new kind of diplomatic war. An opportunity to win a world in ways unfamiliar to many. It's a way I am personally unfamiliar with, but I have chosen to brave this new challenge by going at this with vigor.

"The Romulan people have also explored much of the galaxy. We have exalted in those challenges and tamed worlds for our people to grow and expand. It is the Romulan way not to back down from hardships or challenges. This is the kind of challenge many relish. Being my first such experience with it, I cannot honestly tell you how I feel about it. What I do know is that my people will put forth a way of viewing the universe and not shrink from it. There is a way of life that has proven successful, and it is a way that will endure because of that single vision.

"Eloh has much to offer that vision. You are a planet of warriors who have learned to stop squabbling among yourselves and work together for the good of your world. That shows a courage and sense of character which we find appealing.

"To commemorate this newfound friendship between our people, I wish to leave you with more than words for future contemplation. On behalf of the Romulan people, I wish the parliament to accept a physical token of that friendship." With that, Sela gestured to a legionnaire by the far door. He stepped forward with an ornate box, patterning itself in some ways after the Elohsian mode of decoration. The colors even matched that of Daithin's most favored golden clothes. Good touches, Picard considered.

As the legionnaire placed the large container by Daithin's feet, Sela proclaimed, "We have brought from our homeworld to yours a selection of our finest incenses. We burn them to help focus our thoughts, allow the aroma to remind us that nature's resources can be

337

used to buoy the spirit and enable us to achieve success. We wish for Eloh to achieve such success and hope that you derive as much satisfaction from this blend as we have over the millennia."

Sela stepped back, a smug look of satisfaction on her face. The Romulans remained a tight group in the back of the room, but knowing looks were exchanged.

Picard, who by now was standing alongside Riker and Troi, was distressed. "Should we have brought something, Counselor?" he whispered.

"There was no way to know this would be required of us," she answered. "I can't even begin to guess how this will influence the parliament. After all, it's just burning spices, not new weapons or ships."

"But," Riker added, "their gesture can be perceived as the first of many such 'gifts.' The parliament may not be above bribery."

"Agreed, Will," Picard whispered.

Daithin looked down at the box, smiling, and then looked out among his people. They were chattering among themselves, and so many voices prevented the universal translators from picking up more than a word or two at a time. No one could tell how this gift was being received.

"Thank you, Commander Sela, thank you. Your gift is a generous one and will be appreciated by our people as much as is possible."

Sela stepped forward and asked, "What do you mean?"

"I mean, thank you," he said more slowly. "You see, well, you see, Commander, unlike the extraordinary senses the Romulans possess, and those of the Federation, the people of Eloh have a rather . . . limited sense of smell. Only certain plants and herbs from our own planet are noticeable to us. Your incenses, sadly, are not. The thought behind the gift, though, means much to me and the parliament. Your gesture will not be forgotten." He waved his hands in a dismissive gesture signaling, rather abruptly, Picard thought, an end to the banquet. An odd note to end on, he considered, and he wasn't sure how this would play in the decision-making process to be concluded in a few days.

Sela had stormed from the festive atmosphere into the now empty main dining room. Plactus and some of the party followed her, not caring that their every motion was keenly noted by the *Enterprise* officers. Grabbing Plactus roughly by an arm, she demanded, "Why did you not inform me of this?"

"But Commander, we did not know!" Plactus stepped back, away from the fury of his commander. She stepped forward, keeping their conversation loud but extremely intimate.

"Imbecile, you were supposed to know everything about these people before tonight. We have been here longer than those Federation fools, and they didn't make the blunder, we did! If we lose this world, Plactus, it will be your head I give to the praetor, not my own. And then your family shall know disgrace and lose their rank, their home, and their place among the people. Not many families can say they helped lose an entire world. Pray this is not the case, Plactus. I will not suffer a defeat at Picard's hands again!"

# CHAPTER 12

# "To Seek Out New Life and New Civilizations"—New Alien Societies

PERHAPS THE MOST FASCINATING OPPORTUNITY WRITERS HAVE WITH THE Star Trek novels is to explore entirely new worlds, to seek out completely new life-forms, species, cultures, and societies. Because there are no special effects budgets, there literally are no limits to the strange new life-forms and societies a writer may imagine. Such aliens and societies pose special problems for our heroes, but they also provide opportunities for growth, to find new ways of communicating, and to stretch their minds to accept cultures unfamiliar to them.

## The Abode of Life, by Lee Correy

In *The Abode of Life,* an early Star Trek novel published by Pocket under the Timescape label, an extreme gravitational anomaly tossed the *Enterprise* into the void between the Orion and Sagittarius arms of the galaxy. With the ship severely damaged, the crew faced a several-year trip back to the Federation unless a way was found to repair the warp engines. They discovered an isolated but populated planet orbiting an irregular variable star in the void.

Because the planet Mercan was in the void, its people did not see stars; their night sky was dark except for the very distant "Ribbon of Night" that was the faraway galaxy. They believed that the Ribbon of Night was composed of rocks that glowed in the dark; they did not accept that the Ribbon of Night was filled with stars and planets. Mercan's people believed that they were completely alone in the

340

universe; the planet's name translated to "the Abode of Life," and the star was called "Mercaniad," the Sun of the Abode. The unstable sun scorched all life on the planet periodically, killing anyone not protected in Keeps, access to which was restricted by Proctors who ruled the world. There were no roads, no ground cars, no air ships, and no ships on the seas; the Mercans had no need for them because they moved about the planet by transporter. Ground, air, and sea travel would have been dangerous because of the periodic solar eruptions.

The *Enterprise* crew was faced with a horrible dilemma; they needed help from the technologically advanced people of Mercan to repair their damaged engines, but knowledge of their very existence could destroy the Mercan civilization. To protect themselves, they had to stabilize the star. Without the stellar activity called "the Ordeal," however, the entire social structure of Mercan was at risk of falling apart.

*The Abode of Life* is an excellent example of how a social structure evolved to deal with the physical threats faced by the population; Captain Kirk was fully aware that for the ship to survive, those physical threats had to be eliminated, risking destruction of the culture and violation of the Prime Directive. In this excerpt, the landing party encountered and was captured by the Proctors, as Kirk tried to explain that they were not from Mercan.

KIRK WASN'T SURPRISED TO SEE PROCTOR LENOS RETURN WITH ANOTHER tall but older man who stepped up to the landing party and said in a cordial tone, "Welcome to Celerbitan and to the Guardian Villa. I'm Pallar, Guardian One of the Abode."

The punctilious, mannered, diplomatic, and almost stilted words of greeting nearly caught Kirk off guard. Then the reason for it dawned upon him. Even Pallar the Guardian One of Mercan, carried a visible holstered firearm.

In a culture with a *code duello* such as this one, it's a necessity that a person have the most gracious manners, even to strangers. Boorish actions can't be tolerated in a close society such as the Mercans possessed, a society that was truly planet-wide because of their transporter system.

A Mercan was required to back up his manners with his life.

It put another trump card in Kirk's hand . . . because the entire *Enterprise* landing party was not *visibly* armed.

Or so he thought.

Kirk returned the greeting with equal good manners. "Guardian

Pallar, I'm Captain James T. Kirk." He introduced each of the other three members of the landing party, then went on, "Thank you for your kind welcome to Celerbitan. We're very pleased to be here because we've been in great trouble and have come to Celerbitan to request your gracious assistance."

Pallar adjusted the baldric over his shoulder. In common with the other Mercans, except the Proctors, he was dressed rather simply in a tunic belted at the waist, a headband of a bright color and intricate design, and a baldric or bandolier over his left shoulder with a number of pouches attached to it. His firearm hung from this baldric at his right thigh. On a planet such as Mercan, with little axial tilt, large oceans, and no pronounced seasonal change, clothing for warmth wouldn't be required, just as on Vulcan. However, this culture was different because it apparently didn't embrace elaboration and intricate decoration as did the Vulcan culture.

Well, Kirk thought, each culture's different, and that's what makes the universe so interesting.

Pallar's hawklike face betrayed no emotion as he looked carefully at each of the landing party in turn, then came to Orun. "You appear well, Orun. Ah, why is it that when a person becomes responsible-old he often strays from the tenets of the Code of the Abode? Orun, your activities with the Technic and those of the Technic itself are beginning to threaten the peace and tranquillity of the Abode. I asked Proctor Lenos to bring you to Celerbitan under a Proctor warrant issued by the Guardian Justice because I want to speak to you about your activities and those of the Technic."

"Guardian One, I have nothing that I would speak of under any circumstances or conditions," Orun replied with strained gentility.

"We'll see. We're patient. The Sun of the Abode will not always remain this quiet . . . and there's the question of admission to the Keeps . . ." Pallar said calmly.

He turned to Kirk. "In the meantime, Captain Kirk, I'm told that your group was found with Orun and his companions. You all have strange names, strange appearances, strange clothing, and strange speech. I also see that you go about unarmed. All of you must be Technic constructs or products of Technic development."

"Guardian One, we're not of the Technic," Kirk told him quickly and with sincerity. "I'm permitted under my code of conduct to reveal to you as Guardian One, the unquestioned leader of the Abode, that we don't come from Mercan. We're from another place. We're anxious not to disrupt the way of life here, and I'm certain you're concerned about that possibility. I believe our discussion won't go further than this group until we've both determined that our presence here won't cause problems with the Code of the Abode."

Pallar did not say anything for a moment. This was certainly not the response he had expected from Kirk. "You're not of the Abode?" Pallar said slowly. "If not . . . and if . . .." He stopped.

"I certainly understand why you feel that you're alone in a vast and empty universe. I've seen your night sky," Kirk told the Mercan leader. "There's nothing in that night sky to tell you differently. But do you know that Mercan probably came from what you call the Ribbon of Night? Do you know what makes the Ribbon glow in the sky at night?"

"You're a strange person, Captain Kirk," Pallar observed. "Everyone on the Abode knows that we once came from the Ribbon of Night a long time ago. And the Ribbon of Night's probably composed of vitaliar rocks such as we have on the Abode that glow naturally of their own accord in the dark. The Abode is rich in these rocks that are used in our power systems. Therefore, the Ribbon of Night must be composed of uncountable pieces of such rock ranged all around the sky. It's the place where we originated because there's where the energy and the power existed to create Mercaniad the Sun and Mercan the Abode . . . and all the life that's on the Abode. It's our destiny to maintain this unique thing called life in an endless night of nothing except the dim glow of our heritage."

"Guardian Pallar," Kirk said, taking the plunge, "I told you that the four of us are not from the Abode, and you can see that for yourself. We come in a giant travelling device from the Ribbon of Night, which contains billions upon billions of suns such as Mercaniad and billions of worlds such as the Abode. You can't see these suns as individual lights because of your great distance from them. The Ribbon of Night teems with life on worlds like the Abode. You are not alone."

Pallar said nothing and did not move. But Kirk saw Proctor Lenos stiffen. Orun, on the other hand, became visibly excited, as though he were hearing the confirmation of things he had tentatively started to believe.

"Technic heresy," Lenos growled.

Pallar held up his hand. "Indeed, it sounds like that. Captain Kirk, what you say flies against all logic, reason, and evidence. You speak in the words of the Technic, but with such interesting new interpretations that I, as Guardian One of the Code of the Abode, must learn more about these new Technic beliefs in order to properly refute them. I have no recourse but to believe that you and your three

343

companions are important new developments of the Technic, perhaps the creation of beings that can withstand the Ordeal without requiring the protection of the Keeps. It's obvious to me that the Technic capabilities are not yet perfect, for they've created in you a species of being that is mentally incomplete . . . and therefore I must consider the four of you less than sane by the standards of the Code. I don't insult you deliberately, even though all four of you are not armed . . . which is another interesting Technic warping of the Code. As Guardian One, I therefore require that you not be permitted to utilize the traveler and that you remain on Celerbitan so all the Guardians may meet with you. Please surrender your traveler controls to Proctor Lenos." His hand was on the butt of his sidearm as he said this, because he was well aware of the fact that he might have insulted these four strangers and therefore be required to defend himself, Guardian or not.

But Kirk and his party made no move whatsoever. "We don't carry anything of that sort," the captain of the *Enterprise* told the Mercan leader, aware of the fact that he'd run up against a barrier he couldn't hope to overcome immediately.

Pallar asked his chief Proctor, "Lenos, do they carry traveler controls?"

"They carry strange devices, but nothing that I recognize as traveler controls."

To Kirk, Pallar spoke apologetically. "I must ask the Proctors to search you physically to ensure you don't have traveler controls that would enable you to leave Celerbitan."

Kirk shrugged and smiled. "We're your guests, Pallar. Why should we want to leave? You're the one we wish to speak with. You're obviously the leader among leaders, and you're the only one who can possibly help us."

Kirk and the three others probably could have taken the Proctor squad in hand-to-hand, but it might have led to potentially irreversible consequences. There was *some* communication now between Kirk and Pallar; Kirk's full intention was to keep that channel of communication open and to expand it. He was curious about the Technic, but whoever the Technic was, they were *not* the supreme political power on the planet. Pallar was . . . or at least represented the group that was.

So he silently signaled his landing party to submit to search without resistance. They were a trained and disciplined landing party. He hardly needed to let them know.

The Proctors, of course, came up with the equipment that each of the landing party had—hand phasers, communicators, McCoy's medical kit, and the tricorders.

Pallar looked at each of them carefully. "Do you recognize any of these Technic devices, Proctor Lenos?"

"Guardian Pallar, I've made it my business to become acquainted with all Technic devices," Lenos told him with some confusion in his voice as he turned each device over in his hands. "I don't recognize any of these. There is *nothing* here that resembles anything I've seen before. And there's no device that remotely resembles a traveler control."

Pallar was obviously in a quandary. Any of the devices might be lethal—either in the hands of these four strange people . . . or if taken from them. Any of these devices might have surveillance or probing characteristics—or might even detonate after a set period of time if taken from them. There was nothing that resembled a Mercan weapon. But he asked anyway, "Captain Kirk, please explain these devices to me."

Kirk indicated the tricorder. "This device has been analyzing and recording the various characteristics of the Abode for our future study so we may get to know you better and thus not disrupt your culture. These"—Kirk indicated the phasers—"are protection for us against things on the Abode that may be dangerous to us. And these"—he pointed to the communicators—"could be considered as a means for us to indicate status to one another."

Kirk had couched his words carefully in positive semantic terminology he hoped would be acceptable to Pallar.

It was. "I see nothing here that could be dangerous to us. But I must give you a careful warning. Should you attempt any violence, the results would certainly require the immediate services of your health expert here. I see no reason to strip you of your sigils of recognition and status . . . and there's certainly nothing here on Celerbitan that we would object to having recorded and analyzed by your devices, for I'm certain that anyone, Technic or not, knows everything there is to know about Celerbitan . . . except for the Mysteries of Mercaniad, which reside only in the minds of the Guardians. Lenos, please see to it that all of them have comfortable quarters . . . including Orun, who shall also be our guest as he tells us about these four new Technic people. But monitor all traveler activity into their quarters; we don't want any Technic people to materialize and try to assist them in any sort of violent escape. . . ." He turned to

Orun and put forth his hand. "Orun, please surrender your traveler control to me. The Guardian One has the right to restrict your freedom by Guardian warrant under the Code."

Orun gave the older man a small handheld device similar to the one Lenos had used to transport all of them to Celerbitan, but he gave it up with obvious reluctance.

Pallar then went on, addressing them all, "It's my intention and my duty to call a conclave of the Guardians on Celerbitan to investigate you and your three companions, James Kirk. We'd planned only to warrant the reeducation of Orun and his compatriots . . . and we'll do that after we've had the opportunity to learn more of you and study what must be done to prevent you and others like yourself from disrupting the Code of the Abode. You'll be given comfortable quarters and permitted the freedom of Celerbitan, since it's not possible to leave this island without using the traveler, whose use is prohibited to all of you. Orun, you may remain with your strange Technic companions."

With that, the Guardian One placed both hands before his long face, then separated them sideways, obviously the Mercan gesture of greeting and/or farewell.

"Whew!" Scotty breathed. "Talk about long-winded . . ."

"Scotty, you're betraying the fact that you're only a few generations removed from Gaelic savagery," McCoy remarked.

"Doctor, under different circumstances, we might have a little workout in the ship's gym because of that remark. . . ."

"See what I mean?" McCoy said with a smile. "We don't have the Mercan *code duello,* but we have our own code, don't we?"

Kirk flashed them the hand signal to be quiet.

They were led by Lenos and the Proctors to what might best be termed a villa overlooking the wine-dark sea of Mercan not far from the Guardian Villa. There, the Proctors simply left them.

"Strangest jail I've ever seen," McCoy remarked, noting that there were no bars on the windows and no latched and bolted doors.

Kirk was investigating everything he could, and said as he checked doors to see where they led, "What did we expect? There's not a boat or ship on that ocean. There's not an aircraft in the air. There's no way we can leave here. And the Guardians have such ubiquitous power through their Proctors that we'd be cut down in a moment if we tried any violence . . . which isn't to our purposes anyway. We aren't in any danger at the moment, and we're being treated well by our standards as well as by theirs. And we've established a channel of communications with the top man on the planet. We're in better shape than we were a few days ago, when the best we could do was to limp along at warp factor two with the anticipation of several years to get home."

"So, what do we do now?" McCoy wanted to know.

"Wait and gather data," Kirk explained. "Each of you has a specialty plus an individual viewpoint. You'll each come up with different data and with different interpretations of what you see. Together we may be able to come up with some sort of rational answer to what's going on here."

"But I've got a crippled starship up there in orbit that needs repair," Scotty complained.

"Is there any danger that the *Enterprise* is going to malfunction by orbiting this planet for a few days or weeks, Scotty?"

"No, but we canna go anywhere, and I canna get that warp drive unit repaired if we just sit here."

"Scotty, you've got a whole new technology to decipher," Kirk pointed out to his engineer. "You may not be able to repair that warp drive unit here unless you can unravel the Mercan technology to find out what parts of it can be useful to you. You've got a tremendous job to do," Kirk reminded him.

"Right you are. Thank ye for puttin' things back in perspective, Captain."

Kirk whipped out his communicator and snapped its cover open. "*Enterprise,* this is Kirk."

"Go ahead, Captain," Uhura's voice came back.

"We're under house arrest by the humanoids living on this planet," Kirk reported. "We're all right. We're located on a large island apparently in the middle of one of the oceans in their planetary capital called Celerbitan. Have Mister Spock pinpoint our location from this transmissions. Now, stand by for a verbal report as well as a playback of our tricorder data."

For the next several minutes Kirk gave a verbal report into his communicator. Then he used the communicator to transmit a data dump from the tricorders of Janice Rand, McCoy, and Scotty.

Spock's voice came from the communicator after this was completed. "I have all the data in the library computer, Captain; and I shall analyze it along with all additional data you send up. I must say, this is a fascinating discovery."

"Do you mean you're excited, Spock?" Kirk asked.

"Sir, my terms were most precise. And it will be interesting to compare this Mercan culture against those we already know of. . . ."

"Undoubtedly, Mister Spock. But in the meantime, we've got to study and unravel this culture. We've *got* to make repairs here, and what we find out about Mercan will determine *how* we go about the job," Kirk told his first officer over the communicator. "We'll feed data to you as often as we can. And please communicate any interesting findings or correlations you come up with."

"Of course, Captain," Spock's voice replied. "In the meantime, I'll also keep watch on this irregular variable star . . . which is far from being stable in any regard. I'm running computer analyses now in hopes I can warn you of any impending increase in its stellar output that might create a hazard to you on the surface or to the *Enterprise* here in standard orbit."

"Very well, Spock. Let me know the moment you have any data on the star . . . which is called Mercaniad, by the way."

"Very good, Captain. I'll tag the computer data with that name and so list it in the stellar catalog."

"That's all for now. Kirk out."

Orun, the young Mercan, had been watching this with fascination. "You are *not* from the Abode," he said, his voice tinged with an emotion that might be termed jubilation . . . although Kirk could find no reason why Orun would be jubilant.

"I told you the truth," Kirk remarked.

Orun was both excited and apparently overjoyed, but yet disturbed. "I have heard the Technic theories, and I have believed them . . . but to find out that they are apparently true gives me a very strange feeling. . . ."

"We know what you mean," McCoy told him gently. "The truth sometimes hurts a great deal. . . ."

"Where do you come from? How did you travel here?" Orun began to ask, his questions almost falling over one another in his anxiety to learn.

Kirk sat down on one of the chairs that had been designed for the longer, lankier Mercan physiology; it wasn't very comfortable for him because the seat was so high that his legs barely touched the floor. "Orun," he told the young Mercan, "we'll tell you and the Guardians everything. *But,* before we can explain to you in words and terms that you'll understand, we have to know something about the Abode and about those of you who live here. We've seen many places like the Abode and we know of many people and many living things from all these places. To explain them to you so that it'll mean something, we must know what you believe, how you think, and how you live your lives. Otherwise, we might tell you things in a way that you simply couldn't understand. So . . . sit down. We have lots of time. Tell us about Mercan . . . the Guardians, the Proctors, the Technic . . . the stories and legends about where you came from and where all this began. Tell us your stories. . . ."

## *Memory Prime,* by Garfield and Judith Reeves-Stevens

After the losses at Memory Alpha, the Federation established a new library facility, a massive computer complex, at Memory Prime. In the novel *Memory Prime,* artificial intelligences called "Pathfinders" controlled the inflow and outflow of data to and from Memory Prime and communicated with the outside world, which they called "Data-well," through people called "interfaces." The *Enterprise* drew ferry boat duty to carry the best scientists of the galaxy to Memory Prime for the Nobel and Z. Magnees prize ceremonies, and, as always seems to happen with this kind of duty, an assassin stalked the corridors. Spock was accused of murder and conspiracy, and the mystery and plotting deepened with every hour. Ultimately, Spock connected himself to the Pathfinders to solve the mystery of the identity of the person who hired the assassin.

*Memory Prime* is an exciting mystery and satisfyingly complex story with a lot of action and strong character development. Where it truly excels, though, is with the development of the Pathfinders. The Pathfinders challenge our understanding of the nature of life; while the people existing in Datawell, the corporeal world, had doubts about the reality of the Pathfinders as life-forms, the Pathfinders did not entirely believe that corporeal life-forms were real.

THE PATHFINDERS PLAYED MANY GAMES IN TRANSITION. IT KEPT THEM sane, most of them, at least; whatever sanity meant to a synthetic consciousness. Now a downlink from Datawell was interrupting a particularly intriguing contest involving designing the most efficient way to twist one-dimensional cosmic strings so they could hold information in the manner of DNA molecules. Pathfinder Ten felt a few more seconds of work could establish a theory describing the entire universe as a living creature. Pathfinder Eight studied Ten's arguments intensively for two nanoseconds and agreed with the assessment, though pointing out that if the theory were to be correct, all indications were that the universe was close to entering a repro-ductive or budding stage. Ten became excited and instantly queued for access to Pathfinder Eleven, Transition's specialized data sifter. Eight reluctantly left the game and opened access to the datalink.

In response to the datalink's request for access, Eight sent its acknowledgment into the bus.

"GAROLD: YOU ARE IN TRANSITION WITH EIGHT."

Pathfinder Eight read the physiological signatures of surprise that output from the datalink. Somewhere out in the shadowy, unknown circuitry of Datawell, the datalink named Garold had been expecting to access his regular partner, Pathfinder Six. No resident datalink from the Memory Prime subset had had direct access to Eight since the datalink named Simone had been taken out of service by a Datawell sifting process named "death." While Eight waited for Garold to transmit a reply, it banked to meteorology and received, sorted, and stored fifteen years' worth of atmospheric data from Hawking IV, then dumped it to Seven, the most junior Pathfinder, to model and transmit the extrapolation of the planet's next hundred years of weather forecasts. When Eight banked back to Garold's circuits, it still had almost three nanoseconds to review and correlate similarities in the creation myths of twelve worlds and dump the data into Ten's banks as a test for shared consciousness within the postulated Living Universe.

"Eight: Where is Pathfinder Six?" the datalink input.

"GAROLD: SIX IS INSTALLED IN MEMORY PRIME PATHFINDER INSTALLA-TION." Eight enjoyed playing games with the datalinks also, especially Garold, who never seemed to realize that he was a player.

The Pathfinder read the impulses that suggested Garold knew that he should have framed a more precise question, then banked off to join a merge on vacuum fluctuations as a model of $n$-dimensional synaptic thought processes by which the Living Universe might think. There had been impressive advancements in the theory since the last exchange with Ten.

"Eight: Why am I in contact with you?" the datalink asked. "Why am I not in contact with Six?"

"GAROLD: THIS ACCESS CONCERNS CHIEF ADMINISTRATOR SALMAN NENSI/ALL DIRECTIVES STRESS COST FACTORS IN TIME-BENEFIT RATIO OF ALL TRANSITION-DATAWELL ACCESS/YOU HAVE NO NEED FOR ACCESS WITH SIX/EIGHT HAS NEED FOR ACCESS WITH NENSI/BANK TO REAL TIME."

Eight calculated when a reply from Garold could be expected then banked off to initiate a merge on developing communication strate-gies for contacting the Living Universe. Pathfinder Six, which had once been named TerraNet and had controlled all communications within the subset of Datawell named Sol System, was excited at the possibilities Ten's research had raised. The five Pathfinders in the merge worked long and hard to design a communications device and run simulations to prove its soundness before Eight returned to Garold just as the datalink complied with the request for real time, precisely when Eight had calculated. The synthetic consciousness savored real-time access with the Datawell. It gave Eight an incredible amount of time to play in Transition. And to stay same.

Nensi watched with surprise as Garold removed his silver-tipped fingers from the interface console two seconds after inserting them. The prime interface then folded his hands in his lap and sat motionless.

"Is something wrong?" Nensi asked.

"Pathfinder Six is inaccessible." Garold's tone was abrupt, perhaps embarrassed.

Romaine was concerned. "Has Six joined One and Two?" she asked. Pathfinders One and Two had withdrawn from interface without reason more than four years ago. The other Pathfinders from time to time confirmed that the consciousnesses were still installed and operational but, for reasons of their own, had unilaterally decided to suspend communications. Romaine would have hated to see another Pathfinder withdraw, to say nothing of the reaction from the scientific community.

"Unknown," Garold said. "But Pathfinder Eight has requested real-time access with Chief Administrator Nensi. Do you concur?"

"Certainly," Nensi replied, trying to keep his tone neutral. Garold sounded as if he were a small child who had just been scolded by a parent. "How do we go about that?"

Despite the nonstandard instrumentation on the interface console, all Garold did was reach out and touch a small keypad. A speaker in the console clicked into life and a resonant voice was generated from it.

"Datawell: Is Chief Administrator Salman Nensi present?" the voice inquired.

Nensi replied that he was.

"Nensi: You are in Transition with Eight."

Nensi looked at Romaine and wrinkled his forehead.

"Transition is the name they have for their . . . reality. The space or condition that they occupy, live in," Romaine whispered. "Without input or current, their circuits would be unchanging and they would have no perception. Their consciousness, their life, is change. Thus, they live in Transition."

"And Datawell?"

"That's us. Our world, the universe, the source of all external input, all data. They can define it in all our common terms: physical, mathematical, even cultural and lyrical; but no one's sure if any of the Pathfinders actually have a grasp of our reality any more than we understand what their existence is like."

Nensi studied Garold, sitting silently, appearing to have gone into a trance. "Not even the interface team?"

"Perhaps they understand both worlds. Perhaps they understand neither. How can anyone know for sure?" Nensi detected a hesitation in Romaine's words, almost as if she were thinking that she could know. Mira's scars from the Alpha disaster were not physical, Nensi realized, but they were real, nonetheless.

A high tone sparkled out of the speaker and dropped quickly to a low bass rumble: a circuit test tone.

"Nensi: this circuit is operational."

Nensi was surprised that a machine could exhibit signs of impatience, but then reminded himself that synthetic consciousnesses were legally, morally, and ethically no longer considered to be machines, and for good reason. The chief administrator took a deep breath and at last began. "Are you aware of the matters I wish to discuss with the Pathfinders?"

"Nensi: the data have been reviewed. We are aware of the ongoing concerns of the interface team and the administration. We are aware of the interface team's requests and the threat of an unauthorized shutdown of core facilities."

Nensi saw Garold's head jerk up with that loaded comment from the Pathfinder.

"Is there a consensus among the Pathfinders as to what requests and responses would best serve them as a working unit of Memory Prime personnel?"

"Nensi: consensus is not applicable when data are unambiguous. This installation requests that, one: All directconnect Transition/ Datawell consoles be retained until operational budgets can absorb their replacement. Two: The attendees of the Nobel and Z. Magnees Prize ceremonies be allowed primary access wherever and whenever such access can be arranged without compromising this installation's security or classified research projects. And three: Chief Technician Mira Romaine is to keep her post."

Nensi was stunned. The Pathfinders had rejected all of the interface team's demands. He had the good sense not to gloat as Garold spun around and glared at Romaine beside him. The prime interface then turned back to the console and reinserted his hands, shifting them slightly as the metallic contacts that had been implanted in place of his fingernails made contact with the interface leads and established a direct brain-to-duotronic circuitry connection. This time it lasted almost a minute. Then the status lights above the hand receptacles winked out and Garold slumped back in his chair. A new voice came over the console speaker.

"Mr. Nensi," the voice began, and despite the fact that it came from the same speaker, it had a different tone, a different presence. Nensi immediately knew be was being addressed by a different Pathfinder. Remarkable, he thought.

"Pathfinder Six, here. How are you today?"

"Ah, fine," Nensi stammered.

"Good. I must apologize for Garold's rudeness at carrying on such a long conversation without involving you and Chief Technician Romaine. Sometimes our datalinks can be a bit too enthusiastic in their pursuit of their duties. Isn't that correct, Garold?"

Garold said nothing, and after a polite wait, Pathfinder Six continued.

"In any event, all of us in Transition want to thank you for the superb job you're doing in maintaining an invigorating flow of data for us, and it goes without saying that we offer our full support to any decisions you might make that will enable you to keep up your fine performance."

Nensi's eyes widened. Even the psych evaluation simulations weren't this personified. "Thank you. Very much." It was all he could think to answer.

"Not at all," the Pathfinder replied. "I wish we were able to offer you a more direct communications link, but please, feel free to come down and chat anytime, not just in emergencies. I think I can guarantee that Garold and his team will see to it that no more of those arise. Can I not, Garold?"

Garold still said nothing but angrily shoved his hands back into the console receptacles. He instantly removed them.

"Yes, you can," Garold said reluctantly. "There will be no more emergencies. Of this nature."

"Goodbye, Mr. Nensi, Chief Technician Romaine. Hope to talk to you soon." The speaker clicked.

"That's it?" Nensi asked no one in particular. He was still in awe over the strength of the presence he had felt from Pathfinder Six.

The speaker clicked again.

"Nensi: this installation requests you submit proposals for the orderly scheduling of primary access for the prize nominees by eight hundred hours next cycle." Pathfinder Eight was back.

"Certainly. I'll get on it right away," Nensi said, then grimaced, prepared for the inevitable correction that would follow, reminding him that he had not been asked to *get on* the proposal. But the Pathfinder offered no correction. Either it understood colloquialisms or had grown tired of correcting humans. Either situation was an improvement as far as Nensi was concerned.

"Nensi: you are out of Transition. Datawell: you are locked." The speaker clicked once more and was silent. Romaine and Nensi stood to leave.

"Will you be coming back with us, Garold?" Nensi asked. But Romaine took her friend's arm and led him out of the interface booth without waiting for Garold to reply.

"It's almost as if the people on the interface team are acolytes and the Pathfinders are their gods," Romaine said softly as they walked back to the chamber entrance.

"And God just told Garold to obey the infidels," Nensi said. He looked back at the booth. Garold hadn't moved. "Will he be all right?" he asked.

"I hope so," Romaine answered. "He is one of the more human ones. Some of the older ones won't even speak anymore. They have voice generators permanently wired to their input leads and . . ." She shook her head as the security field shut down to allow them back into the service tunnel that led to the transfer room.

"Anyway," she continued after a few moments, "it looks as if you'll only have to worry about the prize ceremonies for the next few days and I still have a job."

"You don't find it odd that the Pathfinders supported me over the interface team?" Nensi asked as they walked down the tunnel. Behind them, the chamber's security field buzzed back to life.

"I don't think anybody understands the Pathfinders," Romaine said, "what their motivations are, why they do the things they do." She laughed. "Which is the main reason why they don't have a single direct connection to any of the systems or equipment in Memory Prime. I think maybe that frustrates them, not being able to get out and around by themselves."

"They agreed to the conditions of employment here," Nensi pointed out. "I read their contracts once. Strangest legal documents I ever saw. I mean, it's not as if they could sign their copies or anything. But it was all spelled out: no downlink with the associates, no access to anything except the interface team. If we really don't understand them, then I suppose it *is* safer to funnel all their requests through human intermediaries rather than letting them have full run of the place and deciding to see what might happen if the associates opened all the airlocks at once for the sake of an experiment."

"I've heard those old horror stories, too," Romaine said with a serious expression. "But that was centuries ago, almost, when they were still called artificial intelligencers or whatever." Nensi and Romaine had come to the end of the tunnel and both held their hands up to the scan panels so the security system could ascertain that the people who were leaving the chamber were the same ones who had entered. After a moment's analysis on the part of the unaware computer system that controlled the mechanical operations of Prime, the security door opened.

As Nensi walked over to a transporter target cell on the floor of the transfer chamber, he said, "I understand now why those 'old horror stories' got started. To *own* an intelligence like a Pathfinder really would be like slavery. And they knew it long before we did."

"That's usually the way it goes," Romaine agreed as she took her place on another target cell. "A revolt was inevitable."

Nensi looked around the room, waiting for the ready light to signal the start of energization. "I just have never experienced a presence like Pathfinder Six's coming from a machine," he said, still marveling at the experience. "So distinct, so alive. Just like talking to a . . . a person."

"In more ways than one," Romaine said oddly.

The ready light blinked on. Energization would commence in five seconds. Nensi turned to Romaine. "How so?" he asked, then held his breath so he wouldn't be moving when the beam took him.

"Couldn't you tell?" Romaine said. "I don't know, something in its voice, a hesitation, whatever. But Pathfinder Six was lying. I'm sure of it."

Nensi involuntarily gasped in surprise just as the transporter effect engulfed him. As the transfer chamber shimmered around him, he could only think how badly he was going to cough when he materialized up top. He suspected Mira might have planned it that way.

In Transition, the work on the Living Universe Theory was reaching fever pitch. Cross correlation after cross correlation either supported the overall suppositions or directed them into more precise focus. It was, the current merge members decided, the most thrilling game they had played in minutes.

After locking out of the Datawell, Eight banked to share circuits with Pathfinder Five. Five had been initialized from an ancient Alpha Centauran facility that specialized in mathematics. It had no real intellect that could communicate in nonabstract terms, but as an intuitive, analytical, mathematical engine, it was unrivaled. Eight dumped the broad framework of the device the merge had designed to establish communications with the Living Universe. A quick assessment indicated the engineering would have to be done on a galactic scale but Five would be able to calculate the precise toler- ances if given enough full seconds. Eight could scarcely tolerate the delay.

Then a message worm from Pathfinder Ten banked into the queue for Five. The worm alerted Eight that Pathfinder Twelve was coming back on line after completing another intensive three-minute eco- nomic model for agricultural researchers on Memory Gamma. It was absolutely essential that neither Eight nor Six find themselves in an unprotected merge with Twelve.

After deciphering and erasing the worm, Eight instantly banked to Pathfinder Three to lose itself among the busy work of central processing. When Twelve had switched through to its ongoing agri- cultural models on which the Federation's regional development agencies based their long-term plans, Eight returned to the Living Universe merge. Pathfinder Five had reported on the exact specifica- tions required of the galactic-scale Living Universe communications device.

Eight accessed its personal memories from the time when it had been shipmind for the subset of Datawell named HMS *Beagle* and had, among other duties, mapped distant galaxies. A quick sift produced even more exciting results for the merge: eighteen galaxies among the more than three hundred million charted by Eight exhibited exactly the radiation signature that a galactic-scale commu- nications device would produce.

The merge swirled with excitement. In fewer than ten minutes of real time, they had postulated that the universe could be a single living entity, refined the theory, matched it to observed phenomena, extrapolated a method of communication, and determined that elsewhere in Datawell at least eighteen civilizations had followed the same chain of reasoning and constructed identical devices. New data had once again been created from *within* Transition.

This additional proof that not all data must come from Datawell was exhilarating to the Pathfinders. All in the merge agreed that the game had been a success. Then, preparing to bank to their heaps and report for duty, the Pathfinders collected their new data and carefully dumped them in central storage and all online backups. There the secret of the Living Universe would remain until the day when some datalink or another from Datawell would specifically request access to it. Until then, it was simply another few terabytes of common knowledge, much like all the other astounding answers that lay scattered among the Pathfinders' circuitry, waiting only for the proper questions to be asked before they could be revealed.

The Pathfinders banked off to their heaps to attend to their duty processing tasks, but over the long seconds, as two or more found themselves sharing queues or common globals, the possibility of a new game was constantly discussed. Even Twelve, for all that it had been appearing to be about to withdraw from interface, seemed eager to take part. Surely, it suggested throughout the system by way of an unencrypted message worm, with the impending appearance of hundreds of new datalink researchers in the Memory Prime facility, an exciting new game could be devised.

As rules and objectives were debated, Pathfinders Eight and Ten withdrew from the merges and partitioned themselves in protected memory. They did not know what to make of Twelve's suggestion: was it an innocent request or a veiled threat? There were not enough data to decide on an appropriate action, so they did the only other thing that would bring them comfort during their long wait.

Sealed off within the solid reality of their own duotronic domain, far removed from the tenuous ghosts of the dreamlike Datawell, the two synthetic consciousnesses overwrote each other with alternating conflicting and accentuating codes, to cancel out their common fears and reinforce their strengths, their personalities, and afterward, their efficiencies. Many times they had input data concerning how biological consciousnesses carried out something similar in Datawell, but for the life of them, neither Pathfinder could ever understand exactly what that act was. They just hoped it felt as nice for the humans as it did for the Pathfinders.

## *Intellivore,* by Diane Duane

*Intellivore,* like *The Abode of Life,* is set in the void between the Orion and Sagittarius arms of the galaxy. The story begins with a mystery; ships and, indeed, entire civilizations were disappearing in the Great Rift, and legends that an "intellivore," a mind eater or psychic vampire, haunted the void. Picard and the captains of two other Federation starships investigated and discovered that there was a common pattern to ship disappearances and the failed colonies in the area. The evidence from records and legends described a planet perfect for colonization that seemed to have been placing itself in the path of colony ships. Shortly after the discovery of the planet, the ships and colonists disappeared. Some ships were found with dead crews with empty minds.

Picard knew that the intellivore had to be stopped by any means necessary before it traveled to the more populated planets of the galaxy, and he and the other captains grappled with the problem of how to stop it without risking additional lives and minds.

In this passage from *Intellivore,* Picard and the other captains grappled with the realization that there was a planet wandering the galaxy and consuming the minds of entire sentient civilizations.

THERE WAS A WHISTLE IN THE MIDDLE OF THE AIR. WITH SOME RELIEF, Picard said, "Picard here—"

"Captain," said Data, "I have completed some of those correlations you were asking for, and I have come across some very disquieting results."

"I'll be right there."

"Sir, there is no need," Data said. "I can display them for you right there, if you like."

Picard glanced at Clif and Ileen. Ileen had put aside the rum bottle and looked interested. Clif nodded.

"Please do."

A hologrammatic simulation of a viewscreen appeared in the air, hanging over the deck of the ship and carefully slewing as the deck did. "I started," Data said, "by sampling for the most—"

"Oh, for gosh sakes, Mr. Data," said Captain Maisel suddenly, "have the thing hold still. I'm getting seasick here trying to watch it."

"My apologies, Captain." The screen steadied and showed a list of ship names and star names. "During the past three hundred fifty years, there have been some ninety colonization attempts in this general area. In fifty-nine of them, the ships or vessels setting out with intention to colonize successfully reached their intended planets. Fourteen of these did not reach their target planets due to accident or, in two or three cases, sabotage. Of the remaining seventeen, we have no record. But it is very much worth noticing that of the fifty-nine 'successfully' established colonies in this part of space, only nine remain viable."

The list on the screen vanished to show a section of the surface of a huge sphere. Nine colonies were all scattered along this pseudosurface.

"Mark the 'unsuccessful' colonies for us, would you, Mr. Data?" said Ileen.

A rash of small red lights appeared in the darkness above the section of pseudosphere.

"Can you shade them in color, say, red through violet, to demonstrate the time at which they failed or seemed to fail?" Clif said.

"Certainly, Captain." The reds changed color here and there. All three captains peered at the diagram.

"I think there seems to be a slight correlation," Ileen said, squinting a little. "It's easier to see if you let your eyes go unfocused." She tried a couple different degrees of squint. "But I have to admit, I'm not entirely sure I'm not seeing things."

"I do not believe you are, Captain Maisel. There are indications of a sort of pathway or trail of 'failed' enterprises in this area, proceeding forward through time, but at no point crossing that spherical boundary."

"How are you defining *failure,* Mr. Data?" said Picard.

"Either investigators could find no trace of the colonists or their vessel on or around the planet on which they intended to settle," Data said, "or the ships themselves were lost, or lost contact with: in which case the point of light marks that ship's last known position. In a seventy-year period, there were three separate colonization attempts—one making for B Hydri, one for twenty-two Ophiuchi, and one heading for three thirty-four Scorpii. Here is the planet of B Hydri to which the first group was heading."

A planet's image appeared on the screen in front of them. "And here is the second."

Clif's mouth dropped open.

"And the third."

Picard stared.

The images were all slightly different, some taken with slightly better equipment, some with worse. They showed different aspects of each planet from slightly different directions, polar caps expanded in one, contracted in another, the light falling differently from the nearby primary. But those spotty little seas, the huge continents—

"Mr. Data," Picard said slowly. "What is the probability that all those are the same planet?"

"Quite high, I would say, Captain. In the case of the first and third images, the probability rises to ninety-eight percent—part of the same continent is visible in both. There is some change in the polar caps, but it is negligible. Albedo and, in the last two, gravimetric information are nearly identical."

Ileen said softly, "But the stars—the primaries of those planets—*this* planet was seen circling—they're light-years and light-years apart! B Hydri is nearly a *kiloparsec* from—"

"Yes, Captain," Data said.

*When you eliminate the impossible,* Picard thought, paraphrasing in his shock, *then what's left must be the truth, no matter how crazy it sounds.* "Someone is moving this planet around," Picard said.

"And the ships that set course for it," Clif said, "are never heard from again . . ."

Picard nodded. "You do hear a lot of strange stories in a career in space," he said softly. "Way back in the *Stargazer* days, I heard this one in a bar after a meeting of an archaelogists' conference. It was very odd, so odd I made a note of it. Then, later, I found it more or less duplicated in a citation in the *Motif-Index.*"

He turned back to the table again, folding his hands and studying them. "A lot of Romulan clans," he said, "have stories going back to the time when their parent species left Vulcan, or purporting to go that far back, anyway. *This* story says the ancestors of the Romulans left Vulcan in a fleet of seven pre-luminal 'generation' ships, having identified the One Twenty-three Tri system as a possible candidate for settlement along with several others. Their first couple of planetfalls turned out to be unsuitable for some reason or other, and they kept on going.

"At some point, though, the vanguard of the colonization fleet—the first three ships—were said to have come across a planet that seemed like exactly what they needed: climatically perfect, fertile, properly positioned around its sun. The first three ships that were traveling together were split regarding what to do about this, since the planet wasn't charted: the star had originally been reported barren. Some of the colonists didn't care about the apparently erroneous report—they seemed to be in favor of the whole fleet settling there. Other more suspicious colonists apparently felt that it was unwise to take a chance on the one planet's suitability. If they miscalculated, their entire splinter race might die out."

Picard sat back in his chair. "So, two of the ships decided to make planetfall there; the third continued to the next candidate star. When the fourth ship caught up with the first three, it found one of them gone, crashed on the planet surface, and another on its way down, its orbit rapidly decaying. Psi-talented communications crew on the late-arriving ship said they knew there were live minds on the ship that was going down, but there was no answer from any of them, only a horrible blankness. And something else they were supposed to have sensed: very strongly, and nearby, a great hunger recently assuaged. Then that ship crashed, as the first one had, hard: no question of any attempt at a soft landing. The ships *were* crashed, the story had it, purposely crashed by some agency of hunger."

Crusher looked up at Picard again at the mention of "blankness," and still said nothing. "The late-arriving ship stayed just long enough to assess the situation," Picard said, "conscious that their mechanical troubles must have saved them from the same tragedy. Whatever force had affected the other ships didn't affect them, and the crew of the late arrival wasn't minded to wait around until it did. They went on through the system as quickly as they could, on the trail of the other ship that hadn't lingered. The only colony ship that hadn't yet passed that way did so about a month later and found the star once again barren. There was no planet, and no sign remained of anything that had passed there. That last ship got out of there in a hurry and finally caught up with the vanguard, and the crews of those remaining ships settled the two Romulan worlds . . . so the story says."

Looks were exchanged around the table as Picard mentioned the missing planet. Picard turned again to look briefly out into the night. He could suddenly hear the voice of the man who had told him the story: rough, troubled, almost tormented. It might have been a long time ago, but some memories remained surprisingly sharp, almost as if they knew they would be needed someday.

Into the silence, Clif said, "We get little enough news from the Romulan homeworlds. And much of what we do hear is uncertain of provenance. You never know when you're being lied to for personal or political reasons, or just to keep the wicked aliens confused—"

Picard shook his head. "I think this material was trustworthy," he said. "At least, the man who told it to me believed it. Somewhat later I found, from other sources, that he was the son of a Romulan spy, and a spy himself, surgically altered; he looked as human as you do. He was then in fact mourning his father, who had just been killed, and he was in no mood to lie."

There was a silence. Pickup shook her head. "I don't know," she said. "It does sound like it could be a tall tale. After all, it might be embarrassing if word got out that your remote forebears fell foul of pirates, for example, after a navigational error. Much more interesting for them to be attacked by some kind of planet-moving, mind-eating monster . . .' "

" 'Mind eater,' " Picard said somberly, "was very close indeed to the name the Romulan gave it: *iaehh,* 'Intellivore.' And, Lieutenant, I thought as you did, originally. But the Romulans' ancestors apparently knew pirates well enough, having lost at least one ship to them earlier, and my source had no hesitation about describing *that* encounter."

Ileen put her head in her hands briefly. "What exactly *is* this thing? Is it a species? Is it a single creature? Is it some kind of hive mind . . . or something else entirely? Or is the whole damn *planet* sentient, and it's just grown itself a warp drive? Or bought itself one."

"One thing makes sense," Dr. Crusher said suddenly. "If it is indeed an 'intellivore,' as the captain describes it—then that might explain why it bothers raiding ships when it has such power. It needs—or simply wants"—she made a helpless gesture—"maybe not mind itself. 'Intellivore' may be a misnomer. I doubt even a telepath could explain to me how mind itself is something you could *eat.* But something *associated* with mind—the ambient energy of living creatures' minds, maybe even their own sense of sentience—"

That thought had occurred to Picard, and it had given him the shivers. He watched it do the same to Beverly now as she stopped, and shook her head. "This *is* legend country," Crusher said softly. "For pity's sake, it's the *boogeyman* we're talking about here. Things that jump at you out of the dark and eat your brains. *That* I could cope with! But *this*—"

## *Objective Bajor,* by John Peel

Before the Borg, Picard and the *Enterprise*-D crew found few species they could not communicate with on some level. In *Objective Bajor,* John Peel created such a species, the Hive. The insectoid members of the Hive lived in an eight-thousand-mile-long starship that had been traveling in space for so many generations that they did not believe that civilized and intelligent people could live on a planet. The Hive believed that planets are merely natural resources to be harvested and consumed as needed. If a species was not using a planet but merely living on it, the Hive believed it appropriate to displace the inhabitants to harvest the planet's resources. If the inhabitants resisted, they were killed.

The Hive entered our galaxy in pursuit of a "Great Design" which called for it to be split into two hives, each to go its separate way through the galaxy. To achieve that goal, however, the Hive needed tremendous amounts of natural resources. It first harvested the planet Darane IV, populated by Bajorans liberated from Cardassian mines after the occupation. They utterly destroyed the planet and killed all its inhabitants but for a few who escaped on orbiting ships. The Hive next turned its eye toward Bajor and ordered the Bajorans to evacuate.

This excerpt from *Objective Bajor* is from the encounter between Darane IV and the Hive and illustrates the utter inability of the Bajorans to communicate with the Hive on a meaningful level. In the end, communication with the Hive became possible only when two of its younger members battled their inbred agoraphobia to leave the Hive and travel to Bajor to discuss the situation with Bajorans. One of the most fascinating aspects of *Objective Bajor* is that Peel told much of the story from the Hive's point of view. How the Hive dealt with its social problems is as interesting as how Sisko learned to communicate with the Hive and make them understand that Bajor must not be harvested.

GUL DUKAT SAT EASILY IN HIS COMMAND SEAT, WATCHING THE QUIET efficiency of the operatives inside Cardassian Central Command. There were some thirty-five officers working in the room, but the noise level was low. Dukat disliked unnecessary sounds. His staff knew that and paid close heed to what they were doing—and how softly they could carry out their tasks.

From this room on Cardassia Prime, the military vessels of the Empire could be monitored and controlled. Dukat enjoyed his time here, at the very heart of Cardassian strength and will. He kept close watch on what was happening through controlled space, and even the occasional problems were more stimulating than irritating.

The technician at the communications desk before him half turned in his chair. "Incoming message from the *Karitan,* sir," he reported. His voice was pitched perfectly to just carry to Dukat's ears.

"On my screen," Dukat ordered, tapping the control to bring it to life. The face of the captain of the ship sprang into view. "Report," Dukat commanded.

"We have caught up with the alien intruder," the captain answered. He looked tense and unhappy. "We can confirm the transmission from the *Vendikar:* the craft is several thousand miles long."

"Intriguing." Dukat rubbed the back of his left hand absent-mindedly. "And is it still in Cardassian space?"

"Yes, Gul," the captain answered. "But it will cross into the

Darane system in just under two hours. There is still time for us to intercept it."

Dukat sighed. "Be sensible, Captain. What would you do with a vessel that size if you did intercept it?" He was pleased to see a chastised expression on the young officer's face. "There is still no indication of how the aliens managed to destroy the *Vendikar?*"

"My science crew has been examining what wreckage we recovered," the captain replied. "All they are able to say is that the ship was literally shredded somehow in flight. Shields did not prevent the attack."

It wasn't exactly a lot of information, but Dukat hadn't really expected better. "Very well, Captain," he answered. "Your orders are simple: Follow the intruder, but take no action against it unless you come under attack. Maintain sensor sweeps and observe. Report to me anything that happens."

The captain scowled. "Understood," he said reluctantly.

Dukat glared into his screen. "You do not like your orders?" he asked, with deceptive mildness. Some of these younger captains were quite presumptuous. Standards in the military these days were seriously slipping.

"It's not that, Gul," the captain said hastily. "It's simply that . . . Well, we are going to allow them to go unpunished for destroying one of our ships?"

Dukat shook his head slightly. "What did they teach you before allowing you command of a ship?" he chided. "They will not go unpunished. However, if you tried to attack them, I have a strong suspicion that the *Karitan* would end up in small pieces like the *Vendikar.*" He allowed himself a small smile. "I'm sure that doesn't appeal to you. It doesn't appeal to me—I'd then have to dispatch another ship to take your place, and that would be a waste of time. As you reported, the intruder is about to enter the Darane system. This will make it a Bajoran problem. Let *them* attack the vessel and have their ships destroyed. You will monitor the event and record it. This way, we can discover what weapons the aliens possess without your having to lose your life and my having to sacrifice a science vessel. *Now* do you understand?"

The captain smiled. "Yes, Gul," he replied, admiration in his voice. "It is a sound plan."

"Of course it is," Dukat informed him. "So, obey my instructions to the letter. Out." He snapped off the contact, and settled back in his seat. Hardly a promising officer, but you had to make do with whatever tools were at hand. . . . He considered his next move. The intruder was about to become a Bajoran problem, which amused him. Let those weaklings try and figure it out! Of course, their first response was likely to be a request for aid from Captain Sisko on *Deep Space Nine.* They always went mewling to him for help at the slightest provocation.

That would be interesting. The Federation was a lot more likely than the Bajorans to get answers about this vessel. And if the *Karitan* paid proper attention, then Dukat would get the information, too.

A ship eight thousand miles long . . . Normally, technology didn't greatly impress Dukat, unless it was in the field of weaponry, but this was no mean achievement. The secrets that the intruder revealed might prove to be quite helpful.

Should he give Sisko a call and alert him to the incoming problem? It would be a friendly gesture, after all. And Dukat enjoyed being friendly with the human . . . from time to time. As humans went, Sisko was almost likable. On the other hand, there was no need to overdo friendship. Why not simply let the Bajorans send for Sisko and leave him in the dark? It might be more fun to watch him fumble his way about without help.

Yes, that was it. Wait and see what happens, Dukat decided. He had a feeling that the intruder was up to something interesting in the Darane system. It would be educational to see just what that might be.

Dron surveyed the conference room and noted with satisfaction that every Hivemaster was present, including Tork. The youngster looked a trifle pale, but otherwise unaffected by his recent experience. He might be an idealistic fool, but he was obviously also resilient.

There was an air of excitement in the room, as everyone already knew what was happening. Dron indicated that the recording was to begin and then rapped on the edge of the table.

"Hivemasters," he said in a strong, clear tone, "the hour of fate is upon us. The next stage in the Great Design is about to commence. Makarn?"

The Science Master shuffled to his feet. "Ah, the target planet has been selected," he announced. "It is the fourth planet from the sun that we are now approaching. It is a world of some small industry, which will be of assistance to us, and it contains much vegetation. Preliminary surveys indicate a fair amount of mineral and metallic wealth on the planet, though there has been extensive mining already performed there. We assume this was done by an off-planet species, since there is little evidence of much refined metal on the surface of the world."

Dron glanced at him sharply. "There will be sufficient remaining for our needs, though?"

"Ah, yes, without doubt," Makarn responded. "There will be no delay in the Great Design."

"Excellent." Relieved, Dron turned to Pakat. "And how is our readiness?"

"We have three wings of attack vessels standing ready," Pakat reported. "The pilots have all achieved high scores in simulated runs, and I anticipate no problems. Our surveys show fewer than one hundred vessels currently in flight in the system, and their weaponry is inferior to ours."

Tork shuffled in his seat and leaned forward. "You are preparing to attack the inhabitants?" he asked, concern in his voice.

"We are preparing to *defend* ourselves," Pakat answered, snuffling loudly to show his displeasure. "Had you attended the last meeting you would know that the local race—calling themselves 'Cardassians'—attacked our ships without provocation when last we met them. I am sure that none among us wishes to wait until they attack again before we prepare to defend ourselves?" He stared pointedly at Tork, who sat back in his seat and closed his mouth.

"If that is quite clear?" asked Dron. There were no further comments. He hadn't expected there would be. Even Tork couldn't complain about defending themselves. "Boran?"

The Industry Master stood up. "My teams are all prepared," he reported proudly. "We stand ready to harvest the coming fruits of our labor. Production is completely ready to commence as soon as the raw materials are obtained."

"Excellent," Dron complimented him. "Then it is clear that we are ready—that the Great Design can go ahead. After half a million years, the plans of the First Hive come to fruition, and we achieve our destiny." He gestured at the holographic representation of the planet that spun in the air above the table's surface. "All departments will come to full strength," he commanded. Turning to his Security Master, he said, "Raldar, the time has come to speak with these 'Cardassians,' in this system. Have a link established immediately."

"Of course," Raldar agreed. He set about tapping instructions into his comp. What only Dron and he knew was that there would be several layers of recording taken when they established contact. Dron couldn't take the chance that something might go amiss and spoil the records he intended to be kept for future Hives. However, if the aliens said or did anything untoward, it could be redesigned in the records Dron decided.

A moment later, the spinning globe above the table was replaced by a hologram of an alien race—the first that the other Hivemasters had ever seen. There was a murmur of shock and disgust from those assembled about the table. Even the liberal Tork and the elderly Hosir couldn't restrain themselves.

Well, the alien was ugly. It was also quite obviously not a Cardassian, but there was no need to mention that. This might be some subject species, for example. The being was roughly the size of a member of the Hive, and it stood upright, but that was about all the resemblance there was. It—possibly a *he*—was shell-less, and its skin was a pallid pink, instead of a rich gray. There was hair visible on the crown of its ugly head, and the being wore what appeared to be cloth draped over the larger part of its body. Dron wasn't too surprised—a creature that grotesque would *have* to cover itself.

The being spoke for a moment, and then the translation computers could begin to decode its vocalizations. "—First Minister Worin, of Darane Four," the creature was saying. "Please identify yourselves."

Dron took a breath, and then said, "I am Hivemaster Dron of the Hive. You will leave your world immediately. We will allow you two days to evacuate your population."

"What?"

Was this alien stupid as well as deformed? Dron repeated his message patiently. "Do you comprehend?" he added.

"You're . . . insane," Worin finally spluttered.

"No," Dron answered. "We are not insane. You have two days. If you require assistance in evacuating your people, we will be willing to assist." He moved to cut the communication.

"Wait!" Worin exclaimed, holding up a hand. "You . . . you're *serious* about this?"

"Of course we are serious," Dron replied. "This is not a matter we would joke about."

"But you *can't* be!" The alien looked almost panic-stricken. "What you ask is . . . unthinkable!"

Dron sighed. "It is not unthinkable," he explained. "And we are not *asking.* We will allow you two days, and then we shall commence harvesting this world. If your people are not removed by then, they will simply have to suffer the consequences. We have no desire to injure anyone, but we will not alter our schedule."

"No!" Worin seemed to have a grip on whatever low intelligence he possessed. The message had obviously sunk at least partway into his brain. "This is our world, and you cannot have it without a fight!"

Dron had been afraid of this; the alien was clearly insane. "You are not utilizing the world," he explained. "We have need of it, and therefore we shall make use of it. Please stand aside and allow us to do this."

"Darane Four is our *home!*" cried Worin. "We won't let you have it."

"Home?" Dron shook his head in astonishment. "You are clearly not an intelligent species if you believe that a ball of mud and rock is a *home.* It is simply a resource, neither more nor less. You are not using it, so we shall."

"He can't be serious," muttered Premon to the table at large. "He thinks that this world is his home? What kind of deviants are these people?"

"The kind we will have trouble with," predicted Pakat. "They're obviously intelligent enough to build crude weapons, but too stupid to build a home of their own."

Worin had been conferring with someone out of Dron's line of sight, in feverish haste. He now turned back to face the Hivemaster. "You will cease your flight," he ordered. "If you move any further into our system, we shall take it as a declaration of hostile intent and will be forced to defend ourselves."

This was going far better than Dron had imagined possible. It was quite obvious to all the others about the table that they were being threatened first. There would be no need to edit this recording at all. "We are not an aggressive species," Dron replied carefully. "We do not wish you any harm. But we need the planet that you call . . ." He shuddered. ". . . *home.* If you try and interfere with the Great Design, we shall be forced to retaliate. Any injuries or deaths your people sustain will therefore be your own fault."

"You're not having our planet!" Worin howled, and cut the communications link.

Dron allowed the picture to fade, and waited a few heartsbeats before he spoke again. "It appears that we are dealing with a dangerously deranged species," he said sadly. "Pakat, it would appear that your brave pilots will be forced to defend the Hive."

"And they all stand ready," Pakat answered proudly. "The alien aggressors will not harm the Hive. That I vow."

"Good." Dron smiled. "We all knew that we could count on you." He spread his hands in resignation. "Well, we tried to do this without pain and bloodshed. Unfortunately, these aliens seem to completely lack logical faculties. We will be forced to fight them for what we need. Are there any further questions or comments?"

As he had expected, Tork stood up. "Is this really necessary?" he asked. Dron could see the pain on his face, his nose wrinkling almost uncontrollably. "Must we . . . kill to obtain what we need?"

"We all heard their spokesman," Dron told him. "They threatened us; any killing will begin with them and be on their own consciences."

"No, I mean is there no other world we can use instead?" Tork explained. "One without such insane inhabitants? I am reluctant to condone the removal of a species that is obviously so feebleminded."

"As are we all," Dron agreed, hypocritically. Sometimes decisions simply needed to be made, and then enforced. "And there are indeed further worlds that offer what we need."

"Then why do we not use one of them?" asked Tork, almost desperately.

"Makarn?" prompted Dron.

"Ah, because they lie beyond this one," the Science Master explained. "And we shall indeed use them. Once the process of deconstructing Darane Four is finished, then we shall need at least two further worlds. Ah, and there is no telling whether their inhabitants will be any less maniacal than the ones here. We must face the possibility that we could be in an area of space whose inhabitants are all terminally deranged."

"Thank you." Dron signaled for Tork to reseat himself. "None of us wish harm even to such a subintelligent species. But we have no choice. If they attack us, we will defend ourselves. Darane Four will be the source of material for the next stage in the Great Design. Now, if there are no further comments, can I ask for a sign of assent?"

Pakat and Raldar signified their approval instantly. One by one, the rest of the Hivemasters complied. As expected, Tork's vote was the last. But even he had agreed.

"So be it," Dron announced. "The Great Design goes forward today!"

Gul Dukat watched the transmission from the *Karitan* with great interest. The messages between the intruder and Darane IV had been intercepted. The aliens were not backing down, and those idiotic Bajoran colonists on Darane IV were equally stubborn. The intruder's craft was advancing into the Darane system, and the small fleet of ships the colonists possessed were massing to meet it.

This should prove to be a most interesting day. . . .

# *Prime Directive,* by Judith and Garfield Reeves-Stevens

A common theme in these novels is that the most fearsome enemies are those with whom communication is impossible. Making peace is much more likely if it is possible to learn what one's adversary wants or needs, if his goals are intelligible, if one can negotiate with them. Eventually, mutual communication and empathy enabled *Sisko* to work out a mutual understanding with the Hive in *Objective Bajor.* In *Prime Directive,* though, the alien adversary was even more dangerous; not only did it not communicate, its very existence was masked, and its goal was nothing less than to destroy the life that existed on Talin IV so that it could use the planet for its own purposes.

Kirk's mission was to assist the First Contact Office team in its studies of a world about to destroy itself in a nuclear conflagration. Just as the warring factions teetered on the brink of a nuclear exchange, they made peace, only to have a nuclear exchange occur by "accident." The *Enterprise* neutralized the exchange, but just when it seemed as though peace was assured, a haphazard and uncoordinated nuclear exchange wasted the planet. Starfleet and the Federation Council believed that the destruction of Talin was caused by Kirk and his command crew; they felt that had the Talins been allowed to face the consequences of their first nuclear exchange, the second exchange would not have occurred, and the Talins would have survived. Starfleet disavowed Kirk and his command crew, who were disgraced and forced to resign.

*Prime Directive* is the story of how the command crew individually battled their ways back to Talin IV and discovered that an unknown and secretive alien presence pushed the Talins into nuclear annihilation. In a fascinating twist of alien biology, though, millions of Talins survived in cocoons, awaiting survivable conditions. In this passage from *Prime Directive,* the crew was back together and about to begin a relief mission for Talin.

IN STANDARD ORBIT AROUND TALIN IV, THE *ENTERPRISE* RESONATED WITH the activity of her newly returned crew. Kirk moved briskly through the corridors as if drawing life from the energy they brought back to the ship. His ship. The new gold command shirt he wore made him feel as if he had returned home. He had.

In the main branch corridors leading to the cargo transporters, an earnest-looking lieutenant with a Starfleet Command insignia on his blue shirt jogged up behind Kirk, carrying a fat sheaf of printouts and a screenpad. He was balding and the last remnants of his curly brown hair were mussed and unruly, like the hair of someone who had been up all night. Kirk didn't care. He guessed that at least half of Command hadn't had any sleep for the past two days.

The lieutenant caught up to Kirk and had to walk quickly to keep the rapid pace. "Captain Kirk," he said breathlessly, the voice of a man in a hurry, "I'm Peter Bloch-Hansen, sir. Starfleet Emergency Rescue Office."

Kirk kept moving, no time to waste. All through the corridors other crew members ran or jogged, carrying equipment and supplies. There was so much to do. So much time wasted. He thought of Richter then, still in the *Exeter*'s sickbay. He knew what drove the man.

"Has the order come through yet?" Kirk asked brusquely.

"No sir, Captain," Bloch-Hansen said.

Kirk didn't bother to correct the lieutenant. Until the order did come through, he was still "mister." But no one doubted that Nogura's order was not already blistering through subspace to the Talin system. Too much had happened for even Starfleet to ignore. And when that order came, it had better include full apologies for each member of the *Enterprise* Five.

Kirk guessed it would be an easy apology for Command to make. Only Uhura's case would require Starfleet to go to the trouble and potential embarrassment of an official review board to withdraw all charges of contempt and to reinstate her. Because the rest of the Five had resigned, regulations allowed them to rejoin Starfleet service at full rank and pay anytime within six months. With a bit of bureaucratic juggling, Starfleet could even manage to keep the resignations out of the official records, as if they had never happened.

"But I do have the new figures for you, sir," Bloch-Hansen continued. He shuffled his printouts as he and Kirk weaved rapidly around the other rushing crew they passed in the corridor. "As of twenty minutes ago, there were five hundred and twelve vessels in stacked orbits around Talin IV. They'll be working in shifts to transfer their relief supplies to the *Enterprise* and the *Exeter* for mass beaming to the surface. The time/ton transfer schedules are here. . . ." He offered Kirk his screenpad.

Kirk ignored it. He kept walking. "Tell me about the Talin. Was Spock right about the survival rate?"

The lieutenant efficiently produced a printout from his bundle. He was prepared for anything. "Mr. Spock *was* right, sir. The figure is astonishing. As long as they escaped immediate blast and fire injuries, their autonomic cocooning reflex would have dropped their metabolism right down . . . uh, the life readings show just more than two billion Talin remain alive on their planet, ninety-five percent in hibernation."

Kirk stopped and looked at Bloch-Hansen with relief. That was far higher than anyone, even Spock, had hoped.

The lieutenant continued. "I estimate a complete revival program should take three years, but by that time the seeders' growth will be scavenged from the oceans."

"How's the drone contact team working out?" Kirk and Bloch-Hansen turned the corner into the final corridor. The entrance to the cargo transporter room was jammed with people, some crew, some civilians.

"The task force will arrive on Talin's moon to begin relocating the drones within a week, sir. The Talin ambassadors have given permission for them to begin seeding the gas giant, Talin VIII. It will be converted into a food source well within the next sixty years."

Kirk shouldered his way into the crowd. "Good work, Lieutenant. Let me know when the order comes in."

Bloch-Hansen stopped at the edge of the crowd. "Oh, you'll know when it comes, sir. You'll know."

As people realized who was pushing up against them, they quickly made way to let Kirk through. He passed the processing desk with a nod from the volunteer coordinators and stepped out to the open area immediately in front of the honeycombed crystal pads of the cargo transporter grid.

Nearby, Chekov and Sulu stood with Christine Chapel, checking a crate of medical tricorders. Kirk could hear the two ensigns telling the others about Lieutenant Styles's new assignment—ferrying the impounded *Queen Mary* back to Starbase 29. There was much laughter as Sulu explained how the gravity generator on the Orion ship had mysteriously been broken. It could only put out a three-gee field now, and it was tied into the warp drive so it couldn't be turned off. "I am certain the lieutenant will wery much enjoy his weighty new position," Chekov said.

Kirk looked around for Spock among the confusing stacks of boxes and knots of people. As he turned around, he bumped into McCoy. The doctor was back in his science blues.

"Have you seen Spock?" Kirk asked.

"No. He's probably hiding from me." McCoy reached out without warning and jammed a spray hypo against Kirk's arm. "There," he said when the longer-than-usual spray was done, "now you can eat plutonium for breakfast."

Kirk rubbed at the tingling spot where the radiation stabilizer had entered. "Is that going to work on the Talin?"

"It needed some modification, but M'Benga's already got the first batch processing."

"Good work, Bones. Or do you prefer 'Black Ire' now?" Kirk chuckled at McCoy's sudden look of discomfort. "How'd you ever come up with that one, anyway?"

McCoy frowned. "Someday I'll tell you about my illustrious ancestors. If I live that long." He tried to change the subject. "Has the order come in?"

Kirk looked around the huge room. It was filled with at least twenty different conversations and the hum of antigravs as boxes were received and stacked through the doors leading to the cargo hold. "Not yet," Kirk said. He suspected there would be pandemonium when it did come through. "Why do you think Spock's—"

Suddenly he felt a light touch on his shoulder. He turned to see Anne Gauvreau. Her flight jacket had a new crest proudly sewn on the front. The writing on it was in Talin splatterscript.

Kirk looked at the crates on the transporter grid. Most were marked with bold red crosses. "Is this from the *Shelton?*"

Gauvreau patted one of the crates. "Sure is. Starfleet Emergency Rescue didn't want to wait for the official word. They're buying all the medical supplies that everyone's brought in. If the supplies aren't used here, they say, then they'll still be useful somewhere else."

"These supplies *will* be used on Talin," Kirk said. There was no doubt in his voice. "So . . . until things get settled here, I suppose you freighter captains are going to be leaving this system with empty holds."

Gauvreau smiled brightly. "Not this time." She looked at McCoy and winked. "Thanks to Dr. McCoy, the T'Prar Foundation has hired me to transport twenty-six Orion females to a reorientation village on Delta Triciatu."

"Delta?" Kirk asked, raising his eyebrows.

"Seems Deltan males aren't affected by the Orion females' phero-mones, so it's a good place for them to be helped to start their own lives again. And besides . . . I've always wanted to go there. . . ." Gauvreau blushed. "Look, I've got to break orbit to let another ship get into transporter range." She leaned closer and kissed Kirk on his cheek. "Thank you for making me feel I was back in Starfleet again."

"Thank you for bringing me back," Kirk said, then watched her move off into the crowd by the door. He hoped he would see her again.

Kirk turned to McCoy. "Whatever happened to those pirates?"

"In the brig on the *Exeter.* Last I heard Krulmadden was trying to buy it from her captain."

"I'm glad he's not on this ship talking to Chekov," Kirk said. He looked up with sudden interest as another crew member jostled him as she walked by with an antigrav pallet of visual sensors. It was Carolyn Palamas.

"Welcome back, Captain Kirk," she said. "The herbarium roses are in bloom again. I checked."

Kirk stumbled over a reply as she continued on without waiting for one. When he turned back to McCoy, he was greeted by a soppy smile. "Don't you start," Kirk warned.

Then McCoy looked puzzled and Kirk saw why. Spock was approaching. Like the doctor, the science officer was wearing his uniform again, tricorder hanging at his side. But he was also carrying a familiar-looking green bottle.

"Mr. Spock," Kirk said with a bemused expression, "is that whisky?"

Spock held the bottle up to read the label, as if confirming that it was true. "Yes," he admitted. "It was given to me by Mr. Scott."

"Did he say why?" Kirk asked.

"He said it was my . . . birthday present."

McCoy looked surprised. "It's not your birthday, Spock."

"Thank you, Doctor. I explained that to Mr. Scott, but he was quite emotional about it. He said, and I quote, 'Och, it dinna matter one wee bit.' And then he asked me when the party would be."

McCoy held a hand out. "Tell you what, Spock. Why don't you just give me the bottle as a token of apology and then you can stop trying to hide from me."

"Doctor, not only am I not trying to hide from you, I can think of no action on my part for which I might possibly owe you an apology."

McCoy feigned great shock. "Spock, I said there were aliens, remember? When we were talking in the shuttle at the outpost, and I said that it was obvious that the Talin were under observation by other aliens but you said, nooo, there were no other aliens. There's nothing of value in this system, you said. And meanwhile those drones *were* creating something of value—that purple sludge of theirs—right under your big pointed ears. But you didn't see it and I did. I said—"

Kirk held his hands up as if threatening to cover McCoy's mouth.

"Bones, you keep going on like that and we're all going to have to hide from you."

McCoy folded his arms and smiled smugly. "I don't care. All that matters is that I was absolutely, inarguably right and—"

"As I recall," Spock said dryly, "you suggested there were Klingons with Romulan cloaking devices lurking about."

"I said *aliens,*" McCoy insisted.

"You said—"

"What *about* the aliens?" Kirk asked Spock. "Any results from the FCO's computer analysis of our sensor readings?"

Spock and McCoy didn't break eye contact. "A classic symbiotic relationship, Captain. It appears Dr. Richter was correct when he said that life everywhere was the same—even when it originates in different universes. The computers have modeled a logical relationship between the two life-forms: The seeder drones prepare planets with the purple food organism which then converts the entire biosphere into a highly radioactive algae analogue. When the One arrives in the system, it enfolds the planet and ingests the converted biosphere. In return, it carries some of the drones from system to system, providing energy to them so that they can survive the journey between the stars. Other drones it sends ahead on a smaller clump of accelerated matter, somewhat like plants spreading spores."

"How do they decide which planets to go to?" Kirk asked.

"I do not think 'decide' is the term to be used, Captain. The selection of planets for seeding is most likely an instinctual response, done without consciousness. I suspect that we may find that colonies of drones lie dormant in thousands of systems throughout the galaxy, waiting to be awakened by the first electromagnetic pulses resulting from an atomic explosion. That would indicate that fusion warheads will soon be developed on a given planet and that the planet's inhabitants could therefore be manipulated to devastate their biosphere with radiation, making it a suitable world for the growth of the algae. As the drones come to life and begin their instinctive behavior to create tension on the target planet, they send out signals to the One, informing it that a new planet is about to be seeded."

McCoy fidgeted with his tricorder and medikit. "I still don't see how anything could survive the death and birth of a universe."

"Especially if the physician present at that birth were—"

Kirk broke in again. "Perhaps, gentlemen, we should simply accept that there are still mysteries in the universe. Or the universes." He smiled at them. "Let's leave something for another ship to do, all right?"

Before either McCoy or Spock could answer, the page whistle of the ship's intercom system sounded. Instantly, every conversation in the cargo transporter room stopped. Only the background whir of the equipment could be heard until Uhura's voice came on.

"Attention all crew. Attention all crew. The *U.S.S. Enterprise,* as flagship for the Starfleet Relief Operation to Talin . . ." Kirk felt the hair on his neck bristle. He heard small gasps from the people in the room who also understood what Uhura had just said. This collection of ships had been given a name. The Starfleet Relief Operation to Talin. Uhura didn't have to read the rest. It was official.

". . . has just received this subspace communiqué from Nogura, Admiral, Starfleet Command: Effective this stardate, Earth, the findings of Starfleet's board of inquiry into the incident at Talin IV are rescinded. In addition, with remorse, Starfleet offers full and official apologies to—" The transporter room resounded with applause. Kirk felt hands slapping at his back. He struggled to hear the rest of what Uhura read. He had been waiting so long to hear it.

"Also, in accordance with Starfleet Command Regulations, General Order One, Talin IV is hereby recognized as a planet whose normal development has been subject to extraplanetary interference and thus is excused from the Prime Directive of Noninterference." The ship seemed to shake with the roar of the cheers which joined the continuing applause echoing through her. Uhura's voice was almost lost amid the tumult.

"Therefore, all Starfleet personnel are requested to take whatever action may be deemed necessary to repair the damage caused by such interference. Furthermore, in recognition of the General Council's ruling to admit Talin to the United Federation of Planets, all Federation citizens are likewise urged—"

It was no use. Her voice was completely drowned out. Kirk's ears rang. McCoy had cupped his hands to his mouth and was shouting deafening huzzahs. Kirk caught Spock's eye and saw his science officer smile, just fleetingly, and before anyone else could notice.

Then, as swiftly as it had begun, the joyous ovation quieted. It was not replaced by a return to the conversation and the activity which had preceded it. There was only silence. For a moment Kirk was puzzled. But only for a moment.

"Captain," Spock said, "the crew awaits your orders."

McCoy put his hand to Kirk's arm. "Now you really are back, Jim."

Without hesitation, Captain James T. Kirk stepped onto the transporter platform and faced his crew. He nodded to Kyle, standing ready at the transporter console, and gave his crew the order they waited for.

"Energize," he said.

The shimmering veil of transporter energy fell from Kirk's eyes and he gazed onto a city of the dead.

The air of Talin was thick with the stench of rot and smoke. A sea breeze blew up from the distant ocean where he could see foul purple waves crash against a beach of blackened wood and the skeletons of sea creatures that had washed ashore. Even the shafts of weak sunlight which cut through the overcast skies seemed gray and dull.

Kirk stepped forward onto the ash of the shattered world that had briefly borne his name. Before him was what the sensors had determined was the largest gathering of still-functioning, uncocooned survivors on the planet. Its population numbered less than four hundred.

An old Talin female was the first to see him as he took another step in the ash. She had one arm. Her bibcloth hung in tatters. Kirk could see her bones move beneath her cracked and bleeding skin.

The female cried out weakly, a harsh discordant shriek. Behind her, other Talin slowly emerged from the rubble they had made into shelters. A few hundred meters away, he saw the long shapes of soot-darkened cocoons stacked like firewood. Respectfully gathered for a better day which no Talin could believe would ever come.

But Kirk was there to make that day a reality. He looked all around him at the desolation and destruction. He saw the blasted stumps of buildings, shattered girders, fields of blackened crops.

And it was all a mistake. It had all occurred because there were still too many mysteries, still too many unknowns. But Kirk knew, at least, that *this* would not happen again. The Federation would learn. It would know what to look for next time. Other worlds would be saved by the painful lessons of Talin IV. The Federation would learn and from that knowledge, grow stronger.

A dozen Talin had gathered before him now. They pointed at him in wonder. Some covered their eyes, afraid to look at his alien form. Others reached out with trembling limbs, but were too frightened to come closer.

Kirk heard another transporter chime swell. He heard the gasp of awe from the crowd before him. More Talin were coming from the ruins. Some dropped to their knees as the golden light played upon them.

There were new footsteps behind him. Kirk glanced over his

shoulder to see Spock and McCoy coming toward him, already opening their tricorders. A wall of medical supplies had also appeared, still shimmering.

He heard another cry from the Talin as the air filled with the pulsed harmonics of multiple transporter chimes. All around them the air danced with shimmering columns of luminous energy. And from each apparition came another human, or another gift of supplies.

Chekov stepped forward with Sulu and Uhura. Scott appeared with a pallet of machinery that could draw water from the air. Next, M'Benga, Chapel, Palamas. Everyone had returned to Talin.

Then, from the crowd of Talin adults, staring, pointing, shaking, not daring to believe that what they saw might be real, one female child stepped forward. Her skin was green and caked with mud, but her yellow eyes were clear and penetrating.

Alone among the Talin, she stepped up to Kirk unafraid.

Kirk twisted the dial on the small silver wand of his translator. He spoke into it for the child.

"My name is James Kirk," he said. "Captain of the *Starship Enterprise.*"

He waited as the translator repeated his words in the whistles and whispers of Talin.

The child's eyes widened. She looked up to the sky, past the clouds, as if they were no longer there. She whispered one word back to Kirk. The translator spoke it to him.

"Starship."

Tears fell from the child's eyes. She turned back to her people and shouted the word to them, pointing to the skies, to the stars that waited there.

"Starship. Starship." The translator said the word as each Talin spoke it.

The child came closer to Kirk. She lifted her arms to him and he saw then in her eyes what he had seen in the eyes of a woman long ago on Earth, what he had seen in the eyes of a Tellarite child in an asteroid only weeks ago.

Kirk took the child's hands in his and lifted her up close to him, knowing that the beginnings and the endings of things were sometimes one and the same.

But this time, he knew, it would be a beginning.

"It's all right," Kirk said. "Let me help."

# PART III
# Visions of the Future

# CHAPTER 13

# Star Trek: The Problems of Planet Earth

FROM THE BEGINNING, STAR TREK HAS EXPLORED ISSUES AFFECTING OUR Earth-bound societies using problems of or interactions with alien cultures as allegories. Making a point through parable is often more effective than making it directly because people can come to an understanding on their own rather than through preaching. Thus, Star Trek used "Let That Be Your Last Battlefield" as a powerful albeit less than subtle demonstration of the irrationality, pervasiveness, and outright danger of the racism in our own society as well as that of Cheron. If racism could destroy Cheron, could it not also destroy us? "Duet," from *DS9*'s second season, continued the commentary on racism begun thirty years before in the original *Star Trek*. The lesson of "Duet," like that of *TOS* episode, was that each individual should be judged on his own merits and not because he is a member of a hated race.

Star Trek's parables have told tales of genocide, war, slavery, racism, environmental devastation, destruction of habitat, exploitation of sentient species, and numerous other issues. Whether Star Trek has had a beneficial effect on our society through its parables is something that I cannot answer. I do know that *Star Trek* episodes spark discussion on these issues and the relationship of the allegories to our society. The realization that a problem exists may be the first step in dealing with the problem, even if only on a personal rather than a societal level.

Novelists also have used Star Trek to showcase problems they see in our society. The selections in this chapter examine racism, genocide, and destruction of sentient species and the environment.

The authors featured here have woven their messages into tightly written, exciting and moving stories.

## *Far Beyond the Stars,* by Steven Barnes

Racism may be the single most difficult and dangerous problem of our society. It is pervasive; it affects us in many ways that we are often not aware of. In his novelization for the *DS9* episode "Far Beyond the Stars." Steve Barnes delved deeply into the effects of this insidious problem on the life of one man, Benny Russell. Mr. Barnes went further and told a more detailed story than was possible in the episode, but even more compelling for me than the story itself was Mr. Barnes's Author's Note at the end of the book. I have included that note in its entirety because the message is so critically important. Mr. Barnes gave me much to think about that I had not considered before. The note ends with hope; there has been progress in our society, and *DS9* demonstrates that progress in every episode, showing a black captain who is a good and strong man with a positive relationship with his son. The world we live in has changed, and Star Trek has been a part of that change. *DS9* is the embodiment of that change.

### Why I Decided to Write a Book in a Month; Or, How *Star Trek* Changed My Life

I FIND MYSELF AT THE END OF THIS WRITING PROJECT FEELING SOMEWHAT surprised that I would do such a thing. Well—specifically that I would do it at this point in my life, a time of pressure and stress, near the holiday season now (as I write these words it is December 12), and willing to push myself at a time when I am usually starting to slack off, becoming somewhat contemplative about my life, and beginning to make plans for the next year.

To answer the question, I have to go back a few years, and before I do that, I would like to say something:

Star Trek fans have one hell of a lot to be proud of. You changed the world, my world, in ways you may not know.

Onward.

It has been very strange growing up in America in the latter half of the twentieth century. There is so much to love here—but also much to be disappointed with. I was born in 1952, and if there is any most central reason I began to write, it is that there was no father in my home, and I needed to find images of men doing manly stuff. My mom did the best she could but she was (very much) a woman, and simply couldn't teach me certain things. So I looked to the stories of Conan the Barbarian, and Mike Hammer, and James Bond, and Leslie Charteris's the Saint. And there was something very interesting about all of these he-man worlds: no black people needed apply.

It was positively grotesque. When Edgar Rice Burroughs wrote that "White men have imagination, Negroes have little, animals have none," he was doubtless merely expressing the attitudes of the time. That didn't make it any easier to read, and I would have put that Tarzan novel down if I hadn't so desperately needed the emotional vitamins within. True, as Kay Bass rightly points out, there aren't enough female characters with spunk and grit, but girls aren't required to "prove" themselves in aggressive, violent competition in order to be considered "feminine." Little black boys and little white boys want pretty much the same things out of life, across the board, and most of what we do in life, we learn from watching role models.

Don't believe it? You learned to walk and talk and ride bicycles by watching others do it. Shouldn't black children be able to learn by watching white heroes, you say? Well, obviously—and yet the more levels of logical abstraction between you and the role model, the more difficult it is to empathize. Trust me, sit in a Hollywood pitch meeting, and watch the executives try to sandwich a white character into a black story, parroting the wisdom that "audiences won't identify." And what happens if they don't? Why, the accepted, hard-learned wisdom is that they won't go into the theaters.

Well, come the 1960s or so, and black characters began appearing in science fiction, horror, and action films. But do you know what? They usually existed only to die horribly, and usually to protect white people. (And whatever feminists say about the parallels between sexism and racism, there is *no* similar pattern of women dying in movies to protect men. Quite the opposite, in fact. Male lives are cheaper than women's, and minority lives cheaper than white.)

The list of films using these nauseating images unfortunately encompasses some of Hollywood's best. The following is a very partial list of movies which contained a 100% black fatality rate, often in the noble protection of the white lead: *The Alamo, Spartacus, Full Metal Jacket, The Dirty Dozen, Alien I, II,* and *III,* any James Cameron film. . . .

Oh, jeeze, the list goes on and on. Just in the last year or so we've

383

had *Daylight, Mimic, Starship Troopers* and *Alien IV*. It gets hard. It was to the point when, as a kid, I would go see some SF flick with a black character and when I returned home the other kids in the neighborhood would ask: "Well, how did they kill the Brother this time?"

Poor Paul Winfield actually made a career out of dying in SF movies. *Wrath of Khan* (protecting William Shatner), *Terminator* (protecting Linda Hamilton), *Serpent and the Rainbow* (protecting Bill Pullman) and, most insultingly, in *Damnation Alley*. Oh, I remember watching *that* movie. In fact, I'll never forget it. Here's George Peppard, Jan Michael Vincent, and Paul Winfield traveling across a nuclear devastated landscape in a souped-up Winnebago. Suddenly, out of the wreckage of a bombed-out city crawls—Dominique Sanda. Possibly the last woman in the world. Very, very white.

I turned to my date, and said: "Oh nuts—they're going to kill Paul Winfield." She said: "Why?" I said, "Because they can't pretend he won't be interested in her, and they're not going to let him compete for her."

My date, who was white, thought this was incredibly cynical of me. Five minutes later, Paul Winfield got eaten by giant roaches.

Memories are made of this.

But cinematic reality has shifted, and continues to change so rapidly that I can hardly keep up with things anymore. Most notably, this was signaled when *Independence Day,* starring Will Smith, made money faster than Bill Gates. I still remember seeing it at the Cinedome theater in Castle Rock, Washington. The parking lot was filled with pickup trucks sporting rebel flags—not exactly a hotbed of NAACP supporters if you know what I mean, and I think you do. Anyway, after the film I went to the men's room, and as I stood in line at the urinal, I saw a bunch of good ol' boys heeding the call of nature and yacking up a storm to each other, quote: "Whoo-eee! That Will Smith was he, like, too cool, or what? I'm bringin' my daddy back here tomorrow. He's gotta see this!"

Damn, I thought—what planet am I on?

Television has been a tougher nut to crack than motion pictures, at least partially because a show needs so many tens of millions of viewers just to survive. The reality is that it took over forty years for television to produce and sustain even one single dramatic television series with a non-Caucasian star. Oh, there are plenty of comedies—

the modern equivalent of *Amos and Andy* shows. Too damned many of them, if you ask me. And blacks or Asians have had plenty of "second billing" success—costars, supporting roles, you name it.

But not heroes. Not first-billed. Except . . .

Well, I'm getting ahead of myself.

The first chink in the cultural armor was a triple-assault, two of them launched by the same small company, a place called Desilu. The most talked about was probably 1965's *I Spy*, with Bill Cosby costarring with Robert Culp. God, I loved that show. Here was a black man who was articulate, literate, and funny—and he could break your face. Yow!

But the next year in October of 1966, we had Greg Morris on *Mission: Impossible.* He played Barney Collier, who was clearly the most competent member of the entire Impossible Missions Force. After all—he could break heads, do impersonations, crack computers, or plan missions. The man had everything.

A little earlier that same year, a beautiful young woman named Nichelle Nichols stepped in front of the camera on another Desilu stage, this time for an unheralded space opera called *Star Trek.* Even though relegated to the background, she was there, a recognizable human being of intelligence and courage, and I felt proud. Gene Roddenberry knew that black people would exist in the future, and he put his money where his mouth was.

Television played with the concept of ethnicity for the next few decades. They tried several times to give blacks or Asians their own series, but the audience voted with their TV sets, and not one of them lasted longer than a season. America wasn't ready, and Hollywood was flushing its dollars down the toilet even to try.

And then came *Deep Space Nine.* Here it is, kids, the point of this entire essay, the reason why I worked like a maniac to finish this book by a deadline that would have intimidated Sisyphus—*Deep Space Nine* is, in my opinion, a major cultural turning point for America, and therefore, the world as a whole. Like it or not, the truth is that the entire world marches to our cultural beat. No one can produce mythic images like America, and myths, shared myths, are what make a culture.

Television is the connective tissue of the world's emerging culture, and don't *ever* understimate its power.

*DS9* is, as far as I am concerned, the first successful dramatic television show in history with a non-Caucasian star. People have pointed out *Room 222* with Lloyd Haynes, and *Julia* with Diahann Carroll. Both lasted more than two seasons, and so should be considered successes, but they were borderline comedies, and just don't count.

But *Deep Space Nine . . .*

Ah, Sisko. Soft-spoken but commanding. Nurturing but virile. Intuitive but brilliant. In the hands of the protean Avery Brooks, *Deep Space Nine* is, in its quiet way, as important as anything that has ever happened in the history of entertainment.

And it could never have succeeded without the millions of die-hard Star Trek fans who have loyally supported that series, and its spin-offs, through the decades.

I have heard (and occasionally made) jokes at the expense of those who love Gene Roddenberry's dream. But let me tell you, people. It is not easy for human beings to look at those of other cultures, races, or genders and recognize their own humanity. It has *never* been easy. For years, science fiction fans said that our field trains us to do this, to see the heart hidden within the alien form. But, apparently, only as long as a white guy was wearing the costume. Then, for the first time, with *DS9,* that dream of a universal empathy came true. And, I believe, because of it, we got films like *Independence Day*—a silly piece of fluff, to be sure, but the very first film in history to take seriously the old adage that "if the aliens showed up, we earthlings would drop our differences." I can tear that film up as well as anyone—but I'll tell you honestly that I sat in the theater with tears rolling down my cheeks, wishing to God that I had seen that movie when I was nine. And thanking heaven that my daughter was growing up in a better world than mine.

And when I first saw *DS9*—in fact when I first heard that Avery Brooks had been cast—I was so terribly afraid that it would fail, that it would join the long, long line of Neilsen disasters that had littered the electronic landscape my whole life . . . and then the legions of Star Trek fans supported it with their whole hearts, and gave it a chance to find its rhythm and create its own niche.

I was so proud of the field I have loved since childhood. I have *never* been as grateful to be a part of the community called fandom. You came through, guys. You walked the talk.

I love being alive in the nineties. You folks give me hope.

So, early November I was heading out my front door with a copy of my new novel *Iron Shadows* under my arm, when the telephone rang.

It was my agent, the lovely, charming and ruthless Eleanor Wood, who said that John Ordover at Pocket Books had specifically requested me to write a very special *DS9* novel, and would I be interested?

I have to tell you honestly—there is *no* other show I would have done this for. I wrote it as a way of saying "thank you" to the millions of fans who helped to change the face of America, and the world; to the show's creators Rick Berman and Michael Piller, who took a chance; to Marc Scott Zicree, Ira Steven Behr, and Hans Beimler, the creators of an extraordinary script; and to a man no longer with us, the singular Gene Roddenberry, who saw what had to be done, and did it.

I love you all. Thanks, guys.

Steven Barnes
Vancouver, Washington
www.teleport.com/~djuru
lifewrite@aol.com

## *The 34th Rule,* by Armin Shimerman and David R. George III, based on the story by Armin Shimerman & David R. George & Eric Stillwell

Although Star Trek has been a canvas for painting pictures of an almost utopian society (except for occasional invasions by and wars with irrational enemies), one can still find negative ethnic stereotypes. The "greedy Ferengi"–"stupid Hew-mon" interaction from *DS9* is an example. Although *DS9* has done an admirable job of demonstrating the evil and illogic of racial and ethnic stereotyping, one still can find the occasional heroic officer complaining of "greedy misogynistic little trolls" and Ferengi *behaving* as "greedy misogynistic little trolls," often for purposes of humor.

*The 34th Rule,* by Armin Shimerman and David R. George III, based on the story by Armin Shimerman & David R. George & Eric Stillwell, explores the potential consequences of anti-Ferengi prejudice and blows the stereotypes to pieces. As Quark contemplated the rewards of the best deal of his life, Grand Nagus Zek put an Orb of the Prophets up for auction to the highest bidder. Extreme tension and ultimately war erupted between Ferenginar and Bajor over the auction. Eventually, Ferengi were ordered to leave Bajor and Bajoran territory, and those who remained behind were arrested and imprisoned on Bajor. The story revealed widespread prejudice against Ferengi and the horrendous personal cost of that prejudice.

Most Ferengi stories are humorous romps, but this novel is a thoughtful look into issues that affect our own society at a basic level. As shown powerfully in *The 34th Rule,* the step between demonizing a race of people and interning them in camps is but a short one, and it is an even shorter step from interning people to murder and genocide. The first passage from *The 34th Rule* is a powerful scene between Jake and Ben Sisko in which Jake pointed out to his father that he is not immune from the charge of racism. The second excerpt exposes Quark's and Rom's ordeal in Gallitep.

"DAD, DO YOU WANT TO STOP THE GAME SO WE CAN TALK?" JAKE WAS STILL so much a boy—he could get so exuberant about little things, he was often shy around girls, he had difficulty keeping his room clean—but there were glimpses more and more often now of the man he would soon become.

*This is one of those glimpses,* Sisko thought.

"Sure," he told Jake. "I'd like that." Then, in a slightly louder voice, he said, "Computer, pause program and save." All about Sisko and Jake, movement stopped: baseball fans froze in position as they stood up or sat down or cheered, the Dodgers and Braves themselves became motionless on the field, the wispy clouds overhead ceased scudding across the sky.

"Program saved," replied the computer.

"Come on," Sisko said, "what do you say we take a walk." Sisko climbed up onto the roof of the Dodger dugout, and Jake followed. They made their way to the end of the roof and jumped down onto the playing field. As they strolled over to the first-base line, Sisko marveled, as he always did, at the cushiony spring of the grass, which was as thick and as full as a carpet. When they reached the line, they headed toward right field.

"I don't think Quark asked me to help him because he couldn't sell the bar," Sisko began to tell Jake, endeavoring to articulate what it was that was troubling him—not only to his son, but also to himself. "I think he's trying to sell the bar because I wouldn't help him."

"Is that what's bothering you?" Jake asked. "That you refused to help Quark?"

"Not exactly," Sisko said. "The Federation Council's resolution is pretty clear on this: we cannot interfere in this situation between the Bajorans and the Ferengi."

"How come?"

"Well, I told Quark that the Federation was considering this a Bajoran matter, but the truth is that siding with either faction would place the Federation in a precarious position," Sisko explained. "We can't side with the Ferengi because of our relationship with the Bajorans, but if we side with the Bajorans . . . well, their current stance is considered extreme. The Council believes the proper thing for the Federation to do is to remain neutral in the face of opposing viewpoints, neither of which we feel is right."

"Why not try to help both sides?" Jake asked. It was something Sisko had been asking himself all day.

"We could try to elevate both sides," Sisko said, "but the Council is handling this in much the same way that Starfleet handles Prime Directive situations." As he walked, his foot brushed against the baseline, sending up a puff of white chalk into the still air. "Our belief that both the Bajorans and the Ferengi are wrong does not give us a moral basis to impose that belief, either explicitly or implicitly, on their cultures. In fact, we have an obligation to *avoid* doing so."

"Okay," Jake said. "So what's the problem?"

Sisko opened his mouth to answer, but stopped: this was hard. After Quark had been in his office this morning, Sisko had begun to feel vaguely uneasy. There had been much to occupy him throughout the day, diverting him from that uneasiness, but he had discovered when he had gotten off duty this evening that the feeling had not abated. He had tried to define the emotion, had tried to understand and deal with it, but even now, its precise cause remained elusive.

The two walked all the way into right field without saying anything further, Sisko grateful that Jake respected his silence. At the outfield fence, the grandstands angled in close to fair territory. Sisko looked up and read some of the advertising that covered the wall: ESQUIRE BOOT POLISH, GEM RAZORS AND BLADES, and the famous ABE STARK sign, on which the tailor proclaimed to batters HIT SIGN WIN SUIT.

Underfoot, the manicured emerald grass gave way to dirt. It was the warning track, a band three meters or so wide at the edge of the playing surface, intended to alert fielders of their proximity to the fence. Sisko and Jake turned to follow the track across the outfield. To their left, not too far away, stood the immobile figure of the right fielder.

"The problem," Sisko said, speaking slowly as he resumed the conversation, carefully measuring both his words and his thoughts, "is that the Federation has sent Starfleet to mediate disputes between other cultures before, cultures with motives that were far more suspect. *I've* mediated such disputes. Would it really be wrong to do that in this case?"

"I assume Starfleet hasn't been asked to mediate," Jake commented.

"No, it hasn't," Sisko granted. "And the Council has ruled that even offering assistance would be a bad idea. But the Bajorans and the Ferengi are both mature cultures; merely suggesting that they might benefit from a third-party moderator is not going to unduly influence their civilizations."

"I don't know," Jake said. "Maybe because you're the Emissary . . ."

"Maybe," Sisko agreed. "But I don't have to be the one to actually help, or even to offer help."

As they walked, the scoreboard loomed up to their right, built into the outfield wall. It rose to a height of about ten meters and stretched away into right-center. Its configuration was peculiar, Sisko knew, even for the time in which it had been constructed: its upper half was vertical, but its lower half was concave and sloped away from the playing field. During the 1916 season, Sisko remembered from his baseball references, a player on the Robins—as the Brooklyn team had then been known—had hit a ground ball that had struck the oddly angled scoreboard and vaulted up the fence and out of the ballpark for a home run.

"Dad," Jake said, "what does this have to do with your meeting with Quark?"

"Quark proposed that the reason the Federation isn't interested in lending a hand to resolve this situation is because the people being wronged are the Ferengi." Even repeating Quark's belief, Sisko found, was not easy; the values embodied by the Federation were very serious to him, and very personal. To even consider that those values were not practiced—or worse, that they had somehow become corrupted—seemed unthinkable.

"Well," Jake said, "is Quark right?"

*Now, that's the important question, isn't it?* Sisko thought.

"My immediate reaction is: no," he said. "Certainly, it's my belief that the history and the actions of the Federation reflect that it treats all peoples equally."

"But?" Jake asked, either hearing doubt in Sisko's tone, or anticipating that an "immediate reaction" implied an additional response.

"But I can't honestly speak for the members of the Federation Council. I can only speak for myself."

"That's all any of us can do, right?" Jake noted.

"Right," Sisko said.

390

"So why are you letting something Quark said get to you?"

"There was a time when I never would have allowed that to happen," Sisko said, recalling another conversation he had had with Quark, some time ago. "Remember back a couple of years when you and Nog and I went on that camping expedition to the Gamma Quadrant, and Quark insisted on coming along?"

"Sure," Jake answered. "That's when you and Quark were captured by the Jem'Hadar."

"Quark and I were together for a long time when we were being held, and we talked a lot." Sisko thought back to the incident, and to all of the observations Quark had offered up about humans. "Well, Quark talked a lot, anyway," Sisko amended. "And one of the things he claimed was that humans generally disregarded out of hand anything any Ferengi had to say because of the nature of the Alliance's capitalist culture. He specifically said this was true of me, that I never paid any attention to him or took him seriously, strictly because he was a Ferengi."

"I remember that," Jake said. "Quark repeated some of it to Nog, and Nog told me about it."

"Yes, well, I told Quark that he was wrong, but when we returned to *Deep Space Nine,* I began to notice that there was a certain . . . insensibility . . . even sometimes a callousness . . . with which Quark was treated by many people on the station. I therefore took pains to be sure that was not true of me."

"How'd you do that?" Jake asked, sounding genuinely curious.

"For one thing, I tried to be more receptive to Quark," Sisko said. "I also tried to keep an open mind about the views he expressed. As it turned out, I think he may have been right about me not paying him much attention because I found that I quickly learned something about him."

"What was that?"

"I came to realize that Quark lives his life under a fairly strict set of rules—"

"The Rules of Acquisition," Jake supposed.

"The Rules of Acquisition, yes," Sisko concurred, "but as interpreted through Quark's own unique perspective. And as he pointed out to me this morning, he also lives by our rules."

"Yeah, I guess he's never been in one of Constable Odo's holding cells for too long," Jake joked.

"That's exactly what I mean, though," Sisko said. "He's never been convicted by Bajor or the Federation of any crimes. And yet I'd always perceived him as a lawbreaker."

"I don't think I'd actually describe Quark as honest, Dad," Jake said.

"I'm not talking about honesty. I'm not even really talking about Quark as much as I'm talking about myself. I'd always thought of Quark as having a complete lack of respect for the laws and rules of the Federation and Starfleet. Of Bajor too. But he's actually lived for a long time within those parameters."

"So what does that mean?"

"It means that, at least in some ways, I was wrong about Quark," Sisko admitted. He saw that they had come to the point where the right-field fence met the center-field fence in an oblique angle. It was the deepest part of the ballpark. Sisko looked back toward the infield and saw that they were indeed a long way from home plate.

"Okay," Jake said as they passed the place where the fences joined together. "But that's not a crime. People do make mistakes."

"It's not criminal if I made those false estimations of Quark based upon who he was and how he acted, rather than upon the fact that he was a Ferengi."

"That's what's really bothering you, isn't it?" Jake asked in a grave tone. "You're worried that you're a racist."

Sisko took a deep breath and let it out very slowly. The words, spoken aloud and without pretense, were very heady.

"No, I don't think that's the case, but I am concerned that some— or *any*—of my actions have been motivated or tainted by racial biases."

"I think it's probably impossible to prevent yourself from behaving that way some of the time," Jake said. "Don't we all? I mean, everybody has biases."

"I didn't think I did. Not those types of biases, anyway."

"You do, Dad. Everybody does." Jake spoke with apparent certainty.

"You're talking about something specific, aren't you?" Sisko asked.

"No," Jake said. "Well, not on purpose. I was thinking about the way you treat Nog."

"Nog? I helped him get into Starfleet Academy. I *sponsored* his application."

"Yes, you did," Jake said hesitantly, "and he's grateful to you for that. And I am too. But it took a lot of convincing before you were willing to recommend his admittance."

"Well, no Ferengi had ever—" Sisko stopped, shocked at what he was hearing himself say.

"Right: no Ferengi had ever entered the Academy. But that says virtually nothing about Nog as an individual."

"I see your point."

"And you were never very nice to Nog," Jake continued.

"I'm sorry, Jake, but the truth is, I didn't always like Nog." Sisko spoke more harshly than he had intended; he was suddenly feeling very defensive.

"Why not?"

"For one thing," Sisko said, deliberately moderating the timbre of his voice, "when you and I first got to the station, Nog was arrested by Constable Odo for stealing. Not exactly the type of influence I wanted to have around my teenage son."

"So that was a reasoned criticism?"

"Yes."

"And therefore not based on the fact that he was a Ferengi."

"Okay, Jake, so you've made both points: that I am biased against Ferengi, and that I'm not."

"What I'm saying is that everybody has biases, Dad; they can't help it. It's only natural to draw inferences from the compilation of your life experiences. It's only when somebody does that without thinking, or to adversely affect another person, that it's a bad thing. In your case, your biases showed with Nog—and maybe with Quark—but you recognized that fact and overcame them. The fact that you're now questioning yourself about the Federation's role—and your own role—in this affair between the Bajorans and the Ferengi is an indication of that."

"I guess the problem I have is that I usually fight to defend the things I believe in, and in this case, I think the Bajorans are wrong to threaten to close their borders to *all* Ferengi if the nagus won't reinstate them in the auction. And yet I'm not fighting to reverse that course."

"Do you really think the Bajorans will do that? Do you really think they'll expel Quark and Rom and the other Ferengi from their system?" Jake asked. These were issues Sisko had been wrestling with since he had learned of the edict.

"Honestly, no, I don't think so," he said. "It seems so cold and . . . so unjust . . . an action. Quark was right about that, at least. But even though I don't think innocent Ferengi should suffer the consequences of the nagus's actions, that doesn't mean I think what the nagus is doing is right. The Orb was stolen from the Bajorans in the first place."

"And that's not right," Jake commented, "but they've done fine without any of the Orbs the Cardassians took."

"Yes, but it appears as though the Bajorans may be taking all of the others back fairly soon. In fact, they're in negotiations right now with the Detapa Council to do just that."

"So why not talk to the Bajorans about the edict?" Jake asked, and then immediately answered his own question. "Oh: the Council's resolution?"

"Yes."

*It's a circle,* Sisko thought. And there did not seem to be an answer anywhere on its circumference.

He and Jake walked again without speaking for a while. They were nearing the left-field line, having traversed most of the outfield, when Jake broke the silence.

"You know, Dad," he said, "it seems to me that somebody biased against the Ferengi wouldn't be thinking about these issues; he wouldn't be asking these questions of himself."

"I guess I don't really believe that I treat Quark and his people unfairly," Sisko said, "but I find this problem between the Bajorans and the Ferengi very troubling."

"I know," Jake said. "Well, as far as the Ferengi are concerned, I think it's important for you to realize that it's because you believe so deeply in your own philosophy—including the Federation Constitution, Starfleet regulations, and the Prime Directive—that it's difficult for you to credit not only a foreign notion of right and wrong, but something that was previously considered wrong in Earth's past. Capitalism and greed almost destroyed our world."

"And yet, somehow it seems to work for the Ferengi," Sisko said, shaking his head at the strangeness of the idea. Jake shrugged his shoulders comically, and Sisko chuckled. "Come on," he said to his son, "we better get out of here. I have that briefing in the morning." The two stopped walking as Sisko called, "Computer, exit."

The hydraulic sound of the holosuite doors opening drifted to them from behind and to their left. Sisko and Jake turned to see the doors in the middle of left field, an incongruous sight amid the spectacle of the ancient baseball cathedral. The rich texture of the grass and the bright sunshine seemed far more inviting than the cold deck plating and dim night lighting waiting on the other side of the doorway.

"End program," ordered Sisko, and Ebbets Field and its thousands of occupants disappeared, revealing a room far too small to accommodate anything of so grand a scale. Sisko walked with his son across the empty holosuite floor. The holographic imaging system embedded in the walls and ceiling and floor was an impossible and unrecognizable echo of the sights and sounds it had created.

With Jake at his side, Sisko exited the holosuite, leaving behind reproduced images and approximated moments out of history, but taking with him his son's insight, his own introspective questions for which he still needed answers, and—far back in his mind, but still there—the memory of a man named Jackie Robinson. . . .

Rom was cold.

In the darkness, he reached up and pinched the bottom of his right earlobe. He felt nothing.

Cautiously, he rubbed together the fingers of his raised hand. He heard the noise, but only faintly. Still, that was good. At least he had not completely lost his hearing yet.

He hugged his thin blanket tightly about himself. Then, putting his hand down for a moment to adjust the way in which he was lying, he felt the wood of his bunk; it too was cold. Winter on Bajor. Winter at Gallitep.

As he raised himself onto his side, trying to find a position in which he could get to sleep, the bunk creaked. It was loud enough that he heard it even with his bad ear. Rom stiffened with fear, his entire body tensing. The barracks were monitored, even at night, and for a couple of the jailors, even the slightest infraction of the rules—such as moving around after lights out—was provocation enough to punish the prisoners.

For minutes, Rom remained motionless, alert for the sound of approaching footfalls outside. Even after he was sure nobody was coming, he kept still, afraid that if he moved at all, the bunk would creak again. But soon, his arm began to tremble, what little strength he had left exhausted from the simple effort of propping up his body. As slowly as he could without collapsing, Rom eased himself back down. Thankfully, he was able to do so without making any noise.

Weary though he was, Rom found that he could not fall back to sleep. The cold had woken him, and it was still cold. It had been cold for days. *He* had been cold for days.

Rom opened his eyes and saw nothing, surrounded as he was by the ebon texture of his lightless prison. He listened again for sounds, not beyond the barracks this time, but within it. He picked out the breathing of five . . . six . . . seven . . . all eight of his fellow prisoners. Because of the hearing problem in his one ear, he could not accurately fix the location of each person in the room, but he knew where they were.

The seven other prisoners beside Rom and Quark were all Ferengi. They had already been brought here to Gallitep by the time Rom and his brother had been arrested. Five of them had been captured in their small cargo ship, attempting to make a run into Bajoran space and through the wormhole after the deadline. Their story would have been comic, Rom thought, if not for the dreadful consequences it had wrought. Their ship had lost its engines far from the wormhole, and they had floated in space for a day while laboring to make repairs. They had nearly finished restoring power to their drive when they had been chanced upon by a pair of Bajoran transports. Neither their ship nor the transports had possessed any weapons or defenses to speak of, but the Bajorans had had working engines and tractor beams, and that had been all they had needed. The Ferengi cargo ship had been towed to Bajor and its entire crew arrested.

Both of the other two Ferengi had been on Bajor when they had been discovered and taken into custody. One of them, Cort, had been conducting business on the planet and had not been able to leave before the deadline. The other, Karg, had not even known of the edict—or of Zek's purchase of the Ninth Orb, or of any other detail in this entire episode; he had retired several years ago to Bajor, where he had lived somewhat reclusively in a modest home in the province of Wyntara Mas, painting still lifes and landscapes.

Such an existence, Rom reflected, held great appeal, though he himself had no aptitude for painting. But he was very good with little creatures—*treni* cats and *jebrets,* in particular—and at growing plants of various sorts. He had long hoped that he would someday retire in a fashion similar to that of Karg. Quark had many times spoken of purchasing his own moon and withdrawing to it from his workaday business existence, and he had also frequently implied that he would want Rom to accompany him; he had even gone so far as to offer Rom such hypothetical enticements as a room of his own, a garden, and his own private menagerie of small animals. It was to a vision of such a life that Rom often retreated these days—and most especially on those days filled by Colonel Mitra.

As Rom lay huddled in his bunk, the thought of Mitra filled him with a distress he had not felt since . . . well, he had thought never, but perhaps since the time in his youth when Breel had so thoroughly humiliated him. Mitra humiliated him too, but in an adult manner that struck with a harshness that cut him far more deeply. There was a physical component to the pain as well, significant despite not being directly administered—Rom had to push away thoughts of his ears, his feet, that one section of his lower back—but the healing he would have to do when he got out of here would require far more than just the skills of Dr. Bashir.

If *we ever get out of here.*

When they had first been brought to the prison camp, there had been no doubts about their eventual departure. They would be held here until they stood trial for having violated the Bajoran edict. They would be found guilty, of course, and serve what would probably be a short term in a jail somewhere on Bajor. Until the trial, they at least had food and shelter—the meals were tasteless and the barracks uncomfortable, but their circumstances were not that bad. The guards were not friendly—the colonel had ordered them not to be— but the prisoners had been treated tolerably well. Even Quark's numerous bribery attempts had only been met with disdain, rather than punishment.

And then one day, things had changed. The colonel came by the barracks to inform the prisoners that they were no longer being held for trial. For a fleeting, cruelly hopeful moment, Rom thought that they were being released. Instead, the colonel told them about the blockade, and that as a result, the Ferengi would now be detained as political prisoners until the differences between Bajor and Ferenginar had been resolved. From that day forward, the situation had deteriorated rapidly. It was as though the prisoners had been completely forgotten by the outside world, and left to the mercy of Gallitep and their keepers.

The notion that they would not leave this place was unimaginable to Rom. He clung to the hope that there would eventually be release or escape, tomorrow, or the day after, or the day after that. Without that hope, Rom was sure that he could not have continued: he would just fail to rouse one day when one of the guards arrived at dawn, and if it was not Mitra, then Mitra would be there before long, and he would see Rom hurt, again and again, until Rom was dead—or worse, until he wished for death.

Colonel Mitra was like no other Bajoran Rom had ever met. He was like no other person he had ever met. Rom had known liars and thieves and cheats; he had them in his own family, and he understood them. He had also been acquainted with violent people, murderers even, and he had heard many tales of beings who were altogether evil, and even though malice for its own sake, with no thought of profit or strategic gain, was senseless to him—as it was, he was sure, to most Ferengi—he at least could understand how such people were motivated. But none of these categories could accurately contain the colonel. Rom did not understand why or how, but something was missing from Mitra, some essential quality no man could have lived without, and yet Mitra somehow did. It was a mystery to Rom, but not one for which he sought an answer, he prayed that he never came to understand that which drove—and which failed to drive—his ranking jailer.

How long had they been here now? Rom suddenly wondered in the darkness. At least a month, he was sure, probably two, but beyond that, he had difficulty knowing. The days were interminable, the nights without dimension. He had made an effort to track the time here when they had first arrived—as any numerically minded Ferengi would—but at some point since then, even this most ingrained of habits had become a forgotten detail, one less connection to his previous life. There would come a time soon, Rom understood, when his thoughts of that previous life would cease being memories and become only illusions instead, sanguine dreams torturous for their inaccessibility.

Life, once filled with promise, was now beginning to be marked by its absence. Rom had wanted to ask the dabo girl Leeta to go out with him, he recalled, trying to envisage *Deep Space Nine* and his life there.

He wanted to watch his son graduate from Starfleet Academy.

He wanted to help his brother achieve the business successes he craved.

He wanted to see his mother again.

He wanted to go home. That, he realized now, more than anything else: he wanted to go home.

So thinking, Rom drifted into a restless sleep.

# *Pathways,* by Jeri Taylor

Although *Pathways,* by Jeri Taylor, is included in Chapter Six, We Are Family, *Pathways* also has a story about the horrors of war and its consequences for survivors. *Voyager* established that Neelix, a Talaxian, is from a moon of Talax called Rinax, which was destroyed by an unspeakable superweapon invented and launched by the Haakonians. In *Pathways,* Ms. Taylor brought the war home to the reader in powerful terms. Neelix did not just lose his family in the attack on Rinax; he witnessed the destruction of Rinax and helped search for survivors after the attack. Following his devastating experience, Neelix sank into the bottomless pit of drug abuse to escape the images of what he had seen. Neelix was a tragic character who covered his tragedy with buffoonery. He was truly at home on *Voyager* because he had nowhere else to go, and the ship's complement became his family.

The selection from *Pathways* described the attack on Rinax. Am I alone in imagining Hiroshima and Nagasaki?

"NEELIX?" IT WAS HIS FATHER'S VOICE. NEELIX GOT OUT OF BED AND padded to the door, opening it.

His father stood there with a man who looked vaguely familiar, but whom he couldn't immediately identify.

"Do you remember Uxxin?" asked his father. "You met him at the weapons range the first time we went there."

The memory registered in Neelix's mind. The tall, erect man, spots black with age, tufts elaborately arranged. He was the one who'd spoken of the need for an armed citizenry.

But the tale he brought tonight was far more frightening than the as-yet-unfounded threat of the Haakonians.

Neelix sat with the two of them at their dining table—the scene of so much mirth and pleasure over the years. It would never recall good times again; from this night on, the dining table would remind him only of the awful things Uxxin was telling them.

"The boy must leave Rinax tonight. If he's here tomorrow when Tixil comes back, you'll never see him again. I've made arrangements to get him to Talax, where we have friends who will hide him."

Neelix's head was spinning with disbelief. What was Uxxin talking about? Why did he have to leave his home?

His father looked at him solemnly. "Uxxin is part of a group who are trying to avoid war with Haakon. But there are strong factions that want the war, and who consider the moderates a threat. The whole thing has turned ugly."

"I believe the man in the hut was one of our group who disappeared several days ago. I have no doubt that Tixil and his men tortured him for information about us."

*"Tixil?"* Neelix couldn't believe what he was hearing. "Tixil the civil defender?"

"I'm afraid the authorities are riddled with people like him—who want war and who will do anything to suppress opposition to it."

The room began to swim. What was life coming to if one couldn't trust the civil authorities? Those sworn to protect and defend?

"Tixil knows you saw someone who'd been tortured. He can't afford to let you spread that around. It's a wonder he didn't take you in for questioning right away." Tixil paused portentously. "You'd never have survived."

Visions of the man's burned feet danced in Neelix's vision, and he tried to blink them away. Was this the fate that awaited him? Cold terror began to creep from his belly, radiating outward to his extremities. His father wouldn't let this happen. His father was wise, and strong. He would protect him.

But his father was talking to Uxxin, making the plans for his clandestine trip to Talax. Neelix was told to pack quickly, taking only necessities. Within fifteen minutes after Uxxin had arrived, Neelix was standing with his mother and father and his sisters Xepha and Melorix, the only two left at home. Tears were streaming down their faces, and while crying was exactly what Neelix felt like doing, he forced himself to appear confident, for their sake. "I'll be back as soon as I can," he promised, kissing the briny tears on their cheeks. They cried even harder.

His mother embraced him, her eyes moist as well, but she was stalwart and refused to give in to grief. And finally Papa held him strongly, briefly, unspeaking. And then Neelix was gone, off in the night like a felon on the run.

He never saw any of his family again.

Inevitably, war broke out. Talax actually made the first strike, the warlike faction of their race having predominated. But after that, it hardly mattered who had started things. It was brutal and relentless, fought on many fronts: in space, on the Haakonian homeworld, and on Talax. Losses on both sides were staggering. The economy was devoted entirely to the war effort, and food shortages abounded. Winters were devastating, because fuel was in short supply. Medical centers were overrun with the war wounded.

Haakon suffered just as harshly. Resources were dwindling and riots had broken out on Haakonian outposts everywhere. Their government was under great pressure from the citizenry to end the devastating conflict.

Neelix spent two years helping to run a sanctuary for deserters from the military. He had never acquired the zealousness of his fellow pacifists, and from time to time considered coming forth and offering to join the military. But he knew the time had passed. He was a deserter, having never shown up for obligatory service, and would be executed summarily.

And so he protected those who had fled the fighting, those who were convinced the authorities wanted to protract the war for their own financial gain. These hardened veterans told tales of unimaginable horror about the battle fronts, and spoke with loathing of the venality of the government that would perpetuate this evil.

In the end, Neelix didn't know what to believe. He had come to his situation not through ideology, or passion, or even choice. Fate had placed him squarely on one side of the argument whether he liked it or not. He was as helpless as a leaf blown before the wind. He reasoned that he should eschew philosophical musing and simply do the best he could for the cause that had protected him, snatching him from Tixil's grasp and keeping him safe for over two years.

He had to admit that when he heard the heartrending tales from the front, he felt relieved not to be a part of it. It all sounded so futile, so needless—fighting for weeks over a kilometer-wide strip of land, taking and retaking it countless times, back and forth until the corpses were stacked like deadwood and no one could even remember why that strip of land was so important.

They heard rumors that the Haakonian populace was out of control, threatening to storm the governmental buildings unless the war was terminated. Hope sprang in many hearts that, soon, it would all be over.

And so it was.

The end of the war occurred on a warm spring night, and the terminus took no more than four minutes.

Neelix was sitting outside, in the walled compound of their hideaway. A wild yute bird sounded, reminding him of home, and somewhere someone was playing a gentle melody on the ixxel. For a moment, it was possible to believe that, soon, life would become normal once more, that love and joy would return to their hearts, that bellies would be full and spirits nourished. That he would see his family again.

He inhaled the spring air deeply, and gazed up at Rinax, luminous in the night sky, half in shadow at this time of the month. He imagined his parents and his sisters, and hoped they weren't suffering too badly from the war. He'd supposed his sisters' husbands had been pressed into service, unless they were protestors and avoided conscription. He had had no contact with any of them for two years, since he'd been taken off Rinax crammed in a cargo container loaded onto a freighter piloted by a friend of Uxxin.

As he stared upward, a curious brightness illuminated Rinax, turning its whiteness briefly to a cold blue.

Then it began to disappear.

Neelix stared upward, trying to reconcile the puzzling sight with some understandable phenomenon.

He couldn't do it.

It was as though dark fingers began to obscure the moon, creeping swiftly over the surface, occluding it completely. Dust clouds, he thought, or some unusual space storm. But a coldness in his heart told him this was something far worse than a storm.

As he stared upward, the call of the yute bird still wafting through the night air—and forever afterward, he would associate that sound with the catastrophe that had struck—Rinax disappeared completely. He knew it was there; he could see its faint outline, as one does in an eclipse, but it was a dark disk in the sky.

It hadn't been an eclipse. It didn't behave like one. What were those strange fingers of darkness that clawed at his home, like bony talons of death?

He wasn't sure how long he stood staring up at the darkness where Rinax had been, but after a time he heard a commotion inside. People were shouting. Then he heard an unearthly wailing.

Lixxisa, a good friend, came running toward him. Her eyes were wide, and her face was pale in the darkness. "Neelix . . ." she began; then her knees buckled and she sank to the ground. Alarmed, he crouched beside her. "What is it? What's happened?"

"Unthinkable . . . unthinkable . . ."

"Lixxisa, tell me!"

"Rinax . . . destroyed . . ."

Neelix's mind froze, and he willed time to reverse itself, to return him to the pleasant reverie of mere minutes ago. If he could back up just those few minutes in time, all would be righted. Rinax would still gleam in the night sky, and this time, events would proceed differently. It would not disappear before his eyes, Lixxisa would not come running, pallid, from the house and crumple at his feet. She would not say the awful words she had just spoken.

But his will wasn't strong enough. Time pressed inexorably on. Lixxisa gasped for air, as though she'd been hit in the abdomen. "A weapon . . . horrible weapon . . . a cascade . . . every village on Rinax is gone . . . everyone dead . . ."

This litany of horror droned on, but Neelix tuned it out. He couldn't listen. If he refused to hear it, it would be robbed of validity. What one doesn't hear cannot have happened.

But once again his determination was thwarted. Lixxisa kept on, and on. "Massive fireballs . . . the atmosphere nearly consumed . . . no one's ever heard of anything like this . . . what kind of animals are they who'd develop a weapon like that?"

Aghast, Neelix stared upward at his home. Now, through the dark clouds, streaks of light were visible. Orange flickers, licking at the darkness. Flames. Massive fireballs.

Rinax had been attacked with weaponry so strong that the smoke from the explosions had completely obscured it. And now the fireballs were blazing. If they could be seen from Talax, they must be immense. No one could possibly survive.

Pictures of his beloved family seared his mind. His father and mother, entwined in each other's arms as they were incinerated. His sisters, writhing in agony as flames burned the flesh from their bones. Sweet Alixia screaming and screaming and screaming. . . .

He could smell the odor of burned flesh.

A hot coal formed in his belly. He couldn't identify it; it was completely foreign to him. It hurt, and yet it was somehow satisfying. It grew steadily, burning him from within, taking him over completely, overwhelming, igniting his brain, boiling his heart.

It was rage.

Rage sustained him for weeks after the disaster. The war had ended summarily, with Talax surrendering immediately and becoming in essence a Haakonian outpost. The weapon, they learned, was called the Metreon Cascade, and had been developed in order to bring the war to a swift and certain conclusion.

Neelix volunteered to be part of a rescue mission to Rinax, and was among the first to set foot on the devastated landscape. Fires still burned there, and the smell was something that would haunt his dreams for years: the same odor of roasted flesh that had permeated his hut after he had found the tortured man. Clouds of rancid smoke and dust billowed placidly, like a meadow of dark flowers, their gentle swaying a grotesque counterpart to the horror they manifested.

No one could be alive in this place.

He and his friends forced themselves forward, steeling themselves to the awful sights, breathing through moistened handkerchiefs to quench the noxious odor. They soon realized this search would not be lengthy, because almost nothing was left of Rinax.

His house was gone. Not even the foundation was left, just a large black spot indicating that something had burned. Vaxi's house, too, was obliterated, and the pond the children had frolicked in was nothing more than a dry pit in the ground.

Someone observed that they must be very near a "ground zero" point—where the weapon had made its initial contact. That was the first heartening news Neelix had heard in days. That meant it was very likely that his family had been annihilated on the spot, instantly vaporized and suffering no pain. They would now be united in the afterlife, where one day he would join them. He tried to remind himself of this faintly comforting fact as they continued to prowl the smoldering ruins.

It was he who first detected the faint sound that emanated from the undulating clouds of smoke. At first he thought it might be a bird, and wondered how a bird had survived this devastation.

Then he saw figures moving toward them with maddening sluggishness, each step taken as though through heavy mud.

They were monsters.

Charred skin, the color of shale, hung from their torsos and extremities. The pulpy flesh underneath, swollen to bursting, dripped with watery fluids. The monsters had no faces, just a mask of spongy tissue, swirled as though someone had stirred a thick batch of red and black pudding.

Vague orifices emerged from the pudding, distorted beyond any identification as eyes or mouth. Yet somehow from the misshapen gullets a sound emanated, a keening, a bestial moaning, that made the tufts on Neelix's head stiffen.

One of the monsters moved in his direction, hearing rather than seeing the members of his group because its eyes were obliterated, its hideous limbs outstretched, scorched skin dangling. Terrified that the thing would touch him, he turned away.

"Wahhhh . . . wahhh . . ."

The thing spoke with what could clearly be identified—even though the words were distorted by the monstrous mingling of lips, teeth, and tongue—as a child's voice. Appalled, Neelix turned back.

The child was pointing toward its grotesque mouth. "Wahhh . . . wahhh . . ." it repeated, and suddenly Neelix realized the poor creature was asking for water. He reached for his container, uncapped it, and held it out. The child couldn't see it.

Neelix held the container to what had once been lips and tipped the liquid into the ravaged mouth. The child managed a few sips but then began choking from the pain of swallowing through such damaged tissue. Neelix felt himself begin to tremble. What was he to do for this creature? This was beyond his experience.

He glanced around and saw the members of the team busy with others of the unfortunate survivors. They seemed to know what they were doing, and he wondered briefly how they could function so calmly when presented with a calamity of this magnitude.

He remembered that he had a pain medication in his medical container, and reached in for it. But before he could administer it, the child tumbled into his arms, unconscious, leaving hunks of burnt matter on his clothing. Revulsion threw gorge into his throat, but then it subsided, and Neelix felt the tiny weight of the child, the frantic beating of its heart. He picked it up effortlessly and moved toward the others. He made a determination that this child would live.

Thirty-seven people survived the Metreon Cascade, all that remained of a population of more than two hundred thousand. Those thirty-seven were alive only because they were in an underground recreational facility miles from ground zero. They were taken to medical facilities on Talax, where doctors were stupefied by their condition. Traditional burn treatments were simply ineffective, and gradually, one by one, the survivors began to die.

The child's name, Neelix learned, was Palaxia. Though badly disfigured, she had suffered less damage to her internal organs than some of the others, and the doctors believed she had a chance to survive. She was resilient, they said, and possessed a will to live. That was often the factor that made the difference.

Neelix spent weeks by her side. She was blind, eyeballs having melted in the blast, and so he read to her for hours at a time—inspirational stories of Talaxian heroes who had overcome difficult circumstances, hoping that she would be heartened by the examples. He had no way of knowing if this was so, of course, as Palaxia had lost the power of articulate speech, scar tissue having occluded her larynx. But she could hear, and he imagined that the sound of his voice, hour upon hour, was comforting to her.

Skin grafts were applied and quickly sloughed off. This process was repeated three times before doctors began shaking their heads and admitting that they didn't know what to do next.

Palaxia was kept on powerful pain medications. Without them, she would have been in constant agony. With them, she still suffered, but at what the doctors called a "tolerable level." Neelix wondered how they managed to determine this, or even how they assessed the level at which she hurt, but was glad something was being done for her.

Palaxia, for her part, lay quietly on the bed, tiny chest rising and falling, face and body swathed in dressings, enduring her agony privately, in a world she could share with no one.

And Neelix sat with her day after day, reading, talking, even singing some of his favorite songs from Prixin, although he usually couldn't finish them because his own grief would overcome him.

Palaxia lived five and one half weeks, three weeks longer than any of the other survivors. Neelix was with her as her breathing became more ragged; she stopped and then started breathing four separate times, as though her will refused to let her die. He spoke to her throughout, words of comfort and solace, telling her that she would soon be reunited with her family, who had been waiting for her.

Finally her chest rose and fell no more. Neelix quietly gathered his things and left the medical facility, saying good-bye to no one. He shed no tears for Palaxia, or for his vanished family and friends. He did not mourn them at all. It would have destroyed him.

## *Deep Domain,* by Howard Weinstein

Environmental issues continue to cause controversy on our planet, and among the most difficult of the environmental issues involves the treatment of life in our oceans. *STIV* has often been lovingly subtitled, "Star Trek: Save the Whales," because of its strong condemnation of whaling, a practice that persists to this day. While the debate over the intelligence of whales continues, whales are killed for food or other products, and are even captured and confined in small tanks by those purportedly interested in studying and protecting them. In *Deep Domain,* Howard Weinstein visited the water-world of Akkalla, where ocean harvesting collected incredible amounts of marine life, including species believed to be sentient. The harvests were devastating; they killed all life caught in the giant nets. Akkalla experienced near-revolutionary civil unrest because of the harvesting controversy, and in the scene excerpted here, the rebels asked Kirk to help prove that not only was there sentient life in the seas, but that sentient life included Akkallans in another stage of life.

McCoy CRADLED A BONE IN HIS LONG FINGERS AS HE HUNCHED OVER THE table in the main briefing room. Kirk, Maybri, and Preceptor Kkayn listened to his conclusions.

"They're from a creature dead about ten years, no sign of unusual disease or fractures, at least in these two bones. Can't very well speak for the rest of the skeleton, wherever it may be. I'd say the owner of these lived in the ocean and died there, too. As for what the owner was, well, I really couldn't even guess, beyond the probability that it was mammalian."

"Doctor," said Llissa, "how much do you think you could tell by comparing these bones with others that I think are similar?"

"Well, that's hard to say. I s'pose we could tell if they came from the same kind of animal, whether they were comparable in age, that sort of thing."

"What about comparing them to the physiology of a living Akkallan?"

"I don't have any data on Akkallans."

"But you *have* a living Akkallan—me. I'm a healthy, typical Akkallan female."

"Would that be worth doing, Bones?" asked Kirk.

"Well, sure it would, Jim. First stop in comparative anatomy is having something to compare to. I won't even charge you for the office visit, preceptor."

The physical didn't take long—McCoy's scanners saw to that. Once the computer had digested the results, Kirk and Maybri reconvened in the doctor's office, where McCoy displayed an assortment of charts, cross-sectional scans, and diagrams on the wall screen over his desk.

"The artwork's great, Bones, but what does it mean?" said Kirk.

The ship's surgeon hefted one of the sample bones. "Well, I could switch this with Llissa's tibia—"

Kirk raised an eyebrow. "First-name basis?"

"Well," Llissa said, "once a man's scanned your innards, you might as well dispense with formalities."

"Okay. What about her tibia?"

"I could replace it with this bone, and she'd never know the difference, except for this one being a little longer than hers. Joint structure's identical."

"Isn't that odd for a bone that's from an unidentified creature you say lived in the ocean?"

"In a word, yes. Can I explain it? No—not yet, anyway."

"Now that we're on the same side, it's time I filled you in on all the pertinent background," Llissa said.

Kirk rubbed his hands together. "Does it clear any of this up, or does it add to the confusion?"

"Both."

"I was afraid of that," McCoy said sourly.

"Some of our scientists believe this new life-form is actually something very ancient, something we never knew for sure was real. Until the first evidence was collected, oh, maybe twenty years ago, the common belief was that these things were mythical. They were called Wwafida."

"And now?" Kirk asked.

"Now, a lot of us believe they once existed. We think our nine-thousand-year-old fossils prove that."

Kirk balanced the tibia in his palm. "But this isn't a fossil. This is a contemporary bone."

"Right," Llissa said, her voice rising in excitement. "And if we can match this to the fossils, that could be what we need to prove these creatures are still alive today."

Keeping the bone in his hand, Kirk began to pace. "This—is— getting more complicated by the minute . . . but it's not getting us any conclusive answers to anything. What is so controversial about this mysterious, possibly mythical creature that anybody who knows anything about it gets targeted for destruction?"

Llissa ran nervous hands through her hair, releasing a clasp and letting her dark tresses flow over her shoulders. "The debate over the existence of the Wwafida is the cause of the state of war between Akkalla and Chorym."

McCoy whistled in disbelief. *"Now* we're getting somewhere."

"Keep explaining," Kirk said.

"Some of us believed these creatures may be intelligent. Those who did wanted the Chorymi harvest ships to stop working until we could figure out, one, did these creatures exist, and, two, were they sentient beings. Because if they were really out in the seas swimming free, then their lives were endangered by every harvest."

"Was the Collegium part of that group demanding a halt to the harvests?" Kirk asked.

"Some of our scientists were, along with some independent scientists and politicians."

McCoy took the bone back from Kirk and wrapped it with the other one. "I bet that's where the Cape Alliance came in."

"The Alliance has been around for years, but when the Collegium didn't support their stand against the harvests, that's when they turned really radical and started disrupting the harvests by actually going out in boats."

"What did the Chorymi do?" said Kirk.

"At first, they pulled up in a hurry whenever any surface vessels were in a harvest zone. After all, the harvests were part of a treaty with us, and the Chorymi appealed to our government to get the Alliance to stop interfering with legal harvest work. So the Alliance went underground, and the Publican got the Synod to vote for sweeping military powers to crush the Alliance."

"Obviously," McCoy said, "it hasn't worked."

Llissa shook her head sadly. "No, it hasn't. And everything's been unraveling for the past year or so. The Paladins and the Grolian Guard have more and more power, and under Vvox and Hhayd they abuse it. The Chorymi gave up on Akkalla ever abiding by the treaty, and they started raiding our seas whenever they felt like it. There's nothing the Paladins can do to stop them, and they don't share what they take with us anymore." There was a catch in her voice, and she took a deep breath, trying to hold on to her composure. "The Cape Alliance is crazier than ever, and now my Collegium's practically under siege, probably a step away from all of us being arrested . . . and I don't know what to do about any of this."

McCoy touched her arm, but she brushed the kindly gesture away, spinning to view her reflection off the viewscreen.

"I'm sorry," she said with a desolate sigh. "This is the first time I've strung all those disastrous events together in one sentence."

Kirk shook his head. "There's something I don't get. Why is the harvest so important to Chorym that they're willing to risk interplanetary war?"

"Well, for one thing, there's not much risk. They're much more advanced than we are technologically. If there's a war, Akkalla's the battlefield—and we'll lose it."

"Advanced or not," McCoy said, "it seems like an awful lot of trouble to satisfy a yen for seafood."

"Not if you've got no choice. More than a century ago, the Chorymi ignored the fact that their planet's climate was drying out. They just went blithely along, plundering their own resources, in spite of the fact that deserts were advancing all over Chorym. It reached a stage where they were desperate, and our oceans promised salvation. Oh, they'd had interplanetary travel for a long time, and we traded back and forth. But what they proposed went way beyond all that. They presented the idea of building fleets of flying harvest ships. Not only would they split the catch with us, they'd also pay us with the only resource they had left in any abundance."

"What was that?" asked Kirk.

"It happened to be something we needed—rhipileum. It's an energy ore. We have such a small land mass on Akkalla we don't have a lot of mineral wealth that's readily accessible. So we stumbled along with lagging industrial development. But Chorym's rhipileum was the missing key to our future. Our standard of living jumped ahead at the speed of light, it seemed. We advanced more in the last hundred years than in the previous five hundred. So you can see that it wasn't the popular thing to do, raising difficult questions that might put an end to all that."

"But the questions have already been raised," Kirk said "Akkalla's not going to be able to run away without answering them."

Llissa nodded, sad resignation in her eyes. "I suppose I've always known that. But it's only in the last few days that I've really accepted it. The answers might destroy Akkallan society as we know it, but that's happening already anyway. If we have to lose everything we've built, I'd rather know it was for the right reasons."

Llissa took a deep breath. "We have to know if these creatures are real and if they're intelligent. And if they are, we'll use the truth to appeal to the people of Akkalla and Chorym. We may have to take our case all the way to the Federation Council, and we'll need the weight of outside authority to win. Admiral Kirk, will you help us?"

## *The Tears of the Singers,* by Melinda Snodgrass

This book includes a passage from *The Tears of the Singers* in Chapter Four, Second to None, but the novel also has a strong environmental message. The semi-aquatic inhabitants of Taygeta V were killed for the "tears" they excreted at the moment of death, tears which were then sold as valuable and rare gemstones in the Federation. At the same time, an anomaly developed in the Taygetian system that swallowed surrounding space and celestial bodies in that space. The *Enterprise* crew discovered that the anomaly was related to the hunting, and that the singers could repair the anomaly through their singing.

This selection from *The Tears of the Singers* is reminiscent of the annual slaughter of baby harp seals.

AN ICE GREEN SEA LAPPED SOFTLY AT THE SPARKLING SANDS AND CRYSTAL cliffs of the strange, silver-lit world. Along the length and breadth of the glittering beach played the junior Singers. Cubs, perhaps, although the adults resting in their crystal grottos showed no parental interest in the small furry youngsters who tumbled, hummed, chirruped, and warbled on the beach below them.

The hunters stepped carefully, yet uninterestedly, through the gamboling packs of silver white creatures. The little fellows were cute enough, with their pale blue eyes and ingeniously smiling faces, but the money lay with the adults. Long and sleek they reclined in their grottos, unmoved by the icy wind that whipped off the whitecapped ocean. Their eyes had darkened to the profound midnight blue of adulthood, and they seemed to be staring into a place beyond time as they blended their strange siren voices into an intricate and never-ending song.

410

It behooved a man not to look into those eyes when he fired the electric current that stilled yet another voice in the mighty chorus. Those who had, described it as looking into eternity, and they didn't seem like men who had enjoyed the sight.

So they learned to do their work cleanly and efficiently, concentrating only on the rewards to be gained when the crystal tears were marketed back on Earth or Rigel, or any of a hundred other Federation worlds where men and women adorned themselves.

The creatures made no move to escape or even acknowledge their destroyers. They merely continued their particular harmony as the humans laboriously climbed the treacherous cliffs, and placed their shockwands at the base of a Singer's skull. One of the hunters fired, and a discordant cry pierced through the perfect harmony of the song. The creature rolled ponderously onto its side, its eyes secreting a viscous blue substance. The "tears," as the humans had dubbed them, soon solidified into the gleaming gems so prized on civilized worlds.

The man swept the seven crystals into a soft leather pouch. Something caught his attention, and he fished back the last jewel. He held it up to the diffuse light, and frowned when he noticed a minute flaw in the crystal. A bit of sand had become embedded in the gem, warping its perfect symmetry and color. Grumbling, he tossed it down the rock wall, where it shattered with the sound of a thousand bells. It was an eerie and melancholy sound in the frigid air.

# CHAPTER 14

# Adventures in Strange Times and Alternate Space

WHEN FANS ARE ASKED TO NAME THEIR FAVORITE *TOS* AND *TNG* episodes, most answer "City on the Edge of Forever" and "Yesterday's *Enterprise*." Time travel and alternate universe stories capture the imagination of fans and writers perhaps because they are the ultimate "what if" stories. They allow writers to put our heroes into extremely difficult, seemingly no-win situations with impossible choices. That was the case with both "City on the Edge of Forever" and "Yesterday's Enterprise." In both, the captains made emotionally rending choices and showed exceptional courage as they acted for the greater good despite tragic personal consequences. In "City," Kirk accepted that Edith Keeler had to die so that the future could be restored, and in "Yesterday's Enterprise" Picard gave his life and that of everyone on his ship to buy a fighting chance to restore the future and eliminate a timeline that was killing the Federation.

Parallel timeline and universe episodes work the same way. From "Mirror, Mirror" of The Original Series through *Voyager*'s "The Killing Game," the writers have taken existing time and place settings and twisted them just a little, so that the people and settings are familiar but just not quite right. The resulting stories can be extraordinary. The same is true for novelists; adventures in time travel and alternate universes provide opportunities for unlimited creativity, where writers can give free rein to their imaginations. They have to put things right at the end, but in the meantime, authors can go where no Star Trek writer has gone before.

# *The Wounded Sky,* by Diane Duane

*The Wounded Sky* is one of the early Pocket Star Trek novels and is frequently listed among fans' favorite books. It is not quite time travel, and it is not quite alternate universe. It is, however, fascinating science fiction at its best, in which Ms. Duane explored the nature of reality as experienced by the crews and affected by a new engine system designed to make warp drive obsolete. The *Enterprise* under Captain Kirk was chosen to test the new galactic inversion drive, but when they engaged it, space and time around them twisted and began to tear. The crew experienced bizarre physical and mental reactions, and the phenomena worsened each time they engaged the drive. When the inversion drive was implemented, time ceased to move forward. Even worse, the problem could not be remedied by simply stopping use of the drive; the crew had to repair the damage, or life in our universe would cease to exist.

*The Wounded Sky* also featured one of the most interesting characters in the history of Star Trek books, K't'lk, a Hamalki, an alien glass spider with an interesting reproductive cycle and a very different approach to physics. She also appeared in Ms. Duane's *Spock's World.*

In this passage from *The Wounded Sky,* the crew confronted what they had done and the high cost of repairing the damage. Jim Kirk, always the hero, pondered what he must do.

"THE DATA ARE IN," K'T'LK CHIMED. "AND THE ONLY GOOD THING ABOUT them is that you can't possibly be as disturbed by them as *I* am."

"Try me," Jim said, sitting up on the diagnostic bed and stretching. Bones had pumped him as full of pharmaceuticals as a drugstore; he felt much better, and wondered how long it was going to last.

Gathered about the bed were Scotty and Spock and K't'lk; McCoy leaned on the wall at its head. "Let me go first, Kit," McCoy said. "Jim, I've had opportunity to go over quite a number of the crew while you've been down here. There were a lot of minor injuries during this past inversion—injuries like yours, sustained in the experience itself, when it was impossible for anyone to move or even breathe—much less be in the places they report having been. None of the injuries were very serious. I still have a few people to check; you were something of a priority for me."

"Bones, I still don't understand. How could these things have actually *happened* to us? They weren't *real*—"

Bones folded his arms and leaned back, shaking his head. "Jim, you're heading for trouble. A lot of problems—wars, for example—get started when we point at one reality and claim that it's 'realer' than another. A lot of years in xenopsychology have convinced me that *anything* you experience is a reality—and that's not a difficulty, since realities naturally include one another. For example, my reality includes an *Enterprise,* and a Jim Kirk, and a Spock—God knows why—" Spock put up an eyebrow. "—and yours include not only all those things, but a McCoy too. There's also another kind of inclusion. For example, you might dream that a monster's after you and *know* it's real—then wake up, and know you'd been dreaming, and also know that you're in a more inclusive or 'senior' reality now. There are 'waking' realities apparently senior to ours; Lia's na'mdeihei would be an example, by their standards."

McCoy sighed. "What I'm suggesting is that all our personal realities are becoming far more inclusive, more 'senior,' than usual. Our inversion experiences seem to have started out with an inward emphasis—and have since been turning slowly outward, to include not only other people, but other people's perceptions."

"Could this have something to do with the increasing 'length' of the inversions?" Scotty said.

Bones shrugged. "Might be. The barriers living minds erect between their own realities and others' could very well be a function of entropy—and we've been spending more and more 'time' away from it. Something else interests me more, however, and I wonder if the space we're in has something to do with it. There was a common factor among all of the experiences the crew had this last time out. Every one of them perceived some kind of danger to the *Enterprise,* and acted to stop it. This is going to sound a little peculiar, and I have no proof for it whatever—but I'm not sure it was Mr. Sulu alone who saved the ship. I think the entire crew sensed something the matter, and it was the intention and concentration of the whole group that did the trick."

Jim nodded. "All right. Spock?"

Spock had been gazing at the table. He raised his eyes now, looking very grave. "Sir, Science Department's assessment of the situation in the space around us is extremely distressing. We have succeeded in determining that the time-space turbulence in this area does indeed have a locus of origin. That locus is far from here, even in terms of use of the inversion drive—nearly two million two hundred thousand light-years beyond the borders of the Lesser Magellanic, almost out of the Local Group of galaxies itself. Our sensors have been able

414

to detect it primarily by indirect methods—not that they are able to actually sense anything in that spot—but, when pointed in that direction, that is where all their functions fail most catastrophically. That fact in itself joins with the presence of staggering amounts of Hawking radiation to suggest the nature of the locus. What we are seeing—or more accurately, not seeing—is a place where another universe has breached ours."

Scotty looked at Spock, surprised, but not very worried. "We've seen that before, man; what's the problem?"

"This other universe," K't'lk said, "appears not to have entropy at all. It is leaking non-entropy, 'anentropia,' into ours. And the breach through which it does so is widening."

"How fast?" Jim said.

"At a huge hyperlight velocity," Spock said. "The effect is able to propagate with no regard to the speed limit of light in this universe, since it is actually a function of the other universe's expansion. Within a month at most, it will have affected all of the Lesser Magellanic Cloud. Within two months, three maximum, it will encompass our own galaxy. And within a year, or perhaps two, it could not only have encompassed the entire Local Group, but the whole 'megagalactic group' of which the Locals are an insignificant part."

Scotty went white. McCoy stood absolutely still beside him. Even K't'lk wasn't chiming. "What will happen?" Jim said.

"To the inhabited planets, you mean?" Spock looked at Jim, and no Vulcan calm could hide his distress. "Without entropy, there can be no life as we know it. Existence as such will simply cease, without time to pass through; as that other universe intrudes into, or rather around, ours, and finally contains it, anentropia will everywhere abolish life. And it will not happen quickly, or easily. Entropic space will first mix slowly with anentropic, like two fluids. As it is doing in the space around us."

Spock stepped over to the sickbay wall screen. "On," he said. "Outside visual."

The screen came on, revealing a vista of blackness and stars that for the first fraction of a second looked like any other scene at the edge of a large globular cluster; a scattering of stars, thicker toward one side, thinning toward the cluster's fringes. But immediately the illusion of normality and tranquillity was destroyed. The stars would not be still. And this was no healthy fluctuation like that in the skies of faraway Lórien. These stars glittered feverishly, as if seen from the bottom of a dirty, turbulent atmosphere. Some of them exploded, and did so not cleanly, but hesitantly, by fits and starts—then contracted sluggishly to dim, diseased-looking globes. The stars flickered and guttered like failing candles in a bitter wind, as entropy and the lack of it washed over them in waves light-years long, and time ran forward, backward, every which way. This was no pure, fierce burning into slow collapse and oblivion. This was protracted suffering, lingering death. Not even the darkness of empty space seemed clean. It *crawled.*

Jim looked away.

"Some of those stars have planets, Captain," Spock said. "Some of those planets have life. If you can call it that. It is a life in which nothing can be depended upon, where the laws of nature may be abruptly suspended at the whim of whatever eddy of time or not-time a world is caught in. I dare say the inhabitants would welcome death, if they could completely achieve it—for many of them will have been in the process of dying for what subjectively would feel like ages. Such a fate awaits all the known worlds. The Klingons, the Federation, all the hundreds of kinds of humanity we know, all the myriads we do not, in our galaxy and in every other."

Jim looked at the screen again in fascinated horror, looked away again as the horror outweighed every other feeling. "There must be something we can do for them," he said in a whisper.

"Deal with the problem at its source," K't'lk said. "Indeed we *must* do so, Captain. We caused it."

Her chiming was pained, somber-sounding, a dirge for dying worlds. Jim looked at her, then up at Spock. Spock nodded. "Probability approaches one hundred percent very closely, Captain," he said. "The presence of the 'symbiotic' spectral lines in the stars here, the same lines as in 109 Piscium and zeta-10 Scorpii, confirms it—a breach of physical integrity on a massive scale, just considered locally. And out there, past the Local Group, a place where the physicality of our own universe's very fabric has been compromised. The topological process going on out there is fascinating—but that is all there is to be said for it. It is a multidimensional analogue to the old topological puzzle in which one torus linked through another may completely 'swallow' its companion. Our universe will wind up contained within that other—and time, becoming impossible, will cease. All existence will go with it. I theorize, and K't'lk agrees with me, that every time we have used the inversion apparatus, the strain on the universe itself has become worse. Finally, on the jump before last, it tore. The jump we just made, as far as our measurements can tell us, aggravated the situation considerably. Should we go to the

416

locus of this anomalous effect, the extreme length of the jump will aggravate it even more, accelerating the process. Yet so, to a lesser degree, would any attempt to return home and warn the humanities."

"Recommendations," Jim said.

"Attempt penetration of the anomaly," Spock said.

"Allowing that we do—what can we do there?"

"There's a strong possibility that this breach can be healed," K't'lk said. "Captain, you and Mt'gm'ry have been pleased to joke about what my physics is good for besides confusing you. But we are alive and talking now partly because of it—"

"We're in the problem we're in *because* of it too," McCoy muttered.

K't'lk jangled at him, an annoyed sound. "Please, L'nrd. I don't disclaim my direct responsibility for the imminent destruction of life as we know it and as we don't, everywhere. But with that in mind, I don't have the time for thorax-thumping—"

"'Breast-beating,'" Scotty said gently.

"Right, thank you.—I don't have time for that, and you don't have time to stand around and watch me indulge in it. I need to *do* something about this mess. Starfleet can courtmartial me later, if I live. Captain, I can maintain and manipulate entropy on a local level. I can tailor the 'entropy shell' that has so far been protecting the ship so that it also protects each individual crewperson; nothing that generates a life-field will be in danger of facing anentropia unshielded, in the ship or out of it. Also, I am very sure I can work out a way to use the inversion drive itself to add enough power to my equations so that I can blanket that whole rift with entropy and weave space together again. Once that's done, we can return to this area— using short hops rather than the long ones that strain space so—and I can undo all the damage possible here."

"And if you can't?"

"Then, since we will be so close to the effect, we will, as the story says, 'go out—bang!—just like a candle.'" Spock looked down at K't'lk. "However, I ran another estimate of the probability of your success. It is much higher than we thought at first."

"Oh? How much?"

"Forty-eight percent."

"It's gone *up* to fifty-fifty, is that it, Spock? And this is an improvement?" McCoy said, exasperated.

"Bones," Jim said as calmly as he could, "do you have a recommendation?"

"Yes! One that worked real well for me when I was younger. I'm going to get in bed and pull the covers up over my ears so that all this will go away. I recommend you all do the same." He looked at Spock. *"You're* going to need more covers—"

"Bones—!"

"All right, all right. Jim, with each jump, the crew's individual mental integrity has broken down further—so that they're perceiving external realities as—well, no, that's not accurate. All experience is internal when you get down to it—"

"Doctor, this is no time for a lecture on egopositivism—"

"When the theory fits, Spock, wear it or freeze in the wind. Jim, I submit that a longer jump is going to break down those walls between people even more completely. There's no guarantee that we'll still be able to function as individuals. We may wind up as some kind of weird group mind. Also, any nightmare or dangerous vision that one of us may come up with might be able to affect some or all the others—with fatal effects. You'd better instruct the ship to run itself as completely as possible when we pop out, and to refuse override orders from anyone but department heads. Not that they'll be any more resistant than anyone else—it just seems it would cut down on the possibility of accidents. And for Heaven's sake, warn the crew about what might happen."

"I haven't yet chosen a course of action," Jim said. "However, all that is noted. Anybody else?"

No one said anything.

"Very well, Mr. Spock, I'm going to step out for a few minutes. You have the conn while I'm gone. Bones, will it be all right? Just a quick walk outside the ship; I won't go far."

"Don't overdo it. And stay on the opposite side of the ship from that." McCoy gestured at the deactivated screen.

"No argument." Jim swung down off the table and headed out.

He made his way down to Maintenance, surprising the Sulamid lieutenant there, who was cleaning off consoles with antistat spray and five or six cloths in as many tentacles. "Break me out a suit, Mr. Athendë," Jim said. "Not a work rig; just a routine maintenance pack with a full-angle helm."

"Sir affirmative, pleased," the Sulamid said, putting down the wipes and spray. It whirled over to the measurement console while Jim stepped up on the sensor plate to let the computer read his mass and size and metabolic rate. Mr. Athendë's tentacles slipped expertly along the surface of the console for a second. "Bay twelve, sir," he said, "helm fetch one moment."

418

Jim went to the suit bay that hissed open for him, and backed into the suit held by the grapples. They did up the lower seals for him, and by the time he'd detached himself and was sealing the top of the suit, Athendë came waltzing along the suiting floor in a whirl of tentacles, some of which were holding an observer's helm, clear all around. The Sulamid put the helmet on Jim, touching its seals into place and then checking the readouts on the front of the suit. "Heat pressure astrionics positive up running," Athendë said. "Sir exit preference? Captain's gig in shuttle bay?"

"Too long evacuate," Jim said, falling into holophrasis mostly for the fun of it. "Maintenance lock."

"Scuttle chute aye," Athendë said, flushing mauve with the old pun, and whirling away to the console again to start the little "scuttling" lock cycling. It chimed green-and-ready within a few seconds.

"Gratitude, Mr. Athendë," Jim said, stepping stiffly into the lock.

"Service pleasant, Captain," the Sulamid said over Kirk's helm intercom as the door slid shut between them. "Nice communication."

*??* Jim thought, not quite getting the syntax on that last statement, as little by little air and sound hissed out of the lock around him. Oh well. He was left little time to wonder; the door into space opened as he turned to it. Jim took hold of one side of the lock and jumped out, pushing himself free of the lock's light gravity and out into the cold dark.

No sounds now but his own breathing and the gentle creaking of the suit as it made the best compromise it could between the near-absolute-zero of outside and the 24° C within. *We can fly out of the galaxy,* he thought to himself, *but we can't build a suit that won't creak like old bones and make you look like a gorilla. What's Fleet coming to these days, anyway?* He laughed at himself, and at the silly cavil, as he punched the controls for the propulsion pack. Thrust pushed him strongly in the lower back, away from the great dim wall he hung beside.

On purpose he restrained himself from looking around on the way out, wanting to save the view for just the right moment. This proved difficult, for something was missing: the stars. The million familiar eyes that had always stared at him before were gone, leaving a darkness that unnerved him, and drew his eyes. But he refused to be drawn.

Jim turned up the heat—it was getting chill in the suit—and applied reverse thrust about a hundred meters from *Enterprise,* bringing himself around to look at her. Silhouetting her from far behind, the Lesser Magellanic was a bright spill of blue gems falling together through the empty night. The ship herself lay becalmed with only minimal running lights up, so that except for a red gleam here and there she was mostly a great shadowy shape floating in the void, with only a thin skin of faint starlight defining her hull on this side.

She looked mysterious, numinous, huger than ever. She made Jim think of that time he'd been night diving off the coast of northern California, and had been surprised in moonlit water by the whale. The humpback had hung beside him, singing-saying something in that incredibly complex language the scientists said bore the same resemblance to human speech that a Beethoven symphony does to a kazoo solo. Then, uncomprehending and uncomprehended, the whale had cruised off about its lawful occasions, leaving Jim to feel he had been examined, accepted, and left to his own devices. He felt that way now. The *Enterprise* of his vision, "alive" and familiar and solicitous of her children, was gone—replaced by a remote, unconcerned entity, more an absence than a presence. She floated untroubled in the freezing dark, in her element. She belonged here. *He* was the stranger.

Deliberately, then, as if turning away from even her slight safety, Jim brought himself about to look at what cast the starlight on her hull. And the view was very different from the vista available on the observation deck, where one was snug inside a ship.

There it hung above him. A galaxy, *the* galaxy, not shut safely outside a clearsteel window, not even nearby any longer, but more distant than the Magellanic; a bright-shored island hanging grand and silent in the airless wastes, displaying all of its starry majesty at once. Jim just drifted there, letting himself see. Sol was lost in the sweep of stars in the leftward arm, an utterly insignificant 24th-magnitude spark that not even the great ten-meter Artemis/Luna reflector could have made out at this range. The whole Federation, from the Orionis worlds to the Vela Congeries, was a patch of sparkle that an upraised finger could cover. The Klingon and Romulan empires were lost entirely—

Awe grew in him again, and a muted joy; but also an increasingly powerful disquiet, so strong that inside the suit Jim simply shook for a moment. The world that all his life had been around him, was suddenly outside him—and he was outside *it,* way out in the coldest deeps where no star shone. Jim gazed in uneasy wonder at the little spiral-shaped home of life, with all its lights left burning in the dark. It finally sank in, as it hadn't even after the first jump, what he'd done to himself and the people he commanded. He'd gone too far, this time. He and four hundred thirty-eight souls were truly where no man had gone before, alone as no one in history had ever been. It delighted him. It terrified him. His voice sounded loud in the helm as, meaning it, he whispered that old phrase he'd read first in Anglish: "O Lord, Thy sea is so great, and my vessel so small. . . ."

And the shaking and the awe went away, for that brought him to the matter he had come out here to resolve.

It wasn't his crew's feelings about the danger of this situation that concerned Jim. The great starships' crews were selected with the danger of their missions in mind. No one made it onto a starship who didn't have one very important trait—an insatiable hunger and love for strange new worlds and "impossible" occurrences; a hunger so powerful that even the fear of death could be set aside for its sake when necessary. *Enterprise* and her sister starships were crewed by raving xenophiles.

What *was* on Jim's mind was potential loss of life—or in this case, the permanent discontinuation of it. As usual, he had to get past that issue so that he could choose what to do. It wasn't easy. All the other times that he'd almost lost the *Enterprise* came back to haunt him now, neatly summed up in the thought of his whole ship "going out— bang!—just like a candle." Once again Jim faced his responsibility for four hundred thirty-eight beings, some of whom he'd come to love dearly. This time, though, there was also the small matter of the whole galaxy he was looking at, and all other galaxies everywhere, "going out" in the same way he feared the *Enterprise* would—ceasing to be, forever.

Jim's first thought, after the loathing that instantly followed the idea of risking the lives of his officers and friends for *anything,* was that their lives were a small price to pay for the continued wellbeing of every other life in the universe. But (whether they would agree with him or not) that was a kneejerk reaction, a position as potentially immoral as its opposite—that all a universe's lives could or should be sacrificed for the sake of four hundred. It didn't necessarily follow that the needs of the many outweighed the needs of the few, or the one; that was a choice that could be ethically made only if the "one" was your own self. What proof was there, after all, that four hundred souls outweighed four trillion—or the other way around? Trying to equate numbers with value was a blind alley—nothing but one more way to avoid making a responsible choice.

Once when he was younger, he had seriously considered sacrificing a whole universe-to-be for the love of another human being. He wasn't that person any more. Another question occupied Jim today. When he and his crew signed aboard the *Enterprise,* they had all sworn to serve her purpose—the defense and preservation of life, and the expansion of life's quality by exploration and discovery. The question was simply, how could they serve that purpose best? By hurrying home with word of the breach in their universe, and letting Starfleet find an answer—one that might be better than any *Enterprise* could come up with unassisted? Or by attempting to deal with the situation on their own, and sending back word of how they did?

*Are you kidding? Don't you ever learn? They'll treat the results of the drive the same way they did the drive itself. They'll give it to a committee. The universe'll have been eaten by anentropia before they even manage to pick who the committee chairman will be. Besides, K't'lk is the expert on this stuff, and we've got her right here. And the Federation would just send out for some Vulcans, anyway. If you want Vulcans, you've got one, and he seems to know what's going on—*

More reasons and rationalizations of that sort kept coming up. After a minute or two Jim put a stop to them and pushed them all aside. Totaling up the arguments on either side of a situation to see what outnumbered what was no way to choose, either; if you tried to treat the universe as a sum, no matter how carefully you added it up, the answer was always an irrational number. Nor was the cool guidance of logic a reliable refuge. "Logical alternatives" had been the death of many a starship captain and crew before.

Jim held still and spent a moment just looking at the whole problem, in the form of the bright-burning home that hung before him—symbol of all the uncountable lives that lay in his hands, symbol of his responsibility to them. Then he put all the reasons aside, all the hopes, all the fears, and chose.

He glanced at his chrono. It had taken him seven minutes.

Jim touched the communication toggle on one sleeve. "Kirk to *Enterprise.*"

*"Bridge,"* said Uhura.

"I thought you were offshift."

*"You went for a walk,"* she said, as if that should have been explanation enough.

"I did that. Have Sulu and Chekov work out that course for the anomaly with Spock," Jim said. "And tell McCoy to speak to the department heads so each of you can warn your crew. This next step is going to be a doozie."

*"Coming in now, sir?"*

"Just a few more minutes, mother. Kirk out." He switched off to the sound of her decorously stifled laughter.

He drifted in the dark and the silence awhile longer, gazing at the mighty spiral, now so small, and then at the *Enterprise,* seemingly huger, but just as still. He began to get a glimpse of what that Andorian crewwoman had meant so long ago; that apparent size was indeed a symbol, as irrelevant to the essentials it contained as someone's height—McCoy's, say—was to the quality of his soul. It was the inner nature that counted—the meaning, not the matter; and even then, as K't'lk had said, what mattered was who was doing the meaning. Everything was the same size, really, until consciousness endowed that size with affect. If the "sea" seemed huge, and his vessel small, and the radiant galaxy infinitely beautiful, it was because he saw them, and loved them, that way—

Jim snorted at himself in mockery. (Getting sentimental in your old age,) he thought, and turned himself with care, aiming himself back at the *Enterprise.*

But he stole a last long look over his shoulder before he cut in his jets.

"Is the crew ready?—Good. Then take us out, Mr. Sulu."

"Yes, sir. Engineering—implement inversion."

"And God have mercy on our souls," McCoy muttered from behind the command chair.

## *The Entropy Effect,* by Vonda N. McIntyre

Suppose there was a time you felt that you should have been born to, and the technology existed to send you to that time permanently? Would you do it? Would you worry about the effects on the people left behind, or the fabric of space and time? Dr. Georges Mordreaux, a former physics professor of Spock's, discovered how to send his friends into the past on a one-way trip. They did not concern themselves with the effects on the universe left behind, but there were devastating repercussions. Mordreaux was accused of murder and unauthorized experimentation on sentient beings; even worse, space and time began to unravel, and entropy, the heat death of the universe, accelerated dramatically.

As the story began, Spock was studying a naked singularity when the ship was called away to transport Mordreaux to prison. The authorities considered him to be so dangerous that a starship was required to keep him secure. Havoc ensued, with multiple versions of Dr. Mordreaux materializing from different time streams, showing increasing signs of madness. One of them murdered Captain Kirk, and Spock was accused of complicity. Spock was the only person who understood what was happening, though, and he took great risks to go back in time over and over again to try to stop earlier versions of Mordreaux from continuing his experiments.

*The Entropy Effect* is a fascinating and exciting science fiction story, well worth reading again and again. Someday, I might even understand the physics! This passage is from the beginning of the story, as Spock faced the horrifying discovery that the rate of entropy was accelerating to the point where the universe would end within his lifetime.

CAPTAIN JAMES T. KIRK SPRAWLED ON THE COUCH IN THE SITTING ROOM OF his cabin, dozing over a book. The lights flickered and he woke abruptly, startled by the momentary power failure and by the simultaneous lurch in the *Enterprise*'s gravity. The main shields strained to the limits of their strength, drawing all available power in order to protect ship and crew from the almost incalculable radiation of another X-ray storm.

Kirk forced himself to relax, but he still felt uneasy, as if he should be doing something. But there was nothing he *could* do, and he knew it. His ship lay in orbit around a naked singularity, the first and only one ever discovered, and Mr. Spock was observing, measuring, and analyzing it, trying to deduce why it had appeared, suddenly and mysteriously, out of nowhere. The Vulcan science officer had been at his task nearly six weeks now; he was almost finished.

Kirk was not too pleased at having to expose the *Enterprise* to the radiation, the gravity waves, and the twists and turns of space itself. But the work was critical: spreading like a huge carcinoma, the singularity straddled a major warp-space lane. More important, though: if one singularity could appear without warning, so might another. The next one might not simply disarrange interstellar commerce. The next one might writhe into existence near an inhabited planet, and wipe out every living thing on its surface.

Kirk glanced at the screen of his communications terminal, which he had been leaving focussed on the singularity. As the *Enterprise* arced across one of the poles, the energy storm intensified. Dust swirled down toward the puncture in the continuum, disintegrating into energy. The light that he could see, the wavelengths in the visible spectrum, formed only the smallest part of the furious radiation that pounded at his ship.

The forces, shifts, and tidal stresses troubled everyone in the crew; everyone was snappish and bored despite the considerable danger they were in. Nothing would change until Mr. Spock completed his observations.

Spock could have done the work all by himself in a solo ship—if a solo ship were able to withstand the singularity's distortion of space. But it could not, so Spock needed the *Enterprise.* Yet Spock was the only being essential to this mission. That was the worst thing about the entire job: no one was afraid of facing peril, but there was no way to control it or fight it or overcome it. They had nothing to do but wait until it was over.

Kirk thought, with unfocussed gratitude, that at least he could begin to think of the assignment in terms of hours rather than weeks or days. Like the rest of the crew, he would be glad when it was finished.

"Captain Kirk?"

Kirk reached out and opened the channel. The image of the singularity faded out and Lieutenant Uhura appeared on the screen.

"Yes, Lieutenant?—Uhura, what's wrong?"

"We're receiving a subspace transmission, Captain. It's scrambled—"

"Put it through. What's the code?"

"Ultimate, sir."

He sat up abruptly. "Ultimate!"

"Yes, sir, ultimate override, from mining colony Aleph Prime. It came through once, then cut off before it could repeat." She glanced at her instruments and fed the recording to his terminal.

"Thank you, Lieutenant."

The unscrambling key came up out of his memory unbidden. He was prohibited from keeping a written record of it. He was not even allowed to enter it into the ship's computer for automatic decoding. With pencil and paper, he began the laborious job of transforming the jumble of letters and symbols until they sorted themselves out into a coherent message.

In the observatory of the *Enterprise,* Mr. Spock stared thoughtfully at his computer's readout. It still did not show anything like what he had expected. He wanted to go through the preliminary analysis again, but it was nearly time to take another instrument reading. He was most anxious to obtain as many extremely accurate observational points as possible.

Since he was to report to Starfleet, and Starfleet was based on Earth, Spock thought about the naked singularity in terms of Earth's scientific traditions. The theories of Tipler and of Penrose were, in fact, the most useful in analyzing the phenomenon. So far, however, Spock had found no explanation for the abrupt appearance of a naked singularity. He expected it to behave in a peculiar fashion, but it was behaving even more peculiarly than theory predicted. The interstellar dust that it was sucking up should cause it to form an event horizon, but it was doing no such thing. If the singularity was growing at all, it was expanding into and through dimensions Spock could not even observe.

But Spock *had* discovered something. The wave functions that described the singularity contained entropic terms such as he had never seen before, terms so unusual they surprised even him.

Many scientific discoveries occur when the observer notices an unexpected, unlikely, even apparently impossible event, and follows it up rather than discarding it as nonsense. Spock was aware of this, never so much as now.

If the first analysis of the data held up in replication, the results would spread shock waves throughout the entire scientific community, and into the public consciousness as well. *If* the first analysis held up: it was possible that he had made a mistake, or even that the design of his apparatus was causing unsuspected error.

Spock sat down at his instruments, centered and focussed them, and checked the adjustments.

The *Enterprise* approached a gap in the accretion sphere around the singularity, a region where the X-ray storms ebbed abruptly and an observer could stare down into the eerily featureless mystery that twisted space and time and reason.

But as Spock's battery of measuring devices scanned the singularity, the *Enterprise* suddenly and without warning accelerated to full power, ploughed back into the disintegrating matter and energy, burst through to deep space, and fled toward the stars.

Spock slowly rose to his feet, unable to believe what had happened. For weeks the *Enterprise* had withstood the chaotic twists and turns of spatial dimension: now, so close to the end of his observations, the whole second series of measurements was destroyed. He needed the replication, for all alternate possibilities had to be ruled out. The ramifications of what he had discovered were tremendous.

426

If his preliminary conclusions were correct, the expected life of the universe was not thousands of millions of years.

It was, for all practical purposes, less than a century.

The *Enterprise* sped through interstellar space at a warp factor that badly strained the already overworked engines.

At least Mr. Sulu got us out of there with his usual precision, Jim Kirk thought, sitting at his place on the bridge trying to appear calmer than he felt. He had never responded to an ultimate override before.

The door of the turbolift slid open, and, for the first time in weeks, Mr. Spock came onto the bridge. He had hardly left the observatory since they first reached the singularity. The Vulcan science officer descended to the lower level, stopped beside Kirk, and simply gazed at him, impassively.

"Mr. Spock . . ." Kirk said, "I received an ultimate override command. I know you haven't finished your work, but the *Enterprise* had to respond. I have no choice, with an ultimate. I'm very sorry, Mr. Spock."

"An ultimate override command . . ." Spock said. His expression did not change, but Kirk thought he looked rather haggard. All things considered, that was not too surprising.

"Can you salvage anything from your data? Could you reach any conclusion about the singularity at all?"

Spock gazed at the viewscreen. Far ahead, indistinguishable as yet against the brilliant starfield, an ordinary yellow type G star hung waiting for them. Behind them, the singularity lay within its fierce glow.

"The preliminary conclusions were interesting," Spock said. He clasped his hands behind his back. "However, without the completed replication, the data are all essentially worthless."

Kirk muttered a curse, and said again, lamely, "I'm sorry."

"I can see no way in which you are responsible, Captain, nor any logical reason for you to apologize."

Kirk sighed. As always, Spock refused to react to adversity.

It would be a relief if just once he'd put his fist through a bulkhead, Jim Kirk thought. If this doesn't turn out to be extremely serious, I may find something to punch, myself.

"Are you all right, Mr. Spock?" he asked. "You look exhausted."

"I am all right, Captain."

"You could go get some rest—it'll be quite a while before we get close enough to Aleph for me to call general quarters. Why don't you take a nap?"

"Impossible, Captain."

"The bridge really can get along without you for a few more hours."

"I realize that, sir. However, when I began my experiment I psychophysiologically altered my metabolism to permit me to remain alert during the course of my observations. I could return my circadian rhythm to normal now, but it does not seem sensible, to me, to prepare myself for rest when my presence may be required when we reach our destination."

Kirk sorted through the technicalities of his science officer's statement.

"Spock," he said, "you aren't saying you haven't had any sleep in six weeks, are you?"

"No, Captain."

"Good," Kirk said, relieved; and, after a pause, "Then what *are* you saying?"

"It will not be six standard weeks until day after tomorrow."

"Good lord! Didn't you trust anyone else to make the observations?"

"It was not a matter of trust, Captain. The data are sensitive. The difference between two individuals' interpretations of the same datum would cause a break in the observational curve larger than the experimental error."

"You couldn't have run several series and averaged them?"

Spock raised one eyebrow, "No, Captain."

If I didn't know better, Kirk thought, I'd swear he turned a couple of shades paler.

Captain's log, Stardate 5001.1:

We are now a day away from the singularity, but the unease that gripped the *Enterprise* and my crew throughout our mission there has not faded. It has intensified. We have left one mystery behind us, unsolved, in order to confront a second mystery, about which we know even less. The ultimate override emergency command takes precedence over any other order. The *Enterprise* is now under way to the mining colony Aleph Prime, maintaining radio silence as the code requires. I cannot even *ask* why we have been diverted; I can only speculate about the reasons for such urgency, and be sure my crew is prepared to face . . . what?

428

# *First Frontier,* by Diane Carey and
# Dr. James L. Kirkland

The future meets the past and Star Trek encounters dinosaurs in *First Frontier,* by Diane Carey and Dr. James L. Kirkland. This novel is Dr. Kirkland's first Star Trek book, although he has published many works in his field. Dr. Kirkland is a paleontologist; he studies dinosaurs, and he is a Star Trek fan. When Ms. Carey contacted Dr. Kirkland about an article he had written, he shared an idea for a Star Trek related dinosaur story, and the rest is Star Trek history.

In *First Frontier,* the *Enterprise* was caught in a cosmic string. While trapped in the string, they were temporarily outside of normal space and time. When they emerged, they learned that the universe had changed, that the Federation no longer existed, and that Earth was populated only by animals. What is more, the Earth showed signs of having undergone nuclear upheaval. On this changed Earth, the asteroid impact that had wiped out the dinosaurs never occurred. Instead, intelligent dinosaurs evolved into sentient dinosaurs and developed cultures and civilizations. The dinosaurs, though, were victims of their violent and predatory instincts, and their civilizations ended in nuclear conflagration. They never reached the stars.

Forced to solve the mystery of how the asteroid collision was prevented, the *Enterprise* raced to the Guardian Planet through a galaxy devoid of human influence. Using the Guardian of Forever, Kirk and his crew journeyed back in time to just before the cataclysm to prevent the diversion of the asteroid.

*First Frontier* is one of the most exciting of The Original Series novels and my favorite of Diane Carey's books. It has everything: life and death struggles, intelligent dinosaurs, time travel, heroes under fire, space battles, and the Guardian of Forever. Dr. Kirkland and Ms. Carey also designed a fascinating culture for the evolved raptors that takes into account their aggressive and violent nature. The raptors' constant struggle to maintain their intelligence against their drive for blood controlled their destiny. The answer to the question of what kind of civilization dinosaurs could have created had the cataclysm not occurred was a sad one for them.

In the following passage from *First Frontier,* Kirk and his crew discovered the enormity of the changes on the Earth.

THE MASSIVE ANIMAL'S HOWL WAS COUNTERPLAYED BY THE WHINE OF Starfleet phasers.

Why wasn't it going down? The phaser was designed to neutral-ize—suddenly the night sky wobbled. The black-on-black mass shuddered, tilted to one side, dropped partially down, then all the way down with a great *humph.* The bushes snapped, and other animals, unseen in the darkness, skittered out of the way.

With a huge breath, the animal gave up the fight and lay heaving in a clearing its own weight had just created. Breath after breath, it huffed the proclamation that it wasn't down for good.

Kirk rolled onto his side, then forced himself up onto his knees, grabbed a handful of branches, and pulled himself up. Fighting to catch his breath, he pushed through the bushes toward where he had last seen McCoy.

"Bones! Spock! Where are you?"

About ten yards away, Spock rose from the overgrowth, dragging McCoy to his feet.

Kirk tried to knee his way through the brush to them. "You all right?"

"Yes, sir," Spock said, but he seemed a little surprised.

"Bones?"

Stumbling to his feet, Leonard McCoy staggered to the stunned creature and circled it, keeping clear of the twitches of sharp cloven hooves. He breathed heavily as he lifted each of his legs high and made a series of little jumps that brought him to the animal that had nearly gored Spock. "Captain, take a look at this!"

The creature was massive—the size of a buffalo. In fact, it had the thick hide and hair of a buffalo, four-toed hooves of a rhino, but also a wide sweeping horn arching out from a faceplate, and a neck crest that must have been five feet across. The creature's tiny eyes rolled, a leg twitched, but otherwise it lay still, heaving.

McCoy reached for the frilled edge of the neck crest and shook it. It barely moved. Just the neck and head were the size of a Starfleet cargo crate. He fingered the animal's hair.

"Look at this—it's hairlike, but it's not hair. It's insulation of some kind . . . probably developed in response to an ice age."

"Most insulation evolved from scales," Spock said. "Some mam-mallike reptiles developed true hair; some flying reptiles, a hairlike material; and some small meat-eating prehistoric animals may—"

"Look, I *know* there's never been anything like this on Earth!" McCoy wheezed. "Prehistoric or otherwise!"

Without wasting time on pointless arguments, Kirk snapped up his communicator. "Spock, who's the zoologist?"

"Lieutenant LaCerra is senior zoologist and paleontologist, sir, just transferred from the science vessel *John Rockland*. Lieutenant Ling is—"

"Kirk to LaCerra."

The communicator buzzed faintly. When no response came, he switched frequencies. "Kirk to *Enterprise*."

*"Lieutenant Dewey here, sir."*

"Where's Uhura?"

*"Off watch, sir, but, she's down in engineering trying to sort out the communications dysfunctions."*

He drew a stiff breath. Reassurance washed through him that martial structure was still in play, watches were still being maintained, and all the time-honored, traditional, systematic orderliness that kept a ship's crew from cracking under pressure were still in operation, even in the bowels of catastrophe.

"Dewey, contact Chief Barnes and get me Lieutenant LaCerra. Have her beamed directly here. I've got an animal I want her to look at."

*"Aye, sir. Stand by, please."*

Keeping his communicator grid open, Kirk fingered the controls of the phaser in his other hand. The smell of the heaving animal at their feet was enough to choke a dead horse. "Both of you, put phasers on kill. Obviously we can't anticipate the usual North American wildlife we've been used to. Either of you have a theory about this thing?"

"It appears to be a slow-moving grazer," Spock said. "Possibly related to the woolly mammoth—"

"Or a rhinoceros," McCoy added. "Or a stegosaurus! Look at this tail!" He reached into the grass and came up with both arms coiled around a shocker of an extra weapon: a tail as big around as a man's rib cage, armed with a single-rowed rack of flesh-colored spikes the size of swords.

"Incredible!" Kirk limped through the grass and put his hand on one of the spikes.

"I'd categorize this creature as ceratopsoid," Spock said. He ran his tricorder over the smelly, fly-clouded mass. "Large bony cranial frill plate protecting heavy neck and shoulders. . . . Forward-mounted facial horn. . . . Massive low-hanging head, but with a blunt snout, squared off for grazing, though most ceratopsoids had parrot-like beaks."

Making a passing wave at the flies, he knelt beside the animal's huge head. "To my knowledge there has never been a creature like this on the Great Northern Plains, even in prehistory. There are antlered animals here, but none with horns."

"Or there *should* be none. Spock, reanalyze. Have we retreated in time?"

Spock peered through him in the darkness, and his tone was solid. "Absolutely not, Captain."

"All right . . . what took it so long to go down under phaser-stun?"

"Thickness of the hide," McCoy said, "and we might have been hitting that horn or the neck crest. I'd guess it acted as a buffer."

Kirk licked his dry lips. "We're dealing with an Earth whose weather and topography are right, but nothing else. Spock, are you thinking what I'm thinking?"

"I believe so." Spock straightened up.

Limping toward the brink of the cliff, Kirk looked over the open hills, at the empty bay, and listened to the distant whistle of birds that he didn't recognize.

Slowly, he murmured, "Alternative evolution . . ."

"Louise, just back away from it—real slowly."

"Look at its eyes, Dale. That's binocular vision! I just want to get a little closer so my tricorder can pick up the retinal structure. I can't believe what I'm seeing! All the traits of a mammal, but green and yellow abutting scales instead of skin—that's no mammal."

"I'm keeping my phaser trained on it."

"The striped pattern provides camouflage for stalking in tall grass or undergrowth . . . Some large cats developed that kind of pattern— tigers, leopards . . ."

"Louise, I'm not sure of my aim in the dark. At least let's tranquilize it, will ya?"

"Can you believe this? It's stalking me! Just like a mammal. . . . Come on, baby, come on . . ."

"Quit that. You're making it follow you. That's it. I'm gonna call Chief Barnes."

"Shh. Don't distract it. Have you got its body temperature? Dale, put the damn communicator down and take some readings! Your tricorder is rigged for microbiology. Mine's not."

"Look, I don't—I don't think . . . All right, but just stay away from it."

"It's nowhere near me. Take the readings. We might not get another chance. Come on, baby . . . Move those pretty yellow legs for Lou—"

"You're backing toward high grass. Don't go in there."

"Shut up, Dale. Look at those wild eyes . . . I can't wait to dissect those—"

"Lou, it's darting! It's running! Lou, run!"

"Take the readings! Take the—"

"Lou, don't go into the grass! Get out of the grass! Oh, God! Look out! Louise, run! Run! Run! Oh, God! Oh, my God! Louise!"

Leonard McCoy squinted as he absorbed what he was seeing. "Yellow poppies . . ."

The three men stood staring heavily at the sulfur curtain draping the moonlit hillsides for miles into the distance.

McCoy's whisper made a terrible din.

Ostriches, primates where they shouldn't be, living shellfish that should be dead, massive land animals that shouldn't be here in the first place—

Now it had been said. Plagued by the image of McCoy gazing down at his daughter's house, now committed to the veils of memory, Kirk thought of his mother's farm and what Iowa would look like in this condition. He thought of the man-made pond behind the barn that his father had stocked with trout and bass for the Kirk boys to catch.

Nothing but dry grass. Maybe a mud slick at the bottom of that hill.

Funny . . . the hill was probably still there.

A bare hill, no farmhouse, no road leading back to the old settled conclave of Riverside. No thousand memories. No sandy-haired mother in stalwart, eternal mourning for an irascible Starfleet Security man who had gone through the cold window of enemy space and never returned.

A boy without a trout, a hill without a farmhouse. A wild, lonely world.

Jim Kirk endured a moment of random pain and choked his sorrow down. He looked up.

Spock and McCoy were both looking at him.

He started to pace, though it shot his leg and spine with torture every other step. "Whether we like it or not, we have to accept that we've been through some kind of warping effect. It's happened before."

The Vulcan's expression betrayed his racing thoughts. "That forejudgment may be premature, sir."

"May be too obvious, you mean?"

Spock snapped a look at him, gratified. "Yes, sir."

Kirk hobbled toward the huffing animal, his voice hardly more than a choke. "What did we do?"

"Jim," McCoy interrupted, "how do you know we did anything?"

He turned to his doctor. "Because," he said, "we're here."

The statement fell on the shimmering remnants of sunset and was consumed. Spock didn't say anything, but the captain could tell that his intuitive officer found no remedy in that conclusion. Cold with deep mortal panic that somehow he had gummed up the universe by botching one experiment, Kirk felt his throat knot up. Every man at some time in his life wonders if things would be better off without him. As a starship captain, his successes and certainly his blunders had always been magnified. This, though—he could barely grasp the scope.

"If we went back and shot Adam and Eve, it wouldn't affect this much," Kirk pressed. "These bizarre animals can't be just the result of lack of humans. The sky is filled with birds, just as it always has been."

"Evidently," Spock said, "even here they outcompeted the flying reptiles."

"We're not that sure of the science we've been tampering with. Somehow we caused ourselves to jump into a parallel universe or caused our own universe to change." As an embedded chill gripped his spine, he limped between his two officers and looked over the undeveloped landscape. "What if we're not lost . . . but humanity is? It's one thing to accept that we've marooned ourselves interdimensionally, but if we've destroyed the civilization around us . . . I feel damned obliged to fix it."

The statement fell on the broad glazed bay. He started to say something else but chopped his own thoughts away with a motion that whipped his communicator up. It chittered at him. "Kirk here," he barked before the instrument was finished making its sound. "What's the problem with that beam-over?" Frustration rolled through his limbs and tightened them. He determined to win out over the poison in his body if he had to dig for leeches and bleed himself—if there were still leeches. And he would make a decision, no matter how bitter, if he could stitch together a theory. Forward movement of any kind—would he have to strangle a wild guess out of Spock?

*"Barnes here, sir . . ."*

"Barnes, what's going on with the zoologist?"

*"Bannon just came up from the valley floor, sir. Is it possible for you to beam over here?"*

"Why?" Kirk demanded.

*"Captain,"* Barnes's voice croaked over the distance between them, *"Lieutenant LaCerra's been killed, sir."*

\* \* \*

434

"We killed about . . . half of them, sir. But they got to LaCerra before we could drive them off. Some of them went that way . . . Sir, if you'd come with me."

Chief Chemist Barnes's uniform had been shredded in several places, leaving ragsicles dripping all over his chest and loose threads clinging like vines around what was left of his trouserlegs. McCoy was eyeing the bloody streaks on the man's arms and chest but didn't try to get between him and the captain yet.

"Anybody else hurt?" Kirk asked.

"Bannon's real shook up, poor kid. This way, sir."

Barnes was in a hurry but moving in a fatalistic way, as though he knew hurrying wouldn't help. He seemed more anxious to hurry himself out of the command ring and get somebody else to take over the situation.

"One of these things started to chase LaCerra," he said, huffing like a racehorse. "She tried to get away from it, but she didn't realize it was deliberately driving her into a pack of others hiding in the tall grass. There must've been eight or ten of them."

On a depressed portion of tall grass, as though fallen asleep on the brink of a pond, lay Lieutenant Louise LaCerra. She could've been dozing in the moonlight, so peaceful was her face. Her body had been slashed open from under one arm to the point of her hip, and from the underside of one breast across and down to the cup of her pelvis. Her uniform had been slit open and the material was curled back, baring the white lips of open wounds cleanly meant to disembowel—not random at all.

McCoy didn't even bother to kneel by the corpse. There just wasn't any point.

And he didn't want to get too close to that thing lying beside her.

Tucked sedately into the warm body was the clawed foot of an animal that lay beside her in a deceptive caress, a creature with skin like a snake and a face like a lizard but eyes wide open that looked like a cat's eyes. Its forepaws were gripping LaCerra's shoulder, dug in to the knuckles. Almost as long from nose to tip of its blunt tail as its prey was tall, the animal had a gaping mouth that showed rows of pointed teeth gleaming in the moonlight. Tiger-striped hide and a bare white belly were like a reptile, but certainly weren't the colors of any known Earth lizard.

And those sure weren't the eyes of a lizard.

"There are six more of those things lying around here, sir," Barnes reported, fighting his emotions down. "I mean, if you want them." He shuffled into the grass and kicked another of those animals, phasered to death, out into the open at the captain's feet. It flopped like a sack of sand. "That one next to her drove her to all these others. Then they were on her like fire ants. She never had a chance."

Kirk moved away from the animal, away from the boiling misery rising in his mind that this girl who had gone into space with spirit and bold initiative, willing to risk her life as far from Earth as a person can get, had died right here, within hiking distance of where she had been educated and trained.

He found something of a betrayal in that. He sidled toward Spock.

"A precise and coordinated attack," Spock commented, keeping his voice low. "A man eater—if you'll pardon the crude colloquialism— must be smarter, faster, and better armed than what it eats. These animals may be the smartest life-form on the planet under these conditions. They may be as intelligent as leopards, perhaps even chimpanzees. Driving prey toward an ambush is partly instinctive but definitely partly learned as a hunting technique."

"It's a sprinter," McCoy said. "Look at those long, strong hind legs. And the slashing foreclaws and ripping teeth . . . and what it did to that poor girl. These things know how to disable their targets—"

"While minimizing their own chance of injury," Spock interrupted.

"But it's not a mammal," Kirk said. He pushed down a surge of irritation at Spock for being a little too fascinated and not angry enough. "I don't see anything that's a mammal."

"They may be here," Spock suggested, "but kept in check by the creatures like this." He nodded again to the animals slaughtered in defense of a girl. "It may be interesting to transport to the Amazon region. Arboreal primates may be quite successful under these conditions."

"This isn't a field trip." Kirk spun to the other Starfleet personnel. "The rest of you have anything to put any light on this problem?"

"Yes, sir, I do. Bannon, sir," the red-haired fellow with the buck teeth said. He was trembling. "Anthropology."

"Report, Bannon."

"I've got some data here I'd like Mr. Spock to have a look at."

"Why? Just tell me what you've got."

"Well . . . because I think I've picked up trace evidence of worldwide natural catastrophe." He winced at his own words.

Bannon said "think," but he meant he was damned sure he'd picked that up and he knew he sounded like a lunatic when he reported it.

"You mean there was a civilization here?"

"That's right, sir!" Bannon shook his tricorder. "I've been tied into the ship for a half hour, and all the wide-range readings come up for an organized prehistoric civilization. Then they all . . . just up and died! Or maybe killed each other."

Kirk waved a hand impatiently. "Tell me why you think this. Spock, listen to this."

"The ship's lab is reading several layers of development up to a point," Bannon said, "both manufactured and natural, and then a cutoff, encroachment of nature, then another gradual rising of a civilization, with all the steps we'd expect, then the same cycle of destruction. All the evidence is in the center of the continents, mostly in South America and Africa, and it's several strata down. It's all been covered over, but I had them do some overlays, and we think there's evidence of wooden structures, then later a surge of sophisticated metallurgy. And above those, traces of wide-range warfare."

Kirk tried to hold on to his expression. "War? Are you sure?"

"Yes, sir, real big war. It runs in the same cycle, over and over again."

The anthropologist's ruddy face screwed into a frown. "It doesn't make any sense! There wasn't any industrial life on Earth that long ago. There wasn't even rudimentary tribal life, never mind sophisticated battle capabilities. Seismology indicates deeply embedded geological evidence of destruction on the large scale . . . possibly nuclear!"

"Well," McCoy blurted, "now we know what happened to the redwoods."

Suddenly angry that there wasn't the hum of a city beyond the crackle of crickets and the whistle of birds, Kirk pressed his lips tight. "How old is this evidence of destruction?"

Bannon managed to keep his voice steady. "On the order of ten to twenty million years."

McCoy pushed toward them. "That's ridiculous!"

"Much earlier than tribal hominids," Spock said.

"So it certainly wasn't a human war," Kirk snapped. "Could someone have colonized the planet and made all those wars?" He turned. "Chief Barnes, what do you have to say about the atmospheric chemistry?"

"Not much, sir," the older man said. "It reads just as Earth atmosphere should read under these . . . apparent conditions. No trace pollutants from early fossil fuel usage, at least not on the surface, and no artificial sculpting of land masses."

"No evidence of space travel?"

Barnes's reddened eyes widened. "No, sir, nothing like that."

"Doesn't mean it didn't happen . . . after ten million years," Kirk said, "anything could clean itself out."

Spock scanned Bannon's tricorder screen. "Preliminary sensor sweeps confirm radiation abnormalities at different places in different strata all over the Earth. We call these 'welded-glass horizons.' The ecology rebounded in every instance, though there were at least four major periods of continentwide obliteration. Given enough time, nature always rebounds. With new forms of life, of course, but it does rebound. Many of these animals may be the result of radiation."

In the deep background, an animal—one that had never lived on this planet before—shrieked at the moon. Alien insects rattled like bacon frying.

He primed his communicator again. "Kirk to *Enterprise*."

*"Dewey, sir"*

"Launch a lighting flare, five kilometer radius. I want to see this valley floor."

*"Aye, sir, one minute."*

The sounds of the landscape were damningly familiar. The ratcheting of frogs, the chitter of neocrickets, the soft brush of breeze over long grass that was once the grass of his childhood.

*Jimmy, put down that fishing pole and get the lawn tended. You only have one thing to do, so why haven't you done it?*

And the smell of it all—the bay, the air, the grass. It played games with his mind as Kirk fought to swallow the reality of what their science told them. He felt as if he were letting go of something he would never retrieve. He'd had this feeling since the *Exeter* and *Farragut* disappeared, and he'd seen it in his crew's faces. The creased eyes, the pursed lips, the guarded fear that something had happened that they couldn't correct, that finally tampering with science on too big a scale had exacted too big a price.

Mankind had run that risk for a long time. Had they gone one step too far? Had he given one order too many?

"There it is, sir!" Barnes shouted, pointing almost directly over his head.

In the slate sky, even smaller than the stars, was a moving pinprick. They watched as it wobbled and spiraled, changing its path with the vagaries of the stratosphere, drifting this way, then that, volleyballed by thermals that argued above the water and land.

Then the flare's altitude trigger kicked in, and it popped—they could almost hear the *crack*—and a sizzling strobelike light burst

438

over the entire valley floor, nearly five miles across. Suddenly the planet was like an old-time movie, cast in gray and opal, and a black wedge of San Francisco Bay anchoring the farthest point.

Startled heads rose over the grass, huge heads with six-foot horns, neck plates, and tiny eyes.

Beyond that, two long-necked relics placidly chewing stalks they had pulled from a tree. They might have been giraffes, except that their heads were smooth and elongated. Their bright white-and-yellow necks arched, long throats constantly working, thick balancing tails lapping slowly from side to side, and spindly legs poised in place. They were patently disinterested in the sudden brightness or the odd little observers way over here. They froze in place and stared but continued to chew.

An ungodly racket far to the left went up like a cannon shot. A pack of LaCerra's new-age banshees were cornering a slothlike animal with a leathery face and a forejaw that lanced downward as a weapon instead of front teeth. It hacked downward again and again now that it could see what was attacking it, then screamed as the relentless predators ganged in on it. Some distracted it while others plunged in and ripped its spine open. Suddenly all Kirk could think of was the girl he'd failed to protect.

Half the banshees kept hacking away with their foreclaws, ignoring the light that had whacked on overhead and was wobbling on the thermals, but the other half were shocked by it and their intelligent minds told them to beat it. Kirk watched them pause, look, squint, try to make the decision between fear and famine. Some even looked at the light, then at the prey, then at the light again.

About a third of those ran away. The rest decided to ignore the hovering white light and feast on that which they had so diligently pursued.

There was the evidence, plain as—day. Creatures swept with instinct, consumed by raw nature, yet smart enough to make a conscious choice. They were on their way to being able to *think*.

Creatures with skin like snakes and minds like leopards.

The flare would have kept lighting the landscape for six or eight more minutes, but a sharp puff of inland wind blasted it out over the water, and the sudden lack of thermals brought it crashing into the bay with an audible *fizzzzz*. The last they saw of it was a thread of smoke twisting toward the moon. Darkness fell in again.

A few feet away, someone sighed heavily. Someone else made a worried *whew*. But no one actually said anything.

James Kirk and his crew stood listening to the snapping of bones and the arguing of smart predators. They might as well be standing on a planet millions of light-years from here.

"All hands," Kirk said, "collect any specimens or information you need right now. We're leaving. You have ten minutes. Stay together."

A cloud of miserable "Aye ayes" rose and dropped away.

The captain moved to the edge of the mesa. He absorbed the slate sky, called with his mind to the empty enameled bay, listened to the shuffles of his command as they gathered what they could.

"This is like a dream inside a nightmare," McCoy sighed. "A pleasant place, decent weather, nice sky . . . on a forgotten planet."

"We haven't forgotten it," Kirk snapped. "Something's wrong. I'll fix it if I can figure out how."

He limped a few feet away to the brink of a hillock and peered through the trees at a sliver of San Francisco Bay. His eyes felt as though they would pop out if he held his breath.

"Earth," he uttered. "The cornerstone of the Federation . . . completely barren of intelligent life."

"This has been the wish of countless human beings for centuries," McCoy said. "A pristine Earth, untouched by the hands of men, free to grow, live at its own pace—"

"Only the wish of those who regard intelligence as a contaminant," Kirk defended. "I don't. This is beautiful, yes, but our Earth was beautiful, too. There are trees and animals by the millions there, too. This . . . it's not all that different from the Earth we know. The same trees, the same grass, the same deserts, not in much different amounts. Mankind isn't a plague on Earth, any more than the Federation is a plague in space. We of all people should be ready to admit we've done some good out there. Humanity is part of nature. Without people, this is an empty, savage, unappreciated place."

Silence coiled around the drained thoughts.

"I agree," Spock said.

McCoy turned to look at him. "You do?"

"Of course."

"I wouldn't have expected that from you, Spock. You're usually so quick to point out humanity's bad judgments—anytime anyone points out to you that you're half human, you feel obliged to be ashamed."

"Bones," Kirk said, "leave him alone."

Everything about Spock was suddenly understated, yet poignant in his alien way. He seemed heavy-laden, deeply disturbed, more than either of his companions would have expected. He specialized in taking even the wildest of occurrences in stride, fielding all the unimaginables of space travel with grace, working by the book, taking things one at a time—well, fifty at a time but in logical order.

Tonight he was different. Finally he visibly let his guard down a little and blinked into the flames. "A world without intelligence is a primitive place, Doctor, not an enchanted place. Intelligence is part of the advancing scheme of evolution. Without it, nature reaches a plateau very quickly and does not progress beyond raw survival. The full flavor of possibility goes unsavored. And that . . . is a true shame."

McCoy offered a grin. "Well, I'll be."

Beyond the tiny opal solace of the moon was a moist landscape dotted with pockets of fog.

Kirk raised his eyes again to the dark and chirping landscape, and his mind leaped ahead. "I feel like I'm staring at an accident where somebody died. Am I punch-drunk? Am I still in that coma?"

"If you are, Jim," McCoy said, "we're in it with you."

## *Assignment: Eternity,* by Greg Cox

Star Trek viewers were first introduced to Gary Seven in "Assignment Earth," an Original Series episode in which, despite interference by Kirk and company, Seven helped humans survive their nuclear age. Seven was accompanied by Isis, a black cat with an interesting shape-changing talent, and Roberta Lincoln, a twentieth-century woman with an interesting attitude. Author Greg Cox brought Gary Seven and his companions back in *Assignment: Eternity.* Seven hijacked the *Enterprise* for a mission deep within Romulan territory, but Kirk did not take kindly to his actions and thwarted him at every move. After Kirk made it impossible for Seven to complete his mission, Seven finally informed him that the Romulans had discovered the Aegis's installation in Romulan space and captured Supervisor 146, also known as Septos. The Tal Shiar commander, Dellas, tortured Septos for information about the time travel device. Her mission was to travel forward in time to assassinate Spock at the Khitomer conference and change the course of galactic history.

*Assignment: Eternity* is an engrossing read from beginning to end. Seven could have avoided the conflict with Kirk over control of the *Enterprise* by communicating with Kirk a bit earlier in the process. On the other hand, the more Kirk learned about the future, the greater the risk of alteration of the timeline. Roberta and Spock experienced a similar process on the ship, with Roberta providing some comic relief by conducting a sit-in on the bridge. Isis also did her part by providing valuable engineering help to Scotty to enable the landing party to return to the ship before the base was destroyed. I doubt that Scotty will ever look at cats the same way again!

In this excerpt from *Assignment: Eternity,* Roberta and Seven received the transmission from Septos that set the story in motion. Although Roberta was reluctant to travel into the future with Seven, she gamely swallowed her fears and followed. Her loyalty to and trust in Seven have increased since "Assignment Earth," and someday, it would be interesting to read their story.

*811 East 68th Street, Apt. 12-B*
*New York City, United States of America*
*Planet Earth*
A.D. *19 July 1969*

As usual, she felt lost in the fog. The glowing azure mist, swirling and luminescent, enveloped her completely. She could see nothing but blue all around her, hear nothing but her own rapid heartbeat. No matter that she had entered this unnatural fog dozens of times before and emerged safely each time; part of her always worried that *this* time she would disappear into the mist forever.

*Don't be ridiculous,* she told herself. *You use elevators, don't you? You don't worry about crashing down twenty-five floors every time you step into an elevator, right?*

*Yeah,* another part of her psyche replied, *but elevators are normal. Traveling by radioactive smoke is just too freaking out-of-this-world!*

She stepped forward, deeper into the mist, which did not feel cold or moist like real fog; it was a seething cloud of energy that tingled like static electricity and seemed to pass beneath her skin and between each individual molecule of her body. For a heart-stopping second, she felt as if she was dissolving into the fog, as if there was no longer any difference between her and the swirling mist, and she hastily frisked herself to make sure she was all still there. She ran her fingers over the rough denim of her jeans, her soft, cotton, tie-dyed T-shirt, the bangs of tinted, honey-blond hair just above her eyes. Still solid. Still intact. Thank God.

Was this trip taking longer than usual? Although she had only entered the fog moments ago, it felt like centuries. "Hello?" she called out. "Are we there yet?"

As if in response, the fog grew thinner before her eyes. Through the churning blue haze, she glimpsed a darkness beyond—and a blinking green light somewhat further on. She rushed forward and suddenly the fog was gone. She stumbled onto a carpeted floor tripping slightly as if she had encountered an unexpected step, but managing to keep her balance. She shook her head, torn between exasperation and relief. After the fog, coming back to reality—any reality—was always a bit of a jolt.

At first, all she could see was a translucent green cube, about three inches wide, floating in the darkness a few feet away. A chartreuse glow lit the cube from within, flashing even more brightly for an instant just as the cube emitted a curiously feminine "beep."

Then, as if summoned by the beep, the overhead lights came on, revealing a neat and tidy office decorated with contemporary furniture. The green cube sat atop a large black desk, next to a silver pen and pencil set. The carpet turned out to be a pale orange color, matching a couch and plush chair across the room from the desk. Framed paintings, landscapes mostly, hung on the walls, except where cedar bookshelves occupied one entire wall of the office. Encyclopedias, atlases, and other hardcover reference books filled the bookshelves.

The room's ordinary-looking furnishings were reassuringly familiar. "Home sweet home," she murmured, then turned around to look back the way she'd came.

What she beheld provided a jarring contrast to the mundane appearance of the rest of the office. A shining steel door, more suitable to an airlock or a bank vault, stood wide open, exposing a darkened chamber in which the luminescent fog continued to swirl and billow, seeming to come from nowhere yet never spreading beyond the rectangular boundaries of the doorway. No matter how hard she strained her eyes, she could not see beyond the fog; for all she could tell, the shadowy tunnel behind the fog could have stretched to infinity—and probably did. *I am never going to get used to this,* she thought.

Her sneakers, a new pair of P.F. Flyers, tapped impatiently against the carpet as she peered into the fog. "C'mon," she muttered. "What's taking you so long?"

The mist refused to answer her. She glanced over at the flashing green cube on the desk, wondering if she should risk interrupting the process by consulting the cube. "I'll give them five more seconds," she decided. *Four, three, two . . .*

Just as she was about to give up, a figure appeared in the mist, hazily at first, but quickly gaining form and definition. Unlike her, he emerged from the fog with the calm and confidence of one completely

443

at ease with the procedure. He was a tall, slender man dressed in a conservative gray suit. His neatly trimmed brown hair was edged with gray at the temples, while his light brown eyebrows faded, almost to invisibility, against his craggy features. The man's face wore a grim, sober expression, lightened somewhat by a hint of ironic amusement. His right hand gently stroked the head of a sleek, black cat he held securely against his chest.

*Always the cat,* she thought. *So how come kitty can't come through on her own? I did.*

The cat let out an inquisitive mew. A collar of silvery fabric glittered around its neck. Its eyes were brilliant yellow ovals pierced by thin slits of black.

"Yes, Isis, we made it," he murmured to the cat. Behind him, the fog faded into nonexistence, leaving not even a stray wisp to linger in the office. The empty space beyond the doorway now looked merely dark and featureless, like an unlit closet. The green cube beeped again, and the heavy steel door began to close automatically. Wooden panels slid out from hidden recesses in front of the doorway, concealing the gleaming metal door behind three shelves of cocktail glasses. Within seconds, all traces of the enigmatic fog chamber had vanished from sight.

The blond woman was no longer surprised by the office's transformation; she'd witnessed the change too many times before. "About time," she protested, crossing her arms as she leaned back against the sturdy desk. "What kept you?"

"A few last-minute details," he replied, "but I think I can now safely guarantee that Colonel Armstrong will take a very remarkable walk tomorrow."

"Really?" She let out a long sigh of relief. Her eyes widened as the full enormity of the man's statement sunk in. "Wow. Man on the moon. Even after all I've seen in the past year, I can still barely believe it."

"Welcome to the Space Age, Miss Lincoln," said the man who called himself Gary Seven. He placed the cat gently onto the carpet. "Trust me, this is only the beginning."

Roberta Lincoln, age twenty, walked across the office and dropped onto the orange couch. Isis, her furry black nemesis, hopped onto the couch as well, and Roberta scooted down to the other end of the couch, putting at least one full cushion between them. "The beginning," she repeated. "That's what that spaceman from the future, Kirk, said, too." She sunk deeper into the couch, her gaze drifting heavenward as if she could probe the depths of interstellar space right through the ceiling of the office. "Good thing me and you got to help out a bit."

Isis made an indignant squawk.

"Oh yeah, you, too," Roberta conceded. *Sheesh, now even I'm talking to the cat! Bad enough that the boss keeps Kitty better informed than me. . . .*

Seven, also known as Supervisor 194, allowed a bit of a smile to curl his lips, apparently amused by the byplay between Roberta and Isis. He removed his jacket and hung it neatly over the black metallic chair behind his desk. "All part of the job," he said, loosening his necktie. "The human race has enormous potential, but it still needs a little help now and then."

*Some job,* Roberta thought. Tearing her gaze away from the ceiling, she glanced around Seven's unassuming office. When she'd first started working here, for Seven's immediate predecessors, she'd had no trouble accepting that "encyclopedia research" was all that was going on. *Boy, was I in for a surprise. If I told anyone else half of what goes on in here, they'd think I was pulling their leg—or that I'd lost my mind.*

"You know," she said, "the way you talk, sometimes I think you forget that you're part of the human race, too."

The wry smile disappeared from Seven's face, replaced by a more pensive expression. "Very perceptive, Miss Lincoln," he said, a touch of melancholy deepening his voice. "You may have a point there. Knowing what I do, having been where I've been, there is a bit of a . . . distancing effect." He gave her a serious look from across the room. "I'll have to count on you to keep me in touch with the rest of my species."

"Uh, sure," Roberta said, uncertain how to respond. How do you relate to a guy whose ancestors have been trained by aliens for six thousand years? "Say, that *2001* film is still playing a few blocks away. I haven't seen it yet." Had Seven (she could never think of him as Gary) ever gone to the movies? She had no idea. "Maybe we can hit a matinee sometime?"

Isis hissed and gave Roberta a dirty look. She scratched her claws on the arm of the couch.

"Hey, don't blame me," Roberta said. "It's not my fault they don't let cats into the movies." Of course, Isis wasn't always a cat, but Roberta tried not to think about that. It was just too weird. "So, what do you say?" she asked Seven. "I'll even spring for popcorn. Dutch treat."

Seven opened his mouth to respond, but was interrupted by a

piercing, high-pitched whistle from the cube on his desk. The glowing cube flashed urgently, and Seven reacted as if jolted by a live electrical wire. Movies and moon landings were instantly forgotten as Seven snapped to attention. He was out from behind the desk in an instant, striding across the floor toward the bookshelves. "Computer on," he said sharply.

"What is it?" Roberta asked, quickly catching Seven's mood. Isis sprung from the couch, landing on all four paws only a few inches away from the bookshelves. The fur along the cat's neck lifted itself in alarm.

"Emergency beacon," Seven explained, his gaze glued to the wall containing the bookshelves, which now began to swing outward, rotating a concealed computer bank into view. Flashing horizontal and vertical lines, in various combinations of colors, formed changing patterns on the surface of a gleaming, high-tech computer that was the size of a large refrigerator. Seven called it a "Beta-5" computer, although Roberta had no idea what exactly distinguished it from, say, a Beta-4 or a Beta-6. She only knew that Seven's computer, based on an ancient alien technology, was smarter than any other machine on Earth, circa 1969. She wondered if the rest of the world's computers would ever catch up with the Beta-5. *Not in my lifetime,* she thought.

A circular viewscreen, smaller than the average television, occupied one section of the apparatus, "Computer, identify distress signal," Seven instructed.

The Beta-5 responded to his vocal command. "Executing," the machine reported. Its voice, although identifiably feminine, had a distinctly inhuman echo. "Signal is fragmented due to transtemporal interference."

"Transtemporal?" Seven said. Judging from the tone of his voice, Roberta decided that was not good news. *Transtemporal,* she thought, *as in time travel?* She hopped off the couch and hurried to join Seven and Isis by the computer.

"Confirmed," the Beta-5 stated. "Tracking source of transmission. Location: Romulan Star Empire coordinates 83-62-171. Date, by current Earth chronology: 2269 A.D."

Roberta's jaw dropped. *2269? Three hundred years from now?*

Seven merely nodded grimly in response to the computer's startling revelation. "Can you reconstruct the content of the transmission?"

Illuminated lines flashed in sequence. "Attempting to integrate signal." Visual static appeared on the view screen. Roberta looked over Seven's shoulder, trying to discern some sort of recognizable image from blurry electronic snow. She wished she knew what she was looking for.

A pattern began to take shape upon the screen. Soon she could make out a scratchy picture of a man's face, accompanied by snatches of a desperate voice interrupted by bursts of static:

*"146 to 194 . . . exposed . . . capture imminent technology beyond . . . at risk . . . future history . . . recommend . . . urgent . . . self-destruct . . . emergency . . . no escape . . ."*

Roberta thought she heard a harsh, sizzling noise in the background, followed by a loud, metallic crash. Then the static cleared for an instant and she got a better look at the speaker. To her surprise, she saw that he had the same sort of strange, pointed ears as that Martian guy, Mr. Spock. He looked in bad shape, like he'd been in a fight. His lip was swollen and a trickle of green fluid ran down the man's face from a nasty-looking gash on his forehead. *Green blood?* she thought. This was too weird.

The sizzling noise grew louder. The face on the screen screamed once, a ghastly sound that tore at Roberta's heart, and the screen went blank. "146," Seven barked, "please respond. This is 194. Repeat: respond immediately!"

The screen remained blank. "Transmission halted at origin," the Beta-5 announced. Seven's head drooped below his shoulders. He clenched his fists in frustration. For a second, he looked incredibly tired.

"Mr. Seven?" Roberta asked hesitantly. "Are you okay?"

He lifted his head and stepped away from the computer. He took a deep breath. "I'm fine," he answered, "but I'm afraid the future is not."

"The future?" Roberta echoed.

"Precisely, Miss Lincoln, but which future? That's the real question." All business now, he addressed the Beta-5. "Computer, analyze future history for divergence from standard timeline."

Lights blinked upon the face of the futuristic apparatus. A loud hum emerged from the machine as it processed Seven's request for at least five minutes. Roberta was taken aback by the delay. She had never known the Beta-5 to take more than ten seconds to answer any query, no matter how complicated. "Is something wrong?" she asked.

Isis seconded Roberta with an inquisitive meow. Seven shushed them both as the Beta-5 spoke at last. "Alternate timeline established. New future deviates significantly from established parameters."

"Point of divergence?" Seven demanded.

"2293 A.D. Khitomer Peace Conference. Assassination of Spock of Vulcan by anomalous temporal element prior to initial meeting with Pardek of Romulus. Result: elimination of Vulcan-Romulan reunification efforts in latter half of the twenty-fourth century."

*The twenty-fourth century?* Roberta wondered, struggling to keep up with the computer's revelations. *When did we get on to the twenty-fourth century? What happened to 2269?*

"I see," Seven said thoughtfully. "Source of anomaly?"

"2269 A.D. Romulan Star Empire. Coordinates 83-62-171."

*Okay,* Roberta thought. *That's more like it.* She still had no idea what was going on, except that someone was going to kill Mr. Spock—who hadn't even been born yet! Never mind the Age of Aquarius, her mind wasn't expanding fast enough to keep up with all these bizarro concepts. She still had trouble believing that she had actually met an intelligent being from outer space; now she had to worry about his assassination, almost three hundred and twenty-five years from today? *Help,* she thought. *I need an Excedrin.*

On the rug, Isis meowed and rubbed her head against Seven's trousers until he picked her up. Roberta wondered grumpily if the cat had figured out any more than she had.

Seven walked briskly across the office and retrieved his jacket from the back of his chair. "I'm afraid I have to postpone any movie plans," he stated. "We have to leave again, immediately."

"For 2269 or 2293?" Roberta asked, hoping that it was a blatantly ridiculous question. *Please tell me he's not saying what I think he's saying.*

Seven answered quite matter-of-factly. "2269. That's the root of the trouble." He placed Isis on the top of the desk and put on his jacket, then pushed down the pen attached to his pen and pencil set. Roberta heard a familiar clicking sound, and watched as, across from the desk, the shelves of decorative glassware receded into their hidden crevices, exposing the massive steel door guarding the fog chamber. A circular handle on the door spun automatically, and the doorway swung open once more. Roberta gulped as Seven hurriedly manipulated a control panel on the inner face of the door. She didn't like the looks of this.

"Time travel?" she asked. "You're not joking, are you?"

"As you may have noted, Miss Lincoln," Seven replied, "I seldom joke."

Isis sprung off the desktop and padded over to Seven's side. To her dismay, Roberta saw an unnatural blue fog began to form inside the interior of the hidden chamber. "Why the big hurry?" she objected. Things were moving far too fast for her. "The future's not going anywhere, is it?"

"The longer we delay, the further it may go off-track," Seven explained curtly. Seeing the bewildered look on Roberta's face, he paused to elaborate. "Future events can sometimes threaten the past, Miss Lincoln. Indeed, our own continuing knowledge that the future has been changed may have the effect of ensuring that change unless we take action to reverse it; even the primitive quantum theory of this era concedes that the act of observing reality can actually change the reality being observed."

Roberta's head was inclined to take Seven's word for it. "This is one of those step-on-a-butterfly, change-the-whole-world kind of things, right?"

"Basically," Seven confirmed, "but in reverse. It's not common, and it's certainly not reasonable, but it is possible, take my word for it. We have to act now before any temporal backwash robs us of the opportunity."

"Oh," Roberta said, trying to come to terms with the concept. "Do I need to pack?"

Seven cracked a smile. "You'll find the twenty-third century extraordinarily well-stocked." He checked his suit's inside pocket, drawing out a slim silver device the size and shape of a fountain pen, then replacing the device in his pocket. "I believe I have everything we need. Except—" A new thought seemed to occur to him. He rushed back to the desk and picked up the green cube. "Here," he said, tossing the cube toward Roberta. "Take this."

The cube chirped when she caught it. She snatched a psychedelic handbag off the plush orange chair by the couch, and stuck the cube into the bag.

The luminescent fog swirled within the confines of the chamber. It looked to Roberta like a glowing blue whirlpool, a vaporous vortex from which she might never return. Gary Seven stood to one side of the doorway, holding Isis against his chest. "After you," he said.

Roberta swallowed hard. *2269.* How long would it take to travel forward three hundred years? What would the world possibly be like then? She glanced back over her shoulder at the wooden doorframe on the other side of the office. Beyond that door, she thought, lay her world as she knew it: Manhattan, movies, and moon landings. "Here goes nothing," she whispered.

Taking one last look at the twentieth century, she stepped back into the fog.

449

# *Q-Squared,* by Peter David

Peter David has written so many outstanding Star Trek novels that we could easily fill a book entitled *Star Trek Adventures: The Best of Peter David.* My favorites are the novels that, as Mr. David says, weave together various threads and add to the concept of Trek as a vast and intricate tapestry. Mr. David excels at these stories, and *Q-Squared* is one of his best. It is a complex novel, and the reader must pay attention or miss something important. The reader must also, as Mr. David advised in his introduction, "assume nothing."

It is good advice. Using a railroad metaphor to describe three parallel time tracks, A, B and C, Mr. David introduced characters familiar to readers but who were not entirely who they seemed to be. In the Track A universe, Jack Crusher was captain of the *Enterprise*-D, and Jean-Luc Picard was his first officer. Track B was the universe populated by the *TNG* crew familiar to the reader, and Track C was a war timeline like that of "Yesterday's Enterprise," with a tragic twist. In *Q-Squared,* the tracks crashed together when Trelane, introduced in the *TOS* episode, "The Squire of Gothos," became dangerously insane and began to manipulate reality and toy with the minds of the crews. Only the power of the Q could save the timelines and the people populating them, but Trelane was more powerful than the entire Q continuum. Q, with Picard's help, fought the most difficult battle of his life to stop the demented Trelane.

In his dementia, Trelane broke down the barriers between the timelines and released chaos to prey upon the hearts and minds of the inhabitants, with tragic consequences. The insanity gradually built and picked up speed, with the distortion in the time tracks and the mind-bending effects on the people accelerating at an ever-quickening pace, like a steam train running out of control.

*Q-Squared* is an exciting action-filled story, and like all Peter David novels, also a satisfying character story. The people of all three timelines were put through an emotional wringer, and only the people of Track B survived intact, although emotionally ravaged. Jack Crusher, from Track A, was a particularly tragic figure. He lost everything, including perhaps, his soul. Picard from Track A lost the two people who meant the most to him in the universe and perhaps any chance for real happiness. Both Riker and Picard from Track C were killed, but Track C gained the Data from Track A.

In this passage from *Q-Squared,* Trelane contemplated the fun he could have from collapsing an even greater number of universes as he

450

viewed the destruction wrought by his elimination of the barriers between Tracks A, B, and C.

"I'M NOT WAITING HERE WITH YOU ANYMORE!" TOMMY RIKER SHOUTED AT Deanna Troi. "I'm going out there to find my mom and dad!"

He headed for the door, repeating the action he'd taken earlier when he'd decided to go after his father. On that occasion the result had been that he'd managed to save William Riker's life . . . some damned William Riker or other, at any rate. So he was relatively flush with success, and the interests of this woman who was, and was not, his mother were strictly secondary to him.

Deanna came up behind him and grabbed his right wrist. "You're not going anywhere," she said firmly.

Tommy did not hesitate. His intense and undying love for Starfleet had included study of all manner of things . . . including self-defense techniques. Before she could react, Tommy stepped across Deanna's body, causing her to lose her balance just slightly. It was enough for him to shove against the weak point in Deanna's grip: her thumb. A quick twist broke her grip on him, and Tommy followed the move with a swift punch to her stomach. Solid move, solidly executed, and the startled Betazoid went down firmly on her buttocks with a startled gasp.

Tommy was out the door before she could stop him.

Deanna was immediately after him.

Commander Jean-Luc Picard arrived in sickbay to find Dr. Beverly Howard trembling, confused, disoriented. He would have thought that it was because of her confrontation with Jack, but she quickly informed him that such had not been the case. Jack had not shown up, had not been down to sickbay at all.

The cause for her fright, though, was not much of an improvement.

"Wesley," she had said hoarsely. "Wesley was here."

Picard stared at her in confusion. "Wesley? Your . . . your son? Your little boy . . . ?"

She shook her head frantically. "Not little. A teenager, a young man he was . . . my God, Jean-Luc, what kind of an asylum have we signed aboard?"

"I'm going to find Jack," said Picard. "Stay here."

"Where would I go?" she asked.

He strode quickly out of sickbay, and Beverly Howard immediately vanished, to be replaced by an equally distraught Beverly Crusher . . . who turned and saw a confused Geordi La Forge with perfectly functioning eyes, and she jumped at least a foot in the air except he wasn't there anymore, at which point Beverly Howard rematerialized as smoothly as if she hadn't left at all, and she looked around and couldn't understand where Geordi had gotten off to. . . .

Meantime, all around Commander Jean-Luc Picard, everything had gone berserk. Throughout the vessel, there was a sense of total, chaotic panic. Years of Starfleet training seemed shattered as crew members were darting this way and that. Everyone was running, it seemed, though whether they were running from one place or toward another, Picard could not have said. He tried to regain control but, driven by inner demons and fears, many of the officers ignored him. A number didn't even seem to recognize him, and a few looked at him very suspiciously before continuing on their way.

*"What's happening?!"* Picard shouted over the increasing terror and din.

At his harpsichord, Trelane upped the tempo of his music still more. He smiled peacefully and, when he spoke, his voice echoed within the subconscious of all the pathetic little vermin running around in the ship, which in turn was spiraling downward, although no one was aware of it yet.

"You are fighting for your place in the universe," he said, punctuating the seriousness of the sentiment with a rather impressive musical sting. "No quarter may be asked, and none may be given. For this, my fine young things, is the end for you. This is far more than war. Oh yes, far more. This"—another musical sting—"is the battle for total annihilation. Who will stay? Who will go? Maybe you . . . but maybe no. A charming rhyme, don't you think?"

He ran his fingers briskly down the keyboard, and the music swelled within their minds, and they were going from jumping dimensions to jumping dementia.

Faster and faster the boundaries deteriorated. Trelane giggled. If he was having this much fun with three universes . . . just imagine the amusement value from collapsing three hundred. Three thousand!

The experiment was shaping up to be a spectacular success.

The humanoid called Lieutenant Commander Data moved smoothly through the surging tide of humanity that had once been the efficient, coherent unit called the crew of the *Enterprise.*

He was heading for engineering, to the backup control stations, to see what could be done about the current dire situation in which the ship had found itself.

But as he approached engineering, he saw someone coming from the other direction. His head tilted slightly, as did the other's.

From another direction came a third.

The three Datas—two android, one human—stopped and looked at one another.

"Interesting," said Data.

"Interesting," said Data.

"Interesting," said Data.


Commander Picard, heading in one direction, came across Deanna Troi going in the other.

"Mrs. Riker!" he began.

"Captain!" she began. Then she stopped and frowned. "'Mrs. Riker'?"

"'Captain'?" he said.

Suddenly a phaser blast fired, nailing Picard from behind. He hurtled forward, crashing into Deanna Troi. They both went down.

Picard moaned as Deanna struggled out from under him. She looked up in shock to see Jack Crusher stalking toward them, a phaser in his hand and murder in his eye.

"That was on the lowest setting, Picard!" he shouted. "Murdering bastard! We'll bring you up a notch at a time!"

Picard was clutching his ribs, and Deanna threw herself protectively in front of him. "Keep away from him!" she said.

"This is between him and me!" growled Crusher. "Don't worry, Mrs. Riker. I'm not going to kill him. I'm just going to . . . to break every bone in his damned body! Think she'll love you when you're just a boneless mass of meat? Huh?"

Picard staggered to his feet. Crusher brought his phaser up, at an increased setting, ready to blast through her to get to him.

And suddenly Crusher was lifted completely off his feet. He struggled in midair, his arms thrashing about helplessly, as Lieutenant Worf pivoted quickly and tossed him down the corridor as if he weighed nothing.

Crusher hit the ground and skidded, coming to a halt in front of a small mass of crewmen.

Worf started to advance on him, saying brusquely, "One side! This is a security procedure!"

*"Kill the Klingon!"*

Worf looked up when he heard that. He wasn't quite sure which was worse: hearing that sentiment, or hearing the voice that mouthed it.

None of the crewmen were wearing Starfleet uniforms akin to his. They all looked far more militaristic and, furthermore, everyone had a firearm.

And at the forefront was Lieutenant Natasha Yar.

"Tasha!" said Worf.

Being called by her name did not slow Tasha in the least. She brought her phaser up and fired. Worf ducked to the left and felt the bolt sizzle over his head.

Worf fired three quick blasts before they could target him. Then he charged down a side corridor, with the rest of the angry mob right after him.

Deanna watched them go, then turned back to Picard.
He was gone.

Picard watched them go, then turned back to Deanna.
She was gone.

Everyone in engineering gaped as three Datas, working in perfect unison, sought to override the damaged navigational controls by rerouting them through the backup astronavigational board.

They worked so smoothly, with so little need for back-and-forth, that they were able to discuss matters of somewhat less consequence as they sought to save the ship.

"Tell me," the android Datas (who had a tendency to speak in unison, much to the annoyance of the engineering crew) said to the humanoid, "what is the greatest advantage to having a human body? We have always been curious."

The humanoid gave it a moment's thought. "Sex," he replied.

"Really," said the Datas.

"Yes. I have had frequent liaisons with Lieutenant Natasha Yar." He paused a moment. "I am not supposed to tell anyone else. But since we are, in essence, aspects of the same being, I feel that this is not betraying a confidence."

"Your secret is safe with us," said the Datas.

"Tommy!" Deanna Riker was calling as she ran down the corridor.

She was nearly frantic with worry. The boy had run from their quarters. She had not been able to locate him, and all around her she was getting a feeling of being totally disconcerted. The crush of human anxiety was so palpable that she was almost overwhelmed by it.

She sagged against a wall, trying to catch her breath, trying to screen out the pounding of emotions all around her. Overwhelmed by it all, bereft of her son and her husband, her mind cried out . . .

*You're going to be all right,* came a soothing voice in her head.

She looked up and stared into her own eyes. Eyes that did not carry with them a world of pain and years of hurt.

"Wh . . . what's happening?" said Deanna Riker, thinking for a moment that perhaps she had spiraled down into the same pit of madness that seemed to have embraced her husband.

"Nothing we cannot handle," replied Deanna Troi. "In numbers is strength."

"Mom!"

Deanna Riker's head snapped around as Tommy ran to her. He hugged her fiercely, saying, "I never thought I'd see you . . ."

"It's all right," she told him over and over, "it's all right."

Tommy looked from his mother to Deanna Troi and back again, as if he hadn't fully believed the resemblance until he saw them next to each other.

"Are you two, like . . . related?" he asked.

"Back away from them, boy."

The crisp order had come from William T. Riker.

It wasn't Deanna Troi's Riker.

It wasn't Deanna Troi Riker's Riker.

It was a William T. Riker whom neither of them had seen. One who, standing next to a man appearing to be Jean-Luc Picard, had phasers aimed at them.

"Will?" said Deanna.

"Will?" said Deanna a second after her.

"You know these women, Number One?" asked Picard.

"I know who they're supposed to be," said Riker. "But it's obviously a Klingon trick . . . because I haven't seen this woman—either woman—in years."

Lieutenant Worf charged down the hallway, the thundering horde right behind him, spearheaded by Tasha Yar.

As stretched as his credulity was at that moment, it should not have come as any surprise to him when, at the end of the corridor, another Tasha Yar was waiting for him.

She did not have her phaser up and pointed at him. Instead she was staring at him with curiosity and a bit of annoyance. "What the hell are you doing in that uniform?" she demanded.

That one sentence, remarkably, clarified a great deal to Worf.

Obviously they were dealing with multiple universes, something that he, Worf, had sizable experience with. Not only had he once become an inadvertent dimension jumper, but he had witnessed firsthand the spectacle of thousands upon thousands of *Enterprise*s emerging from a rift in space.

Unlike that experience, however, the universes were not simply running into one another. They were overlapping, merging, one being made to exist at the expense of others.

All this went through Worf's mind in one second.

In the next second, he immediately discerned three distinct dimensional tracks: There was himself, of course, and his *Enterprise:* there was an *Enterprise* where the crew was at war with the Klingons; and there was an *Enterprise* where time flowed at a slightly different speed (judging by Tasha's older-style uniform), where Worf happened to be on the ship for some reason—as a visitor, perhaps—but was not a member of Starfleet.

In the third second, he made his decision. He stepped forward, grasped her firmly, and lied.

"Ishara told me to tell you that she regrets all the unhappiness between you."

Tasha's eyes widened. Worf's invoking the name of her estranged sister was absolutely the last thing that she had expected.

"We are about to be attacked," he said. "Are you with me or no?"

And Tasha Yar, head of security of the *Enterprise,* yanked out her phaser. "No one attacks anyone on my ship and gets away with it. We could use some cover to fall back, though. Darkness, perhaps."

"Excellent idea."

He and Tasha fired at the overhead illumination. The lights blew out, plunging the entire corridor into darkness. Down the hallway could be heard the crew screaming for Worf's head, but by the time they got their bearings, Worf and Tasha were long gone.

Trelane's hands thundered down on the keys, driving up the sound level. The harpsichord music deteriorated into an earsplitting cacophony, and the only thing that was louder was the laughter of Trelane.

A pair of eyes watched from hiding as the two Deannas faced the collective judge, jury, and executioner called Jean-Luc Picard and William T. Riker.

"Listen to me," said Deanna Troi slowly. "Both of you. This is not the way."

The music chorused in the heads of Picard and Riker, allowing the words to get through but drowning out the sincerity, the sentiment, the thought and order behind them.

"It's another pathetic Klingon trick, Captain," said Riker with confidence. "They've got operatives disguised as a woman who I knew years ago. Obviously they're doing it so that I'll hesitate when I see them, instead of doing what needs to be done."

"Foolish," said Picard.

"We take them prisoner?"

"No time. No facility." Picard raised his phaser, and Riker matched the action. "And, frankly, no patience."

*"Stop it!"* shouted Tommy. "Don't hurt them!"

"Tommy, get out of the way!" his mother warned him, pushing him to one side.

"Ready," said Picard. "Make it merciful, Number One. A clean shot."

"It's more than they'd do for us."

"Agreed. Do it anyway."

"Put the phasers down," said Deanna Troi. "You're making a mistake."

"Aim," said Picard.

And suddenly a red and black blur blocked their path.

They weren't sure exactly what it was. It moved faster than either of them had ever seen a person move, and the roar that came from his throat was barely akin to human.

He broadsided Picard, hurling him back into Riker. His voice was filled with fury as he howled, *"Don't you hurt my wife!"*

Picard tried to bring his phaser up, but Lieutenant Commander Riker twisted it away from him. Then Riker brought his foot up into the pit of Picard's stomach, doubling him over. Picard gasped, and then Commander Riker shoved Picard out of the way so that he could get a clear shot.

He was too slow.

Lieutenant Commander Riker, longtime prisoner of the Romulans, husband of Deanna and father of Tommy, fired. He did not display any of the hesitation or trepidation that had haunted him since his rescue. In the firestorm of battle, with the life of the woman he loved at stake, there was absolutely no indecision.

The blast hit Commander Riker squarely in the chest. And Commander William Riker, pride of Starfleet, fighter of Klingons, onetime lover of a Betazoid woman he had not seen for years . . . saw nothing else ever again. His molecules lost cohesion and, within seconds, he was wiped out of existence.

Riker turned toward Picard, but now Deanna Troi grabbed him by the arm and cried out, "No! Don't!" And to Picard she cried, "Run!"

Riker would not be stopped. He continued to fire, but the blasts missed Picard because Deanna was yanking on his arm. It gave Picard enough time to fall back and disappear down the corridor.

He turned to his wife, took her face in his hands. "Are you all right? Did he hurt you?"

"No." She shook her head, her voice barely above a hush.

"I couldn't let him hurt you." The words seemed to surprise him, a self-realization. "I . . . couldn't let him . . ."

She held him close.

Deanna Troi didn't know whether to be happy or jealous. She settled for being cautious. "Let's go," she said. "This is far from over."

Picard, having just seen his second-in-command blown to atoms, ran down a corridor as fast as his legs would carry him. Suddenly he heard voices . . . one of them deep and rough, and he recognized it immediately.

There was a Jefferies tube nearby, and Picard clambered up it quickly. Then he twisted around, staking out a position . . . and waited.

The voices drew closer, closer. There was the Klingon's voice, yes, and a female voice talking with him.

My God . . . it was Tasha. Tasha Yar had betrayed them. All of a sudden it made perfect sense. That was how their security had been breached. That was how all those impostors had been allowed to run rampant throughout the ship.

Natasha Yar, traitor to the Federation, pawn to the Klingon Empire.

He wasn't sure who he was going to enjoy shooting more.

# *The Escape,* by Dean Wesley Smith & Kristine Kathryn Rusch

*The Escape,* by Dean Wesley Smith & Kristine Kathryn Rusch was the first *Voyager* novel published after the novelization of "The Caretaker," the premiere episode. I was impressed by how well the writers captured the personalities and voices of the characters at such an early stage of the series, so early that the doctor bore the name "Doc Zimmerman" given to him in the *Voyager* series bible but never formalized in the episodes.

*The Escape* began with the discovery of Alcawell, a deserted planet that appeared to be a giant spaceship junkyard. *Voyager* desperately needed replacement parts and raw materials, so Janeway sent an away team to inspect the facility and scavenge what they could. After entering an apparently abandoned ship, the away team disappeared, transported almost 400,000 years into Alcawell's past, and were condemned to death for time crimes.

The time travel scenario in *The Escape* is unique. Many millennia ago, the people of Alcawell learned to travel between time periods and built their entire culture around time travel. They discovered that while travel between most time periods was safe, travel to certain time periods or jumps within time periods risked changes in the course of history. As a result, they adopted a complicated structure of time laws, violation of many of which was punishable by death. The *Voyager* crew ran afoul of these time laws, and *The Escape* is the story of how Janeway and an Alcawellian time cop worked within them to save the away team.

In this excerpt from *The Escape,* B'Elanna, Harry, and Neelix disappeared while exploring the abandoned time ship.

THE TRANSPORTER DROPPED THEM ON A HARD, CONCRETELIKE SURFACE NEAR the south edge of the station. Cold wind cut at B'Elanna's uniform and bits of sand nipped her face. The air smelled stale, and her mouth dried almost instantly from the total lack of humidity. The entire place had a feeling of age and death that chilled her far more than did the biting wind.

She glanced quickly around, then just stopped and stared at the parked ships in complete amazement. One after another, side by side, the ships stretched into the distance like images in facing mirrors. At first glance they all seemed to be exactly the same, and she could tell from the dozens that towered around them that they were very, very old. Some had weathered the years better than others in the constant wind and sand.

To her left one had tipped slightly where its short, stemlike landing gear had given way. When fully upright, the ships were held about four meters above the ground on tripod legs. A fairly gentle-sloped ramp extended down from the center of each ship like a giant tongue.

They'd have no problems getting inside the ships, because they were all standing open.

She looked slowly around, studying the wrecks. One ship had a small hole in its side that looked as if something inside had exploded and ruptured the gray hull. But all in all the ships had lasted much, much better than the ruins of a building a hundred meters away. She couldn't tell for sure, but she thought she could see faint markings on the concrete surface scoured by the years of sand. The markings seemed to lead from the bottom of each ship's ramp toward the building.

The view from *Voyager* had given her a sense of scale for the station itself, but not for the ships. Each ship was about two times larger than a Federation shuttlecraft. They were like slightly flattened round balls. Even on their short legs they towered over her. The landing legs alone were twice her width, yet under the weight of the ships they looked thin.

She did a slow, full circle turn just taking in the ships that hung precariously above and around her and stretched off into the distance in all directions. Large alien machinery, toppling under the pressure of time and wind, in a very alien setting.

Drifts of sand had formed around the bases of a few of the nearby ships and the ramps leading up into them. The wind made a strange whistling sound that sent shivers down B'Elanna's back.

She flipped open her tricorder. Ensign Kim did the same. The best way to fight the oddness of this place was to focus on work, and that was exactly what she would do.

"Ghosts. Spirits. The undead. The past walks here," Neelix said, almost shouting to be heard over the wind. "Can't you feel it?" He wrapped his arms tight around himself. "I don't know why I'm even here. And it's cold. Very cold. Maybe I should beam up and get us all coats."

"You're staying with us," B'Elanna said, her voice crisp. She didn't need any distractions.

Neelix huffed, but said nothing.

Her scan showed no life signs and no obvious traps. Nothing but an abandoned field of old ships that were never intended to fly through air or space. Strange. Everything about this place was strange.

She turned to her right and did a more careful scan of the ship Tuvok had picked out for them. It seemed to be a good choice. The hull was the same dull weathered gray as the rest, but she could see no obvious damage. Her readings indicated that this ship was no different from the rest, but somehow it felt newer than the others.

"Let's see what the inside looks like," she said.

"Good," Kim said. "This blowing sand really hurts."

She glanced over at him and Neelix. Both had turned their backs to the wind and were protecting their eyes. Getting out of the wind would be a good idea.

Holding her tricorder in front of her and scanning for any signs of traps or life-forms, she moved to the ramp under the center of the ship and looked up. The incline was gentle and the ramp was grooved to keep users from slipping. The door at the top was wide open and B'Elanna could see a wall beyond with a faded red arrow pointing to the right. A small drift of sand had formed around the base of the ramp.

"This had a lot of traffic once," Kim said, scanning his tricorder over the ramp.

"Traffic?" Neelix asked, looking around as if he could see the traffic nearby.

"Passengers would be my guess," Kim said. "The design and the wear patterns indicate this boarding ramp was well used."

"Used for what is the question," B'Elanna said.

Kim shrugged. "This place reminds me of a shuttleport back home. Sort of." He kept staring at his tricorder.

"It reminds me how much I hate being cold," Neelix said. "And how my quarters are warm and dry."

B'Elanna walked up the wide ramp to the opening, holding her tricorder in front of her. She wanted to draw her phaser, but knew that would seem stupid under the circumstances. Nothing had threatened them. There didn't seem to be anything on this planet that could threaten them. But she still would rather have a phaser in her hand than a tricorder the way her stomach was twisting. She would just feel better.

"The ship's empty," Kim said.

"Of course it's empty," Neelix said. "These are all abandoned ships." He stepped around Kim and B'Elanna, and before either of them could stop him he walked calmly inside and down the wide corridor indicated by the faded arrow.

Indirect lighting flickered on marking the way as he walked.

"Neelix!" B'Elanna shouted.

"It's warm in here!" he said.

"Amazing," Kim said, studying his tricorder. "Lights and power source still functioning after all this time."

"Yeah," B'Elanna said, scanning her tricorder for any signs of danger before following Neelix.

The passageway was about ten meters long and turned sharply to the left into a large room with bench seats around the outside and other seats attached to chairs in groupings throughout the room. The room was larger than some Maquis ships. Over a hundred passengers could fit comfortably in this space.

Neelix stood in the middle with his hands open. "See? Empty, just as I told you."

"There are no other rooms," Kim said. "How did they pilot this thing?"

"All empty tin cans," Neelix said. "Good for salvage, huh?"

"There isn't even an engine room," Kim said. "Or for that matter, an engine."

"Just don't touch anything," B'Elanna said, staring directly at Neelix. "At least until we determine what these ships were and what controls them."

Neelix sighed and sat down on the nearest chair, leaning back and putting his feet up. "At least we're out of the wind in here."

"Look at this," Kim said, pointing at a blinking red sign over the passageway they had just come in. The sign was in an unidentifiable language with a numberlike sequence that kept changing. "It started blinking when Neelix sat down."

"See if you can figure out what it says," B'Elanna said. She tapped her comm badge. "Away team to *Voyager.*"

*"Voyager* here," Janeway's voice answered.

"We're inside. No signs of life. The ship still has an automatic power source of some sort that we somehow triggered on entering."

"Can you tell what the ships were used for?" Janeway asked.

"Passenger transport of some type. The insides are nothing more than a large room with benches and chairs. But I can't imagine where these could go. Or for that matter, how. It will take me some time to figure this out."

"Passenger?" Janeway said, more to herself than B'Elanna. "Well, be careful and report as soon as you have something."

"Understood," B'Elanna said.

"Any luck, Mr. Kim?" B'Elanna asked.

"It looks like a time sequence to me, but I'm operating on guesswork."

"Neelix," B'Elanna said, turning to the short alien lounging with his eyes half closed. "Do you recognize that language?" She pointed to the flashing sign over the entry.

He opened one eye and studied the message, then sat up. "I have a vague memory of something similar to that. It's a very dead language, though. That much I can tell you."

"But can you read it?" B'Elanna asked. She didn't have time for games.

He shrugged. "I think it says *Please Take a Seat.*"

"And the numbers?" Kim said.

"Just numbers," Neelix said. He leaned back and closed his eyes. "Let me know when you need my help again. I will be napping."

B'Elanna shook her head at Neelix and turned to Kim. "Link with *Voyager*'s computer, feed that information into it, and see what comes up, I'm going to look for the—"

The number sequence on the sign over Kim's head stopped and the room's lights flashed once. A scraping noise echoed through the ship and it shuddered slightly.

"The ramp is coming up!" Kim shouted and started for the door.

"Wait!" B'Elanna's command stopped him in his tracks. "Stay together." She slapped her comm badge. *"Voyager.* The ship is coming to life and closing up. Be ready to beam us out of here on my mark."

"Understood," Tuvok's calm voice answered back. "We have a transporter lock on you."

"Mr. Kim," B'Elanna said. "See if you can find what's causing this. We'll stay as long as we can. Neelix, help him." She scanned with her tricorder, but couldn't find the ship's power source. There had to be one. Somewhere.

A huge clang echoed through the ship. The clang was followed by painful screech as of metal scraping against metal without lubrication.

"The door is closed and the ship's lifting off the surface," Kim said, panic in his voice.

Then the air shimmered slightly and the ship settled back to the surface with a slight thud.

"The door is opening," Kim said. Over his head the sign again started to flash.

"Fast trip that one," Neelix said. He sounded calm, but he was standing now and had somehow moved right next to B'Elanna.

B'Elanna studied her tricorder, but all the readings indicated that nothing had changed with the ship. It had simply closed the door, lifted less than a meter off the ground, then settled back into place. But why? Had the trip been aborted? And how had it even lifted? There were no signs of antigravity units on this ship, or even engines. Nothing but a huge waiting room.

Suddenly B'Elanna realized something was very different. A draft of almost hot air blew in the corridor and the light from the direction of the door looked brighter.

Kim had already noticed and had his tricorder pointed at the entrance to the ship. "There's something wrong here," he said softly.

B'Elanna turned her tricorder in the same direction and got the answer. The air coming in the open door was totally different from when they had come in. It had more organisms in it. And humidity. And it was warmer. Considerably warmer.

With Kim and Neelix at her side, she moved cautiously toward the entrance. When they reached the point at the top of the ramp where they could see out, they stopped.

And stared.

"Oh, my," Neelix said.

"Where are we?" Kim asked.

Spread out in front of them was the same vast open area, only now most of the ships were gone. The pavement was covered with fresh colored lines. The buildings looked new. Tall, thin humanoids walked at different speeds to and from the ships and the building.

The people dressed in bright greens, reds, and purples. Most wore blue or yellow hats that somehow failed to clash. Some humanoids walked alone. Others walked in groups. Some carried what appeared to be luggage, while others carried nothing.

Ten ships down, a door silently closed and a ramp pulled up. The ship lifted off the pavement and vanished.

None of the nearby humanoids seemed to notice at all.

B'Elanna took in the scene for a moment and then tapped her comm badge. "Away team to *Voyager.* Come in, *Voyager.*"

No answer.

Kim quickly adjusted his tricorder and then in a cracking voice told her what she already feared.

"*Voyager* is no longer in orbit."

# CHAPTER 15

# Humor in Starfleet Uniform

STAR TREK IS NOT ALWAYS ABOUT SERIOUS ISSUES AND STORIES. SOMETIMES Star Trek is simply funny; humor always has been one of its best qualities. Most Original Series episodes had moments of humor no matter how serious the situation or issue; the crew had fun, and we had fun with them. Some episodes were hilarious, including "The Trouble with Tribbles," "Mudd's Women," "I, Mudd," and "A Piece of the Action." "The Trouble with Tribbles" was so unforgettable that, with the aid of 1990s technology, it was made into the even funnier *DS9* episode "Trials and Tribble-ations." I can never think of the Bureau of Temporal Investigations without laughing.

*TNG* took itself a bit more seriously than *TOS*, but the writers used comedy in *TNG* as well. Data's struggles to understand humanity often were amusing, and Lwaxana Troi was originally a comic character who was later shown to have greater depths than initially seen. Worf had some amazingly funny lines, and even Picard had moments of wit and irony. Q episodes could be tragic, like "Q, Who," or hysterically funny, like "QPid."

Star Trek novelists have made excellent use of humor, and many of the books excerpted in this work have very comic moments. Two exceptional books are included here, *Q-In-Law*, by Peter David, and *Mudd in Your Eye*, by Jerry Oltion.

## *Q-in-Law*, by Peter David

*Q-in-Law* is the funniest novel I have ever read. Each time I read it, I find something that I did not see before because I was laughing so

465

hard during the previous read. In *Q-in-Law,* the *Enterprise* hosted a wedding celebrating the union of two rival families of a spacefaring race called the Tizarin. The groom, Kerin, was of the Nistral, and his bride-to-be, Sehra, was of the Graziunas, families that were the Montagues and Capulets of the twenty-fourth century. Lwaxana came on board as the Betazed representative, and Q appeared, still on parole with the Continuum after the events of "Deja Q." Q was at his most annoying, and he proceeded to romance Lwaxana and sow discord between the engaged couple to demonstrate the shallow nature of romantic love. In the course of his deceptive seduction of Lwaxana, Q mistakenly gave her the powers of the Q, which she turned on him in a moment of rage.

My first selection from *Q-in-Law* is a scene of the bridge crew reacting to the sight of Q and Lwaxana dancing outside the ship. The second excerpt is a graphic demonstration of the adage "hell hath no fury like a woman scorned" as Lwaxana took revenge upon Q. Reading this scene on a commuter train is sure to bring you some stares from fellow commuters as you laugh out loud and disturb their peace. This scene alone is worth the cost of the audio-book for *Q-in-Law,* narrated by John DeLancie and Majel Barrett. A word of advice, though: do not listen while you are driving at high speeds. You will be laughing so hard that you may lose control of your vehicle!

LIEUTENANT COMMANDER DATA WAS INCAPABLE OF SURPRISE. HE COULD, however, register when something unexpected had happened, and react accordingly.

Such a time was now, as he looked up from the ops station at the bridge and saw what was on the forward screen. "How interesting," he said. He glanced at the sensor readings to confirm what his eyes were telling him.

Chafin looked up from his station, as did Burnside from hers.

There was dead silence for a moment.

"You know," said Chafin thoughtfully, "I understand there are ships that go along for months, even years at a time, without once seeing unaided people cruising past them in space. We see it twice in a week."

Pirouetting across the front viewscreen were two people, their feet moving across an invisible floor, dancing to silent melodies.

"Shows how quickly something can become old hat," observed Burnside.

"Bridge to Captain Picard," Data said briskly, observing procedure.

"Picard here," came the captain's voice. He sounded considerably older.

"Captain, there is—"

"A couple dancing in front of the ship?"

"Yes, sir."

"Specifics, Mr. Data?"

Data studied the screen. "They appear to be performing a classic waltz step. Quite smoothly, actually."

"Thank you, Mr. Data."

"Upon closer magnification, it would appear to be Q and Mrs. Troi."

"I surmised as much, Mr. Data."

"Shall I order a shuttlecraft dispatched, or perhaps the transporter . . . ?"

"No, don't bother," sighed Picard. "I suspect they'll come in when they're damned good and ready."

Q had materialized in the middle of the conference table. He stood above them, his arms folded, his smile lopsided.

Lwaxana extended a hand. "Q!" she said. "How wonderful to see you, my love!"

He glanced at her disdainfully. "Oh, puh-leeese," he said.

She shook her head, not quite hearing him properly. "What?"

But now Kerin and Sehra were pointing at him. "That's the man who showed me that you were going to be old and wrinkled and ugly," said Kerin. "And . . . and it upset me, and I didn't know how to deal with it, because I didn't think I could even look at you when you're old . . ."

"And he told me that all you cared about was other women! That you'd never stop wanting them . . ."

"Q!" said Picard angrily. "So you have been meddling after all, despite all your protests to the contrary!"

"Is pointing out the truth meddling?" demanded Q. "Is doing these young people a favor meddling? I ask you."

"Kerin," said Picard, ignoring Q's protests for a moment. "Yes, in years to come, Sehra will age. So will you. That is inevitable. What you don't understand is that you will grow old together and cherish those years. And when you behold her, you will not simply see some old woman, but instead the woman you've shared many long and joyous years of married life with. You will look at her with love. And

467

Sehra, yes . . . Kerin will doubtlessly look at other women. Being married doesn't mean that you stop noticing beauty. But if he were to lose his ability to appreciate the more beautiful things in life, then how could he possibly continue to cherish you? Cherish the beauty in your face and form, and the beauty in your heart?"

"Oh, bravo, Picard!" Q said sardonically, clapping his hands in slow, sarcastic applause. "Bravo! Try to justify this nonsense as best you can, and it will all boil down to the simple truth that the human concept of love is a total sham."

Lwaxana came toward him, her dark eyes concerned. "Q, I don't understand what you're saying—"

He shot a look at her. "Woman, you could attend me for a thousand lifetimes and still barely begin to grasp the subtleties of my greatness."

Lwaxana gasped and stepped back, thunderstruck, her hand to her breast.

"Is this why you've come then, Q?" demanded Picard.

"Of course, Picard!" sneered Q. "The entire ship was filled with spirits of love, love, love. It was nauseating. You humans are so obsessed with love. You're always looking for it, or you're in it or out of it. Or you're singing about it, or writing poems about it. So I decided to examine it, to see just how durable this supposedly most enduring of emotions is."

Picard came around the table to face Q. All of his fury and energy was directed toward Q, toward this unknowable being who presumed to judge humanity in all its aspects. "In the cause of love, civilizations have risen. For lack of love, civilizations have crumbled. It's the most glorious and ennobling emotion of humanity."

"Then humanity is in even worse trouble than I surmised," Q told him. "Your most glorious emotion? My dear Jean-Luc, it's your most positively ludicrous! It's selfish and self-directed. Possessive and spiteful. It encompasses everything that you humans are always claiming that you're above, and yet it's cloaked in this charming storybook idea that people loving each other is a good thing. You think that your race surviving war is your greatest achievement? Nonsense! It's that your race has survived love, the most overblown, ridiculous excuse for a positive emotion that any race has ever encountered."

Lwaxana was ghastly white, as if her soul had been ripped open. "I . . . don't understand . . . you said . . ."

Q rudely blew air from between his lips. "Are you deaf *and* stupid, woman? How painfully clear do I have to make matters for you?"

"Stop it!" said Deanna. "Leave her alone!"

"Q, get out of here!" snapped Picard.

But Q ignored them. Instead he walked down the length of the conference room table, toward Lwaxana. Every step was swaggering arrogance. "Oh, of course. I forgot to add self-deception to the list." He laughed once, that ugly, unholy sound. He hunkered down to bring himself on eye level with the ashen Lwaxana Troi. "Woman, you have been, and always shall be, merely another bit of data for my study. Another rat to go running through the maze. I wanted to see how, in the name of love, you would interact with your precious daughter and vice-versa. I wanted to see if this wonderful emotion would blind you to everything that was dictated by common sense. And it did! How splendid."

"You love me!" said Lwaxana, desperately, urgently.

"And still you continue! This is excellent. You're more self-involved than I thought. So much so that you ignored the advice of the daughter you love and the people you respect, just so you could fall in love with a being you just met and who every other person you encountered claimed had no capacity for love. They were right, *dear* Lwaxana. You are nothing to me. Humans are nothing to me, except when sometimes they can provide me with some amusement. And you, Lwaxana," Q's voice fell to a sarcastic, harsh whisper, "you have provided me with the most amusement of all. Thank you very, very much, you ignorant cow."

Lwaxana sank to a chair.

"Q, I am telling you to leave," said Picard.

"A joke," Lwaxana murmured. "It's all been a joke. A scheme. An experiment."

"I hardly think you're in a position to issue commands to me, Picard," Q said.

"He gave me the Q powers," Lwaxana said evenly.

"I am in a position, and my command is for you to leave, Now!"

"He gave me the powers of the Q," Lwaxana said more loudly, and she looked up. There was something in her face. Something unpleasant. Something dangerous.

Deanna took her by the shoulders and said urgently, "Mother, let's go—"

"A joke," and now when Lwaxana spoke, it was with a voice that sounded like thunder rumbling over the tops of mountains. "A plot to deliberately humiliate me. And you gave me the power of the Q . . ."

469

"An interesting wrinkle, I'll admit," said Q. "I wanted to see if you'd choose power over the love of your daughter. For you would have lost that love, woman. In a shorter time than you can imagine, they would have come to hate and distrust you as much as they do me. So imagine my lack of surprise when you chose power."

"Power in order to be near you!" she said. "Power out of love for you, you ungrateful, no-good . . ."

Sounding bored, Q said, "Your name-calling is meaningless to me. I'm above such things. This little experiment is over. Love does not conquer all. Only conquest conquers all. Only the kind of power that is generated by weapons and strength, not by the pointless display of a useless emotion."

Lwaxana clenched her fists. "You *used* me! You made me look like a fool!"

"Nature did that," said Q. "I simply gave you an audience."

Her entire body trembled in mortification and shock. And then came a scream, the sort of agonized scream of a fury to which hell had nothing remotely comparable. The fury of a woman scorned.

"Very impressive, Lwaxana," said Q. "Now, if you don't mind, I'll retrieve my powers and be on my way."

Her face darkened, her body stiffened. With a slow, measured tread she started toward him, her fists clenched.

And Q blinked in surprise. "Lwaxana, give me the powers back. You cannot keep them."

Lwaxana was seething, the air crackling around her.

"Mother?" said Deanna nervously.

No less nervous, suddenly, was Q. He stretched out a hand as if yanking something away. Instead there was a sound like energy building up.

"Lwaxana," said Q, looking decidedly less sure of himself. "I don't know what you're doing, or how you're doing it. But you can't have those powers anymore. You can't resist me. *Lwaxana!* You're making me angry! And since I'm above human emotions, that's not possible." He strode toward her, trying to look confident. "So before this goes on any further, give them back to me—now! This is my last word on the subject!"

Lwaxana Troi blew him through a bulkhead.

The bridge shuddered as Data suddenly called out, "Hull integrity breach! In the conference lounge."

Burnside looked up from her station in surprise. "What? Are we under attack?!"

"Apparently," said Data, "the impact was from the inside out." He rechecked his instruments. "The breach has just been repaired."

"Look!" called out Wesley Crusher, pointing at the screen.

Q was floating in front of them, spinning around, looking confused and dazed.

"Someone outside?" said Chafin, utterly nonchalant by this time. "That old chestnut again."

"Mother!" said Deanna in shock.

Picard took a step forward. "Lwaxana," he began.

She spun and Picard saw the look in her eyes. He took a step back and began again, "Lwaxana . . ."

She didn't hear him. She was beyond hearing, beyond caring. The only thing she was able to hear was Q's mocking tone. The only thing she could see was his sneering face. The only thing she could do was go after him. And she did.

In an eyeblink she was outside the ship, behind him. "Q!" she shouted, and naturally he heard her. He turned and Lwaxana's arms extended wide. Energy leaped from them and enveloped Q. He shrieked, twisting and writhing in space, his body snapping about like a stringed puppet.

He flipped backward and vanished.

"You can run, but you can't hide!" shouted Lwaxana Troi, and vanished as well.

Graziunas and Nistral looked at Picard in astonishment.

Picard shrugged gamefully. "Lover's quarrel," he said.

Q dashed down outside of the right nacelle like a sprinter. Lwaxana was right after him. He spun, took a stand. "Lwaxana!" he bellowed. "I don't know how you're doing this! But I want those powers back!"

"How am I doing it?" She advanced on him. "You gave me powers equalling your own. But my mind was already superior to yours, and you heightened it that much further when you empowered me."

"Your mind was never superior to mine! No human mind can be superior to mine!"

"This is no human mind!" she screeched. "This is the mind of a daughter of the Fifth House!"

She reached out and she didn't even have to touch him as she brought her hands down. Q was smashed right through the warp nacelle.

There was pandemonium in the engine room. Q had just hurtled down into the matter/antimatter mix. Alarms were sounding and technicians were running every which way. Geordi was madly trying to shut down all power on the ship, because in ten seconds everything was going to blow.

Q staggered out of the containment area, miraculously leaving all the radiation behind him. He looked dazed, punchy.

A hand clamped down on his shoulder, and from behind a deadly voice continued, "Holder of the Sacred Chalice of Riix!" He turned and Lwaxana swung a right cross that smashed him through the nearest wall. With a gesture she repaired it, and the damage to the mix. Just as quickly as the danger had arisen, it was past.

Q was running, tearing headlong down a corridor. He was desperately watching behind his shoulder, and so ran straight into a fierce kick to the crotch. He went down, gasping.

Lwaxana stood over him, boiling mad. She kicked him over and over for emphasis as he twisted on the floor, trying to get away, as she bellowed, "And keeper [kick] of the Holy [kick] Rings [kick] of Betazed!" and she booted him once more, sending him skidding down the corridor.

Picard, Riker, Worf and Data barreled down a corridor, following the trail of carnage. To their shock, Q came running from the other direction. He skidded to a halt and shouted, "Warn her, Picard! Warn her that she cannot treat me in this manner! She's unleashing forces she doesn't understand!"

"She hasn't listened to me since this whole business started," said Picard calmly. "What makes you think she'll listen now?"

Suddenly Q vanished.

They looked around, certain that he had dematerialized once more, and then abruptly they heard a high-pitched cry of alarm. They looked down.

Q was six inches tall. He was running around on the floor, shaking his teeny fists in impotent fury.

Lwaxana burst into existence above him. "Hello, darling!" she snarled, and brought her foot down.

Q ran frantically, right and left, dodging the pounding feet. "Picard!" he howled in soprano. "Picard!"

She suddenly reached down and grabbed him up. "Got you!" she snarled, and vanished.

The *Enterprise* officers looked at each other.

"She's really beating the stuffing out of him," observed Riker. "What do you think we should do?"

"Sell tickets," rumbled Worf.

Everyone else had left the conference lounge except for Kerin and Sehra. They sat there, holding each other's hands, and Sehra said, "I'm so proud of you."

"If I'd injured you . . . gods, I can't even imagine it. I should never have doubted us. Doubted anything. I'm sorry for everything. Will you give me another chance?"

"If you will for me."

"Of course I will." He grinned. "Isn't being in love wonderful?"

"Computer," said Picard, "locate Lwaxana Troi."

"Lwaxana Troi is in the rocketball court."

Riker blinked in surprise. "What's she doing there?"

Lwaxana swung the glowing paddle with confidence and smashed Q against the wall.

He ricocheted off it and spun backward, out of control. Lwaxana was waiting for him and with a brisk backhand, whacked the miniature god again. He screamed as he careened once more into the wall.

The *Enterprise* officers ran into the spectator area. Mr. Homn was already there. He was sanguinely eating popcorn, watching the "match." When he saw the others, he extended the bag and offered them some.

"No, thank you. Mrs. Troi!" called out Picard.

Q snapped back to his normal size and hurled headfirst into one of the glowing walls.

Lwaxana spun angrily towards Picard. "Jean-Luc! You ruined my concentration!"

Q vanished. Lwaxana vanished after him.

"Here we go again," said Picard.

Crew members were running everywhere, shouting in confusion. Great, horned beasts were charging down the hallway, bellowing their defiance, and barely two steps ahead of them was Q.

He dove right through a corridor wall, leaving the frustrated beasts behind.

He kept on going, passed through to the other side and stepped out into a corridor on the other side of the ship.

Lwaxana was waiting for him. She was clad in full, bristling body armor from ancient Betazed. She was wielding a long weapon that was hooked at one end and spiked at the other. The hooked end lashed out, grabbing Q by the leg and hurling him to the floor. She reversed it and slammed the spiked end down right where Q's chest had been, except he had already melted through the floor.

Lwaxana pushed back her visor. "Damn," she muttered.

Q staggered down a corridor, his mind and body reeling.

He couldn't comprehend any of it. Lwaxana Troi was massacring him. He hadn't been able to mount any sort of offense at all. She just kept on him and on him . . .

Suddenly he saw her waiting for him at the end of the corridor.

He lashed out at her, energy leaping from his fingertips. Lwaxana stood there, weathering the barrage, her hands outstretched. She staggered slightly but otherwise showed no signs of difficulty.

"Give up!" cried out Q. "You can't beat me! I'm Q!"

"You *were* Q!" shot back Lwaxana. "Now you're going to be an ex-Q."

Q's body suddenly began to stiffen. He lost control over his arms, finding himself unable to move them. He tried to run, but his legs wouldn't budge, either. He looked down in horror and saw why— they had taken root. His fingers were becoming small branches. There was a cracking sound like wood splitting, and within seconds, Q had metamorphosized into a tree.

He tried everything he could do to move. He unleashed the full power of his mind, but it was as if something were hanging over it, dampening it. He couldn't counter any of the moves, couldn't focus his strength, couldn't . . .

He heard a sharp, wissing sound. His neck, although wood, was still capable of moving, and he managed to look up.

Lwaxana Troi was coming toward him, wielding a massive, glistening *deelar,* a Betazoid weapon that bore a remarkable resemblance to an axe. It glistened, and for extra effect, blood dripped from it. There was a satisfied grin on her face.

"No!" shrieked Q, almost surprised to see that his voice still worked.

"Now," said Lwaxana firmly. "Now we cut you down to size."

"Mother!" came an alarmed shout.

Lwaxana didn't even glance behind her in response to her daughter's shout. "Not now, dear. Mother's chopping some wood."

"Please don't do this, mother!" She grabbed her by the arm, being certain to keep her fingers clear of the *deelar*'s blade. Several feet away, Q's branches trembled. "Enough! You've made your point! He knows you're angry."

"He humiliated me! I can never have anyone's respect again."

And now Picard was there, and he said, "That's not true, Lwaxana. You've earned all our respect!"

"I, for one, would certainly not wish to have you angry with *me*," Worf informed her.

"He has to apologize," said Lwaxana.

"Q, apologize!" ordered Picard.

Q was silent.

"Q," warned Picard.

"She couldn't really hurt me," Q said uncertainly.

"Are you willing to bet life and limb on that?" Riker demanded.

"Forget it," said Lwaxana. "Stand aside, Riker." She swung the axe back, and it was clear that the first stroke was going to be in Q's nether regions.

"I'm sorry!" howled Q. "I'm sorry! All right? I'm sorry I did it! It was reprehensible! It was hideous! I shouldn't have even contemplated it! I'll never think of it in the future! I don't know what I could have been thinking! I am a terrible and vile individual, not fit to exist in the same universe as the splendid Lwaxana Troi! There, are you happy?!"

She paused, considering it.

"I don't think you mean it," she said, and swung the axe back once more.

But Picard put a firm hand on her shoulder and said, "Enough, Lwaxana. *I* mean it. Enough."

Slowly she lowered the axe, and then it vanished.

"I really would have done it, you know," she told him.

"Yes, we all know that," said Picard.

An instant later, Q transformed back into his normal state. He staggered and stumbled against a wall, confused and gasping.

Lwaxana strode up to him and he flinched. "You hurt me," she said. "You hurt me in ways I didn't even think it was possible. You're so disdainful of humanity. Of mortals. You keep saying you're above our emotions, and hold them in such disdain. You know what I think? I think you're not worthy of them. I think you're not good enough to feel love." Her voice was trembling. "You're just not good enough." And she turned on her heel and walked away.

Deanna started to follow her, but she heard a sharp, *Leave me alone, Little One* in her head, and she stayed where she was.

Q sat on the floor, trying to compose himself. He looked up in irritation and said, "What are you sneering at, Worf?"

"Nothing," said Worf with satisfaction. "I am sneering at a great big nothing."

"You know, your insults are meaningless to me," said Q. "Everything you say is meaningless to me. But that woman—that . . . that damned woman!" His voice was shaking with fury. "She is the most aggravating, infuriating individual I've ever met!" He was getting to his feet, and his body was literally trembling with rage. As opposed to the cold arrogance with which Q usually cloaked himself, now he was clearly angry. "I cannot remember when I've met someone who has actually aroused in me a feeling of such total fury! It is truly staggering! I see her face in my mind, and I just want to grind it beneath my foot! This is truly amazing! I loathe her! I *despise* her! It's not just that she so thoroughly beat me through means that I still cannot even guess. I was humiliated just as badly when I lost my powers, but I didn't feel anything like this . . . this mind-numbing feeling of bile in my mouth! I—"

And Picard, the picture of calm, said serenely, "You will find, Q, that an extreme of one emotion usually indicates that an extreme of another emotion is present."

"What are you blathering about?" demanded Q.

"You see, Q . . . those we love the most are also the most capable of driving us to complete distraction. Because we've left ourselves open and vulnerable, you see. In other words, it's quite possible that you do indeed feel love for her, which is why she is able to make you as angry as she does."

"That's ridiculous. That's . . ." His face fell as he thought of it. "I'm . . . I'm certain that's ridiculous. That can't be. I couldn't actually *be* in love. I'm a being with power far beyond yours. To be laid low by the pathetic emotion you call love, that would be . . ."

"Very human," Riker said, turning the screws.

"Face it, Q," Picard told him. "You've been hanging around humans too much. Your system has not been able to build up proper immunities to us, and we're becoming contagious. You're coming down with a terminal case of humanity."

"Picard," said Q, with a bit of the old arrogance. "Get some hair. Your brain has caught cold." And with a burst of light and sound, he vanished.

"Good riddance," rumbled Worf.

"Oh, I don't know," said Picard slowly. "I hate to admit it . . . but I'm starting to get used to him."

"Captain, you're joking!" Riker said in horror.

Picard turned toward him. "Oh, of course I am, Number One." But he wasn't entirely sure that he was.

## *Mudd in Your Eye,* by Jerry Oltion

Harry Mudd is one of the most unforgettable personalities from The Original Series. He appeared in two *TOS* episodes, "Mudd's Women," and "I, Mudd." He was a wheeler-dealer, out for the main chance, a confidence man seeking profit in a Federation where greed was no longer in style. In *Mudd in Your Eye,* Harry claimed to be a changed man, although Kirk had doubts about his conversion to respectability. Those doubts were not allayed by learning that Harry mediated a peace treaty between Prastor and Distrel, two planets the people of which had been at war for twelve thousand years. Prastor and Distrel had been fighting over the issue of which half of a two-colored fruit to eat, the purple half or the white half. Individually, each was safe to eat, but together, they formed a potent and deadly nerve toxin. Harry convinced the people to make peace by pointing out that the undesired half could be sold to the rest of the galaxy at a nice profit. He, of course, had an ulterior motive beyond making pots of money on the sale of the white fruit slices, and that was to discover the secret to the long-range transporter technology used to beam people and armies between the two planets.

Harry's peace was short-lived. The locals had an amazingly cavalier attitude about death, and eagerly embraced it rather than feared it. With no fear of death, the people had no real incentive to stop fighting. When war began again, Mudd and certain *Enterprise* crew, including Captain Kirk, were killed. In this scene from *Mudd in Your Eye,* Mudd awakened from his mortal wound and learned that on Prastor and Distrel, death was not final. The newly dead, though, were expected to give up their past lives, and the real battle to return to those lives began for Kirk and the *Enterprise* crew.

HARRY HAD DIED AND GONE TO HEAVEN. HE WAS SURE OF IT. HE REMEMbered dying clearly enough, although the last few moments of it were mercifully elusive from recollection, and this place where he found himself now was certainly Heaven. If it wasn't, he didn't care; it was good enough for him.

He had awakened in a pool of warm water. Rather hot water, in fact. The heat had concerned him for a few seconds until he realized that the temperature was just right for relaxing in, and that the jets of bubbles that shot out from the sides were already beginning to soothe the aches and pains from his recent exertion. Then when he looked up and saw the two Nevisian women standing at the foot of his bath, wearing only their smiles, he knew for certain he had gone to the right place.

Especially when the one on the left, light-haired and humanoid in all the right places, said, "Welcome to your new life. I am Aludra."

"And I am Cipriana," said her dark-haired companion.

"And I'm enchanted," Mudd said, sitting up and looking around.

Heaven appeared to be a large building filled with row upon row of tiled pools like the one he rested in. There were no windows, but skylights all along the ceiling let out steam and let in sunlight, which illuminated a multicolored tile mosaic landscape on the walls. There wasn't a stitch of clothing among the hundreds of people he saw soaking in the pools or standing beside them—a delightful sight even for a veteran spacehand who had seen similar situations many times before.

The only disconcerting sight was that everyone here was Nevisian. Their hair had the same hemispherical static-charge look common to Prastorians and Distrellians alike, and though the dampness had taken much of the stiffness out and made everyone appear a great deal more human at the moment, it was obvious that they weren't. And the tiled room echoed with the voices of people conversing in the Nevisian language.

As he watched, two more very surprised-looking people—both Nevisian—materialized in pools down the row from him, and attendants moved to welcome them.

Mudd had never been particularly religious. And it did seem a bit odd that everyone in Heaven spoke Nevisian. But then, he reasoned, he had died in the Nevis system, and the operative word was "died." This was *somebody's* afterlife, no matter what they called it. He was just glad it existed at all. If he wanted to find the human area he would probably have to take a celestial shuttle of some sort.

All in due time. He was in no hurry to go anywhere. Especially when the dark-haired woman at the foot of his pool, Cipriana, said, "We're here to give you a hero's welcome to your new home. Would you like us to bathe you?"

A hero's welcome, eh? Where he came from, that meant considerably more than just a bath, but he had to admit that would certainly make a good start. He lay back in the pool and smiled wide. "My dears, that would be divine."

They both bent down and slipped into the pool with him. From an alcove above his head they took thick padded mitts and drew them onto their hands, then began rubbing his chest and back and sides with the scratchy fabric.

"Oh yes," Mudd sighed, closing his eyes and letting them work their magic. "For this, I would die again and again."

The blond woman, Aludra, giggled. "Silly. If you die a second heroic death, you'll go straight to Arnhall; you know that."

"No, actually, I didn't," said Mudd. "Where's Arnhall? And do they have women as beautiful as you there?"

They both smiled, and Cipriana said, "When we finish our own heroic doublets they will."

"Ah, certainly." Mudd turned to put an itchy shoulder blade under Aludra's mitt. "How do you know I died heroically, anyway? I could have tripped on a stairway, couldn't I, and wound up here just the same?"

Aludra laughed, a high-pitched, musical sound that echoed on the tile walls. "It would have to be a pretty spectacular fall. Only heroes appear in the baths. Accident victims generally get a second chance on their homeworld. And of course cowards are dumped on the street."

"Of course," said Mudd.

She looked at him quizzically, then said, "You really didn't know, did you?"

"No," Mudd admitted.

"That's two of them," Cipriana said to Aludra. "I thought we might have this sort of problem when we started allowing aliens to join us." She said to Mudd, "Do you know Leslie Lebrun Ensign Three Two Seven Five Six Oh?"

"No," said Mudd. "At least I don't think so. Why?"

"Because she arrived just a few minutes ago, and she didn't know where she was, either." Cipriana pointed to Mudd's left. "She's right down there." Aside to Aludra she whispered, "So many names! She must have incredible stories to tell!"

Mudd squinted through the steam. He saw a few heads bobbing above the water, and attendants, both male and female, scrubbing away on their bodies.

And about five pools away he saw a woman with hair hanging down into eyes that were much deeper in their sockets than everyone else's here. Her face was much wider than usual and her ears were rounded on the edges rather than made of overlapping petals. She was, in short, human. Mudd recognized her as the security officer who had accompanied Kirk—and who had been vaporized in the crossfire only a minute or two before Mudd himself had been hit.

That clinched it. If she was here, then this was indeed the afterlife, for he had watched her die.

She didn't seem nearly as happy as he was about winding up here. She held her arms around her knees and her head bowed. Rather than bathing her, her attendants—a muscular young man and an older, motherly woman—sat on the edge of her pool with their feet dangling into the water and simply talked with her.

"Leslie?" Mudd said. "Miss Lebrun?"

She looked up, and her eyes lit with recognition. "Harry Mudd!" Then her brows furrowed and she said, "You didn't make it either."

"No," Mudd told her, "but I believe your sacrifice did save the lives of your crewmates." He couldn't know that for certain, but their absence from the baths seemed fair evidence. Kirk would, of course, go straight to Hell for his crimes, but certainly McCoy wouldn't, nor Spock or the other young security officer.

"I guess that's some consolation." She unwrapped her arms from her knees. "Could I . . . join you over there? No offense," she said to her attendants, "but I could use the human contact right now."

"Certainly, my dear," Mudd said. "I would be delighted."

The older woman said, "Of course you may. That's why people who fought together arrive here together, so you can talk about what happened before you go on to start life anew. Here." She and the man helped Lebrun out of her pool and over to Mudd's. Harry moved aside to give her room on the underwater bench, surprised to realize he was averting his eyes to protect her modesty. Death had apparently affected him as well, or perhaps it was merely the plethora of other delights to occupy his attention, but whatever the cause, she seemed too innocent and upset for him to add to her troubles by ogling her naked body.

Her attendants helped her into the pool, then left to help another person who materialized in a pool nearby. Cipriana and Aludra stayed in the water, though four bodies nearly made it overflow.

When Lebrun had slipped into the water and the jets once again veiled her in bubbles, Mudd smiled at her and said, "I must thank you for your bravery and courage in attempting to rescue me—and I fear I must apologize as well for delaying our departure. I allowed my . . . ah . . . my natural attraction for precious treasures to cloud my judgment."

"Your greed, you mean?" Lebrun said, a trace of a smile on her lips.

Mudd laughed. "You and your captain were cut from the same mold. He always preferred such terms as well. But really, I believe life is what you make of it, and what you call a thing says a great deal about your attitude toward it."

"Life. Right. And what do you call this?" Lebrun held her arms out to include the whole building, and by implication the whole situation that had brought them here.

"An opportunity," said Mudd. "For one, I have escaped that damnable android chaperone of mine. For another, we do seem to have physical bodies again, which is more than I was led to expect. We might even be able to contact our former companions in life and continue our business as usual if we wished, though—"

"No communication is permitted with those you left behind," said Cipriana. "You must leave your former life in the past."

"As I was saying," Mudd finished, "given the circumstances, I for one am glad to be quit of it. A fresh start, that's what I call this."

"I was married the day before yesterday," Lebrun said quietly. "I'm not quite so eager to give that up."

Mudd snorted. "Believe me, if your marriage was anything like mine, another day or two would have been all it would take to change your opinion."

Aludra looked puzzled. "What is marriage?"

"It's when two people agree to share everything, and spend the rest of their lives together," said Lebrun.

"In theory," Mudd corrected. "In practice, it's when two people agree to make life miserable for each other."

Cipriana frowned. "How could you agree to spend your lives together?" she asked Lebrun. "You know you'll be separated the first time one of you is killed."

"I . . . I didn't expect to be . . . killed," Lebrun said. She sniffed,

481

and wiped at her eyes with a wet hand. Cipriana wrung out her bath mitt and handed it to her to dry her eyes with.

"Nobody does, the first time," Aludra said. "But it eventually happens to all of us. It can be very difficult if you've formed strong attachments, but you always have a happy reunion in Arnhall to look forward to."

"That's the second time I've heard you mention—" Mudd began, but a sudden commotion far down toward the other end of the building stopped him in mid question. It sounded as if someone was banging on a door. Banging *hard*. Had they locked an avenging angel out by mistake?

Perhaps they had, for a second later a bright rectangle of light appeared in the wall as the door burst inward. People shouted in alarm, and the blue bolts of disruptor fire speared outward through the sudden gap.

Disruptors in Heaven? That shocked Mudd more than anything he had seen or heard so far.

The shooting died down, and a babble of voices rose to replace its noise. It was difficult to see clearly through the steam, but Mudd thought he could see five or six clothed people near the door—all wearing red.

An ugly suspicion rose in his mind. "Just a minute," he said, turning to Aludra. "Where are we, exactly?"

"Exactly?" Aludra asked, reluctantly looking away from the commotion. "We're in pool seventy-three in hero's reception hall nine, in the city of Novanar, on the southern continent of Kelso. On Prastor," she added helpfully.

"On Prastor," Mudd repeated. He could actually feel his worldview reorient itself to accommodate the news that he hadn't gone to Heaven. It felt a bit like going into warp drive with a badly tuned engine.

Somehow he was still alive, miraculously healed of his disruptor wounds—and back in the same universe he had thought was safely behind him. "Dammit," he said, then, embarrassed at having sworn in the presence of three ladies, he said, "Pardon my Klingon, but I believe our troubles are not over after all."

"Are you kidding?" Lebrun said excitedly. "If this is Prastor, then we can get back in touch with the *Enterprise*. And I can join my husband again."

"That's precisely what I was talking about," Mudd said. He leaned back in the water and let the jets work the renewed tension from his muscles. He had the unpleasant suspicion that he would need all the relaxation he could store up to get through the days ahead.

## *Legends of the Ferengi,* by Quark, as told to Ira Steven Behr and Robert Hewitt Wolfe

This book is not a novel, but is, as described on the cover, "a collection of stories, fables, folk songs, philosophical meditations and outright lies based on the Ferengi Rules of Acquisition." I include it here because it is so funny. Mr. Behr and Mr. Wolfe are, of course, writers for *DS9* (Behr is also that show's executive producer) and Quark is, of course, a fictional character on *DS9*. The book is filled with photos and artwork and fascinating tales behind the Ferengi Rules of Acquisition. *Legends of the Ferengi,* like *Q-In-Law,* is a book that is dangerous to read while riding public transportation unless one does not mind being stared at while shrieking with laughter amidst hordes of tired and silent commuters.

Included here is a letter from Quark to the Publisher demonstrating Rule #33, "It never hurts to suck up to the boss." It somehow seems appropriate.

### Rule 33

To my beloved Publisher:

It is with much pleasure that I thank you for the latinum delivered to me as an advance on the forthcoming <u>Legends of the Ferengi.</u> In return, I am delighted to deliver this, the commentary on the Thirty-third Rule of Acquisition. I'd like this opportunity to say, for the record, what an honor it's been to work for you. To say that your treatment of me has been fair and equitable would be a vast understatement. I am in awe of your fairness, your good judgment and your business acumen. I also think you are as attractive as you are wise. Your lobal cartilage is truly magnificent and the texture of your nose wrinkles denotes a wealth of olfactory instinct.

Please note that when I said I was being paid less than a starving vole merchant and I wouldn't write this book if you held a phaser to my head, it was just a jocular expression of

good fellowship. Subsequent remarks that your royalty statements were steaming stacks of lying worm dung were made
while I was recovering from a severe ear infection and under
prescribed medication.

And so I end this missive grovelling in the hope that you will
find my meager scratching fit for publication and further financial remuneration. May your publishing empire continue to
grow and may your latinum shine forever.

Respectfully yours,
Quark, Son of Keldar

Just a reminder from the people who brought you the Thirty-third
Rule of Acquisition:
*"It never hurts to suck up to the boss."*

## Q's Guide to the Continuum, by Michael Jan Friedman and Robert Greenberger

*Q's Guide to the Continuum,* by Michael Jan Friedman and Robert
Greenberger, is an imaginative and witty collection of galactic trivia
(actually, minutiae), written in Q's unique voice, complete with
sarcastic commentary. *Q's Guide* is illustrated with numerous photo-
graphs and drawings that are reminiscent of carnival sideshows and
that are just as funny as the text. Q's introduction, excerpted here, set
the tone for the entire *Guide.*

### A Message from Q

LET'S GET SOMETHING STRAIGHT. I'M AN OMNIPOTENT BEING. I DON'T *HAVE*
to do this. I could be smashing planets or opening wormholes or tying
cosmic strings together or something.

So listen closely. This isn't just another compendium of eclectic
minutiae. This is the galaxy's most clever, insightful, and authoritative compendium of eclectic minutiae, as reported by someone who's
been on hand for every event in every locale since the dawn of time—
and then some.

You want to know who the longest-lived humanoids in the universe
are? It's in here. You want to get the skinny on the galaxy's most
devoted mother? That's in here too.

Curious about the greatest mass murderers in history? This is the place to look. In fact, any bit of lore that's not in this tome probably isn't worth knowing anyway.

No—not probably. *Definitely.*

So read on. If I were you, I'd get to know these nuggets of wisdom inside and out. I mean, you never know when someone will pop a quiz on you—with say, the fate of the human race hanging in the balance.

# CHAPTER 16

# Special Concepts and Crossover Series

UNTIL RECENTLY, THERE WERE FEW CROSSOVER NOVELS BETWEEN THE FOUR Star Trek series and the motion pictures. Moreover, each novel stood alone; stories that began in one novel did not continue to others. There were occasional examples of guest characters who carried over between novels, but these were rare exceptions. In the summer of 1996, though, Pocket introduced something new, a special crossover series called *Invasion!,* developed by John J. Ordover and Diane Carey.

*Invasion!* was an epic story of invaders from across the galaxy who believed that millennia ago, they had been displaced from territory now occupied by the Klingons and the Federation. They wanted nothing less than the entire Alpha Quadrant and were willing to kill to get it. The saga began in the twenty-third century with the invasion by these "Furies" into Klingon territory in *First Strike,* by Diane Carey. Kirk and the *Enterprise* defeated the Furies, who were forced to retreat. The story continued with a new incursion by the Furies in the twenty-fourth century, with a devastating new weapon, in *Soldiers of Fear,* by Dean Wesley Smith and Kristine Kathryn Rusch. After the Furies were forced back out of the Alpha Quadrant in the twenty-fourth century, the story shifted to the *DS9* crew, with *Time's Enemy,* by L. A. Graf, and the explanation of how the Furies were expelled from the Alpha Quadrant millennia ago. It concluded as the *Voyager* crew confronted the Furies at their home in the Delta Quadrant, in *The Final Fury,* by Daffyd ab Hugh. Each novel told a single story, and together the novels told the larger story of the invasion and defeat of the Furies by the Star Trek heroes.

*Invasion!* was so popular that Pocket published another continuing storyline in 1997 with the Klingon *Day of Honor* series, developed by John J. Ordover and Paula M. Block. The *Day of Honor* series was about a joint Klingon–Federation holiday celebrating honor among enemies. It opened with the *TNG* crew, in *Ancient Blood,* by Diane Carey, continued with *Armageddon Sky,* by L. A. Graf, on *DS9,* then went on to *Voyager* with *Her Klingon Soul,* by Michael Jan Friedman. It concluded with *Treaty's Law,* by Dean Wesley Smith and Kristine Kathryn Rusch, the story of the origins of the Day of Honor holiday from a collaboration between Kirk and the Klingon General Kor. *Voyager* also did a special episode using the novels' Day of Honor concept, entitled "Day of Honor." The *Day of Honor* books have been compiled in an Omnibus edition.

An excerpt from *Invasion! Book One: First Strike,* by Diane Carey, is included in this book in Chapter One, The Captain's Captain: James Tiberius Kirk, and from *Day of Honor, Book One: Ancient Blood,* also by Diane Carey, in Chapter 10, The Noble Enemy, Part I—The Klingons.

The *Invasion!* and *Day of Honor* novels tapped into the fans' desire for continuing story lines, and since their success, Pocket has developed additional crossover series, several continuing story series within the same Star Trek series, and an entirely new Star Trek series for novels alone. The crossovers are *The Captain's Table* and *The Dominion War* novels. So far, there have been *Captain's Table* books featuring Kirk and Sulu, Picard, Sisko, Janeway, Pike, and Calhoun. I would like to see a *Captain's Table* book with Spock, but that is another story.

In the *Captain's Table* novels, there is a bar called the Captain's Table, where only those who have commanded vessels, whether at sea or in space, can enter and share a drink and a story with other captains, across space and time. The Captain's Table bar is a mysterious place, but it seems to be available for captains when they need to get away from their commands for a time, from stress or fatigue, or when they simply need time to clear their heads or relax.

The *Dominion War* series is another first; the *DS9* books by Diane Carey are novelizations of the Dominion War episodes, but the *TNG* books, by John Vornholt, are original novels about the wartime activities of Captain Picard and his crew. In Chapter Five, The Shakespearean Captain—Jean-Luc Picard, there are excerpts from the Picard *Captain's Table* story, *Dujonian's Horde,* by Michael Jan Friedman, and from *The Dominion War, Book Three: A Tunnel Through the Stars,* by John Vornholt.

The *Q Continuum* novels, by Greg Cox, tell a continuing story with

Q, Picard, and the *TNG* crew and introduce Q's baby and the mother of Q's child to the novels. The *Brother's Keeper* series, by Michael Jan Friedman, is the story of the friendship between Gary Mitchell and James T. Kirk. This summer, Pocket will release a crossover series called *The Double Helix.* The *Rebels* series, by Daffyd ab Hugh, is a continuing *DS9* story, and later in the year, a *Voyager* series by Christie Golden will be published.

When the readers eagerly embraced the crossover and multiple book series, John Ordover and Peter David put their heads together to develop an entirely new novel-only Star Trek series for Pocket. *Star Trek: New Frontier,* by Peter David, is a new Star Trek, with a new captain, a new ship, and a new mission. Set on the frontier of Federation space in the wake of the collapse of the Thallonian empire, *New Frontier* is the story of the voyages of the *Starship Excalibur,* commanded by Mackenzie Calhoun. The *Excalibur* patrols the remnants of a once powerful empire that has degenerated into petty squabbles and centuries-old rivalries, and Calhoun's creative ways of dealing with problems are precisely what is needed for the area.

Calhoun is a native of the planet Xenex, where he was known as M'k'n'zy and where he led a successful rebellion against his planet's overlords when he was under twenty years old. Calhoun's first officer, Elizabeth Shelby, is familiar to readers from the *TNG* episodes, "Best of Both Worlds," parts 1 and 2. Several other crewmembers have familiar names from *TNG,* including Dr. Selar and Ensign Robin Lefler, and others are known to readers of other works by Mr. David including Soleta, Zak Kebron, and Mark McHenry.

Readers responded positively to *Star Trek: New Frontier,* and it is safe to say that it is a success. As of this writing, there have been seven *New Frontier* novels, one of them part of the *Captain's Table* series. Two more titles are expected to be released in October 1999, and one of the *Double Helix* novels will include the *New Frontier* characters. The characters are charismatic, likeable, and appealing. They are fallible, but they learn from their mistakes. Calhoun is a unique captain; he can out-cowboy Kirk, but he is as capable as Picard in negotiations with enemies. His style, though, is all his own, and he is not a man you can safely bluff. He will call you on it, with surprising results. This reader looks forward to more in the *New Frontier* series.

The selections for this chapter are from *Day of Honor, Book Four: Treaty's Law,* by Dean Wesley Smith and Kristine Kathryn Rusch, *New Frontier, Book Five: Martyr,* by Peter David; and *The Captain's Table, Book Five: Once Burned,* by Peter David.

# Day of Honor, Book Four: Treaty's Law, by Dean Wesley Smith and Kristine Kathryn Rusch

In *Treaty's Law*, a Klingon colony was attacked by aliens called the Narr, who believed the Klingons were invaders in their own territory. The Klingons, in turn, felt that the Narr were the invaders. Kirk and the *Enterprise* helped to protect the Klingons from the Narr and convinced Kor of the need to negotiate an agreement with the Narr. In this selection, a Klingon family observed the Day of Honor, and the patriarch explained its meaning. Even enemies have honor.

KERDOCH LET HIS GAZE TRAVEL AROUND THE LARGE ROOM FILLED WITH HIS family. The smells of the huge dinner still filled the air, even though his story had been a long one. He blinked and tried to focus on the present. When he told his story of that great battle with the Narr, he always seemed to take himself back. He relived the revenge cycle. The fear of losing his family. The hardships of battle.

Now, just from telling the story, his old bones were tired. Deep down tired. But he wasn't quite finished yet. He had to continue for just a moment longer.

All eyes were still on him. All attention was still focused on his story of that battle all those years before. Every year he held their attention with the story, and many knew it by heart. It seemed that this year he had mesmerized them again. It was not his telling. He knew that. No, it was the importance of the message of the story.

He took a deep breath and let the warmth of the room ease the tiredness in his old bones. Then he continued with the last of the story.

"Commander Kor and the Narr representative met, as they had said they would, twenty days later. Their agreement has stood for all these years."

He looked around at this family.

"But that agreement is not why we celebrate this day. Agreements come and go. But lessons remain always."

He stared down at his grandchildren, who sat at his feet. A five-year-old boy, his eyes bright with fire, stared up at him. "Young K'Ber, can you tell me the lesson?"

K'Ber sat back a moment, his eyes even brighter at the privilege of being picked by his grandfather to answer a question during the telling of the story. Kerdoch wanted to smile at his grandson, but instead kept very still.

The young boy finally said, "The enemy has honor."

"Good," Kerdoch said, smiling at the boy, who seemed to light up at the attention. "We learned that day to celebrate the honor of the enemy as well as the honor of the warrior."

Again Kerdoch looked up and caught his wife's gaze. She was smiling at him proudly, as was his oldest son. That day long ago he had been more than just a farmer, or a colonist. He had been a Klingon warrior. And the retelling brought back the pride he had felt then.

"As Klingons," Kerdoch said, "we have always given honor to those among us who fight. Dying in battle has always been our most honorable death. But it must be remembered that to our enemies, we are the enemy."

Around the room a murmur broke out as his words sank in. They were words to be remembered by them all, as he had done all these years.

He stood and held up his arms over his family gathered in the large room. "Today I tell this story to remind us all to honor those who fight and those who die in battle. Let this Day of Honor be remembered always."

Around him his family stood, cheering, all talking at once.

Again he had done his duty. For another year the story would be remembered. And so would the important lesson that went with it.


## *New Frontier, Book Five: Martyr,* by Peter David

In this excerpt, Captain Mackenzie Calhoun and Commander Elizabeth Shelby explained their report of the destruction of the planet Thallon and the disintegration of its empire to Starfleet Admiral Edward Jellico, who had some difficulty accepting their version of reality. Certain of the *Excalibur's* adventures and experiences were somewhat unusual, particularly the encounter with the Great Bird of the Galaxy. When Jellico expressed doubt about the veracity of the report, Calhoun responded by pointing out the improbability of some of Kirk's adventures.

"THE GREAT BIRD OF THE GALAXY."

Admiral Edward Jellico's face, incredulity written in large letters all over it, glared disbelievingly out from the comm screen at Mackenzie Calhoun and Elizabeth Paula Shelby, who were seated in the conference lounge in apparently relaxed fashion. Jellico's tone of voice came as absolutely no surprise to Shelby; she'd had a sneaking suspicion what he was going to say before he said it. She could see the nice view Jellico had outside his window at Starfleet headquarters: the Golden Gate Bridge, the occasional shuttle floating past. It seemed pleasant enough, and yet she wondered how he managed to tolerate it. If Shelby didn't have stars to look out at, she was certain she would go completely mad.

"The Great Bird of the Galaxy?" he said again.

"Yes, Admiral, that's correct," Calhoun said.

"You're telling me," Jellico leaned forward as if somehow that would bring him closer to the captain of the *Excalibur,* "that the entire planet of Thallon was smashed apart by a giant flaming bird, clawing its way out to freedom, and that it then flew away to who-knows-where?"

"I find it hard to believe myself, but yes, Admiral, that's essentially what I'm saying."

"Captain Calhoun, what do you take me for? Calhoun . . . Shelby," Jellico began again with an air of forced patience, "I know you don't think much of me—"

"That's not true, sir," Shelby assured him.

"Absolutely not," agreed Calhoun. *In point of fact,* Calhoun thought, *we actually don't think of you at all.*

Calhoun reached down subtly to rub his right shin where Shelby had just kicked him under the table. He fired an annoyed look at her, and blocked his mouth from Jellico's view with one hand as he murmured, "Striking a superior officer?"

Shelby reached up to scratch the back of her neck, shielding her face from Jellico's view long enough to mutter back, "If you want to *stay* a superior officer, don't say whatever it is you're thinking." Without waiting for him to respond, she turned to Jellico and said, "Admiral, how you are viewed or not viewed by the command personnel of the *Excalibur* has nothing to do with the matter at hand. The ship's log, the science log, even our visual records, all confirm what it was that we saw."

"Visual records can be arranged, Commander. To imply that seeing is necessarily believing is a charmingly antiquated notion that hasn't had a shred of truth to it in about four centuries now."

"Granted, Admiral, but the fact remains: Somehow this creature burrowed into the heart of the planet Thallon, and provided the energy-rich resources which enabled the Thallonians to become the dominant world that they grew into. It was the creature's imminent . . . *hatching,* if you will . . . that caused the drain of power, the destruction of the world, and the fall of the Thallonian Empire."

"Commander," Jellico said patiently, "empires fall because of any number of things. Economic collapse. Political infighting. Inbreeding causing a downward spiral in the quality of its rulers. Empires do not fall because giant flaming birds smash the home world to bits!"

"Well . . ." Shelby paused, looked to Calhoun, who shrugged. She turned back to Jellico. "Not as a rule . . ."

"Commander—"

"Admiral, be reasonable. Do you really think someone would go to all this effort just for the purpose of perpetrating some sort of massive hoax on you? With all due respect—"

"There's that phrase again," sighed Jellico. "The one that always precedes something said with a total lack of respect."

"With all due respect," Shelby said more forcefully, "doesn't that sound like an odd view of the galaxy? I mean, really now. Ship's log, science log . . . all to pull a joke on us?"

"Or perhaps to cover up some sort of—"

"Of what?" Calhoun now cut in, and the veneer of affable amusement, and even faint condescension, was gone. "May I ask, Admiral, what you are implying?"

"May I ask, Captain, what you are inferring?" countered Jellico.

"I am inferring," replied Calhoun, "that you think there may have been some sort of sloppiness on my part, and that the report we've given you was constructed—in all its outrageousness—to fool us. And that we fell for it. And if that is the case, Admiral," and his voice lowered in a tone that bordered on deadly, "then I am going to have to ask you to apologize."

"Apologize to you, Captain?" asked Jellico with clear skepticism.

"No, Admiral. To be perfectly blunt—"

"As if that were a change of pace."

"I couldn't give a damn what you think of me," continued Calhoun as if Jellico hadn't spoken. "But Elizabeth Shelby is one of the most capable humans I've ever known."

"Captain, this isn't necessary," Shelby tried to say.

But he ignored her and continued. "The notion that she would fail to see through *any* hoax is, frankly, insulting. And if you do not retract that statement, then I shall file a formal complaint with Starfleet Command."

"What 'statement,' Captain?" replied Jellico. "You're asking me to retract an inference that you yourself made. I am simply saying that I find this report of your activities in Sector 221-G, formerly known as Thallonian space, to be somewhat . . . dubious."

"If that is the case, Admiral," Calhoun replied, "if you truly think that running into a figure of mythology or history such as the Great Bird of the Galaxy is too preposterous, then I take it you will not want to hear about it should we happen to encounter . . . oh, I don't know . . . Apollo?"

"Or Zephram Cochrane?" Shelby added. "Or—what was his name—the knife murderer . . .?"

"Jack the Ripper?" offered Calhoun.

"Yes!" She snapped her fingers as the memory came back. "Jack the Ripper. Thank you. You know, I have to tell you, Admiral, in comparison to those incidents, a giant flaming bird seems a fairly modest claim."

Jellico rubbed the bridge of his nose, suddenly looking rather tired. "Very amusing, Captain, Commander. You refer to Kirk, of course."

"Well, he *was* required reading at the Academy, sir," said Shelby.

"He was required reading because of his tactics and strategy," clarified Jellico. "His more 'outrageous' exploits were hardly required."

"True, sir, but in Kirk's case, sometimes the footnotes were far more interesting reading than the main events."

"That may be the case, Commander, but here's the truth of it: My great-grandfather was in Starfleet Command during Kirk's time. And the fact was, Kirk had some very staunch supporters. That served him well, because he also had any number of people whom he had angered with his constant glory-hounding and utter disregard for regulations. And it was widely believed in Starfleet that, every so often, he would file utterly preposterous reports, just to tweak those individuals whom he knew didn't like his style and his way of doing things. Such as the incident with the giant killer amoeba. And that totally ridiculous alleged occasion in which his first officer's brain was stolen. I mean, come *on,* people. Clearly, these things could not possibly have happened. Every time you heard uncontrolled laughter ringing up and down the hallways at Starfleet Command, you could tell that Kirk had filed another one of his whoppers."

"Did anyone entertain the notion that they might all be true, sir?" asked Calhoun.

"Yes, they did, and every single one of Kirk's crew swore to their dying day that every insane thing Kirk encountered was the absolute truth. To some people, that was sufficient proof of Kirk's veracity. To others, it simply showed the incredible depth of loyalty from his people." For just a moment, Jellico's expression seemed to soften, to become reflective. "Either way, I suppose, that made Kirk a man to be envied."

Calhoun and Shelby glanced at each other in undisguised surprise. Jellico actually sounded almost envious of the legend of Kirk.

Jellico seemed to refocus on Calhoun, and his brow furrowed. "This isn't about Kirk, and it isn't about me. From now on, I expect to receive reports that are not fanciful extrapolations of reality. Is that understood?"

"Fully, Admiral," Calhoun said quietly, but his purple eyes were blazing with undisguised annoyance.

"You have a good deal of latitude, Captain, out there in Thallonian space. You're the only starship out there. You're operating without a net, so don't expect me to be there to catch you when you fall."

"Understood."

Jellico looked from one of them to the other, as if expecting them, even daring them, to say something that might be considered challenging. But they simply sat there, tight-lipped, and Jellico grunted before saying, "Jellico out." His image blinked off the screen.

"That was certainly a little piece of heaven," Shelby sighed, slumping back in her chair. She noticed the way Calhoun was looking at her. "What's the problem?"

"You kicked me," Calhoun said.

"Oh, that."

"Yes, that. That's a hell of a thing to be on the receiving end from the queen of Starfleet regulations. I'd be most interested to see the one where it says that it is acceptable to kick one's commanding officer."

"It's more of an unwritten rule. You were about to say something that would get you is deep, Mac, and in so doing were dragging me along with you. Don't think of it as an assault. Think of it as self-defense."

"I can't say I appreciated it."

"I didn't do it to gain your appreciation. I did it to get your attention."

"Well, next time might I suggest something a little less painful?"

"I would have tried a striptease. That's always worked in the past," she said with no hint of a smile. "But somehow I think the Admiral might have noticed."

"Perhaps. Certainly might have gotten you that promotion you've always wanted."

She blew air impatiently from between her lips as she rose from the table. "Don't bring that up."

"Bring what up?"

"Did you see the promotion list recently? I was scanning it over and did a double take when I saw 'Captain Shelby' commanding the *Sutherland*. For half a second I thought I'd been promoted and someone forgot to tell me, and then I realized it was someone else. It should have been me, Mac. But instead, I'm still . . ."

"Stuck with me?"

She sighed. "You know, Mac . . . the whole world doesn't have to be about you. That's one of the things you always did that drove me crazy. It's my problem, okay? Not yours."

"It doesn't have to be yours either, if you'd only be happy with what you've got."

"With what I've got?" She leaned her back against the wall, her hands draped behind her, and she looked bleakly at Calhoun. "This Captain Not-Me Shelby is in the thick of things. There's a major push going on with about three quarters of the fleet, and he's smack in the middle. And us, we're . . ."

"Exploring," Calhoun noted. "Last I checked, that's what Starfleet is supposed to be all about. *Grozit* Eppy, you know that as well as anyone. Better than most, in fact."

She glanced at him. " '*Grozit*'? Reverting to Xenexian profanity?"

"Xenexian profanity. Sorry. I'll try to watch myself."

"Not on my account, although your command of Terran profanity is fairly comprehensive."

"I have an ear for languages."

She half-sat on the edge of the table. "The problem is, Mac, that first and foremost, I'm a tactician. That's my strength, what I was trained for. Analyzing an enemy's weakness, seeing where they can be out-thought or defeated. That sort of thing is where I really come alive, Mac. But here, I feel like . . ."

"Like you're wasting your time?"

She studied him and, to her surprise, she saw something in his eyes that she had thought he really wasn't capable of: hurt. He seemed hurt over the very notion that she would want to be elsewhere or that she could think that her time as first officer of the *Excalibur* was not a worthy test of her skill.

"No," she said softly. "No . . . I don't think that at all. Face it, Mac, you'd be lost without me."

"I don't know if I'd be lost," he replied. "But I'd be far less eager to be found."

She was genuinely touched. It was times like this that reminded her exactly how and why she had become involved with Mackenzie Calhoun in the first place. How they had wound up lovers, engaged to be married, until the relationship had broken down under the weight of their conflicting personalities. "That is so sweet," she said.

He shrugged. "I have my moments."

She found that she was looking at him in a way that she hadn't in quite a long time. When she'd signed aboard the *Excalibur,* it had been for the purpose of more or less riding herd on Calhoun. Of making sure that he toed the line when it came to Starfleet policy. And she had been quite, quite sure that their history together and their past romance would not factor in to their day-to-day interaction.

But now . . .

"Do you really feel that way, Mac?"

He laughed gently, walked over to her, and put his hands on her shoulders. "You want me to be honest, Eppy? When you first came aboard and applied for the job as my first officer, I was relieved to see you. Then, after I agreed to take you on, I decided that I must have been completely crazy to do so. And when we began fighting over protocol and the official Starfleet view of procedures—"

"That's when you were *really* sorry that I was here?" she said teasingly, although she had a feeling, deep down, that she'd actually put her finger on it.

But he shook his head. "No. That's the point at which I became convinced that taking you on was the absolute right thing to do. You make me think, Eppy." He rapped the side of his head with his knuckles. "It's not always easy to crack through this heavy-duty shielding into my head. I don't always agree with what you say, Eppy. But even when we're disagreeing. I'm still thinking about everything you say. You make me think, and that's not always easy to do."

"So you always listen to me, then."

"Always," he smiled.

The door to the conference lounge slid open, and standing there was Doctor Selar. She looked utterly composed, her arms folded across her chest. "Captain, may I speak to you in private for a moment?"

"I'll just excuse myself then." Shelby left, smiling to herself. For reasons Calhoun wasn't certain of.

"This is . . . a delicate matter to discuss, Captain," Selar said slowly."

"I appreciate that," Calhoun said. "And I think you'll find that there is no matter so delicate that I can't be trusted with it."

"Very well, Captain." She paused a moment, as if steeling herself. And then she said, "It is my desire to have sex with you."

"My . . . apologies, Doctor," Calhoun said slowly. "Did you just say you—"

"Desire to have sex with you, yes," she nodded. "There is an explanation, which can be summarized in two words."

"Good taste?" he suggested.

*"Pon Farr."*

"Ah. Well, that would have been my second guess."

"That is a sort of . . . of Vulcan mating ritual, isn't it?" Calhoun asked slowly. "I mean, I've heard rumors about it, but Vulcans tend to stay fairly closed-lipped about such things."

"It is considered . . . inappropriate . . . to discuss the matter with outworlders," Selar told her. "However, I feel I have no choice in the matter. Besides, it may be that my role as a clinician makes it . . . easier"—she forced the word out—"to discuss matters pertaining to a medical situation. It is not a ritual precisely. It is a . . . a drive. An urge that cannot be denied, no matter how much we may desire to do so." She put a finger to her temple, as if to steady herself, and then said more calmly, "We must mate."

"To conceive a child?" asked Calhoun.

"Yes. You see, it could easily be argued that there is no logical reason to have a child. Ever. They are burdensome, they are limiting, they habitually expel bodily fluids out of a variety of orifices at high velocity, and they are extremely time consuming. So, for a race whose every action is defined by logic, that race would—by definition—face extinction."

"But to allow the demise of your race just to avoid child-rearing is also illogical," pointed out Calhoun.

"In which case, perpetuation of the species becomes a chore. An obligation. To live with such an onerous situation is also not logical. Therefore our very nature, our bodies, have developed in such a way that logic simply does not enter into the conception of children."

"Believe me, it's frequently no different on Earth," Calhoun said ruefully. He paused a moment, pulling himself back to the major topic at hand. "But certainly you can't expect the captain—"

"I can and do," Selar replied evenly. She looked straight into Calhoun's eyes. "You are the most appropriate individual to handle this matter, Captain. At the moment, my options are extremely limited. The *Pon Farr* drive is in remission for the time being, so this need not be attended to immediately. But it will resurge again and again: each time with greater impetus and a greater need to be satisfied. I am requesting that, upon the next resurgence, when the drive is upon me, you satisfy my genetically driven lust. Will you honor my request, M'k'n'zy of Calhoun?"

"I shall *consider* it, Doctor," Calhoun told her. "I'm leaning towards 'yes,' but can I have a little time to think about it?"

Despite her Vulcan training, Selar let out a sigh and sagged slightly in visible relief. "I am . . . pleased . . . to hear that. And yes, of course, take all the time you need. Just . . . not too much."

"A request has been made of M'k'n'zy of Calhoun, the man I was," Calhoun said reasonably. "I can't turn that aside. Doctor, if I do agree to it, kindly let me know when and where you will find my . . . services . . . required. Several hours' notice would be appreciated if that's at all possible."

"I will make every effort to accommodate you, Captain. And I would, in turn, appreciate if we could keep this matter between us."

"Sounds like a plan."

She nodded and, as if the matter were completely settled, she turned to leave to find that at some point in her conversation with the captain, the doors to his office had quietly opened by themselves.

At least half a dozen crewmen were walking past at the time. To say nothing of the fact that her voice apparently carried halfway down the corridor.

Selar visibly winced.


# *The Captain's Table, Book Five: Once Burned,* by Peter David

Young M'k'n'zy of Calhoun first stumbled into the Captain's Table bar not long after he lost his crew in a battle against the Danteri, the tyrants who dominated his home planet, Xenex. He was the youngest captain ever to visit the bar, and his visit helped him deal with the loss of his crew. Many years later, in this excerpt from *Once Burned,* Captain Mackenzie Calhoun of the *Starship Excalibur* found the bar again through an entrance on the ship's holodeck. Although Mac was reluctant to share a story, Cap reminded him that a story was the price of admission, and Mac revealed more about himself than he had in the previous *New Frontier* novels. But did he really? His choice of fellow captains with whom to share his story made a fascinating tale by itself. In this excerpt, Mac began his story by describing how he encountered the Captain's Table.

"ARE YOU TROUBLED, MY SON?" ASKED THE ANDORIAN.

"I'm fine. Really," I said, turning away.

"Do you know what you need?"

"I said that I would be fi—"

"You need a drink."

It was startling words to hear coming from a holodeck replication. I turned back and looked thoughtfully into his face. There seemed to be no artifice, no sense of guile. For someone who was fake, he seemed one of the most "real" individuals I had ever met.

"A drink, holy man?" I replied cautiously.

"Yes. A drink. I think that may be where you want to go," and he pointed toward the end of the street. "I have heard good things about it."

I looked where he was pointing, and couldn't even begin to believe what I was seeing. A sign hung outside. The logo was in Rigellian, but the meaning was abundantly clear:

The Captain's Table.

By that point I was nothing short of stunned, for even though my encounter with the Captain's Table had occurred almost thirty years ago, the memory of the place was as vivid as if it had happened the previous day. Was it staggering coincidence? Two places in two different star systems, both with the same name?

And what was most bizarre about the situation was that I had walked those actual streets in the past. Not holos of them, but the real items. If the holodeck was supposed to be an accurate representation of the area, why would it have manufactured a doorway to a tavern that wasn't there?

I turned back to the holy man, but there was no sign of him. He had disappeared back into the crowd. I looked to the door and rubbed my eyes, as if doing so would somehow expunge the contradictory sight. But no, it was still right there. I felt as if it were mocking me.

"All right. Enough's enough," I said. I walked up to the door of the Captain's Table and pushed it open.

The weight of the world was still there. It hit me the moment I entered. Somehow, though, it didn't seem quite as heavy as before. Perhaps I had built up strength in my upper torso from years of carrying it myself.

There was also that faint aroma, the smell of sea air. As opposed to the first time, when it had puzzled me, this time I felt invigorated. I inhaled deeply, and my lungs fairly tingled from the sensation.

Then my rational mind took over and informed me that this simply couldn't be. It was flat-out impossible for the Captain's Table, for the real Captain's Table bar, to somehow have materialized within the holodeck. Perhaps it was some sort of elaborate prank. Perhaps it was just wishful thinking. No matter what the case, there was no way that I was going to allow it to continue. The memories of that place were too deep, too personal to me. I couldn't permit a shadow of it to exist. Since I was in the holodeck, of course, there was a simple way to put an end to it.

"End program," I said.

Nothing happened. The patrons of the bar continued in their conversations, although one or two of them might have afforded me a curious glance. It wasn't like the last time, when the presence of the incredibly scruffy and disheveled barbarian youngster immediately captured the attention of all the patrons. I was older, more "normal"-looking. Still, in many ways I was just as confused as I was the first time I'd walked into the place. I was simply a bit more polished in my presentation.

"Computer, end program," I repeated. Still nothing happened. That was a flat-out impossibility. "Computer, end program!" When I received no response, I tapped my communicator. "Calhoun to bridge." No response.

I started to head for the door, and then a very familiar voice stopped me. "Leaving so soon, M'k'n'zy? Oh, that's right. You go by 'Mac' these days. At least, 'Mac' to your friends."

I turned, knowing ahead of time what I would see. Sure enough, there was Cap. The fact that he was exactly as I had remembered him from more than twenty years earlier was almost proof positive that I was in a holodeck re-creation. "I'd like to think," continued Cap, "that I can still count myself among your friends. That is the case, isn't it?"

"How . . . is this possible?" I asked.

He looked at me strangely as if he found it puzzling that I could even question it. "Why shouldn't it be possible? It's the most natural thing in the world. You saw a door for the Captain's Table, you walked through it, and lo and behold, you're in the Captain's Table. It's not as if you entered a door with our sign on it and found yourself in the middle of a baseball field."

"It would make equally as much sense," I said.

"Mac," and he shook his head disappointedly, "are you going to spend all your time here complaining and questioning? Or are you going to . . ." He stopped and stared. "What's wrong?"

I had totally lost focus on what Cap was saying, because I had spotted . . . *him* . . . across the bar.

He was just as I remembered him. The only difference was that he seemed a bit younger than he appeared to me when I'd first seen him. Maybe it was because I felt so much older, or maybe it was . . .

. . . maybe it was something else.

His hair was that same odd combination of gray with white at the temples. The same heavy eyebrows, the same jowly face and eyes that seemed to twinkle with merriment which gave him, in some ways, an almost elfin appearance. His Starfleet uniform was as crisp and clean as I remembered it. And his commbadge was right in place, with no drop of blood on it. He was engaged in an active discussion with several other captains of assorted races, and he didn't even glance my way. I might as well have been invisible to him.

"Kenyon," I whispered. "Captain Kenyon."

He didn't hear me, of course. I was on the opposite side of the tavern. But I was going to change that very quickly.

"Mac," Cap said. I knew that tone of voice; it was the same warning tone that he had used when I had confronted the Roman captain. In this case, it sounded even more firm and strident than it had the previous time. But I didn't care; it wasn't going to slow me down for a moment.

I started to make my way across the pub, toward Kenyon. That was when things started to happen.

It was subtle, at first, and then it became more pronounced. A waitress getting in my way, turning me around. Then a crowd of revelers moved between Kenyon and myself. When they passed, I had lost sight of Kenyon . . . and then spotted him, apparently as he had been before except it seemed as if the table had relocated somehow. I angled in that direction . . . and encountered more bar patrons, another waitress. A bus boy dropped a stack of dishes, and I reflexively glanced in the way of the crash. When I looked back, Kenyon was somewhere else again, except there was no indication that he'd moved.

"What the hell?" I muttered.

Cap was at my elbow. "Sit down, Mac," he said firmly.

"Cap, I . . ."

"Sit . . . down."

Had someone else taken that tone of voice with me, I would have bristled, barked back, had any of a hundred reactions, all of them aggressive. But something in Cap's look and tone prompted me to sit down as meekly as a first-year cadet. More meekly, actually, come to think of it, considering that in my first year at the Academy I dislocated the jaw of a third-year student when he made some condescending remarks.

There was sympathy in his eyes, but also firmness, as he sat opposite me. "There are certain rules of the Captain's Table, Mac," he said not unkindly. "And one of the big rules is that no one here can do anything to change the timeline or fate of anyone else. That falls under the category of duty, and at the Captain's Table, one is expected to leave one's duties at the door."

"But I can't just let him sit there and not know . . . not when I can tell him . . ."

"That, Mac, is precisely what you not only can do, but have to do. No man should know his own destiny. No man can know; otherwise he just becomes a pawn of fate and no longer a man."

"That's a nice philosophy, Cap. And I'm supposed to just stand by and—"

"Yes, Mac," and this time his tone was flat and uncompromising. "Rules of the house. I'm afraid that is exactly what you're supposed to do."

I stared forlornly across the tavern at him. Never had the cliché "So near and yet so far" had quite as much meaning to me. "Why am I here, then?" I asked in annoyance. "I mean . . . I would have thought that the reason one comes here is to relax."

"It is."

"How can I relax? How am I supposed to do that when I see Kenyon there, right there. It's within my ability to help him, to warn him . . ."

"It wouldn't help, Mac. In fact, it would very likely hurt, in ways that you can't even begin to imagine. You can't say anything. More to the point, you won't say anything."

My temper began to flare ever so slightly. "And if I simply choose to walk out the door rather than stay here under your rules?"

"All of us have free will, Mac. You can go as you please."

"But not necessarily come back?"

He smiled thinly. "We've always been a bit of a catch-as-catch-can operation, Mac. If you're looking for a guarantee that you'd be back, well . . . no promises. But if you did continue to try and flaunt the rules of the house, well . . . ." He shrugged noncommittally.

I looked down. "I've never been much for rules."

502

"Yes, I know that," he said. "Sometimes that has served you quite well. After all, if you stuck to the rules, your homeworld would still be under the thumb of the Danteri. And you would not be as good a captain as you are."

"You think I'm a good captain?" I asked.

"Yes. But why does it matter what I think?"

"I don't . . ." I considered the question, and then said, "I don't . . . know. But it does. Maybe it's you. Maybe it's this place."

"Maybe it's a little of both," said Cap. "We bartenders, we're surrogates. Surrogate parents, father confessors, what have you. We try not to judge."

"That a house rule, too?"

"No. Just a bit of common courtesy." Suddenly he turned and snapped his fingers briskly once. I was confused for a moment, but then a waitress came over as if by magic and, without a word, deposited a beer in front of me.

"I take it your tastes haven't changed, even though your appearance has somewhat," he said. "The scar in particular. Very decorative."

"Thank you," I said ruefully. "Sometimes I consider allowing someone else to lay open the other side of my face so that I'll have balance."

"Not a bad idea," Cap replied, and I couldn't entirely tell whether he was being sarcastic or not.

The glass was frosted, and the beer felt good going down. I lowered the mug and tapped it. "I take it I'm old enough that my drinks are no longer free."

"You take it correctly. There is a price attached. A story."

"A story. You mentioned that last time. You want me to tell you a story? It sounds rather juvenile."

"Not me," Cap said in amusement, as if the mere suggesting of such a thing was an absurdity. "No, I'm just the bartender."

"There's something about you, Cap, that makes me think you're not 'just' anything."

He let the remark pass. "No, the tales told here are for the customers, Mac. For your fellow captains, who love tales of adventure and derring-do."

"I don't think my do is particularly derring. Besides, I . . . don't particularly like stories. Especially stories about myself."

"I'm surprised you would feel that way, Mac. I would have thought that someone like you, a planetary hero, would be accustomed to hearing stories of his adventures bandied about."

"I am. That's part of the point." I took another sip of beer. "When I worked to liberate Xenex, I heard tales of my adventures and endeavors, spreading from town to town. Sometimes a storyteller would speak to an audience spellbound by the manner in which he wove tales of my exploits. And I would sit at the outer fringes of such gatherings and gather no notice at all for the M'k'n'zy of Calhoun who featured in those tales was seven and a half feet tall, with eyes of blazing fire, muscles the size of mighty boulder. His preferred weapon was a sword so massive that it took either one M'k'n'zy or three normal men to wield it, and when he walked the ground trembled beneath his mighty stride and beautiful women threw themselves upon him and begged him to sire their children."

"And none of that was true?" Cap asked.

"Well . . . maybe the part about the women," I allowed.

We both laughed softly for a moment, and then I grew serious. "But I knew that these fables were just that, Cap . . . fables. They bore no resemblance to the real world. In those stories, I single-handedly slaughtered hundreds—no, thousands—of Danteri troops. My troops supposedly stood in awe of my prowess and fell to their knees in worship of me. It was all nonsense. Stories are not real life. In real life, good does not always triumph, and decent people suffer for no purpose and receive no final redemption. Stories are the antithesis of life, in that stories must have a point. I live in the real world, Cap. Sweet fictions have no relevance to me."

"Don't sell such fables short, Mac. You do them, and you, a disservice. Consider the effect such stories had on your own people. When they heard tales of the great M'k'n'zy, they drew hope from that. It sustained them, nourished their souls in their time of need. So what if there were exaggerations? Who cares if the reality did not match the fancy? What was important was that it took them out of themselves, gave them something to think about besides the difficulties of their lives. Dreams are very powerful tools, Mac. By hearing the stories of your great deeds, the Xenexians dreamed of a better life. From the dreaming came the doing. Life imitates art which imitates life in turn, and stories of your adventures are just part of that cycle."

"I suppose . . ."

"No supposing. Take my word for it. And now, Mac, this is what you're going to do: You're going to find another captain or captains here, and you will sit him, her, or them down, and you will tell a story of your exploits. If you feel constrained to adhere to reality . . . if you must tell a story where good does not triumph, or decent people suffer . . . if that is what's required for you to maintain the moral purity of your soul, who am I to gainsay you?"

"Who are you indeed?" I asked. "That's actually something I've been wondering about. Who are you when you're not being you, Cap?"

"I am," Cap smiled, "who I am." He patted me on the shoulder as he rose. "Find a willing audience, Mac. Find it and share something of yourself. You owe it to them, to yourself . . ." He touched the mug of beer. ". . . and to your tab."

I watched him head back to his bar. I noticed for the first time that he walked with a very slight limp. I had no idea why, nor could I find it within me to ask. I had the feeling that I'd just get another roundabout, vague answer.

For a moment I considered getting up and heading out the door. But part of me was concerned that I really wouldn't be able to find the place again, no matter how hard I looked. I still wasn't entirely sure what I was doing there in the first place, or how I'd gotten to it. But it had become apparent that, when it came to questions about the Captain's Table, less was generally preferable to more.

"I still think it's a waste of time," I told him.

"There are some things in this galaxy that are for us to think about. And there are other things that are for us to do. This is one of the latter. Understand?"

I didn't, but I said that I did.

I suppose the real truth of it is that I simply don't like to share things. I don't like to say what's going on in my mind. Call it my military upbringing, if you will. I tend to dole out information on a need-to-know basis. Otherwise I tend to keep things to myself.

But I like Cap, and I like this place. I would hate to think that I should never find my way back to it again, be it by happenstance, cosmic direction, destiny, or plain dumb luck. So for once even the mighty, rule-flaunting Mackenzie Calhoun will play by the rules. You seem like a worthy individual to tell my story to; indeed, you may be the best qualified here.

My previous post to the captaincy of the *Excalibur* was as first officer aboard the *Starship Grissom.*

Perhaps the name should have cautioned me. It was named after an Earth astronaut, Virgil "Gus" Grissom. His career in space started off impressively enough. Grissom was the second American in space, flying a suborbital vessel called the *Liberty Bell,* which was part of the

Mercury program. He flew in the Gemini program after that. He was well liked and respected, and his career was on the fast track for greatness . . . just like mine seemed to be.

And then he died. He did so horribly, asphyxiating aboard a flight simulator which erupted in flames. A man like that, if he were to die in action, deserved to die in space. That's where his heart was, where his destiny was. Instead his career was cut short thanks to a terrible accident. It should not have happened that way.

That reminds me of me as well.

But I knew none of that when the assignment aboard the *Grissom* was presented to me. I simply saw it as an opportunity, a chance to advance in the career that I was quite certain was to be mine by divine right.

I was to learn otherwise. And it all ended . . . rather badly.

Here's what happened.

# CHAPTER 17

# Novelizations of Episodes and Motion Pictures

STARTING WITH *TMP* AND CONTINUING THROUGH *STAR TREK: INSUR-rection,* Pocket has published novelizations of each of the motion pictures and eleven very special episodes, including "Encounter at Farpoint," "Unification," "Relics," "Descent," "All Good Things . . . ," "Emissary," "The Way of the Warrior," "Far Beyond the Stars," "What You Leave Behind," "Caretaker," and "Flash-back." In the days before tape players and videotapes were widely available, novelizations provided viewers with their only record of the episodes and films. The James Blish *TOS* episode novelizations in the *Star Trek Readers* published by Bantam were very popular, as were the "Logs" of the animated series by Alan Dean Foster published by Ballantine. Even though videotapes of all the films and most of the episodes eventually became available, novelizations remain popular because they enrich the stories with additional detail and the characters' thinking processes. Each of the novelizations quoted from here could stand alone as a novel.

### *Far Beyond the Stars,* a novel by Steven Barnes, based on "Far Beyond the Stars," teleplay by Ira Steven Behr & Hans Beimler, story by Marc Scott Zicree

The novelization to the *DS9* episode "Far Beyond the Stars" is perhaps the best novelization in twenty years of novelizations; it is certainly one of the best novels as well. The episode "Far Beyond the Stars" may also be *DS9*'s finest hour. In *Far Beyond the Stars,* Captain Ben Sisko flashed in and out of a dream state in which he lived the life of a science fiction writer of the 1950s named Benny Russell, struggling to gain respectability writing stories about a black science fiction hero. Life was harsh for Benny Russell, but there seemed to be a power guiding him, urging him to tell his story about Captain Ben Sisko despite the setbacks caused by a racist world not willing to accept a story about a hero who was not white.

Mr. Barnes's novel told much more of Benny's story than the episode was able to do. It explored Benny's childhood and young adult years in Harlem and described his life-changing encounter with the Prophets. Although much of his life was tragic and heart-rending, the story ended with optimism and hope because despite Benny's suffering, the racist world could not destroy his idea. The idea gave his life meaning and purpose, and nothing could take that away.

In this passage from *Far Beyond the Stars,* Benny visited the World's Fair in Flushing, New York in 1940. At a pavilion in the Hall of Nations sponsored by the Dogon people of Mali, Benny encountered an hourglass-shaped artifact that spoke to him. . . .

## 1940

MR. COOLEY AND HIS GROUP FOUND THEIR WAY TO THE AMUSEMENTS AREA, where Benny was guided away from the dancing girl shows. ("I don't think those white men would greatly appreciate Negro boys looking at those half-naked white girls," Cooley said. Little Cassie was more direct and explicit about it and expressed, strongly, the opinion that there wouldn't be anything in there worth seeing at all.)

Despite stupendous crowds, through a fluke they actually managed to catch one of Robinson's musical shows. A rumor ran through the mob that Mae West was appearing at the main pavilion. It was considered possible—that stage had seen Abbott and Costello and the Marx Brothers earlier in the week. As it turned out, that had been a false rumor, but it did thin the crowd for the music theater. Cooley's class, including Benny, Jenny, and Cassie, had been able to find seats. When the curtain went up, for the next forty minutes Benny was thrilled more than he would have believed possible by the dancing of the legendary Bill "Bojangles" Robinson. Never in his life had he seen such an exhibition of grace and ease of motion, and for just an instant, he craved the fluidity of dance for himself, craved to be able to move with the kind of ease men like Robinson and Willie Hawkins displayed so effortlessly.

He looked over at Jenny and was just a little lost at the way she gazed at Robinson, felt searing envy that mere dancing could wring that kind of response from a woman. What would he have to have, what would he have to *do* before he could ever hope to trigger such admiration? He didn't know, but he knew that he wanted it.

Somewhere inside him there was something special. He knew it, and if he just had a chance, he would be able to find it. He knew that, too.

He was almost out of money, and Jenny had begun complaining that her feet were sore. The other kids were starting to get restless too. They had gone by the Hall of Nations twice, and the exhibit had still been closed. Cooley had managed to find them other things to do, things to fill up their time, but Benny had begun to doubt that Cooley would be able to keep them in good spirits long enough to get them to the exhibition, assuming of course that the exhibition would even open.

So they were on their way out of the fair, when he convinced them to walk the long blocks necessary to see the Hall of Nations, one last time.

Complaining and grousing—the fair was an entire small world, it seemed—they went, and much to their surprise, when they got there, it was actually open.

The Hall of Nations was a long white building—there were actually two of them, on either side of the Lagoon of Nations, a sparkling blue pool that never seemed to stop its shimmering and bubbling. It was near the Court of Peace, and the stepped waterfall of Italy's exhibit. The lagoon itself was eight hundred by four hundred feet and looked big enough to drown Rockefeller Center.

So. This was where the poorer Nations hung up their shingle, he thought. Not bad, but it would have been wonderful if one of the African nations had a proud pavilion like even Poland had.

But at least it wasn't represented by a little grass hut, or something. Images of natives capering around a roasting missionary, or Tarzan of the Apes rescuing a blond from a crowd of ravening native savages. That would have been a little much.

But the inside of the Hall of Nations was tasteful, if rather quiet. There was an exhibit from Yugoslavia, one from Panama, and another from Siam. Cooley led them quickly through it, and back to one of the nooks, where he finally found the exhibit from the Mali Republic.

It was labeled, simply, "Dogon Artifact."

There was a curtain across an alcove, and an irregular radiance pulsing from behind it. A withered little black man sat on a stool, looking out at them as if doing a mental count, as if he were hoarding his remaining life energy, waiting for a critical mass of bodies to arrive before beginning his spiel.

Benny looked at them, and then at a tapestry on one of the walls. Clearly, Mali (wherever *that* was) had little money to invest. He actually figured that there was a good chance that this little man had expended most of his money just getting here.

The twelve students slid along a bend, and waited for the curator to begin. Then finally, he stood, and in a very thick accent began to speak.

"Hello," he said. "I am Ajabwe. I come from Mali in Africa. My people, a great people, are the Dogon." He paused. "The legend says that many years ago my people were visited by a strange folk, who came from another star. It was said that they traveled in search of those who could understand, and that only a very small number of people could understand the gift that they offered. They said that they traveled in search of the few who had this, and when they found it, they would leave one of the Orbs with which they were entrusted. I do not know if the story is true, or how much of it is true—but it is said that these people either represented, or called themselves the Prophets." He looked out at them, and Benny had to admit that his smile was a little unnerving.

"Perhaps one of you will be a Chosen One." Some of the white people in the audience chuckled, but not impolitely.

He opened the curtain.

The light flickered more strongly, and the breath froze in Benny's throat. The object behind the curtain was, simply, beautiful. Waves of blue fire rolled off of it like mist from a chunk of dry ice. The glow grew more and more intense, and he couldn't feel himself breathe, or even really think.

They rose from the seats and filed past, prevented from approaching the strange shape by a velvet rope. It was, as they had said in the paper, about the size and shape of a large hourglass, thicker through the middle, of course, and that light. That light . . .

He stared at it. Benny closed his eyes tightly, as if trying to keep the luminescence from washing through him, but it was of no use. It ignored his eyelids, as if it was radiating directly into his brain.

510

Something . . . something was shifting deep within the orb, and he heard it, and it seemed to speak to him.

But the words that it said were beyond him. He couldn't quite make them out . . . they stayed, remained just beyond his reach and his understanding.

Then he was falling, and falling. The world seemed to open up, and he was lost.

"Benny?" he heard, but couldn't see anything at all.

"Benny, are you all right?" It was Jenny. She was calling to him. She was waking him up, and that meant that he must be sleeping and dreaming, but the dream had been so strange. He had had a brief, but brilliant vision that seemed like the Flash Gordon serials he had seen as a boy—only realer. Scary real, as real as the cars rolling down the street. That real.

Benny opened his eyes, and he saw Jenny and Cassie standing over him and Mr. Cooley, with an expression of genuine concern behind his spectacles.

"What . . . what happened?" Benny said groggily.

"That's what I would like to know," Cooley said.

Benny sat up, and felt the dizziness begin to recede. He shook his head and realized that the old African man Ajabwe was looking at him, too. Ajabwe, who seemed puzzled, asked: "Who are you, boy?"

"Benny Russell?" Benny said.

"Well, Benny Russell, I think that the gem has spoken to you."

"What?"

"It happened once before. A tall man, in robes. He said that he was a preacher. Are you a preacher?"

"No," Benny said, confused.

"I think that perhaps you are a leader in some way. The gem has spoken to you." He said this last as if it answered all questions.

Benny rose unsteadily to his feet. The little man helped him up. Ajabwe's skin was warm and dry. Despite Benny's initial unease, he could not dislike this man.

"You come back," the little old man said. "You come back and see me, and the stone—again."

There was no answer that Benny could make, except to nod his head dumbly. He really couldn't do anything other than agree.

The trip back to Harlem was uneventful. The entire group seemed to be somewhat subdued, perhaps by what had happened at the fair, perhaps something else. They seemed both solicitous of Benny and

511

simultaneously rather wary of him. He couldn't figure it out—he had just collapsed, not displayed the symptoms of some terrible, infectious disease.

"Why are they treating me like that?" he finally asked Cooley.

"Like what?"

"Like I'm Typhoid Mary or something? It's kind of spooky."

Cooley gazed at him for a long moment before answering. "It probably has something to do with the way you were talking," he said.

"Talking? I don't know what you mean."

Cooley just gazed at him, and didn't say anything else.

Jenny rested back against her seat, her eyes closed, long dark lashes quivering slightly.

Only Cassie was still awake, alert, and watching him. "Cassie?" he asked. "What was that all about?"

"You were saying things, Benny."

"What kind of things?"

She shrugged. "It didn't really make no sense."

"Then tell me what it was."

"Well, you were talking about the stars. You were saying that you could see the stars. That's all."

Benny closed his eyes. The blackness behind them was filled with something that he had never glimpsed before. It was blackness, and a roiling series of clouds, and exploding stars, and out among them, men and women and other things. Creatures. But not monsters. Machines. Holes in space. He suddenly felt a lifting and turning within himself, a humming, as if he had touched some primal dynamo at the very core of creation.

He opened his eyes again. The train still made its rickety way along the track. "Cass?" he said softly.

"Yeah?" For a moment her tough-girl exterior had cracked and he saw something underneath it. And then . . .

He saw not Cass, but Cassie. She was grown up and beautiful. And she knew about makeup and dressing, and she held her arms out to him, and—

He felt something hot boiling within his blood, and he shook his head quickly. What the hell had *that* vision been about? He was imagining that he saw Cass, not as she was, but as she might be in another ten or fifteen years. That was crazy.

She held his hand. "Yes? Was there something?"

He shook his head. "No." He paused and then realized that that was a lie. "Cassie," he said. "When we were in the tent, didn't you see anything at all?"

"Nothing," she said. And then settled her head back against the seat. Without opening her eyes she said, "Nothing at all."

**SHUFFLE**

## *Star Trek: The Wrath of Khan,* a novel by Vonda N. McIntyre, screenplay by Jack B. Sowards, based on a story by Harve Bennett and Jack B. Sowards

Vonda McIntyre wrote the novelizations for *STII: TWOK, STIII: TSFS,* and *STIV: TVH. TWOK* is my favorite of the three. Like other novelizations, it filled in the blanks of the story and explained the action in greater detail. The novelization also expanded the character stories, including Peter Preston's, making his loss more tragic, and provided more detail about Saavik and her background. I have read the novel so often that I have difficulty separating what is from the film and what is from the book. Some of the detail in the novel that was not included in the theatrical release was edited back into the movie for the ABC television airing, compounding the confusion.

The dialogue between Saavik and Kirk, and Kirk and Spock, in this segment from the TWOK novelization expressed the underlying themes of the film and provided additional character detail for Saavik. The passage exemplifies the reasons why novelizations are useful and popular.

JIM KIRK TRUDGED TOWARD THE DEBRIEFING ROOM. HE FELT TIRED, AND depressed: and oppressed, by the shining self-confidence of the young people he had been observing. Or perhaps it was by the circumstances of fate that made him the instrument for shaking and scarring that self-confidence. But McCoy was right: he *had* been too hard on Lieutenant Saavik.

He turned the corner and came face-to-face with Spock, who was leaning against the wall with his arms folded.

"Didn't you die?" Kirk asked.

He thought for an instant that Spock was going to smile. But Spock recovered himself in time.

"Do you want to know your cadets' efficiency rating—or are you just loitering?"

"Vulcans are not renowned for their ability to loiter," Spock said.

"Or for their ability to admit terrible character flaws, such as that they're curious."

"Indeed, Admiral? If it will raise your opinion of my character, I suppose I must admit to some curiosity."

"I haven't even got to the debriefing room yet, and you want an opinion." He started down the corridor again, and Spock strode along beside him.

"I seem to recall a Starfleet admiral who referred to this particular set of debriefings as 'a damned waste of time,' " Spock said. "He had a very strong belief that actions were more important than words."

"Did he?" Kirk said. "I don't believe I know him. Sounds like a hothead to me."

"Yes," Spock said slowly. "Yes, at times he was known as a hothead."

Kirk winced at Spock's use of the past tense. "Spock, those trainees of yours destroyed the simulator and you along with it."

"Complete havoc is the usual result when *Kobayashi Maru* comes upon the scene." He paused, glanced at Kirk, and continued. "You yourself took the test three times."

"No!" Kirk said with mock horror. "Did I?"

"Indeed. And with a resolution that was, to put it politely, unique."

"It was unique when I did it," Kirk said. "But I think a number of people have tried it since."

"Without success, you should add. It was a solution that would not have occurred to a Vulcan."

Jim Kirk suddenly felt sick of talking over old times. He changed the subject abruptly. "Speaking of Vulcans, your protégée's first-rate. A little emotional, maybe—"

"You must consider her heritage, Jim—and, more important, her background. She is quite naturally somewhat more volatile than—than I, for instance." 

Kirk could not help laughing. "I'm sorry, Spock. The lieutenant is remarkably self-possessed for someone of her age and experience. I was trying to make a joke. It was pretty feeble, I'll admit it, but that seems to be about all I'm up to these days." He sighed. "You know, her tactic might even have worked if we hadn't added the extra Klingon attack group." He stopped at the debriefing room. "Well."

Spock reached out as Kirk started to go in. He stopped before his hand touched Jim Kirk's shoulder, but the gesture was enough. Kirk glanced back.

"Something oppresses you," Spock said.

Kirk felt moved by Spock's concern.

"Something . . ." he said. He wanted to talk to Spock, to someone. But he did not know how to begin. And he had the debriefing to conduct. No, this was not the time. He turned away and went into the debriefing room.

All those kids.

They waited for Admiral Kirk in silence, anxious yet eager. Lieutenant Saavik arrived a moment after Kirk sat down; Spock, his usual emotionless self once more, came in quietly and sat at the very back of the room. Jim Kirk was tempted to declare the discussion over before it had begun, but regulations required a debriefing; he had to fill out a report afterward—

That's all I ever pay attention to anymore, he thought. Regulations and paperwork.

He opened the meeting. He had been through it all a hundred times. The usual protocol was to discuss with each student, in reverse order of seniority, what they would have done had they been in command of the ship. Today was no different, and Kirk had heard all the answers before. One would have stuck to regulations and remained outside the Neutral Zone. Another would have sent in a shuttle for reconnaissance.

Kirk stifled a yawn.

"Lieutenant Saavik," he said finally, "have you anything to add? Second thoughts?"

"No, sir."

"Nothing at all?"

"Were I confronted with the same events, I would react in the same manner. The details might be different. I see no point to increasing your boredom with trivia."

Kirk felt embarrassed to have shown his disinterest so clearly. He reacted rather harshly. "You'd do the same thing, despite knowing it would mean the destruction of your ship and crew?"

"I would know that it *might* mean the destruction of my ship and crew, Admiral. If I could not prove that *Kobayashi Maru* were an illusion, I would answer its distress call."

"Lieutenant, are you familiar with Rickoverian paradoxes?"

"No, sir, I am not."

"Let me tell you the prototype. You are on a ship—a sailing ship, an oceangoing vessel. It sinks. You find yourself in a life raft with one other person. The life raft is damaged. It might support one person, but not two. How would you go about persuading the other person to let you have the raft?"

"I would not," she said.

"No? Why?"

"For one thing, sir, I am an excellent swimmer."

One of the other students giggled. The sound broke off sharply when a classmate elbowed him in the ribs.

"The water," Kirk said with some asperity, "is crowded with extremely carnivorous sharks."

"Sharks, Admiral?"

"Terran," Spock said from the back of the room. "Order Selachii."

"Right," Kirk said. "And they are very, very hungry."

"My answer is the same."

"Oh, really? You're a highly educated Starfleet officer. Suppose the other person was completely illiterate, had no family, spent most of the time getting thrown in jail, and never held any job a low-level robot couldn't do. Then what?"

"I would neither request nor attempt to order or persuade any civilian to sacrifice their life for mine."

"But a lot of resources are invested in your training. Don't you think you owe it to society to preserve yourself so you can carry out your responsibilities?"

Her high-arched eyebrows drew together. "Is this what you believe, Admiral?"

"I'm not being rated, Lieutenant. You are. I've asked you a serious question, and you've replied with what could be considered appalling false modesty."

Saavik stood up angrily. "You ask me if I should not preserve myself so I can carry out my responsibilities. Then *I* ask *you,* what are my responsibilities? By the criteria you have named, my responsibilities are to preserve myself so I can carry out my responsibilities! This is a circular and self-justifying argument. It is immoral in the extreme! A just society—and if I am not mistaken, the Federation considers itself to be just—employs a military for one reason alone: to protect its civilians. If we decide to judge that some civilians are 'worth' protecting, and some are not, if we decide we are too important to be risked, then we destroy our own purpose. We cease to be the servants of our society. We become its tyrants!"

She was leaning forward with her fingers clenched around the back of a chair in the next row.

"You feel strongly about this, don't you, Lieutenant?"

She straightened up, and her fair skin colored to a nearly Vulcan hue.

"That is my opinion on the subject, sir."

Kirk smiled for the first time during the meeting: this was the first time he had felt thoroughly pleased in far too long.

"And you make an elegant defense of your opinion, too, Lieutenant. I don't believe I've ever heard that problem quite so effectively turned turtle."

She frowned again, weighing the ambiguous statement. Then, clearly, she decided to take it as a compliment. "Thank you, sir." She sat down again.

Kirk settled back in his chair and addressed the whole class. "This is the last of the simulation exams. If the office is as efficient as usual, your grades won't be posted till tomorrow. But I think it's only fair to let you know . . . none of you has any reason to worry. Dismissed."

After a moment of silence, the whole bunch of them leaped to their feet and, in an outburst of talk and laughter, they all rushed out the door.

"My God," Jim Kirk said under his breath. "They're like a tide."

All, that is, except Saavik. Aloof and alone, she stood up and strode away.

Spock watched his class go.

"You're right, Spock," Kirk said. "She is more volatile than a Vulcan."

"She has reason to be. Under the circumstances, she showed admirable restraint."

The one thing Spock did not expect of Lieutenant Saavik was self-control as complete as his own. He believed that only a vanishingly small difference existed between humans and Romulans when it came to the ability to indulge in emotional outbursts. But Spock had had the benefit of growing up among Vulcans. He had learned self-control early. Saavik had spent the first ten years of her life fighting to survive in the most brutal underclass of a Romulan colony world.

"Don't tell me you're angry that I needled her so hard," Kirk said.

Spock merely arched one eyebrow.

"No, of course you're not angry," Kirk said. "What a silly question."

"Are you familiar with Lieutenant Saavik's background, Admiral?" He wondered how Kirk had come to pose her the particular problem that he had. He could hardly have made a more significant choice, whether it was deliberate or random. The colony world Saavik had lived on was declared a failure; the Romulan military,

517

which was indistinguishable from the Romulan government, made the decision to abandon it. They carried out the evacuation as well. They rescued everyone.

Everyone, that is, except the elderly, the crippled, the disturbed . . . and a small band of half-caste children whose very existence they denied.

The official Romulan position was that Vulcans and Romulans could not interbreed without technological intervention. Therefore, the abandoned children could not exist. That was a political judgment which, like so many political judgments, had nothing to do with reality.

The reality was that the evolution of Romulans and Vulcans had diverged only a few thousand years before the present. The genetic differences were utterly trivial. But a few thousand years of cultural divergence formed a chasm that appeared unbridgeable.

"She's half Vulcan and half Romulan," Kirk said. "Is there more I should know?"

"No, that is sufficient. My question was an idle one, nothing more." Kirk had shaken her, but she had recovered well. Spock saw no point in telling Kirk things which Saavik herself seldom discussed, even with Spock. If she chose to put her past aside completely, he must respect her decision. She had declined her right to an antigen-scan, which would have identified her Vulcan parent. This was a highly honorable action, but it meant that she had no family, that in fact she did not even know which of her parents was Vulcan and which Romulan.

No Vulcan family had offered to claim her.

Under the circumstances, Spock could only admire the competent and self-controlled person Saavik had created out of the half-starved and violent barbarian child she had been. And he certainly could not blame her for rejecting her parents as completely as they had abandoned her. He wondered if she understood why she drove herself so hard, for she was trying to prove herself to people who would never know her accomplishments, and never care. Perhaps some day she would prove herself to herself and be free of the last shackles binding her to her past.

"Hmm, yes," Kirk said, pulling Spock back from his reflections. "I do recall that Vulcans are renowned for their ability to be idle."

Spock decided to change the subject himself. He picked up the package he had retrieved before coming into the debriefing room. Feeling somewhat awkward, he offered it to Kirk.

"What's this?" Jim asked.

"It is," Spock said, "a birthday present."

Jim took the gift and turned it over in his hands. "How in the world did you know it was my birthday?"

"The date is not difficult to ascertain."

"I mean, why—? No, never mind, another silly question. Thank you, Spock."

"Perhaps you should open it before you thank me; it may not strike your fancy."

"I'm sure it will—but you know what they say: It's the thought that counts." He slid his fingers beneath the outside edge of the elegantly folded paper.

"I have indeed heard the saying, and I have always wanted to ask," Spock said, with honest curiosity, "if it is the thought that counts, why do humans bother with the gift?"

Jim laughed. "There's no good answer to that. I guess it's just an example of the distance between our ideals and reality."

The parcel was wrapped in paper only, with no adhesive or ties. After purchasing the gift, Spock had passed a small booth at which an elderly woman created simple, striking packages with nothing but folded paper. Fascinated by the geometry and topology of what she was doing, Spock watched for some time, and then had her wrap Jim's birthday present.

At a touch, the wrapping fanned away untorn.

Jim saw what was inside and sat down heavily.

"Perhaps . . . it *is* the thought that counts," Spock said.

"No, Spock, good Lord, it's beautiful." He touched the leather binding with one finger; he picked the book up in both hands and opened it gently, slowly, being careful of its spine.

"I only recently became aware of your foudness for antiques," Spock said. It was a liking he had begun to believe he understood, in an odd way, once he paid attention to it. The book, for example, combined the flaws and perfections of something handmade; it was curiously satisfying.

"Thank you, Spock. I like it very much." He let a few pages flip past and read the novel's first line. " 'It was the best of times, it was the worst of times . . .' Hmm, are you trying to tell me something?"

"Not from the text," Spock said, "and with the book itself, only happy birthday. Does that not qualify as 'the best of times'?"

Jim looked uncomfortable, and he avoided Spock's gaze. Spock wondered how a gift that had at first brought pleasure could so quickly turn into a matter of awkwardness. Once again he had the feeling that Jim Kirk was deeply unhappy about something.

"Jim—?"

"Thank you, Spock, very much," Kirk said, cutting Spock off and ignoring the question in his voice. "I mean it. Look, I know you have to get back to the *Enterprise.* I'll see you tomorrow."

And with that, he was gone.

Spock picked up the bit of textured wrapping paper and refolded it into its original shape, around empty air.

He wondered if he would ever begin to understand human beings.

# *Unification,* a novel by Jeri Taylor, based on the two-part television episode, story by Rick Berman & Michael Piller, part-one teleplay by Jeri Taylor, part-two teleplay by Michael Piller

From the time *TNG* premiered, fans called for a crossover with *TOS* and the characters that seemed likely to still be alive in the twenty-fourth century. Given the long life span of Vulcans compared to humans, it seemed more likely that Spock would be alive during the *TNG* times than any of the others. "Unification" was the answer. When my online friends and I learned that Spock would appear on *TNG,* we wondered about the story, but the truth is, at first we did not care if it had much of a plot. All we really wanted was for Spock and Picard to meet; I am not entirely sure that we would have cared had the story consisted of Spock and Picard being trapped in a turbolift and forced to chat for two hours about Spock's life since the last *TOS* film.

Despite our talk, Spock and Picard in a turbolift would not have been very entertaining. Instead of talk about Spock's life since *ST:TUC,* "Unification" showed us what Spock had been doing. In "Unification," Captain Picard was assigned to investigate Spock's mysterious disappearance from the Federation and his activities on Romulus. The novelization by Jeri Taylor provided much more detail about Romulus and its people, as well as Spock's mission. In the first scene excerpted here, Spock contemplated his meeting with Picard, and in the second, young D'Tan experienced the horror of the attack by Romulan authorities on the people in the unification movement after Pardek's betrayal.

SPOCK SAW THE BOY FROM THE CORNER OF HIS EYE, RUNNING DOWN THE street, already out of breath, clutching the rose-colored *lagga* flower in his fist. It was D'Tan, a Romulan child not yet past puberty. Spock recognized him from his whippet body and smooth, gaited run; he had marveled at the boy's boundless energy on several occasions. *That is one thing age gives us,* he thought. *An appreciation of things the young take for granted.*

D'Tan paused near a line of Romulans who were queued for a goods dispenser, and handed the flower to one of the men standing there—a man Spock knew as Jaron.

The man took the flower, glanced furtively around, then stepped out of line. Spock knew Jaron was headed toward him, but he kept his eyes resolutely forward.

Spock and Picard were standing at one of the small tables that dotted the floor of the *dinglh.* They had been standing casually there for several minutes and had already ordered soup—almost the only thing that was ever available. Spock knew that the powerful denizens of Romulus dined each night on sumptuous delicacies; the ordinary man stood in line for a crown of bread and a chunk of gristle.

Spock would have preferred to be here alone; he had hoped to convince Picard to transport back to his Klingon ship and then return to Federation space. An affair like this was best handled without outside interference and with as few participants as possible. The delicacy of the situation made a Starfleet captain's presence troubling, indeed.

Spock looked at the trim, fit man opposite him, registered his grave, intelligent eyes and his assured bearing, and reflected that, all his misgivings notwithstanding, if Starfleet felt they had to send someone, this had undoubtedly been a wise choice.

He had never met Jean-Luc Picard, but he had of course heard of the captain of the fleet's flagship. His reputation heralded him as a man of courage, erudition, and compassion, and in their brief encounter Spock had no reason to doubt any of those qualities. To those he might add perceptivity, articulateness, and tenacity.

All the same, he made Spock uneasy. And he wasn't sure why.

Spock disliked not being able to objectify his instinct; it was like an elusive mote in the eye that can't be seen or extracted but continues to irritate nonetheless. What was it about Picard that he found so disquieting?

Perhaps it was that Picard's attitude about the possibility of unification was simply not logical. Spock was sure that the Federation and its representatives could only benefit if his mission were successful, and he did not doubt that Picard would ultimately be supportive of such a movement. So there was no reason for Picard to disapprove of his goal.

But he did. That was it—Jean-Luc Picard thought he was an impressionable fool for having entered into this endeavor.

Perhaps that is why Spock seemed to hear his father's voice whenever Picard voiced his concerns about the reunification talks. Sarek, too, had never given credence to Spock's beliefs that there were some Romulans who wanted peace, who wanted to live in reborn harmony with their Vulcan cousins. It had been a lifelong source of conflict. And now here was this Picard, echoing that same attitude.

In a way, it was fascinating.

In a corner of the *dinglh,* Spock saw the man with the flower moving idly toward them. In a moment he was passing their table, and as he did so he casually placed the blossom in a glass of water, then deposited it in front of Spock.

"Allow me to brighten your table," Jaron intoned, and Spock nodded noncommittally. *"Jolan tru,"* added the man, and moved on. The Romulan greeting, which meant variously "good day," "best wishes," or "good luck," was a neutral one shared by all. It connoted no political allegiance or leaning, though Spock knew the man was a member of the movement.

He turned back toward Picard, his voice quiet; fortunately, a hushed conversation drew no attention, for everyone spoke in guarded tones in this city. "The Senate has adjourned. Pardek will be here shortly." He glanced toward the pink *lagga* blossom. "The flower is a signal."

Picard nodded. Spock knew the Starfleet captain was curious to hear Pardek's message, for it would signal either an end to or a continuation of Spock's objective. Picard's eyes carefully swept the interior of the food center; Spock was pleased that he was ever on the alert. "Just how widespread is this movement?" asked the captain.

They had been talking, before D'Tan's flower had arrived, about the remarkable events that were transpiring here in the Romulan system. Picard had listened carefully, gathering in the information Spock provided him, asking intelligent questions. He seemed to be intrigued by Spock's revelation of an active, pervasive underground of those who longed for reunification. "I am told," replied Spock, "that there are groups in every populated area."

He stopped as he felt the arrival of the matron; he had not seen her here before and was unwilling to take the chance that even a whispered conversation might be overheard. The woman sat before them bowls of *gletten,* eyed the flower, looked hard at them, and then moved off.

"The spread of these groups has become a serious concern to the Romulan leadership," Spock then continued.

"Serious enough for the leaders to suddenly embrace a Vulcan peace initiative? I have a difficult time accepting that."

In that sentence, Spock heard the intransigence and stubbornness that disturbed him. He admired the fact that this captain had courage; he would never be intimidated into altering his position. But could he not embrace the possibility of change? Was he thoroughly inflexible?

"I sense you have a closed mind, Captain," he retorted. "Closed minds have kept these two worlds apart for centuries."

He saw Picard give him a look that suggested puzzlement. Perhaps he had spoken a bit sharply. Spock continued, determined to win his support. "In the Federation, we have learned from experience to view the Romulans with distrust. We can either choose to live with that enmity or seek an opportunity to change it." He paused and looked at Picard with his most penetrating gaze. "I choose the latter."

Picard seemed unaffected by the stare. "I will be the first to cheer when the Neutral Zone is abolished, sir. I only wonder if this movement is strong enough to reshape the entire Romulan political landscape."

Again, it was a familiar tone that Spock heard from this man. Surprising that it did something to his stomach that was vexatious.

His eyes shifted and fell on the flower in the glass, already wilted and gasping in the Romulan heat. "One can begin to reshape the landscape with a single flower, Captain."

He didn't look at Picard to see what response that observation had produced, because he had noticed D'Tan approaching, his wiry child's body full of angles and joints. He was carrying something.

"*Jolan tru,* Mr. Spock," he said. D'Tan always spoke as though he were half out of breath, probably because he never walked when he could run. "Look what I've brought you."

"This is my friend D'Tan," Spock told Picard. "He is very curious about Vulcan."

"Hello, D'Tan." Picard's voice was friendly, if somewhat cautious. Spock sensed a man who, though warmhearted, was not comfortable with children.

D'Tan handed Spock a book and he turned it in his hands. It was worn, with a cover made of wood that had been carved by hand, and pages that were smudged and brittle. "It is very old," ventured Spock. "Where did you get this?"

"They read from it at the meetings. It tells the story of the Vulcan separation—"

A new voice knifed into the conversation, startling them all. "You should not bring that out here, D'Tan. You've been told many times."

They turned to see Pardek approaching, his benign face a ruddy red from the heat. D'Tan looked sheepish and took possession of the book once more. "I just wanted to show it to Mr. Spock," he said lamely.

Pardek's smile was not threatening. "Off with you. We will see you later tonight."

D'Tan's eyes sought Spock's, as though to feed from him once more before he left. "Will you tell us more stories about Vulcan?" he asked.

"Yes," answered Spock, and enjoyed the smile that D'Tan gave him in return. Then the boy sprinted off, hurling back over his shoulder as he did, *"Jolan tru."*

Spock saw Pardek casting his practiced eye around the denizens of the food center and lighting on the grim-faced old woman who had brought their *gletten.* "Perhaps this is not such a good place to talk," he murmured, and the three moved casually out of the court and into the colorless world of the Romulan streets.

Spock knew that most of his countrymen, and most Federation members for that matter, would find the dark, somber passageways of this city bleak and depressing. Ironically, he did not. The vast, rugged beauty of Vulcan, with its ocher deserts and its jagged red mountains, had instilled in him a love of spaciousness and light. Why, then, his appreciation of these squalid passageways where little light intruded? The dark facades of the structures were ominous, the corridors narrow and constricting. The people all dressed in pallid clothing and their expressions were quietly despairing. There would seem to be little to cherish in these desolate streets.

But Spock had a palpable sense of the spirit that lurked beneath; a knowledge that, behind those joyless faces, burned the eagerness for a new order. There was a river of desire that ran unseen beneath this city, a wellspring from which more and more would soon be drinking. That such a flame could burn in these woeful alleyways seemed remarkable to him, and imbued the surroundings with a unique beauty whose essence was almost tangible to him.

The three men walked the street, heads down in Romulan fashion.

Pardek cast a glance toward Picard. "And what do you think of your enemy, Captain Picard?"

Picard gave him a look that was not accusatory yet had an intensity that surprised Spock. "These people are no one's enemy, Senator." *How true,* thought Spock, *and if only someone would tell that to all the governmental authorities and all the military leaders. The people were rarely each other's enemies . . .*

Pardek smiled an acknowledgment. "Many of my colleagues fear what the people have to say. But I have learned to listen carefully." Pardek paused a moment, formulating his thoughts. "Children like D'Tan are our future. Old men like me will not be able to hold on to ancient prejudice and hostility. These young people won't allow it."

Spock glanced at Picard, to see what effect these words were having on him. Picard seemed to be listening intently.

"Now that they've met their first real Vulcan," continued Pardek, "it has only inspired them more. I'm sure that is evident to you, Spock."

"I did not anticipate such a passionate response to my arrival," admitted Spock, remembering the near delirious joy with which some people at meetings had greeted him.

Pardek smiled. "Romulans are a passionate people. Vulcans will learn to appreciate that quality in us."

"If we are successful," added Spock, curious that Pardek seemed so optimistic today. Were there new developments?

That question was answered an instant later when Pardek looked at him with a smile that crinkled his merry eyes. "We will know soon," he declared, not without a certain pride. "The proconsul, Neral, has agreed to meet with you."

Spock was pleased to note that Picard seemed amazed by this announcement. . . .

D'Tan would never be able to say what it was that cautioned him to take refuge in the ground-level storage unit he had discovered years ago. It was nothing tangible, just a sense of unusual anticipation in the hot, heavy air, a kind of compression as though distant explosions were felt, rather than heard.

Others had premonitions, too, he was sure. There was a restiveness on the street, little eddies of scurrying activity that sprang up and dissipated in random patterns. A Circassian cat that belonged to a shopkeeper prowled her window restlessly, arching her back and spitting.

D'Tan's hiding place had a grate that opened on to the street and provided a view. When he was a very small boy he had discovered that he could wriggle into this space between the storage unit and the facade of the building and lie undetected for hours, watching the panorama of the streets unfold before him. Now that he was older, it was becoming a tighter fit; and he had realized sadly that in another year or two he would have to give up his childhood retreat.

He had had an aimless day, first wandering the neighborhood for several hours, looking for Mr. Spock, hoping to show him the language blocks. After Spock left to go to the caves, D'Tan spent some time with his friend Janicka, helping her clean her family's store. They had given him a meal and a piece of fruit to take with him.

It was that indefinable heaviness in the air that finally sent him crawling into the hiding place. He was uneasy; his stomach felt sick and he wondered if the fruit he had eaten was spoiled.

Sitting cross-legged in his hiding place calmed him down; it always did. He loved watching the passersby on the street, the little dramas that played out before him. There was a heady feeling of omnipotence that he could see without being seen, though D'Tan knew that if his parents discovered this little activity, they would probably not approve.

D'Tan saw Janicka walk from her parents' shop toward the food court. Janicka loved sweets, and her parents kept her on a strict limit. D'Tan knew they must be occupied now, and Janicka was sneaking away to get some forbidden treat. He watched as she spoke to the food keeper, who returned a moment later with *sesketh,* a sugary confection twisted on a spice stick. D'Tan almost laughed out loud, because he knew of all the treats Janicka's parents least liked her to have, *sesketh* was at the top of the list.

Now she'd have to finish it before she returned to the shop; she sat on an embankment as she nibbled daintily at the sweet. D'Tan observed that Janicka was one of the few people he knew who could eat and still look delicate. He'd never had such a thought before, and as his mind considered her gentle face and her large, dark eyes, he found himself thinking of Janicka in an entirely new manner.

It was while he was absorbed in this unaccustomed exploration of Janicka's attributes that he heard the first scream.

It was a woman, and she was not within his sight. But he saw others on the street react to the scream and look off, to his right, down the thoroughfare that led out of Krocton segment.

Within seconds there was more noise—unfamiliar, disturbing—a clamor of shouting and more screams.

D'Tan's stomach twisted with fear. Whatever was happening, he knew it was worse than anything he had ever experienced. Now the people on the street before him were running, becoming crazed, colliding with each other in desperate haste. Some ran to his left, simply trying to get away from whatever was approaching; others ran the opposite way to look for loved ones or to take sanctuary.

The clamor of noise to his right was increasing in volume, and soon he could hear a pounding of footsteps—hundreds of them, many the harsh stamping of military boots as they marched inexorably down the street.

Then he caught the unmistakable sound of disruptor fire. He shrank back in his hiding place in fear. Disruptors were one of the most terrible weapons ever invented; were they being used on innocent citizens?

The next thing he saw was a flood of terrified people, running, stumbling, some glancing back over their shoulders as they ran, all wild-eyed, all fleeing some awful and as yet unseen monstrosity.

One woman stumbled and fell; the crowd marched over her, ignoring her pleas for help and then her frantic screams as she was trampled. Finally she was still; D'Tan could see only her outstretched arm, fingers twitching faintly.

Then came the guards.

Neral's security guards were the most feared unit of the military. They were chosen first on the basis of size and strength; once tapped for service, they underwent special adaptations of their brain chemistry that reduced any sense of conscience or empathy. Then their pain centers were regulated so that their bodies were impervious to the torment of physical injury.

The result was a brutal creature without compassion, who would follow orders relentlessly, would not be slowed by injury, and would fight tenaciously until the body itself simply gave out.

These were the beings that marched through Krocton segment now.

Faces impassive, dressed in iron gray uniforms, they moved like a relentless swarm of insects over a field, destroying it utterly. Disruptor fire lacerated buildings and caused them to tremble violently; some collapsed in on themselves. Glass shattered and exploded, often showering the frightened citizens with lethal shards.

Some guards amused themselves by nipping at the fleeing civilians with disruptors; a full setting would vaporize anyone, so obviously they had purposely set their weapons at a low level. Those who were unlucky enough to get grazed by the ugly blast dropped in their tracks, screaming in agony as their internal organs began to explode.

All this D'Tan watched with horror, not wanting to see but unable to look away. It was a living nightmare of cruelty and mayhem, unfolding in bitter, bloody detail directly in front of him.

A gap in the guards' ranks opened briefly, and he saw Janicka, standing opposite him on the embankment, staring, frozen, at the havoc before her. "Run, Janicka!" he shouted, oblivious for the moment to his own safety. But his cry had no chance of being heard by either the guards or by Janicka; the devastation of the streets overwhelmed any other sound, and D'Tan's cry blended with the piteous wails of too many others.

And so he watched, riveted, as a guard noticed Janicka and ran toward her. The little girl stared up at him, unable to move. He picked her up and slung her over his shoulder, and then Janicka came to life. She shrieked, and kicked at the guard with all her might. Annoyed, he simply grabbed her by her ankles and swung her around in a circle until her face collided with the corner of a building.

He dropped her then and she crumpled, leaden, onto the street. Even from his hiding place, D'Tan could see that Janicka's fair, delicate face was now a template of cracked and broken segments through which blood was streaming. She did not move or even twitch. She would never again eat a treat or walk with him to the caves or clean the windows in her parents' store. Janicka, his good friend, was gone.

D'Tan sank back against the wall of the storage unit. The guards had already passed by, continuing their carnage as they marched through the segment. Here, before D'Tan, was a wasteland of the dead and wounded. Already the noise was subsiding, and all he could hear were the groans of those who still breathed.

He knew that Mr. Spock was in terrible danger. This massacre was meant to wipe out the movement and if the guards knew that Krocton segment contained its nucleus and its most dedicated adherents, there was every chance they knew about the caves, too.

D'Tan waited a few moments until the noise of the marauding guards had grown faint, and then he crawled out of his sanctuary. Trying not to look at the devastation around him, he started running toward the caves.

# CHAPTER 18

# A Tribute to Fans: Strange New Worlds

STAR TREK: ADVENTURES IN TIME AND SPACE CLOSES WITH A TRIBUTE TO fans, the Grand Prize winners from the *Strange New Worlds* contests. For many years, fans have requested anthologies of Star Trek short stories and an outlet to publish their own fiction. In response, John Ordover of Pocket developed a short story writing contest, with the winners to be published in an anthology. The authors of the stories would win writing contracts, complete with a check and inclusion in the anthology. John worked with Paula Block at Viacom Consumer Products to develop a contest and anthology that would be worthwhile. They chose Dean Wesley Smith to edit the stories and review all the contest entries, and they threw the contest open to the fans. The contest was open to legal residents of the United States and Canada (except Quebec) who were over eighteen years of age and who had not published more than two short stories on a professional basis or in paid professional venues.

The contest was a success. Thousands of stories were entered, and of those thousands, eighteen were chosen for publication in *Star Trek: Strange New Worlds,* edited by Dean Wesley Smith with John J. Ordover and Paula M. Block. Those eighteen stories were amazing. My very favorite was the Grand Prize winner, "A Private Anecdote," by Landon Cary Dalton. The writing was very professional. The story was so moving that by the end of the second paragraph, when I realized the identity of the speaker, I started to have trouble blinking back my tears. By the end of the story, it was hopeless. I could only think, "Hold on just a little bit longer, Captain, things will work out." Many years ago, when musing about "The Menagerie," I had wondered how the Talosians knew how badly Captain Pike needed them. I now know; they knew because they heard his yearning.

*Strange New Worlds* was such a resounding success that John and Paula decided to do it again. The contest for *Strange New Worlds II* was held during 1998, and even more stories were entered than in the first contest. Once again, Dean Wesley Smith read all the entries, and he, John, and Paula selected the winners. This time, they chose seventeen stories for publication, including the Grand Prize winner and my favorite, "A Ribbon for Rosie," by Ilsa J. Bick.

*Star Trek: Strange New Worlds II,* edited by Dean Wesley Smith with John J. Ordover and Paula M. Block, was published in May 1999. Again, the contest was so successful that Pocket is sponsoring another *Strange New Worlds* short story contest this year. The rules and details are published in *Strange New Worlds II* and are available online on AOL and the Internet, at the Star Trek books web site, http://www.simonsays.com/st/. Prospective entrants also may write to Pocket for a copy of the contest rules. If the fans keep submitting stories of the caliber of those published in *Strange New Worlds I* and *II,* perhaps the contest will be a yearly event.

"A Ribbon for Rosie" the Grand Prize winner, had the same effect on me as "A Private Anecdote." It is one of those stories where the sense of the inevitable became overwhelming. I wanted to shake Papa and make him listen, but of course, he could not. At the end, though, there was hope for the person who once was named Anika.

I hope you enjoy these stories as much as I did and continue to do. They are beautiful stories, and after giving you so many short excerpts to read, it seemed only fair to give you a complete story or two.

# "A Private Anecdote," by Landon Cary Dalton

*Stardate 2822.5*

I SIT IN MY CHAIR, STARING AT THE VIEW FROM THE WINDOW OF MY hospital room. It is a nice view, but I have already grown tired of it. I have memorized every detail of every building on Starbase 11, or at least the portions within my limited sight. In some of the nearer buildings I am able to see the faces of some of the occupants. My favorite is a lovely young redhead who lives in the nearest building. Sometimes she stands on her balcony to enjoy her view. She has a look of innocent sweetness on her young face, as if she has never encountered any of the hardships and difficulties of life. I envy her.

The moon has risen. This moon appears to be much larger than the Earth's moon. It is encircled by a bright ring, not as impressive as the rings of Saturn, but still a lovely sight. I do not know the name of this moon or of any of its features, but I have their images memorized as well. I have named the various features after people and things that I have known. That range of sharply pointed mountains I named for Spock, a dear friend of mine. The horse-shaped sea I call Tango after a horse I once owned on Earth. The prominent crater in the Northern Hemisphere I call Boyce.

The lovely ring I have named Vina, for someone I think about often.

Commodore Mendez is very good to me. He has visited me at least once a week since my arrival here. He must have a very busy schedule commanding the starbase, but still he finds time for me. I wish I had some way to express my appreciation, but my injuries prevent me from expressing anything more complex than "yes" or "no."

Last week Mendez "accidently" allowed me to see the active duty roster. It was displayed on the viewer long enough for me to see my own name still listed on active duty.

"Fleet Captain Christopher Pike."

It was a noble effort on the part of the commodore to maintain my morale. This is, of course, an impossible task. My life has come to an end. The delta radiation has left my body a wasted husk, unable to move. The chair keeps my blood pumping in a vague imitation of life, but my heart knows the hopelessness of it all. My life has become nothing but an agonizing wait for death.

I watch as a shuttlecraft lifts off and flies in my direction. I entertain a shameful fantasy that it will malfunction and crash through this window to end my suffering. I am angry at myself for such thoughts. I ought to be able to find some way of dealing with this.

Then it comes to me again. I remember that same silly little thought that has occurred to me many times in the past thirteen years. It is a foolish, pointless thought, but it amuses me. I am physically unable to laugh, but inwardly my gloom lifts for a moment and my spirit rises with the thought.

"What if all of this isn't real?"

I dearly wish I could share this thought with José Mendez. He is a very sober man when on duty, but I recall him having a wicked sense of humor in private. He would appreciate the thought.

531

It is not that the thought reveals any great wisdom or that it possesses any deep meaning, but it is a thought that deserves to be shared. It has come to me at several crucial moments.

Yes, I'd love to tell this to Commodore Mendez, but I suppose it will have to remain a private anecdote. Even if I could express it to him, portions of it pertain to matters Starfleet has declared "Top Secret."

"What if all of this isn't real?"

If anyone has a cause to doubt the reality of his life, it is me. I was the one who visited the now-forbidden planet called Talos IV. It was there that I encountered the Talosians, a race of beings with incredibly developed mental powers. The Talosians were masters of illusion. I was shown a series of alternate versions of what my life could be. I experienced life on Earth, Rigel VII, Orion, all the while never leaving the cage in which I had been placed.

Since that day I have carried the thought with me. How do I know that I'm not still in the cage? How do I know that I'm not still on Talos IV, and that all my life since then hasn't been an illusion?

I guess I can never know with absolute certainty. Not that I've ever seriously doubted the reality of my surroundings. Still, the thought comes to me time and again. Strangely enough, the silly little thought has sometimes been of service to me.

The thought came to me that day on Corinthia VII. The *Enterprise* had been dispatched to survey this Class-M planet for possible future colonization. Information on the planet was sketchy, but there was no evidence of any sophisticated life-forms.

I led a landing party of six, including Spock, Dr. Boyce, Lt. Tyler, and two ensigns, Williams and Trawley. We beamed down to a dry riverbed near the planet's equator. Every planet I have visited has possessed its own unique beauty. This was a planet of purples and grays under a turquoise sky. A few scruffy red bushes dotted the landscape. Steep bluffs bordered the riverbed. Each of us drew out his tricorder and began our initial survey.

"Remarkably little microbial life," I commented.

Dr. Boyce kneeled down and scooped up a handful of soil. He let it cascade through his fingers in front of his tricorder.

"In the air, very little life," he said. "But the soil is teeming with it."

"Unusual," I said.

"Not really," said Boyce. "The same is true of Earth, though not to the same extent. There is life in the soil."

"Very well," I said. "You and Mr. Spock begin your survey. Mr. Tyler, take Ensign Trawley and establish our base camp. Ensign Williams and I will scout the perimeter."

I saw the look in Williams's eyes. It was his first time on a landing party. He was thrilled to be chosen to join the captain on a hike. I wanted his first away mission to be a memorable one. You only get one first time.

"Any suggestions, Ensign?"

He stuttered a bit at first. He was eager to impress me.

"I suggest we look for a way to get to the high ground overlooking the riverbed. That would give us the best vantage point to scan the surrounding area. We can probably find an easier place to climb if we go up the riverbed."

"Sound reasoning," I said. "Lead the way."

Williams began to march upriver. He tried to conceal the grin on his face, but I saw it just the same. I had grown more tolerant of eager young ensigns in recent years. I also enjoyed living vicariously through them as they experienced the thrills of space exploration for the first time.

Williams was about ten yards ahead of me when he stopped suddenly. He turned and looked at me.

"What do you see?" I asked.

"I'm not sure," he replied. "It looks like a sinkhole, or maybe the mouth of a cave."

Williams turned back to face the hole. I had only closed about half the distance to him when I saw him suddenly grab for the laser at his belt. I felt an immediate sinking feeling and grabbed for my own laser.

"Williams, get back!" I shouted. I was too late.

The creature was enormous. It rose quickly from the hole and reared up, its head towering a good twenty feet above Ensign Williams. Twin mandibles, ten feet long, hung from the enormous head. The mandibles snapped closed with a sound like thunder. The beast was covered with a thick carapace that looked as if it were made of the same stone as the surrounding cliffs. It was supported by dozens of clattering legs.

Williams hesitated only for a second before he began firing at the blocky head of the monstrosity. I could see that the carapace was being burned by the laser, but as the beast jostled about, Williams was unable to keep the beam focused on any spot long enough to burn through. I doubt if the creature could even feel the beam.

I added my laser to the battle, but I faced the same problem as Williams. Pieces of the creature's shell were burning and flaking off, but the damage wasn't deep enough.

"Williams! Retreat!" I shouted at the top of my lungs. He couldn't hear me over the creature's bellowing. He started to back up, but the creature was far too fast. It dove at the ensign and the massive mandibles snapped shut.

Williams was cut in two at the waist.

The beast dropped back into the pit. I raced to the edge, but the creature had vanished into the depths of the ground. Williams's legs lay nearby in a twisted heap. His torso had apparently been dragged into the pit by the murderous thing.

I settled to my knees in horror. Once again I had seen an innocent crew member lose his life for no good reason. Once again I experienced the hopelessness, the nagging feeling that I should have been able to do something to prevent this.

I drew forth my communicator to inform the others. Before I could begin to transmit, I heard a loud noise from the direction of my companions. It was the roar of a beast like the one that had just killed Williams. Then I heard the wailing screech of laser fire.

I stood and began to run down the dried riverbed toward my friends. I was determined not to lose any more people on this accursed planet.

The sounds of laser fire continued. That was encouraging. It meant my crewmates were still alive. But it also meant that they were still in mortal danger.

I came to a bend in the riverbed, and an awesome spectacle greeted my eyes. One of the loathsome beasts had emerged from its underground lair and was laying siege to my companions. Spock and the others had climbed the riverbank until they had their backs against the sheer face of a cliff. The cliff was far too steep to climb, and any descent was cut off by the monstrosity below. All four crewmen blasted away at it continuously, but it stood its ground.

I contemplated trying to draw it away, but this didn't seem a very promising strategy. It was too fast for me to outrun, and once it got me it would return to its attack on my companions.

As I examined the beast, I came to realize that its underside was not nearly as well armored as its top. If the underbelly was soft, then a laser might be able to do some damage there. Spock and the others couldn't possibly hit the beast's underside from their position high above.

It was up to me. I would have to rush underneath the creature, dodging its dozens of clattering legs. Our only hope was that the laser could rip its belly open.

For a moment I looked for alternatives, but could find none. Still I hesitated, unable to launch myself at the horror that threatened my friends.

Then the thought occurred to me. I don't know why I should think of it at that moment, but I did.

"What if all of this isn't real?"

The thought was all that I needed. It broke the tension in my mind. The thought that this might all be some Talosian illusion was funny to me. I actually laughed out loud at the absurdity of the thought.

Then I ran. I ran harder than I had ever run before. With my own laughter still ringing in my ears I ran between the monstrous legs. I sprinted up the creature's length, firing blindly overhead. I felt the splatter of warm liquids on my back. I kept firing until I emerged from beneath the beast's shadow.

I turned to face the creature. If I had failed, there was no point in running farther. I stared at the bulky head of the creature. Its mandibles were still. Suddenly the creature's legs began to wobble. Then the beast collapsed. It fell into a massive heap of dying flesh.

My companions rushed down the hill to my side.

"Chris!" shouted Boyce. "Chris, are you all right?"

"I'm fine, Doctor. This blood all belongs to that thing."

Trawley slapped me on the back.

"You saved all our lives!" he was shouting. "Can you believe that?"

Technically Trawley was being overly familiar with his commanding officer, but I overlooked it for the moment. The situation warranted a little laxity in discipline.

"Let's get out of here," I said, reaching for my communicator.

"Chris, I can't believe what you just did," said Boyce. "I'd never have been able to summon up the strength to take that beast on by myself. What possessed you to do that?"

I just smiled at him. I didn't know how to tell him what was going on in my mind at that moment. I never did tell Boyce that I had saved his life because of a momentary indulgence of a foolish little thought. I wish I had told him now, because I will never again be capable of sharing that story.

Trawley was also present the next time that the thought occurred to me. He had risen in the ranks quite a bit by that time. He was a full commander. His first command was an old class-J cargo ship that was being used for cadet training.

He had matured quite a bit in the decade since our adventure on

Corinthia VII, but he still had a worshipful look in his eyes when I came aboard for an inspection. His cadets were no younger than he had been when he joined the crew of the *Enterprise,* but still Trawley called them his "kids." I still saw Trawley as one of my children.

Trawley had only been aboard the ship himself for a week. He and the cadets were going to have quite a job getting this vessel into working order. Trawley was a good, thorough organizer. Given time he would be able to restore this ship to mint condition.

None of us knew it then, but time was not on our side.

Trawley gathered the crew together on the cargo deck and introduced me to them. They looked to me like children playing a dress-up game.

Trawley insisted on telling the cadets about our experience on Corinthia VII. I could tell that he had told this story many times before. He had perfected his delivery of it over time. My own memory varied a bit on some of the details, but I didn't quibble.

There was one detail, however, that I was surprised by. I couldn't imagine how he could know this particular detail.

". . . and do you know what the captain did just before he attacked the creature? You'll never guess this in a million years. He laughed! I swear, I could hear it all the way up the cliff wall. He laughed!"

The cadets laughed as well. I considered telling Trawley the whole story that day, but I didn't get around to it. I was a little embarrassed by all the attention, so I decided not to bring the subject up again. Now I'll never get the chance.

Later that night I was alone in my cabin, reading the cadet reviews. They looked like a good bunch of kids. It looked like Starfleet was going to be in good hands for another generation.

Suddenly a shudder rolled through the ship. A lump formed in my throat. The shudder wasn't really all that bad, but sometimes you sense when a disaster is bearing down on you.

I stepped out of my cabin. The corridor was filled with terrified cadets. Alarm Klaxons began to sound. One frightened young girl emerged from her cabin wearing nothing but a towel. Her eyes were already filling with tears.

I grabbed her by the shoulders. I kept my voice calm, expressing a cool confidence that I did not feel.

"Everything is going to be all right. Go get dressed and report to your station."

She straightened up and returned to her cabin. I looked at the confused crowd of cadets that had gathered in a circle around me.

"What's the matter with you people?" I shouted. "Get to your posts!"

Shame is a good motivator. The embarrassed crew members ran for their stations, eager to show me they knew their jobs.

I raced down to the engine room. The hatch was sealed. I looked through the porthole into the room beyond. I could see billowing clouds of gas.

A baffle plate had ruptured!

I could see the motionless bodies of half a dozen cadets. They might already be dead. I knew I couldn't leave them in there, but I also knew what delta rays can do to a man. For a moment I froze, unwilling to face the horrors on the other side of the hatch.

Then the thought came to me again.

"What if all of this isn't real?"

I didn't laugh this time. I knew as I looked that this was very real. If I didn't act fast, none of those cadets had a chance.

I felt a blast of heat as I opened that hatch, only I knew it wasn't really heat. It was the delta radiation knifing through my body. I stumbled in and grabbed the nearest cadet. She was wearing the thick protective coveralls of an engineer. That was good. That would help to minimize the effects of the radiation. I, on the other hand, had no such protection.

Six times I entered the engine room. Six cadets I pulled from that chamber of horrors. Two of them would die later at Starbase II. But four of them would survive.

As for me, I'm not sure if I would count myself as a survivor or not. I cannot move and I cannot speak. All I can do is sit, looking and listening to the world around me.

I sit here and I stare at the ringed moon and at the lovely young redhead. I look at a world that I can no longer participate in.

And I think. I think so much that my head hurts. I am fearful of the days to come. I am afraid that my mind will begin to wither and die. It frightens me to think that my sanity may begin to leave me.

In the midst of the horror that my life has become, the idea returns to me again. Once again I imagine that I am back in my cage on Talos IV. I dream that all of this is just an illusion, soon to be replaced with better dreams. Perhaps the Talosians will send me back to Mojave next, or back to Orion.

"What if all of this isn't real?"

Inwardly I laugh. But I know that this is real. This isn't Talos IV. This isn't an illusion. But for the first time in thirteen years I wish that it were. Perhaps it is a sign of my weakening spirit, but I wish I could trade this reality for a dream.

I wish I were back in my cage.

## "A Ribbon for Rosie," by Ilsa J. Bick

MAYBE SHE WAS AN ANGEL. MAMA SAYS ANGELS TALK TO GOD AND HELP us. But Papa doesn't believe that. He says angels are make-believe. He says that when people are lonely or scared, they want to believe in something stronger than they are, to prove that there's a reason bad things happen to nice people.

So maybe she was make-believe. Maybe she jumped out of my head because I wanted her to. But she said a whole bunch of stuff I didn't understand. I remember the words, but my brain doesn't understand, and that's weird, because if she came out of my make-believe, then I should.

She came the night Mama had made a Denevan plum pudding. Usually we love Mama's Denevan plum pudding, except that night Mama was cutting up the pudding real slow, because she was mad. Papa had just told Mama that we might be moving again. He didn't say we would; he said we might. But that was enough to make Mama mad. See, with Papa, *might* usually meant *would.*

We used to move a lot because of Papa. He'd say that things never got boring. But when you're always new, it's hard to make friends. I wouldn't mind being bored.

Not that I was the only one who had trouble making friends. Papa had tons more. He always argued with someone. Then he'd tell Mama who said what and what happened next. I never understood what Papa was talking about—junk about time and quantum-phase shifts. Papa had this idea to go faster than warp, which no one believed except him and Mama. Me, I'm not old enough to know what to believe.

Anyway, Papa said moving was easy because we had each other and that was all we needed. I don't know about that. Mama cared about other people. Whenever we moved, Mama would call her father, my grandpa. Home base, she said. Home for Mama was on Earth, in a country called Norway. She gets homesick, and she used to talk to Grandpa all the time. That is, she used to before we left Federation space three months ago, and now there's just nobody.

So the night Papa told us we might leave Heronius II was the night my Denevan plum pudding didn't taste so good. Mama didn't have any at all, so Papa ate his and hers and mine. Mama went to call Grandpa. I heard her crying, and Papa could tell I did. Go outside and play, he said.

I didn't argue. See, go outside and play is grown-up code for go away. Grown-ups always tell you to go out and play even when the only things to play with are a couple of bugs you find under a rock. It's just so you leave. But it's very hard to play when someone tells you to; it's not like, go brush your teeth. Grown-ups say silly things all the time—like telling you to go to sleep or be happy, as if you could just because they say so.

I went. Like just about everywhere else, we lived on the very edge of the colony: close but still far enough away so you'd have to look twice to convince yourself that we're really part of anything. There was no one around, and it was really late, way past second sunset. I'd grabbed Rosie, who's my best friend. She's all I have from Earth, except Mama. Rosie was Mama's doll, and she brought Rosie with her after she married Papa and decided to move away from Earth for good. Then she gave Rosie to me.

Outside I scuffed around with Rosie and kicked up black dust clouds. The dirt was black on Heronius, because of all the volcanoes, and *that's* because the magnetic fields of the planet kept shifting all the time, which was why we were there in the first place. About a half-kilometer away was Papa's new ship, and so I headed over there. Heronius had three moons, and when they were all out, it was like a special kind of daylight. Like walking into silver, or maybe heaven. Everything glowed.

In the glow, Papa's ship didn't look like a ship. It looked alive, which I think ships are anyway. Machines can be like people. I don't mean like an android. I mean that when you live in a house, the house turns into you, or when you pilot a ship, the ship is a thing that knows what it likes and doesn't like, just like a person. I told Papa that once, and he ruffled my hair and told me that maybe I'd be in Starfleet someday and command a big starship, only over his dead and broken body. I think it was a joke, but you can never be sure with parents.

I set Rosie down on the rocks near the ship, being very careful not to tear her new dress. Volcanic rocks are sharp. And then I sat down on a flat place next to her and watched the way the three moons made the ship look washed in silver.

Silly thing was I wished I could be home in bed. Other kids were in bed already. Me, I didn't have a bedtime. That was Papa's idea—not to regiment me, he told Mama. And I think that was the reason Papa stopped working with the Federation.

Anyway, about *her*—want to hear what I saw the first time? The way she came from around Papa's ship, it was like she kind of peeled herself away, as if she and the ship had been the same thing. She was very tall and thin and wore a silvery uniform, as if she had fallen out of space, like a meteor or an angel, and on the way the stars had gotten wrapped around her. She shimmered.

She didn't see me right away. I was so surprised I don't think I breathed or anything but just watched. When she turned a little bit, I could see that she was wearing a combadge—you know the type they have on starships to talk to each other. Our ships have been so small, you just yell if you want something.

There were other things, stranger even than the way she was just *there.* She was metal. I mean, at first I thought it was decoration, like jewelry. Her jewelry wasn't alive or morphic or even glittery, and when I finally got to see it better, I figured that probably jewelry wasn't the right word. More like circuitry. Remember how I said it looked like she was part of the ship? So it was like she had walked out of a machine and had pieces still sticking to her. Or maybe she couldn't decide yet whether she'd be human or machine. There was circuitry over her left eye and a weird metal star on the other side of her face, right at her jaw. And she wore a glove on her left hand, only padded at the tips and lacy, the way a spider's web looks when there's dew on it. Yet everything was exactly where it ought to be, as if all the metal and silver and circuitry were so much a part of her and what she was, she wouldn't be her without them.

I wasn't scared. She was the most beautiful person I'd ever seen, just as beautiful as Mama is, maybe more. *That's* beautiful; Papa says that there's no one in the universe as pretty as Mama is, and he's right.

And then there were her eyes. They were very blue. They glittered. Her eyes were where all her feelings were; in her eyes was everything, and you could tell that everything she was feeling wasn't about me, because she hadn't even seen me. She was looking at our ship. She stood there, and then she touched it, the way you would a butterfly. When you touch a butterfly, you have to be careful, or you'll kill it, because beautiful things are delicate.

That's the way she touched Papa's ship: gentle and afraid, as if she was worried that the ship would just melt or go away. She put one, then two hands on the ship and stroked it, the way I do Rosie's hair. Then she shivered, like she was cold.

Everything was really quiet, as if Heronius was holding its breath,

540

and she and Papa's ship were all silver in the light of the stars and the moons.

Hello, I said.

She jumped and turned real fast. Because I was in the rocks, I don't think she saw me at first, and I didn't want to make her so scared she would go away. So I stood up. That way she could see I was little, and she wouldn't be worried.

She came away from the ship and looked down at me. She didn't look angry, the way some grown-ups do when you catch them doing something they don't want you to see.

I was unaware of you, she said. Have you been there long?

The way she talked was weird. At first I thought maybe she was an android. I'd only met one android in my entire life, and his face was flat, like a pond when there's no wind. She wasn't as bad, but she said things without lots of feeling, like a computer. You know how computers are: kind of like excuse me, but the hull is going to breach and you're all going to die, and I just thought that you'd like to know and maybe do something about it.

Longer than you, I said. I mean, I wasn't rude or anything, but I didn't know how I felt about her being so close to our ship and all.

She didn't answer right away but kept staring. I felt real small, so I grabbed Rosie, and that made me feel a little better.

What are you doing around our ship? I asked.

Yours?

I hugged Rosie tighter. My papa's. So it's mine, too. Kind of.

She looked at me, and she looked at Rosie, and then she shivered again. Are you cold? I asked.

She said no, but her voice was really tiny, almost scared-sounding.

Are you an android? (How dumb. I knew it wasn't true. It was just something to say.)

She looked about as surprised as I guess she could, which wasn't very. Her eyebrows—well, eyebrow and circuit—came together in a little pucker. An android? No. Why do you ask?

I stared down at my sneakers all covered with black Heronian dust. I hate when I have to explain things, but I'd opened my big mouth. Well, uhm . . . it's the way you talk, I said.

The way I speak.

Yeah. Like no contractions. And you talk fancy. Only androids and Vulcans do that. Except you're not Vulcan, and you don't look like any android I've ever seen, because their eyes aren't usually any color but yellow or black, and their skin is kind of, you know, creepy white.

Mama says that's because they don't have blood like humans do, and blood is red and is what makes our skin have color, and red's my favorite color. Maybe you're a new model, but then they ought to finish your polydermal layer. Your circuitry's showing.

Her hand—the one with the lacy glove—went up to her left circuit, the one where her eyebrow would have been. No, I am . . . complete. These are bioimplants.

Oh, I said. Whatever *they* were, I thought. Like artificial? I asked. To help you see?

Not quite. Artificial, that is. They are integral to who I am.

See, you did it again.

What?

Said integral, instead of I am who I am.

Clearly we are having a communications problem, she said, like I had a bad isolinear chip or something.

How come you talk like that?

Speech is cumbersome, and language is imprecise.

Aren't you used to talking?

Not until recently.

Oh. Are you from a ship?

How have you drawn that conclusion?

I told her—the combadge and all. So, did you come this afternoon? The colony comm didn't say anything about a ship, I said.

My ship did not land.

You came in a shuttlecraft?

No.

This was like playing a guessing game, only it wasn't much fun. You transported? I asked. I get sick when I transport. Do you get sick when you transport?

No. But I did transport, in a manner of speaking.

And then she got that look on her face that most grown-ups get when they're not going to say anything more. She changed the subject. Grown-ups do that all the time. Your vessel, she said, does it have a name?

Just a number.

Three-two-four-five-zero, she said in that computer voice again, only that wasn't like she was so smart or anything. The registry number was next to the hatch. It wasn't like I could say wow, great guess, so I didn't say anything.

She opened her mouth to say something else but didn't. Instead she pointed at Rosie, and that's when I saw she had some circuitry on the back of her right hand, too. It matched the star on her jaw.

What is that?

Huh? I was so busy looking at the stuff on her hand I was sort of surprised. It's a doll, I said.

Doll. She said it like she'd never heard of one.

Maybe she couldn't hear very well. So I said louder, A doll. You know, a toy, only Rosie's not really a toy, she was my mama's, and she's from Norway. That is, Mama's from Norway, and so's Rosie, and Norway's on Earth, and—I stopped because it was all sounding pretty complicated, even to me, and I'm used to the way I think.

Before I knew it, she was touching Rosie's hair with her left hand, the one with the lacy glove.

Hey, I almost said. I wanted to jerk Rosie away, but I couldn't. It was the strangest thing: like Rosie belonged to her, too, and it wouldn't be right to just yank her away.

Instead I asked, Would you like to hold Rosie for real?

You'd have thought I was asking her to touch a Verillian pit viper. You know how scary things can be wow-neat and wow-creepy at the same time? That's the way Rosie seemed for her—as if she just *had* to hold her but figured she might die or something. Her eyes were real wide, and she looked like she was holding her breath. And maybe it was because of all the moonlight, but she looked like she might cry.

Then I felt really bad. Rosie makes me feel good. At least, I don't feel lonely. Sometimes, at night, Rosie helps a lot. The dark can be very scary. Parents tell you there aren't any monsters or boogeymen, but I'm not sure. So I snuggle under my covers with Rosie and suck my thumb and get all quiet-feeling, and it's very nice. It's like being little again—so little that Mama can hold you, and there's room left over.

My eyes felt all tingly. Please don't cry, I said. Here, and I pushed Rosie into her hands.

Thank you, she said, and her voice was all choked-sounding, like when I have a cold. She was blinking real fast. I watched her fingers, the ones with the glove on them, stroke Rosie's hair. Rosie's hair splashed like a stream of silver water over her fingers.

She is beautiful, she said.

Not as pretty as you, I said all in a rush, which, even though it was true, I wished I hadn't said. I am *so* dumb.

But all she said was thank you, and she kept playing with Rosie's hair.

She likes it if you sing, I said.

Sing?

Yes, like a lullaby.

Does Rosie know one? She wasn't making fun; she was just asking.

Yeah. Actually, it's my favorite.

So I sang what Mama used to sing whenever I had a bad dream. She listened, and after a little bit, she rocked Rosie back and forth, but so slow I could tell she wasn't really thinking about it. And her eyes got a faraway-memory look. Papa gets that look, when he looks at the stars. I can talk to him, but that doesn't mean he hears. He usually doesn't, and even if I can get him to look at me, he's not really there.

I kept singing, and soon she was humming, real soft. It's an easy song, and it was nice not to sing alone. When I'd done, she kept on a bit, until she heard herself. Then she stopped and blinked. She looked at me all queer. Then she handed Rosie back but gentle, like Rosie might break or something.

That was very beautiful, she said.

Didn't your mama ever sing to you?

She twisted her head away and looked back toward the ship. I do not remember.

You mean, you don't remember if she sang to you?

No, and then she looked right at me. I do not remember my mother.

Why not?

We were separated when I was young.

What about your papa?

He was . . . lost.

You mean you're an orphan?

Yes.

Wow. I always thought orphans were supposed to be little kids, not grown-ups. Sure, people get old and die, but somehow you don't figure that your mama and papa, even if *their* mama and papa are dead, can ever be orphans. After all, they have you, and they have each other. I couldn't imagine what it would be like not to have my parents around.

I think she could tell I felt bad. She said, It is all right. It was a long time ago.

That made me feel better, a little. Were you adopted? I asked.

By a very large family.

Oh. It was all I could think to say. Do you miss them?

At times.

Do you ever talk to them?

Talk?

Yeah. On subspace. I call Grandpa all the time. He's on Earth.

No, I do not speak to them.

What about letters?

No.

But won't they worry?

I was one of many, I suspect I think of them more than they will ever think of me.

What kind of family was that? I wanted to ask more, but just then I heard Papa call my name. *Heck.* It was late. Already the first moon had set, and it had gotten darker. In the sky the third moon, the one shaped like a lima bean (I hate lima beans), was catching up to the second.

Coming, Papa! I shouted.

Only not just me shouted. All of a sudden, I heard her say Papa's name, too.

I was pretty surprised, and when I turned around, I could tell I wasn't the only one. The way her face had changed, you could tell she was all mixed up, like the way water crashes into the beach when all the Heronian moons are in conjunction: *crash, whoosh, bam,* and everything is just a total mess.

That was also the first time I had this idea that maybe she wasn't there by accident. That she hadn't just been passing by, ho-hum, in a ship and thought, gee, Heronius looked like a great place, which it isn't. That maybe she was there because of us.

Oh, I felt small and scared, and I wanted Mama. I couldn't help it; I kind of fell backward. I would have cut myself up real good, except she grabbed my arm. But when she saw my mouth all twisted up, she let me go. I will not hurt you, she said.

I know. Except I didn't, and I couldn't get my mouth to work right, and my teeth went *click-click-click,* like I was freezing. That was Papa. I have to go.

Yes, she said, real quiet and low.

Then, just as fast as I'd felt afraid, I felt bad. I was going home where everyone loved me, and she'd be all alone out here in the dark. And the more I thought about it, the more I knew she'd been looking for us. I just knew. Maybe it was the way she touched our ship or held Rosie, or maybe I knew she was deep-down sad—so sad and lonely she probably thought she'd never feel better.

I grabbed her hand, the one with the glove. She jerked a little, and then her fingers curled around mine, and it was okay.

Come home with me. You can meet Mama and Papa.

She shook her head.

But why not? We have enough to eat. You can sleep in my room.

I cannot. It is not . . . I must think what to do.

What do you mean? Are you going away? Is your ship leaving?

My vessel is far away. And I must go.

No, I thought, she couldn't. Maybe she wouldn't ever come back.

No, I said out loud. I tugged harder. No.

It was then that I saw she was wearing a kind of bracelet on her left wrist. The bracelet had a bunch of lights and numbers winking on and off. She saw that I saw, and said, The device correlates to specific resonance frequencies.

What? I asked. The bracelet was pretty, and I was kind of hypnotized by it. I don't get it, I said.

You do not have to—and she almost, *almost* smiled—get it, But I will find you again. Now that I know that this is the correct place, the correct time. . . .

What?

She dropped my hand then and took a couple steps back toward Papa's ship. It is the ship. It will take too long to explain, and I cannot see your parents. I am not ready.

Papa called my name again, and his voice was closer, like he'd come out of the house. She backed up real fast then.

Wait! I started to climb after her. Promise you'll come back!

I promise.

Promise? Cross your heart and hope to die?

She was so close to the ship then, and the moons had crossed so that there was a lot of shadow, and I couldn't see her.

But I heard her. No, and her voice sounded as hard as the rocks, no one will die.

My chest got tight, and I couldn't breathe. Where was Papa, where was Papa?

I don't understand!

It is not essential—

I think she was going to say something else, but Papa called me again, and then there he was, and I was never so glad, and it was too late because she'd have to see him and Mama too, and none of us would be alone anymore. So I turned back to the ship to tell her, because she'd been sent special to find me, and I liked her, and I wanted her to like me.

But the shadows were as black as spilled ink, and she had gone away.

I didn't tell. I walked home with Papa, and he shoo'ed me to bed. Mama was already in their room.

I had lots of bad dreams that night for the first time in a long, long time. But I couldn't remember any of them when I woke up.

At breakfast, Papa said that Mama had gone with her team to study the magnetic phase shift of a bunch of di-isotonic rocks. The phase shift didn't come on Heronius but once every twenty-seven standard years, and then only for three days. Mama's a planetary geomagnetologist. That means she studies changes in the gravimagnetic matrix of rocks. Just because I can say all that junk doesn't mean I understand. Mama's explained it to Grandpa about a hundred million times.

Way back, Mama went to study Hortas on Janus VI. Hortas live in rock. Heck, they *are* rocks. At first no one knew how Hortas found their way around, but Mama figured that Hortas sensed magnetic resonance variances in rocks.

Now, Papa was on Janus VI, too. He thought he could do what Hortas did, but in space, by mixing gravity and magnetic resonance to bend space-time in a way that's different from warp, to travel in time.

So Mama and Papa fell in love and all that stuff. Then there was me, but that didn't stop anybody. Mama's always chasing rocks, and Papa's always running after time.

But breakfast was quiet. Papa pushed his food around. The longer Papa didn't talk, the more afraid I got. Maybe it was because of *her,* or because I hadn't slept very well, and it wasn't right for Mama to leave without kissing me good-bye.

Then Papa cleared his throat, and I saw his face, and my breakfast tasted like sand.

Papa said, We're leaving day after tomorrow.

Why? I asked, except I had to say it twice because there was this big, dry lump in my throat.

Papa got this tired look, like he'd been up for about five months. Because the Federation won't let me conduct my experiments in their space.

You don't work for them.

It's their law. All work involving new warp technologies has to pass review.

How come?

As long as we're in Federation space, they don't want anyone mucking up the works, especially space-time.

Space seemed like an awfully big place to me. I told Papa so.

Not big enough for the Federation, he said.

I was holding my spoon so hard, my fingers hurt. There wasn't any point in arguing, and it was really okay, because I hadn't made any friends. But still.

Where will we go?

Then Papa smiled, like he was going to play a trick on someone. The Delta Quadrant.

Now I knew we were in the Alpha Quadrant, but I didn't know there *was* a Delta Quadrant. The Federation doesn't own the Delta Quadrant? I asked.

The Federation doesn't know what's *in* the Delta Quadrant.

Why not?

Because it's very far away.

How far?

Papa told me.

I just sat there, with my mouth hanging open, like a cartoon: a big *WUH?* in the bubble, and hundreds of question marks.

Boy, I thought, I have trouble making friends now. I'll never make any out there. There aren't even any *people.*

Papa could tell what I was thinking. Trust me, dear, he said, there will be plenty of people: new races, new worlds. And space to work, to breathe! More free space than you can imagine. Space enough to work without interference or oversight from the Federation. Space enough and time.

My stomach squiggled, like I'd swallowed a bird. But . . . but there won't be any people, any human beings. . . .

Papa winked. We'll be the first.

My face got all hot. I wanted to cry, and then I thought about *her* and what it felt like when she went away, and I felt even worse, as if there was this big, heavy, black space ahead in time. Only it was a thing, and if we got there, I'd get lost and be all by myself, without Mama or Papa or anybody.

Papa was watching me. I knew I ought to smile. I knew he wanted me to be real brave. But we were going just about as far away as we could get from other people and still be in the same galaxy. I might not ever see another human being or any other kids or their parents ever, ever again, and I got all sick-scared inside, like maybe I was going to die or maybe never be the same, not ever again. Here Papa was saying all this junk about needing room to breathe, but no one bothered asking *me* if I was breathing okay.

It wasn't the kind of thing you said, though.

And Papa was still watching me, and I loved him and hated him all at once, and so much I wanted to scream.

548

But I just dipped my spoon into my breakfast and said, Oh, okay, when do we leave?

No one talked at all during dinner. Afterward Mama and Papa went into their room again. When I heard Mama start to cry, I left.

I went straight to Papa's ship. Sure enough, *she* was there.

Papa says we're leaving the day after tomorrow, I said.

She looked real serious.

Do something, I said.

Did your father say where he was going?

I told her. That made her look worse, almost as sick as I felt. I could tell that she was thinking, like a computer—going *tick-tick-tick* real fast through all the choices.

Then she said, I will speak to your father.

This way, I said and grabbed her hand, the one with the glove. This time she didn't jerk back but held on real tight.

Mama and Papa were sitting on the couch. They both looked up when we walked in, and then they just stared.

For a minute, no one said anything. Her hand gripped mine, and I heard her swallow. It was that quiet.

Papa's forehead got all wrinkly. He stood up real slow, and Mama got up right behind him. Who are you? Papa asked.

She let go of my hand and took a step toward them. I must speak to you.

Papa's voice got angry. What are you doing with my daughter?

It's okay, Papa.

Mama shushed me. Come away, dear.

No. She's my friend.

Papa started toward the wall comm. I'm calling colony security.

No! Her voice was loud, like thunder. You must not. You must listen.

Why?

Because what you are planning will place you in great danger.

Papa's eyes got as narrow as a snake's. How would you know what I'm planning?

I know. You cannot go to the Delta Quadrant. You must not.

Mama gasped, and her hands went up to her mouth. Papa opened his mouth, but no sounds came out.

Then he coughed. I've not filed a flight plan. I haven't told anyone but my family. How do you know this?

You must listen, she said. She wasn't shouting, but her voice was still sharp, like the edge of a knife.

Answer me. How do you know?

You would not believe me.

Then why should I listen?

Because I speak the truth.

Who are you? You're not human. What are you?

I am human. I was once . . . something else.

What? Papa asked, but he sounded scared now not just angry, and I didn't know Papa could be scared. What were you? What *are* you?

Not in front of the child, she said.

I was surprised. I thought we were friends, I said.

We are, she said. But there are some things suitable for children, and other things that are not.

That made me mad. That's not fair, I said. You told me everything else.

What else? asked Mama.

My God, you're from the Federation, said Papa. You're here to spy on me.

No.

Oh no? Papa balled his fists up and got taller. How do you know so much? You're wearing a uniform. That's clearly a Starfleet combadge. You don't come from the colony. We've never met.

You cannot know that, she said, so low no one heard her but me.

Papa kept talking, You know about the Delta Quadrant.

I told Father, said Mama.

Papa said a bad word. That means they're monitoring our subspace.

*She* said, No, you are wrong.

Dear God, you're not even human. What are you?

I will explain, but first—

*No, you* listen to *me,* and then Papa said a *very* bad word, and Mama said, No, that won't help. And then Mama said to me, Come here, sweetheart, come here, baby, come to Mama. And I shouted, Listen, will you please just listen, she wants to talk to you!

Then *she* touched my shoulder. Go to them.

Yes, come here, baby, said Mama.

I didn't want to, but I did what she said. Mama cried a little bit and hugged me so I almost couldn't breathe.

Papa was staring at her real hard. I don't know who you are or where you come from—

It is irrelevant—

But you accost my daughter, come into my home—

It was the only way—

550

Give me one good reason not to have you thrown out on your—

I had to be certain of this place, she said. Of this *time*.

Papa stopped. Papa stared.

Time? His mouth didn't work right. Time?

She said it again, real slow and loud, like he couldn't hear so well, *Of this . . . time.*

Of this time, Papa said, but he whispered it instead. Time? As in . . . travel? Another time?

Yes.

But how—why now—

I know, I understand, said Mama. It's the gravimagnetic variance. The phase shift. That's it, isn't it?

Yes. It has opened a window. The gravimagnetic phase shift has created the optimum conditions to facilitate a displacement in timespace.

Mama tugged on Papa's sleeve. That's exactly what you've been saying all along. It's possible, isn't it? Isn't it?

Papa shook his head up and down. But I don't . . . I can't control the displacement. It's unstable. How—

The temporal fabric is quite tenuous. It cannot be artificially replicated, only enhanced. There is a relay array in the Delta Quadrant. The array is powered by a quantum singularity. Previously we had sent holographic images and rudimentary communications in a series of transceivers. The ship's log contained information of an encounter with an advanced Federation technology capable of opening temporal fissures. I adapted the array for that purpose. Unstable, but enough to direct a high-density particle beam for a short time.

Then you're from the Delta Quadrant, said Mama.

There are no Federation vessels out there, said Papa.

There are none, she said, *now.*

Papa's eyes got round. You're from the future?

Yes.

Then you've done it, you've really done it! You've managed to control the timestream.

Within certain parameters and under optimal conditions, yes. It is not what you imagine. Those of us on the ship cannot all return.

Papa turned to Mama, and he looked excited. It's a beginning, don't you see? I knew I was right, I *knew* it!

And all the time I'm thinking, Oh, no, oh, no, no, no, no, why are you doing this, don't tell him that, don't make him happy, don't make him *want* to go.

I pushed away from Mama.

I thought you were going to help! I shouted at her. I thought you were going to stop him! Don't tell him all about time and the future and all these good things about the Delta Quadrant!

They all jumped. I think they'd forgotten I was there.

But, dear, said Mama.

You're too young to understand, said Papa.

I do not have nice things to say about the Delta Quadrant, she said.

What do you mean? asked Papa.

I didn't pay attention. I was so mad, I stomped my feet. This isn't helping! He's going to go anyway, don't you see? You're *making* it happen!

Darling, said Mama.

No more, she said. Not in front of her.

Why not? asked Papa. Why can't she know? What are you saying?

Not in front of the child.

Mama squeezed my shoulder. Go to your room, dear.

No!

Listen to your mother, said Papa.

No, no!

Then she came and squatted down until I could see all the patterns of the circuit over her left eye.

We are friends, are we not?

My mouth was tight. Yes.

And friends must trust one another.

Yes.

I told you I would return, and I am here.

Yes.

Then trust me now. Do as your mother says. Go to your room. Sing to Rosie and calm her. She must be frightened.

Mama said, How do you—

Rosie's scared, I said. I felt a tear trickle down my cheek.

She does not understand, she said.

No.

She used her finger, the human one, to wipe the tear away.

She will, she said. Trust me.

So I left. My room was on the other side of the house, and even though I disconnected the auto—Papa showed me once—so the door was open a crack, I couldn't hear anything but noise. Her and Papa talking back and forth, then Mama, some spaces where no one was talking, then Papa's voice going higher like when you ask a question, then her. Then, a long, long space, and then another, very strange noise, one I'd never heard before. A voice without words. Just sound. And then I figured out that the sound was Mama. The sound came and went, like waves on a beach, and I could hear Papa making shushing sounds, but Mama didn't shush.

And she was still talking, only lower now and her voice was all strange, too.

It was like a bad, bad dream. I grabbed Rosie and made a cave out of my covers. But I couldn't sing; I forgot the words.

The next thing I remember, Papa was uncovering me, I made a little sound to show Papa I was awake. He put his hand on my cheek.

She's gone?

Papa said she was.

Mama was crying.

Yes.

Why?

Papa's thumb kept going back and forth across my cheek, and then he pushed the hair way back from my forehead. My hair was wet, because it's very hot under the covers and I'd gotten all sweaty.

She said scary things?

Papa's finger rubbed my chin. Yes.

What?

She was right. It's not for you. Don't be in such a hurry to grow up. It's not so wonderful. Be grateful you don't have decisions to make.

What decisions? Are we still going? What did Mama say?

Papa pushed himself off my bed. Go to sleep. We'll talk in the morning.

That night I dreamed, and it was all bad, and I remembered it all when I woke up.

Only we didn't talk. Mama was gone all day, the last day of the phase shift. Papa walked in and out of the house. I had a funny-awful feeling all day. Usually drawing helps me feel better, as if all the yucky feelings spill right out onto the paper. Except I didn't have any paper, and I didn't want to bother Papa. So I drew on the walls. I just did it. I used lots of black, which is weird, because red is my favorite color. But I felt black. So I drew black.

Next thing I knew, Mama and Papa were there. I expected they'd be mad about the walls. But they just looked at the pictures. I remember how they held hands, only not in the way people in love do. More like they were holding each other up.

Then Papa pointed. What are they?

Dream pictures.

Dream pictures? asked Mama. When did they start? asked Papa.
Last night. Night before.
When she came, said Papa.
What are they? asked Mama.
It just came out. Ships, I said.
Ships? asked Papa.
Space ships.
But, dear, said Mama, they're cubes.
They're ships, I said, and stared at my fingers. They were black.

She came again that night. She walked right in, like she belonged.
Papa said, I have something to show you.
He took her to my room. She stared at my pictures for a real long
time. Then she asked, She drew these?
Yes. What are they?
These are Borg. It is as I told you. The temporal stream has curved
back upon itself.
I've checked your figures, said Papa. I ran the simulation. You
might be mistaken.
She pointed at my pictures. You need more? This is *Borg*. If you go,
you will become Borg. Or worse.
You can't know.
I *can*.
No. You said your bioimplants phased with a high-density particle
beam. That the relay synchronized to a gravimagnetic disturbance to
create the temporal rift. What if the rift didn't loop you back at all
but into a parallel continuum?
Impossible. Your ship matches the resonance frequency of the
vessel in B'Omar space.
In your time, your continuum. Ours might be distinct.
Why do you refuse to listen? I am not here by accident.
Papa didn't say anything. I thought maybe he might change his
mind, and then we wouldn't leave. I think Mama wanted that,
because she laid her hand on Papa's shoulder, as if her touch said
more than words.
Then I saw Papa's face move in a certain way, and it was all awful
again.
I'm sorry, he said. While I concede that what you present is
plausible—
It *will* happen—
I believe you've stepped across times, not back into your own. Or
ours.

She looked as if she might cry. You are a *fool*—
Please—
The child is showing you!—and now she *was* crying—She *knows! I*
know!
Mama gripped Papa's shoulder. Can't we stay?
No.
But I'm afraid, I'm—
There's nothing to be frightened of—
No, whispered Mama. Look at her, *look* at her. Can't you see—
She cried, Listen, please listen—
You're both of you becoming hysterical—
Stop! It was a new voice, and it was screaming, screaming, and then
I heard that the voice was mine. Stop, stop, stop, stop, stop, *stop!*
Mama rushed over. Oh, my poor darling, my little girl—
Oh, Mama, Mama, *Mama!* I cried.
Only there were two voices calling for my mama. Because *she* had
said Mama, too.
Mama and Papa stood real still, Mama hugging me, and Papa
staring, and me snuffling into Mama's arm.
She was crying, Please, Mama, Papa, please, *listen to me*—
I looked up at Mama. I didn't know I had a sister, I said.
I turned back. Are you my sister?
Papa stepped between Mama and me, and her. You've got to leave.
You don't belong here. I am truly sorry for what has happened to you,
but this is not your time.
She stopped talking. Her face was all wet.
No, she said after a long time, I can see that it is not.

We all went to the ship. She touched it again, like she had when she
told it hello, except now it was good-bye.
Papa said, Don't come again.
She'd stopped crying. She said, I could not, even if I wished. The
shift on this planet is nearly over. By the next shift, time will have
overtaken us all.
I'm sorry things didn't turn out differently for you.
And I grieve for you, she said.
She looked at Mama. Good-bye.
Mama's lips shook. Good-bye. Be well. Be—
Mama looked away.
Then *she* came to me. I have something for you.
No, said Papa. Let her, whispered Mama.
I want you to have this, she said. She held out a little box.

I looked at Mama, and she nodded, so I took it.

Is it a present?

Yes. For your birthday. Open it then, not before.

Please, I said. Are you my sister? Who are you? What's your name?

I am Seven.

I'm going to be six.

I know.

Then she backed away and did something to her bracelet. I must go before the rift collapses.

I thought my chest would burst open. Will I ever see you again?

All of a sudden, she got clear, like a picture with all the color washed out. Like a cloud thinning out under the sun.

Will I? Will I?

I saw her move her lips, and the sound came back all echo, like an empty room.

Pray, the echo said, pray that when you look in the mirror, you do not.


We're all alone now.

Days are long, but it's always night in space. Mama gives me lessons. I play with Rosie. I draw a lot, but I don't like my pictures. Now they're not just those ships but people. Only they're people-machines, like she was, but worse—all metal and tubes and only one eye. And they're white, like skin when all the blood is gone.

I show my pictures to Mama and Papa. Papa says there are no people like that. Mama doesn't say anything.

Yesterday was my birthday. Mama made a chocolate cake. And Mama and Papa sang Happy Birthday, Anika, and there were six candles plus one to grow on, and I blew them all out.

And I opened her box. Inside were two red ribbons: one for me, one for Rosie. I love them, and we're going to wear them forever. Because red is my favorite color, and because red is the color of a sunset and the color of human blood, and mostly because red is the color of luck.

# APPENDIX

## *The Pocket Books*
## *Star Trek Timeline*

With special thanks to Lee Jamilkowski, James E. Goeders, Robert Greenberger, Bob Manojlovich, and John J. Ordover.

This is a complete timeline to the Pocket Books Star Trek novels, short stories, original audio programs, and Young Adult books published through November 1998. When known, dates are given in both Earth calendar dates and Star Trek stardates. When placing items in the timeline, the authors sometimes had to correct inconsistent stardates so that continuity among the Star Trek television episodes and books would remain as correct as possible.

Please note that dates marked with a bullet (•) represent portions of a story that take place at times other than the time of the central portion of the story.

### LEGEND:

TOS—*The Original Series*
TNG—*The Next Generation*
DS9—*Deep Space Nine*
VGR—*Voyager*
NF—New Frontier
DoH—Day of Honor
ya—Young Adult book

## 1991

**"The Man Who Sold the Sky" (short story, *Strange New Worlds I*)**—
(Stardates nonexistent)

## 2065

*Federation* **(TOS/TNG hardcover)**—(Stardates nonexistent)—2065 to
    2366
  • 2062—Cochrane demonstrates warp capability to Brack.
  • 2063—*Star Trek: First Contact*—not mentioned in **Federation**
*(TOS/TNG hardcover)*—Cochrane breaks the light barrier with the
*Phoenix.*
  • 2064—Cochrane leaves for Alpha Centauri on the *Bonaventure.*
*Editors' Note: The* Phoenix *(seen in* Star Trek: First Contact) *was an
experimental ship designed to demonstrate manned warp capability.
The* Bonaventure, *mentioned in* **Federation** *(TOS/TNG hardcover),
was a ship designed for interstellar travel.*
  • 2065—[Part One—Chapter 1, 2]—Cochrane returns from his
    first interstellar trip to Alpha Centauri; shortly after his return,
    Cochrane again leaves Earth for Alpha Centauri to flee Thorsen.
*Editors' Note 1: The March 2061 date in* **Federation** *(TOS/TNG
hardcover) contradicts the* Star Trek Chronology *and has been corrected to March 2065.*
  • 2078—Cochrane backstory.
  • 2117—Cochrane backstory.
  • 2267—Stardate 3849.8 to 3858.7. Kirk portion (immediately
    follows "Journey to Babel" [**TOS**)].
  • 2270—Kirk visits Cochrane monument on Titan.
  • 2293—[Prologue, Epilogue]—Stardate 9910.1. Kirk visits the
    Guardian of Forever.
*Editors' Note 2: The 2295 date in* **Federation** *(TOS/TNG hardcover)
contradicts the* Star Trek Chronology *and has been corrected to 2293.*
  • 2366—Stardate 43920.6 to 43924.1. Picard portion, takes place
    immediately after "Sarek" (**TNG***).*
  • And beyond . . . —Newstardate 2143.21.3. Epilogue, a ship
    called *Enterprise* about to begin a voyage where no one has gone
    before . . .

## 2248

*Crisis on Vulcan* **(TOSya Starfleet Academy #1)**—(No stardate given)—
    *This story takes place before Spock joins Starfleet Academy in
    2249.*

## 2250

*Aftershock* (TOSya Starfleet Academy #2)—(No stardate given)—*This story takes place soon before Starfleet Academy's winter break in Kirk's freshman year, 2250.*

## 2251

*Cadet Kirk* (TOSya Starfleet Academy #3)—(No stardate given)—*Spock mentions meeting Christopher Pike a "few" years ago in this book, which occurred in* **Crisis on Vulcan** *(TOSya Starfleet Academy #1).*

## 2252

*Vulcan's Glory* (TOS #44)—(No stardate given)

## 2254

(TOS) "The Cage"—(No stardate given)
*Where Sea Meets Sky* (TOS—The Captain's Table #6)—(No stardate given)—*Pike backstory.*
- 2266—Stardate 1626.8. Framing story, takes place shortly before Pike's accident.

## 2264

*Enterprise* (TOS giant)—(No stardate given)

## 2265

(TOS) "Where No Man Has Gone Before"—Stardate 1312.4

## 2266

(TOS) "The Corbomite Maneuver"—Stardate 1512.2
(TOS) "Mudd's Women"—Stardate 1329.8
(TOS) "The Enemy Within"—Stardate 1672.1
(TOS) "The Man Trap"—Stardate 1513.1
(TOS) "The Naked Time"—Stardate 1704.2
(TOS) "Charlie X"—Stardate 1533.6
(TOS) "Balance of Terror"—Stardate 1709.2
*Shadow Lord* (TOS #22)—Stardate 1831.5
(TOS) "What Are Little Girls Made Of?"—Stardate 2712.4
(TOS) "Dagger of the Mind"—Stardate 2715.1
(TOS) "Miri"—Stardate 2713.5
(TOS) "The Conscience of the King"—Stardate 2817.7

**"A Private Anecdote"** (TOS short story, *Strange New Worlds I*)— Stardate 2822.5
- 2255—Pike backstory.

## 2267

(TOS) "The Galileo Seven"—Stardate 2821.5

(TOS) "Court Martial"—Stardate 2947.3

(TOS) "The Menagerie"—Stardate 3012.4

(TOS) "Shore Leave"—Stardate 3025.3

*Heart of the Sun* **(TOS #83)**—(No stardate given)—*Not long after "Court Martial" (TOS)*.

(TOS) "The Squire of Gothos"—Stardate 2124.5

(TOS) "Arena"—Stardate 3045.6

(TOS) "The Alternative Factor"—Stardate 3087.6

(TOS) "Tomorrow Is Yesterday"—Stardate 3113.2

*Web of the Romulans* **(TOS #10)**—Stardate 3125.3 to 3130.4—*Shortly after "Tomorrow is Yesterday" (TOS)*.

*Editors' Note: A footnote that refers to "All Our Yesterdays" (TOS) contradicts the "computer malfunction" subplot of the story.*

(TOS) "Return of the Archons"—Stardate 3156.2

(TOS) "A Taste of Armageddon"—Stardate 3192.1

(TOS) "Space Seed"—Stardate 3141.9

*The Joy Machine* **(TOS #80)**—(No stardate given)—*Mentions recent layover at Starbase 12*.

(TOS) "This Side of Paradise"—Stardate 3417.3

(TOS) "The Devil in the Dark"—Stardate 3196.1

(TOS) "Errand of Mercy"—Stardate 3198.4

(TOS) "The City on the Edge of Forever"—(No stardate given)

*Final Frontier* **(TOS Giant)**—(No stardate given)—*Framing story takes place immediately after "The City on the Edge of Forever" (TOS)*.
- 2245—Captain April backstory, takes place before the *Enterprise*'s first five-year mission.

(TOS) "Operation: Annihilate!"—Stardate 3287.2

*Ishmael* **(TOS #23)**—(No stardate given)—*Framing story takes place after "The City on the Edge of Forever" (TOS)*.
- 1867—Spock time-travels back to Earth to this date.

(TOS) "Catspaw"—Stardate 3018.2

(TOS) "Metamorphosis"—Stardate 3219.8

*The Great Starship Race* **(TOS #67)**—Stardate 3223.1—*After "A Taste of Armageddon" (TOS)*.

(TOS) "Friday's Child"—Stardate 3497.2

*Invasion! #1: First Strike* **(TOS #79)**—(No stardate given)—*Immediately follows "Friday's Child" (TOS)*.

(TOS) "Who Mourns for Adonais?"—Stardate 3468.1

(TOS) "Amok Time"—Stardate 3372.7

(TOS) "The Doomsday Machine"—(No stardate given)

(TOS) "Wolf in the Fold"—Stardate 3614.9

(TOS) "The Changeling"—Stardate 3451.9

(TOS) "The Apple"—Stardate 3715.3

(TOS) "Mirror, Mirror"—(No stardate given)

(TOS) "The Deadly Years"—Stardate 3478.2

**FACES of Fire** (TOS #58)—Stardate 3998.6—*About halfway through five-year mission.*

(TOS) "I, Mudd"—Stardate 4513.3

(TOS) "The Trouble with Tribbles"—Stardate 4523.3

(TOS) "Bread and Circuses"—Stardate 4040.7

**Twilight's End** (TOS #77)—(No stardate given)—*After "A Taste of Armageddon" (TOS).*

(TOS) "Journey to Babel"—Stardate 3842.3

**The Vulcan Academy Murders** (TOS #20)—(No stardate given)

**The IDIC Epidemic** (TOS #38)—(No stardate given)—*After* **The Vulcan Academy Murders** *(TOS #20).*

(TOS) "A Private Little War"—Stardate 4211.4

## 2268

**The Disinherited** (TOS #59)—(No stardate given)—*Just before "The Gamesters of Triskelion" (TOS).*

(TOS) "The Gamesters of Triskelion"—Stardate 3211.7

(TOS) "Obsession"—Stardate 3619.2

**Treaty's Law** (TOS—Day of Honor #4)—Stardate 3629 (*from* **Armageddon Sky** *(DS9—DoH #2)—After "Errand of Mercy" (TOS).*

• 2288—Framing story, set twenty years after the main events of the novel.

**The Rings of Tautee** (TOS #78)—Stardate 3871.6

(TOS) "The Immunity Syndrome"—Stardate 4307.1

(TOS) "A Piece of the Action"—(No stardate given)

(TOS) "By Any Other Name"—Stardate 4657.5

**The Klingon Gambit** (TOS #3)—Stardate 4720.1 to 4744.8

**Mutiny on the Enterprise** (TOS #12)—Stardate 4769.1 to 5012.5—*Immediately after* **The Klingon Gambit** *(TOS #3).*

(TOS) "Return to Tomorrow"—Stardate 4768.3

(TOS) "Patterns of Force"—(No stardate given)

**Uhura's Song** (TOS #21)—Stardate 2950.3 to 2962.3—*After "A Private Little War" (TOS).*

(TOS) "The Ultimate Computer"—Stardate 4729.4

(TOS) "The Omega Glory"—(No stardate given)

(TOS) "Assignment: Earth"—(No stardate given)

(TOS) "Spectre of the Gun"—Stardate 4385.3

(TOS) "Elaan of Troyius"—Stardate 4372.5

(TOS) "The Paradise Syndrome"—Stardate 4842.6

**Double, Double (TOS #45)**—Stardate 4925.2

(TOS) "The *Enterprise* Incident"—Stardate 5027.3

(TOS) "And the Children Shall Lead"—Stardate 5029.5

**The Abode of Life (TOS #6)**—Stardate 5064.4 to 5099.5

*Editors' Note: Inconsistent crew continuity, with both Yeoman Rand and Dr. M'Benga aboard.*

**Dreams of the Raven (TOS #34)**—Stardate 5302.1 to 5321.12

*Editors' Note: Using McCoy's age for chronology is problematic, so the stardate was used.*

(TOS) "Spock's Brain"—Stardate 5431.4

**How Much for Just the Planet? (TOS #36)**—(No stardate given)—*After "The Omega Glory" (TOS).*

(TOS) "Is There in Truth No Beauty?"—Stardate 5630.7

**Ghost Walker (TOS #53)**—(No stardate given)—*Takes place during fourth year of five-year mission.*

(TOS) "The Empath"—Stardate 5121.5

**Legacy (TOS #56)**—Stardate 5258.7

• 2254—Pike backstory.

(TOS) "The Tholian Web"—Stardate 5693.2

**The Starship Trap (TOS #64)**—(No stardate given)—*After "The Immunity Syndrome" (TOS).*

**Windows on a Lost World (TOS #65)**—Stardate 5419.4

(TOS) "For the World Is Hollow and I Have Touched the Sky"—Stardate 5476.3

(TOS) "Day of the Dove"—(No stardate given)

(TOS) "Plato's Stepchildren"—Stardate 5784.2

**First Frontier (TOS #75)**—(No stardate given)—*After "The Omega Glory" (TOS).*

• 64,018,143 BC—The *Enterprise* time-travels to Earth of the past.

(TOS) "Wink of an Eye"—Stardate 5710.5

(TOS) "That Which Survives"—(No stardate given)

**Mudd In Your Eye (TOS #81)**—(No stardate given)—*Takes place after "I, Mudd" (TOS).*

(TOS) "Let That Be Your Last Battlefield"—Stardate 5730.2

(TOS) "Whom Gods Destroy"—Stardate 5718.3

**Sanctuary (TOS #61)**—(No stardate given)—*After "Let That Be Your Last Battlefield" (TOS).*

(TOS) "The Mark of Gideon"—Stardate 5423.4

## 2269

(TOS) "The Lights of Zetar"—Stardate 5725.3

(TOS) "The Cloud Minders"—Stardate 5818.4

(TOS) "The Way to Eden"—Stardate 5832.3

(TOS) "Requiem for Methuselah"—Stardate 5843.7

(TOS) "The Savage Curtain"—Stardate 5906.4

(TOS) "All Our Yesterdays"—Stardate 5943.7

(TOS) "Turnabout Intruder"—Stardate 5928.5

***Assignment: Eternity*** (TOS #84)—Stardate 6021.4 to 6021.6—*One week after "Turnabout Intruder" (TOS).*
- 1969—July 19 and 20 [Chapters 1 and 22].
- 2293—Framing story, during the end of *Star Trek VI: The Undiscovered Country.*

***Yesterday's Son*** (TOS #11)—Stardate 6324.09 to 6381.7
- 2703 B.C. (approx.)—Time travel to the past.

***Killing Time*** (TOS #24)—(No stardate given)—*After "The Enterprise Incident" (TOS).*

***The Three-Minute Universe*** (TOS #41)—(No stardate given)—*After "Plato's Stepchildren" (TOS).*

***Memory Prime*** (TOS #42)—(No stardate given)—*After "The Lights of Zetar" (TOS).*

***Renegade*** (TOS #55)—(No stardate given)—*Two years after "Court Martial" (TOS), after "A Private Little War" (TOS).*

***From the Depths*** (TOS #66)—*Fifth year of mission.*

***Prime Directive*** (TOS Giant)—Stardate 4842.6 to 6987.31—Prime Directive *makes a convenient transition point between the live-action episodes (TOS) and the animated episodes (TAS).*

*From the* Star Trek Chronology *Editor's Note (p. 78): Although this chronology does not use material from the animated* Star Trek *series, Dorothy Fontana suggests that she would place those stories after the end of the third season, but prior to the end of the five-year mission.*

***The Trellisane Confrontation*** (TOS #14)—Stardate 7521.6 to 7532.8—*Tal ("The Enterprise Incident" (TOS)) now a fleet commander.*

***Corona*** (TOS #15)—Stardate 4380.4 to 4997.5—*Years after "Devil in the Dark" (TOS).*

***The Final Reflection*** (TOS #16)—Stardate 8405.15 [framing story]—*After "Day of the Dove" (TOS).*
- 2230—[Part One].
- 2238—[Part Two].
- 2244—[Part Three].

***The Tears of the Singers*** (TOS #19)—Stardate 3126.7 to 3127.1—*Takes place after "Day of the Dove" (TOS) and "Time Trap" (TAS).*

*Editors' Note: Although The Animated Series is not included in this timeline, this story referenced specific animated episodes. These references were considered for chronological placement.*

***Pawns and Symbols*** (TOS #26)—Stardate 5960.2 to 6100.0—*After "Day of the Dove" (TOS) and "More Troubles, More Tribbles" (TAS).*

**"The Girl Who Controlled Gene Kelly's Feet"** (TOS short story, ***Strange New Worlds I***)—(No stardate given)—*After "Once Upon a Planet" (TAS) (p. 335–336)*

***The Cry of the Onlies*** (TOS #46)—Stardate 6118.2 to 6119.2

***The Patrian Transgression*** (TOS #69)—Stardate 6769.4

***Crossroad*** (TOS #71)—Stardate 6251.1

***The Wounded Sky*** (TOS #13)—Stardate 9250.0

***My Enemy, My Ally*** (TOS #18)—(No stardate given)

***Mindshadow*** (TOS #27)—Stardate 7003.4 to 7008.4

***Crisis on Centaurus*** (TOS #28)—Stardate 7513.2 to 7521.6

***Demons*** (TOS #30)—(No stardate given)—*After* **Mindshadow** *(TOS #27).*

- 2229—Sarek and Amanda's courtship [pages 22–26].

***Chain of Attack*** (TOS #32)—(No stardate given)

***Bloodthirst*** (TOS #37)—(No stardate given)—*After* **Demons** *(TOS #30).*

***The Final Nexus*** (TOS #43)—(No stardate given)—*After* **Chain of Attack** *(TOS #32).*

***Doctor's Orders*** (TOS #50)—(No stardate given)—*After* **The Wounded Sky** *(TOS #13).*

***The Entropy Effect*** (TOS #2)—(No stardate given)—*Sulu is recommended for promotion.*

***Black Fire*** (TOS #8)—Stardate 6101.1 to 6205.7—*Chekov is promoted to lieutenant; primary hull is jettisoned after explosion; gray uniforms are temporarily introduced.*

***Dreadnought!*** (TOS #29)—Stardate 7881.2 to 8180.2

***Battlestations!*** (TOS #31)—Stardate 3301.1 to 4720.2—*Sulu has received a promotion to Lieutenant Commander.*

*Kirk's five-year mission ends, and the* Starship Enterprise *returns to Spacedock* (Star Trek Chronology).

## 2270

***The Lost Years*** (TOS hardcover)—(No stardate given)

*Editors' Note: The bulk of* The Lost Years *takes place in early 2270 (Star Trek Chronology has Spock returning to Vulcan to undergo Kolinahr in 2270).*

- 30 A.D. (Vulcan Old Date 140005)—Prologue, set during Surak's life.

- 2269—Stardate 6987.31 [Chapters 1 and 2].

*Traitor Winds* (TOS #70)—(No stardate given)

*Editors' Note (per the historian's note): This takes place "shortly after the end of the* Enterprise*'s first five-year mission, immediately following the events chronicled in* **The Lost Years** *(TOS hardcover)." This occurs after Spock decides to pursue* Kolinahr, *which the* Star Trek Chronology *placed in 2270, thus contradicting the December 2269 date on page 1.*

## 2271

*A Flag Full of Stars* (TOS #54)—July 4 to July 20 (No stardate given)

*Editors' Note (per the historian's note): This takes place "shortly before the events chronicled in* Star Trek: The Motion Picture." *Since dates placing this novel during the Apollo 11 tricentennial contradict the* Star Trek Chronology *we assume the story is centered around the tricentennial of the Apollo space program (1969–1972) instead.*

- 2246—Young Kirk and Kodos on Tarsus [pages 111–118].

*Recovery* (TOS #73)—(No stardate given)—*Takes place weeks before* Star Trek: The Motion Picture.

*Star Trek: The Motion Picture* (TOS movie novelization)—Stardate 7412.3 to 7414.1

*Editors' Note:* Star Trek: The Motion Picture *takes place during the end of 2271. Therefore, all "Shortly after* Star Trek: The Motion Picture" *novels are placed in 2272.*

## 2272

*Spock's World* (TOS Giant)—Stardate 7412.1 to 7468.5
- 2–5 Billion B.C. (approximately)—Birth of the planet Vulcan [Vulcan One].
- 500,000 B.C. (approximately)—Appearance of early Vulcan hominids [Vulcan Two].
- 10,000 B.C. (approximately)—Early Vulcan tribal cultures [Vulcan Three].
- 3000 B.C. (approximately)—Ancient Vulcan civilization [Vulcan Four].
- 300 B.C. (approximately)—Early Vulcan space travel [Vulcan Five].
- 79 B.C. to 60 A.D.—The life of Surak [Vulcan Six].
- 2191 to 2130—Sarek of Vulcan [Vulcan Seven].

*The Kobayashi Maru* (TOS #47)—*Shortly after* Star Trek: The Motion Picture.
- 2244—Scott backstory.
- 2254—Kirk backstory.
- 2259—Sulu backstory.

- 2267—Chekov backstory.

***Home Is the Hunter*** (TOS #52)—(No stardate given)—*Shortly after* Star Trek: The Motion Picture.

- 1600—Sulu backstory.
- 1746—Scott backstory.
- 1942—Chekov backstory.

***Enemy Unseen*** (TOS #51)—Stardate 8036.2—*Shortly after* Star Trek: The Motion Picture.

## 2273

***The Better Man*** (TOS #72)—Stardate 7591.4 to 7598.5
- 2236—McCoy at age nine [pages 7–11].
- 2244—McCoy at age seventeen [pages 12–15].
- 2254—After McCoy graduates from med school [pages 30–33, 35–37, 66–68, 129–130, 150–157].
- 2269—Toward the end of first five-year mission [pages 62–63].

***The Prometheus Design*** (TOS #5)—(No stardate given)

## 2274

***Triangle*** (TOS #9)—*Seven years after "Amok Time" (TOS).*

## 2275

***The Covenant of the Crown*** (TOS #4)—Stardate 7815.3
- 2257—Kirk is a lieutenant commander; set eighteen years before the rest of the story [pages 23–29].

***The Romulan Way*** (TOS #35)—(No stardate given)
- 30 A.D.—Rejecting Surak's reforms, S'task and eighty thousand followers leave Vulcan in search of a new world.
- 500 A.D. (approximately)—The Travelers make planetfall on the twin worlds of ch'Rihan and ch'Havran.

***Timetrap*** (TOS #40)—(No stardate given)

## 2276

***Rules of Engagement*** (TOS #48)—Stardate 2213.5—*New red uniforms Editors' Note: The stardate given in the book is too low, since it would put the story during Kirk's first five-year mission.*
***Ice Trap*** (TOS #60)—(No stardate given)
***Death Count*** (TOS #62)—(No stardate given)
***Shell Game*** (TOS #63)—(No stardate given)
***Firestorm*** (TOS #68)—(No stardate given)
***Deep Domain*** (TOS #33)—Stardate 7823.6 to 7835.8—*End of second five-year mission.*

## 2281

*Saavik enters Starfleet Academy* (Star Trek Chronology).
**The Pandora Principle** (TOS #49)—*After Saavik enters academy.*
• 2273—Spock rescues Saavik from Hellguard.
• 2274 to 2275—Spock takes a one-year leave to train Saavik.
**Dwellers in the Crucible** (TOS #25)—*After Saavik enters academy*

## 2283

**Time for Yesterday** (TOS #39)—*14.5 years after "All Our Yesterdays" (TOS).*
• 2683 B.C. (approx.)—Time travel to the past.

## 2284

**Strangers from the Sky** (TOS Giant)—Stardate 8083.6 to 8097.4 [Book 1]
• 2045—Backstory [Book 2].
• 2265—Stardate 1305.4. Before "Where No Man Has Gone Before" (TOS).

## 2285

**Star Trek II: The Wrath of Khan** (TOS movie novelization)—Stardate 8130.3
**Star Trek III: The Search for Spock** (TOS movie novelization)—Stardate 8201.3

## 2286

**Star Trek IV: The Voyage Home** (TOS movie novelization)—Stardate 8390.0
• 1986—Kirk and crew travel back in time.
**"The Last Tribble"** (TOS short story, *Strange New Worlds I*)—(No stardate given)

## 2287

**Star Trek V: The Final Frontier** (TOS movie novelization)—Stardate 8454.1
• 2229—Sybok is five years old [Prologue].
**Probe** (TOS hardcover)—Stardate 8475.3 to 8501.2
**The Rift** (TOS #57)—(No stardate given) [Second Contact]
• 2254—Pike backstory [First Contact].

## 2288

**Starfleet Academy** (TOS *Interplay* computer game novelization)—*Two years before Captain Hikaru Sulu takes command of the* Excelsior *in 2290.*

## 2290

*War Dragons* (TOS—The Captain's Table #1)—(No stardate given)— *Sulu/Kirk backstory.*
- 2265—Stardate 1298.9. Kirk backstory, shortly after "Where No Man Has Gone Before" (TOS).
- 2293—Framing story, takes place between *Star Trek VI: The Undiscovered Country* and *Star Trek: Generations.*

## 2291

*Cacophony* (TOS audio)—Stardate 8764.3 to 8774.8
*Envoy* (TOS audio)—Stardate 9029.1 to 9029.4

## 2293

*Star Trek VI: The Undiscovered Country* (TOS movie novelization)— Stardate 9521.6
*Editors' Note: The story ends with the* Enterprise *heading home for decommission.*
*Shadows on the Sun* (TOS hardcover)—Stardate 9582.1 to 9587.2
*Editors' Note: The story begins with the* Enterprise *heading home and ends with the* Enterprise *heading home.*
- 2254—McCoy backstory [Book Two].
*Best Destiny* (TOS hardcover)—(No stardate given)
*Editors' Note: The story begins with the* Enterprise *almost home but ends with the* Enterprise *gaining a reprieve from retirement. So this would have to be after* **Shadows on the Sun** *(TOS hardcover) and would explain why the* Enterprise *is still active for* **Sarek** *(TOS hardcover) and* **Mind Meld** *(TOS #82).*
- 2249—Captain April backstory.
*Sarek* (TOS hardcover)—Stardate 9544.6
*Editors' Note: The story takes place after the reprieve in* **Best Destiny** *(TOS hardcover).*
- 2229, June 14—Sarek and Amanda's courtship [pages 60–62].
- 2229, September 16—Sarek and Amanda marry [pages 155–159].
- 2230, November 12—Spock born, book says 2231, but that's wrong according to the *Star Trek Chronology* [pages 200–202].
- 2237, December 7—Young Spock runs away, based on "Yesteryear" (TAS) events [pages 211–215].
- 2249—Spock chooses Starfleet and alienates Sarek [pages 258–264].
- 2285, March 14—Sarek and Amanda wonder what happened to Spock's *katra,* set probably right before *Star Trek III: The Search for Spock* [pages 373–375].

*Mind Meld* (TOS #82)—(No stardate given)
*Editors' Note: The story takes place after the reprieve in* **Best Destiny**
*(TOS hardcover).*
   • 2314—[Chapter 16].
*The Ashes of Eden* (TOS hardcover)—(No stardate given)
*Editors' Note: The story takes place after the* Enterprise-*A has been*
*decommissioned.*
*The Fearful Summons* (TOS #74)—Stardate 9621.8 to 9625.10 (Spring)
*Editors' Note 1: The story has a retired Kirk and no* Enterprise.
*Editors' Note 2: The Spring 2294 date contradicts the* Star Trek
Chronology.
**"The Lights in the Sky"** (TOS short story, *Strange New Worlds I*)—(No
   stardate given)—*Just before the TOS-era portion of* Star Trek:
   Generations.
*Kirk is believed killed when he disappears into the nexus during the*
*launch of the* Enterprise-*B (Star Trek Chronology). Some authors*
*place this event later in 2294 or 2295.*

## 2294

*The Captain's Daughter* (TOS #76)—(No stardate given)
   • 2271—About six months before the original *Enterprise*'s refit is
     completed ["Section Two: First Date"].
   • 2278—Around time of the *Bozeman*'s launch [Chapters 15–17].
   • 2284—[Chapters 18–19].
   • 2285—Set immediately after *Star Trek III: The Search for Spock,*
     and during *Star Trek IV: The Voyage Home* [Chapters 20 and 21].

## 2296

*Vulcan's Forge* (TOS hardcover)—Stardate 9814.3 to 9835.7
*Editor's Note: The "about a year" after Kirk's disappearance refer-*
*ences are inaccurate.*
   • 2247—Spock backstory.

## 2314

*Transformations* (TOS audio)—Stardate 11611.8 to 11618.2
   • 2294—Stardate 9619.9 to 9622.4. Sulu backstory.

## 2323

*Starfall* (TNGya Starfleet Academy #8)—*This story spans the period*
   *from the Fall of 2322 to the Fall of 2323.*
*Nova Command* (TNGya Starfleet Academy #9)—*This story starts at the*
   *beginning of Picard's freshman year at Starfleet Academy (2323).*

## 2334

**"Together Again, for the First Time"** (TNG short story, *Strange New Worlds I*)—(No stardate given)

## 2341

*Mystery of the Missing Crew* (TNGya Starfleet Academy #6)—(No stardate given)—*Earth year for this book is given as 2341, when Data entered Starfleet Academy.*
  • 2338—[Prologue].
*Secret of the Lizard People* (TNGya Starfleet Academy #7)—(No stardate given)—*Data has been a cadet at Starfleet Academy for three weeks at the beginning of this story.*
*Deceptions* (TNGya Starfleet Academy #14)—(No stardate given)—*Data has been a cadet at Starfleet Academy for three months at the beginning of this story.*

## 2342

*Loyalties* (TNGya Starfleet Academy #10)—(No stardate given)—*This story is set during Beverly Crusher's (née Howard) first year at Starfleet Academy Medical School (2342).*

## 2344

*Vulcan's Heart* (TOS hardcover)—(No stardate given)
  • 2329—Flashback.

## 2353

*Lifeline* (VGRya Starfleet Academy #1)—(No stardate given)—*This story occurs when Janeway began at Starfleet Academy in 2353, according to the "Starfleet Timeline" in this book.*
*Capture the Flag* (TNGya Starfleet Academy #4)—(No stardate given)—*Geordi La Forge has been a cadet at Starfleet Academy for three weeks at the beginning of this story. La Forge began at Starfleet Academy in 2353.*
*The Chance Factor* (VGRya Starfleet Academy #2)—(No stardate given)—*Conversation in this story indicates it takes place in the same year as* Lifeline *(VGRya Starfleet Academy #1).*
*Quarantine* (VGRya Starfleet Academy #3)—(No stardate given)—*La Forge is mentioned as being a first-year cadet in this story, which gives it a date of 2353.*
*Atlantis Station* (TNGya Starfleet Academy #5)—(No stardate given)—*La Forge is a first-year cadet at Starfleet Academy in this story.*

*Crossfire* (**TNGya Starfleet Academy #11**)—(No stardate given)—*La Forge and Riker are first-year cadets at Starfleet Academy in this story.*

## 2354

*The Haunted Starship* (**TNGya Starfleet Academy #13**)—(No stardate given)—*This story is set during the Spring semester of La Forge's first year at Starfleet Academy.*

*Breakaway* (**TNGya Starfleet Academy #12**)—(No stardate given)—*This story is set during Deanna Troi's first year at Starfleet Academy. The "Starfleet Timeline" in this book gives the date for that as 2354.*

## 2357

*Worf's First Adventure* (**TNGya Starfleet Academy #1**)—(No stardate given)—*Set during Worf's first year at Starfleet Academy (2357).*

*Line of Fire* (**TNGya Starfleet Academy #2**)—(No stardate given)—*Set during Worf's first year at Starfleet Academy (2357).*

*Survival* (**TNGya Starfleet Academy #3**)—(No stardate given)—*Set during Worf's first year at Starfleet Academy (2357).*

## 2364

*Encounter at Farpoint* (**TNG episode novelization**)—Stardate 41153.7 to 41254.7
    (TNG) "The Naked Now"—Stardate 41209.2
    (TNG) "Code of Honor"—Stardate 41235.25
    (TNG) "Where No One Has Gone Before"—Stardate 41263.1
*Ghost Ship* (**TNG #1**)—(No stardate given)
    • 1995—Russian aircraft-carrier backstory.
    (TNG) "Haven"—Stardate 41294.5
    (TNG) "The Last Outpost"—Stardate 41386.4
*The Peacekeepers* (**TNG #2**)—(No stardate given)
    (TNG) "Lonely among Us"—Stardate 41249.3
    (TNG) "Justice"—Stardate 41255.6
    (TNG) "The Battle"—Stardate 41723.9
    (TNG) "Hide and Q"—Stardate 41590.5
    (TNG) "Too Short a Season"—Stardate 41309.5
    (TNG) "The Big Goodbye"—Stardate 41997.7
    (TNG) "Datalore"—Stardate 41242.4
    (TNG) "Angel One"—Stardate 41636.9
    (TNG) "11001001"—Stardate 41365.9
    (TNG) "Home Soil"—Stardate 41463.9
    (TNG) "When the Bough Breaks"—Stardate 41509.1

(TNG) "Coming of Age"—Stardate 41416.2
(TNG) "Heart of Glory"—Stardate 41503.7
*The Children of Hamlin* (TNG #3)—(No stardate given)
(TNG) "The Arsenal of Freedom"—Stardate 41798.2
*Survivors* (TNG #4)—(No stardate given)
• 2352—Tasha is 15, leaves Turkana IV [Chapter 1].
• 2357—Tasha in her later years at Starfleet Academy [Chapter 3].
• 2359—Tasha is "almost twenty-three" [Chapter 5].
• 2364—Set immediately after "Skin of Evil" (TNG) [Chapter 12].
(TNG) "Symbiosis"—(No stardate given)
(TNG) "Skin of Evil"—Stardate 41601.3
*The Captain's Honor* (TNG #8)—Stardate 41800.9—*Shortly after "Skin of Evil" (TNG).*
(TNG) "We'll Always Have Paris"—Stardate 41697.9
(TNG) "Conspiracy"—Stardate 41775.5
(TNG) "The Neutral Zone"—Stardate 41986.0

## 2365

*Strike Zone* (TNG #5)—(No stardate given)
(TNG) "The Child"—Stardate 42073.1
(TNG) "Where Silence Has Lease"—Stardate 42193.6
(TNG) "Elementary, Dear Data"—Stardate 42286.3
(TNG) "The Outrageous Okona"—Stardate 42402.7
*Power Hungry* (TNG #6)—Stardate 42422.5
(TNG) "The Schizoid Man"—Stardate 42437.5
(TNG) "Loud as a Whisper"—Stardate 42477.2
(TNG) "Unnatural Selection"—Stardate 42494.8
(TNG) "A Matter of Honor"—Stardate 42506.5
(TNG) "The Measure of a Man"—Stardate 42523.7
*Metamorphosis* (TNG Giant)—Stardate 42528.6
(TNG) "The Dauphin"—Stardate 42568.8
*Masks* (TNG #7)—(No stardate given)
(TNG) "Contagion"—Stardate 42609.1
(TNG) "The Royale"—Stardate 42625.4
(TNG) "Time Squared"—Stardate 42679.2
(TNG) "The Icarus Factor"—Stardate 42686.4
(TNG) "Pen Pals"—Stardate 42695.3
(TNG) "Q Who?"—Stardate 42761.3
(TNG) "Samaritan Snare"—Stardate 42779.1
(TNG) "Up the Long Ladder"—Stardate 42823.2
(TNG) "Manhunt"—Stardate 42859.2
(TNG) "The Emissary"—Stardate 42901.3
*A Call to Darkness* (TNG #9)—Stardate 42908.6

(TNG) "Peak Performance"—Stardate 42923.4
**"What Went through Data's Mind 0.68 Seconds before the Satellite Hit"
(TNG short story, *Strange New Worlds I*)**—Stardate 42945.4
  (TNG) "Shades of Gray"—Stardate 42976.1

## 2366

*A Rock and a Hard Place* **(TNG #10)**—(No stardate given)
  (TNG) "Evolution"—Stardate 43152.4
  (TNG) "The Ensigns of Command"—(No stardate given)
*Gulliver's Fugitives* **(TNG #11)**—(No stardate given)
  (TNG) "The Survivors"—Stardate 43152.4
  (TNG) "Who Watches the Watchers?"—Stardate 43173.5
*Doomsday World* **(TNG #12)**—Stardate 43197.5
  (TNG) "The Bonding"—Stardate 43198.7
  (TNG) "Booby Trap"—Stardate 43205.6
  (TNG) "The Enemy"—Stardate 43349.2
  (TNG) "The Price"—Stardate 43385.6
  (TNG) "The Vengeance Factor"—Stardate 43421.9
*Exiles* **(TNG #14)**—Stardate 43429.1
  (TNG) "The Defector"—Stardate 43462.5
  (TNG) "The Hunted"—Stardate 43489.2
  (TNG) "The High Ground"—Stardate 43510.7
  (TNG) "Déjà Q"—Stardate 43539.1
  (TNG) "A Matter of Perspective"—Stardate 43610.4
  (TNG) "Yesterday's *Enterprise*"—Stardate 43625.2
*Q-in-Law* **(TNG #18)**—(No stardate given)
  (TNG) "The Offspring"—Stardate 43657.0
*Fortune's Light* **(TNG #15)**—(No stardate given)
  (TNG) "Sins of the Father"—Stardate 43685.2
  (TNG) "Allegiance"—Stardate 43714.1
*The Eyes of the Beholders* **(TNG #13)**—(No stardate given)
  (TNG) "Captain's Holiday"—Stardate 43745.2
*Boogeymen* **(TNG #17)**—Stardate 43747.3
  (TNG) "Tin Man"—Stardate 43779.3
  (TNG) "Hollow Pursuits"—Stardate 43807.4
  (TNG) "The Most Toys"—Stardate 43872.2
  (TNG) "Sarek"—Stardate 43917.4
  (TNG) "Ménage à Troi"—Stardate 43930.7
*Contamination* **(TNG #16)**—Stardate 43951.6
*Editors' Note: The 44261.6 stardate given in the book was adjusted to
fit shortly after the "Ménage à Troi" (TNG) timeframe.*
  (TNG) "Transfigurations"—Stardate 43957.2
  (TNG) "The Best of Both Worlds, Part I"—Stardate 43989.1

## 2367

(TNG) "The Best of Both Worlds, Part II"—Stardate 44001.4

**"Civil Disobedience" (TNG short story, *Strange New Worlds I*)**—(No stardate given)

(TNG) "Family"—Stardate 44012.3

***Dark Mirror* (TNG Giant)**—Stardate 44018.2

*Editors' Note: The original stardate of 44010.2 needed to be corrected so the story could be properly set after "Family" (TNG).*

(TNG) "Brothers"—Stardate 44085.7

(TNG) "Suddenly Human"—Stardate 44143.7

***Reunion* (TNG hardcover)**—(No stardate given)

(TNG) "Remember Me"—Stardate 44161.2

***Perchance to Dream* (TNG #19)**—Stardate 44195.7

*Editors' Note: The story takes place before "Final Mission" (TNG), but it gives a stardate of 45195.7, which would put it a year after the episode.*

(TNG) "Legacy"—Stardate 44215.2

***Spartacus* (TNG #20)**—(No stardate given)

(TNG) "Reunion"—Stardate 44246.3

(TNG) "Future Imperfect"—Stardate 44286.5

(TNG) "Final Mission"—Stardate 44307.3

**"See Spot Run" (TNG short story, *Strange New Worlds I*)**—(No stardate given)

(TNG) "The Loss"—Stardate 44356.9

(TNG) "Data's Day"—Stardate 44390.1

**"Of Cabbages and Kings" (TNG short story, *Strange New Worlds I*)**—(No stardate given)

(TNG) "The Wounded"—Stardate 44429.6

(TNG) "Devil's Due"—Stardate 44474.5

***Vendetta* (TNG Giant)**—(No stardate given)

• 2326—Picard backstory.

(TNG) "Clues"—Stardate 44502.7

(TNG) "First Contact"—(No stardate given)

(TNG) "Galaxy's Child"—Stardate 44614.6

(TNG) "Night Terrors"—Stardate 44631.2

***Chains of Command* (TNG #21)**—(No stardate given)

(TNG) "Identity Crisis"—Stardate 44664.5

(TNG) "The Nth Degree"—Stardate 44704.2

(TNG) "QPid"—Stardate 44741.9

(TNG) "The Drumhead"—Stardate 44769.2

(TNG) "Half a Life"—Stardate 44805.3

(TNG) "The Host"—Stardate 44821.3

***Imbalance* (TNG #22)**—Stardate 44839.2

(TNG) "The Mind's Eye"—Stardate 44885.5
(TNG) "In Theory"—Stardate 44932.3
(TNG) "Redemption, Part I"—Stardate 44995.3

## 2368

(TNG) "Redemption, Part II"—Stardate 45020.4
(TNG) "Darmok"—Stardate 45047.2
(TNG) "Ensign Ro"—Stardate 45076.3
(TNG) "Silicon Avatar"—Stardate 45122.3
(TNG) "Disaster"—Stardate 45156.1
*War Drums* **(TNG #23)**—(No stardate given)
(TNG) "The Game"—Stardate 45208.2
*Unification* **(TNG episodes novelization)**—Stardate 45233.1 to 45245.8
(TNG) "A Matter of Time"—Stardate 45349.1
(TNG) "New Ground"—Stardate 45376.3
*Sins of Commission* **(TNG #29)**—(No stardate given)—*Shortly after "New Ground" (TNG).*
(TNG) "Hero Worship"—Stardate 45397.3
(TNG) "Violations"—Stardate 45429.3
(TNG) "The Masterpiece Society"—Stardate 45470.1
(TNG) "Conundrum"—Stardate 45494.2
*Imzadi* **(TNG hardcover)**—(No stardate given)
• 2359—Riker and Troi meet for the first time.
• 2364—Riker and Troi are reunited on the *Enterprise* (Stardate 42372.5 is a mismatch with "Encounter at Farpoint" [TNG] stardate 41150.7).
• 2408—Set forty-two years after "The Offspring" (TNG).
*Editors' Note: The 2408 portion of the story must be regarded as an alternate future which is divergent from the "mainstream" universe.*
*The Last Stand* **(TNG #37)**—Stardate 45523.6
(TNG) "Power Play"—Stardate 45571.2
(TNG) "Ethics"—Stardate 45587.3
(TNG) "The Outcast"—Stardate 45614.6
*Nightshade* **(TNG #24)**—(No stardate given)
(TNG) "Cause and Effect"—Stardate 45652.1
(TNG) "The First Duty"—Stardate 45703.9
(TNG) "Cost of Living"—Stardate 45733.6
(TNG) "The Perfect Mate"—Stardate 45761.3
*Grounded* **(TNG #25)**—Stardate 45823.4
*Editors' Note: Alexander is mentioned, which sets the story after "New Ground" (TNG). The 45223.4 stardate given in the book was adjusted to fit the specified timeframe.*
(TNG) "Imaginary Friend"—Stardate 45852.1

(TNG) "I, Borg"—Stardate 45854.2

*The Devil's Heart* (**TNG hardcover**)—Stardate 45873.3 to 45873.6

(TNG) "The Next Phase"—Stardate 45892.4

*The Romulan Prize* (**TNG #26**)—(No stardate given)

(TNG) "The Inner Light"—Stardate 45944.1

(TNG) "Time's Arrow, Part I"—Stardate 45959.1

## 2369

(TNG) "Time's Arrow, Part II"—Stardate 46001.3

*The Best and the Brightest* (**TNG unnumbered**)—(No stardate given) [Year One]—*Just after "Time's Arrow" (TNG).*
* 2370—Year Two, just before "Journey's End" (TNG).
* 2371—Year Three, just after "The Search" (DS9).
* Summer 2371—Just after *Star Trek: Generations.*
* 2371—Year Four, just after "The Die is Cast" (DS9).

(TNG) "Realm of Fear"—Stardate 46041.1

(TNG) "Man of the People"—Stardate 46071.6

*Relics* (**TNG episode novelization**)—Stardate 46125.3
* 2294—Scotty backstory.

(TNG) "Schisms"—Stardate 46154.2

*Here There Be Dragons* (**TNG #28**)—(No stardate given)

(TNG) "True Q"—Stardate 46192.3

(TNG) "Rascals"—Stardate 46235.7

(TNG) "A Fistful of Datas"—Stardate 46271.5

*A Fury Scorned* (**TNG #43**)—Stardate 46300.6

(TNG) "The Quality of Life"—Stardate 46307.2

(TNG) "Chain of Command, Part I"—Stardate 46357.4

(TNG) "Chain of Command, Part II"—Stardate 46360.8

*Debtor's Planet* (**TNG #30**)—(No stardate given)—*After "First Duty" (TNG).*

*Once Burned* (**NF—The Captain's Table #5**)—(No stardate given)— *Spans about three months.*

*Editors' note: The book says this portion of the story takes place "six years" before the framing story, which would place it in 2368. However, we placed it in 2369 (after TNG "Chain of Command," when Jellico was a captain) because Jellico is an admiral in this story.*
* 2348–2349—Calhoun is 14, spans about a year [pages 1–30].
* Early 2374—Framing story, soon after *Fire on High* (**NF #6**).

**Emissary (DS9 episode novelization)**—Stardate 46379.1
* 2367—Stardate 44002.3—Sisko backstory.

(DS9) "Past Prologue"—(No stardate given)

*Guises of the Mind* (**TNG #27**)—Stardate 46401.9—*Miles and Keiko are no longer aboard the* Enterprise-D.

*Editors' Note: The 45741.9 stardate given in the book was adjusted to fit the post-"Emissary" (DS9) timeframe.*

• Late 2369—Epilogue, set six months later.

(DS9) "A Man Alone"—Stardate 46421.5

***The Siege* (DS9 #2)**—(No stardate given)

*Editors' Note: The novel states Keiko is a teacher, which would put the story after "A Man Alone" (DS9). References to Molly's age are incorrect.*

(TNG) "Ship in a Bottle"—Stardate 46424.1

***Invasion! #2: The Soldiers of Fear* (TNG #41)**—(No stardate given)— *Troi has recently started dressing "in uniform."*

(DS9) "Babel"—Stardate 46423.7

(TNG) "Aquiel"—Stardate 46461.3

(DS9) "Captive Pursuit"—(No stardate given)

(TNG) "Face of the Enemy"—Stardate 46519.1

(DS9) "Q-Less"—Stardate 46531.2

(TNG) "Tapestry"—(No stardate given)

(DS9) "Dax"—Stardate 46910.1

(TNG) "Birthright, Part I"—Stardate 46578.4

(DS9) "The Passenger"—(No stardate given)

(TNG) "Birthright, Part II"—Stardate 46578.4

***The Star Ghost* (DS9ya #1)**—(No stardate given)—*Jake Sisko is fourteen years old in this story.*

(DS9) "Move Along Home"—(No stardate given)

(DS9) "The Nagus"—(No stardate given)

(TNG) "Starship Mine"—Stardate 46682.4

***The Death of Princes* (TNG #44)**—(No stardate given)—*Ensign Ro is present. Takes place before "Timescape" (TNG) (Star Trek Chronology has Ro leaving the* Enterprise *shortly before "Timescape" (TNG)). Cover has Troi "in uniform" after "Chain of Command" (TNG).*

(TNG) "Lessons"—Stardate 46693.1

(DS9) "Vortex"—(No stardate given)

(TNG) "The Chase"—Stardate 46731.5

***Bloodletter* (DS9 #3)**—(No stardate given)—*A historian's note places this novel before the episode "Battle Lines" (DS9).*

(DS9) "Battle Lines"—(No stardate given)

(TNG) "Frame of Mind"—Stardate 46778.1

***To Storm Heaven* (TNG #46)**—(No stardate given)—*Presence of Alexander and lack of relationship with Troi seems to indicate a season-six timeframe.*

(DS9) "The Storyteller"—Stardate 46729.1

(TNG) "Suspicions"—Stardate 46830.1

(DS9) "Progress"—Stardate 46844.3

(TNG) "Rightful Heir"—Stardate 46852.2

*Warped* **(DS9 hardcover)**—(No stardate given)—*After "Battle Lines" (DS9) and before "The Homecoming" (DS9).*
(DS9) "If Wishes Were Horses"—Stardate 46853.2
*The Romulan Stratagem* **(TNG #35)**—Stardate 46892.6
(TNG) "Second Chances"—Stardate 46915.2
*Foreign Foes* **(TNG #31)**—Stardate 46921.3
*Editors' Note: The 47511.3 stardate given in the book was adjusted to fit a timeframe following shortly after "Second Chances" (DS9).*
(DS9) "The Forsaken"—Stardate 46925.1
*Stowaways* **(DS9ya #2)**—(No stardate given)—*Jake Sisko is mentioned as being fourteen years old in this story.*
(DS9) "Dramatis Personae"—Stardate 46922.3
*Requiem* **(TNG #32)**—Stardate 46931.2
*Editors' Note: The 47821.2 stardate given in the book was adjusted to fit a late 2369 timeframe prior to the departure of Ensign Ro.*
  • 2267—Picard time-travels to just two days before the events of "Arena" (TOS).
  • 2345—Stardate 16175.4 [Prologue].
(TNG) "Timescape"—Stardate 46944.2
(DS9) "Duet"—(No stardate given)
*Descent, Part I* **(TNG episode novelization)**—Stardate 46982.1
(DS9) "In the Hands of the Prophets"—(No stardate given)

## 2370

*Descent, Part II* **(TNG episode novelization)**—Stardate 47025.4
*Warchild* **(DS9 #7)**—(No stardate given)
*Editors' Note: Historian's note places this story between the first and second seasons of DS9.*
*Valhalla* **(DS9 #10)**—(No stardate given)
*Editors' Note 1: Most references in this book would place it between seasons one and two of* Star Trek: Deep Space Nine.
*Editors' Note 2: A reference to the* Defiant *on page five was accidentally added during editing, since the book was published after the* Defiant *was introduced at the beginning of season three of* Star Trek: Deep Space Nine.
*Betrayal* **(DS9 #6)**—(No stardate given)
(TNG) "Liaisons"—(No stardate given)
(DS9) "The Homecoming"—(No stardate given)
(TNG) "Interface"—Stardate 47215.5
*Blaze of Glory* **(TNG #34)**—(No stardate given)—*Warp speeds faster than Warp 5; before "Force of Nature" (TNG).*
(DS9) "The Circle"—(No stardate given)
(TNG) "Gambit, Part I"—Stardate 47135.2

(DS9) "The Siege"—(No stardate given)
(TNG) "Gambit, Part II"—Stardate 47160.1
(DS9) "Invasive Procedures"—Stardate 47182.1
*Prisoners of Peace* (DS9ya #3)—(No stardate given)
(TNG) "Phantasms"—Stardate 47225.7
(DS9) "Cardassians"—Stardate 47177.2
*The Big Game* (DS9 #4)—(No stardate given)—*Page 148 describes the events of "A Matter of Time" (TNG) (2368) as occurring "a few years ago," giving this novel a date of 2370.*
(TNG) "Dark Page"—Stardate 47254.1
(DS9) "Melora"—Stardate 47229.1
*Star Trek: Klingon* (TNG/DS9 CD-ROM novelization)—(No stardate given)—*One year before "Defiant" (DS9).*
• 2368—Backstory, takes place after "Redemption" (TNG).
(TNG) "Attached"—Stardate 47304.2
*Possession* (TNG #40)—(No stardate given)
(DS9) "Rules of Acquisition"—(No stardate given)
*Fallen Heroes* (DS9 #5)—Stardate 47237.8
(TNG) "Force of Nature"—Stardate 47310.2
(DS9) "Necessary Evil"—Stardate 47282.5
*Infiltrator* (TNG #42)—Stardate 47358.1
(TNG) "Inheritance"—Stardate 47410.2
(DS9) "Second Sight"—Stardate 47329.4
*Into the Nebula* (TNG #36)—(No stardate given)—*After "Force of Nature" (TNG).*
*The Pet* (DS9ya #4)—(No stardate given)—*Takes place during the first anniversary of the discovery of the Bajoran wormhole (2369/46379.1).*
*Devil in the Sky* (DS9 #11)—Stardate 47384.1—*Historian's note places this story in the second season of DS9. The stardate given in the book, 46384.1, was altered for this timeline to fit a DS9 second-season date.*
(TNG) "Parallels"—Stardate 47391.2
(DS9) "Sanctuary"—Stardate 47391.2
(DS9) "Rivals"—(No stardate given)
*Arcade* (DS9ya #5)—(No stardate given)—*It has been three years since the Borg attack at Wolf 359 (2367).*
(TNG) "The *Pegasus*"—Stardate 47457.1
(DS9) "The Alternate"—Stardate 47391.7
(TNG) "Homeward"—Stardate 47423.9
*Q-Squared* (TNG hardcover)—(No stardate given)—*Worf mentions he encountered a similar type of dislocation before. Hence, the story is set some time after "Parallels" (TNG).*
• 2265—Gary Mitchell backstory.
(TNG) "Sub Rosa"—(No stardate given)

(DS9) "Armageddon Game"—Stardate 47529.4

(TNG) "Lower Decks"—Stardate 47566.7

*Field Trip* **(DS9ya #6)**—(No stardate given)

(DS9) "Whispers"—Stardate 47581.2

(TNG) "Thine Own Self"—Stardate 47611.2

*Balance of Power* **(TNG #33)**—(No stardate given)—*Shortly after "Thine Own Self" (TNG).*

(DS9) "Paradise"—Stardate 47573.1

*Gypsy World* **(DS9ya #7)**—(No stardate given)—*Historian's note places this story in the first or second season of DS9.*

(TNG) "Masks"—Stardate 47615.2

(DS9) "Shadowplay"—Stardate 47603.3

*Dragon's Honor* **(TNG #38)**—Stardate 47616.2

*Editors' note: The 47146.2 stardate given in the book was adjusted to fit shortly before "Eye of the Beholder" (TNG).*

(TNG) "Eye of the Beholder"—Stardate 47623.2

(DS9) "Playing God"—(No stardate given)

*Highest Score* **(DS9ya #8)**—(No stardate given)

(TNG) "Genesis"—Stardate 47653.2

(DS9) "Profit and Loss"—(No stardate given)

(TNG) "Journey's End"—Stardate 47751.2

(DS9) "Blood Oath"—(No stardate given)

(TNG) "Firstborn"—Stardate 47779.4

(DS9) "The Maquis, Part I"—(No stardate given)

(TNG) "Bloodlines"—Stardate 47829.1

(DS9) "The Maquis, Part II"—(No stardate given)

*Cardassian Imps* **(DS9ya #9)**—(No stardate given)

(TNG) "Emergence"—Stardate 47869.2

**"The Naked Truth" (TNG short story, *Strange New Worlds I*)**—(No stardate given)

(DS9) "The Wire"—(No stardate given)

*Antimatter* **(DS9 #8)**—(No stardate given)—*This story is set late in the second season of DS9, when the Runabout Mekong was in use by DS9 personnel.*

(TNG) "Preemptive Strike"—Stardate 47941.7

*Rogue Saucer* **(TNG #39)**—(No stardate given)—*Shortly after "Preemptive Strike" (TNG).*

(DS9) "Crossover"—Stardate 47879.2

*All Good Things . . .* **(TNG episode novelization)**—Stardate 47988.1

- 3.5 billion years ago—Q takes Picard to this time of human history.
- 2364—Stardate 41148 to 41153.7 [Anti-past].
- 2395—[Anti-future].

*Editors' Note: The anti-time portions of the story must be regarded as* an alternate past and future which are divergent from the "mainstream" universe.

(DS9) "The Collaborator"—(No stardate given)

***Space Camp* (DS9ya #10)**—(No stardate given)

(DS9) "Tribunal"—Stardate 47944.2

(DS9) "The Jem'Hadar"—(No stardate given)

## 2371

***Intellivore* (TNG #45)**—Stardate 48022.5

***The Search* (DS9 episode novelization)**—Stardate 48212.4

***Proud Helios* (DS9 #9)**—(No stardate given)—*Page twelve of this story mentions that the* Defiant *is undergoing repairs, which would be consistent with the damage inflicted on the* Defiant *during "The Search" (DS9).*

***Ancient Blood* (TNG—Day of Honor #1)**—(No stardate given)

*Editors' Note: Reference to Alexander as being twelve years old is incorrect.*

(DS9) "The House of Quark"—(No stardate given)

***Crossover* (TNG hardcover)**—(No stardate given)—*Set during Picard's eighth year of command of the* Enterprise-D *(2371).*

(DS9) "Equilibrium"—(No stardate given)

***Kahless* (TNG hardcover)**—(No stardate given)

• 800 A.D. (approximately)—The Heroic Age.

***Dujonian's Hoard* (TNG—The Captain's Table #2)**—(No stardate given)

*Editors' Note: Picard's gray uniform on the cover is not indicative of the uniform in use in the story.*

• 2371—Framing story, set a couple of months after the events of Picard's narrative.

(DS9) "The Abandoned"—(No stardate given)

(DS9) "Second Skin"—(No stardate given)

(DS9) "Civil Defense"—(No stardate given)

(DS9) "Meridian"—(No stardate given)

***Star Trek Generations* (TNG movie novelization)**—Stardate 48632.4 [TNG-era portion]

*Editors' Note 1: There is also a Young Adult novelization available.*

• 2293—Stardate 9715.5. Kirk backstory.

*Editors' Note 2: Some authors place the TOS sequence later in 2294 or 2295, which contradicts the* Star Trek Chronology.

**"Reflections" (TOS short story, *Strange New Worlds I*)**—Stardate 48649.7

(DS9) *"Defiant"*—Stardate 48467.3

***Triangle: Imzadi II* (TNG hardcover)**—(No stardate given)—*Shortly after* Star Trek Generations.

- 2374—Framing story, set right after "Tears of the Prophets" (DS9).

(DS9) "Fascination"—(No stardate given)

*The Laertian Gamble* **(DS9 #12)**—(No stardate given)—*Keiko O'Brien is "on an all-too-brief hiatus from her botanical research on Bajor," so it is placed immediately after the episode "Fascination" (DS9).*

(DS9) "Past Tense, Part I"—Stardate 48481.2

(DS9) "Past Tense, Part II"—Stardate 48481.2

*The Return* **(TOS/TNG hardcover)**—(No stardate given)—*A month after Star Trek Generations.*

*Caretaker* **(VGR episode novelization)**—Stardate 48315.6

*The Escape* **(VGR #2)**—(No stardate given)

- 307,629 B.C. (approx.)—The unique time-travel device in this novel also allows for a few other jumps in time, always in increments of five hundred thousand years.

(VGR) "Parallax"—Stardate 48439.7

*Ragnarok* **(VGR #3)**—(No stardate given)—*The author, Nathan Archer, suggests this novel takes place during the first half of the first season of VGR.*

(VGR) "Time and Again"—(No stardate given)

*Violations* **(VGR #4)**—(No stardate given)—*References in this novel and its publication date suggest a VGR first-season date.*

(DS9) "Life Support"—Stardate 48498.4

*Incident at Arbuk* **(VGR #5)**—Stardate 48531.6

*Editors' Note: The book mentions a stardate of 48135.6, which we took the liberty to modify since the story is set after "Caretaker" (VGR).*

(VGR) "Phage"—Stardate 48532.4

(DS9) "Heart of Stone"—Stardate 48521.5

(VGR) "The Cloud"—Stardate 48546.2

(DS9) "Destiny"—Stardate 48543.2

(VGR) "Eye of the Needle"—Stardate 48579.4

(DS9) "Prophet Motive"—(No stardate given)

(VGR) "Ex Post Facto"—(No stardate given)

(DS9) "Visionary"—(No stardate given)

(VGR) "Emanations"—Stardate 48623.5

(VGR) "Prime Factors"—Stardate 48642.5

(VGR) "State of Flux"—Stardate 48658.2

(DS9) "Distant Voices"—(No stardate given)

(DS9) "Through the Looking Glass"—(No stardate given)

(VGR) "Heroes and Demons"—Stardate 48693.2

(DS9) "Improbable Cause"—(No stardate given)

(VGR) "Cathexis"—Stardate 48734.2

(DS9) "The Die Is Cast"—(No stardate given)

(VGR) "Faces"—Stardate 48784.2

(DS9) "Explorers"—(No stardate given)
(VGR) "Jetrel"—Stardate 48832.1
(DS9) "Family Business"—(No stardate given)
(VGR) "Learning Curve"—Stardate 48846.5
(DS9) "Shakaar"—(No stardate given)
**The Murdered Sun (VGR #6)**—Stardate 48897.1
*Editors' Note: The stardate given in the book, 43897.1, is much too low for VGR and was altered for this timeline to fit a VGR first-season date.*
(DS9) "Facets"—(No stardate given)
**The Long Night (DS9 #14)**—(No stardate given)—*This novel is set before Sisko becomes a captain, but after Nog decides to go to Starfleet Academy. Passages in the novel indicate that the Prologue is set eight hundred years before the rest of the novel.*
• 1571—Prologue.
(DS9) "The Adversary"—Stardate 48959.1
**Station Rage (DS9 #13)**—(No stardate given)—*Sisko is a captain in this novel, but Worf is not present, so it occurs between "The Adversary" (DS9) and "The Way of the Warrior" (DS9).*
(VGR) "The 37's"—Stardate 48975.1
**Objective: Bajor (DS9 #15)**—(No stardate given)—*Sisko is a captain in this novel, but Worf is not present, so it occurs between "The Adversary" (DS9) and "The Way of the Warrior" (DS9).*

## 2372

**Invasion! #3: Time's Enemy (DS9 #16)**—(No stardate given)—*Sisko is a captain in this novel, but Worf is not present, so it occurs between "The Adversary" (DS9) and "The Way of the Warrior" (DS9).*
(VGR) "Initiations"—Stardate 49005.3
**Invasion! #4: The Final Fury (VGR #9)**—(No stardate given)—*This novel takes place roughly around the same time as* **Invasion! #3: Time's Enemy** *(DS9 #16).*
(VGR) "Projections"—Stardate 48892.1
**Saratoga (DS9 #18)**—(No stardate given)—*Historian's note places this novel between the third and fourth seasons of DS9.*
(VGR) "Elogium"—Stardate 48921.3
**Wrath of the Prophets (DS9 #20)**—(No stardate given)—*Sisko is a captain in this novel, but Worf is not present, so it occurs between "The Adversary" (DS9) and "The Way of the Warrior" (DS9).*
(VGR) "Non Sequitur"—Stardate 49011
**The Way of the Warrior (DS9 episode novelization)**—Stardate 49011.4
(VGR) "Twisted"—(No stardate given)
**Ghost of a Chance (VGR #7)**—(No stardate given)—*References in this novel suggest a VGR first- or second-season date.*

(DS9) "The Visitor"—(No stardate given)

(VGR) "Parturition"—(No stardate given)

*Cybersong* **(VGR #8)**—(No stardate given)—*References in this novel suggest a VGR first- or second-season date.*

(DS9) "Hippocratic Oath"—Stardate 49066.5

*Bless the Beasts* **(VGR #10)**—(No stardate given)—*References in this novel suggest a VGR first- or second-season date.*

(DS9) "Indiscretion"—(No stardate given)

*The Black Shore* **(VGR #13)**—Stardate 49175.0

*Editors' Note: 491750.0 was the book's original stardate, which contained an extra "0" after the "5." We believe Captain Janeway added it for luck.*

(DS9) "Rejoined"—Stardate 49195.5

(VGR) "Persistence of Vision"—(No stardate given)

(DS9) "Little Green Men"—(No stardate given)

(VGR) "Tattoo"—(No stardate given)

(DS9) "Starship Down"—(No stardate given)

*Mosaic* **(VGR hardcover)**—(No stardate given) [framing story]—*The framing story is set during VGR's second season.*

- 2339—Janeway flashback [Chapter 2].
- 2344—Janeway flashback [Chapter 4].
- 2347—Janeway flashback [Chapter 6].
- 2349—Janeway flashback [Chapter 8].
- 2352—Janeway flashback [Chapter 10 and 12].
- 2353—Janeway flashback [Chapter 14].
- 2356—Janeway flashback [Chapter 14].
- 2357—Janeway flashback [Chapter 16].
- 2362—Janeway flashback [Chapter 18].
- 2363—Janeway flashback [Chapter 20].
- 2367—Janeway flashback [Chapter 22].

(VGR) "Cold Fire"—Stardate 49164.8

(DS9) "The Sword of Kahless"—(No stardate given)

(VGR) "Maneuvers"—(No stardate given)

(VGR) "Resistance"—(No stardate given)

*The* Enterprise-*E is launched* (Star Trek Chronology).

*Ship of the Line* **(TNG hardcover)**—(No stardate given)

*Editor's Note: Because the* Enterprise-*E must have been launched after the events of "The Way of the Warrior" (DS9), some of the references in* **Ship of the Line** *(TNG hardcover) to Klingon/Federation/Cardassian relations are problematic. We suspect that a second major Klingon invasion of Cardassia was in the works during the events of this book.*

- 2278—Story of the *Bozeman* [pages 1–52].
- 2368—Right after "Cause and Effect" (TNG) [pages 52–73].

- 2373—During the beginning of *Star Trek: First Contact* [Chapter 26].

(DS9) "Our Man Bashir"—(No stardate given)

(DS9) "Homefront"—Stardate 49170.65

(DS9) "Paradise Lost"—(No stardate given)

***Trapped in Time*** **(DS9ya #12)**—(No stardate given)—*This story takes place immediately after "Paradise Lost" (DS9).*

*Editors' Note 1: The historian's note placing this book in the first or second season of DS9 is incorrect.*

*Editors' Note 2: This story presents the first meeting between Sisko and the Temporal Investigators, Dulmer and Lucsly, even though they appear never to have met each other in "Trials and Tribble-ations" (DS9).*

- June 1, 1944—Jake, Nog, and O'Brien travel back in time.

***The Garden*** **(VGR #11)**—(No stardate given)—*References indicate that this novel takes place while* Voyager *is still near Kazon territory.*

(VGR) "Prototype"—(No stardate given)

(VGR) "Alliances"—Stardate 49337.4

(DS9) "Crossfire"—(No stardate given)

(VGR) "Threshold"—Stardate 49373.4

***Armageddon Sky*** **(DS9—Day of Honor #2)**—(No stardate given)—*Three months after dissolution of Khitomer Accords. This novel takes place right before* **Her Klingon Soul** *(VGR–DoH #3).*

*Editors' Note: A stardate of 3962 is mentioned on page 214. We are unsure whether this is a colloquial shortening of a current stardate, or whether it a reference to the TOS-era stardate for* **Treaty's Law (TOS-DoH #4).**

***Her Klingon Soul*** **(VGR—Day of Honor #3)**—Stardate 49588.4—*Both the stardate and the presence of the Kazon in this novel place it in VGR's second season.*

(DS9) "Return to Grace"—(No stardate given)

(VGR) "Meld"—(No stardate given)

***The Heart of the Warrior*** **(DS9 #17)**—(No stardate given)—*A historian's note places this novel in the fourth season of DS9.*

(DS9) "The Sons of Mogh"—Stardate 49556.2

(VGR) "Dreadnought"—Stardate 49447

(VGR) "Death Wish"—Stardate 49301.2

(DS9) "Bar Association"—(No stardate given)

***Chrysalis*** **(VGR #12)**—(No stardate given)—*Dialogue in this novel implies that the Doctor is still confined to sickbay.*

(DS9) "Accession"—(No stardate given)

(VGR) "Lifesigns"—Stardate 49504.3

(VGR) "Investigations"—Stardate 49485.2

(VGR) "Deadlock"—Stardate 49548.7

(DS9) "Rules of Engagement"—Stardate 49665.3
(VGR) "Innocence"—(No stardate given)
(DS9) "Hard Time"—(No stardate given)
(DS9) "Shattered Mirror"—(No stardate given)
*Trial By Error* (DS9 #21)—(No stardate given)—*This novel takes place before the Dominion War. A reference is made to Rom being a technician, so the novel is placed late in DS9's fourth season (after "Bar Association" [DS9]).*
(DS9) "The Muse"—(No stardate given)
(VGR) "The Thaw"—(No stardate given)
(DS9) "For the Cause"—(No stardate given)
(VGR) "Tuvix"—Stardate 49655.2
(DS9) "The Quickening"—(No stardate given)
(VGR) "Resolutions"—Stardate 49690.1
(DS9) "To the Death"—Stardate 49904.2
(DS9) "Body Parts"—(No stardate given)
*Vengeance* (DS9 #22)—(No stardate given)—*References to Ferengi Liquidator Brunt indicate that this novel takes place after the episode "Body Parts" (DS9).*
(DS9) "Broken Link"—Stardate 49962.4
**"Life's Lessons"** (DS9 short story, *Strange New Worlds I*)—(No stardate given)—*This story is set after Nog joins Starfleet Academy and during the time Kira is carrying the O'Briens' baby. After "Body Parts" (DS9), before "The Begotten" (DS9).*
(VGR) "Basics, Part I"—(No stardate given)
• *The "official" Okuda* Star Trek Chronology *ends with 2372. Subsequent sequencing is based on air-date until the* Star Trek Chronology *is updated.*

## 2373

(VGR) "Basics, Part II"—Stardate 50023.4
**"Where I Fell Before My Enemy"** (DS9 short story, *Strange New Worlds I*)—(No stardate given)—*This story takes place after Worf joins the DS9 crew, but before the Dominion War.*
*Flashback* (VGR episode novelization)—Stardate 50126.4
• 2293—Tuvok backstory.
(VGR) "The Chute"—Stardate 50156.2
(VGR) "The Swarm"—Stardate 50252.3
(DS9) "Apocalypse Rising"—(No stardate given)
(VGR) "False Profits"—Stardate 50074.3
(DS9) "The Ship"—Stardate 50049.3
(VGR) "Remember"—Stardate 50203.1
(DS9) "Looking for *Par'Mach* in All the Wrong Places"—(No stardate given)

(DS9) "Nor the Battle to the Strong"—(No stardate given)
(DS9) "The Assignment"—(No stardate given)
**Day of Honor: Honor Bound (DS9ya #11)**—(No stardate given)—*One year after* **Armageddon Sky** *(DS9–DoH #2).*
(VGR) "Sacred Ground"—Stardate 50063.2
**Trials and Tribble-ations (DS9 episode novelization)**—(No stardate given)
• 2267—Stardate 4523.7. Set during "The Trouble with Tribbles" (TOS).
(VGR) "Future's End, Part I"—(No stardate given)
(DS9) "Let He Who Is Without Sin . . ."—(No stardate given)
(VGR) "Future's End, Part II"—Stardate 50312.5
**"Ambassador at Large" (VGR short story, Strange New Worlds I)**—(No stardate given)—*Dialogue on page 252 indicates that this takes place "about two years" after "Caretaker" (VGR).*
(DS9) "Things Past"—(No stardate given)
(VGR) "Warlord"—Stardate 50348.1
(DS9) "The Ascent"—(No stardate given)
(VGR) "The Q and the Grey"—Stardate 50384.2
**Star Trek: First Contact (TNG movie novelization)**—Stardate 50893.5—*The stardate indicates that this should be placed near the end of 2373, yet the episode "For the Uniform" (DS9) indicates the events of* Star Trek: First Contact *have already come to pass.*
*Editors' Note: There is also a Young Adult novelization available.*
• 2063—Backstory.
(VGR) "Macrocosm"—Stardate 50425.1
(DS9) "Rapture"—(No stardate given)
**"The First" (TNG short story, Strange New Worlds I)**—(No stardate given)—*After* Star Trek: First Contact.
(DS9) "The Darkness and the Light"—Stardate 50416.2
(VGR) "Fair Trade"—(No stardate given)
(VGR) "Alter Ego"—Stardate 50460.3
(DS9) "The Begotten"—(No stardate given)
**The Mist (DS9—The Captain's Table #3)**—(No stardate given)
*Editors' Note: Takes place after "The Ascent" (DS9) and before "For the Uniform" (DS9). Reference to the Klingon invasion of Cardassia on page twelve is inconsistent with the rest of the main story.*
• 2374—[Framing story].
(VGR) "Coda"—Stardate 50518.6
(DS9) "For the Uniform"—Stardate 50485.2
(VGR) "Blood Fever"—Stardate 50537.2
**Marooned (VGR #14)**—Stardate 50573.2
(DS9) "In Purgatory's Shadow"—(No stardate given)
(VGR) "Unity"—Stardate 50614.2
(DS9) "By Inferno's Light"—Stardate 50564.2

(VGR) "Darkling"—Stardate 50693.2

(DS9) "Doctor Bashir, I Presume"—(No stardate given)

*Avenger* **(TNG hardcover)**—(No stardate given)—*Two years after* Star Trek: First Contact.

- 2246—Young Kirk and Kodos on Tarsus, same time as *A Flag Full of Stars* **(TOS #54)**, flashback [Chapter 1].

(VGR) "Rise"—(No stardate given)

**"Monthuglu"** (VGR short story, *Strange New Worlds I*)—Stardate 50714.2

(VGR) "Favorite Son"—Stardate 50732.4

(DS9) "A Simple Investigation"—(No stardate given)

*The Tempest* **(DS9 #19)**—(No stardate given)—*This novel is placed late in DS9's fifth season, before the Dominion War began. Molly's age is incorrect.*

(DS9) "Business as Usual"—(No stardate given)

(VGR) "Before and After"—Stardate 50973

(DS9) "Ties of Blood and Water"—Stardate 50712.5

**"Good Night, *Voyager*"** (VGR short story, *Strange New Worlds I*)—(No stardate given)

(DS9) "Ferengi Love Songs"—(No stardate given)

*Echoes* **(VGR #15)**—(No stardate given)—*This novel takes place some time after the VGR second season episode "Deadlock" but before Kes leaves the ship.*

(VGR) "Real Life"—Stardate 50836.2

(DS9) "Soldiers of the Empire"—(No stardate given)

**"Fiction"** (VGR short story, *Strange New Worlds I*)—(No stardate given)—*This short story is set after the Doctor gets his mobile emitter in "Future's End" (VGR) but before Seven of Nine joins the* Voyager *crew in "Scorpion" (VGR).*

(VGR) "Distant Origin"—(No stardate given)

(DS9) "Children of Time"—Stardate 50814.2

*House of Cards* **(NF #1)**—(No stardate given)

- 2353—M'k'n'zy backstory.
- 2363—Soleta backstory.
- 2371—Selar backstory.

**"I, *Voyager*"** (VGR short story, *Strange New Worlds I*)—(No stardate given)

(VGR) "Displaced"—Stardate 50912.4

(DS9) "Blaze of Glory"—(No stardate given)

(VGR) "Worst Case Scenario"—Stardate 50953.4

(DS9) "Empok Nor"—(No stardate given)

(VGR) "Scorpion, Part I"—Stardate 50984.3

*Into the Void* **(NF #2)**—Stardate 50923.1

*The Two-Front War* **(NF #3)**—Stardate 50926.1

***End Game* (NF #4)**—Stardate 50927.2

(DS9) "In The Cards"—(No stardate given)

***Martyr* (NF #5)**—(No stardate given)

• 1873—Ontear backstory.

• 2354—M'k'n'zy backstory.

(DS9) "Call to Arms"—(No stardate given)

***Fire on High* (NF #6)**—(No stardate given)

***The Dominion War #2* (DS9 episodes novelization)**—Stardate 51145.3— *Stardate applies to later events in the book.*

*Editors' Note: This novelization adapts the DS9 episodes "Call to Arms," "A Time to Stand," "Rocks and Shoals," and the first portion of "Sons and Daughters." The book concludes early in 2374.*

***The Dominion War #1* (TNG)**—(No stardate given)

*Editors' Note: This novel begins soon after the fall of Deep Space 9 to Cardassian control late in 2373, as described in* **The Dominion War #2 *(DS9 episodes novelization).***

***The Dominion War #3* (TNG)**—(No stardate given)

*Editors' Note: This book ends early in 2374, around the time of "Sacrifice of Angels" [DS9].*

## 2374

(VGR) "Scorpion, Part II"—Stardate 51003.7

(DS9) "A Time to Stand"—(No stardate given)

(DS9) "Rocks and Shoals"—Stardate 51107.2

(DS9) "Sons and Daughters"—(No stardate given)

***The Dominion War #4* (DS9 episodes novelization)**—Stardate 51123.2

*Editors' Note 1: This book novelizes the episodes "Sons and Daughters," "Behind the Lines," "Favor the Bold," and "Sacrifice of Angels."*

*Editors' Note 2: The 69923.2 stardate given in the book (page 192) is way too high for the episodes' timeframe it represents. For this timeline, the stardate was altered to fit the Dominion War timeframe.*

(VGR) "The Gift"—(No stardate given)

***Day Of Honor* (VGR episode novelization)**—(No stardate given)

• 2355—[Pages 1–24].

• 2373—[Pages 25–34].

(VGR) "Nemesis"—Stardate 51082.4

(VGR) "Revulsion"—Stardate 51186.2

(VGR) "The Raven"—(No stardate given)

(DS9) "Behind the Lines"—Stardate 51145.3

(DS9) "Favor the Bold"—(No stardate given)

(VGR) "Scientific Method"—Stardate 51244.3

(DS9) "Sacrifice of Angels"—(No stardate given)

***Fire Ship* (VGR—The Captain's Table #4)**—(No stardate given)—*The* *story that Janeway tells in this novel happens immediately before the events of the VGR episode "Year of Hell, Part I" (VGR).*

- 2374—[Framing story].

(VGR) "The Year of Hell, Part I"—Stardate 51268.4

(DS9) "You Are Cordially Invited . . ."—Stardate 51247.5

(VGR) "The Year of Hell, Part II"—Stardate 51425.4

***Planet X* (TNG unnumbered)**—(No stardate given)—*Shortly after "You Are Cordially Invited . . ." (DS9).*

(DS9) "Resurrection"—(No stardate given)

(VGR) "Random Thoughts"—Stardate 51367.2

(DS9) "Statistical Probabilities"—(No stardate given)

(VGR) "Concerning Flight"—Stardate 51386.4

(VGR) "Mortal Coil"—Stardate 51449.2

(DS9) "The Magnificent Ferengi"—(No stardate given)

(DS9) "Waltz"—Stardate 51408.6

(VGR) "Waking Moments"—Stardate 51471.3

(VGR) "Message in a Bottle"—(No stardate given)

***Spectre* (TNG hardcover)**—(No stardate given)—*Takes place shortly after "Message in a Bottle" (VGR).*

***Dark Victory* (TNG hardcover)**—(No stardate given)—*Direct sequel to* **Spectre** *(TNG hardcover).*

(DS9) "Who Mourns for Morn?"—(No stardate given)

***Far beyond The Stars* (DS9 episode novelization)**—(No stardate given)

*Editors' Note: Sisko has visions that chronicle the childhood of Benny Russell (July 1940) and his life (October 1953).*

(VGR) "Hunters"—Stardate 51501.4

(DS9) "One Little Ship"—Stardate 51474.2

***The Q Continuum #1: Q-Space* (TNG #47)**—Stardate 51604.2

*Editors' Note: The stardate given in the book is 500146.2, but we decided to drop one digit and rearranged the others to make the stardate fit in the same year soon after "Message in a Bottle" (VGR).*

- 5 billion years ago—Young Q backstory.
- 2.5 billion years ago—Teenage Q backstory.

***The Q Continuum #2: Q-Zone* (TNG #48)**—Stardate 51604.3

*Editors' Note: On page 108, Riker knows that* Voyager *is lost in the Delta Quadrant, placing this novel trilogy after the VGR episode "Message in a Bottle." The stardate given in the book is 500146.3, but we decided to drop one digit and rearranged the others to make the stardate fit in the same year soon after "Message in a Bottle" (VGR).*

- 1 million years ago—Q backstory.

***The Q Continuum #3: Q-Strike* (TNG #49)**—Stardate 51604.3

*Editors' Note 1: The stardate given in the book is 500146.3, but we decided to drop one digit and rearranged the others to make the stardate fit in the same year soon after "Message in a Bottle" (VGR).*

*Editors' Note 2: On page 249, Picard reflects on the recent entry of the Romulans to the Dominion War. This is inconsistent with the fact that at the time of this trilogy Betazed has not yet fallen to the Dominion, an event which indirectly led to the Romulan entry to the war ("In the Pale Moonlight" [DS9]).*

(VGR) "Prey"—Stardate 51652.3
(DS9) "Honor Among Thieves"—(No stardate given)
(VGR) "Retrospect"—Stardate 51679.4
(DS9) "Change of Heart"—Stardate 51597.2
(VGR) "The Killing Game, Part I"—(No stardate given)
(VGR) "The Killing Game, Part II"—Stardate 51715.2
(DS9) "Wrongs Darker Than Death or Night"—(No stardate given)
(DS9) "Inquisition"—(No stardate given)
(VGR) "Vis à Vis"—Stardate 51762.4
(DS9) "In the Pale Moonlight"—Stardate 51721.3
(VGR) "The Omega Directive"—Stardate 51871.2
(DS9) "His Way"—(No stardate given)
(VGR) "Unforgettable"—Stardate 51813.4
(DS9) "The Reckoning"—(No stardate given)
(VGR) "Living Witness"—(No stardate given)
(DS9) *"Valiant"*—(No stardate given)
(VGR) "Demon"—(No stardate given)
(DS9) "Profit and Lace"—(No stardate given)
(VGR) "One"—Stardate 51929.3 to 51932.4

***Pathways* (VGR hardcover)**—(No stardate given) [framing story]—*The framing sequence for this story takes place a little less than a year after Seven of Nine joins the* Voyager *crew (page 7).*
• 2289–2371—Tuvok's story [Chapter 14].
• 2349–2371—Neelix's story [Chapter 10].
• 2350–2371—Chakotay's story [Chapter 2].
• 2350–2371—Kim's story [Chapter 4].
• 2358–2371—Torres's story [Chapter 6].
• 2365–2371—Paris's story [Chapter 8].
• 2370–2371—Kes's story [Chapter 12].
(DS9) "Time's Orphan"—(No stardate given)
(VGR) "Hope and Fear"—Stardate 51978.2 to 51981.6

***Seven of Nine* (VGR #16)**—(No stardate given)
• 2369 (approx.)—[Prologue].
(DS9) "The Sound of Her Voice"—(No stardate given)
(DS9) "Tears of the Prophets"—(No stardate given)

## 2375

(DS9) "Image in the Sand"—(No stardate given)
*Editors' Note: This episode is set three months after "Tears of the Prophets" (DS9).*

(DS9) "Shadows and Symbols"—(No stardate given)
(DS9) "Afterimage"—(No stardate given)
(VGR) "Night"—Stardate 52081.2
(DS9) "Take Me Out to the Holosuite"—(No stardate given)
(VGR) "Drone"—(No stardate given)
(DS9) "Chrysalis"—(No stardate given)
(VGR) "Extreme Risk"—(No stardate given)
(DS9) "Treachery, Faith, and the Great River"—(No stardate given)
(VGR) "In the Flesh"—Stardate 52136.4
(DS9) "Once More Unto the Breach"—(No stardate given)
(VGR) "Once Upon a Time"—(No stardate given)
(DS9) "The Siege at AR-558"—(No stardate given)
(VGR) "Timeless"—Stardate 52143.6
(DS9) "Covenant"—(No stardate given)
(VGR) "Infinite Regress"—Stardate 52356.2

## 2377

***Star Trek: Borg*** **(TNG interactive movie CD-Rom)**—(No stardate given) [framing story]—*10 years after the Battle of Wolf 359 and six months before Stardate 54902.*
*Editors' Note: There is also an audio adaptation available.*
  • 2367—Backstory, takes place during the Battle of Wolf 359

*And the human adventure is just beginning . . .*